# The Brothers Karamazov

# THE BROTHERS KARAMAZOV

A novel in four parts & epilog
by FYODOR DOSTOEVSKY

The translation by CONSTANCE GARNETT revised, with
an introduction, by AVRAHM YARMOLINSKY. Illustrated
with lithographs by FRITZ EICHENBERG.
New York: The Heritage Press

# INTRODUCTION

Of the nineteenth century novelists, none have worn so well as the Russians, but whereas the passage of time has given Turgenev a slightly old-fashioned air, and has neither subtracted from nor yet added to the excellences of Tolstoy, it has only served to bring out the profundity and imaginative power of Dostoevsky's work. Within the last two or three decades his reputation has climbed to dizzying heights. For one thing, the malaise through which our civilization is passing has brought us closer to a man who, we must admit, foresaw pretty clearly the progress of our spiritual disease, even though he would have medicined us with a religion which we cannot swallow. Further, a better and more widely diffused knowledge of mental processes has made this generation more appreciative of the first novelist to have such an astonishing insight into human motives and into all the contradictions and confusions of the mind. His present extraordinary vogue may suffer an eclipse abroad, for causes not necessarily the same as those that have weakened his influence at home, where both his convictions and his perplexities are out of harmony with the practical temper of the times. Yet his greatness as a novelist is one of the few certainties in an uncertain world.

Dostoevsky's crowning achievement was "The Brothers Karamazov." Few novels of any time and any country have been so heartily praised in our own day, and by connoisseurs so diverse. Marcel Proust, himself a mas-

ter builder in the field of fiction, allowed it a mysterious beauty, a sculptural grandeur. Arnold Bennett classed it as "one of the supreme marvels of the world." Sigmund Freud, who brings to his judgment of literature the acumen of a pioneer psychologist, does not hesitate to call it "the most magnificent novel ever written." Translated into practically every civilized language, broadcast in inexpensive editions, the book is finding its way to a widening circle of readers. And yet, though it carries the thrills of a detective story, the elementary interest of melodrama and romance, the persuasiveness of realistic fiction, it will always be, to some degree, caviar to the general. Its psychological subtleties, its passionate philosophizing, will inevitably limit its deepest appeal to the mature and the discriminating.

"The Brothers Karamazov" was at once the culmination and the close of Dostoevsky's career: when he put finis to it, in November, 1880, he had only two months to live. He had been occupied with the actual writing of it for three years, but some of its elements had been present in his mind before he set pen to paper, and indeed are discoverable in his earliest writings. As though he feared that the sands were running out for him, he gave more of himself to the book than to any previous work. He put into it the affirmation which was the difficult yield of so many doubts; he put into it the doubts, too, along with his understanding of character, his intimate knowledge of the obscure ways of the human soul, his sense of life, with its burden of mystery, terror and pity, and its core of pure joy. The book bears witness to the strength of a creative power miraculously preserved in a body racked by disease and distress, by the accumulated fatigues of nearly sixty lacerating years.

It is far from obvious precisely how Dostoevsky's personal fortunes shaped his novels, and particularly "The Brothers Karamazov," yet a glance at the more significant among the author's experiences and private opinions, and at the influences that worked upon him, may contribute something to the appreciation of the book.

Fyodor Dostoevsky was born in 1821, in the pious old city of Moscow, where he spent his childhood and early youth. He was the son of an army doctor, a stern, moody, irascible man, who belonged to the gentry, and the growing family led a shabby-genteel existence in a corner of the charity hospital where he served. A religious atmosphere prevailed in the home, and the memory of childhood pilgrimages to a neighboring monastery must have fed the imagination of the man who wrote the scenes from monastic life in "The Brothers Karamazov." From the first, Dostoevsky's taste for reading was encouraged by his parents, who were not without literary interests, and who were at pains to give him a good schooling. As a boy he spent several summers on his father's modest property in the provinces, but the spacious manorial setting in which Turgenev and Tolstoy, his two famous contemporaries, grew up, was alien to him. His mind was at home in the city, and practically all his characters have the urban stamp upon them.

His mother died just before he left Moscow, at the age of sixteen, to attend a military engineering school in what was then St. Peters-burg. There, his unaccustomed surroundings, the severity of the discipline, the roughness and vulgarity of his schoolmates, the uncongenial character of his studies, his humiliating poverty (his tuition had been paid by a well-to-do relative), combined to make a brooding solitary of the proud, dreamy, high-strung boy. He was in his second year at school when news reached him that his father had been murdered. The doctor had retired to his country place and given himself up to drink, and the killing was no doubt an act of vengeance on a brutal master perpetrated by his own serfs. The psychoanalytic view of the matter is that the effect of the tragedy on Dostoevsky, who allegedly harbored a strong unconscious death-wish against his father, was a shattering one, and indeed, brought out his latent tendency to epilepsy. Posthumous psychoanalysis is admittedly guess-work, but it is at least noteworthy that Dostoevsky's last and greatest novel revolves around the murder of a repulsive old sot by his servant, who is also his bastard, while two other sons of his commit the crime of parricide in their minds, and that one of the major themes is the problem of moral responsibility for a crime which is a wish rather than an act.

The profession of engineering held no attractions for the young man, and within a year of graduation he retired from the service, determined to make his living by his pen, even if he had to starve for it. From then on almost to the end of his days he lived in the grip of crushing poverty, enduring for a while a kind of literary peonage, and always writing desperately against time. He broke into print at the age of twenty-four with "Poor Folk," a short novel, which had an immediate and dazzling success. He followed it up with a story called "The Double," a striking and penetrating study of the split personality, a theme which was to haunt his mind and to recur again in his last work. He was hailed as a prodigy by Belinsky, and was welcomed into the circle over which this influential critic presided. Here Dostoevsky was exposed to liberal and even radical views, and more particularly to the ideas of the Westernists, who wished to see Russia follow the lead of Europe. A break soon took place between him and his new-found friends, partly owing to his touchiness and arrogance — his success had gone to his head — and partly to intellectual incompatibility. His fame seemed to be withering as rapidly as it had bloomed, the stories he was now writing being coldly received; his earnings were of the meagrest; and to add to his harassments, he was ill: he had various nervous symptoms and seems to have already become subject to epileptic seizures.

Although living under the iron rule of a paternalistic autocrat, a handful of young Russian intellectuals were sensitive to the movement that prepared the revolutions of 1848 abroad. Dostoevsky was one of these young men: he followed eagerly the events in Europe, he read the books of the French socialists, and he attended Friday night gatherings at which opinions directed against church and state were aired. At the same time, paradoxically enough, he seems to have entertained some nationalistic and pietistic notions which were then being popularized by the Slavophils. At all events, it is highly doubtful whether he subscribed to the more subversive views of his companions; he was certainly no atheist, and a socialist of only the mildest variety; if he uttered some wild words it was because he was carried away by a generous im-

pulse toward social justice. The result of it all was that on the morning of Holy Saturday in 1849 he, as well as dozens of other young men who had attended the Fridays, was arrested and thrust into prison. Charged with having attended the meetings and with having read aloud a seditious letter, he was condemned, and sentenced to four years of hard labor in Siberia, to be followed by service in the ranks. But together with the other prisoners, he was taken to a public square, where a sentence of capital punishment was read aloud, and the preliminaries to execution by shooting were carried out. For some interminable minutes Dostoevsky believed that he was about to die. Suddenly, in accordance with the grim comedy prearranged by the czar, who had a taste for theatricals, the true sentence was announced.

Dostoevsky endured four years of penal servitude in a foul prison, shaven and fettered like the common criminals who were his constant companions, without the merest decencies of existence, without privacy, without any book but the New Testament, without a word from home. Furthermore, he now came to recognize for the first time that he was an epileptic. On his release he became a private in a Siberian regiment largely recruited from ex-convicts and stationed in a miserable frontier town thousands of miles from civilization. He accepted his punishment as though he deserved it, and did not shrink from his brutish fellows. He was later to assert that his intimate contact with the common people had opened his eyes to the ancient treasure of the Russian folk: their Orthodox faith and their childlike confidence in the czar. His experiences no doubt helped to stimulate his preoccupation with crime, which was to him a token of man's spiritual nature. His exile lasted ten years in all, and when he returned to Petersburg in 1859, he was not only toughened in soul and body, but a firmer adherent of the Russian Christ and a loyal subject of his emperor. He was moreover a married man, having allied himself with a widow, a delicate and destitute gentlewoman, for whom he had conceived a passion not unmixed with pity.

Dostoevsky, now approaching forty, had to start again at the bottom. He had brought from Siberia two rather mediocre tales, which he had difficulty in placing. The problem of how to earn enough to support himself, his wife, and his stepson was acute. The rôle of a publicist had always fascinated him, and now, with the quickening of Russia's intellectual and political life, prior to the great reforms of the sixties, it seemed more attractive than ever. Although he knew that fiction was his métier, he had a strong impulse to make his influence felt in a more direct fashion. With his brother Mikhail, who was himself something of a littérateur and who had besides a head for business, he launched a monthly review. It was a conservative periodical waging war against the nihilists, and just tinged with liberalism to suit the times. Through a misunderstanding it was suppressed in 1863, and was resumed shortly under another name. It was to these magazines that Dostoevsky contributed, besides some miscellaneous papers, an inferior novel, and a remarkable chronicle of his prison days, as well as "Notes From the Underground," that disturbing mixture of controversy and confession which, both in its probing of a sick soul and its implied aspiration toward spiritual health, is the true preamble to his great novels.

During these years his personal life was an agitated one. There was a peaceful interval when he fulfilled his long cherished dream of visiting Western Europe. The trip confirmed him in the prejudices he took with him against the West and also in his faith in Russia's manifest destiny. He went abroad unaccompanied by his wife. His marriage had turned out badly. The two seem to have been bound to each other by the double ties of love and hate, which he was to represent in his novels so often as the basis of the passional relation. His devotion to her did not prevent him from having a brief liaison with a young student, who took the initiative in terminating their intimacy. In 1863, while his wife lay desperately ill with consumption, he went abroad for the second time, ostensibly to be treated for epilepsy, actually to be with his fickle mistress, and it was on this trip that he contracted the gambling fever which was to be the curse of his existence for years. The following spring his wife died, and a few months later his brother Mikhail, too, passed away suddenly, leaving a mass of debts incurred in connection with the magazine, and a family without visible means of support. Dostoevsky took over the magazine, sank in it his share of his aunt's fortune, only to see the review fail within a few months, and to find himself, an ailing, middle-aged man, deep in debt, with his own stepson and his brother's family on his hands, and no one and nothing to live for.

And yet he sometimes felt, strangely enough, that his life was just beginning, and indeed, his best work was still to come. One evening in Wiesbaden, in September, 1865, after he had lost everything at roulette, the main outline of his first important novel, "Crime and Punishment," suddenly crystallized in his brain. In this "psychological account of a crime," as Dostoevsky himself described his superb work, the author expresses his fascinated horror at a mind which allows itself to be guided by reason alone, and which in its aberration dares to set itself beyond good and evil. Ideas of this order recur.

He was forced to interrupt the writing of the novel and to dash off another story in order to fulfill an onerous contract into which he had entered in a moment of utter penury. In this short novel, "The Gambler," he drew upon his experiences at the tables and also upon his unhappy liaison. He had to work at record speed and so resorted to the services of a stenographer, probably an unprecedented occurrence in the history of Russian letters. The girl — she was only twenty — was not the first to whom he proposed after becoming a widower, but she was the first to accept him. His marriage, early in 1867, to this steadfast, brave, humdrum young person, won him a loving wife, a devoted helpmate, and a capable manager of his affairs. A few weeks after the wedding the couple went abroad, partly to escape creditors, but more particularly to save their union, seemingly so incongruous, from the attacks upon it made by his relatives.

The couple stayed abroad, chiefly in Germany, four years, and at times this second exile seemed to him worse than his Siberian captivity. They were constantly in want, often not knowing where the next meal was to come from, and reduced to pawning even their necessaries. His periodic and disastrous gambling fits contributed not a little to their misery. Two children were born to them here, but the parents knew the sorrow of leaving their first-born in a foreign cemetery. Dostoevsky's seizures, though less frequent, persisted. His homesickness was made acute by his hatred of the alien scene, but more by the feeling that

he was losing touch with his country and so with the source of his art and the springs of life itself. Under these harassing circumstances, Dostoevsky wrote "The Idiot," a work of great originality and power, in which for the first time he made the attempt, repeated in "The Brothers Karamazov," to depict the perfect Christian confronting the world, the flesh, and the devil. He also began "The Possessed," a huge novel which savagely attacks the revolutionary movement, then still in its infancy, and which is further concerned with the tragedy of a rootless soul, unable to lay hold of anything on earth or in heaven which gives validity to life, — another motif which Dostoevsky resumes in his last novel.

"The Possessed" was finished in 1872, when he was again settled in Petersburg. In his last decade his life was uneventful and less irregular than it had ever been before. There were still creditors to satisfy, his health was worse, and what with the needs of a growing family, he had to drive his pen harder and faster than ever, but thanks to the business sense of his energetic wife, toward the end he knew relative security and ease. The winters were spent in the capital and the summers in a provincial town, which Dostoevsky used as the setting for "The Brothers Karamazov." The great sorrow of these latter years was the loss of his youngest child, Alyosha — only two of his four children survived — and there are echoes of it in that moving passage of his last novel in which the peasant woman bereaved of her child pours out her heart to the elder Zosima.

He occupied himself alternately with journalism and fiction, giving almost equal time to each. For a while he edited a conservative weekly, to which he contributed, besides comment on foreign politics, informal miscellaneous feuilletons dealing with matters of current interest, which he called "A Writer's Diary." He gave up the burdensome editorial task to write "A Raw Youth," which first appeared in 1875, serially, like all his novels. This sprawling narrative, which is the least integrated of Dostoevsky's works, has for one of its dominant themes the father-son relation which is touched upon again in "The Brothers Karamazov." Both the assent to life arrived at by the adolescent hero, who had been possessed by a withering cerebral dream, and the inner peace found by his father, the divided soul, announce Dostoevsky's final work. Having completed "A Raw Youth," he resumed his "Writer's Diary," this time as a monthly miscellany, of which he was the publisher and to which he was the sole contributor. He made this the vehicle for the expression of his belief in the messianic destiny of his country, and of other views as vehement as they were contradictory. His forensic writings, added to his novels, won him a wide reputation even among those who were hostile to his nationalistic and pietistic opinions, and he was looked to for spiritual guidance by many, so that the speech which he delivered at the unveiling of a statue of Pushkin in Moscow was the occasion of a public ovation approximating that tendered the aged Voltaire on his final visit to Paris. The Pushkin festival occurred in the summer of 1880.

The most obvious claim that this book makes upon the reader's attention is its excellence as a crime novel. Dostoevsky was not averse to using the tricks of his trade, and in this story of parricide he contrived suspense and surprise with extraordinary skill. It owes much of its effectiveness to its dramatic qual-

ity. It exhibits the tempo and tension of high tragedy: there are prolixities and interpolations, but the main action is crowded into a few days; the protagonists are observed not in the sober light of common day but in the flash of the thunderbolt; a sense of impending catastrophe broods over the scenes.

The characters — there are some fifty men and women in the book — are drawn with that understanding of emotional ambivalence and the rôle of the unconscious which distinguishes Dostoevsky's art. They are not transcripts of ordinary humanity. Their ecstasies and agonies are too intense, their soul-searchings too keen, their tossings between good and evil, between love and hatred, too abrupt, their impulses too perverse. Yet they have a compelling reality. The inwardness and authority with which Dostoevsky portrayed the Karamazovs may be due to the fact that they are projections of the several elements at war within his own breast. They are creatures of flesh and blood, endowed with a distinct life of their own, but they may also be taken as symbols. The old man Karamazov seems to be the pattern of the sensualist in all his unredeemable animalism; his bastard, Smerdyakov, the moral idiot, being the evil growth of his blind lust. It is with the three legitimate sons that we reach the human plane, and the violent Dmitri, the subtle Ivan, the gentle Alyosha, appear respectively as the body, the mind, and the spiritual member. It belongs to the substance of Dostoevsky's thinking that he should represent the body as striving toward union with the spirit, the intellect as cruelly divided against itself and fundamentally inimical to life.

The book derives further significance from the fact that it is concerned with ideas. The crime novel is also a philosophical novel, but that does not mean that the author engages in dry abstract disquisitions. With Dostoevsky, intellection has the force and heat of emotion. The ideas either grow naturally out of the situations, or are formulated in the course of those absorbing arguments which are among the high points of the narrative. They revolve around the whole complex of problems that cluster about morality and religion. "The Brothers Karamazov" may be viewed as a vast parable, or, better still, as a religious disputation, such as is carried on, with a difference, in the Book of Job. Ivan, the dialectician, upholds the negative: if God can allow the suffering of the innocent, of children, above all, even though this be the price of some future beatitude, then the world is meaningless and unacceptable. His blasphemies go further. In his fantasy, "The Grand Inquisitor," he shows the Catholic Church at the height of its power serving not Christ, but the Evil One who tempted Him in the desert; the church is using the means that Christ had spurned, in order to make men happy and save them from His terrible gift of freedom. It is Ivan's tragedy that he cannot wholeheartedly side with Christ against Satan and the Grand Inquisitor. To understand Dostoevsky's intention here one must remember that among his favorite ideas was the dubious notion that Catholicism, in arrogating to itself temporal power, had betrayed Christ, and so become the mother of socialism. The latter Dostoevsky abhorred as a crass destructive doctrine which set the nourishment of man's body above the well-being of his soul, and which would result in the establishment of a sane, safe, social order, orphaned of God. Ivan's own fate, no less than Dmitri's regeneration, the serene faith which guides Alyosha, and the saintly life and Orthodox teachings of his master, Zosima, all indirectly refute Ivan's argument and proclaim a religious acceptance of life. The reader must decide for himself who wins the debate. As for Dostoevsky, he was, consciously at least, on the side of the angels, as the final scene emphatically attests.

Often after completing a novel, Dostoevsky was left with a feeling of the inadequacy of what he had set down. Some such feeling must have haunted him when he finished his last work, for the end of the book was by no means the end of the story of the Karamazovs. Indeed, the novel closes before he has fairly launched the youngest brother, the novice, on his career in the world. As is indicated in the author's foreword, which the present edition offers for the first time in English, "The Brothers Karamazov" was to have had a second part, with Alyosha as the hero. Dostoevsky did not live to write it, so that, in a sense, the novel is a torso, not unlike that other Russian masterpiece, Gogol's "Dead Souls." Little is known of the author's plans for the sequel. It is said that Alyosha was to have become involved with revolutionists and to have committed a political crime, — it will be recalled that during Dostoevsky's last years the terrorists were increasingly active and, indeed, his own death antedated by one month the assassination of the czar. The possibilities of such a novel as this projected sequel fairly dazzle the imagination. But there is no need to speak of might-have-beens. The work as it stands is sufficient to engage profoundly the mind and the emotions of the reader, and to leave him shaken by a sense of the large potentialities of the soul.

AVRAHM YARMOLINSKY

*xiii*

Verily, verily, I say unto you, Except a corn of wheat fall into the ground and die, it abideth alone: but if it die, it bringeth forth much fruit. JOHN XII. 24.

# THE TABLE OF CONTENTS

# THE TABLE OF CONTENTS

# A LIST OF THE LITHOGRAPHS

xix

# The Brothers Karamazov

In commencing the life-story of my hero, Alexey Fyodorovich Karamazov, I find myself somewhat perplexed: although I call Alexey Fyodorovich my hero, nevertheless I myself know that he is by no means a great man, and hence I foresee that there will inevitably arise such questions as these: "What is so remarkable about your Alexey Fyodorovich, that you have chosen him as your hero? What has he accomplished? For what is he known, and by whom? Why should a reader like myself spend time over the facts of his life?"

The last question is the most embarrassing one, for I can answer it only by saying: "Perhaps you will see for yourself from the novel." And what if you do read it, and fail to see, and so do not agree that my Alexey Fyodorovich is remarkable? I say this because unhappily I anticipate such an eventuality. To my mind he is remarkable, but I doubt very much if I shall succeed in proving it to the reader. The fact is that he is perhaps a leader, but a leader in the making, still unformed. Indeed, it would be strange to require in an age like ours that a man should have a clearly defined viewpoint. One thing perhaps is plain: he is a queer character, indeed an original. But queerness and oddity are more apt to repel than to command attention, especially at a time when all are striving to eliminate differences and to find some unifying principle in the general

confusion. But an original is in most cases the very essence of what is particular and apart from the commonalty. Isn't that so?

Should you disagree with this notion and answer: "No, it isn't so," or "It isn't always so," then I might feel more encouraged about the significance of my hero, Alexey Fyodorovich. For not only is an original "not always particular and apart from the commonalty," but, on the contrary, it happens sometimes that such a person is near the very heart of the commonalty, and the rest of the men of his age have temporarily been swept away from it, as by a gust of wind. . . .

I should not have entered into these uninteresting and vague explanations and should have begun simply without any introduction, saying to myself: "If they like it, they will read it," but the trouble is that while there is one life-story, there are two tales here. The main narrative is the second one, — it has to do with the activity of my hero in our own day, precisely at the present moment. As for the first tale, it deals with events of thirteen years ago, and properly speaking, it is not an entire novel, but only the description of one episode in my hero's early youth. I cannot do without this first tale, because much in the second tale would become unintelligible without it. But in this way my original embarrassment is rendered even greater: if I, that is, the biographer himself, find that my immature and modest hero seems not to deserve even one tale, why appear with two, and how can I justify such presumption?

At a loss as to how to answer these questions, I choose to evade them. Of course, the perspicuous reader has long since guessed that such was my intention from the first, and was only vexed with me for wasting words and time. To this, here is my direct reply: I was wasting words and time, first, out of courtesy, second, out of shrewdness: at least I gave my readers fair warning. Besides, I am even glad that my book has of itself split into two narratives, without injury, however, to its essential unity: having perused the first tale, the

reader will decide for himself whether it is worth his while to attempt the second. Of course, there is no obligation in the matter, — you may throw the book aside after the first two pages and never open it again. But there are readers so conscientious that they will certainly wish to read the book to the end, so as to form a judicious estimate of it. Such, for instance, are all the Russian critics. It is by this type of reader that I feel I have done my duty. I have given these scrupulous and conscientious folk a legitimate pretext for tossing the book aside at the outset. Well, here is my whole foreword. I fully agree that it is altogether useless, but as it has been written, let it stand. And now to business.

PART
I

# A
## NOTE
## ON THE
## TEXT

*A word should be said about the present text of the novel. In revising Mrs. Garnett's version, the effort was — aside from correcting the errors which mar a generally admirable performance— to bring the translation closer to the original. No attempt was made to gloss over the imperfections of an author who, at his worst, lumbers along in a helpless fashion, and whose very awkwardness is an earnest of his terrible sincerity, his need for utterance by any means. To give the style a finish which the original does not possess would be for the translator to betray his trust. Certainly authenticity seemed to be demanded in presenting a version of what has come to be recognized as a major work of literature.* A.Y.

# BOOK I

## THE HISTORY OF A FAMILY

### CHAPTER I
#### FYODOR PAVLOVICH KARAMAZOV

ALEXEY FYODOROVICH KARAMAZOV was the third son of Fyodor Pavlovich Karamazov, a landowner well known in our district in his own day, and still remembered among us owing to his tragic and obscure death, which happened just thirteen years ago, and of which I shall speak in its proper place. For the present I will only say that this "landowner"—for so we used to call him, although he hardly spent a day of his life on his estate—was a strange sort, yet one pretty frequently to be met with, a worthless and dissolute and at the same time senseless type of man. But he was one of those senseless persons who are very well able to look after their worldly affairs, and, apparently, after nothing else. Fyodor Pavlovich, for instance, began with next to nothing; his estate was of the smallest; he ran to dine at other men's tables, and was on the look-out for a chance to become a hanger-on, yet at his death it appeared that he had a hundred thousand roubles in hard cash. At the same time, he was all his life one of the most senseless eccentrics in the whole district. I repeat, it was not stupidity—the majority of these eccentrics are shrewd and intelligent enough—but just senselessness, and a peculiar national form of it.

He was married twice, and had three sons, the eldest, Dmitri, by his first wife, and two, Ivan and Alexey, by his second. Fyodor Pavlovich's first spouse, Adelaïda Ivanovna, belonged to the gentry, coming of a fairly rich and distinguished family, also landowners in our district, the Miüsovs. How it came to pass that a girl with a dowry, who was also a beauty, and moreover one of those lively, intelligent girls, so common in this generation, but sometimes also to be found in the last, could have married such a seedy nonentity, as everybody called him then, I won't attempt to explain. I knew a young lady of the last "romantic" generation who after some years of an enigmatic passion for a gentleman, whom she might quite easily have married at any moment, invented insuperable obstacles to their union, and ended by throwing herself one stormy night into a rather deep and rapid river from a high bank, almost a precipice, and so perished, entirely to satisfy her own caprice, and to be like Shakespeare's Ophelia. Indeed, if this precipice, a chosen and favourite spot of hers, had been less picturesque, if there had been a prosaic flat bank in its place, most likely the suicide would never have occurred. This is a fact, and probably there have been not a few similar instances in Russia in the last two or three generations. Adelaïda Ivanovna Miüsov's action was likewise, no doubt, an echo of other people's ideas, and was due to the "chafing of imprisoned thought." She wanted, perhaps, to show her feminine independence, to defy social conventions and the despotism of her family. And a pliable imagination persuaded her, we must suppose, for a brief moment, that Fyodor Pavlovich, in spite of his parasitic position, was one of the bold and ironical spirits of that progressive epoch, though he was, in fact, an ill-natured buffoon and nothing more. What gave the marriage piquancy was that it was preceded by an elopement, and this greatly captivated Adelaïda Ivanovna's fancy. Fyodor Pavlovich's position at the time made him specially eager for any such enterprise, for he was passionately anxious to make a career in one way or another. To attach himself to a good family and obtain a dowry was an alluring prospect. As for love, apparently the bride felt none for the groom, nor, in spite of Adelaïda Ivanovna's beauty, he any for her. This was, perhaps, a unique case in the life of Fyodor Pavlovich, who was always of a sensuous temperament, and ready to run after any petticoat on the slightest encouragement. She seems to have been the only woman who made no particular appeal to his senses.

Immediately after the elopement Adelaïda Ivanovna discerned in a flash that she had no feeling for her husband but contempt. The marriage accordingly showed itself in its true colours with extraordinary rapidity. Although the family became reconciled to the event pretty quickly and apportioned the runaway bride her dowry, the husband and wife began to lead a most unseemly life, and there were everlasting scenes between them. It was said that the young wife showed incomparably more nobility and high-mindedness than Fyodor Pavlovich, who, as is now known, got hold of all her money up to twenty-five thousand roubles as soon as she received it, so that those thousands were lost to her for ever. The little village and the rather fine town house which formed part of her dowry he did his utmost for a long time to transfer to his name, by means of some deed of conveyance. He would probably have succeeded, merely because of her moral fatigue and desire to get rid of him, and because of the contempt and loathing he aroused in her by his persistent and shameless importunity. But, fortunately, Adelaïda Ivanovna's family intervened and restrained the shark. It is known for a fact that frequent fights took place between the husband and wife, but, according to legend, it was not Fyodor Pavlovich but Adelaïda Ivanovna who did the beating, for she was a hot-tempered, bold, dark-browed, impatient woman, possessed of remarkable physical strength. Finally, she left the house and ran away from Fyodor Pavlovich with a destitute divinity student, leaving Mitya, a child three years old, on her husband's hands. Immediately Fyodor Pavlovich introduced a regular harem into the house, and abandoned himself to orgies of drunkenness. In the intervals he used to drive all over the province, complaining tearfully to each and all of Adelaïda Ivanovna's having left him, going into details too disgraceful for a husband to mention in regard to his own married life. What seemed to gratify him most and flatter him was to play the ridiculous part of the injured husband, and to parade his woes.

"One would think that you'd got a promotion, Fyodor Pavlovich, you seem so pleased in spite of your sorrow," scoffers said to him.

Many added that he was glad of a new comic part in which to play the buffoon, and that it was simply to make it funnier that he pretended to be unaware of his ludicrous position. But, who knows, it may indeed have been simplicity. At last he succeeded in getting on the track of his runaway wife. The poor woman turned out to be in Petersburg, where she had gone with her divinity student, and where she had thrown herself into a life of complete emancipation. Fyodor Pavlovich at once began bustling about, making preparations to go to Petersburg, with what object he could not himself have said. He would perhaps really have gone; but having determined to do so he felt at once entitled to fortify himself for the journey by another bout of reckless drinking. And just at that time his wife's family received the news of her death in Petersburg. She had died quite suddenly in a garret, according to one story, of typhus, or, as another version had it, of starvation. Fyodor Pavlovich was drunk when he heard of his wife's death, and the story is that he ran out into the street and began shouting with joy, raising his hands to heaven: "Lord, now lettest Thou Thy servant depart in peace," but others say he wept without restraint like a little child, so much so that people were sorry for him, in spite of the disgust he inspired. It is quite possible that both versions were true, that he rejoiced at his release, and at the same time wept for her who released him. As a general rule, people, even the wicked, are much more naïve and simple-hearted than we suppose. And we ourselves are, too.

## CHAPTER II
### HE GETS RID OF HIS ELDEST SON

You can easily imagine what a father such a man could be and how he would bring up his children. His behaviour as a father was exactly what might be expected. He completely abandoned the child of his marriage with Adelaïda Ivanovna, not from malice, nor because of his grievances as a husband, but simply because he forgot him altogether. While he was wearying every one with his tears and complaints, and turning his house into a sink of debauchery, a faithful servant of the family, Grigory, took the three-year-old Mitya into his care. If he hadn't looked after him there would have been no one even to change the child's little shirt.

It happened moreover that the child's relations on his mother's side also forgot him at first. His grandfather was no longer living, the widow, Mitya's grandmother, had moved to Moscow, and was seriously ill, while his aunts were married, so that Mitya remained for almost a whole year in old Grigory's charge and lived with him in the servant's cottage. But even if his father had remembered him (he could not, indeed, have been altogether unaware of his existence), he would have sent him back to the cottage, as the child would only have been in the way of his debaucheries. But a cousin of Mitya's mother, Pyotr Alexandrovich Miüsov, happened to return from Paris. He was afterwards to reside abroad for many years, and at that time, still quite a young man, he was distinguished among the Miüsovs as a person of enlightened ideas of European culture, who had lived in the capitals and abroad. Towards the end of his life he became a Liberal of the type common in the forties and fifties. In the course of his career he had come into contact with many of the most liberal men of his epoch, both in Russia and abroad. He had known Proudhon and Bakunin personally, and in his declining years was very fond of describing the three days of the Paris Revolution of February 1848, hinting that he himself had almost taken part in the fighting on the barricades. This was one of the most grateful recollections of his youth. He had an independent property of about a thousand souls, to reckon in the old style. His splendid estate lay on the outskirts of our little town and bordered on the lands of our famous monastery, with which Pyotr Alexandrovich began an endless lawsuit, almost as soon as he came into the estate, concerning the rights of fishing in the river or wood-cutting in the forest, I don't know exactly which. He regarded it as his duty as a citizen and a man of culture to bring an action against the "clericals." Hearing all about Adelaïda Ivanovna, whom he, of course, remembered, and in whom he had at one time been interested, and learning of the existence of Mitya, he intervened, in spite of all his youthful indignation and his contempt for Fyodor Pavlovich. It was then that he made the latter's acquaintance for the first time, and told him directly that he wished to undertake the child's education. He used long afterwards to tell, as a characteristic touch, that when he began to speak of Mitya, Fyodor Pavlovich looked for some time as though he did not understand what child he was talking about, and even as though he was surprised to hear that he had a little son in the house. The story may have been exaggerated, yet it must have been something like the truth. But Fyodor Pavlovich was all his life fond of acting, of suddenly playing an unex-

pected part, sometimes without any motive for doing so, and even to his own direct disadvantage, as, for instance, in the present case. This habit, however, is characteristic of a very great number of people, some of them very clever ones, not like Fyodor Pavlovich.

Pyotr Alexandrovich carried the business through vigorously, and was appointed, with Fyodor Pavlovich, joint guardian of the child, because, after all, he had a small property, a house and land, left him by his mother. Mitya did, in fact, pass into this cousin's keeping, but as the latter had no family of his own, and after securing the revenues of his estates was in haste to return at once to Paris, he left the boy in charge of one of his cousins, a lady living in Moscow. It came to pass that, settling permanently in Paris, he, too, forgot the child, especially when the February revolution broke out, making an impression on his mind that he remembered all the rest of his life. The Moscow lady died, and Mitya passed into the care of one of her married daughters. I believe he changed his home a fourth time later on. I won't enlarge upon that now, as I shall have much to tell later of Fyodor Pavlovich's firstborn, and must confine myself now to the most essential facts about him, without which I could not begin my story.

In the first place, this Mitya, or rather Dmitri Fyodorovich, was the only one of Fyodor Pavlovich's three sons who grew up in the belief that he had property, and that he would be independent on coming of age. He spent an irregular boyhood and youth. He did not finish his studies at the gymnasium, got into a military school, then went to the Caucasus, was promoted, fought a duel, and was degraded to the ranks, earned promotion again, led a wild life, and spent a good deal of money.

He did not begin to receive any income from Fyodor Pavlovich until he came of age, and until then kept getting into debt. He saw and got to know his father, Fyodor Pavlovich, for the first time on coming of age, when he visited our neighbourhood on purpose to settle with him about his property. Even then he seems not to have liked his father. He did not stay long with him, and made haste to get away, having only succeeded in obtaining a certain sum of money, and entering into an agreement for future payments from the estate, of the revenues and value of which he was unable (a fact worthy of note), upon this occasion, to get a statement from his father. Fyodor Pavlovich remarked for the first time then (this, too, should be noted) that Mitya had an exaggerated and mistaken idea of his property. Fyodor Pavlovich was very well satisfied with this, as it fell in with his own designs. He gathered that the young man was frivolous, unruly, of violent passions, impatient, and dissipated, and that if he could only obtain ready money he would be satisfied, although only, of course, for a short time. So Fyodor Pavlovich began to take advantage of this, sending him from time to time small doles, irregular remittances. In the end, when, four years later, Mitya, losing patience, came a second time to our little town to settle up once for all with his father, it suddenly turned out to his amazement that he had nothing, that it was even difficult to get an account, that he had received the whole value of his property in sums of money from Fyodor Pavlovich, and was perhaps even in debt to him, that by various agreements into which he had, of his own desire, entered at various previous dates, he had no right to demand anything more, and so on, and so on. The young man was over-whelmed, suspected dishonesty and cheating, was almost beside himself, and, as it were, lost his head. It was indeed this circumstance that led to the catastrophe, the account of which forms the subject of my first introductory story, or rather the external side of it. But before I pass to that story I must tell about Fyodor Pavlovich's other two sons, and of their origin.

## CHAPTER III
### THE SECOND MARRIAGE
### AND THE SECOND FAMILY

VERY shortly after getting the four-year-old Mitya off his hands Fyodor Pavlovich married a second time. His second marriage lasted eight years. He took this second wife, Sofya Ivanovna, also a very young girl, from another province, where he had gone upon some small piece of business in company with a Jew. Though Fyodor Pavlovich was a drunkard and a lecher he never neglected investing his capital, and managed his business affairs very successfully, though, no doubt, not over-scrupulously. Sofya Ivanovna was the daughter of an obscure deacon, and was left from childhood an orphan without relations. She grew up in the house of a wealthy old lady, General Vorohov's widow, who was at once her benefactress and tormentor. I do not know the details, but I have only heard that the orphan girl, a meek, gentle, long-suffering creature, was once cut down from a halter in which she was hanging from a nail in the lumber-room, so terrible were her sufferings from the crotchets and everlasting nagging of this old woman, who was apparently not bad-hearted but had become an insufferable tyrant through idleness.

Fyodor Pavlovich offered her his hand; inquiries were made about him and he was sent packing. But again, as in his first marriage, he proposed an elopement to the orphan. There is very little doubt that she would not on any account have married him if she had learned a little more about him in time. But he came from another province; besides, what could a little girl of sixteen know about it, except that she would be better off at the bottom of the river than remaining with her benefactress. So the poor child exchanged a benefactress for a benefactor. Fyodor Pavlovich did not get a penny this time, for the general's widow was furious. She gave them nothing and cursed them both into the bargain. But this time he had not even reckoned on a dowry; what allured him was the remarkable beauty of the innocent girl, above all her innocent appearance, which made a deep impression on a vicious sensualist who had hitherto admired only the coarser types of feminine beauty.

"Those innocent eyes slit my soul up like a razor," he used to say afterwards, with his loathsome snigger. In a man so depraved this might, of course, mean no more than sensual attraction. As he had received no dowry with his wife, and had, so to speak, taken her "from the halter," he did not stand on ceremony with her. Making her feel that she had "wronged" him, he took advantage of her phenomenal meekness and submissiveness to trample on the elementary decencies of marriage. He gathered loose women into his house, and carried on orgies of debauchery in his wife's presence. To show what a pass things had come to, I may mention that Grigory, the gloomy, stupid, obstinate, argumentative servant, who had hated his first mistress, Adelaïda Ivanovna, took the side of his new mistress. He championed her cause, abusing Fyodor Pavlovich in a manner

little befitting a servant, and on one occasion broke up the revels and drove all the disorderly women out of the house by main force. In the end this unhappy young woman, kept in terror since childhood, fell a victim to that kind of nervous disease which is most frequently found in peasant women who are said to be possessed by devils. At times, after terrible fits of hysterics, she even lost her reason. Yet she bore Fyodor Pavlovich two sons, Ivan and Alexey, the elder in the first year of marriage and the second three years later. When she died, little Alexey was in his fourth year, and, strange as it seems, I know that he remembered his mother all his life, like a dream, of course. At her death almost exactly the same thing happened to the two little boys as to their elder brother, Mitya. They were completely forgotten and abandoned by their father. They were looked after by the same Grigory and lived in his cottage, where they were found by the tyrannical old lady who had brought up their mother. She was still alive, and had not, all those eight years, forgotten the insult done her. All that time she had been getting exact information as to her Sofya's manner of life, and hearing of her illness and hideous surroundings she declared aloud two or three times to her retainers:

"It serves her right. God has punished her for her ingratitude."

Exactly three months after Sofya Ivanovna's death the general's widow suddenly appeared in our town, and went straight to Fyodor Pavlovich's house. She spent only half an hour in the town but she accomplished a great deal. It was evening. Fyodor Pavlovich, whom she had not seen for those eight years, came in to her tipsy. The story is that instantly upon seeing him, without any sort of explanation,

8

FYODOR'S SECOND MARRIAGE

she gave him two good, resounding slaps in the face, seized him by a tuft of hair, and shook him three times up and down. Then, without a word, she went straight to the cottage to the two boys. Seeing, at the first glance, that they were unwashed and in dirty linen, she promptly gave Grigory, too, a slap in the face, and announcing that she would carry off both the children she wrapped them just as they were in a plaid, put them in the carriage, and drove off to her own town. Grigory accepted the blow like a devoted slave, without a rude word, and when he escorted the old lady to her carriage he made her a low bow and pronounced impressively that, "God would repay her for the orphans." "You are a blockhead all the same," the old lady shouted to him as she drove away.

Fyodor Pavlovich, thinking it over, decided that it was a good thing and did not refuse his formal consent to having his children brought up by the general's widow. As for the slaps she had given him, he drove all over town telling the story.

It happened that the old lady died soon after this, but she left the boys in her will a thousand roubles each "for their instruction, and so that all be spent on them without fail, with the condition that it be so portioned out as to last till they are of age, for even a pittance of this sort is sufficient for such children, and if other people wish to open up their purses, let them." I have not read the will myself, but I heard that it did contain something queer of the sort, very whimsically expressed. The old woman's principal heir, Yefim Petrovich Polenov, the Marshal of Nobility of the province, turned out, however, to be an honest man. Having communicated with Fyodor Pavlovich, and discerning at once that he could

extract nothing from him for his children's education (though the latter never directly refused but only procrastinated as he always did in such cases, and was, indeed, at times effusively sentimental), Yefim Petrovich took a personal interest in the orphans. He became especially fond of the younger, Alexey, who lived for a long while as one of his family. I beg the reader to note this from the beginning. And to Yefim Petrovich, a man of a nobility and kindness rarely to be met with, the young men were more indebted for their education and bringing up than to any one. He kept the two thousand roubles left to them by the general's widow intact, so that by the time they came of age their portions had been doubled by the accumulation of interest. He educated them both at his own expense, and certainly spent far more than a thousand roubles upon each of them. I won't enter into a detailed account of their boyhood and youth, but will only mention a few of the most important circumstances. Of the elder, Ivan, I will only say that he grew into a somewhat morose and reserved, though far from timid, boy. At ten years old he had realised that they were living not in their own home but on other people's charity, and that their father was a man of whom it was disgraceful to speak. This boy began very early, almost in his infancy (so they say at least), to show a brilliant and unusual aptitude for learning. I don't know precisely why, but he left the family of Yefim Petrovich when he was hardly thirteen, entering a Moscow gymnasium, and boarding with an experienced and celebrated teacher, an old friend of Yefim Petrovich. Ivan used to declare afterwards that this was all due to the "ardour for good works" of Yefim Petrovich, who was captivated by the idea that a boy of

9

genius should be trained by a teacher of genius. But neither Yefim Petrovich nor this teacher was living when the young man graduated from the gymnasium and entered the university. As Yefim Petrovich had made no provision for the payment of the tyrannical old lady's legacy, which had grown from one thousand to two, it was delayed, owing to formalities inevitable in Russia, and the young man was in great straits for the first two years at the university, as he was forced to keep himself all the time he was studying. It must be noted that he did not even attempt to communicate with his father, perhaps from pride, from contempt for him, or perhaps because of his cool common sense, which told him that from such a father he would get no assistance worth mentioning. However that may have been, the young man was by no means despondent and succeeded in getting work, at first doing miserably paid tutoring and afterwards getting paragraphs on street incidents into the newspapers under the signature of "Eye-Witness." These paragraphs, it was said, were so interesting and piquant that they were snapped up. This alone showed the young man's practical and intellectual superiority over the masses of needy and unfortunate students of both sexes who hang about the offices of the newspapers and magazines, from morning till night, unable to think of anything better than everlasting entreaties for copying and translations from the French. Having once got into touch with the editors Ivan Fyodorovich always kept up his connection with them, and in his latter years at the university he published brilliant reviews of books upon various special subjects, so that he became well known in literary circles. But only in his last year he suddenly succeeded in attracting the attention of a far wider circle of readers, so that a great many people noticed and remembered him. It was rather a curious incident. When he had just left the university and was preparing to go abroad upon his two thousand roubles, Ivan Fyodorovich published in one of the larger newspapers a strange article, which attracted general notice, on a subject of which he might have been supposed to know nothing, as he was a student of natural science. The article dealt with a subject which was being debated everywhere at the time — the question of the ecclesiastical courts. After discussing several opinions on the subject he went on to explain his own view. What was most striking about the article was its tone, and its unexpected conclusion. Many of the Church party regarded him as decidedly on their side. And yet not only the anti-clericals but even atheists joined them in their applause. Finally some sagacious persons opined that the article was nothing but an impudent satirical burlesque. I mention this incident particularly because in due time this article reached the famous monastery in our neighbourhood, where the brethren, being particularly interested in the question of the ecclesiastical courts, were completely bewildered by it. Learning the author's name, they were interested in his being a native of the town and the son of "that Fyodor Pavlovich." And just then it was that the author himself made his appearance among us.

Why Ivan Fyodorovich had come amongst us I remember asking myself at the time with a certain uneasiness. This fateful visit, which was the first step leading to so many consequences, I never fully explained to myself. It seemed strange on the face of it that a young man so learned, so proud, and apparently so cautious, should suddenly visit such an infamous house and a father who had ignored him all his life, hardly knew him, did not remember him, and would not under any circumstances have given him money, though he was always afraid that his sons Ivan and Alexey would come to ask him for it. And here the young man was staying in the house of such a father, had been living with him for two months, and they were on the best possible terms. This last fact was a special cause of wonder to many others as well as to me. Pyotr Alexandrovich Miüsov, of whom I have spoken already, the cousin of Fyodor Pavlovich's first wife, happened to be in the neighbourhood again on a visit to his estate. He had come from Paris, which was his permanent home. I remember that he was more surprised than any one when he made the acquaintance of the young man, who interested him extremely, and with whom he sometimes argued and not without an inner pang compared himself in acquirements.

"He is proud," he said to us at the time, "he will never be in want of money; he has got enough to go abroad now. What does he want here? Every one can see that he hasn't come for money, for his father would never give him any. He has no taste for drink and dissipation, and yet his father can't do without him. They get on so famously together!"

That was the truth; the young man had an unmistakable influence over the old man, who, though often extremely and even spitefully perverse, positively appeared to be behaving more decently and even seemed at times ready to obey his son.

It was only later that we learned that Ivan had come partly at the request of, and in the interests of, his elder brother, Dmitri, whom he saw for the first time on this very visit, though before leaving Moscow he had been in correspondence with him about an important matter of more concern to Dmitri than to himself.

What that business was the reader will learn fully in due time. Yet even when I did know of this special circumstance I still felt Ivan Fyodorovich to be an enigmatic figure, and thought his visit rather puzzling.

I may add that Ivan appeared at the time in the light of a mediator between his father and his elder brother Dmitri, who was in open quarrel with his father and even planning to bring an action against him.

The little family, I repeat, was now united for the first time, and some of its members met for the first time in their lives. The younger brother, Alexey, had already been a year among us, having been the first of the three to arrive. It is of that brother Alexey I find it most difficult to speak in this introduction before I have brought him on the scene. Yet I must give some preliminary account of him, if only to explain one queer fact, which is that I have to introduce my future hero to the reader wearing the cassock of a novice. Yes, he had been for the last year in our monastery, and seemed willing to be cloistered there for the rest of his life.

## CHAPTER IV
### THE THIRD SON, ALYOSHA

He was only twenty, his brother Ivan was in his twenty-fourth year at the time, while their elder brother Dmitri was in his twenty-eighth year. First of all, I must explain that this young man, Alyosha, was not a fanatic, and, in my opinion, at least, was not even a mystic. I may as well state my full opinion from the beginning. He was simply an early lover of humanity, and if he adopted the monastic way of life it was simply because at that time it struck him, so to say, as the ideal escape for his soul struggling as it was from the darkness of worldly wickedness to the light of love. And the reason this way of life struck him thus was that he found here at that time an extraordinary being, as he thought, our celebrated elder, Zosima, to whom he became attached with all the first ardour of his unappeasable heart. But I do not dispute that he was very strange even at that time, and had been so indeed from his cradle. I have mentioned already, by the way, that though he lost his mother in his fourth year he remembered her all his life — her face, her caresses, "as though she stood living before me." Such memories may persist, as every one knows, from an even earlier age, even from two years old, but only standing out through a whole lifetime like spots of light out of darkness, like a corner torn out of a huge picture, which has all faded and vanished except that fragment. That is how it was with him. He remembered one still summer evening, an open window, the slanting rays of the setting sun (that he recalled most vividly of all); in a corner of the room the holy image, before it a lighted lamp, and on her knees before the image his mother, sobbing hysterically with shrieks and moans, snatching him up in both arms, squeezing him close till it hurt, and praying for him to the Mother of God, holding him out in both arms to the image as though to put him under the Mother's protection . . . and suddenly a nurse runs in and snatches him from her in terror. That was the picture! And Alyosha remembered his mother's face at that minute. He used to say that it was frenzied but beautiful, as he remembered. But he rarely cared to speak of this

memory to any one. In his childhood and youth he was by no means expansive, and talked little indeed, but not from distrust or shyness or a sullen unsociability; quite the contrary, from something different, from a sort of inner preoccupation entirely personal and unconcerned with other people, but so important to him that he seemed, as it were, to forget others on account of it. But he was fond of people: he seemed throughout his life to put implicit trust in people: yet no one ever looked on him as a simpleton or a naïve person. There was something about him which made one feel at once (and it was so all his life afterwards) that he did not care to be a judge of others — that he would never take it upon himself to criticise and would never condemn any one for anything. He seemed, indeed, to accept everything without the least condemnation, though often grieving bitterly: and this was so much so that no one could surprise or frighten him even in his earliest youth. Coming at twenty to his father's house, which was a very sink of filthy debauchery, he, chaste and pure as he was, simply withdrew in silence when to look on was unbearable, but without the slightest sign of contempt or condemnation. His father, who had once been in a dependent position, and so was sensitive and ready to take offence, met him at first with distrust and sullenness. "He does not say much," he used to grumble, "and thinks the more." But soon, within a fortnight indeed, he took to embracing him and kissing him terribly often, with drunken tears, with sottish sentimentality, yet he evidently felt a real and deep affection for him, such as he had never been capable of feeling for any one before.

Every one, indeed, loved this young man wherever he went, and it was so from his earliest childhood. When he entered the household of his patron and benefactor, Yefim Petrovich Polenov, he gained the hearts of all the family, so that they looked on him quite as their own child. Yet he entered the house at such a tender age that he could not have acted from design or artfulness in winning affection. So that the gift of making himself loved directly and naturally was inherent in him, in his very being so to speak. It was the same at school, though he seemed to be just one of those children who are distrusted, sometimes ridiculed, and even hated by their schoolfellows. He was dreamy, for instance, and rather solitary. From his earliest childhood he was fond of creeping into a corner to read, and yet he was a general favourite all the while he was at school. He was rarely playful or merry, but any one could see at the first glance that this was not from any sullenness. On the contrary, he was serene and even-tempered. He never tried to show off before his schoolfellows. Perhaps because of this, he was never afraid of any one, yet the boys immediately understood that he was not proud of his fearlessness and seemed to be unaware that he was brave and fearless. He never bore a grudge. It would happen that an hour after the offence he would address the offender or answer some question with as trustful and open an expression as though nothing had happened between them. And it was not that he seemed to have forgotten or intentionally forgiven the affront, but simply that he did not regard it as an affront, and this completely conquered and captivated the boys. He had one characteristic which made all his schoolfellows from the bottom class to the top want to make fun of him, not from malice but because it amused them. This characteristic was a wild frantic bashfulness and chastity. He could not bear to hear certain words and certain conversations about women. It is unfortunately impossible to eradicate these words and conversations in schools. Boys pure in mind and heart, almost children, are fond of talking in school among themselves, and even aloud, of things, pictures, and images of which even soldiers would sometimes hesitate to speak. More than that, much that soldiers have no knowledge or conception of is familiar to quite young children of our intellectual and higher classes. There is no moral depravity, no real corrupt inner cynicism in it, but there is the appearance of it, and it is often looked upon among them as something refined, subtle, smart, and worthy of imitation. Seeing that Alyosha Karamazov put his fingers in his ears when they talked of "that," they used sometimes to crowd round him, pull his hands away, and shout nastiness into both ears, while he struggled, slipped to the floor, tried to hide himself without uttering one word of abuse, enduring their insults in silence. But at last they left him alone and gave up taunting him with being a "regular girl," and what's more they looked upon it with compassion. And by the way, he was always one of the best in the class but was never first.

After Yefim Petrovich's death, Alyosha spent two more years at the provincial gymnasium. Almost immediately after the man's decease the inconsolable widow went for a long visit to Italy with her whole family, which consisted only of persons of the female sex. Alyosha found himself in the house of two distant relations of Yefim Petrovich, ladies whom he had never seen before. On what terms he lived with them he did not know himself. It was very characteristic of him, indeed, that he never cared at whose expense he was living. In that respect he was a striking contrast to his elder brother Ivan, who struggled with poverty for his first two years in the university, maintained himself by his own efforts, and had from childhood been bitterly conscious of living at the expense of his benefactor. But this strange trait in Alyosha's character must not, I think, be condemned too severely, for at the slightest acquaintance with him any one would have perceived that Alyosha was one of those youths, verging on the "fool in Christ" type, who, if they were suddenly to come into possession of a large fortune, would not hesitate to give it away for the asking, either for good works or perhaps to a clever rogue. In general he seemed scarcely to know the value of money, not, of course, in a literal sense. When he was given pocket-money, which he never asked for, he was either terribly careless of it so that it was gone in a moment, or he kept it for weeks together, not knowing what to do with it.

In later years Pyotr Alexandrovich Miüsov, a man very sensitive on the score of money and bourgeois honesty, pronounced the following judgment, after getting to know Alyosha:

"Here is perhaps the one man in the world whom you might leave alone without a penny, in the centre of an unknown town of a million inhabitants, and he would not come to harm, he would not die of cold and hunger, for he would be fed and sheltered at once; and if he were not, he would find a shelter for himself, and it would cost him no effort or humiliation. And to shelter him would be no burden, but, on the contrary, would probably be looked on as a pleasure."

He did not finish his studies at the gymnasium. A year before the end of the course he suddenly announced to the ladies that he was going to see his father about a plan which had occurred to him. They were sorry and unwilling to let him go. The journey was not an expensive one, and the ladies would not let him pawn his watch, a parting present from his benefactor's family. They provided him liberally with money and even fitted him out with new clothes and linen. But he returned half the money they gave him, saying that he intended to go third class. On his arrival in the town he made no answer to his father's first inquiry why he had come before completing his studies, and seemed, so they say, unusually pensive. It soon became known that he was looking for his mother's grave. He practically acknowledged at the time that that was the only object of his visit. But it can hardly have been the whole reason for it. It is more probable that he himself did not understand and could not explain what had suddenly arisen in his soul and drawn him irresistibly into a new, unknown, but inevitable path. Fyodor Pavlovich could not show him where his second wife was buried, for he had never visited her grave since her coffin had been covered with earth, and in the course of years had entirely forgotten where she was buried.

Fyodor Pavlovich, by the way, for some time previously had not been living in our town. Three or four years after his wife's death he had gone to the south of Russia and finally turned up in Odessa, where he spent several years. He made the acquaintance at first, in his own words, "of a lot of low Jews, Jewesses, and Jewkins," and ended by being received by "Jews high and low alike." It may be presumed that at this period he developed a peculiar faculty for making and squeezing out money. He finally returned to our town

ALYOSHA THE BOY

only three years before Alyosha's arrival. His former acquaintances found him looking terribly aged, although he was by no means an old man. He behaved not exactly with more dignity but with more effrontery. The former buffoon showed an insolent propensity for making buffoons of others. His vile behaviour with women was not simply what it used to be, but even more revolting. In a short time he opened a great number of new pot-houses in the district. It was evident that he was worth perhaps a hundred thousand roubles or not much less. Many of the inhabitants of the town and district were soon in his debt, and, of course, had given good security. Of late, too, he looked somehow bloated and seemed more irresponsible, more uneven, had sunk into a sort of incoherence, used to begin one thing and end with another, as though he were falling to pieces. He was more and more frequently drunk, and, if it had not been for the same servant Grigory, who by that time had aged considerably, too, and used to look after him sometimes almost like a nurse, Fyodor Pavlovich might have got into terrible scrapes. Alyosha's arrival seemed to affect him even morally, as though something had awakened in this prematurely old man which had long been dead in his soul.

"Do you know," he used often to say, looking at Alyosha, "that you are like her, 'the possessed woman' " — that was what he used to call his dead wife, Alyosha's mother. Grigory it was who pointed out the "possessed woman's" grave to Alyosha. He took him to our town cemetery and showed him in a remote corner a cast-iron tombstone, cheap but decently kept, on which were inscribed the name and age of the deceased and the date of her death, and below something by way of a

funerary quatrain, such as are commonly used on old-fashioned middle-class tombs. To Alyosha's amazement this tombstone turned out to be Grigory's doing. He had put it up on the poor "possessed woman's" grave at his own expense, after Fyodor Pavlovich, whom he had often pestered about the grave, had gone to Odessa, abandoning the grave and all his memories. Alyosha showed no particular emotion at the sight of his mother's grave. He only listened to Grigory's sententious and solemn account of the erection of the tombstone; he stood with bowed head and walked away without uttering a word. It was perhaps a year before he visited the cemetery again. But this little episode was not without an influence upon Fyodor Pavlovich — and a very peculiar one. He suddenly took a thousand roubles to our monastery to pay for requiems for the soul of his wife; but not for the second, Alyosha's mother, the "possessed woman," but for the first, Adelaïda Ivanovna, who used to thrash him. In the evening of the same day he got drunk and abused the monks to Alyosha. He himself was far from being religious; he had probably never put a five-copeck candle before the image of a saint. Strange impulses of sudden feeling and sudden thought are common in men of that sort.

I have mentioned already that he had come to look bloated. His countenance at this time testified unmistakably to the character of the life he had led. Besides the long fleshy bags under his little eyes, always full of insolence, suspicion, and mockery; besides the multitude of deep wrinkles in his small fat face, below his sharp chin the Adam's apple hung fleshy and long, like a purse, which gave him a peculiar, repulsive, sensual appearance; add to that a voluptuary's wide mouth with full lips, between which could be seen little stumps of black decayed teeth. He slobbered every time he began to speak. He was fond indeed of making fun of his own face, though, I believe, he was well satisfied with it. He used particularly to point to his nose, which was not very large, but very delicate and conspicuously aquiline. "A regular Roman nose," he used to say; "with my Adam's apple I've quite the countenance of an ancient Roman patrician of the decadent period." He seemed proud of it.

Not long after visiting his mother's grave Alyosha suddenly announced to him that he wanted to enter the monastery, and that the monks were willing to receive him as a novice. He explained that this was his strong desire, and that he was solemnly asking his consent as a father. The old man knew that the elder Zosima, who was living in the monastery hermitage, had made a special impression upon his "gentle boy."

"That is the most honest monk among them, of course," he observed, after listening in thoughtful silence to Alyosha, and seeming scarcely surprised at his request. "H'm! . . . So that's where you want to go, my gentle boy?"

He was half drunk, and suddenly he grinned his slow half-drunken grin, which was not without a certain cunning and tipsy slyness. "H'm! . . . I had a presentiment that you would end in something like this. Would you believe it? You were making straight for it. Well, to be sure you have your own two thousand. That's a dowry for you. And I'll never desert you, my angel. And I'll pay what's wanted for you there, if they ask for it. But, of course, if they don't ask, why should we worry them? What do you say? You know, you spend money like a canary, two grains a

week. H'm! . . . Do you know that near one monastery there's a place outside the town where every baby knows there are none but 'the monks' wives' living, as they are called. Thirty women, I believe. I have been there myself. You know, it's interesting in its own way, of course, for a change. The worst of it is, it's awfully Russian. There are no French women there. Of course they could be gotten, there is plenty of money there. If they get to hear of it they'll come along. Well, there's nothing of that sort here, no 'monks' wives,' and two hundred monks. They're honest. They keep the fasts. I admit it. . . . H'm. . . . So you want to be a monk? And do you know I'm sorry to lose you, Alyosha; would you believe it, I've really grown fond of you? Well, it's a good opportunity. You'll pray for us sinners; we have sinned too much here. I've always been thinking who would pray for me, and whether there's any one in the world to do it. My dear boy, I'm awfully stupid about that. You wouldn't believe it. Awfully. You see, however stupid I am about it, I keep thinking, I keep thinking—from time to time, of course, not all the while. It's impossible, I think, for the devils to forget to drag me down to hell with their hooks when I die. Then I wonder—hooks? Where would they get them? What of? Iron hooks? Where do they forge them? Have they a factory there of some sort? The monks in the monastery probably believe that there's a ceiling in hell, for instance. Now I'm ready to believe in hell, but without a ceiling. It makes it more refined, more enlightened, more Lutheran that is. And, after all, what does it matter whether it has a ceiling or not? But, do you know, there's a damnable question involved in it? If there's no ceiling there can be no hooks, and if there

are no hooks it all breaks down, which is unlikely again, for then there would be none to
drag me down to hell, and if they don't drag
me down what justice is there in the world?
*Il faudrait les inventer*, those hooks, on purpose for me alone, for, if you only knew, Alyosha, what a loose fish I am."

"There are no hooks there," said Alyosha,
looking gently and seriously at his father.

"Yes, yes, only the shadows of hooks. I
know, I know. That's how a Frenchman described hell: '*J'ai vu l'ombre d'un cocher qui
avec l'ombre d'une brosse frottait l'ombre
d'une carosse.*' How do you know there are no
hooks, darling? When you've lived with the
monks you'll sing a different tune. But go and
get at the truth there, and then come and tell
me. Anyway it's easier going to the other
world if one knows for a fact what there is
there. Besides, it will be more seemly for you
with the monks than here with me, with a
drunken old man and his wenches . . . though
you're like an angel, nothing touches you. And
I dare say nothing will touch you there. That's
why I give you my permission, because I hope
it will be so. You've got all your wits about
you. Go ahead and get over it; you will be
cured and come back again. And I will wait
for you. I feel that you're the only creature in
the world who has not condemned me. My
dear boy, I feel it, you know. I can't help feeling it."

And he even began blubbering. He was sentimental. He was vicious and sentimental.

## CHAPTER V
### ELDERS

SOME of my readers may imagine that my
young man was a sickly, ecstatic, poorly developed creature, a pale dreamer, a feeble,
consumptive little fellow. On the contrary,
Alyosha was at this time a well-grown, red-
cheeked, clear-eyed lad of nineteen, radiant
with health. He was very handsome, too,
graceful, moderately tall, with hair of a dark
brown, with a regular, rather long, oval-
shaped face, and wide-set dark grey, shining
eyes; he was very thoughtful, and apparently
very serene. I shall be told, perhaps, that red
cheeks are not incompatible with fanaticism
and mysticism; but I fancy that Alyosha was
more of a realist than any one. Oh! no doubt,
in the monastery he fully believed in miracles,
but, to my thinking, miracles are never a stumbling-block to the realist. It is not miracles
that dispose realists to belief. The true realist,
if he is an unbeliever, will always find strength
and ability to disbelieve in an actual miracle,
and if he is confronted with a miracle as an
irrefutable fact he would rather disbelieve his
own senses than admit the fact. Even if he admits it, he admits it as a natural phenomenon
till then unknown to him. Faith does not, in
the realist, spring from the miracle but the
miracle from faith. If the realist once believes,
then he is bound by his very realism to admit
the miraculous also. The Apostle Thomas said
that he would not believe till he saw, but when
he did see he said, "My Lord and my God!"
Was it the miracle forced him to believe?
Most likely not, but he believed solely because
he desired to believe and possibly he fully believed in his secret heart even when he said,
"I do not believe till I see."

I shall be told, perhaps, that Alyosha was
stupid, undeveloped, had not finished his studies, and so on. That he did not finish his studies
is true, but to say that he was stupid or foolish
would be a great injustice. I'll simply repeat
what I have said above. He entered upon this

path only because, at that time, it alone struck his imagination and presented itself to him as offering an ideal means of escape for his soul from darkness to light. Add to that that he was to some extent a youth of our own time — that is, honest in nature, demanding the truth, seeking it and believing in it, and seeking to serve it at once with all the strength of his soul, demanding immediate action, and ready to sacrifice everything, life itself, for it. Though these young men unhappily fail to understand that the sacrifice of life is, in many cases, the easiest of all sacrifices, and that to sacrifice, for instance, five or six years of their seething youth to hard and tedious study, if only to multiply ten-fold their powers of serving the truth and the cause they have set before them as their goal — such a sacrifice is utterly beyond the strength of many of them. The path Alyosha chose was a path going in the opposite direction, but he chose it with the same thirst for swift and noble action. As soon as he reflected seriously he was convinced of the existence of God and immortality, and at once he naturally said to himself: "I want to live for immortality, and I will accept no compromise." In the same way, if he had decided that God and immortality did not exist, he would at once have become an atheist and a socialist. For socialism is not merely the labour question, or the question of the so-called fourth estate, it is above all things the atheistic question, the question of the form taken by atheism to-day, the question of the tower of Babel built without God, not to mount to heaven from earth but to bring heaven down to earth. Alyosha found it strange and impossible to go on living as before. It is written: "Give all that thou hast to the poor and follow Me, if thou wouldst be perfect." Alyosha

said to himself: "I can't give two roubles instead of 'all,' and only go to mass instead of 'following Him.'" Perhaps his memories of childhood brought back our monastery, to which his mother may have taken him to mass. Perhaps the slanting sunlight and the holy image to which his poor "possessed" mother had held him up still acted upon his imagination. Brooding on these things, he may have come to us perhaps only to see whether here he could sacrifice all or only "two roubles," and in the monastery he met this elder. . . .

This elder was, as I have already explained, elder Zosima. I must digress to say a few words about what an "elder" is in Russian monasteries, and I am sorry that I do not feel very competent to do so. I will try, however, to give a superficial account of it in a few words. Authorities on the subject assert that the institution of "elders" is of recent date, not more than a hundred years old in our monasteries, though in the orthodox East, especially at Sinai and Athos, it has existed over a thousand years. It is maintained that the institution existed in ancient times in Russia also, but owing to the calamities which befell Russia — the Tatars, civil war, the interruption of relations with the East after the destruction of Constantinople — it fell into oblivion and "elders" disappeared. It was revived among us towards the end of the last century by one of the great "ascetics," as they called him, Païssy Velichkovsky, and his disciples. But to-day, even after a hundred years, it exists in a few monasteries only, and has sometimes been almost persecuted as an innovation unheard of in Russia. It flourished especially in the celebrated Kozelski Optin Monastery. When and how it was introduced into our monastery I cannot say. There had already been three such elders and Zosima was the last of them. But he was almost dying of weakness and disease, and they had no one to take his place. The question for our monastery was an important one, for it had not been distinguished by anything in particular till then: they had neither relics of saints, nor wonder-working ikons, nor glorious traditions, nor historical exploits in the service of the country. It had flourished and been glorious all over Russia through its elders, to see and hear whom pilgrims had flocked for thousands of miles from all parts.

What then is an elder? An elder is one who takes your soul, your will, into his soul and his will. When you choose an elder, you renounce your own will and yield it to him in complete submission, complete self-abnegation. This novitiate, this terrible discipline, is undertaken voluntarily, in the hope of self-conquest, of self-mastery, in order, after a life of obedience, to attain perfect freedom, that is, from self; to escape the lot of those who have lived their whole lives without finding their true selves in themselves. This institution of elders is not founded on theory, but was derived in the East from the practice of a thousand years. The obligations due to an elder are not the ordinary "obedience" which has always existed in our Russian monasteries. What is involved here is continual confession to the elder by all who have submitted themselves to him, and an indissoluble bond between him and them.

The story is told, for instance, that in the early days of Christianity one such novice, failing to fulfil some command laid upon him by his elder, left his monastery in Syria and went to Egypt. There, after great exploits, he was found worthy at last to suffer torture and a martyr's death for the faith. When the Church, regarding him as a saint, was burying him, suddenly, at the deacon's exhortation, "Depart all ye unbaptized," the coffin containing the martyr's body left its place and was cast forth from the church, and this took place three times. And only at last they learnt that this holy man had broken his vow of obedience and left his elder, and, therefore, could not be forgiven without the elder's absolution in spite of his great deeds. Only after this could the funeral take place. This, of course, is only an old legend. But here is a recent and true occurrence.

In our own day a monk who was dwelling at Athos was suddenly commanded by his elder to quit the place, which he loved as a sacred and tranquil haven of refuge, and to go, first to Jerusalem to do homage to the Holy Places and thence north to Siberia: "There is the place for thee and not here." The monk, overwhelmed with sorrow, went to the Œcumenical Patriarch at Constantinople and besought him to release him from his vow of obedience. But the Patriarch replied that not only was he unable to release him, but there was not and could not be on earth a power which could release him except the elder who had himself laid that vow upon him. In this way the elders are endowed in certain cases with unbounded and unfathomable authority. That is why in many of our monasteries the institution at first met with extreme hostility. Meantime the elders gained high respect among the masses. Simple people as well as men of the highest station flocked, for instance, to the elders of our monastery to confess their doubts, their sins, and their sufferings, and ask for counsel and admonition. Seeing this, the opponents of the elders added to other accusations this, that the sacrament of confession was being arbitrarily and frivolously degraded, though the continual opening of the heart to the elder by the novice or the layman had nothing of the character of the sacrament. In the end, however, the institution of elders has been retained and is gradually becoming established in Russian monasteries. It is true, perhaps, that this tried and tested thousand-year-old instrument for the emancipation of man from slavery and his moral regeneration may become a two-edged tool and it may lead some not to humility and complete self-control but to the most satanic pride, that is, to bondage and not to freedom.

The elder Zosima was about sixty-five. He came of a family of landowners, had been in the army in his early youth, and served in the Caucasus as an officer. He had, no doubt, struck Alyosha by some peculiar quality of his soul. Alyosha lived in the cell of the elder, who grew very fond of him and made him his intimate. It must be noted that at that time Alyosha was not as yet bound by any obligation and could go where he pleased and be absent for whole days. If he wore the monastic dress it was voluntarily, so as not to be different from the other inhabitants of the monastery. No doubt he liked it, too. Possibly his youthful imagination was deeply stirred by the power and fame of his elder. It was commonly said that so many people had for years past come to open their hearts to Father Zosima and to entreat him for words of advice and healing, he had taken into his soul so many revelations and confessions, so much contrition, that he had acquired the keenest intuition and could tell from a stranger's face what he wanted, and what pain was tearing at his conscience. He sometimes astounded and almost alarmed his visitors by his knowledge of their secrets before they had spoken a word.

Alyosha noticed that many, almost all, went in to the elder for the first time with apprehension and uneasiness, but came out with bright and happy faces. Alyosha was particularly struck by the fact that Father Zosima was not at all stern. On the contrary, he was always almost gay in his dealings with people. The monks said that he was drawn precisely to those who were more sinful, and the greater the sinner the more he loved him. There were, no doubt, up to the end of his life, among the monks some who hated and envied him, but they were becoming fewer and they held their peace, though among them were several of high standing in the monastery, for instance, one of the oldest monks distinguished for his long periods of silence and strict fasting. But the majority were on Father Zosima's side and very many of them loved him with all their hearts, warmly and sincerely. Some were almost fanatically devoted to him, and declared, though not quite aloud, that he was a saint, beyond any doubt, and, seeing that his end was near, they anticipated miracles and great glory to the monastery in the immediate future from his relics. Alyosha believed unquestioningly in the miraculous power of the elder, just as he had unquestioning faith in the story of the coffin that flew out of the church. He saw many who came with sick children or relatives and besought the elder to lay hands on them and to pray over them, return shortly after — some the next day — and, falling in tears at the elder's feet, thank him for healing their sick.

Whether they had really been healed or were simply better in the natural course of the disease was a question which did not exist for Alyosha, for he fully believed in the spiritual power of his master and rejoiced in his fame, in his glory, as though it were his own triumph.

His heart beat loudest, and he beamed, as it were, all over when the elder came out to the gates of the hermitage into the waiting crowd of pilgrims of the humbler class who had flocked from all parts of Russia to see the elder and obtain his blessing. They fell down before him, wept, kissed his feet, kissed the earth on which he stood, and wailed, while the women held up their children to him and brought him the sick "possessed of devils." The elder spoke to them, read a brief prayer over them, blessed them, and dismissed them. Of late he had been so weakened by attacks of illness that he was sometimes unable to leave his cell, and the pilgrims waited several days for him to come out. Alyosha did not wonder why they loved him so, why they fell down before him and wept with emotion merely at seeing his face. Oh! he understood that for the humble soul of the Russian commoner, worn out by grief and toil, and still more by the everlasting injustice and everlasting sin, his own and the world's, it was the greatest need and comfort to find some one or something holy to fall down before and worship: "Among us there is sin, unrighteousness, and temptation, but yet, somewhere on earth there is some one holy and exalted. He possesses righteousness; he knows what righteousness is; so it is not dead upon the earth; so it will come one day to us, too, and rule over all the earth according to the promise."

Alyosha knew that this was just how the people felt and even reasoned. He understood it, but that the elder Zosima was this saint and custodian of God's justice — of that he had no more doubt than the weeping peasants and the sick women who held out their children to the elder. The conviction that after his death the elder would bring extraordinary glory to the monastery was even stronger in Alyosha than in any one there, and, of late, a kind of deep burning inner ecstasy flamed ever higher in his heart. He was not at all troubled at this elder's standing as a solitary example before him.

"No matter. He is holy. He carries in his heart the secret of renewal for all: that power which will, at last, establish righteousness on earth, and all men will be holy and love one another, and there will be neither rich nor poor, neither exalted nor humbled, but all will be as the children of God, and the true Kingdom of Christ will come." That was the dream in Alyosha's heart.

The arrival of his two brothers, whom he had not known till then, seemed to make a great impression on Alyosha. He more quickly made friends with his half-brother Dmitri (though he arrived later) than with his own brother Ivan. He was extremely interested in his brother Ivan, but when the latter had been two months in the town, though they had met fairly often, they were still not intimate. Alyosha was naturally reserved, and he seemed to be expecting something, ashamed of something, while his brother Ivan, though Alyosha noticed at first that he looked long and curiously at him, seemed soon to have left off thinking about him. Alyosha noticed it with some embarrassment. He ascribed his brother's indifference at first to the disparity of their age and education. But he also wondered whether the absence of interest and sympathy in Ivan might be due to some other cause entirely unknown to him. He kept fancying that Ivan was absorbed in something — something inward and important — that he was striving towards some goal, perhaps very hard to attain, and that that was why he had no thought for him. Alyosha wondered, too, whether there was not some contempt on the part of the learned atheist for him — a silly novice. He knew for certain that his brother was an atheist. He could not take offence at this contempt, if it existed; yet, with an uneasy embarrassment which he did not himself understand, he waited for his brother to come nearer to him. Dmitri used to speak of Ivan with the deepest respect and with a peculiar emotion. From him Alyosha learnt all the details of the important affair which had of late formed such a close and remarkable bond between the two elder brothers. Dmitri's enthusiastic references to Ivan were the more striking in Alyosha's eyes since Dmitri was, compared with Ivan, almost uneducated, and the two brothers were such a contrast in personality and character that it would be difficult to find two men more unlike.

It was at this time that the meeting, or rather gathering, of the members of this ill-assorted family took place in the cell of the elder who had such an extraordinary influence on Alyosha. The pretext for this gathering was really a false one. It was at this time that the difference between Dmitri and his father with regard to money matters seemed at its acutest stage and their relations had become insufferably strained. Fyodor Pavlovich seems to have been the first to suggest, apparently in jest, that they should all meet in Father Zosima's cell, and that, without resorting directly to his mediation, they might more decently come to an understanding under the conciliating influence of the elder's presence. Dmitri, who had never seen the elder, naturally supposed that his father was trying to intimidate him, but, as he secretly blamed himself for his outbursts of temper with his father on several

recent occasions, he accepted the challenge. It must be noted that he was not, like Ivan, staying with his father, but living apart at the other end of the town. It happened that Pyotr Alexandrovich Miüsov, who was staying in the district at the time, caught eagerly at the idea. A Liberal of the forties and fifties, a free-thinker and an atheist, he may have been led on to take a hand in the affair by boredom or the hope of frivolous diversion. He was suddenly seized with the desire to see the monastery and the holy man. As his lawsuit with the monastery still dragged on, he made a pretended attempt to settle it amicably the pretext for seeing the Father Superior. A visitor coming with such laudable intentions might be received with more attention and consideration than if he came from simple curiosity. Pressure from within the monastery was brought to bear on the ailing elder, who of late had scarcely left his cell, and had been forced by illness to deny even his ordinary visitors. In the end he consented to see them, and the day was fixed. "Who has made me a judge over them?" was all he said, smilingly, to Alyosha.

Alyosha was much perturbed when he heard of the proposed visit. Of all the wrangling, quarrelsome party, Dmitri was the only one who could regard the interview seriously. All the others would come from frivolous motives, perhaps insulting to the elder. Alyosha was well aware of that. Ivan and Miüsov would come from curiosity, perhaps of the coarsest kind, while his father might be contemplating some piece of buffoonery. Though he said nothing, Alyosha thoroughly understood his father. The boy, I repeat, was far from being as simple as every one thought him. He awaited the day with a heavy heart. No doubt he was always deeply worried in his heart as to how the family discord could be ended. But his chief anxiety concerned the elder. He trembled for him, for his reputation, and dreaded any affront to him, especially the refined, courteous irony of Miüsov and the supercilious half utterances of the highly educated Ivan. He even wanted to venture on warning the elder, telling him something about them, but, on second thoughts, said nothing. He only sent word the day before, through a friend, to his brother Dmitri, that he loved him and ex-pected him to keep his promise. Dmitri wondered, for he could not remember what he had promised, but he answered by letter that he would do his utmost not to let himself be provoked "by vileness," but that, although he had a deep respect for the elder and for his brother Ivan, he was convinced that the meeting was either a trap for him or an unworthy farce. "Nevertheless I would rather swallow my tongue than be lacking in respect to the sainted man whom you reverence so highly," he wrote. Alyosha was not greatly cheered by the letter.

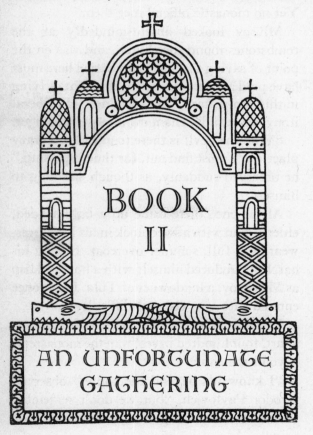

# BOOK II

# AN UNFORTUNATE GATHERING

## CHAPTER I
### THEY ARRIVE AT THE MONASTERY

IT was a warm, bright day at the end of August. The interview with the elder had been fixed for half-past eleven, immediately after late mass. Our visitors were not present at the service, but arrived just as it was over. First an elegant open carriage, drawn by two valuable horses, drove up with Miüsov and a distant relative of his, a young man of twenty, called Pyotr Fomich Kalganov. This young man was preparing to enter the university. Miüsov, with whom he was staying for the time, was trying to persuade him to go abroad to the university of Zürich or Jena. The young man was still undecided. He was thoughtful and absent-minded, as it were. He had a pleasant face, was strongly built, and rather tall. There was a strange fixity in his gaze at times. Like all very absent-minded people he would sometimes stare at a person for quite a while without seeing him. He was silent and rather awkward, but sometimes, when he was alone with some one, he became very talkative in a spasmodic fashion, and would laugh at anything or nothing. But his animation vanished as quickly as it appeared. He was always well and even elegantly dressed; he had already some independent fortune and expectations of much more. He was a friend of Alyosha's.

In an ancient, creaking, but roomy, hired carriage, with a pair of old pinkish-grey horses, a long way behind Miüsov's carriage, came Fyodor Pavlovich, with his son Ivan. Dmitri was late, though he had been informed of the time the evening before. The visitors left their carriage at the hostelry, outside the precincts, and entered the gates of the monastery on foot. Except Fyodor Pavlovich, none of the party had ever seen the monastery, and Miüsov had probably not even been to church for some thirty years. He looked about him with curiosity, and with assumed ease. But, aside from the church and the living quarters, though these too were ordinary enough, he found nothing of interest in the interior of the monastery. The last of the worshippers were coming out of the church, bareheaded and crossing themselves. Among the humbler people were a few of higher rank — two or three ladies and a very old general. They were all staying at the hostelry. Our visitors were at once surrounded by beggars, but none of them gave them anything, except young Kalganov, who took a ten-copeck piece out of his purse, and, nervous and embarrassed — God knows why! — hurriedly gave it to an old woman, saying:

"Divide it equally." None of his companions made any remark upon it, so that he had no reason to be embarrassed; but, perceiving this, he was even more overcome.

It was strange that their arrival did not seem expected, and that they were not received with special honour, though one of them had recently made a donation of a thousand roubles, while another was a very wealthy and highly cultured landowner, upon whom the monastery might become dependent for its fishing-rights if the lawsuit took a certain turn. Yet no monastic official met them.

Miüsov looked absent-mindedly at the tombstones round the church, and was on the point of saying that the dead buried here must have paid a pretty penny for the right of lying in this "holy place," but refrained. His liberal irony was rapidly changing almost into anger.

"Who the devil is there to ask in this crazy place? We must find out, for time is passing," he observed suddenly, as though speaking to himself.

All at once there came up a bald-headed, elderly man with a sweet look in his little eyes, wearing a full, summer overcoat. Lifting his hat, he introduced himself with a honeyed lisp as Maximov, a landowner of Tula. He at once entered into our visitors' difficulty.

"Father Zosima lives in the hermitage, apart, four hundred paces from the monastery, beyond the copse."

"I know it's beyond the copse," observed Fyodor Pavlovich, "but we don't remember the way. It is a long time since we've been here."

"This way, through this gate, and straight across the copse . . . the copse. Come with me, won't you? I'll show you. I have to go . . . I am going myself. This way, this way."

They came out of the gate and turned towards the copse. Maximov, a man of sixty, ran rather than walked, turning sideways to stare at them all, with an incredible degree of nervous curiosity. His eyes bulged.

"You see, we have come to the elder upon business of our own," observed Miüsov severely. "That personage has granted us an audience so to speak, and so, though we thank you for showing us the way, we cannot ask you to accompany us."

"I've been there. I've been already; *un chevalier parfait*," and Maximov snapped his fingers in the air.

"Who is a *chevalier?*" asked Miüsov.

"The elder, the splendid elder, the elder! The honour and glory of the monastery, Zosima. Such an elder!"

But his incoherent talk was cut short by a very pale, wan-looking monk of medium height, wearing a monk's hood, who overtook them. Fyodor Pavlovich and Miüsov stopped.

The monk, with an extremely courteous, profound bow, announced:

"The Father Superior invites all of you gentlemen to dine with him after your visit to the hermitage. At one o'clock, not later. And you also," he added, addressing Maximov.

"That I certainly will, without fail," cried Fyodor Pavlovich, hugely delighted at the invitation. "And, believe me, we've all given our word to behave properly here. . . . And you, Pyotr Alexandrovich, will you go, too?"

"Yes, of course. What have I come for but to study all the customs here? The only thing that embarrasses me is your company. . . ."

"Yes, Dmitri Fyodorovich isn't here yet."

"It would be a capital thing if he didn't turn up. Do you suppose I like all this business, and in your company, too? So we will come to dinner. Thank the Father Superior," he said, turning to the monk.

"No, it is my duty now to conduct you to the elder," answered the monk.

"If so I'll go straight to the Father Superior — to the Father Superior," chirped Maximov.

"The Father Superior is engaged just now. But as you please——" the monk hesitated.

"A most annoying old man!" Miüsov observed aloud, while Maximov ran back to the monastery.

"He's like von Sohn," Fyodor Pavlovich said suddenly.

"Is that all you can think of? . . . In what way is he like von Sohn? Have you ever seen von Sohn?"

"I've seen his portrait. It's not the features, but something indefinable. He's a second von Sohn. I can always tell from the physiognomy."

"Ah, I dare say you are a connoisseur in that. But, look here, Fyodor Pavlovich, you said just now that we had given our word to behave properly. Remember it. I advise you to control yourself. But if you begin to play the buffoon I don't intend to be associated with you here. . . . You see what a man he is" — he turned to the monk — "I'm afraid to go among decent people with him." A thin, subtle smile, not without a certain slyness, came to the pale, bloodless lips of the monk, but he made no reply, and it was evident that he held his peace from a sense of his own dignity. Miüsov frowned more than ever.

"Oh, devil take them all! It's just surface polish kept up for centuries, and nothing but charlatanism and nonsense underneath," flashed through Miüsov's mind.

"Here's the hermitage. We've arrived,"

cried Fyodor Pavlovich. "The gates are shut."

And he began ostentatiously to make the sign of the cross before the saints painted above and on the sides of the gates.

"In Rome do as the Romans do. Here in this hermitage there are twenty-five saints being saved. They look at one another, and eat cabbage. And not one woman goes in at this gate. That's what is remarkable. And that really is so. But I did hear that the elder receives ladies," he remarked suddenly to the monk.

"Women of the people are here, too, now, lying in the portico there waiting. But for ladies of rank two rooms have been built adjoining the portico, but outside the precincts — you can see the windows — and the elder goes out to them by an inner passage when he is well enough. They are always outside the precincts. There is a Harkov lady, Madame Hohlakov, waiting there now with her ailing daughter. Probably he has promised to come out to her, though of late he has been so weak that he has hardly shown himself even to the people."

"So then there are loopholes, after all, to creep out of the hermitage to the ladies. Don't suppose, holy father, that I mean any harm. But do you know that at Athos not only the visits of women are prohibited, but no creature of the female sex is allowed — no hens, nor turkey-hens, nor young cows."

"Fyodor Pavlovich, I warn you I shall go back and leave you here. They'll turn you out when I'm gone."

"But I'm not interfering with you, Pyotr Alexandrovich. Look," he cried suddenly, stepping within the precincts, "what a vale of roses they live in!"

Though there were no roses now, there were numbers of rare and beautiful autumn flowers growing wherever there was space for them, and evidently tended by a skilful hand; there were flower-beds round the church, and between the tombs; and the one-storeyed wooden house where the elder lived was also surrounded with flowers.

"And was it like this in the time of the last elder, Varsonofy? That one didn't care for such elegance. They say he used to jump up and thrash even ladies with a stick," observed Fyodor Pavlovich, as he went up the steps.

"The elder Varsonofy did sometimes act rather queerly, but a great deal that's told is foolishness. He never thrashed any one," answered the monk. "Now, gentlemen, if you will wait a minute I will announce you."

"Fyodor Pavlovich, for the last time, remember our agreement, do you hear? Behave properly or I will pay you out!" Miüsov had time to mutter again.

"I can't think why you are so agitated," Fyodor Pavlovich observed sarcastically. "Are you uneasy about your sins? They say he can tell by one's eyes what one has come about. And what a lot you think of their opinion! you, a Parisian, and so advanced. I'm surprised at you."

But Miüsov had no time to reply to this sarcasm. They were asked to come in. He walked in, somewhat annoyed.

"Now, I know myself, I am irritated, I shall lose my temper and begin to argue — and lower myself and my ideas," he reflected.

## CHAPTER II
### THE OLD BUFFOON

THEY entered the room almost at the same moment that the elder came in from his bedroom. There were already in the cell, awaiting the elder, two monks of the hermitage, one the

26

Father Librarian, and the other Father Païssy, a very learned man, so they said, in delicate health, though not old. There was also a tall young fellow, who looked about two and twenty, standing in the corner throughout the interview. He had a broad, fresh face, and clever, observant, narrow brown eyes, and was wearing ordinary dress. He was a divinity student, and a future theologian, who was for some reason befriended by the monks. His expression was one of unquestioning, but self-respecting, reverence. Being in a subordinate and dependent position, and so not on an equality with the guests, he did not greet them with a bow.

Father Zosima was accompanied by a novice, and by Alyosha. The two monks rose and greeted him with a very deep bow, touching the ground with their fingers; then kissed his hand, asking his benediction. Blessing them, the elder replied with as deep a reverence to them, and asked the blessing of each of them. The whole ceremony was performed very gravely, not as though it were an everyday rite, but with some emotion. But Miüsov fancied that it was all done with intentional impressiveness. He stood in front of the other visitors. He ought — he had reflected upon it the evening before — from simple politeness, since it was the custom here, to have gone up to receive the elder's blessing, even if he did not kiss his hand. But when he saw all this bowing and kissing on the part of the monks he instantly changed his mind. With dignified gravity he made a rather deep, conventional bow, and moved away to a chair. Fyodor Pavlovich did the same, mimicking Miüsov like an ape. Ivan bowed with great dignity and courtesy, but he too kept his hands at his sides, while Kalganov was so confused that he did

not bow at all. The elder let fall the hand raised to bless them, and, bowing to them again, asked them all to sit down. The blood rushed to Alyosha's cheeks. He was ashamed. His forebodings were coming true.

Father Zosima sat down on a very old-fashioned mahogany sofa, upholstered in leather, and made his visitors sit down in a row along the opposite wall on four mahogany chairs, covered with shabby black leather. The monks sat, one at the door and the other at the window. The divinity student, the novice, and Alyosha remained standing. The cell was by no means spacious and had a faded look. It contained nothing but the most necessary furniture, of coarse and poor quality. There were two pots of flowers in the window, and a number of ikons in the corner. Before one huge ancient ikon of the Virgin a lamp was burning. Near it were two other holy pictures in shining settings, and, next them, carved cherubim, china eggs, a Catholic cross of ivory with a Mater Dolorosa embracing it, and several foreign engravings of the works of the great Italian artists of past centuries. Next to these costly and artistic engravings were several of the crudest Russian lithographs of saints and martyrs, such as are sold for a few copecks at all the fairs. On the other walls were portraits of Russian bishops, past and present.

Miüsov cast a cursory glance at all these "conventional" ornaments and bent an intent look upon the elder. He had a high opinion of his own insight, a weakness excusable in him, as he was fifty, an age at which a clever man of the world of established position can hardly help taking himself rather seriously. At the first moment he did not like the elder. There was, indeed, something in the elder's face which many people besides Miüsov might not have liked. Zosima was a short, bent, little man, with very weak legs, and, though he was only sixty-five, he looked at least ten years older. His face was very thin and covered with a network of fine wrinkles, particularly numerous about his eyes, which were small, light-coloured, quick, and shining like two bright points. He had a sprinkling of grey hair about his temples. His pointed beard was small and scanty, and his lips, which smiled frequently, were as thin as two threads. His nose was not long, but sharp, like a bird's beak.

"To all appearances a malicious, small soul, full of petty pride," thought Miüsov. He felt altogether dissatisfied with himself.

A cheap little clock on the wall struck twelve hurriedly, and helped to start the conversation.

"Precisely the hour," cried Fyodor Pavlovich, "but no sign of my son, Dmitri. I apologise for him, sacred elder!" (Alyosha shuddered all over at "sacred elder.") "I am always punctual myself, to the minute, remembering that punctuality is the courtesy of kings . . ."

"But you are no king, anyway," Miüsov muttered, losing his self-restraint at once.

"Yes; that's true. I'm not a king, and, would you believe it, Pyotr Alexandrovich, I was aware of that myself. But, there! I always say the wrong thing. Your reverence," he cried, with sudden pathos, "you behold before you a buffoon, a buffoon in good sooth! I introduce myself as such. It's an old habit, alas! And if I sometimes talk nonsense out of place it's with an object, with the object of amusing people and making myself agreeable. One must be agreeable, mustn't one? I was seven years ago in a little town where I had business, and I made friends with some merchants there.

We went to the *ispravnik* [captain of police] because we had to ask a favour of him, and to invite him to dine with us. He was a tall, fat, fair, sullen man, the most dangerous type in such cases. It's their liver. I went straight up to him, and with the ease of a man of the world, you know, 'Mr. Ispravnik,' said I, 'be our Napravnik, so to speak.' 'What do you mean by Napravnik?' said he. I saw, at the first half-second, that it had missed fire. He stood there so glum. 'I wanted to make a joke,' said I, 'for the general diversion, as Mr. Napravnik is our well-known Russian orchestra conductor and what we need for the harmony of our undertaking is some one of that sort.' And I explained my comparison very sensibly, didn't I? 'Excuse me,' said he, 'I am an *ispravnik*, and I do not allow puns to be made on my calling.' He turned and walked away. I followed him, shouting, 'Yes, yes, you are an *ispravnik*, not a Napravnik.' 'No,' he said, 'since you called me a Napravnik I am one.' And would you believe it, it ruined our business! And I'm always like that, always like that. Always injuring myself with my amiability. Once, many years ago, I said to an influential, you might say, person: 'Your wife is a ticklish lady,' in an honourable sense, of the moral qualities, so to speak. And what do you suppose he asked me, 'Why, have you tickled her?' I thought I'd be polite, so I couldn't help saying, 'Yes, I have,' and he gave me a fine tickling on the spot. Only that happened long ago, so I'm not ashamed to tell the story. I'm always injuring myself like that."

"You're doing it now, too," muttered Miüsov, with disgust.

Father Zosima scrutinised them both in silence.

"Am I? Would you believe it, I was aware

of that, too, Pyotr Alexandrovich, and let me tell you, indeed, I foresaw I should as soon as I began to speak. And do you know I foresaw, too, that you'd be the first to remark on it. The minute I see my joke isn't coming off, your reverence, both my cheeks feel as though they were cleaving to the lower jaw and there is almost a spasm in them. That's been so since I was young, when I used to be a hanger-on, and made my living that way in the houses of the gentry. I am an inveterate buffoon, and from my birth, your reverence, there's been a crazy streak in me. I do not deny that there may be an unclean spirit in me. But only a little one. A more important one would have chosen another lodging. But not your soul, Pyotr Alexandrovich; you're not a lodging worth having either. But I do believe — I believe in God, it's only of late that I had doubts. But now I sit and await words of wisdom. I'm like the philosopher, Diderot, your reverence. Did you ever hear, most holy father, how Diderot went to see the Metropolitan Platon, in the time of the Empress Catherine? He went in and said straight out, 'There is no God.' Whereat the exalted and holy dignitary lifted up his finger and answered, 'The fool hath said in his heart there is no God.' The philosopher fell down at his feet on the spot. 'I believe,' he cried, 'and will be christened.' And so he was. Princess Dashkov was his godmother, and Potyomkin his godfather."

"Fyodor Pavlovich, this is unbearable! You know you're telling lies and that that stupid anecdote isn't true. Why are you playing the fool?" cried Miüsov in a shaking voice, quite unable to control himself.

"I suspected all my life that it wasn't true," Fyodor Pavlovich cried with conviction. "But I'll tell you the whole truth, gentlemen. Great

elder! Forgive me; the last thing about Diderot's christening I made up just now. I never thought of it before. I made it up to add piquancy. I play the fool, Pyotr Alexandrovich, to make myself agreeable. Though I really don't know myself, sometimes, what I do it for. And as for Diderot, I heard as far as 'the fool hath said in his heart' twenty times from the gentry about here when I was young. Among others I heard your aunt tell the story, Pyotr Alexandrovich. They all believe to this day that the infidel Diderot came to dispute about God with the Metropolitan Platon. . . ."

Miüsov got to his feet, so thoroughly out of patience that he forgot himself. He was furious, and conscious that as a result he was ridiculous himself.

What was taking place in the cell was really incredible. For forty or fifty years past, since the times of former elders, no visitors had entered that cell without feelings of the profoundest veneration. Almost every one admitted to the cell felt that a great favour was being shown him. Many remained kneeling during the whole visit. Of those visitors, many had been men of high rank and learning, some even free-thinkers, attracted by curiosity, but all without exception, whether coming singly or in groups, felt called upon to show the profoundest reverence and delicacy, all the more so since here there was no question of money, but only, on the one side, love and grace, and on the other penitence and eager desire to resolve some spiritual problem or crisis. So that Fyodor Pavlovich's buffoonery amazed and bewildered the spectators, or at least some of them. The monks, with unchanged countenances, waited, with earnest attention, to hear what the elder would say, but seemed on the point of getting up, like Miüsov. Alyosha stood, with hanging head, on the verge of tears. What seemed to him strangest of all was that his brother Ivan, on whom alone he had rested his hopes, and who alone had such influence on his father that he could have stopped him, sat now quite unmoved, with downcast eyes, apparently waiting with interest to see how it would end, as though he were altogether an outsider. Alyosha did not even dare to look at Rakitin, the divinity student, whom he also knew very well, indeed, almost intimately. For he knew Rakitin's thoughts — he was the only one in the monastery who did.

"Forgive me," began Miüsov, addressing Father Zosima, "for perhaps I seem to be taking part in this unworthy foolery. I made a mistake in believing that even a man like Fyodor Pavlovich would understand what was due on a visit to a person so highly esteemed. I did not suppose I should have to apologise simply for having come with him. . . ."

Pyotr Alexandrovich could say no more, and was about to leave the room, overwhelmed with confusion.

"Don't distress yourself, I beg." The elder suddenly got on to his feeble legs, and taking Pyotr Alexandrovich by both hands made him sit down again. "I beg you not to disturb yourself. I particularly beg you to be my guest." And with a bow he went back and sat down again on his little sofa.

"Great elder, speak out! Do I annoy you by my vivacity or not?" Fyodor Pavlovich cried suddenly, clutching the arms of his chair in both hands, as though ready to leap up from it if the answer were unfavourable.

"I earnestly beg you, too, not to disturb yourself, but to be at your ease," the elder said impressively. "Be at your ease. Make yourself quite at home. And, above all, do not be so ashamed of yourself, for that is at the root of it all."

"Quite at home? To be my natural self? Oh, that is much too much, but I accept it with feeling. Do you know, blessed father, you'd better not invite me to be my natural self. Don't risk it. . . . I will not go so far as that myself. I warn you for your own sake. Well, the rest is still wrapped in the mists of uncertainty, though there are people who'd be pleased to give you a complete picture of me. I mean that for you, Pyotr Alexandrovich. But as for you, most holy one, let me tell you, I am brimming over with ecstasy."

He started to get up and, lifting his hands, declaimed, "Blessed be the womb that bare thee, and the paps that gave thee suck — the paps especially. When you said just now, 'Don't be so ashamed of yourself for that is at the root of it all,' you pierced right through me with that remark, and read me to the core. Indeed, I always feel when I meet people that I am lower than all, and that they all take me for a buffoon. So I say, 'Let me really play the buffoon. I am not afraid of your opinion, for you are every one of you worse than I am.' That is why I am a buffoon. It is from shame, great elder, from shame; it's simply over-sensitiveness that I run riot. If I were only sure that every one would accept me as the kindest and wisest of men, oh, Lord, what a good man I should be then! Master!" he fell suddenly on his knees, "what shall I do to inherit eternal life?"

It was difficult even now to decide whether he was joking or really moved.

Father Zosima, lifting his eyes, looked at him, and said with a smile:

"You have known for a long time what you

THE OLD BUFFOON

must do. You have sense enough: don't give way to drunkenness and incontinence of speech; don't give way to sensual lust; and, above all, to the love of money. And close your pot-houses. If you can't close all, at least two or three. And, above all — don't lie."

"You mean about Diderot?"

"No, not about Diderot. Above all, don't lie to yourself. The man who lies to himself and listens to his own lie comes to such a pass that he cannot distinguish the truth within him, or around him, and so loses all respect for himself and for others. And having no respect he ceases to love, and in order to occupy and distract himself without love he gives way to passions and coarse pleasures, and sinks to bestiality in his vices, all from continual lying to other men and to himself. The man who lies to himself can be more easily offended than any one. You know it is sometimes very pleasant to take offence, isn't it? A man may know that nobody has insulted him, but that he has invented the insult for himself, has lied and exaggerated to make it picturesque, has caught at a word and made a mountain out of a molehill — he knows that himself, yet he will be the first to take offence, and will revel in his resentment till he feels great pleasure in it, and so pass to genuine vindictiveness. But get off your knees, sit down, I beg you. All this, too, is deceitful posturing . . ."

"Blessed man! Give me your dear hand to kiss."

Fyodor Pavlovich skipped up, and imprinted a rapid kiss on the elder's thin hand. "It is, it is pleasant to take offence. You said that so well, as I never heard it before. Yes, I have been all my life taking offence, to please myself, taking offence on æsthetic grounds, for to be insulted is not only a matter of pleas-ure, but sometimes a matter of beauty — that you had forgotten, great elder, of beauty! I shall make a note of that. But I have been lying, lying positively my whole life long, every day and hour of it. Truly, I am a lie, and the father of lies. Though I believe I am not the father of lies. I am getting mixed in my texts. Say, the son of lies, and that will be enough. Only . . . my angel . . . I may sometimes talk about Diderot! Diderot will do no harm, though sometimes a word will do harm. Great elder, by the way, I was forgetting, though I had been meaning for the last two years to come here on purpose to ask and to find out something. Only do tell Pyotr Alexandrovich not to interrupt me. Here is my question: Is it true, great father, that the story is told somewhere in the 'Lives of the Saints' of a holy miracle-worker martyred for his faith who, when his head was cut off at last, stood up, picked up his head, and 'fondly kissed it'? He walked a long way, carrying it in his hands, and kissing it. Is that true or not, honoured fathers?"

"No, it is untrue," said the elder.

"There is nothing of the kind in all the lives of the saints. What saint do you say the story is told of?" asked the Father Librarian.

"I do not know what saint. I do not know, and can't tell. I was deceived. That was the way I was told the story. I had heard it, and do you know who told it? Pyotr Alexandrovich Miüsov here, who was so angry just now about Diderot. It was he who told the story."

"I have never told it you, I never speak to you at all."

"It is true you did not tell me, but you told it when I was present. It was three years ago. I mentioned it because by that ridiculous story you shook my faith, Pyotr Alexandrovich.

You knew nothing of it, but I went home with my faith shaken, and I have been getting more and more shaken ever since. Yes, Pyotr Alexandrovich, you were the cause of a great fall. That was worse than Diderot!"

Fyodor Pavlovich got excited and pathetic, though it was perfectly clear to every one by now that he was playing a part again. Yet Miüsov was stung to the quick by his words.

"What nonsense, and it is all nonsense," he muttered. "I may really have told it, some time or other . . . but not to you. I was told it myself. I heard it in Paris from a Frenchman. He told me it was read at our mass from the 'Lives of the Saints' . . . he was a very learned man who had made a special study of Russian statistics and had lived a long time in Russia. . . . I have not read the 'Lives of the Saints' myself, and I am not going to read them . . . all sorts of things are said at dinner — we were dining then."

"Yes, you were dining then, and so I lost my faith!" said Fyodor Pavlovich, teasing him.

"What do I care for your faith?" Miüsov was on the point of shouting, but he suddenly checked himself, and said with contempt, "You literally defile everything you touch."

The elder suddenly rose from his seat. "Excuse me, gentlemen, for leaving you a few minutes," he said, addressing all his guests. "I have visitors awaiting me who arrived before you. But don't you tell lies all the same," he added, turning to Fyodor Pavlovich with a good-humoured face. He went out of the cell. Alyosha and the novice flew to escort him down the steps. Alyosha was breathless: he was glad to get away, but he was glad, too, that the elder was good-humoured and not offended. Father Zosima was going towards the portico to bless the people waiting for him

there. But Fyodor Pavlovich persisted in stopping him at the door of the cell.

"Most blessed man!" he cried, with feeling. "Allow me to kiss your dear hand once more. Yes, with you I could still talk, I could still get on. Do you think I always lie and play the fool like this? Believe me, I have been acting like this all the time on purpose to try you. I have been testing you all the time to see whether I could get on with you. Is there room for my humility beside your pride? I am ready to give you a testimonial that one can get on with you! But now, I'll be quiet; I will keep quiet all the time. I'll sit in a chair and hold my tongue. Now it is for you to speak, Pyotr Alexandrovich. You are the principal person left now — for ten minutes."

## CHAPTER III
### PEASANT WOMEN WHO HAVE FAITH

NEAR the wooden portico below, built on to the outer wall of the precinct, there was a crowd of about twenty peasant women. They had been told that the elder was at last coming out, and they had gathered together in anticipation. Two ladies, Madame Hohlakov and her daughter, had also come out into the portico to wait for the elder, but in a separate part of it set aside for ladies of rank.

Madame Hohlakov was wealthy, still young and attractive, and always dressed with taste. She was rather pale, and had lively black eyes. She was not more than thirty-three, and had been five years a widow. Her daughter, a girl of fourteen, was partially paralysed. The poor child had not been able to walk for the last six months, and was wheeled about in a chair. She had a charming little face, rather thin from illness, but full of gaiety. There was a gleam of mischief in her big dark eyes with their long lashes. Her mother had been intending to take her abroad ever since the spring, but they had been detained all summer by business connected with their estate. They had been staying a week in our town, where they had come more for purposes of business than devotion, but had visited Father Zosima once already, three days before. Though they knew that the elder saw scarcely any one, they had now suddenly turned up again, and urgently entreated "the happiness of looking once again on the great healer."

The mother was sitting on a chair by the side of her daughter's wheel-chair, and two paces from her stood an old monk, not of our monastery, but a visitor from an obscure religious house in the far north. He, too, sought the elder's blessing.

But Father Zosima, on entering the portico, went first straight to the peasant women who were crowded at the foot of the three steps that led up into the portico. Father Zosima stood on the top step, put on his stole, and began blessing the women who thronged about him. One "possessed" woman was led up to him. As soon as she caught sight of the elder she began shrieking, hiccuping, and writhing in convulsions. Laying the stole on her forehead, he read a short prayer over her, and she was at once soothed and quieted.

I do not know how it may be now, but in my childhood I often happened to see and hear these "possessed" women in the villages and monasteries. They used to be brought to mass; they would squeal and bark like a dog so that they were heard all over the church. But when the sacrament was carried in and they were led up to it, at once the "possession" ceased, and the sick women were always soothed for a time. I was greatly impressed and amazed at this as a child; but then I heard from country neighbours and from my town teachers that the whole illness was simulated to avoid work, and that it could always be cured by suitable severity; various anecdotes were told to confirm this. But later on I learnt with astonishment from medical specialists that there is no pretence about it, that it is a terrible illness to which women are subject, specially prevalent among us in Russia, and that it is due to the hard lot of the peasant women. It is a disease, I was told, arising from exhausting toil too soon after hard, abnormal, and unassisted labour in childbirth, and from the hopeless misery, from beatings, and so on, which some women were not able to endure like others. The strange and instant healing of the frantic and struggling woman as soon as she was led up to the holy sacrament, which had been explained to me as due to malingering and the trickery of the "clericals," arose probably in the most natural manner. Both the women who supported her and the invalid herself fully believed as truth beyond question that the evil spirit in possession of her could not hold out if the sick woman were brought to the sacrament and made to bow down before it. And so, with a nervous and psychically deranged woman, a sort of convulsion of the whole organism always took place, and was bound to take place, at the moment of bowing down to the sacrament, a convulsion aroused by the expectation of the miracle of healing and the implicit belief that it would come to pass; and it did come to pass, though only for a moment. It was exactly the same now as soon as the elder touched the sick woman with the stole.

Many of the women in the crowd were moved to tears of ecstasy by the effect of the moment; some strove to kiss the hem of his garment; others wailed in sing-song voices.

He blessed them all and talked with some of them. The "possessed" woman he knew already. She came from a village only six versts from the monastery, and had been brought to him before.

"But here is one from afar." He pointed to a woman by no means old but very thin and wasted, with a face not merely sunburnt but almost blackened by exposure. She was kneeling and gazing with a fixed stare at the elder; there was something almost frenzied in her eyes.

"From afar off, father, afar off! Two hundred miles from here. From afar off, father, from afar off!" the woman began in a sing-song voice as though she were chanting a dirge, swaying her head from side to side with her cheek resting in her hand.

There is among the masses silent and long-suffering sorrow. It withdraws into itself and is quiet. But there is a grief that breaks out in tears and from then on finds vent in wailing. This is particularly common with women. But it is no lighter a grief than the silent kind. Lamentation comforts only by lacerating the heart still more. Such grief does not desire consolation. It feeds on the sense of its hopelessness. Lamentation springs only from the constant craving to keep the wound green.

"You are of the townspeople?" said Father Zosima, looking curiously at her.

"Townfolk we are, father, townfolk. We work the land though we live in the town. I have come to see you, oh, father! We heard of you, father, we heard of you. I have buried my little son, and I have come to pray to God. I have been in three monasteries on my pilgrimage, but they told me, 'Go, Nastasya, go to this place' — that is to you, little dove, to you. I

have come; I was yesterday at the service, and to-day I have come to you."

"What are you weeping for?"

"It's my little son I'm grieving for, father. He was three years old — three years all but three months. For my little boy, father, I'm in anguish, for my little boy. He was the last one left. We had four, my Nikita and I, but we don't keep our children, my dear, we don't keep them. I buried the first three without grieving overmuch, and now I have buried the last I can't forget him. It's as though he were standing before me. He doesn't leave me. He has dried up my heart. I look at his little clothes, his little shirt, his little boots, and I cry. I lay out all that is left of him, all his little things. I look at them and cry. I say to Nikita, my husband, let me go on a pilgrimage, master. He is a driver. We're not poor people, father, not poor; we are independent. It's all our own, the horses and the carriage. And what good is it all to us now? My Nikita has begun drinking while I am away. I'm sure of it. It used to be so before. As soon as I turn my back he gives way to it. But now I don't think about him either. It's three months since I left home. I've forgotten him. I've forgotten everything. I don't want to remember. And what would our life together be now? I've done with him, I've done. I've done with them all. I don't care to look upon my house and my goods. I don't care to see anything at all!"

"Listen, mother," said the elder. "Once in olden times a great saint saw in church a mother like you weeping for her little one, her only one, whom God had called to him. 'Knowest thou not,' said the saint to her, 'how bold these little ones are before the throne of God? Verily there are none bolder than they in the Kingdom of Heaven. "Thou didst give us life, O Lord," they say, "and scarcely had we looked upon it when Thou didst take it back again." And so boldly they ask and ask again that God gives them at once the rank of angels. Therefore,' said the saint, 'thou, too, woman, rejoice and weep not, for thy little one is now with the Lord in the host of his angels.' That's what the saint said to the weeping mother of old. He was a great saint and he could not have spoken falsely. Therefore you, too, mother, know that your little one is surely before the throne of God, is rejoicing and happy, and praying to God for you. Therefore do you also weep, but rejoice." The woman listened to him with downcast eyes, leaning her cheek on her hand. She sighed deeply.

"My Nikita tried to comfort me with the same words as you. 'Foolish one,' he said, 'why weep? Our son is no doubt chanting with the angels before God.' He says that to me, but he weeps himself. I see that he cries like me. 'I know, Nikita,' said I. 'Where could he be if not with the Lord God? Only, he is not here with us, sitting beside us as he used to before.' And if only I could look upon him one little time, if only I could peep at him just once, without going up to him, without speaking, if I could hide myself in a corner and only see him for one little minute, hear him playing in the yard. He used to come and call in his little voice, 'Mammy, where are you?' If only I could hear him just once, only once, pattering about the room on his little feet, pit-a-pat, with his little feet, so quick, quick; I remember how he used to run to me and shout and laugh, if only I could hear his little feet, hear them, recognise them! But he's gone, father, he's gone, and I shall never hear him again. Here's his little sash, but he isn't here, him I shall never see or hear now."

She drew out of her bosom her boy's little sash, with braid on it, and as soon as she looked at it she began shaking with sobs, hiding her eyes with her fingers through which the tears flowed in a sudden stream.

"It is Rachel of old," said the elder, "weeping for her children, and will not be comforted because they are not. Such is the lot set on earth for you mothers. Be not comforted. Consolation is not what you need. Weep and be not consoled, but weep. Only every time that you weep be sure to remember that your little son is one of the angels of God, that he looks down from there at you and sees you, and rejoices at your tears, and points at them to the Lord God; and a long while yet will you keep that great mother's grief. But it will turn in the end into quiet joy, and your bitter tears will be only tears of tender sorrow that purifies the heart and delivers it from sin. And I shall pray for the peace of your child's soul. What was his name?"

"Alexey, father."

"A sweet name. After Alexey, the man of God?"

"Yes, father."

"What a saint he was! I will remember him in my prayers, mother, and your grief, and I will pray for your husband's health. It is a sin for you to leave him. Your little one will see from heaven that you have forsaken his father, and will weep over you. Why do you trouble his happiness? He is living, for the soul lives for ever, and though he is not in the house he is near you, unseen. How can he go into the house when you say that the house is hateful to you? To whom is he to go if he find you not together, his father and mother? He comes to you in dreams now, and you are tormented. But then he will send you gentle dreams. Go

35

to your husband, mother; go this very day."

"I will go, father, at your word. I will go. You've touched my heart. Nikita, my Nikita, you are waiting for me," the woman began in a sing-song voice; but the elder had already turned away to a very old woman, dressed like a townswoman, not like a pilgrim. Her eyes showed that she had come with an object, and in order to ask a question. She said she was the widow of a non-commissioned officer, and lived close by in the town. Her son Vasenka was in the commissariat service, and had gone to Irkutsk in Siberia. He had written twice from there, but now a year had passed since he had written.

She did inquire about him, but she did not know whether she had inquired in the proper place.

"Only the other day Stepanida Ilyinishna Bedryagin — she's a rich merchant's wife — said to me, 'You go, Prohorovna, and put your son's name down for prayer in the church, that they may pray for the peace of his soul as though he were dead. His soul will be troubled,' she said, 'and he will write you a letter.' And Stepanida Ilyinishna told me it was a certain thing and well-tried. Only I am in doubt. . . . Oh, light of our lives! is it true or isn't it, and would it be right?"

"Don't think of it. It's shameful to ask the question. How is it possible to pray for the peace of a living soul as though for the dead? And his own mother, too! It's a great sin, akin to sorcery. Only for your ignorance it is forgiven you. Better pray to the Queen of Heaven, our swift defence and help, for his good health, and that she may forgive you for your erring thought. And another thing I will tell you, Prohorovna. Either he will soon come back to you, your son, or he will be sure to send

a letter. Go, and henceforward be in peace. Your son is alive, I tell you."

"God reward you, dear father, our benefactor, who prays for all of us and for our sins!"

But the elder had already noticed in the crowd two burning eyes fixed upon him. An exhausted, consumptive-looking peasant woman, still young, was looking at him in silence. Her eyes besought him, but she seemed afraid to approach.

"What is it, my child?"

"Absolve my soul, father," she articulated softly and slowly, sank on her knees and bowed down at his feet. "I have sinned, father. I fear my sin."

The elder sat down on the lower step. The woman crept closer to him, still on her knees.

"I am a widow these three years," she began in a half-whisper, with a sort of shudder. "I had a hard life with my husband. He was an old man. He used to beat me cruelly. He lay ill; I thought looking at him, if he were to get well, if he were to get up again, what then? And then the thought came to me — "

"Stay!" said the elder, and he put his ear close to her lips.

The woman went on in a low whisper, so that it was almost impossible to catch anything. She had soon done.

"Three years ago?" asked the elder.

"Three years. At first I didn't think about it, but now I've been taken ill, and the thought never leaves me."

"Have you come a distance?"

"Over three hundred miles."

"Have you told it in confession?"

"I have confessed it. Twice I have confessed it."

"Have you been admitted to Communion?"

WOMEN OF GREAT FAITH

"Yes. I am afraid. I am afraid to die."

"Fear nothing and never be afraid; and don't fret. If only your penitence fail not, God will forgive all. There is no sin, and there can be no sin on earth, which the Lord will not forgive to the truly repentant! Man cannot commit a sin so great as to exhaust the infinite love of God. Can there be a sin which could exceed the love of God? Think only of repentance, continual repentance, but dimiss fear altogether. Believe that God loves you inconceivably; that He loves you with your sin, in your sin. It has been said of old that over one repentant sinner there is more joy in heaven than over ten righteous men. Go, and fear not. Be not bitter against men, be not angry if you are wronged. Forgive the dead man in your heart what wrong he did you. Be reconciled with him in truth. If you are penitent, you love. And if you love you belong to God. All things are redeemed, all things are saved by love. If I, a sinner, even as you are, am tender with you and have pity on you, how much more will God. Love is such a priceless treasure that you can purchase the whole world with it, and expiate not only your own sins but the sins of others. Go, and do not fear."

He signed her three times with the sign of the cross, took from his own neck a little ikon and put it upon her. Without a word, she bowed down to the earth before him.

He got up and looked cheerfully at a healthy peasant woman with a tiny baby in her arms.

"From Vyshegorye, dear father."

"Five miles you have dragged yourself with the baby. What do you want?"

"I've come to look at you. I have been to you before — or have you forgotten? You've no great memory if you've forgotten me. They told us you were ill. Thinks I, I'll go and see him for myself. Now I see you, and you're not ill! You'll live another twenty years. God bless you! There are plenty to pray for you; how should you be ill?"

"I thank you for all, daughter."

"By the way, I have a thing to ask, not a great one. Here are sixty copecks. Give them, dear father, to some one poorer than me. I thought as I came along, better give through him. He'll know whom to give to."

"Thanks, my dear, thanks! You are a good woman. I love you. I will do so certainly. Is that your little girl?"

"My little girl, father, Lizaveta."

"May the Lord bless you both, you and your babe Lizaveta! You have gladdened my heart, mother. Farewell, dear children, farewell, dear ones."

He blessed them all and bowed low to them.

## CHAPTER IV
### A LADY OF LITTLE FAITH

A LADY, watching the scene between the elder and the peasant women and his blessing them, shed silent tears and wiped them away with a dainty handkerchief. She was a sentimental society lady with a disposition genuinely good in many respects. When the elder went up to her at last she met him enthusiastically.

"Ah, what I have been feeling, as I watched this touching scene! . . . " She could not go on for emotion. "Oh, I understand the people's love for you. I love the people myself. I want to love them. And who could help loving them, our splendid Russian people, so simple in their greatness!"

"How is your daughter's health? You wanted to talk to me again?"

"Oh, I have been urgently begging for it,

I have prayed for it! I was ready to fall on my knees and remain kneeling for three days at your windows until you let me in. We have come, great healer, to express our ardent gratitude. You have healed my Lise, healed her completely, merely by praying over her last Thursday and laying your hands upon her. We have hastened here to kiss those hands, to pour out our feelings and our homage."

"What do you mean by healed? But she is still lying in her chair."

"But her night fevers have entirely ceased ever since Thursday," said the lady with nervous haste. "And that's not all. Her legs are stronger. This morning she got up well; she had slept all night. Look at her rosy cheeks, her bright eyes! She used to be always crying, but now she laughs and is gay and happy. This morning she insisted on my letting her stand up, and she stood up for a whole minute without any support. She wagers that in a fortnight she'll be dancing a quadrille. I've called in Dr. Herzenstube. He shrugged his shoulders and said, 'I am amazed; I can make nothing of it.' And would you have us not disturb you, not fly here to thank you? Lise, thank him — thank him!"

Lise's pretty little laughing face became suddenly serious. She rose in her chair as far as she could and, looking at the elder, clasped her hands before him, but could not restrain herself and broke into laughter.

"It's at him," she said, pointing to Alyosha, with childish vexation at herself for not being able to repress her mirth.

If any one had looked at Alyosha standing a step behind the elder, he would have caught a quick flush mantling his cheeks in an instant. His eyes flashed and fell.

"She has a message for you, Alexey Fyo-dorovich. How are you?" the mother went on, holding out her exquisitely gloved hand to Alyosha.

The elder turned round and all at once looked attentively at Alyosha. The latter approached Lise and, smiling in a strangely awkward way, held out his hand to her, too. Lise assumed an important air.

"Katerina Ivanovna has sent you this through me." She handed him a little note. "She particularly begs you to go and see her as soon as possible; that you will not fail her, but will be sure to come."

"She asks me to go and see her? Me? What for?" Alyosha muttered in great astonishment. His face at once looked anxious.

"Oh, it all has to do with Dmitri Fyodorovich and — with what has happened lately," the mother explained hurriedly. "Katerina Ivanovna has made up her mind, but she must see you about it without fail. . . . Why? Of course, I can't say. But she asks you to come as soon as possible. And you will do it, you will surely do it. Your feelings as a Christian will make you."

"I have only seen her once," Alyosha protested with the same perplexity.

"Oh, she is such a noble, exalted creature! Her sufferings alone . . . Think what she has gone through, what she is enduring now! Think what awaits her! It's all terrible, terrible!"

"Very well, I will come," Alyosha decided, after rapidly scanning the brief, enigmatic note, which consisted of an urgent entreaty that he would come, without any sort of explanation.

"Oh, how sweet and how splendid that would be of you!" cried Lise with sudden animation. "And I told mamma: he is sure not to go, he is saving his soul. How splendid you are! I've always thought you were splendid. How glad I am to tell you so now!"

"Lise!" said her mother impressively, but at once broke into a smile.

"You have quite forgotten us, Alexey Fyodorovich," she said; "you never come to see us. Yet Lise has told me twice that she is never happy except with you."

Alyosha raised his downcast eyes and again flushed, and again smiled without knowing why. But the elder was no longer watching him. He had engaged in conversation a monk who, as mentioned before, had been awaiting his entrance by Lise's chair. He was evidently a monk of the humblest, that is of the peasant, class, of a narrow outlook, but a true believer, and, in his own way, a stubborn one. He announced that he had come from the far north, from Obdorsk, from St. Sylvester, and was a member of a poor monastery, consisting of only nine monks. The elder gave him his blessing and invited him to come to his cell whenever he liked.

"How can you presume to do such deeds?" the monk asked suddenly, pointing solemnly and significantly at Lise. He was hinting at her "cure."

"It's too early, of course, to speak of that. Relief is not complete cure, and may proceed from other causes. But if there has been any healing, it is by no power but God's will. It's all from God. Visit me, father," he added to the monk. "It's not always I can see visitors. I am ill, and I know that my days are numbered."

"Oh, no, no! God will not take you from us. You will live a long, long time yet," cried the lady. "And in what way are you ill? You look so well, so gay and happy."

"I am extraordinarily better to-day. But I know that it's only for a moment. I understand my disease now thoroughly. If you say that I seem so cheerful to you, you could never tell me anything that would please me more. For men are made for happiness, and any one who is completely happy has a right to say to himself, 'I have done God's will on earth.' All the righteous, all the saints, all the holy martyrs were happy."

"Oh, how you speak! What bold and lofty words!" cried the lady. "You seem to pierce with your words. And yet — happiness, happiness — where is it? Who can say of himself that he is happy? Oh, since you have been so good as to let us see you once more to-day, let me tell you what I could not utter last time, what I dared not say, all I am suffering and have been for so long! I am suffering! Forgive me! I am suffering!"

And in a rush of fervent feeling she clasped her hands before him.

"From what specially?"

"I suffer . . . from lack of faith."

"Lack of faith in God?"

"Oh, no, no! I dare not even think of that. But the future life — it is such an enigma! And no one, no one can solve it. Listen! You are a healer, you are deeply versed in the human soul, and of course I dare not expect you to believe me entirely, but I assure you on my word of honour that I am not speaking lightly now. The thought of the life beyond the grave agitates me to the point of suffering, of fright, of terror. And I don't know to whom to appeal, and have not dared to all my life. And now I am so bold as to ask you. Oh, God! What will you think of me now?"

She struck her hands together.

"Don't distress yourself about my opinion

of you," said the elder. "I quite believe in the sincerity of your anguish."

"Oh, how thankful I am to you! You see, I shut my eyes and ask myself: if every one has faith, where did it come from? They say that it all comes from terror at the menacing phenomena of nature, and that none of it's real. And I say to myself, 'I've been believing all my life, and what if, when I come to die, there's nothing but burdocks growing on the grave? — as I read in some book.' It's awful! How — how can I get back my faith? But really I only believed when I was a little child, mechanically, without thinking of anything. How, how is one to prove it? I have come now to lay my soul before you and to ask you about it. If I let this chance slip, no one all my life will answer me. How can one prove it? How can one convince oneself? Oh, how unhappy I am! I stand and look about me and see that scarcely any one else cares; no one troubles his head about it, and I'm the only one who can't stand it. It's deadly — deadly!"

"No doubt. But there's no proving it, though you can be convinced of it."

"How?"

"By the experience of active love. Strive to love your neighbour actively and tirelessly. In so far as you advance in love you will grow surer of the reality of God and of the immortality of your soul. If you attain to perfect self-forgetfulness in the love of your neighbour, then you will believe without doubt, and no doubt can possibly enter your soul. This has been tried. This is certain."

"In active love? There's another question — and such a question! You see, I so love humanity that — would you believe it? — I often dream of forsaking all that I have, leaving Lise, and becoming a sister of mercy. I close my eyes and think and dream, and at that moment I feel full of strength to overcome all obstacles. No wounds, no festering sores could at that moment frighten me. I would bind them up and wash them with my own hands. I would nurse the afflicted. I would be ready to kiss such wounds."

"It is much, and well that your mind is full of such dreams and not others. Sometime, unawares, you may do a good deed in reality."

"Yes. But could I endure such a life for long?" the lady went on fervently, almost frantically. "That's the chief question — that's my most agonising question. I shut my eyes and ask myself, 'Would you persevere long on that path? And if the patient whose wounds you are washing did not meet you with gratitude, but worried you with his whims, without valuing or remarking your charitable services, began abusing you and rudely commanding you, and complaining to the superior authorities of you (which often happens when people are in great suffering) — what then? Would you persevere in your love, or not?' And do you know, I came with horror to the conclusion that, if anything could dissipate my active love for humanity, it would be ingratitude. In short, I am a hired servant, I expect my payment at once — that is, praise, and the repayment of love with love. Otherwise I am incapable of loving any one."

She was in a very paroxysm of self-castigation, and, concluding, she looked with defiant resolution at the elder.

"It's just the same story as a doctor once told me," observed the elder. "He was a man getting on in years, and undoubtedly clever. He spoke as frankly as you, though in jest, in sorrowful jest. 'I love humanity,' he said, 'but I wonder at myself. The more I love humanity in general, the less I love man in particular, that is, as separate individuals. In my dreams,' he said, 'I have often come to making enthusiastic schemes for the service of humanity, and perhaps I might actually have faced crucifixion if it had been suddenly necessary; and yet I am incapable of living in the same room with any one for two days together, as I know by experience. As soon as any one is near me, his personality disturbs my self-importance and restricts my freedom. In twenty-four hours I begin to hate the best of men: one because he's too long over his dinner; another because he has a cold and keeps on blowing his nose. I become hostile to people the moment they come close to me. But it has always happened that the more I detest men individually the more ardent becomes my love for humanity in general."

"But what's to be done? What can one do in such a case? Must one despair?"

"No. It is enough that you are distressed by it. Do what you can, and it will be reckoned unto you. Much is done already in you since you can so deeply and sincerely know yourself. If you have been talking to me so sincerely, simply to gain approbation for your frankness, as you did from me just now, then of course you will not attain to anything in the achievement of real love; it will all get no further than dreams, and your whole life will slip away like a phantom. In that case you will naturally cease to think of the future life, too, and will of yourself grow calmer after a fashion in the end."

"You have crushed me! Only now, as you speak, I understand that I was really only seeking your approbation for my sincerity when I told you I could not endure ingratitude. You have revealed me to myself. You have seen through me and explained me to myself!"

"Are you speaking the truth? Well, now, after such a confession, I believe that you are sincere and good at heart. If you do not attain happiness, always remember that you are on the right road, and try not to leave it. Above all, avoid falsehood, every kind of falsehood, especially lying to yourself. Watch over your own deceitfulness and look into it every hour, every minute. Avoid also being scornful, both of others and of yourself. What seems to you abominable within you is purified by the very fact of your observing it in yourself. Avoid fear, too, though fear is only the consequence of every sort of falsehood. Never be frightened at your own faint-heartedness in the attainment of love. Don't be frightened overmuch even at your evil actions. I am sorry I can say nothing more consoling to you, for love in action is a harsh and dreadful thing compared with love in dreams. Love in dreams thirsts for immediate action, rapidly performed and in the sight of all. Men will even give their lives if only the ordeal does not last long but is soon over, with all looking on and applauding as though on the stage. But active love is labour and fortitude, and for some people, too, perhaps, a whole science. But I predict that just when you see with horror that in spite of all your efforts you are getting further from your goal instead of nearer to it — at that very moment I predict that you will reach it and behold clearly the miraculous power of the Lord who has been all the time loving and mysteriously guiding you. Forgive me for not being able to stay longer with you. They are waiting for me. Good-bye."

The lady was weeping.

"Lise, Lise! Bless her — bless her!" she cried, starting up suddenly.

"She does not deserve to be loved. I have seen her naughtiness all along," the elder said jestingly. "Why have you been laughing at Alexey?"

Lise had in fact been occupied in mocking at him all the time. She had noticed before that Alyosha was shy and tried not to look at her, and she found this extremely amusing. She waited intently to catch his eye. Alyosha, unable to endure her persistent stare, was irresistibly and suddenly drawn to glance at her, and at once she smiled triumphantly in his face. Alyosha was even more disconcerted and vexed. At last he turned away from her altogether and hid behind the elder's back. After a few minutes, drawn by the same irresistible force, he turned again to see whether he was being looked at or not, and found Lise almost hanging out of her chair to peep sideways at him, eagerly waiting for him to look. Catching his eye, she laughed so that the elder could not help saying, "Why do you tease him like that, naughty girl?"

Lise suddenly and quite unexpectedly blushed. Her eyes flashed and her face became terribly serious. She began speaking quickly and nervously in a warm and resentful voice:

"Why has he forgotten everything, then? He used to carry me about when I was little. We used to play together. He used to come to teach me to read, do you know it? Two years ago, when he went away, he said that he would never forget me, that we were friends for ever, for ever, for ever! And now he's afraid of me all at once. Am I going to eat him? Why doesn't he want to come near me? Why doesn't he talk? Why won't he come and see us? It's not that you won't let him. We know that he goes everywhere. It's not good

manners for me to invite him. He ought to have thought of it first, if he hasn't forgotten me. No, now he's saving his soul! Why have you put that long gown on him? If he runs he'll fall."

And suddenly she hid her face in her hand and went off into irresistible, prolonged, nervous, inaudible laughter, that fairly shook her. The elder listened to her with a smile, and blessed her tenderly. As she kissed his hand she suddenly pressed it to her eyes and began crying.

"Don't be angry with me. I'm silly and good for nothing . . . and perhaps Alyosha's right, quite right, in not wanting to come and see such a ridiculous girl."

"I will send him without fail," said the elder.

## CHAPTER V
### SO BE IT! SO BE IT!

THE elder's absence from his cell had lasted for about twenty-five minutes. It was more than half-past twelve, but Dmitri, on whose account they had all met there, had still not appeared. But he seemed almost to be forgotten, and when the elder entered the cell again, he found his guests engaged in eager conversation. Ivan and the two monks took the leading share in it. Miüsov, too, was trying to take a part, and apparently very eagerly, in the conversation. But he was unsuccessful in this also. He was evidently in the background, and his remarks were treated with neglect, which increased his irritability. He had had intellectual encounters with Ivan before and he could not endure with equanimity a certain carelessness Ivan showed him.

"Hitherto at least I have stood in the front ranks of all that is progressive in Europe, and here the new generation positively ignores us," he thought.

Fyodor Pavlovich, who had given his word to sit still and be quiet, had actually been quiet for some time, but he watched his neighbour Miüsov with an ironical little smile, obviously enjoying his discomfiture. He had been waiting for some time to pay off old scores, and now he could not let the opportunity slip. Bending over his shoulder, he began teasing him again in a whisper.

"Why didn't you go away just now, after the 'fondly kissing'? Why did you consent to remain in such unseemly company? It was because you felt insulted and injured, and you remained to vindicate yourself by showing off your intelligence. Now you won't go till you've displayed your intellect to them."

"You again? . . . On the contrary, I'm just going."

"You'll be the last, the last of all to go!" Fyodor Pavlovich delivered him another thrust. At that moment Father Zosima returned.

The discussion died down for a moment, but the elder, seating himself in his former place, looked at them all as though cordially inviting them to go on. Alyosha, who knew every expression of his face, saw that he was fearfully exhausted and forcing himself to keep up. Of late he had been liable to fainting fits from exhaustion. His face had the pallor that was common before such attacks, and his lips were white. But he evidently did not want to break up the gathering. He seemed to have some special object of his own in acting thus. What object? Alyosha watched him intently.

"We are discussing this gentleman's most interesting article," said Father Iosif, the librarian, addressing the elder, and pointing to Ivan. "He brings forward much that is new, but I think the argument cuts both ways. It is an article written in answer to a book by an ecclesiastical authority on the question of the ecclesiastical jurisdiction and its scope."

"I'm sorry I have not read your article, but I've heard of it," said the elder, looking keenly and intently at Ivan.

"He takes a most interesting position," continued the Father Librarian. "As far as Church jurisdiction is concerned he is apparently quite opposed to the separation of Church from State."

"That's interesting. But in what sense?" Father Zosima asked Ivan. The latter, at last, answered him, not condescendingly, as Alyosha had feared, but with modesty and reserve, with evident goodwill and apparently without the slightest mental reservation.

"I start from the thesis that this confusion of elements, that is, of the essential principles of Church and State, taken separately, will, of course, go on for ever, in spite of the fact that it is impossible, and that the confusion of these elements cannot be reduced to any order or harmony, for there is falsity at the very root of the thing. Compromise between Church and State in such questions as, for instance, jurisdiction, is, to my thinking, impossible in any real sense. My clerical opponent maintains that the Church holds a precise and definite position in the State. I argued, on the contrary, that the Church ought to contain within itself the whole State, and not simply occupy a corner in it, and, if this is, for some reason, impossible at present, then it ought, in reality, to be set up as the direct and chief goal of the future development of Christian society!"

"Perfectly true," Father Païssy, the silent and learned monk, assented nervously but firmly. "The purest Ultramontanism!" cried Miüsov, impatiently crossing his legs.

"Oh, but we have no mountains," cried Father Iosif, and turning to the elder he continued: "the gentleman replies to the following 'fundamental and essential' propositions of his opponent, who is, you must note, an ecclesiastic. First, that 'no social organisation can or ought to arrogate to itself power to dispose of the civil and political rights of its members.' Secondly, that 'criminal and civil jurisdiction ought not to belong to the Church, and is inconsistent with its nature, both as a divine institution and as a union of men for religious purposes,' and, finally, in the third place, 'the Church is a kingdom not of this world.'"

"A most unworthy play upon words for an ecclesiastic!" Father Païssy could not refrain from breaking in again. "I have read the book to which you made reply," he added, addressing Ivan, "and was astounded at the words 'the Church is a kingdom not of this world.' If it is not of this world, then it cannot exist on earth at all. In the Gospel, the words 'not of this world' are not used in that sense. To play with such words is indefensible. Our Lord Jesus Christ came precisely to set up the Church upon earth. The Kingdom of Heaven, of course, is not of this world, but in heaven; but it is entered only through the Church which has been founded and established upon earth. And so a frivolous play upon words in such a connection is unpardonable and improper. The Church is, in truth, a kingdom and is ordained to rule, and in the end must undoubtedly become the kingdom embracing all the earth. For that we have divine promise."

He ceased speaking suddenly, as though checking himself.

After listening to him attentively and respectfully, Ivan went on, addressing the elder with perfect composure but as before with ready cordiality:

"The whole point of my article is that during the first three centuries Christianity existed on earth only in the Church and was nothing but the Church. When the pagan Roman State desired to become Christian, it inevitably happened that, by becoming Christian, it merely included the Church within it, but remained a pagan State in very many of its functions. In the nature of things, this was bound to happen. But Rome as a State retained too much of the pagan civilisation and culture, as, for example, the very objects and fundamental principles of the State. As for the Christian Church, on entering into the State it could, of course, surrender no part of its fundamental principles — the rock on which it stood — and could pursue no aims but its own, those which have been ordained and revealed by God Himself, and among them that of transforming the whole world, and therefore the ancient pagan State itself, into the Church. In that way (that is, with a view to the future) it is not the Church that should seek a definite position in the State, like 'every social organisation,' or as 'a union of men for religious purposes' (as my opponent calls the Church), but, on the contrary, every earthly State should be, in the end, completely transformed into the Church and should become nothing else but a Church, rejecting every purpose incongruous with the aims of the Church. All this will not degrade it in any way or take from its honour and glory as a great State, nor from the glory of its rulers, but only turns it from a false, still pagan, and mistaken path to the true and rightful path, which alone leads to the eternal goal. This is why the author of the book 'On the Foundations of Church Jurisdiction' would have judged correctly if, in seeking and laying down those foundations, he had looked upon them as only a temporary compromise inevitable in our sinful and imperfect days. But as soon as the author ventures to declare that the foundations which he predicates now, part of which Father Iosif just enumerated, are the unshakable, primal, and eternal foundations, he is going directly against the Church and its sacred, eternal, and unshakable destiny. That is the gist of my article."

"That is, in brief," Father Païssy began again, laying stress on each word, "according to certain theories only too clearly formulated in the nineteenth century, the Church ought to be transformed into the State, as though this would be an advance from a lower to a higher form, so as subsequently to disappear into it, making way for science, for the spirit of the age, and civilisation. And if the Church resists and is unwilling, some corner is set apart for her in the State, and even that under surveillance — and this is so everywhere in all modern European countries. But Russian thinking, Russian hopes and conceptions demand not that the Church should pass as from a lower into a higher type into the State, but, on the contrary, that the State should end by being worthy to become only the Church and nothing else. So be it! So be it!"

"Well, I confess you've reassured me somewhat," Miüsov said smiling, again crossing his legs. "So far as I understand then, the realisation of such an ideal is infinitely remote, and will take place only at the second coming of Christ. That's as you please. It's a beautiful Utopian dream of the disappearance of war, diplomacy, banks, and so on — something after the fashion of socialism, indeed. But I imagined that it was all meant seriously, and that the Church might be *now* going to try criminals, and sentence them to beating, prison, and even death."

"But if there were even now none but the ecclesiastical court, the Church would not sentence a criminal to prison or to death. Crime and the way of regarding it would inevitably change, not all at once of course, but fairly soon," Ivan replied calmly, without flinching.

"Are you serious?" Miüsov glanced keenly at him.

"If everything became the Church, the Church would excommunicate all the criminal and disobedient, and would not cut off their heads," Ivan went on. "I ask you, what would become of the excommunicated? He would be cut off then not only from men, as now, but from Christ. By his crime he would have transgressed not only against men but against the Church of Christ. This is so even now, of course, strictly speaking, but it is not clearly enunciated, and very, very often the criminal of to-day compromises with his conscience: 'I steal,' he says, 'but I don't go against the Church, I'm not an enemy of Christ.' That's what the criminal of to-day is continually saying to himself, but when the Church takes the place of the State it will be difficult for him, in opposition to the Church all over the world, to say: 'All men are mistaken, all in error, all mankind are the false Church. I, a thief and a murderer, am the only true Christian Church.' It will be very difficult to say this to himself; it requires a rare combination of unusual circumstances. Now, on the other hand, take the Church's own view of crime: is it not bound to renounce the present almost pagan attitude, and instead of mechanically cutting off its tainted member for the preservation of society, as at present, to adopt completely and honestly the idea of the regeneration of the man, of his resurrection and salvation?"

"What do you mean? I fail to understand again," Miüsov interrupted. "Some sort of dream again. Something shapeless and even incomprehensible. What do you mean by excommunication? What sort of excommunication? I suspect you are simply amusing yourself, Ivan Fyodorovich."

"Yes, but you know, in reality it is so now," said the elder suddenly, and all turned to him at once. "If there were no Church of Christ now, there would be nothing to restrain the criminal from evil doing, no real chastisement for it afterwards; none, that is, but the mechanical punishment spoken of just now, which in the majority of cases only embitters the heart; and not the real punishment, the only effectual one, the only deterrent and softening one, which lies in the recognition of sin by one's own conscience."

"How is that, may one inquire?" asked Miüsov, with lively curiosity.

"Why," began the elder, "all these punishments, — hard labour, and formerly flogging also, reform no one, and what's more, deter hardly a single criminal, and the number of crimes does not diminish but is continually on the increase. You must admit that. Consequently the security of society is not preserved, for, although the obnoxious member is mechanically cut off and sent far away out of sight, another criminal always comes to take his place at once, and perhaps two of them. If anything does preserve society, even in our time, and does regenerate and transform the criminal, it is only the law of Christ speaking with the voice of his conscience. It is only by recognising his guilt as a member of Christ's society — that is, of the Church — that he recognises his guilt before society — that is, before the Church. Thus, the criminal of to-day can recognise his guilt only before the Church, and not before the State. Now, if jurisdiction belonged to society as a Church, then it would know whom to recall from exclusion and bring back into the fold. But at present the Church, having no active jurisdiction, but only the power of moral condemnation, refrains of her own accord from imposing active punishment on the criminal. She does not excommunicate him but merely does not deprive him of fatherly exhortation. What is more, the Church even tries to preserve all Christian communion with the criminal. She admits him to church services, to the holy sacrament, gives him alms, and treats him more as a captive than as a convict. And what would become of the criminal, O Lord, if the Christian society too — that is, the Church — were to reject him even as the civil law rejects him and cuts him off? What would become of him if the Church, too, punished him with her excommunication as the immediate and automatic consequence of the punishment inflicted by secular law? There could be no more terrible despair, at least for a Russian criminal, for Russian criminals still have faith. Though, who knows, perhaps then a fearful thing would happen, perhaps the despairing heart of the criminal would lose its faith and then what would become of him? But the Church, like a tender, loving mother, refrains from active punishment herself, as the sinner is too severely punished already by the State court, and there must be some one to have pity on him. The Church holds aloof, above all, because its judgment is the only one that contains the truth, and therefore cannot either from a practical or a moral standpoint ally itself with any other judgment even as a temporary compromise. No compact is possible here. The foreign criminal, they say, rarely repents, for the very doctrines of to-day confirm him in the idea that his crime is not a crime, but only a rebellion against an unjustly oppressive force. Society cuts him off completely by a force that triumphs over him mechanically and (so at least they say of themselves in Europe) accompanies this exclusion with hatred, forgetfulness, and the most profound indifference as to the ultimate fate of the erring brother. In this way, it all takes place without the compassionate intervention of the Church, for in many cases there are no churches there at all, for though ecclesiastics and splendid church buildings remain, the churches themselves have long ago striven to pass from Church into State and to disappear in it completely. So it seems at least in Lutheran countries. As for Rome, it was proclaimed a State instead of a Church a thousand years ago. And so the criminal is no longer conscious of being a member of the Church and, having been excommunicated, sinks into despair. If he returns to society, often it is with such hatred that he, as it were, cuts himself off from society. You can judge for yourself how it must end. In many cases it would seem to be the same with us, but the difference is that besides the established law courts we have the Church, too, which always keeps up relations with the criminal as a dear and still precious son. And besides that, there is still preserved, though only in thought, the judgment of the Church, which though at present in a state of suspension is still living as a dream for the future, and is, no doubt, instinctively recognised by the criminal in his soul. What was said here just now is true, too, that is, that if the jurisdiction of the Church were introduced in practice in its full force, that is, the whole of society were turned into the Church, not only the judgment of the Church would have influence on the reformation of the criminal such as it never has now, but possibly also the crimes themselves would be incredibly diminished. And there can be no doubt that the Church would look upon the criminal and the crime of the future in many cases quite differently and would succeed in restoring the excluded, in restraining those who plan evil, and in regenerating the fallen. It is true," said Father Zosima, with a smile, "Christian society now is not ripe and is only resting on some seven righteous men, but as they are never lacking, it will continue still unshaken in expectation of its complete transformation from a society almost heathen in character into a single universal and regnant Church. So be it, so be it. Even though at the end of the ages, for it is ordained to come to pass! And there is no need to be troubled about times and seasons, for the secret of the times and seasons is in the wisdom of God, in His foresight, and His love. And what in human reckoning seems still afar off, may by the Divine ordinance already be, on the eve of its appearance, standing at the gates. And so be it, so be it!"

"So be it, so be it!" Father Païssy repeated austerely and reverently.

"Strange, extremely strange!" Miüsov pronounced it, not so much with heat as with latent indignation.

"What strikes you as so strange?" Father Iosif inquired cautiously.

"Why, it's beyond anything!" cried Miüsov, suddenly breaking out, "the State is eliminated and the Church is raised to the position of the State. It's not simply Ultramontanism, it's arch-ultramontanism! It's beyond the dreams of Pope Gregory the Seventh!"

"You are completely misunderstanding it," said Father Païssy sternly; "understand the Church is not to be transformed into the State. That is Rome and its dream. That is the third temptation of the devil. On the contrary, the State is transformed into the Church, ascends to the Church and becomes a Church over the whole world — which is the complete opposite of Ultramontanism and Rome, and your interpretation, and is only the glorious destiny ordained for the Orthodox Church. This star will arise in the east!"

Miüsov was significantly silent. His whole figure expressed extraordinary personal dignity. A supercilious and condescending smile played on his lips. Alyosha watched it all with a throbbing heart. The whole conversation stirred him profoundly. He glanced casually at Rakitin, who was standing immovable in his place by the door listening and watching intently though with downcast eyes. But from the colour in his cheeks Alyosha guessed that Rakitin was probably no less excited, and he knew what caused his excitement.

"Allow me to tell you one little anecdote, gentlemen," Miüsov said impressively, with a peculiarly important air. "Some years ago, soon after the *coup d'état* of December, I happened to be calling in Paris on an extremely influential personage in the Government, and I met a very interesting man in his house. This individual was not precisely a detective but was a sort of superintendent of a whole regiment of political detectives — a rather powerful position in its own way. I was prompted by curiosity to seize the opportunity of conversation with him. And as he had not come as a visitor but as a subordinate official coming to present a report, and as he saw the reception given me by his chief, he deigned to speak with some openness, to a certain extent only, of course. He was rather courteous than open, as Frenchmen know how to be courteous, especially to a foreigner. But I thoroughly understood him. The subject of our talk was the socialist revolutionaries who were at that time persecuted. I will quote only one most curious remark dropped by this person. 'We are not particularly afraid,' said he, 'of all these socialists, anarchists, infidels, and revolutionists; we keep watch on them and know all their moves. But there are a few peculiar men among them who believe in God and are Christians, but at the same time are socialists. Those are the people we are most afraid of. They are terrible people! The socialist who is a Christian is more to be dreaded than a socialist who is an atheist.' The words struck me at the time, and now they have suddenly come back to me here, gentlemen."

"You apply them to us, and look upon us as socialists?" Father Païssy asked directly, without beating about the bush.

But before Pyotr Alexandrovich could think what to answer, the door opened, and the guest so long expected, Dmitri Fyodorovich, came in. They had, in fact, given up expecting him, and his sudden appearance caused some surprise for a moment.

## CHAPTER VI
### WHY IS SUCH A MAN ALIVE?

DMITRI FYODOROVICH, a young man of eight and twenty, of medium height and agreeable countenance, looked much older than his years. He was muscular, and showed signs of considerable physical strength. Yet there was something almost sickly in his face. It was rather thin, his cheeks were hollow, and there was an unhealthy sallowness in their colour. His rather large, prominent, dark eyes had an expression of firm determination, and yet there was a vague look in them, too. Even when he was excited and spoke irritably, his eyes somehow did not obey his mood, but expressed something else, sometimes quite incongruous with what was passing. "It's hard to tell what he's thinking," those who talked to him sometimes declared. People who saw something pensive and sullen in his eyes were startled by his sudden laugh, which bore witness to mirthful and light-hearted thoughts at the very time when his expression was so gloomy. A certain unhealthy look in his face was easy to understand at this moment. Every one knew or had heard of the extremely restless and dissipated life which he had been leading of late, as well as of the violent anger to which he had been roused in his quarrels with his father about money. There were several stories current in the town about it. It is true that he was irritable by nature, "of an unstable and faulty mind," as our justice of the peace, Semyon Ivanovich Kachalnikov, happily described him at a gathering.

He was dressed stylishly and irreproachably in a carefully buttoned frock-coat. He wore black gloves and carried a top hat. Having only lately left the army, he still had moustaches and no beard. His dark brown hair was cropped short, and combed forward on his temples. He had the long determined stride of a military man. He stood still for a moment on the threshold, and glancing at the whole party went straight up to the elder, guessing him to be their host. He made him a low bow, and asked his blessing. Father Zosima, rising in his chair, blessed him. Dmitri kissed his hand respectfully, and with intense agitation, almost anger, he said:

"Be so generous as to forgive me for having kept you waiting so long, but Smerdyakov, my father's valet, in reply to my insistent inquiry, told me twice over that the appointment was for one o'clock. Now I suddenly learn — "

"Don't be upset," interposed the elder. "No matter. You are a little late. It's of no consequence. . . ."

"I'm extremely obliged to you, and expected no less from your kindness."

Dmitri spoke curtly and bowed once more. Then, turning suddenly towards his father, made him, too, a similarly low and respectful bow. He had evidently decided upon it beforehand, and made this bow in all sincerity, thinking it his duty to show his respect and good intentions.

Although Fyodor Pavlovich was taken unawares, he was equal to the occasion. In response to Dmitri's bow he jumped up from his chair and made his son a bow as low in return. His face was suddenly solemn and impressive, which gave him, however, a positively malignant look. Dmitri then bowed to all present, and without a word walked to the window with his long, resolute stride, sat down on the only empty chair, near Father Païssy, and, bending forward, prepared to

49

listen to the conversation he had interrupted.

Dmitri's entrance had taken no more than two minutes, and the conversation was resumed. But this time Miüsov thought it unnecessary to reply to Father Païssy's persistent and almost irritable question.

"Allow me to withdraw from this discussion," he observed with a certain well-bred nonchalance. "It's a subtle question, too. Here Ivan Fyodorovich is smiling at us. He must have something interesting to say about that also. Ask him."

"Nothing special, except one little remark," Ivan replied at once. "European Liberals in general, and even our liberal dilettanti, often mix up the final results of socialism with those of Christianity. This absurd conclusion is, of course, a characteristic feature. But it's not only Liberals and dilettanti who confuse socialism and Christianity, but, in many cases, it appears, the police, too — that is, the foreign police, of course. Your Paris anecdote is rather to the point, Pyotr Alexandrovich."

"I ask your permission to drop this subject altogether," Miüsov repeated. "I will tell you instead, gentlemen, another interesting and rather characteristic anecdote about Ivan Fyodorovich himself. Only five days ago, at a gathering here, principally of ladies, he solemnly declared in argument that there was nothing in the whole world to make men love their neighbours. That there was no law of nature that man should love mankind, and that, if there had been any love on earth hitherto, it was not owing to a natural law, but simply because men have believed in their immortality. Ivan Fyodorovich added in parenthesis that the whole natural law lies in that faith, and that if you were to destroy in mankind the belief in immortality, not only

love but every living force maintaining the life of the world would at once be dried up. Moreover, nothing then would be immoral, everything would be permitted, even cannibalism. That's not all. He ended by asserting that for every individual, like ourselves, who does not believe in God or immortality, the moral law of nature must immediately be changed into the exact contrary of the former religious law, and that egoism, even to the point of crime, must become, not only permissible but even recognised as the inevitable, the most rational, all but honourable outcome of his position. From this paradox, gentlemen, you can judge the rest of the theories which our eccentric and paradoxical friend, Ivan Fyodorovich, has set forth or intends to offer."

"Excuse me," Dmitri cried suddenly, "if I've heard aright: crime must not only be permitted but even recognised as the inevitable and the most logical outcome of his position for every atheist! Is that so or not?"

"Quite so," said Father Païssy.

"I'll remember it."

Having said this, Dmitri ceased speaking as suddenly as he had flung himself into the conversation. Every one looked at him with curiosity.

"Is that really your conviction as to the consequences of the disappearance of the belief in immortality?" the elder asked Ivan suddenly.

"Yes. That was my contention. There is no virtue if there is no immortality."

"You are blessed in believing that, or else most unhappy."

"Why unhappy?" Ivan asked smiling.

"Because in all probability you don't believe yourself in the immortality of your soul, nor in what you have written in your article on the Church and on the Church question."

"Perhaps you are right! . . . But I wasn't altogether joking," Ivan suddenly and strangely confessed, flushing quickly.

"You were not altogether joking. That's true. The question is not settled and is still fretting your heart. But even the martyr likes sometimes to divert himself with his despair, as it were driven to it by despair itself. Meanwhile, in your despair, you, too, divert yourself with magazine articles, and drawing-room discussions, though you don't believe your own arguments, and with an aching heart mock at them inwardly. . . . That question you have not settled, and it is your great grief, for it clamours for an answer."

"But can it be answered by me? Answered in the affirmative?" Ivan went on asking strangely, still looking at the elder with the same inexplicable smile.

"If it can't be decided in the affirmative, it will never be decided in the negative. You know that that is the peculiarity of your heart, and all its suffering is due to it. But thank the Creator who has given you a lofty heart capable of such suffering; of thinking and seeking higher things, for our dwelling is in the heavens. God grant that your heart will attain the answer on earth, and may God bless your ways."

The elder raised his hand and would have made the sign of the cross over Ivan from where he stood. But the latter rose from his seat, went up to him, received his blessing, and kissing his hand went back to his place in silence. His expression was firm and earnest. This action and all the preceding conversation with the elder, which was so surprising coming from Ivan, impressed every one by its strangeness and a certain solemnity, so that all were silent for a moment, and there was a look almost of apprehension in Alyosha's face. But Miüsov suddenly shrugged his shoulders. And at the same moment Fyodor Pavlovich jumped up from his seat.

"Divine and most holy elder," he cried, pointing to Ivan, "that is my son, flesh of my flesh, the dearest of my flesh! He is my most dutiful Karl Moor, so to speak, while this son who has just come in, Dmitri, against whom I am seeking a judgment from you, is the undutiful Franz Moor — they are both out of Schiller's *Robbers*, and so I am no less than *regierender* Graf von Moor! Judge and save us! We need not only your prayers but your prophecies!"

"Speak without buffoonery, and don't begin by insulting the members of your family," answered the elder, in a faint, exhausted voice. He was obviously getting more and more fatigued, and his strength was visibly failing.

"An unseemly farce which I foresaw when I came here!" cried Dmitri indignantly. He leapt up. "Forgive it, reverend father," he added, addressing the elder. "I am not a cultivated man, and I don't even know how to address you properly, but you have been deceived and you have been too good-natured in letting us meet here. All my father wants is a scandal. Why he wants it only he can tell. He always has some motive. But I believe I know why ——"

"They all blame me, all of them!" cried Fyodor Pavlovich in his turn. "Pyotr Alexandrovich here blames me, too. You have been blaming me, Pyotr Alexandrovich, you have!" he turned suddenly to Miüsov, although the latter was not dreaming of interrupting him. "They all accuse me of having hidden the children's money in my boots, and cheated them, but allow me, isn't there a court of law? There they will reckon out for you, Dmitri Fyodorovich, from your receipts, your letters, and your agreements, how much money you had, how much you have spent, and how much you have left. Why does Pyotr Alexandrovich refuse to pass judgment? Dmitri is not a stranger to him. Because they are all against me, while Dmitri Fyodorovich is in debt to me, and not a little, but some thousands, of which I have documentary proof. The whole town is ringing with his debaucheries. And where he was stationed before, he would spend a thousand or two to seduce some respectable girl; we know all about that, Dmitri Fyodorovich, the most secret details of it. I'll prove it. . . . Would you believe it, holy father, he has captivated the heart of the most honourable of young ladies of good family and fortune, the daughter of a gallant and distinguished colonel, formerly his superior officer, who had been decorated with the Order of Anna. He promised to marry the girl and now she is here, an orphan; she is betrothed to him, yet before her very eyes he is paying court to a certain local enchantress. And although this enchantress has lived in, so to speak, civil marriage with a respectable man, yet she is of an independent character, an impregnable fortress, so to speak, for everybody, just like a lawful wife — for she is virtuous, yes, holy fathers, she is virtuous. And Dmitri Fyodorovich wants to open this fortress with a golden key, and that's why he is insolent to me now, trying to get money from me, though he has wasted thousands on this enchantress already. He's continually borrowing money for the purpose. From whom do you think? Shall I say, Mitya?"

"Hold your tongue!" cried Dmitri; "wait till I'm gone. Don't dare in my presence to asperse the good name of a most honourable girl! That you should utter a word about her is an outrage, and I won't permit it!"

He was choking.

"Mitya! Mitya!" cried Fyodor Pavlovich nervously, squeezing out a tear. "And is your father's blessing nothing to you? If I curse you, what then?"

"Shameless hypocrite!" growled Dmitri furiously.

"He says that to his father! his father! What would he do to others? Gentlemen, only fancy; there's a poor but honourable man living here, burdened with a numerous family, a captain who got into trouble and was discharged from the army, but not publicly, not by court-martial, with no slur on his honour. And three weeks ago, Dmitri seized him by the beard in a tavern, dragged him out into the street and beat him publicly, and all because he is an agent, on the quiet, in a little business of mine."

"It's all a lie! Outwardly it's the truth, inwardly it's a lie!" Dmitri was trembling with rage. "Father, I don't justify my action. Yes, I confess it publicly, I behaved like a brute to that captain, and I regret it now, and I'm disgusted with myself for my brutal rage. But this captain, this agent of yours, went to that lady whom you call an enchantress, and suggested to her from you that she should take IOU's of mine which were in your possession, and should sue me for the money so as to get me into prison by means of them, if I persisted in claiming an account of my property from you. Now you reproach me for having a weakness for that lady when you yourself incited her to captivate me! She told me so to my face. . . . She told me the story and laughed at you. . . . You want to put me in prison only because you are jealous of me on her account, because you'd begun to force your attentions upon her; and I know all about that, too; she laughed at you for that as well — you hear — she laughed at you as she described it. So here, holy fathers, you have this man, this father who reproaches his profligate son! Gentlemen, forgive my anger, but I foresaw that this crafty old man had only brought you together to create a scandal. I had come to forgive him if he held out his hand; to forgive him, and ask forgiveness! But as he has just this minute insulted not only me, but an honourable young lady for whom I feel such reverence that I dare not take her name in vain, I have made up my mind to show up his game, though he is my father. . . ."

He could not go on. His eyes were glittering and he breathed with difficulty. But every one in the cell was stirred, too. All except Father Zosima rose in alarm from their seats. The monks looked austere but waited for the elder to make his will known. He sat still, very pale, not from excitement but from the weakness of disease. An imploring smile lighted up his face; from time to time he raised his hand, as though to check the storm, and, of course, a gesture from him would have been enough to end the scene; but he seemed to be waiting for something and watched them intently as though trying to make out something which was not perfectly clear to him. At last Miüsov felt completely humiliated and disgraced.

"We are all to blame for this scandalous scene," he said hotly. "But I did not foresee it when I came, though I knew with whom I had to deal. This must be stopped at once! Believe me, your reverence, I had no precise knowledge of the details that have just come to light, I was unwilling to believe them, and I learn for the first time. . . . A father is jealous of his son's relations with a woman of loose behaviour and intrigues with the creature to get his son into prison! This is the company in which I have been forced to appear here! I was deceived. I declare to you all that I was as much deceived as any one."

"Dmitri Fyodorovich," yelled Fyodor Pavlovich suddenly, in an unnatural voice, "if you were not my son I would challenge you this instant to a duel . . . with pistols, at three paces . . . across a handkerchief, across a handkerchief," he ended, stamping with both feet.

With old liars who have been acting all their lives there are moments when they enter so completely into their part that they tremble or shed tears of emotion in earnest, although at that very moment, or a second later, they are able to whisper to themselves, "You know you are lying, you shameless old sinner! You're play-acting now, in spite of your 'holy' wrath."

Dmitri frowned terribly, and looked with unutterable contempt at his father.

"I thought . . . I thought," he said, in a soft and, as it were, controlled voice, "that I was coming to my native place with the angel of my heart, my betrothed, to cherish his old age, and I find nothing but a depraved sensualist, a despicable clown!"

"A duel!" yelled the old wretch again, breathless and spluttering at each syllable. "And you, Pyotr Alexandrovich Miüsov, let me tell you that there has never been in all your family a loftier, and more honest — you hear — more honest woman than this 'creature,' as you have dared to call her! And you,

Dmitri Fyodorovich, have given up your betrothed for that 'creature,' so you must yourself have thought that your betrothed wasn't worth her little finger. That's the woman called a 'creature'!"

"Shameful!" broke from Father Iosif.

"Shameful and disgraceful!" Kalganov, flushing crimson, cried in a boyish voice, trembling with emotion. He had been silent till that moment.

"Why is such a man alive?" Dmitri, beside himself with rage, growled in a muffled voice, hunching up his shoulders till he looked almost deformed. "No, but tell me, should he be allowed to go on defiling the earth?" He looked round at every one and pointed at the old man. He spoke evenly and deliberately.

"Listen, listen, monks, to the parricide!" cried Fyodor Pavlovich, rushing up to Father Iosif. "That's the answer to your 'shameful'! What is shameful? That 'creature,' that 'woman of loose behaviour' is perhaps holier than you are yourselves, you monks who are seeking salvation! She fell perhaps in her youth, ruined by her environment. But she loved much, and Christ himself forgave the woman 'who loved much.'"

"It was not for such love Christ forgave her," broke impatiently from the gentle Father Iosif.

"Yes, it was for such, monks, it was! You save your souls here, eating cabbage, and think you are the righteous. You eat gudgeons, a gudgeon a day, and you think you bribe God with gudgeon."

"This is unendurable!" was heard on all sides in the cell.

But this unseemly scene was cut short in a most unexpected way. Father Zosima rose suddenly from his seat. Almost distracted with anxiety for the elder and every one else, Alyosha succeeded, however, in supporting him by the arm. Father Zosima moved towards Dmitri and reaching him sank on his knees before him. Alyosha thought that he had fallen from weakness, but this was not so. Having knelt, the elder distinctly and deliberately bowed down at Dmitri's feet till his forehead touched the floor. Alyosha was so astounded that he failed to assist him when he got up again. There was a faint smile on the elder's lips.

"Farewell! Forgive me, all of you!" he said, bowing on all sides to his guests.

Dmitri stood for a few moments in amazement. Bowing down to him — what did it mean? Suddenly he cried aloud, "Oh, God!" hid his face in his hands, and rushed out of the room. All the guests flocked out after him, in their confusion not saying good-bye, or bowing to their host. Only the monks went up to him again for a blessing.

"What did it mean, falling at his feet like that? Was it symbolic or what?" said Fyodor Pavlovich, suddenly quieted and trying to reopen conversation without daring to address anybody in particular. They were all passing out of the precincts of the hermitage at the moment.

"I can't answer for a madhouse and for madmen," Miüsov answered at once ill-humouredly, "but I will spare myself your company, Fyodor Pavlovich, and, trust me, for ever. Where's that monk?"

"That monk," that is, the monk who had invited them to dine with the Superior, did not keep them waiting. He met them as soon as they came down the steps from the elder's cell, as though he had been waiting for them all the time.

"Reverend father, kindly do me a favour. Convey my deepest respects to the Father Superior, apologise for me, Miüsov, personally, to his reverence, telling him that I deeply regret that owing to unforeseen circumstances I am unable to have the honour of being present at his table, greatly as I should desire to do so," Miüsov said irritably to the monk.

"And that unforeseen circumstance, of course, is myself," Fyodor Pavlovich cut in immediately. "Do you hear, father; this gentleman doesn't want to remain in my company or else he'd come at once. And you shall go, Pyotr Alexandrovich, pray go to the Father Superior and good appetite to you. I will decline, and not you. Home, home, I'll eat at home, I don't feel equal to it here, Pyotr Alexandrovich, my amiable relative."

"I am not your relative and never have been, you contemptible man!"

"I said it on purpose to madden you, because you always disclaim the relationship, though you really are a relation in spite of your shuffling. I'll prove it by the church calendar. As for you, Ivan, stay if you like. I'll send the horses for you later. Propriety requires you to go to the Father Superior, Pyotr Alexandrovich, to apologise for the disturbance we've been making. . . ."

"Is it true that you are going home? Aren't you lying?"

"Pyotr Alexandrovich! How could I dare after what's happened! Forgive me, gentlemen, I was carried away! And upset besides! And, indeed, I am ashamed. Gentlemen, one man has the heart of Alexander of Macedon and another the heart of the little dog Fido. Mine is that of the little dog Fido. I am abashed! After such an escapade how can I go to dinner, to gobble up the monastery's sauces? I am ashamed, I can't. You must excuse me!"

"The devil only knows, what if he deceives us," thought Miüsov, still hesitating, and watching the retreating buffoon with distrustful eyes. The latter turned round and, noticing that Miüsov was watching him, waved him a kiss.

"Well, are you coming to the Superior?" Miüsov asked Ivan abruptly.

"Why not? I was especially invited yesterday."

"Unfortunately I feel myself compelled to go to this confounded dinner," said Miüsov with the same irritability, regardless of the fact that the monk was listening. "We ought, at least, to apologise for the disturbance, and explain that it was not our doing. What do you think?"

"Yes, we must explain that it wasn't our doing. Besides, Father won't be there," observed Ivan.

"Well, I should hope not! Confound this dinner!"

They all walked on, however. The monk listened in silence. On the road through the copse he made one observation however — that the Father Superior had been waiting a long time, and that they were more than half an hour late. He received no answer. Miüsov looked with hatred at Ivan. "Here he is, going to the dinner as though nothing had happened," he thought. "A brazen face, and the conscience of a Karamazov!"

## CHAPTER VII
### A DIVINITY STUDENT BENT ON A CAREER

ALYOSHA helped his elder to his bedroom and seated him on his bed. It was a little room furnished with the bare necessities. There was a narrow iron bedstead, with a strip of felt for a mattress. In the corner, under the ikons, was a reading-desk with a cross and the Gospel lying on it. The elder sank exhausted on the bed. His eyes glittered and he breathed hard. He looked intently at Alyosha, as though considering something.

"Go, my dear boy, go. Porfiry is enough for me. Make haste, you are needed there, go and wait on the Father Superior's table."

"Allow me to stay here," Alyosha entreated.

"You are more needed there. There is no peace there. You will wait on them, and be of service. If evil spirits rise up, repeat a prayer. And remember, my boy (the elder liked to call him that), this is not the place for you in the future. When it is God's will to call me, leave the monastery. Go away for good."

Alyosha started.

"What is it? This is not your place for the time being. I consecrate you to a great novitiate in the world. Yours will be a long pilgrimage. And you will have to take a wife, too, you must. You will have to bear *all* before you come back. There will be much to do. But I don't doubt of you, and so I send you forth. Christ is with you. Do not abandon Him and He will not abandon you. You will see great sorrow, and in that sorrow you will be happy. This is my last message to you: in sorrow seek happiness. Work, work unceasingly. Remember my words, for although I shall talk with you again, not only my days but my hours are numbered."

Alyosha's face again betrayed strong emotion. The corners of his mouth quivered.

"What is it again?" Father Zosima asked, smiling gently. "The worldly may follow their dead with tears, but here we rejoice over the father who is departing. We rejoice and pray for him. Leave me, I must pray. Go and make haste. Be with your brothers. And not with one only, but with both."

Father Zosima raised his hand to bless him. It was impossible to protest, though Alyosha had a great longing to remain. He longed, moreover, to ask what was the significance of this bow to Dmitri; indeed, the question was on the tip of his tongue, but he dared not ask it. He knew that the elder would have explained it unasked if he had thought fit. But evidently such was not his pleasure. That gesture had made a terrible impression on Alyosha; he believed blindly that it had a mysterious significance. Mysterious, and perhaps dreadful.

As he hastened out of the hermitage precincts to reach the monastery in time to wait on the Father Superior's table, he felt a sudden pang at his heart, and stopped short. He seemed to hear again Father Zosima's words, foretelling his approaching end. What he had foretold so exactly must infallibly come to pass. Alyosha believed that implicitly. But how could he be left without him? How could he live without seeing and hearing him? Where should he go? He had told him not to weep, and to leave the monastery. Good God! It was long since Alyosha had known such anguish. He hurried through the copse that divided the hermitage from the monastery and, unable to bear the burden of his thoughts, he gazed at the ancient pines beside the path. He had not far to go — about five hundred paces. He expected to meet no one at that hour, but at the first turn of the path he noticed Rakitin. He was waiting for some one.

"Are you waiting for me?" asked Alyosha, overtaking him.

THE BLESSING OF FATHER ZOSIMA

"Yes," grinned Rakitin. "You are hurrying to the Father Superior, I know; he has a banquet. There's not been such a banquet since the Superior entertained the Bishop and General Pahatov, do you remember? I shan't be there, but you go and hand the sauces. Tell me one thing, Alexey, what does that dream mean? That's what I want to ask you."

"What dream?"

"That bowing to your brother, Dmitri. And didn't he tap the ground with his forehead, too!"

"You speak of Father Zosima?"

"Yes, of Father Zosima."

"Tapped the ground?"

"Ah, I have expressed myself irreverently? Well, what of it? Anyway, what does that dream mean?"

"I don't know what it means, Misha."

"I knew he wouldn't explain it to you! There's nothing wonderful about it, of course, only the usual holy mummery. But the hocus-pocus was not without a purpose. All the bigots in the town will talk about it and spread the story through the province, wondering what it meant. To my thinking the old man really has a keen nose; he sniffed a crime. Your house stinks."

"What crime?"

Rakitin evidently had something he was eager to speak of.

"It'll be in your family, this crime. Between your brothers and your rich old father. So Father Zosima flopped down to be ready for what may turn up. If something happens later on, it'll be: 'Ah, the holy man foresaw it, prophesied it!' though it's a poor sort of prophecy, flopping like that. 'Ah, but it was symbolic,' they'll say, 'an allegory,' and the devil knows what all! It'll be remembered to his glory: 'He predicted the crime and marked the criminal!' That's always the way with these pious ecstatics; they cross themselves at the pot-house and throw stones at the church. Your elder's that sort: he takes a stick to a just man and falls at the feet of a murderer."

"What crime? What murderer? What do you mean?"

Alyosha stopped dead. Rakitin stopped, too.

"What murderer? As though you didn't know! I'll bet you've thought of it before. That's interesting, too, by the way. Listen, Alyosha, you always speak the truth, though you're always between two stools. Have you thought of it or not? Answer."

"I have," answered Alyosha in a low voice. Even Rakitin was taken aback.

"What? Have you really?" he cried.

"I . . . I've not exactly thought of it," muttered Alyosha, "but directly you began speaking so strangely, I fancied I had thought of it myself."

"You see (and how well you expressed it!), you see? Looking at your father and your brother Mitya to-day you thought of a crime. Then I'm not mistaken?"

"But wait, wait a minute," Alyosha broke in uneasily; "what has led you to see all this? Why does it interest you? That's the first question."

"Two questions, disconnected, but natural. I'll deal with them separately. What led me to see it? I shouldn't have seen it, if I hadn't suddenly understood your brother Dmitri, seen right into the very heart of him all at once. I caught the whole man from one trait. These very honest but passionate people draw a line which mustn't be crossed. If it were, he'd stick a knife even into his father. But his father's a drunken and abandoned old sinner, who has never known how to restrain himself — they'll both let themselves go, and they'll come to grief."

"No, Misha, no. If that's all, you've reassured me! It won't come to that."

"But why are you trembling all over? Let me tell you; he may be honest — your Mitya (he is stupid, but honest), but he's — a sensualist. That's the very definition and inner essence of him. It's your father has handed him on his low sensuality. Do you know, I simply wonder at you, Alyosha, how you can have kept your purity. You're a Karamazov, too, you know! In your family sensuality is carried to a disease. But now, these three sensualists are watching one another, with their knives in their boots. The three of them are knocking their heads together, and you may be the fourth."

"You are mistaken about that woman. Dmitri — despises her," said Alyosha, with a sort of shudder.

"Grushenka? No, brother, he doesn't despise her. Since he has openly given up his betrothed for her, he doesn't despise her. There's something here, my dear boy, that you don't understand yet. A man will fall in love with some beauty, with a woman's body, or even with a part of a woman's body (a sensualist can understand that), and he'll surrender his own children for her, sell his father and mother, and his country, Russia, too. If he's honest, he'll steal; if he's humane, he'll murder; if he's faithful, he'll deceive. Pushkin, the poet of women's feet, sang of their feet in his verse. Others don't sing their praises, but they can't look at women's feet without a thrill — and it's not only their feet. Contempt's no help here, brother, even if he

did despise Grushenka. He does, but he can't tear himself away."

"I understand that," Alyosha jerked out suddenly.

"Really? Well, I dare say you do understand, since you blurt it out at the first word," said Rakitin, malignantly.

"That escaped you unawares, and the confession's the more precious. So it's a familiar subject; you've thought about it already, about sensuality, I mean! Oh, you virgin soul! You're a quiet one, Alyosha, you're a saint, I know, but the devil only knows what you've thought about, and what you know already! You are pure, but you've been down into the depths. . . . I've been watching you a long time. You're a Karamazov yourself; you're a thorough Karamazov — no doubt birth and selection have something to answer for. You're a sensualist through your father, a saintly fool through your mother. Why do you tremble? Is it true, then? Do you know, Grushenka has been begging me to bring you along; 'I'll pull off his cassock,' she says. You can't think how she keeps begging me to bring you. I wondered why she took such an interest in you. Do you know, she's an extraordinary woman, too!"

"Thank her and say I'm not coming," said Alyosha, with a crooked smile. "Finish what you were saying, Misha. I'll tell you my idea after."

"There's nothing to finish. It's all clear. It's the same old tune, brother. If even you are a sensualist at heart, what of your brother Ivan? He's a Karamazov, too. What is at the root of all you Karamazovs is that you're all grasping sensualists and saintly fools! Your brother Ivan writes theological articles in jest, for some idiotic, unknown reason of his own, though he's an atheist, and he admits it's a fraud himself — that's your brother Ivan. Besides, he's trying to get Mitya's betrothed for himself, and I fancy he'll succeed, too. And what's more it's with Mitya's consent. For Mitya will surrender his betrothed to him to be rid of her, the sooner to run to Grushenka. And he's ready to do that in spite of all his nobility and disinterestedness. Observe that. Those are the most fatal people! Who the devil can make you out? He recognises his vileness and goes on with it! Let me tell you, too, the old man, your father, is now crossing Mitya's path. He has suddenly gone crazy over Grushenka. His mouth waters at the sight of her. It's simply on her account he made that scene in the cell just now, simply because Miüsov called her an 'abandoned creature.' He's worse than a tom cat in love. At first she was only employed by him in connection with his pot-houses and in some other shady business, but now he has suddenly realised all she is and has gone wild about her. He keeps pestering her with his offers, not honourable ones, of course. And they'll clash, the precious father and son, on that path! But Grushenka favours neither of them, she's still playing with them, and teasing them both, considering which she can get most out of. For though she could filch a lot of money from the papa he wouldn't marry her, and maybe he'll turn stingy in the end and pull his purse-strings tight. That's where Mitya's value comes in, he has no money, but he's ready to marry her. Yes, ready to marry her! to abandon his betrothed, a rare beauty, Katerina Ivanovna, who's rich, and the daughter of a colonel, and to marry Grushenka, the former kept woman of a dissolute old merchant, Samsonov, a coarse, uneducated, provincial mayor. Some

murderous conflict may well come to pass from all this, and that's what your brother Ivan is waiting for. It would suit him down to the ground. He'll carry off Katerina Ivanovna, for whom he is languishing, and pocket her dowry of sixty thousand. That's very alluring to start with, for a man of no consequence and a beggar. And, take note, he won't be wronging Mitya, but doing him the greatest service. For I know for a fact that Mitya, only last week, when he was with some gipsy girls drunk in a tavern, shouted that he was unworthy of his betrothed, Katya, but that his brother Ivan, he was the man who deserved her. And Katerina Ivanovna will not in the end refuse such a fascinating man as Ivan. She's hesitating between the two of them already. And how has that Ivan won you all, so that you all worship him? He is laughing at you, and enjoying himself at your expense."

"How do you know? How can you speak so confidently?" Alyosha asked sharply, frowning.

"Why do you ask, and why are you frightened at my answer in advance? It shows that you know I'm speaking the truth."

"You don't like Ivan. Ivan wouldn't be tempted by money."

"Really? And the beauty of Katerina Ivanovna? It's not only the money, though a fortune of sixty thousand is an attraction."

"Ivan is above that. He wouldn't be tempted by thousands. It is not money, it's not comfort Ivan is seeking. Perhaps it's suffering he is seeking?"

"What wild dream now? Oh, you — aristocrats!"

"Ah, Misha, he has a stormy spirit. His mind is in bondage. He is haunted by a great, unresolved idea. He is one of those who don't want millions, but an answer to their questions."

"That's plagiarism, Alyosha. You're paraphrasing your elder. Ah, Ivan has set you a riddle!" cried Rakitin, with undisguised malice. He even changed colour, and his lips twitched. "And the riddle's a stupid one. It isn't worth guessing at it. Think a bit — and you'll see through it. His article is absurd and ridiculous. And did you hear his stupid theory just now: if there's no immortality of the soul, then there's no virtue, and everything is permissible. (And by the way, do you remember how your brother Mitya cried out: 'I will remember!') An attractive theory for scoundrels! — (I'm being abusive, that's stupid.) Not for scoundrels, but for sophomoric poseurs, 'haunted by profound, unsolvable problems.' He's showing off, and what it all comes to is, 'on the one hand we cannot but admit' and 'on the other, it must be confessed'! His whole theory is vile! Humanity will find in itself the power to live for virtue even without believing in immortality. It will find it in the love of freedom, of equality, of fraternity."

Rakitin could hardly restrain himself in his heat, but, suddenly, as though remembering something, he stopped short.

"Well, that's enough," he said, with a still more crooked smile. "Why are you laughing? Do you think I'm a vulgarian?"

"No, I never dreamed of thinking you a vulgarian. You are clever but . . . never mind, I was silly to smile. I understand your getting hot about it, Misha. I guess from your warmth that you are not indifferent to Katerina Ivanovna yourself; I've suspected that for a long time, brother, that's why you don't like my brother Ivan. Are you jealous of him?"

"And jealous of her money, too? Won't you add that?"

"I'll say nothing about money. I am not going to insult you."

"I believe it, since you say so, but confound you, and your brother Ivan with you. Don't you understand that one might very well dislike him, apart from Katerina Ivanovna? And why the devil should I like him? He condescends to abuse me, you know. Why haven't I a right to abuse him?"

"I never heard of his saying anything about you, good or bad. He doesn't speak of you."

"And I heard that the day before yesterday at Katerina Ivanovna's he was abusing me for all he was worth — you see what an interest he takes in your humble servant. And which is the jealous one after that, brother, I can't say. He was so good as to express the opinion that, if I don't go in for the career of an archimandrite in the immediate future and don't take orders, I shall be sure to go to Petersburg and get on to some solid magazine as a critic, that I shall write for the next ten years, and in the end become the owner of the magazine. Then, he said, I'll go on editing it, in a liberal and atheistic spirit, with a socialistic tinge, with a tiny gloss of socialism, but keeping a sharp look-out all the time, that is, keeping in with both sides and hoodwinking the fools. According to your brother's account, the tinge of socialism won't hinder me from laying by the proceeds and investing them under the guidance of some Jew, till at the end of my career I build a large house in Petersburg and move my publishing offices to it, and let out the rest to lodgers. He has even chosen the place for it, near the new stone bridge which they say is to be built across the Neva at Liteinaya Street."

"Ah, Misha, perhaps that's just what will really happen, every word of it," cried Alyosha, unable to restrain a good-humoured smile.

"You are pleased to be sarcastic, too, Alexey Fyodorovich."

"No, no, I'm joking, forgive me. I've something quite different in my mind. But, excuse me, who can have told you all this? You can't have been at Katerina Ivanovna's yourself when he was talking about you?"

"I wasn't there, but Dmitri Fyodorovich was; and I heard him tell it with my own ears; if you want to know, he didn't tell me, but I overheard him, unintentionally, of course, for I was sitting in Grushenka's bedroom and I couldn't go away because Dmitri Fyodorovich was in the next room."

"Oh, yes, I'd forgotten she was a relation of yours."

"A relation! That Grushenka a relation of mine!" cried Rakitin, turning crimson. "Are you mad? You're out of your mind!"

"Why, isn't she a relation of yours? I heard so."

"Where can you have heard it? You Karamazovs brag of being an ancient, noble family, though your father used to run about playing the buffoon at other men's tables, and was only admitted to the kitchen as a favour. I may be only a priest's son, and dirt in the eyes of gentlemen like you, but don't insult me so lightly and wantonly. I have a sense of honour, too, Alexey Fyodorovich, I couldn't be a relation of Grushenka, a common wench. I beg you to understand that!"

Rakitin was intensely irritated.

"Forgive me, for goodness' sake, I had no idea . . . besides . . . how can you call her that? Is she . . . that sort of woman?" Alyosha flushed suddenly. "I tell you again, I heard that she was a relation of yours. You often go to see her, and you told me yourself you're not having a love affair with her. I never dreamed that you of all people had such contempt for her! Does she really deserve it?"

"I may have reasons of my own for visiting her. That's not your business. But as for relationship, your brother, or even your father is more likely to make her yours, than mine. Well, here we are. You'd better go to the kitchen. Hullo! what's wrong, what is it? Are we late? They can't have finished dinner so soon! Have the Karamazovs been making trouble again? No doubt they have. Here's your father and your brother Ivan after him. They've broken away from the Father Superior's party. And look, Father Isidor's shouting after them from the steps. And your father's shouting and waving his arms. I expect he's swearing. Bah, and there goes Miüsov driving away in his carriage. You see, he's going. And there's old Maximov running!—but this is a scandal! There can't have been any dinner. Have they beaten up the Father Superior? Or have they, perhaps, been beaten up? It would serve them right!"

There was reason for Rakitin's exclamations. Indeed, there had been an unprecedented and unheard-of scandal. It had all happened on the spur of the moment.

## CHAPTER VIII
### THE SCANDALOUS SCENE

Miüsov, as a man of breeding and delicacy, could not but feel some inward qualms, when he reached the Father Superior's quarters with Ivan: he felt ashamed of having lost his temper. He felt that he ought to have disdained that despicable wretch, Fyodor Pavlovich, too much to have been upset by him in Father Zosima's cell, and so to have forgotten himself. "The monks were not to blame, in any case," he decided, on the steps. "And if they're decent people here, too (and the Father Superior, I understand, is of the gentry), why not be courteous and friendly with them? I won't argue, I'll fall in with everything, I'll win them by politeness, and . . . and . . . show them that I've nothing to do with that Æsop, that buffoon, that Pierrot, and have merely been taken in over this affair, just as they have."

He determined to drop his litigation with the monastery, and relinquish his claims to the wood-cutting and fishery rights once and for all that very day. He was the more ready to do this because the rights had become much less valuable, and he had indeed the vaguest idea where the wood and river in question were.

These excellent intentions were strengthened when they entered the Father Superior's dining-room, though, strictly speaking, it was not a dining-room, for the Father Superior had only two rooms altogether; they were, however, much larger and more comfortable than Father Zosima's. But there was no great luxury about the furnishing of these rooms either. The furniture was of mahogany, upholstered in leather, in the old-fashioned style of the twenties; the floor was not even stained, but everything was shining with cleanliness, and there were many choice flowers in the windows; the most sumptuous thing in the room at the moment was, of course, the luxuriously appointed table. The cloth was clean, the service shone; there were three kinds of well-baked bread, two bottles of wine, two of excellent mead, and a large glass jug of kvass — both the latter made in the monastery, and

famous in the neighbourhood. There was no vodka. Rakitin related afterwards that the dinner included five courses: fish soup made of sterlets, served with little fish patties; delicious boiled fish served in a special way; salmon cutlets; ice cream and compote; and finally, blanc-mange. Rakitin nosed out all these good things, for he could not resist peeping into the kitchen, where he already had connections. He had connections everywhere, and got information about everything. He had a restless and envious heart. He was well aware of his own considerable abilities, but nervously exaggerated them in his self-conceit. He knew he would play a prominent part of some sort, but Alyosha, who was strongly attached to him, was distressed to see that his friend Rakitin was dishonourable, and quite unconscious of being so, considering, on the contrary, that because he would not steal money left on the table he was a man of the highest integrity. Neither Alyosha nor any one else could have done anything about that.

Rakitin, of course, was a person of too little consequence to be asked to the dinner, to which Father Iosif, Father Païssy, and only one other monk had been invited. They were already waiting in the dining-room when Miüsov, Kalganov, and Ivan Fyodorovich arrived. The other guest, Maximov, stood a little aside, waiting also. The Father Superior stepped into the middle of the room to receive his guests. He was a tall, thin, but still vigorous old man, with black hair streaked with grey, and a long, grave, ascetic face. He bowed to his guests in silence. But this time they approached to receive his blessing. Miüsov even tried to kiss his hand, but the Father Superior drew it back in time to avoid the salute. But Ivan Fyodorovich and Kalganov went through the ceremony in the most simple-hearted and complete manner, kissing his hand as peasants do.

"We must apologise most humbly, your reverence," began Miüsov, simpering affably, and yet speaking in a dignified and respectful tone. "Pardon us for having come alone without the other gentleman you invited, Fyodor Pavlovich. He felt obliged to decline the honour of your hospitality, and not without reason. In the reverend Father Zosima's cell he was carried away by the unhappy dissension with his son, and let fall words which were quite out of keeping . . . in fact, quite unseemly . . . as" (he glanced at the monks) "your reverence is, no doubt, already aware. And therefore, recognising that he had been to blame, he felt sincere regret and shame, and begged me, and his son Ivan Fyodorovich, to convey to you his apologies, regrets, and contrition. In brief, he hopes and desires to make amends later. For the present, he asks your blessing, and begs you to forget what has taken place."

As he uttered the last word of his tirade, Miüsov completely recovered his self-complacency, and all traces of his former irritation disappeared. He fully and sincerely loved humanity again.

The Father Superior listened to him with dignity, and, with a slight bend of the head, replied:

"I sincerely deplore his absence. Perhaps at our table he might have learnt to like us, and we him. Pray join us in our repast, gentlemen."

He stood before the holy image, and began to say grace, aloud. All bent their heads reverently, and Maximov stepped forward, clasping his hands before him, with peculiar fervour.

It was at this moment that Fyodor Pavlovich played his last prank. It must be noted that he really had meant to go home, and really had felt the impossibility of going to dine with the Father Superior as though nothing had happened, after his disgraceful behaviour in the elder's cell. Not that he was so very much ashamed of himself or that he felt himself much at fault — quite the contrary perhaps. But still he felt it would be unseemly to go to dinner. Yet his creaking carriage had hardly been brought to the steps of the hostelry, and he had hardly got into it, when he suddenly stopped short. He remembered his own words at the elder's: "I always feel when I meet people that I am lower than all, and that they all take me for a buffoon; so I say let me play the buffoon, for you are, every one of you, stupider and lower than I." He had the sudden desire to revenge himself on every one for his own vileness. He suddenly recalled how he had once in the past been asked, "Why do you hate so and so, so much?" And he had answered them, in a fit of clownish impudence, "I'll tell you. He has done me no harm. But I played him a dirty trick, and ever since I have hated him."

Remembering that now, he smiled quietly and malignantly, hesitating for a moment. His eyes flashed, and his lips positively began to quiver. "Well, since I have begun, I may as well finish," he decided suddenly. His inmost thought at that moment might be expressed in the following words, "Well, there is no clearing myself now. So I'll go the limit. I will show them I have no shame before them — that's all!"

He told the coachman to wait, while with rapid steps he returned to the monastery and went straight to the Father Superior's quarters. He had no clear idea what he would do, but he knew that he was no longer in control of himself, and that a touch might drive him to the utmost limits of obscenity, but only to obscenity, to nothing criminal, nothing for which he could be legally punished. In the last resort, he could always restrain himself, and indeed had marvelled at himself, on that score, sometimes. He appeared in the Father Superior's dining-room, just at the moment when the prayer was over, and all were moving to the table. Standing in the doorway, he scanned the company and, with a prolonged, impudent, malicious chuckle, looked them all boldly in the face. "They thought I had gone, and here I am again," he shouted so that the room rang.

For one moment every one stared at him without a word; and at once every one felt that something revolting, grotesque, positively scandalous, was about to happen. Miüsov passed immediately from the most benevolent frame of mind to the most savage. All the feelings that had subsided and died down in his heart revived instantly.

"No! this I cannot endure!" he cried. "I absolutely cannot! and . . . I certainly cannot!" The blood rushed to his head. He positively stammered, but he was beyond thinking of style; and he seized his hat.

"What is it he cannot?" cried Fyodor Pavlovich, "that he absolutely cannot and certainly cannot? Your reverence, am I to come in or not? Will you receive me as your guest?"

"You are heartily welcome," answered the Superior. "Gentlemen!" he added, "may I venture to beg you most earnestly to lay aside your dissensions, and to be united in love and family harmony — with prayer to the Lord — at our humble table."

"No, no, it is impossible!" cried Miüsov, beside himself.

"Well, if it is impossible for Pyotr Alexandrovich, it is impossible for me, and I won't stop. That is why I came. I will stay with Pyotr Alexandrovich everywhere now. If you will go away, Pyotr Alexandrovich, I will go away, too; if you remain, I will remain. You stung him by what you said about family harmony, Father Superior, he does not admit he is my relation. That's right, isn't it, von Sohn? Here's von Sohn. How are you, von Sohn?"

"Do you mean me?" muttered Maximov, puzzled.

"Of course I mean you," cried Fyodor Pavlovich. "Who else? The Father Superior could not be von Sohn."

"But I am not von Sohn either. I am Maximov."

"No, you are von Sohn. Your reverence, do you know who von Sohn was? It was a famous murder case. He was killed in a house of harlotry — I believe that is what such places are called among you — he was killed and robbed, and in spite of his venerable age, he was nailed up in a box and sent from Petersburg to Moscow in the luggage van. And while they were nailing him up, the harlots sang songs and played the harp, that is to say, the piano. So this is that very von Sohn. He has risen from the dead, haven't you, von Sohn?"

"What can this mean? What is this?" voices were heard in the group of monks.

"Let us go," cried Miüsov, addressing Kalganov.

"No, permit me," Fyodor Pavlovich broke in shrilly, taking another step into the room. "Allow me to finish. There in the cell I was blamed for behaving disrespectfully just because I mentioned gudgeon. Pyotr Alexandrovich Miüsov, my relation, prefers to have *plus de noblesse que de sincérité* in his words, but I prefer in mine *plus de sincérité que de noblesse*, and — damn the noblesse! That's right, isn't it, von Sohn? Allow me, Father Superior, though I am a buffoon and play the buffoon, yet I am the soul of honour, and I want to speak my mind. Yes, I am the soul of honour, while in Pyotr Alexandrovich there is wounded vanity and nothing else. I had come perhaps to have a look round and speak my mind. My son, Alexey, is here, saving his soul. I am a father; I care for his welfare, and it is my duty to care. While I've been playing the fool, I have been listening and having a look on the sly; and now I want to give you the last act of the performance. You know how things are with us? As a thing falls, so it lies. As a thing once has fallen, so it must lie for ever. Not a bit of it! I want to get up again. Holy fathers, you revolt me. Confession is a great sacrament, before which I am ready to bow down reverently; but there in the cell, they all kneel down and confess aloud. Can it be right to confess aloud? The holy fathers ordained that confession should be whispered into the ear: only then your confession will be a sacrament, and so it has been since olden times. But this way how can I explain to him before every one that I did this and that, for instance. . . . I mean, this and that, you understand? Sometimes it would not be proper to talk about it — why, it's a scandal! No, fathers, this way lies sectarian heresy, I dare say. . . . At the first opportunity I shall write to the Synod, and I shall take my son, Alexey, home."

We must note here that Fyodor Pavlovich knew where to look for the weak spot. There had been at one time malicious gossip which had even reached the Archbishop (not only

regarding our monastery, but also others where the institution of elders existed) that too much respect was paid to the elders, even to the detriment of the authority of the Superior, that the elders abused the sacrament of confession, and so on and so on — absurd charges which had died away of themselves everywhere. But the spirit of devilish folly, which had caught up Fyodor Pavlovich, and was spurring him on in his wrongheadedness to lower and lower depths of ignominy, prompted him with this old slander. Fyodor Pavlovich did not understand a word of it, and he could not even put it sensibly, for on this occasion no one had been kneeling and confessing aloud in the elder's cell, so that he could not have seen anything of the kind. He was only speaking from confused memory of old slanders. But as soon as he had uttered his foolish tirade, he felt he had been talking absurd nonsense, and at once longed to prove to his audience, and above all to himself, that he had not been talking nonsense. And, though he knew perfectly well that with each word he would be adding more and more absurdity, he could not restrain himself, and plunged forward blindly.

"How abominable!" cried Pyotr Alexandrovich.

"Pardon me!" said the Father Superior. "It was said of old, 'Many have begun to speak against me and have uttered wicked words. And hearing it I have said within me: it is the medicine of the Christ, and He has sent it to heal my vainglorious soul.' And so we humbly thank you, precious guest!" and he made Fyodor Pavlovich a low bow.

"Tut-tut-tut! Bigotry and stock phrases! Stock phrases and stock gestures. The old lies and formal prostrations. We know all about them. A kiss on the lips and a dagger in the heart, as in Schiller's *Robbers*. I don't like sham, fathers, I want the truth. But the truth is not to be found in gudgeon, and that I proclaim aloud! Father monks, why do you fast? Why do you expect reward in heaven for that? Why, for reward like that I will come and fast, too! No, saintly monk, you try being virtuous in the world, be useful to society, without shutting yourself up in a monastery at other people's expense, and without expecting a reward up aloft for it — you'll find that a bit harder. I can talk sense, too, Father Superior. What have they got here?" He went up to the table. "Old port wine, mead brewed by the Eliseyev Brothers. Fie, fie, fathers! That's better than gudgeon. Look at the bottles the fathers have brought out, he! he! he! And who has provided it all? The Russian peasant, the toiler, brings here the groat earned by his horny hand, wringing it from his family and the tax-gatherer! You bleed the people, you know, holy fathers."

"This is altogether disgraceful, coming from you," said Father Iosif.

Father Païssy kept obstinately silent. Miüsov rushed from the room, and Kalganov after him.

"Well, father, I will follow Pyotr Alexandrovich! I am not coming to see you again. You may beg me on your knees, I shan't come. I sent you a thousand roubles, so you're casting sheep's-eyes at me again. He, he, he! No, you won't get any more from me. I am taking my revenge for my youth, for all the humiliation I endured." He thumped the table with his fist in a paroxysm of simulated feeling. "This monastery has played a great part in my life! It has cost me many bitter tears. You used to set my wife, the possessed one, against me.

You cursed me with bell and book, you spread stories about me all over the place. Enough, fathers! This is the age of Liberalism, the age of steamers and railways. Neither a thousand, nor a hundred roubles, no, nor a hundred copecks will you get out of me!"

It must be noted again that our monastery had never played any great part in his life, and he had never shed a bitter tear because of it. But he was so carried away by his simulated emotion that for one moment he almost believed it himself. He almost wept with emotion. But at that very instant, he felt that it was time to draw back.

The Father Superior bowed his head at his malicious lie, and again spoke impressively:

"It is written again, 'Bear circumspectly and gladly dishonour that cometh upon thee by no act of thine own, be not confounded and hate not him who hath dishonoured thee.' And so will we."

"Tut-tut-tut! Church lingo and all that rigmarole. Farewell, fathers, I am going. But I will take my son, Alexey, away from here for ever, on my parental authority. Ivan Fyodorovich, my most dutiful son, permit me to order you to follow me. Von Sohn, what are you staying here for? Come to my place now. It is fun there. It is only one short verst; instead of lenten oil, I will give you sucking-pig and kasha. We will have dinner with French brandy and liqueurs. I've cloudberry wine. . . . Hey, von Sohn, don't lose your chance." He went out, shouting and gesticulating.

It was at that moment Rakitin saw him and pointed him out to Alyosha.

"Alexey!" his father shouted, from far off, catching sight of him. "You come home to me to-day, for good, and bring your pillow and mattress, and leave no trace behind."

Alyosha stood rooted to the spot, watching the scene in silence. Meanwhile, Fyodor Pavlovich had got into the carriage, and Ivan was about to follow him in grim silence without even turning to say good-bye to Alyosha. But at this point another almost incredible scene of grotesque buffoonery gave the finishing touch to the episode. Suddenly, beside the footboard of the carriage, Maximov appeared. He ran up, panting, afraid of being too late. Rakitin and Alyosha saw him running. He was in such a hurry that in his impatience he put his foot on the step on which Ivan's left foot was still resting, and clutching the carriage he kept trying to jump in. "I am going with you!" he kept shouting, laughing a thin mirthful laugh with a look of reckless glee in his face. "Take me, too."

"There!" cried Fyodor Pavlovich, delighted. "Did I not say he was von Sohn? It is von Sohn himself, risen from the dead. Why, how did you tear yourself away? What were you *vonsohning* in there? And how could you get away from the dinner? You must really be brazen-faced! I am that myself, but I am surprised at you, brother! Jump in, jump in! Let him in, Ivan. It will be fun. He can lie somewhere at our feet. Will you, von Sohn? Or perch on the box with the coachman. Skip onto the box, von Sohn!"

But Ivan, who had by now taken his seat, without a word gave Maximov a violent punch in the breast and sent him flying. It was pure luck that he did not fall. "Drive on!" Ivan shouted angrily to the coachman.

"Why, what are you doing, what are you about? Why did you do that?" Fyodor Pavlovich protested.

But the carriage had already driven away. Ivan made no reply.

"Well, you are a fellow," Fyodor Pavlovich said again.

After a pause of two minutes, looking askance at his son, "Why, it was you got up all this monastery business. You put me up to it, you approved of it. Why are you angry now?"

"You've talked rot enough. You might rest a bit now," Ivan snapped sullenly.

Fyodor Pavlovich was silent again for two minutes.

"A drop of brandy now would go to the right spot," he observed sententiously, but Ivan made no response.

"You shall have some, too, when we get home."

Ivan was still silent. Fyodor Pavlovich waited another two minutes.

"But I will take Alyosha away from the monastery, though you will dislike it so much, most respectful Karl von Moor."

Ivan shrugged his shoulders contemptuously, and turning away stared at the road. And they did not speak again all the way home.

# BOOK III

## THE SENSUALISTS

### CHAPTER I

#### IN THE SERVANTS' QUARTERS

THE Karamazov house was far from being in the centre of the town, but neither was it on the outskirts. It was a pleasant-looking old house of two storeys, painted grey, with a red iron roof. It was roomy and snug, and might still last many years. There were all sorts of unexpected little cupboards and closets and staircases. There were rats in it, but Fyodor Pavlovich did not altogether dislike them. "One doesn't feel so lonesome when one's left alone in the evening," he used to say. It was his habit to send the servants away to the lodge for the night and to lock himself up alone. The lodge was a spacious and solid building in the yard. Fyodor Pavlovich used to have the cooking done there, although there was a kitchen in the house; he did not like the smell of cooking, and, winter and summer alike, the dishes were carried in across the courtyard. The house was built for a large family; there was room for five times as many, with their servants. But at the time of our story there was no one living in the house but Fyodor Pavlovich and his son Ivan. And in the lodge there were only three servants: old Grigory, his old wife Marfa, and the servant Smerdyakov, still a young man. Of these three we must say a few words. Of Grigory Vasilyevich Kutuzov we have said something already. He was firm and determined and went stubbornly and undeviatingly towards his goal, if once he had been brought by any reasons (and they were often amazingly illogical ones) to believe that it was the right one. He was honest and incorruptible. His wife, Marfa Ignatyevna, had obeyed her husband's will implicitly all her life, yet she had pestered him terriby after the emancipation of the serfs. She was set on leaving Fyodor Pavlovich and opening a little shop in Moscow with their small savings. But Grigory decided then, once for all, that "the woman's talking nonsense, for every woman is without honour," and that they ought not to leave their old master, whatever he might be, "for that was now their duty."

"Do you understand what duty is?" he asked Marfa Ignatyevna.

"I know about duty, Grigory Vasilyevich, but why it's our duty to stay here, that I can't understand," Marfa answered firmly.

"Well, don't understand then. But so it shall be. And you hold your tongue."

And so it was. They did not go away, and Fyodor Pavlovich named a sum, a small one, as wages, and paid it regularly. Grigory knew, too, that he had an indisputable influence over his master. It was true, and he was aware of

68

it. Fyodor Pavlovich was an obstinate and cunning buffoon, yet, though his will was strong enough "in some of the affairs of life," as he expressed it, he found himself, to his surprise, of a somewhat weak character when it came to certain other emergencies. He knew his weaknesses and was afraid of them. There are positions in which one has to keep a sharp look-out. And that's not easy without a trustworthy man, and Grigory was a most trustworthy man. Many times in the course of his life Fyodor Pavlovich had only just escaped a sound thrashing through Grigory's intervention, and on each occasion the old servant gave him a lecture. But it wasn't only thrashings that Fyodor Pavlovich was afraid of. There were graver situations, and very subtle and complicated ones, in which Fyodor Pavlovich felt an inexplicable and extraordinary craving for some one faithful and devoted, which sometimes unaccountably came upon him all in a moment. It was almost a morbid condition. Dissolute and often cruel in his lust, like some noxious insect, Fyodor Pavlovich was sometimes, in moments of drunkenness, overcome by a spiritual terror and a moral convulsion which took an almost physical form. "My soul's simply quaking in my throat at such times," he used to say. At such moments he liked to feel that there was near at hand, in the lodge if not in the room, a steady, devoted soul, a man untainted by vice, and indeed, totally unlike himself, one who had seen all his debauchery and knew all his secrets, but was ready in his devotion to overlook all that, not to oppose him, above all, not to reproach him or threaten him with anything, either in this world or in the next, and, in case of need, to defend him — from whom? From somebody unknown, but terrible and dangerous. What he needed was to feel that there was *another* human being, an old and tried friend, that he might call him in his sick moments merely to look at his face, or, perhaps, exchange some quite irrelevant words with him. And if this person were not angry, he felt comforted, and if he were angry, he was more dejected. It happened even (very rarely however) that Fyodor Pavlovich went at night to the lodge to wake Grigory and fetch him for a moment. When the old man came, Fyodor Pavlovich would begin talking about the most trivial matters, and would soon dismiss him, sometimes even with mockery and a jest. And then Fyodor Pavlovich would spit, get into bed, and sleep the sleep of the just. Something of the same sort had happened to Fyodor Pavlovich on Alyosha's arrival. Alyosha "pierced his heart" by "living with him, seeing everything and condemning nothing." Moreover, Alyosha brought with him something his father had never known before: a complete absence of contempt for him and an invariable kindness, a perfectly natural unaffected devotion to the old man who deserved it so little. All this was a complete surprise to the old lecher, who had been leading a bachelor's life. It was a new and startling experience for him, who had till then loved nothing but "evil." When Alyosha had left him, he confessed to himself that he had learnt something he had not till then been willing to learn.

I mentioned already at the beginning of my tale that Grigory had detested Adelaïda Ivanovna, the first wife of Fyodor Pavlovich and the mother of Dmitri, and that he had, on the contrary, protected Sofya Ivanovna, the poor "possessed woman," against his master and any one who chanced to speak ill or lightly of her. His sympathy for this unhappy woman had become something sacred to him, so that even now, twenty years after, he could not bear a slighting allusion to her from any one, and would at once check the offender. Externally, Grigory was a cold, dignified, and reserved man, whose words, when he did speak, were weighty and grave. It was impossible to tell at first blush whether he loved his meek, obedient wife; but he really did love her, and she knew it.

Marfa Ignatyevna was by no means stupid; indeed, she was probably cleverer than her spouse, or, at least, more prudent than he in worldly affairs, and yet she had given in to him in everything without question or complaint ever since her marriage, and respected him for his spiritual superiority. It was remarkable how little they spoke to one another in the course of their lives, and only of the most necessary daily affairs. Grave and dignified, Grigory thought over all his affairs and troubles alone, so that Marfa Ignatyevna had long grown used to knowing that he did not need her advice. She felt that her husband prized her silence, and took it as a sign of her good sense. He had never beaten her but once, and then only slightly. Once during the year after Fyodor Pavlovich's marriage to Adelaïda Ivanovna, the village girls and women — at that time serfs — were called together before the house to sing and dance. They were beginning "In the Green Meadows," when Marfa, at that time a young woman, skipped forward and danced "the Russian Dance," not in the village fashion, but as she had danced it when she was a servant in the service of the rich Miüsov family, in their private theatre, where the actors were taught to dance by a dancing master from Moscow. Grigory saw how his wife danced, and, an hour later,

at home in their cottage he gave her a lesson, pulling her hair a little. But there it ended: the beating was never repeated, and Marfa Ignatyevna gave up dancing.

God had not blessed them with children. One child was born but it died. Grigory was fond of children, and was not ashamed of showing it. When Adelaïda Ivanovna had run away, Grigory took Dmitri, then a child of three, combed his hair and washed him in a tub with his own hands, and looked after him for almost a year. Afterwards he had looked after Ivan and Alyosha for which the general's widow had rewarded him with a slap in the face; but I have already related all that. The only happiness his own child had brought him had been in the anticipation of its birth. When it was born, his heart was stricken with grief and horror. The baby had six fingers. Grigory was so crushed by this that he was not only silent till the day of the christening, but kept away in the garden. It was spring, and he spent three days digging the kitchen garden. The third day was fixed for christening the baby: meantime Grigory had reached a conclusion. Going into the cottage where the clergy were assembled and the visitors had arrived, including Fyodor Pavlovich, who was to stand godfather, he suddenly announced that the baby "ought not to be christened at all." He announced this quietly, briefly, speaking through his teeth, and gazing with dull intentness at the priest.

"Why not?" asked the priest with good-humoured surprise.

"Because it's a dragon," muttered Grigory.

"A dragon? What dragon?"

Grigory did not speak for some time. "It's a confusion of nature," he muttered vaguely, but firmly, obviously unwilling to say more.

GRIGORY AND THE CHILD

They laughed, and of course christened the poor baby. Grigory prayed earnestly at the font, but his opinion of the new-born child remained unchanged. Yet he did not interfere in any way. As long as the sickly infant lived he scarcely looked at it, tried indeed not to notice it, and for the most part kept out of the cottage. But when, at the end of a fortnight, the baby died of thrush, he himself laid the child in its little coffin, looked at it in profound grief, and when they were filling up the shallow little grave he fell on his knees and bowed down to the earth. He did not for years afterwards mention his child, nor did Marfa speak of the baby before him, and, even if Grigory were not present, she never spoke of it above a whisper. Marfa observed that, from the day of the burial, he devoted himself to "religion" and took to reading the "Lives of the Saints," for the most part sitting alone and in silence, and always putting on his big, round, silver-rimmed spectacles. He rarely read aloud, only perhaps during Lent. He was fond of the book of Job, and had somehow got hold of a copy of the discourses and sermons of "our godly Father Isaac the Syrian," which he read persistently for years together, understanding practically nothing of it, but perhaps prizing and loving it the more for that. Of late he had begun to listen to the doctrines of the sect of Flagellants settled in the neighbourhood. He was evidently shaken by them, but judged it unfitting to go over to the new faith. His habit of edifying reading gave him an expression of still greater gravity.

He was perhaps predisposed to mysticism. And the birth of his deformed child, and its death, had, as though by special design been accompanied by another strange and marvellous event, which, as he said later, had left an "imprint" upon his soul. It happened that, on the very night after the burial of his child, Marfa was awakened by the wail of a new-born baby. She was frightened and waked her husband. He listened and said he thought it was more like some one groaning, "it might be a woman." He got up and dressed. It was a rather warm night in May. As he went down the steps, he distinctly heard groans coming from the garden. But the gate from the yard into the garden was locked at night, and there was no other way of entering it, for it was enclosed all round by a strong, high fence. Going back into the house, Grigory lighted a lantern, took the garden key, and taking no notice of the hysterical terror of his wife, who was still persuaded that she heard a child crying, and that it was her own baby crying and calling for her, went into the garden in silence. There he heard at once that the groans came from the bath-house that stood near the garden gate, and that they were the groans of a woman. Opening the door of the bath-house, he saw a sight which petrified him. An idiot girl, who wandered about the streets and was known to the whole town by the nickname of Lizaveta Smerdyashchaya (Stinking Lizaveta), had got into the bath-house and had just given birth to a child. She lay dying with the baby beside her. She said nothing, for she had never been able to speak. But her story needs a chapter to itself.

## CHAPTER II
### LIZAVETA

THERE was one circumstance which struck Grigory particularly, and confirmed a very unpleasant and revolting suspicion. This Lizaveta was a dwarfish creature, "not five foot within a wee bit," as many of the pious old women said pathetically about her, after her death. The broad, healthy, red face of the twenty-year old girl had a look of blank idiocy and the fixed stare in her eyes was unpleasant, in spite of their meek expression. She wandered about, summer and winter alike, barefooted, wearing nothing but a hempen smock. Her coarse, almost black hair curled like lamb's wool, and formed a sort of huge cap on her head. It was always crusted with mud, and had leaves, bits of stick, and shavings clinging to it, as she always slept on the ground and in the dirt. Her father, a homeless, sickly drunkard, called Ilya, had lost everything and lived many years as a workman with some well-to-do tradespeople. Her mother had long been dead. Spiteful and ailing, Ilya used to beat Lizaveta inhumanly whenever she returned to him. But she rarely did so, for every one in the town was ready to look after her as being an idiot, and so specially dear to God. Ilya's employers, and many others in the town, especially of the tradespeople, tried to clothe her better, and always rigged her out with high boots and a sheepskin coat for the winter. But, although she allowed them to dress her up without resisting, she usually went away, preferably to the cathedral porch, and taking off all that had been given her — kerchief, sheepskin, skirt, or boots — she left them there and walked away barefoot in her smock as before. It happened on one occasion that a new governor of the province, making a tour of inspection in our town, saw Lizaveta, and was wounded in his tenderest feelings. And though he was told she was an idiot, he pronounced that for a young woman of twenty to wander about in nothing but a smock was a breach of the proprieties, and must not occur again. But the governor went his way, and

Lizaveta was left as she was. At last her father died, which endeared her, being thus orphaned, even more to the pious people of the town. In fact, every one seemed to love her; even the boys did not tease her, and the boys of our town, especially the schoolboys, are a mischievous set. She would walk into strange houses and no one drove her away. On the contrary, every one was kind to her and gave her a groat. If she were given a copper, she would take it, and at once drop it in the alms-jug of the church or the prison. If she were given a roll or a bun in the market, she would hand it to the first child she met. Sometimes she would stop one of the richest ladies in the town and give it to her, and the lady would be pleased to take it. She herself never tasted anything but black bread and water. If she went into a fine shop, where there were costly goods or money lying about, no one kept watch on her, for they knew that if she saw thousands of roubles overlooked by them, she would not have touched a groat. She scarcely ever went to church. She slept either on a church porch or, having climbed over a hurdle (to this day there are many hurdles instead of fences in our town), in a kitchen garden. She used at least once a week to turn up "at home," that is at the house of her father's former employers, and in the winter went there every night, and slept either in the passage or the cowhouse. People were amazed that she could stand such a life, but she was accustomed to it, and, although she was so tiny, she was of a robust constitution. Some of the townspeople declared that she did all this only from pride, but that is hardly credible. She could hardly speak, and only from time to time uttered an inarticulate grunt. How could she have been proud?

Now it happened one clear, warm, moonlight night in September (a long time ago) that five or six drunken revellers were returning from the club at a very late hour, according to our provincial notions. They passed through the "back-way," which led between the back gardens of the houses, with hurdles on either side. This way leads out on to the bridge over the long, stinking pool which we were accustomed to call a river. Among the nettles and burdocks beside the hurdle our revellers saw Lizaveta asleep. They stopped to look at her, laughing, and began jesting with unbridled licentiousness. It occurred to one young gentleman to make the whimsical inquiry whether any one could possibly look upon such an animal as a woman, and so forth. . . . They all pronounced with lofty repugnance that it was impossible. But Fyodor Pavlovich, who was of the company, thrust himself forward and declared that it was by no means impossible, and that, indeed, there was a certain piquancy about it, and so on. . . . It is true that at that time he was overdoing his part as a buffoon. He liked to put himself forward and entertain the company, ostensibly on equal terms, of course, though in reality he was on a servile footing with them. It was just at the time when he had received the news of his first wife's death in Petersburg, and, with crape upon his hat, was drinking and behaving so shamelessly that even the most reckless among us were shocked at the sight of him. The revellers, of course, laughed at this unexpected opinion; and one of them even began encouraging him to act upon it. The others repelled the idea even more emphatically, although still with the utmost hilarity, and at last they went on their way. Later on, Fyodor Pavlovich swore that he had gone with them, and perhaps it was so, no one

knows for certain, and no one ever knew. But five or six months later, all the town was talking, with intense and sincere indignation, of Lizaveta's condition, and trying to find out who was the miscreant who had wronged her. Then suddenly a terrible rumour was all over the town that this miscreant was no other than Fyodor Pavlovich. Who set the rumour going? Of that drunken band five had left the town and the only one still among us was an elderly and estimable civil councillor, the father of grown-up daughters, who could hardly have spread the tale, even if there had been any foundation for it. But rumour pointed straight at Fyodor Pavlovich, and persisted in pointing at him. Of course this was no great grievance to him: he would not have troubled to contradict a set of tradespeople. In those days he was proud, and did not condescend to talk except in his own circle of officials and gentlemen, whom he entertained so well.

At the time, Grigory stood up for his master vigorously. He provoked quarrels and altercations in defence of him and succeeded in bringing some people round to his side. "It's the wench's own fault," he asserted, and the culprit, according to him, was none but "Karp with the Screw," a dangerous convict, who had escaped from prison and who had hidden in our town. This conjecture sounded plausible, for it was remembered that Karp had been in the neighbourhood just at that time in the autumn, and had robbed three people. But this affair and all the talk about it did not estrange popular sympathy from the poor idiot. She was better looked after than ever. A well-to-do merchant's widow named Kondratyeva arranged to take her into her house at the end of April, meaning not to let her go out until after the confinement. They kept a constant watch over her, but in spite of their vigilance she escaped on the very last day, and made her way into Fyodor Pavlovich's garden. How, in her condition, she managed to climb over the high, strong fence, remained a mystery. Some maintained that she must have been lifted over by somebody; others hinted at something more uncanny. The most likely explanation is that it happened naturally — that Lizaveta, accustomed to clambering over hurdles to sleep in gardens, had somehow managed to climb this fence, in spite of her condition, and had leapt down, injuring herself.

Grigory rushed to Marfa and sent her to Lizaveta, while he ran to fetch an old midwife who lived close by. They saved the baby, but Lizaveta died at dawn. Grigory took the baby, brought it home, and making his wife sit down, put it on her lap. "A child of God, an orphan, is akin to all," he said, "and to us above others. Our little lost one has sent us this infant who has sprung from the devil's son and a holy innocent. Nurse him and weep no more."

So Marfa brought up the child. He was christened Pavel, to which people were not slow in adding Fyodorovich (son of Fyodor). Fyodor Pavlovich did not object to any of this, and thought it amusing, though he persisted vigorously in denying his responsibility. The townspeople were pleased at his adopting the foundling.

Later on, Fyodor Pavlovich invented a surname for the child, calling him Smerdyakov, after his mother's nickname.

So this Smerdyakov became Fyodor Pavlovich's second servant, and was living in the lodge with Grigory and Marfa at the time our story begins. He was employed as cook. I ought to say something of this Smerdyakov, but I am ashamed of keeping my readers' attention so long occupied with these common menials, and I will go back to my story, hoping to say more of Smerdyakov in the course of it.

## CHAPTER III
### THE CONFESSION
#### OF AN ARDENT HEART — IN VERSE

ALYOSHA remained for some time irresolute after hearing the command his father shouted to him from the carriage. But in spite of his uneasiness he did not stand still. That was not his way. He went at once to the kitchen to find out what mischief his father had been doing upstairs. Then he set off, trusting that on the way to town he would find some answer to the question tormenting him. I hasten to add that his father's shouts, commanding him to return home "with his mattress and pillow," did not frighten him in the least. He understood perfectly that those peremptory shouts were merely "a flourish" to produce an effect. In the same way a tradesman in our town who was celebrating his name-day with a party of friends, getting angry at being refused more vodka, smashed up his own crockery and furniture and tore his own and his wife's clothes, and finally broke his windows, all for the sake of effect. Next day, of course, when he was sober, he regretted the broken cups and saucers. Alyosha knew that his father would let him go back to the monastery next day, possibly even that evening. Moreover, he was fully persuaded that his father might injure any one else, but would not injure him. Alyosha was certain that no one in the whole world ever would want to injure him, and, what is more, he knew that no one could injure him. This was for him an axiom, assumed once for all without question, and he went his way without hesitation, relying on it.

But at that moment a fear of a different sort disturbed him, and worried him the more because he could not define it. It was the fear of a woman, of Katerina Ivanovna, who had so urgently entreated him in the note handed to him by Madame Hohlakov to come and see her about something. This request and the necessity of going had at once aroused an uneasy feeling in his heart, and this feeling had grown more and more painful as the morning wore on, in spite of the scenes at the hermitage and at the Father Superior's. He was not uneasy because he did not know what she would say and what he would answer. And he was not afraid of her simply as a woman. Though he knew little of women, he had spent his life, from early childhood till he entered the monastery, entirely with women. He was afraid of that particular woman, Katerina Ivanovna. He had been afraid of her from the first time he saw her. He had only seen her two or three times, and had only chanced to say a few words to her. He remembered her as a beautiful, proud, imperious girl. It was not her beauty which troubled him, but something else. And the vagueness of his apprehension increased the apprehension itself. The girl's aims were of the noblest, he knew that. She was trying to save his brother Dmitri simply through generosity, though he had already behaved badly to her. Yet, although Alyosha recognised and did justice to all these fine and generous sentiments, a shiver began to run down his back when he drew near her house.

He reflected that he would not find Ivan, who was so intimate a friend, with her, for Ivan was certainly now with his father. Dmitri he was even more certain not to find there, and he had a foreboding of the reason. And so his conversation would be with her alone. He had a great longing to run and see his brother Dmitri before that fateful interview. Without showing him the letter, he could have a talk with him. But Dmitri lived a long way off, and he was sure to be away from home, too. Standing still for a minute, he reached a final decision. Crossing himself with a rapid and accustomed gesture, and at once smiling, he turned resolutely in the direction of his terrible lady.

He knew her house. If he went by Bolshaya Street and then across the market-place, it would be a long way round. Though our town is small, the houses are far apart, and the distances are rather great. And meanwhile his father was expecting him, and perhaps had not yet forgotten his command. He might be unreasonable, and so he had to make haste to get there and back. So he decided to take a short cut by the back-way, for he knew every inch of the ground. This meant skirting fences, climbing over hurdles, and crossing other people's back-yards, where every one he met knew him and greeted him. In this way he could reach Bolshaya Street in half the time.

He had to pass the garden adjoining his father's, and belonging to a little tumbledown house with four windows. The owner of this house, as Alyosha knew, was a bedridden old woman, living with her daughter, who had been a genteel maid-servant in generals' families in Petersburg. Now she had been at home a year, looking after her sick mother. She always dressed up in fine clothes, though her old mother and she had sunk into such poverty that they went every day to Fyodor Pavlovich's kitchen for soup and bread, which Marfa gave readily. Yet, though the young woman came for soup, she had never sold any of her dresses, and one of these even had a long train — a fact which Alyosha had learned from Rakitin, who always knew everything that was going on in the town. He had forgotten it as soon as he had heard it, but now, on reaching the garden, he remembered the dress with the train, raised his head, which had been bowed in thought, and came upon something quite unexpected.

Over the hurdle in the garden, Dmitri, mounted on something, was leaning forward, gesticulating violently, beckoning to him, obviously afraid to utter a word for fear of being overheard. Alyosha ran up to the hurdle.

"It's a good thing you looked up. I nearly shouted to you," Mitya said in a joyful, hurried whisper. "Climb in here quickly! How splendid that you've come! I was just thinking of you!"

Alyosha was delighted, too, but he did not know how to get over the hurdle. Mitya put his powerful hand under his elbow to help him jump. Tucking up his cassock, Alyosha leapt over the hurdle with the agility of a bare-legged street urchin.

"Well done! Now come along," said Mitya in an enthusiastic whisper.

"Where?" whispered Alyosha, looking about him and finding himself in a deserted garden with no one in it but themselves. The garden was small, but the house was at least fifty paces away.

"There's no one here. Why do you whisper?" asked Alyosha.

"Why do I whisper? Deuce take it!" cried Dmitri at the top of his voice. "Why, indeed? You see what silly tricks nature plays one. I am here in secret, and on the watch. I'll explain later on, but, knowing it's a secret, I be-

gan whispering like a fool, when there's no need. Let us go. Over there. Till then be quiet. I want to kiss you.

*Glory be to God in heaven,*
*Glory be to God in me . . .*

I was just repeating that, sitting here, before you came."

The garden was about three acres in extent, and planted with trees along the fence on all four sides. There were apple-trees, maples, limes, and birch-trees. The middle of the garden was a bare grass-plot, which yielded several loads of hay in the summer. The garden was leased in the spring for a few roubles. There were also patches of raspberries and currants and gooseberries along the fences; a kitchen garden had been planted lately near the house.

Dmitri led his brother to the most secluded corner of the garden. There, in a thicket of lime-trees and old bushes of black currant, elder, snowball-tree, and lilac, there stood a tumbledown green summer-house, blackened with age. Its walls were of lattice-work, but there was still a roof which could give shelter. God knows when this summer-house was built. There was a tradition that it had been put up some fifty years before by a retired colonel called von Schmidt, who owned the house at that time. It was all in decay, the floor was rotting, the planks were loose, the wood smelled musty. In the summer-house there was a green wooden table fixed in the ground, and round it were some green benches upon which it was still possible to sit. Alyosha had at once observed his brother's exalted condition, and on entering the arbour he saw half a bottle of cognac and a wineglass on the table.

"That's cognac," Mitya laughed. "I see

THE FINDING OF LIZAVETA

your look: 'He's drinking again!' Distrust the phantom.

*Distrust the vapid, lying crowd,*
*And lay aside thy doubts.*

I'm not drinking, I'm only 'indulging,' as that pig, your Rakitin, says. He'll be a councillor of state one day, but he'll always talk about 'indulging.' Sit down. I could take you in my arms, Alyosha, and press you to my bosom till I crushed you, for in the whole world — really — re-al-ly (can you take it in?) — I love no one but you!"

He uttered the last words in a sort of ecstasy.

"No one but you and one 'jade' I have fallen in love with, to my ruin. But being in love doesn't mean loving. You may be in love with a woman and yet hate her. Remember that! I can still talk about it cheerfully. Sit down here at the table and I'll sit beside you and look at you, and go on talking. You shall keep quiet and I'll go on talking, for the time has come. But on reflection, you know, I'd better speak quietly, for here — here — you can never tell what ears are listening. I will explain everything, as they say, 'to be continued.' Why have I been longing for you? Why have I been thirsting for you all these days, and just now? (It's five days since I've cast anchor here.) Because it's only to you I can tell everything; because I must, because I need you, because to-morrow I shall fly from the clouds, because to-morrow life will end and begin. Have you ever experienced, have you ever dreamt of falling down a precipice into a pit? That's just what I'm doing now, but not in a dream. And I'm not afraid, and don't you be afraid. At least, I am afraid, but it's sweet. It's not pleasure though, but ecstasy. Damn it all,

whatever it is! A strong spirit, a weak spirit, a womanish spirit — whatever it is! Let us praise nature: look at all the sunshine, how clear the sky is, the leaves are all green, it's still summer; four o'clock in the afternoon, and the stillness! Where were you going?"

"I was going to see father, but I meant to go to Katerina Ivanovna's first."

"To her, and to father! Oo! what a coincidence! Why was I waiting for you? Hungering and thirsting for you in every cranny of my soul and even in my ribs? Why, to send you to father and to her, Katerina Ivanovna, so as to have done with her and with father. To send an angel. I might have sent any one, but I wanted to send an angel. And here you are on your way to see father and her."

"Did you really mean to send me?" cried Alyosha with a pained expression.

"Stay! You knew it! And I see that you have understood it all at once. But be quiet, be quiet for a time. Don't be sorry, and don't cry."

Dmitri stood up, thought a moment, and put his finger to his forehead.

"She's asked you, written you a letter or something, that's why you're going to her? You wouldn't be going except for that?"

"Here is her note." Alyosha took it out of his pocket. Mitya glanced through it quickly.

"And you were going the back-way! Oh, gods, I thank you for sending him by the back-way, and he got into my hands like the golden fish to the silly old fisherman in the fairy-tale. Listen, Alyosha, listen, brother! Now I mean to tell you everything, for I must tell some one. An angel in heaven I've told already; but I want to tell an angel on earth. You are an angel on earth. You will hear and judge and forgive. And that's what I need, that some one above me should forgive. Listen! If two people break away from everything on earth and fly off into the unknown, or at least one of them, and before flying off or going to ruin he comes to some one else and says, 'Do this for me' — some favour never asked before that could only be asked on one's deathbed — would that other refuse, if he were a friend or a brother?"

"I will do it, but tell me what it is, and make haste," said Alyosha.

"Make haste! H'm! . . . Don't be in a hurry, Alyosha, you hurry and worry yourself. There's no need to hurry now. Now the world has turned a corner. Ah, Alyosha, what a pity you can't understand ecstasy. But what am I saying to him? As though you didn't understand it. What an ass I am, what am I saying: 'Be noble, oh, man!' Whose verse is that?"

Alyosha made up his mind to wait. He felt that, perhaps, indeed, his work lay here. Mitya sank into thought for a moment, with his elbow on the table and his head in his hand. Both were silent.

"Alyosha," said Mitya, "you're the only one who won't laugh. I should like to begin — my confession — with Schiller's 'Hymn to Joy,' *An die Freude!* I don't know any German, I only know it's called that. Don't think I'm talking nonsense because I'm drunk. I'm not a bit drunk. Brandy's all very well, but I need two bottles to make me drunk:

*Silenus with his rosy phiz*
*Upon his stumbling ass.*

But I've not drunk even a quarter of a bottle, and I'm not Silenus. I'm not Silenus, but I am strong,\* for I've made a decision once for all.

\*In Russian, "silen."

Forgive me the pun; you'll have to forgive me a lot more than puns to-day. Don't be uneasy. I'm not spinning it out. I'm talking sense, and I'll come to the point in a minute. I won't keep you in suspense. Stay, how does it go?"

He raised his head, thought a minute, and began ecstatically:

*"In the craggy clefts deep-hidden*
*Crouched the fearful troglodyte;*
*And the nomad left but barren*
*Traces, in his desert flight.*
*Savage spear and keen-tipped arrow*
*Through the woods the hunter bore;*
*Woe unto the wave-tossed stranger*
*Flung upon the luckless shore!*

*"On her way sad Ceres greeted*
*Mournfully a coast so bare,*
*Seeking still her daughter's footsteps,*
*Where was nothing green or fair!*
*Not an omen there of comfort,*
*Not a welcome where she trod,*
*Not one temple's shining columns*
*Spoke of reverence due a god.*

*"There no fruit of sweetest harvest*
*Bade her share the meal serene;*
*On the horrid altars smoking*
*Human sacrifice was seen.*
*Yea, as far as she might wander*
*Only misery met her gaze,*
*Deep within her mighty spirit*
*She bewailed man's fallen ways."*

Mitya sobbed and seized Alyosha's hand.

"My dear, my dear, in degradation, in degradation now, too. There's a terrible amount of suffering for man on earth, a terrible lot of grief. Don't think I'm only a brute in an officer's uniform, who swills cognac and wallows in debauchery. I hardly think of anything but

78

of that degraded man — if only I'm not lying. God keep me from lying and boasting. I think about that man because I am such a man.

*That man's soul might rise from vileness,*
*And attain to light and worth,*
*He did frame a pact eternal*
*With primeval Mother Earth.*

Only here is the difficulty: how am I to frame an eternal pact with Mother Earth? I don't kiss her. I don't cleave to her bosom. Am I to become a peasant or a shepherd? I go ahead and I don't know whether I'm on my way to stench and shame or to light and joy. That's the trouble, for everything in the world is a riddle! And whenever I've happened to sink to the lowest depths of depravity (and that's all I've been doing) I always read that poem about Ceres and man. Has it reformed me? Never! For I'm a Karamazov. For when I do leap into the abyss I pitch in head foremost and heels up, and am positively pleased to be falling in that degrading attitude, and pride myself upon it. And in the very depths of that degradation I suddenly begin a hymn. Let me be accursed. Let me be vile and base, but let me, too, kiss the hem of the garment in which my God is clothed. Though I may be following the devil, I am Thy son, O Lord, and I love Thee, and I feel the joy without which the world cannot exist and have its being.

*Joy, each blade of grass announces,*
*Nature's precept to rehearse,*
*Joy, 'tis joy that turns the wheeling*
*Watchworks of the universe.*
*Flowers from the bud she beckons,*
*Stars and suns she brings to pass,*
*Filling space with worlds undreamed of,*
*Hidden from the seer's glass.*
*Joy all creatures drink unstinting*

*From great Nature's bounteous breast,*
*All the virtuous, all the wicked,*
*Seek her rosy path with zest.*
*Wine and kisses both she gave us,*
*Friendship, faithful to its trust;*
*To the cherub, sight of Godhead,*
*To the insect — sensual lust.*

But enough poetry! I am in tears; let me cry. It may be foolishness that every one would laugh at. But you won't laugh. Your eyes are shining, too. Enough poetry. I want to tell you now about the insects to whom God gave 'sensual lust.'

*To the insect — sensual lust.*

I am that insect, brother, and the words are said of me specially. And all of us Karamazovs are the same kind, and, angel as you are, that insect lives in you, too, and stirs up tempests in your blood. Tempests, because sensual lust is a tempest — worse than a tempest! Beauty is a terrible and awful thing! It is terrible because unfathomable; and it cannot be fathomed, because God sets us nothing but riddles. Here the boundaries meet and all contradictions dwell together. I am not a cultivated man, brother, but I've thought a lot about this. What a terrible lot of mysteries there are! Too many riddles weigh men down on earth. We must solve them as best we can, and try to keep a dry skin in the water. Beauty! I can't endure the thought that a man of lofty mind and heart begins with the ideal of the Madonna and ends with the ideal of Sodom. What's still more dreadful is that a man with the ideal of Sodom in his soul does not renounce the ideal of the Madonna, and his heart is on fire with that ideal, genuinely on fire, just as in the days of his youth and innocence. Yes, man is broad, too broad, indeed. I'd have him nar-

warmly (obviously the idea was not a new one). "It's like the rungs of the same ladder. I'm on the bottom rung, and you're above, somewhere about the thirteenth. That's how I see it. But it's all the same. Absolutely the same in kind. Any one on the bottom step is bound to go up to the top one."

"Then one ought not to step on at all."

"Any one who can help it had better not."

"But can you?"

"I think not."

"Hush, Alyosha, hush, darling! I could kiss your hand, you touch me so. That hussy, Grushenka, is a judge of men. She told me once that she'd devour you one day. There, there, I won't! From this field of corruption, this place fouled by flies, let's pass to my tragedy, also befouled by flies, that is by every sort of vileness. Although the old man told lies abut my seducing innocence, there really was something of the sort in my tragedy, though it was only once, and then it did not come off. The old man who has reproached me with what never happened does not even know of this fact; I never told any one about it. You're the first, except Ivan, of course — Ivan knows everything. He knew about it long before you. But Ivan's a tomb."

"Ivan's a tomb?"

"Yes."

Alyosha listened with great attention.

"I was lieutenant in a line regiment, but still I was under surveillance, like a kind of exile. Yet I was awfully well received in the little town. I spent money right and left. I was thought to be rich; I thought so myself. But I must have pleased them in other ways as well. Although they shook their heads over me, they liked me. My colonel, who was an old man, took a sudden dislike to me. He was always down on me, but I had powerful friends, and, moreover, all the town was on my side, so he couldn't get me into trouble. I was at fault myself for refusing to treat him with proper respect. I was proud. This obstinate old fellow, who was really a very good sort, kind-hearted and hospitable, had had two wives, both dead. His first wife, who was of a humble family, left a daughter as unpretentious as herself. She was a young woman of four and twenty when I was there, and was living with her father and an aunt, her mother's sister. The aunt was a simple, silent woman; the niece was simple, too, but lively. When I look back, I like to say a good word about people. I never knew a woman of more charming character than Agafya — fancy, her name was Agafya Ivanovna! And she wasn't bad-looking either, in the Russian style: tall, stout, with a full figure, and beautiful eyes, though a rather coarse face. She had not married, although she had had two suitors. She refused them, but was as cheerful as ever. I was intimate with her, not in 'that' way, it was pure friendship. I have often been friendly with women quite innocently. I used to talk to her with shocking frankness, and she only laughed. Many women like such freedom, and she was a girl, too, which made it very amusing. Another thing, one could never think of her as a young lady. She and her aunt lived in her father's house with a sort of voluntary humility, not putting themselves on an equal footing with other people. She was a general favourite, and of use to every one, for she was a clever dressmaker. She had a talent for it. She gave her services freely without asking for payment, but if any one offered her payment, she didn't refuse. The lieutenant-colonel, of course, was a very different matter. He was one of the chief personages in the district. He kept open house, entertained the whole town, gave suppers and dances. At the time I arrived and joined the battalion, all the town was talking of the expected return of the lieutenant-colonel's second daughter, a great beauty, who had just left a fashionable school in the capital. This second daughter is this very Katerina Ivanovna, and she was the child of the colonel's second wife, who belonged to a distinguished family, being the daughter of a general; although, as I learnt on good authority, she brought the lieutenant-colonel no money. She had connections, and that was all. There may have been expectations, but they had come to nothing.

"Yet, when the young lady came from boarding-school on a visit, the whole town revived. Our most distinguished ladies — two 'Excellencies' and a colonel's wife — and all the rest following their lead, at once took her up and gave entertainments in her honour. She was the belle of the balls and picnics, and they got up *tableaux vivants* in aid of distressed governesses. As for me, I took no notice, I went on as wildly as before, and one of my exploits at the time set all the town talking. I saw her eyes taking my measure one evening at the battery commander's, but I didn't go up to her, as though I disdained her acquaintance. I did go up and speak to her at an evening party not long after. She scarcely looked at me, and compressed her lips scornfully. 'Wait a bit. I'll have my revenge,' thought I. I behaved like an awful rowdy on many occasions at that time, and I was conscious of it myself. The main thing was that I felt that 'Katenka' was not an innocent boarding-school miss, but a person of character, proud and really high-principled; above

all, she had education and intellect, and I had neither. You think I meant to make her an offer? No, I simply wanted to revenge myself, because I was such a capital fellow and she didn't seem to notice it.

"Meanwhile, I spent my time in drink and riot, till the lieutenant-colonel put me under arrest for three days. Just at that time father sent me six thousand roubles in return for my sending him a deed giving up all claims upon him — settling our accounts, so to speak, and saying that I wouldn't demand anything more. I didn't understand a word of it at the time. Until I came here, Alyosha, till the last few days, indeed, perhaps even now, I haven't been able to make head or tail of my money affairs with father. But let all that go to the deuce, we'll talk of it later.

"Just as I received the money, I got a letter from a friend telling me something that interested me immensely. The authorities, I learnt, were dissatisfied with our lieutenant-colonel. He was suspected of irregularities; in fact, his enemies were preparing a surprise for him. And then the commander of the division arrived, and kicked up the devil of a shindy. Shortly afterwards he was ordered to retire. I won't tell you how it all happened. He had enemies certainly. Suddenly there was a marked coolness in the town towards him and all his family. His friends all turned their backs on him. Then I took my first step. I met Agafya Ivanovna, with whom I'd always kept up a friendship, and said, 'Do you know there's a deficit of 4,500 roubles of government money in your father's accounts?'

" 'What do you mean? What makes you say so? The general was here not long ago, and everything was all right.'

" 'Then it was, but now it isn't.'

III: THE SENSUALISTS

"She was terribly scared.

" 'Don't frighten me!' she said. 'Who told you so?'

" 'Don't be uneasy,' I said, 'I won't tell any one. You know I'm as silent as the grave. I only wanted, in view of "possibilities," to add, that when they demand that 4,500 roubles from your father, and he can't produce it, he'll be tried, and demoted to the ranks in his old age. But you just send me your boarding-school miss secretly. I've received some money lately. I'll give her four thousand, maybe, and keep the secret religiously.'

" 'Ah, you scoundrel!' that's what she said. 'You vicious scoundrel! How dare you!'

"She went away furiously indignant, while I shouted after her once more that the secret should be kept sacred. Those two simple creatures, Agafya and her aunt, I may as well say at once, behaved like innocent angels all through this business. They genuinely adored their 'Katya,' thought her far above them, and waited on her, hand and foot. But Agafya told her of our conversation. I found that out afterwards. She didn't keep it back, and of course that was just what I wanted.

"Suddenly the new major arrived to take command of the battalion. The old lieutenant-colonel was taken ill at once, couldn't leave his room for two days, and didn't hand over the government money. Dr. Kravchenko declared that he really was ill. But I knew for a fact, and had known for a long time, that for the last four years the money had never been in his hands except when the Commander made his visits of inspection. He used to lend it to a trustworthy person, a merchant of our town called Trifonov, an old widower, with a big beard and gold-rimmed spectacles. He used to go to the fair, do a profitable business

with the money, and return the whole sum to the colonel, bringing with it a present from the fair, as well as interest on the loan. But this time (I heard all about it quite by chance from Trifonov's son and heir, a drivelling youth and one of the most vicious in the world) — this time, I say, Trifonov brought nothing back from the fair. The lieutenant-colonel flew to him. 'I've never received any money from you, and couldn't possibly have received any.' That was all the answer he got. So now our lieutenant-colonel is confined to the house, with a towel round his head, while they're all three busy putting ice on it. All at once an orderly arrives on the scene with a book and an order to 'hand over the government money immediately, within two hours.' He signed his name in the book (I saw the signature in the book afterwards), stood up, saying he would put on his uniform, ran to his bedroom, loaded his double-barrelled gun with a service bullet, took the boot off his right foot, fixed the gun against his chest, and began feeling for the trigger with his foot. But Agafya, remembering what I had told her, had her suspicions. She stole up and peeped into the room just in time. She rushed in, flung herself upon him from behind, threw her arms round him, and the gun went off, but the bullet hit the ceiling, and hurt no one. The others ran in, took away the gun, and held him by the arms. I heard all about this afterwards. I was at home, it was getting dusk, and I was just preparing to go out. I had dressed, brushed my hair, scented my handkerchief, and taken up my cap, when suddenly the door opened, and there in my lodging facing me stood Katerina Ivanovna.

"It's strange how things happen sometimes. No one had seen her in the street, so that no

83

one knew of it in the town. I lodged with two decrepit old ladies, who looked after me. They were most obliging old things, ready to do anything for me, and at my request were as silent afterwards as two cast-iron posts. Of course I grasped the situation at once. She walked in and looked straight at me, her dark eyes determined, even defiant, but on her lips and round her mouth there was an expression of uncertainty.

" 'My sister told me,' she began, 'that you would give me 4,500 roubles if I came to you for it — myself. I have come . . . give me the money!'

"She couldn't keep it up. She choked, frightened, her voice failed her, and the corners of her mouth and the lines round it quivered. Alyosha, are you listening, or are you asleep?"

"Mitya, I know you will tell the whole truth," said Alyosha in agitation.

"I am telling it. If I tell the whole truth just as it happened I shan't spare myself. My first thought was a — Karamazov one. Once I was bitten by a centipede, brother, and laid up for a fortnight with fever from it. Well, I felt as though a centipede stung my heart then — a noxious insect, you understand? I looked her up and down. You've seen her? She's a beauty. But she was beautiful in another way then. At that moment she was beautiful because she was noble, and I was a scoundrel; she in all the grandeur of her generosity and sacrifice for her father, and I — a bug! And, scoundrel and bug that I was, she was altogether at my mercy, body and soul. She was hemmed in. I tell you frankly, that thought, that venomous thought, so possessed my heart that it almost swooned. It seemed as if there could be no resisting it; that I would act like a bug, like a venomous spider, without a spark of pity. My breath failed me. Understand, I should have gone next day to ask for her hand, so that it might end honourably, so to speak, and that nobody would or could know. For though I'm a man of base desires, I'm honest. And at that very second some voice seemed to whisper in my ear, 'But when you come to-morrow to make your proposal, that girl won't even see you; she'll order her coachman to kick you out of the yard. "Publish it through all the town," she would say, "I'm not afraid of you." ' I looked at the young lady, my voice had not deceived me. That is how it would be, not a doubt of it. I could see from her face now that I should be turned out of the house. My spite was roused. I longed to play her the nastiest swinish cad's trick: to look at her with a sneer, and on the spot where she stood before me to stun her with a tone of voice that only a shopman could use.

" 'Four thousand! What do you mean? I was joking. You've been reckoning without your host, madam. Two hundred, perhaps, yes, with pleasure. But four thousand is not a sum to throw away on such frivolity. You've put yourself out to no purpose.'

"I should have lost the game, of course. She'd have run away. But it would have been an infernal revenge. It would have been worth it all. I'd have howled with regret all the rest of my life, only to have played that trick. Would you believe it, it has never happened to me with any other woman, not one, to look at her at such a moment with hatred. But, on my oath, I looked at her for three seconds, or five perhaps, with fearful hatred — that hate which is only a hair's-breadth from love, from the maddest love!

"I went to the window, put my forehead

THE ARDENT HEART

against the frozen pane, and I remember the ice burnt my forehead like fire. I did not keep her long, don't be afraid. I turned round, went up to the table, opened the drawer and took out a bank-note for five thousand roubles (it was lying in a French dictionary). Then I showed it her in silence, folded it, handed it to her, opened the door into the passage, and, stepping back, made her a deep bow, a most respectful, a most impressive bow, believe me! She shuddered all over, gazed at me for a second, turned horribly pale — white as a sheet, in fact — and all at once, also without a word, not impetuously but softly, gently, bowed down to my feet — not a boarding-school curtsey, but a Russian bow, with her forehead to the floor. She jumped up and ran away. I was wearing my sword. I drew it and nearly stabbed myself with it on the spot; why, I don't know. It would have been frightfully stupid, of course. I suppose it was out of ecstasy. Can you understand that one might kill oneself out of ecstasy? But I didn't stab myself. I only kissed my sword and put it back in the scabbard — which there was no need to have told you, by the way. And I fancy that in telling you about my inner conflict I have laid it on rather thick to glorify myself. But let it pass, and to hell with all who pry into the human heart! Well, so much for that 'adventure' with Katerina Ivanovna. So now Ivan knows of it, and you — no one else."

Dmitri got up, took a step or two in his excitement, pulled out his handkerchief and mopped his forehead, then sat down again, not in the same place as before, but on the opposite side, so that Alyosha had to turn quite round to face him.

## CHAPTER V
### THE CONFESSION
#### OF AN ARDENT HEART — "HEELS UP"

"Now," said Alyosha, "I understand the first half."

"You understand the first half. That half is a drama, and it was played out there. The second half is a tragedy, and it will be enacted here."

"And I understand nothing of that second half so far," said Alyosha.

"And I? Do you suppose I understand it?"

"Stop, Dmitri. There's one important question. Tell me, you were betrothed, you are betrothed still?"

"We weren't betrothed at once, not for three months after that adventure. The next day I told myself that the incident was closed, concluded, and that there would be no sequel. It seemed to me caddish to make her an offer. On her side she gave no sign of life for the six weeks that she remained in the town; except, indeed, for one action. The day after her visit the maid-servant slipped round with an envelope addressed to me. I tore it open; it contained the change out of the bank-note. Only 4,500 was needed, but there was a discount of about 200 on changing it. She only sent me about 260 roubles, I don't remember exactly, but not a note, not a word of explanation. I searched the packet for a pencil mark — n-nothing! Well, I spent the rest of the money on such an orgy that the new major was obliged to reprimand me.

"Well, the lieutenant-colonel produced the government money, to the astonishment of every one, for nobody believed that he had the money intact. He'd no sooner paid it than he fell ill, took to his bed, and, three weeks later, softening of the brain set in, and he died five days afterwards. He was buried with military honours, for he had not had time to receive his discharge. Ten days after his funeral, Katerina Ivanovna, with her aunt and sister, went to Moscow. And, behold, on the very day they went away (I hadn't seen them, didn't see them off or take leave) I received a tiny note, a sheet of blue lace-edged paper, and on it only one line in pencil: 'I will write to you. Wait. K.' And that was all.

"I'll explain the rest now, in two words. In Moscow their fortunes changed with the swiftness of lightning and the unexpectedness of an Arabian fairy-tale. That general's widow, their nearest relation, suddenly lost the two nieces who were her heiresses and next-of-kin — both died in the same week of small-pox. The old lady, prostrated with grief, welcomed Katya as a daughter, as her one hope, pounced upon her, altered her will in Katya's favour. But that concerned the future. Meanwhile she gave her, for present use, eighty thousand roubles, as a marriage portion, to do what she liked with. She was an hysterical woman. I saw something of her in Moscow, later.

"Well, suddenly I received by post four thousand five hundred roubles. I was speechless with surprise, as you may suppose. Three days later came the promised letter. I have it with me now. I always keep it, and shall keep it till I die. Shall I show you? You must read it. She offers to be my wife, offers herself to me. 'I love you madly,' she says, 'even if you don't love me, never mind. Be my husband. Don't be afraid. I won't hamper you in any way. I will be your chattel. I will be the carpet under your feet. I want to love you for ever. I want to save you from yourself.' Alyosha, I am not worthy to repeat those lines in my vile words and in my vile tone, my everlastingly vile tone, that I can never cure myself of. That letter stabs me even now. Do you think I don't mind — that I don't mind even now? I wrote her an answer at once, as it was impossible for me to go to Moscow. I wrote to her with tears. One thing I shall be ashamed of for ever. I referred to her being rich and having a dowry while I was only a stuck-up beggar! I mentioned money! I ought to have borne it in silence, but it slipped from my pen. Then I wrote at once to Ivan, and told him all I could about it in a letter of six pages, and sent him to her. Why do you look like that? Why are you staring at me? Yes, Ivan fell in love with her; he's in love with her still. I know that. I did a stupid thing, in the world's opinion; but perhaps that one stupid thing may be the saving of us all now. Oo! Don't you see what a lot she thinks of Ivan, how she respects him? When she compares us, do you suppose she can love a man like me, especially after all that has happened here?"

"But I'm convinced that she does love a man like you, and not a man like him."

"She loves her own *virtue*, not me." The words broke involuntarily, and almost maliciously, from Dmitri. He laughed, but a minute later his eyes flashed, he flushed crimson and struck the table violently with his fist.

"I swear, Alyosha," he cried, with intense and genuine anger at himself; "you may not believe me, but as God is holy, and as Christ is our Lord, I swear that though I mocked at her lofty sentiments just now, I know that I am a million times baser in soul than she, and that these lofty sentiments of hers are as sincere as a heavenly angel's. That's the tragedy of it — that I know that for certain. What if one does show off a bit? Don't I do it myself?

And yet I'm sincere, sincere. As for Ivan, don't I understand how he must be cursing Fate now — with his intellect, too! To see the preference given — to whom, to what? To a monster who, though he is betrothed and all eyes are fixed on him, can't restrain himself from debauchery — and before the very eyes of his betrothed! And a man like me is preferred, while he is rejected. And why? Because a girl wants to ruin her life and future out of gratitude. Absurd! I've never said a word of this to Ivan, and Ivan of course has never dropped a hint of the sort to me. But destiny will take its course, and the worthy man will come into his own, while the undeserving one will vanish into his back-alley for ever — his filthy back-alley, his beloved back-alley where he is at home, and there in filth and stench he will perish, of his own free will and with joy. I've been talking foolishly. I've worn out all my words. I use them at random, but it will be as I have said. I shall drown in the back-alley, and she will marry Ivan."

"Stop, brother," Alyosha interrupted again with great anxiety. "There's one thing you haven't made clear yet: you are still betrothed all the same, aren't you? How can you break off the engagement if she, your betrothed, doesn't want to?"

"Yes, formally and solemnly betrothed. It was all done on my arrival in Moscow, with great ceremony, with ikons, all in fine style. The general's widow blessed us, and — would you believe it? — congratulated Katya. 'You've made a good choice,' she said, 'I see right through him.' And, would you believe it, she didn't like Ivan, and hardly greeted him? I had a lot of talk with Katya in Moscow. I told her about myself — sincerely, honourably. She listened to everything.

*There was sweet confusion,*
*There were tender words.*

Though there were proud words, too. She wrung out of me a mighty promise to reform. I gave my promise, and here ——"

"What?"

"Why, I called to you and brought you out here to-day, this very day — remember it — to send you — this very day again — to Katerina Ivanovna, and ——"

"What?"

"To tell her that I shall never come to see her again, and that I send her my compliments."

"But is that possible?"

"That's just the reason I'm sending you in my place, because it's impossible. How could I tell her myself?"

"And where will you go?"

"To the back-alley."

"To Grushenka then!" Alyosha exclaimed sorrowfully, striking his hands together. "Can Rakitin really have told the truth? I thought that you had just visited her, and that was all."

"Can a betrothed man pay such visits? Is such a thing possible and with such a betrothed, and before the eyes of all the world? Confound it, I have some honour! As soon as I began visiting Grushenka, I ceased to be betrothed, and to be an honest man. I understand that. Why do you look at me? You see, I went in the first place to give her a beating. I had heard, and I know for a fact now, that that captain, father's agent, had handed Grushenka an IOU of mine for her to sue me for payment, so as to put a spoke in my wheels. They wanted to scare me. I set out to thrash Grushenka. I had had a glimpse of her before.

She doesn't strike one at first sight. I knew about her old merchant, who's lying ill now, paralysed; but he will leave her a decent little sum, anyhow. I knew, too, that she was fond of money, that she hoarded it, and lent it at a wicked rate of interest, that she's a merciless cheat and swindler. I went to thrash her, and I stayed. A storm broke, — a plague struck me. I'm plague-stricken still, and I know that everything is over, that there will never be anything more for me. The cycle of time is accomplished. That's my position. And though I'm a beggar, as fate would have it, I had three thousand just then in my pocket. I drove with Grushenka to Mokroye, a place twenty-five versts from here. I got gipsies there and champagne and made all the peasants there drunk on it, and all the women and girls. I sent the thousands flying. In three days' time I was stripped bare, but a hero. Do you suppose the hero had gained his end? Nothing of the sort. I tell you: it's a curve. That hussy, Grushenka, has a certain curve to her body. You can see it even in her little foot, even in the little toe of her left foot. I saw it, and kissed it, but that was all, I swear! 'I'll marry you, if you like,' she said, 'you're a beggar, you know. Say that you won't beat me, and will let me do anything I choose, and perhaps I will marry you.' She laughed, and she's laughing still!"

Dmitri leapt up in a sort of fury. It seemed all at once as though he were drunk. His eyes became suddenly bloodshot.

"And do you really mean to marry her?"

"At once, if she is willing. And if she isn't, I shall stay all the same. I'll be the porter at her gate, Alyosha!" he cried. He stopped short before him, and taking him by the shoulders began shaking him violently. "Do you know, you innocent boy, that this is all delirium, senseless delirium, for there's a tragedy here. Let me tell you, Alexey, that I may be a low man, with low and degraded passions, but a thief, a pickpocket, a housebreaker, Dmitri Karamazov can never be. Well, then; let me tell you that I am a thief and a pickpocket. That very morning, just before I went to thrash Grushenka, Katerina Ivanovna sent for me, and in strict secrecy (why I don't know, I suppose she had some reason) asked me to go to the city and to post three thousand roubles to Agafya Ivanovna in Moscow, so that nothing should be known of it in the town here. So I had that three thousand roubles in my pocket when I went to see Grushenka, and it was that money we spent at Mokroye. Afterwards I pretended I had been to the city, but did not show her the post office receipt. I said I had sent the money and would bring the receipt, and so far I haven't brought it. I've forgotten it. Now what do you think you'll answer her to-day when you say: 'He sends his compliments,' and she asks you, 'What about the money?' You could still have said to her, 'He's a degraded sensualist, and a low creature, with uncontrollable passions. He didn't send your money then, but embezzled it, because, like a low brute, he couldn't restrain himself.' But still you might have added, 'He isn't a thief though. Here is your three thousand; he sends it back. Send it yourself to Agafya Ivanovna. But he told me to say "he sends his compliments." ' But, as it is, she will ask, 'But where is the money?' "

"Mitya, you are unhappy, yes! But not as unhappy as you think. Don't kill yourself with despair, don't."

"What, do you suppose I'd shoot myself because I can't get three thousand to pay back? That's just it. I shan't shoot myself. I haven't

88

the strength now. Afterwards, perhaps. But now I'm going to Grushenka. The hell with it."

"And what will you do there?"

"I'll be her husband if she deigns to have me, and when her lover comes, I'll go into the next room. I'll clean her friends' goloshes, fan the coals for the samovar, run errands."

"Katerina Ivanovna will understand it all," Alyosha said solemnly. "She'll understand the depth of your sorrow and will forgive you. She has a lofty mind, and no one could be more unhappy than you. She'll see that for herself."

"She won't be reconciled to everything," said Dmitri, with a grin. "There's something in it, brother, that no woman could reconcile herself to. Do you know what would be the best thing to do?"

"What?"

"Pay back the three thousand."

"Where can we get it from? I say, I have two thousand. Ivan will give you another thousand — that makes three. Take it and pay it back."

"And when would you get it, your three thousand? You're not of age, besides, and you must — you absolutely must — convey my farewell to her to-day, with the money or without it, for I can't drag on any longer, things have come to such a pass. To-morrow is too late. I shall send you to father."

"To father?"

"Yes, to father first. Ask him for three thousand."

"But, Mitya, he won't give it."

"As though he would! I know he won't. Do you know the meaning of despair, Alexey?"

"Yes."

"Listen. Legally he owes me nothing. I've had it all from him, I know that. But morally he owes me something, doesn't he? You know he started with twenty-eight thousand of my mother's money and made a hundred thousand with it. Let him give me back only three out of the twenty-eight thousand, and he'll draw my soul out of hell, and it will atone for many of his sins. With that three thousand — I give you my solemn word — I'll make an end of everything, and he shall hear nothing more of me. For the last time I give him the chance to be a father. Tell him God Himself sends him this chance."

"Mitya, he won't give it for anything."

"I know he won't. I know it perfectly well. Now, especially. That's not all. I know something more. Now, only a few days ago, perhaps only yesterday, he found out for the first time *in earnest* (underline *in earnest*) that Grushenka is perhaps really not joking, and may indeed leap into marriage with me. He knows her character; he knows the cat. And do you suppose he's going to give me money to help to bring that about when he's crazy about her himself? And that's not all, either. I can tell you more than that. I know that for the last five days he has had three thousand drawn out of the bank, changed into notes of a hundred roubles, packed into a large envelope, sealed with five seals, and tied across with red tape. You see how well I know all about it! On the envelope is written: 'For my angel, Grushenka, if she will come to me.' He scrawled it himself in silence and in secret, and no one knows that the money's there except the valet, Smerdyakov, whom he trusts like himself. So now he has been expecting Grushenka for the last three or four days; he hopes she'll come for the money. He has sent her word of it, and she has sent him word that perhaps she'll come. And if she does go to the old man, can I marry her after that? You understand now why I'm here in secret and what I'm on the watch for."

"For her?"

"Yes, for her. Foma has a room in the house of these sluts here. Foma comes from our parts; he was a soldier in our regiment. He does jobs for them. He's watchman at night and goes grouse shooting in the day-time; and that's how he lives. I've established myself in his place. Neither he nor the women of the house know the secret — that is, that I am on the watch here."

"No one but Smerdyakov knows, then?"

"No one else. He will let me know if she goes to the old man."

"It was he told you about the money, then?"

"Yes. It's a dead secret. Even Ivan doesn't know about the money, or anything. The old man is sending Ivan to Chermashnya for a stay of two or three days. A purchaser has turned up for the copse: he'll give eight thousand for the timber. So the old man keeps asking Ivan to help him by going there to arrange it. It will take him two or three days. That's what the old man wants, so that Grushenka can come while he's away."

"Then he's expecting Grushenka to-day?"

"No, she won't come to-day; there are signs. She's certain not to come," cried Mitya suddenly. "Smerdyakov thinks so, too. Father's drinking now. He's sitting at table with Ivan. Go to him, Alyosha, and ask for the three thousand."

"Mitya, dear, what's the matter with you?" cried Alyosha, jumping up from his place, and looking keenly at his brother's frenzied face. For one moment the thought struck him that Dmitri had gone mad.

"What is it? I'm not insane," said Dmitri, looking intently and earnestly at him. "No fear. I am sending you to father, and I know what I'm saying. I believe in miracles."

"In miracles?"

"In a miracle of Divine Providence. God knows my heart. He sees my despair. He sees the whole picture. Surely He won't let something awful happen. Alyosha, I believe in miracles. Go!"

"I am going. Tell me, will you wait for me here?"

"Yes. I know it will take some time. You can't go at him point blank. He's drunk now. I'll wait three hours — four, five, six, seven. Only remember you must go to Katerina Ivanovna to-day, if it has to be at midnight, *with the money or without the money*, and say, 'He sends his compliments to you.' I want you to say that line to her: 'He sends his compliments to you.'"

"Mitya! And what if Grushenka comes to-day — if not to-day, to-morrow, or the next day?"

"Grushenka? I shall see her. I will rush out and prevent it."

"And if —— ?"

"If there's an if, it will be murder. I couldn't endure it."

"Who will be murdered?"

"The old man. I shan't kill her."

"Brother, what are you saying?"

"Oh, I don't know. . . . I don't know. Perhaps I shan't kill him, and perhaps I shall. I'm afraid that his face will suddenly become so loathsome to me at that moment. I hate his throat, his nose, his eyes, his shameless snigger. I feel a physical repulsion. That's what I'm afraid of. That's what may be too much for me."

"I'll go, Mitya. I believe that God will order things for the best, that nothing awful may happen."

"And I will sit and wait for the miracle. And if it doesn't come to pass ——"

Alyosha went thoughtfully towards his father's house.

## CHAPTER VI
### SMERDYAKOV

HE did in fact find his father still at table. Though there was a dining-room in the house, the table was laid as usual in the drawing-room, which was the largest room, and furnished with old-fashioned ostentation. The furniture was white and very old, upholstered in worn red silky material. In the spaces between the windows there were mirrors in elaborate white and gilt frames, with old-fashioned carving. On the walls, covered with a white paper, which was cracked in many places, there hung two large portraits — one of some prince who had been governor of the district thirty years before, and the other of a bishop, also long since deceased. In the right-hand corner there were several ikons, before which a lamp was lighted at nightfall . . . not so much for devotional purposes as to light the room. Fyodor Pavlovich used to go to bed very late, at three or four o'clock in the morning, and would wander about the room at night or sit in an armchair, thinking. This had become a habit with him. He often slept quite alone in the house, sending his servants to the lodge; but usually Smerdyakov remained, sleeping on a bench in the hall.

When Alyosha came in, dinner was over, but coffee and preserves had been served. Fyodor Pavlovich liked sweet things with cognac after dinner. Ivan was also at table, having coffee. The servants, Grigory and Smerdyakov, were standing by. Both the gentlemen and the servants seemed in singularly good spirits. Fyodor Pavlovich was roaring with laughter. Before he entered the room, Alyosha heard the shrill laugh he knew so well, and could tell from the sound of it that his father had reached only the good-humoured stage, and was far from being completely drunk.

"Here he is! Here he is!" yelled Fyodor Pavlovich, highly delighted at seeing Alyosha. "Join us. Sit down. Coffee is a lenten dish, but it's hot and good. I don't offer you cognac, you're keeping the fast. But would you like some? No; I'd better give you some liqueur, — it's fine. Smerdyakov, go to the cupboard, the second shelf on the right. Here are the keys. Look sharp!"

Alyosha refused the liqueur.

"Never mind. If you won't have it, we will," said Fyodor Pavlovich, beaming. "But hold on — have you dined?"

"Yes," answered Alyosha, who had in truth eaten only a piece of bread and drunk a glass of kvass in the Father Superior's kitchen. "Though I should like to have some hot coffee."

"Bravo, my darling! He'll have some coffee. Does it want warming? No, it's boiling. It's capital coffee: Smerdyakov's making. My Smerdyakov's an artist at coffee and at fish patties, and at fish soup, too. You must come one day and have some fish soup. Let me know beforehand. . . . But hold on, hold on; didn't I tell you this morning to come home with your mattress and pillow and all? Have you brought your mattress? He, he, he!"

"No, I haven't," said Alyosha, smiling, too.

"Ah, but you were frightened, you were frightened this morning, weren't you? There, my darling, would I do anything to vex you? Do you know, Ivan, I can't resist the way he looks one straight in the face and laughs. I can't. It makes me shake with-laughter. I just love him. Alyosha, let me give you my paternal blessing."

Alyosha rose, but Fyodor Pavlovich had already changed his mind.

"No, no," he said, "I'll just make the sign of the cross over you, now. Sit still. Now we've a treat for you, in your own line, too. It'll make you laugh. Balaam's ass has begun talking here — and how he talks! How he talks!"

Balaam's ass, it appeared, was the valet, Smerdyakov. He was a young man of about four and twenty, terribly unsociable and taciturn. Not that he was shy or bashful. On the contrary, he was conceited and seemed to despise everybody.

We must say a few words about him now. He was brought up by Grigory and Marfa, but the boy grew up "with no sense of gratitude," as Grigory expressed it; he was an unfriendly boy, and seemed to look at the world distrustfully. In his childhood he was very fond of hanging cats, and burying them with great ceremony. He used to dress up in a sheet as though it were a surplice, and sang, and waved some object over the dead cat as though it were a censer. All this he did on the sly, with the greatest secrecy. Grigory caught him once at this diversion and gave him a sound beating. He shrank into a corner and sulked there for a week. "He doesn't care for you or me, the monster," Grigory used to say to Marfa, "and he doesn't care for any one. Are you a human being?" he said, addressing the boy directly. "You're not a human being. You grew from bath-house slime. That's what you are." Smerdyakov, it appeared afterwards, could never

forgive him those words. Grigory taught him to read and write, and when he was twelve years old began teaching him the Scriptures. But this teaching came to nothing. At the second or third lesson the boy suddenly grinned.

"What's the matter?" asked Grigory, looking at him threateningly over his spectacles.

"Oh, nothing. God created light on the first day, and the sun, moon, and stars on the fourth day. Where did the light come from on the first day?"

Grigory was thunderstruck. The boy looked sarcastically at his teacher. There was something positively haughty in his expression. Grigory could not restrain himself. "I'll show you where!" he cried, and gave the boy a violent slap on the cheek. The boy took the slap without a word, but withdrew into his corner again for some days. A week later he had his first attack of the disease to which he was subject all the rest of his life — epilepsy. When Fyodor Pavlovich heard of it, his attitude to the boy seemed changed at once. Till then he had taken no notice of him, though he never scolded him, and always gave him a copeck when he met him. Sometimes, when he was in good humour, he would send the boy something sweet from his table. But as soon as he heard of his illness, he showed an active interest in him, sent for a doctor, and tried remedies, but the disease turned out to be incurable. The fits occurred, on an average, once a month, but at various intervals. The fits varied, too, in violence: some were light and some were very severe. Fyodor Pavlovich strictly forbade Grigory to use corporal punishment on the boy, and began allowing him to come upstairs to him. He forbade him to be taught anything whatever for a time, too. One day when the boy was about fifteen, Fyodor Pavlovich noticed him lingering by the bookcase, and reading the titles through the glass. Fyodor Pavlovich had a fair number of books — over a hundred — but no one ever saw him reading. He at once gave Smerdyakov the key to the bookcase. "Come, read. You shall be my librarian. It'll be better for you to sit reading than to wander about the courtyard. Come, read this," and Fyodor Pavlovich gave him "Evenings in a Cottage near Dikanka."

He read a little, but didn't like it. He did not smile once, and ended by frowning.

"Why? Isn't it funny?" asked Fyodor Pavlovich.

Smerdyakov did not speak.

"Answer, stupid!"

"It's all untrue," mumbled the boy, with a grin.

"Then go to the devil! You have the soul of a lackey. Stay, here's Smaragdov's 'Universal History.' That's all true. Read that."

But Smerdyakov did not get through ten pages of Smaragdov. He thought it dull. So the bookcase was closed again.

Shortly afterwards Marfa and Grigory reported to Fyodor Pavlovich that Smerdyakov was gradually beginning to show an extraordinary fastidiousness. He would sit before his soup, take up his spoon and look into the soup, bend over it, examine it, take a spoonful and hold it to the light.

"What is it? A beetle?" Grigory would ask.

"A fly, perhaps," observed Marfa.

The squeamish youth never answered, but he did the same with his bread, his meat, and everything he ate. He would hold a piece on his fork to the light, scrutinise it as through a microscope, and only after long deliberation decide to put it in his mouth.

"Ach! What fine gentlemen's airs!" Grigory muttered, looking at him.

When Fyodor Pavlovich heard of this development in Smerdyakov he determined to make him his cook, and apprenticed him to a chef in Moscow. The apprenticeship lasted several years and he came back remarkably changed in appearance. He looked extraordinarily old for his age. His face had grown wrinkled, yellow, and he resembled a eunuch. In character he seemed almost exactly the same as before he went away. He was just as unsociable, and showed not the slightest inclination for any companionship. In Moscow, too, as we heard afterwards, he had always been silent. Moscow itself had little interest for him; he saw very little there, and took scarcely any notice of anything. He went once to the theatre, but returned silent and displeased with it. On the other hand, he came back to us from Moscow well dressed, in a clean coat and clean linen. He invariably brushed his clothes most scrupulously twice a day, and was very fond of cleaning his smart calf boots with a special English polish, so that they shone like a mirror. He turned out a first-rate cook. Fyodor Pavlovich paid him a salary, almost the whole of which Smerdyakov spent on clothes, pomade, perfumes, and such things. But he seemed to have as much contempt for the female sex as for men; he was sedate, almost unapproachable, with them. Fyodor Pavlovich began to regard him rather differently. His fits were becoming more frequent, and on the days he was ill Marfa cooked, which did not suit Fyodor Pavlovich at all.

"Why are your fits getting worse?" Fyodor Pavlovich would ask, looking askance at his new cook. "Would you like to get married? Shall I find you a wife?"

But Smerdyakov would turn pale with vexation, and make no reply. Fyodor Pavlovich would leave him with a gesture of surrender. The great thing was that he had absolute confidence in his honesty. It happened once, when Fyodor Pavlovich was drunk, that he dropped in the muddy courtyard three hundred-rouble notes which he had only just received. He missed them only the next day, and was just hastening to search his pockets when he saw the notes lying on the table. Where had they come from? Smerdyakov had picked them up and brought them in the day before.

"Well, my lad, I've never met any one like you," Fyodor Pavlovich said shortly, and gave him ten roubles. We may add that he not only believed in his honesty, but had, for some reason, a liking for him, although the young man looked as morosely at him as at every one and was always silent. He rarely spoke. If it had occurred to any one to wonder at the time what the young man was interested in, and what was in his mind, it would have been impossible to tell by looking at him. Yet he used sometimes to stop suddenly in the house, or even in the yard or street, and stand still for ten minutes, lost in thought. A physiognomist studying his face would have said that there was no thought in it, no reflection, but only a sort of contemplative look. There is a remarkable picture by the painter Kramskoy, called "Contemplation." It shows a forest in winter, and on a roadway through the forest, in absolute solitude, stands a peasant in a torn kaftan and bast shoes. He stands, as it were, lost in thought. Yet he is not thinking; he is "contemplating." If one touched him he would start and look at one as though awakening but bewildered. It's true he would come to himself immediately; but if he were asked what he had

been thinking about, he would remember nothing. Yet probably he has hidden within himself the impression which had dominated him during the period of contemplation. Those impressions are dear to him and no doubt he hoards them imperceptibly, and even unconsciously. How and why, of course, he does not know either. He may suddenly, having accumulated impressions for many years, abandon everything and go off to Jerusalem on a pilgrimage for his soul's salvation, or perhaps he will suddenly set fire to his native village, or perhaps do both. There are a good many "contemplatives" among the peasantry. Well, Smerdyakov was probably one of them, and he probably was greedily hoarding up his impressions, hardly knowing why.

## CHAPTER VII
### CONTROVERSY

BUT Balaam's ass had suddenly spoken. The subject was a strange one. Grigory had gone in the morning to make purchases, and had heard from the shopkeeper Lukyanov the story of a Russian soldier which had appeared in the newspaper that day. This soldier had been taken prisoner in some remote part of Asia, and was threatened with an immediate agonising death if he did not renounce Christianity and embrace Islam. He refused to deny his faith, and was tortured, flayed alive, and died, praising and glorifying Christ. Grigory had related the story at table. Fyodor Pavlovich always liked, over the dessert after dinner, to laugh and talk, if only with Grigory. This afternoon he was in a particularly good-humoured and expansive mood. Sipping his cognac and listening to the story, he observed that a soldier like that should be immediately canonised and his skin dispatched to some monastery. "That would bring the crowds and the money."

Grigory frowned, seeing that Fyodor Pavlovich was by no means touched, but, as usual, was beginning to blaspheme. At that moment, Smerdyakov, who was standing by the door, grinned. Smerdyakov often waited at table towards the end of dinner, and since Ivan's arrival in our town he had done so every day.

"What are you grinning at?" asked Fyodor Pavlovich, catching the smile instantly, and knowing that it referred to Grigory.

"Well, my opinion is, sir," Smerdyakov began suddenly and unexpectedly in a loud voice, "that if that soldier's praiseworthy exploit was so very great there would have been, to my thinking, no sin in it if he had in such an emergency renounced, so to speak, the name of Christ and his own christening, to save by that same his life, for good deeds, by which, in the course of years to expiate his cowardice."

"How could it not be a sin? You're talking nonsense. For that you'll go straight to hell and be roasted there like mutton," put in Fyodor Pavlovich.

It was at this point that Alyosha came in, and Fyodor Pavlovich, as we have seen, was highly delighted at his appearance.

"We're on your subject, your subject," he chuckled gleefully, making Alyosha sit down to listen.

"As for mutton, sir, that's not so, and there'll be no punishment there for this, and there shouldn't be either, in all justice, sir," Smerdyakov maintained sedately.

"How do you mean 'in all justice'?" Fyodor Pavlovich cried still more gaily, nudging Alyosha with his knee.

"He's a rascal, that's what he is!" burst from Grigory. He looked Smerdyakov wrathfully in the face.

"As for being a rascal, wait a little, Grigory Vasilyevich," answered Smerdyakov with perfect composure. "You'd better consider yourself that, once I am taken prisoner by the enemies of the Christian race, and they demand that I curse the name of God and renounce my holy baptism, I am fully empowered by my own reason to do so, for there would be no sin in it."

"But you've said that before. Don't waste words. Prove it," cried Fyodor Pavlovich.

"Bouillon-maker!" muttered Grigory contemptuously.

"As for being a bouillon-maker, wait a bit, too, and consider for yourself, Grigory Vasilyevich, without abusing me. For as soon as I say to those torturers, 'No, I'm not a Christian, and I curse my true God,' then at once, by God's high judgment, I become immediately and specially anathema accursed, and am cut off from the Holy Church, exactly as though I were a heathen, so that at that very instant, not only when I say it aloud, but when I think of saying it, before a quarter of a second has passed, I am cut off. Is that so or not, Grigory Vasilyevich?"

He addressed Grigory with obvious satisfaction, though he was really answering Fyodor Pavlovich's questions, and was well aware of it, and intentionally pretending that the questions had come from Grigory.

"Ivan," cried Fyodor Pavlovich suddenly, "stoop down, I must whisper something to you. He's got this all up for your benefit. He wants you to compliment him. Compliment him."

Ivan listened with perfect seriousness to his father's excited whisper.

"Wait, Smerdyakov, be quiet a minute," cried Fyodor Pavlovich once more. "Ivan, your ear again."

Ivan bent down again with a perfectly grave face.

"I love you as I do Alyosha. Don't think I don't love you. Some cognac?"

"Yes." But you're rather drunk yourself, thought Ivan, looking steadily at his father.

He was watching Smerdyakov with great curiosity.

"You're anathema accursed, as it is," Grigory suddenly burst out, "and how dare you argue, you rascal, after that, if . . ."

"Don't scold him, Grigory, don't scold him," Fyodor Pavlovich cut him short.

"You should wait, Grigory Vasilyevich, if only a short time, and listen, for I haven't finished all I had to say. For at the very moment I become accursed of God, at that same highest moment, I become exactly like a heathen, and my baptism is removed and becomes of no avail. Isn't that so?"

"Make haste and finish, my boy," Fyodor Pavlovich urged him, sipping from his wine-glass with relish.

"And if I've ceased to be a Christian, then I told no lie to the torturers when they asked whether I was a Christian or not a Christian, seeing I had already been relieved by God Himself of my Christianity by reason of the thought alone, before I had time to utter a word to the torturers. And if I have already been demoted, in what manner and with what sort of justice can I be held responsible as a Christian in the other world for having denied Christ, when, through the very thought alone, before denying Him I had been relieved of my baptism? If I'm no longer a Christian, then I can't renounce Christ, for I've nothing then to

renounce. Who will hold an unclean Tatar responsible, Grigory Vasilyevich, even in heaven, for not having been born a Christian? And who would punish him for that, considering that you can't take two skins off one ox? For God Almighty Himself, even if He did make the Tatar responsible, when he dies would give him the smallest possible punishment, I imagine (since he must be punished), judging that he is not to blame if he has come into the world an unclean heathen, from heathen parents. The Lord God can't surely take a Tatar and say he was a Christian? That would mean that the Almighty would tell a real untruth. And can the Lord of heaven and earth tell a lie, even in one word?"

Grigory was thunderstruck and looked at the orator, his eyes nearly starting out of his head. Though he did not clearly understand what was said, he had caught something in this rigmarole, and stood, looking like a man who has just hit his head against a wall. Fyodor Pavlovich emptied his glass and went off into his shrill laugh.

"Alyosha! Alyosha! What do you say to that! Ah, you casuist! He must have been with the Jesuits somewhere, Ivan. Oh, you stinking Jesuit, who taught you? But you're talking nonsense, you casuist, nonsense, nonsense, nonsense. Don't cry, Grigory, we'll reduce him to smoke and ashes in a moment. Tell me this, oh, ass; you may be right before your torturers, but you have renounced your faith all the same in your own heart, and you say yourself that in that very hour you became anathema accursed. And if once you're anathema they won't pat you on the head for it in hell. What do you say to that, my fine Jesuit?"

"There is no doubt, sir, that I have renounced it in my own heart, sir, but there was no special sin in that. Or if there was sin, sir, it was of the most ordinary kind."

"How's that, the most ordinary kind?"

"You lie, accursed one!" hissed Grigory.

"Consider yourself, Grigory Vasilyevich," Smerdyakov went on, staid and unruffled, conscious of his triumph, but, as it were, generous to the vanquished foe. "Consider yourself, Grigory Vasilyevich; it is said in Scripture that if you have faith, even as a mustard seed, and bid a mountain move into the sea, it will move without the least delay at your bidding. Well, Grigory Vasilyevich, if I'm without faith and you have so great a faith that you are continually swearing at me, you try yourself telling this mountain, not to move into the sea, for that's a long way off, but even to our stinking little river which runs beyond our garden. You'll see for yourself that it won't budge, but will remain just where it is however much you shout at it, and that shows, Grigory Vasilyevich, that you haven't faith in the proper manner, and only abuse others about it. Again, taking into consideration that no one in our day, not only you, but actually no one, from the highest person to the lowest peasant, can shove mountains into the sea — except perhaps some one man in the world, or, at most, two, and they most likely are saving their souls in secret somewhere in the Egyptian desert, so you wouldn't find them — if so it be, if all the rest have no faith, will God curse all the rest? that is, the population of the whole earth, except about two hermits in the desert, and in His well-known mercy will He not forgive one of them? And so I trust that though I may once have doubted I shall be forgiven if I shed tears of repentance."

"Wait!" cried Fyodor Pavlovich, in a transport of delight. "So you do suppose there are two who can move mountains, that they do exist? Ivan, make a note of it, write it down. There you have the Russian all over!"

"You're quite right in saying it's characteristic of the people's faith," Ivan assented, with an approving smile.

"You agree. Then it must be so, if you agree. It's true, isn't it, Alyosha? That's the Russian faith all over, isn't it?"

"No, Smerdyakov has not the Russian faith at all," said Alyosha firmly and gravely.

"I'm not talking about his faith. I mean those two in the desert, only that idea. Surely that's Russian, isn't it?"

"Yes, that's purely Russian," said Alyosha, smiling.

"Your words are worth a gold piece, oh, ass, and I'll give it to you to-day. But as for the rest, you talk nonsense, nonsense, nonsense. Let me tell you, stupid, that we here are all of little faith, only from carelessness, because we haven't time; in the first place, things are too much for us, and, in the second place, the Lord God has given us so little time, only twenty-four hours in the day, so that one hasn't even time to get sleep enough, much less to repent of one's sins. But you there, you denied your faith to your torturers when you'd nothing else to think about but your faith and nothing else to do but show your faith. So I consider, brother, that it constitutes a sin."

"Constitute a sin it may, but consider yourself, Grigory Vasilyevich, that it only extenuates it, if it does constitute it. If I had believed then in very truth, as I ought to have believed, then it really would have been sinful if I had not faced tortures for my faith, and had gone over to the filthy Mohammedan faith. But, of course, it wouldn't have come to torture then, because I should only have had to say at that instant to the mountain, 'Move and crush the tormentor,' and it would have moved and at the very instant have crushed him like a black-beetle, and I should have walked away as though nothing had happened, praising and glorifying God. But, suppose at that very moment I had tried all that, and cried to that mountain, 'Crush these tormentors,' and it hadn't crushed them, how could I have helped doubting, pray, at such a time, and at such a dread hour of mortal terror? And apart from that, I should know already that I could not attain to the fulness of the Kingdom of Heaven (for since the mountain had not moved at my word, they could not think very much of my faith up aloft, and there could be no very great reward awaiting me in the world to come). So why should I let them flay the skin off me as well, and to no good purpose? For, even though they had flayed my skin half off my back, even then the mountain would not have moved at my word or at my cry. And at such a moment not only doubt might come over one, but one might lose one's reason from fear, so that one would not be able to think at all. And, therefore, how should I be particularly to blame, if, not seeing my advantage or reward there or here, I should, at least, save my skin? And so trusting fully in the grace of the Lord I should cherish the hope that I might be altogether forgiven, sir."

## CHAPTER VIII
### OVER THE COGNAC

THE controversy was over. But strange to say Fyodor Pavlovich, who had been so gay, suddenly began frowning. He frowned and gulped some cognac, and it was already a glass too much.

"Get along with you, Jesuits!" he cried to the servants. "Get out, Smerdyakov. I'll send you the gold piece I promised you to-day, but be off! Don't cry, Grigory. Go to Marfa. She'll comfort you and put you to bed. The rascals won't let me sit in peace after dinner," he snapped peevishly, as the servants promptly withdrew at his word.

"Smerdyakov always pokes himself in now, after dinner. It's you he's so interested in. What have you done to fascinate him?" he added to Ivan.

"Nothing whatever," answered Ivan. "He's pleased to have a high opinion of me; he's a lackey and a mean soul. Worms'-meat of progress, however, when the time comes."

"Of progress?"

"There will be others and better ones. But there will be some like him as well. His kind will come first, and better ones after."

"And when will the time come?"

"The rocket will go off and fizzle out, perhaps. The people are not very fond of listening to these bouillon-makers, so far."

"Ah, brother, but a Balaam's ass like that thinks and thinks, and the devil knows where he'll end."

"He's storing up ideas," said Ivan, smiling.

"You see, I know he can't bear me, nor any one else, even you, though you fancy that he has a high opinion of you. Worse still with Alyosha, he despises Alyosha. But he doesn't steal, that's one thing, and he's not a gossip, he holds his tongue, and doesn't wash our dirty linen in public. He makes capital fish patties, too. But, damn him, is he worth talking about so much?"

"Of course he isn't."

"And as for the ideas he may be hatching, the Russian peasant, generally speaking, needs

98

flogging. That I've always maintained. Our peasant is a swindler, and doesn't deserve to be pitied, and it's a good thing he's still thrashed sometimes. Russia's strength is in the birch. If they destroy the forests, Russia will perish. I stand up for the clever people. We've left off thrashing the peasants, we've grown so clever, but they go on thrashing themselves. And a good thing, too. 'For with what measure ye mete it shall be measured to you again,' or how does it go? Anyhow, it will be measured out. But Russia's all swinishness. My dear, if you only knew how I hate Russia. . . . That is, not Russia, but all this vice! But maybe I mean Russia. *Tout cela c'est de la cochonnerie.* . . . Do you know what I like? I like wit."

"You've had another glass. That's enough."

"Wait. I'll have one more, and then another, and then I'll stop. No, stop, you interrupted me. At Mokroye I was talking to an old peasant, and he told me: 'There's nothing we like so much as sentencing girls to be thrashed, and we always give the lads the job of thrashing them. And the girl he has thrashed to-day, the young man will ask in marriage to-morrow. So it quite suits the girls, too,' he said. There's a set of de Sades for you! But it's clever, anyway. Shall we go over and have a look at it, eh? Alyosha, are you blushing? Don't be bashful, child. I'm sorry I didn't stay to dinner at the Father Superior's and tell the monks about the girls at Mokroye. Alyosha, don't be angry that I offended your Superior this morning. I lost my temper. If there is a God, if He exists, then, of course, I'm to blame, and I shall have to answer for it. But if there isn't a God at all, don't they deserve worse, your fathers? It's not enough to cut their heads off, for they keep back progress. Would you believe it, Ivan,

that this hurts my feelings? No, you don't believe it, as I see from your eyes. You believe what people say, that I'm nothing but a buffoon. Alyosha, do you believe that I'm nothing but a buffoon?"

"No, I don't believe it."

"And I believe you don't, and that you speak the truth. You look sincere and you speak sincerely. But not Ivan. Ivan's supercilious. . . . I'd make an end of your monastery, though, all the same. I'd take all that mystic stuff and suppress it, once for all, all over Russia, so as to bring all the fools to reason. And the gold and the silver that would flow into the mint!"

"But why suppress it?" asked Ivan.

"That Truth may prevail the sooner."

"Well, if Truth were to prevail, you know, you'd be the first to be robbed and . . . suppressed."

"Bah! I dare say you're right. Ah, I'm an ass!" burst out Fyodor Pavlovich, striking himself lightly on the forehead.

"Well, your monastery may stand then, Alyosha, if that's how it is. And we clever people will sit snug and enjoy our cognac. You know, Ivan, it must have been so ordained by the Almighty Himself. Ivan, speak, is there a God or not? Wait: speak the truth, speak seriously. Why are you laughing again?"

"I'm laughing because you made a clever remark just now about Smerdyakov's belief in the existence of two saints who could move mountains."

"Why, am I like him now, then?"

"Very much."

"Well, that shows I'm a Russian, too, and I have a Russian trait. And you may be caught in the same way, though you are a philosopher. Shall I catch you? What do you bet that I'll catch you to-morrow. Speak, all the same, is there a God, or not? Only, be serious. I want you to be serious now."

"No, there is no God."

"Alyosha, is there a God?"

"There is."

"Ivan, and is there immortality, some sort of immortality, just a little, just a tiny bit?"

"There is no immortality either."

"None at all?"

"None at all."

"There's absolute nothingness then. Perhaps there is just something? Not altogether nothing!"

"Absolute nothingness."

"Alyosha, is there immortality?"

"There is."

"God and immortality?"

"God and immortality. In God is immortality."

"H'm! It's more likely Ivan's right. Good Lord! to think what faith, what force of all kinds, man has lavished for nothing, on that dream, and for how many thousand years. Who is it that is making a mock of man this way? Ivan! For the last time, once for all, is there a God or not? I ask for the last time!"

"And for the last time, there is not."

"Who is laughing at man, then, Ivan?"

"The devil, perhaps," said Ivan, smiling.

"And the devil? Does he exist?"

"No, he doesn't."

"It's a pity. Damn it all, what wouldn't I do to the man who first invented God! Hanging on a bitter aspen tree would be too good for him."

"There would have been no civilisation if they hadn't invented God."

"Wouldn't there have been? Without God?"

"No. And there would have been no cognac either. But I must take your cognac away from you, anyway."

"Stop, stop, stop, dear boy, one more little glass. I've hurt Alyosha's feelings. You're not angry with me, Alyosha? My dear little Alexey!"

"No, I am not angry. I know your thoughts. Your heart is better than your head."

"My heart better than my head, is it? Oh, Lord! And that from you. Ivan, do you love Alyosha?"

"I do."

"You must love him." (Fyodor Pavlovich was getting very drunk.) "Listen, Alyosha, I was rude to your elder this morning. But I was excited. But there's wit in that elder, don't you think, Ivan?"

"Very likely."

"There is, there is. *Il y a du Piron là dedans.* He's a Jesuit, a Russian one, that is. As he's an honourable person there's a hidden indignation boiling within him at having to pretend and affect holiness."

"But, of course, he believes in God."

"Not a bit of it. Didn't you know? Why, he tells every one so, himself. That is, not every one, but all the clever people who come to him. He said straight out to Governor Schultz not long ago: '*Credo,* but I don't know in what.'"

"Really?"

"He really did. But I respect him. There's something of Mephistopheles about him, or rather of 'The hero of our time.' . . . Arbenin, or what's his name? . . . You see, he's a sensualist. He's such a sensualist that I should be afraid for my daughter or my wife if she went to confess to him. You know, when he begins telling stories . . . The year before last he invited us to tea, tea with liqueur (the ladies send him liqueur), and began telling us about old times till we nearly split our sides. . . . Especially how he once cured a paralysed woman. 'If my legs were not bad I know a dance I could dance you,' he said. What do you say to that? 'I've played plenty of tricks in my time,' said he. He did Demidov, the merchant, out of sixty thousand."

"What, he stole it?"

"He brought him the money as a man he could trust, saying, 'Take care of it for me, brother, the police will be searching my place to-morrow.' And he kept it. 'You have given it to the Church,' he declared. I said to him: 'You're a scoundrel,' I said. 'No,' said he, 'I'm not a scoundrel, but I'm broad-minded.' But that wasn't he, that was some one else. I've muddled him with some one else . . . without noticing it. Come, another glass and that's enough. Take away the bottle, Ivan. I've been telling lies. Why didn't you stop me, Ivan, and tell me I was lying?"

"I knew you'd stop of yourself."

"That's a lie. You did it from spite, from simple spite against me. You despise me. You have come to me and you despise me in my own house."

"Well, I'll leave. It's the cognac working in you."

"I've begged you for Christ's sake to go to Chermashnya for a day or two, and you don't go."

"I'll go to-morrow if you're so set up on it."

"You won't go. You want to keep an eye on me. That's what you want, you spiteful soul. That's why you won't go."

The old man persisted. He had reached that state of drunkenness when the drunkard who has till then been inoffensive tries to pick a quarrel and to assert himself.

"Why are you looking at me? Why do you look like that? Your eyes look at me and say, 'The drunken mug!' Your eyes are suspicious, they're contemptuous. . . . You've come here with some design. Alyosha, here, looks at me and his eyes shine. Alyosha doesn't despise me. Alexey, you mustn't love Ivan."

"Don't be cross with my brother. Leave off insulting him," Alyosha said suddenly and with emphasis.

"Oh, all right. Ugh, my head aches. Take away the cognac, Ivan. It's the third time I've told you."

He mused, and suddenly a slow, cunning grin spread over his face.

"Don't be angry with a feeble old man, Ivan. I know you don't love me, but don't be angry all the same. There's nothing to love me for. You go to Chermashnya. I'll come to you myself and bring you a present. I'll show you a little wench there. I've had my eye on her a long time. She's still running about barefoot. Don't be afraid of bare-footed wenches — don't despise them — they're pearls!"

And he kissed his hand with a smack.

"To me . . ." he revived at once, seeming to grow sober the instant he touched on his favourite topic. "To me . . . Ah, you boys! You children, little sucking pigs, to me . . . all my life a woman has never seemed ugly — that's been my rule! Can you understand that? How could you understand it? You've still milk in your veins, not blood. You're not hatched yet. My rule has been that you can always find something devilishly interesting in every woman that you wouldn't find in any other. Only, one must know how to find it, that's the point! That's a talent! To my mind there are no homely women. The very fact that she is a woman is half the battle . . . but how could you understand that? Even in *vieilles filles*, even in them you may discover something that makes you simply wonder that men have been such fools as to let them grow old without noticing them. Bare-footed girls or unattractive ones, you must take by surprise. Didn't you know that? You must astound them till they're fascinated, pierced, ashamed that such a gentleman should fall in love with such a little slut. It's a jolly good thing that there always are and always will be masters and slaves in the world, so there always will be a little maid-of-all-work and her master, and you know, that's all that's needed for happiness. Wait . . . listen, Alyosha, I always used to astonish your late mother, but in a different way. I used to neglect her completely, but all at once, when the moment came, I'd be all devotion to her, crawl on my knees, kiss her feet, and I always, always — I remember it as though it were to-day — reduced her to that tinkling, quiet, nervous, queer little laugh. It was peculiar to her. I knew her attacks always used to begin like that, the next day she would begin shrieking hysterically, and this little laugh was not a sign of delight, but it made a very good counterfeit. That's what it means to be able to find the right thing in every one. Once Belyavsky — he was a handsome fellow, and rich — he courted her and made a habit of coming here — suddenly gave me a slap in the face in my own house and in her presence. And she — such a sheep — why, I thought she would have knocked me down for that blow. How she set on me! 'You're beaten, beaten now,' she said. 'You've taken a blow from him. You have been trying to sell me to him,' she said. . . . 'And how dared he strike you in my presence! Don't dare come near me again, never, never! Run

at once, challenge him to a duel!' . . . I took her to the monastery then to bring her to her senses. The holy fathers prayed over her. But I swear, by God, Alyosha, I never harmed my poor possessed girl! Only once, perhaps, in the first year; she was already very fond of praying. She used to keep the feasts of Our Lady particularly and used to turn me out of her room then. I'll knock that mysticism out of her, thought I! 'Here,' said I, 'you see your holy image. Here it is. Here I take it down. You believe it's a miracle-working ikon, but here, I'll spit on it directly and nothing will happen to me for it!' . . . When she saw it, good Lord! I thought she would kill me. But she only jumped up, struck her hands together, then suddenly hid her face in them, began trembling all over and fell on the floor . . . fell all of a heap. Alyosha, Alyosha, what's the matter?"

The old man jumped up in alarm. From the time he had begun speaking about his mother, a change had gradually come over Alyosha's face. He flushed crimson, his eyes glowed, his lips quivered. The old sot had gone spluttering on, noticing nothing, till the moment when something very strange happened to Alyosha. Precisely what he was describing in the possessed woman was suddenly repeated in Alyosha. He jumped up from his seat exactly as his mother was said to have done, struck his hands together, hid his face in them, and dropped into the chair, shaking all over in an hysterical paroxysm of sudden, violent, silent weeping. His extraordinary resemblance to his mother particularly startled the old man.

"Ivan, Ivan! Water, quickly! It's like her, exactly as she used to be then, his mother. Spurt some water on him from your mouth, that's what I used to do to her. He's upset about his mother, his mother," he muttered to Ivan.

"But she was my mother, too, I believe, his mother. Was she not?" said Ivan, with uncontrolled anger and contempt. The old man shrank before his flashing eyes. But something very strange had happened, though only for a second; it seemed really to have escaped the old man's mind that Alyosha's mother actually was Ivan's mother, too.

"Your mother?" he muttered, not understanding. "What do you mean? What mother are you talking about? Was she? . . . Why, damn it! of course she was yours, too! Damn it! My mind's gone back on me, that never happened to me before. Excuse me, why, I was thinking, Ivan . . . He, he, he!" He stopped. A broad, drunken, half senseless grin overspread his face.

At that moment a fearful noise and clamour was heard in the hall, there were violent shouts, the door was flung open, and Dmitri burst into the room. The old man rushed to Ivan in terror.

"He'll kill me! He'll kill me! Don't let him get at me!" he screamed, clinging to the skirt of Ivan's coat.

## CHAPTER IX
### THE SENSUALISTS

GRIGORY and Smerdyakov ran into the room right after Dmitri. They had been struggling with him in the passage, refusing to admit him, acting on instructions given them by Fyodor Pavlovich some days before. Taking advantage of the fact that Dmitri stopped a moment on entering the room to look about him, Grigory ran round the table, closed the double doors on the opposite side of the room leading to the inner apartments, and stood before the closed doors, stretching wide his arms, prepared to defend the entrance, so to speak, with the last drop of his blood. Seeing this, Dmitri uttered a scream rather than a shout and rushed at Grigory.

"Then she's there! She's hidden there! Out of the way, scoundrel!"

He tried to pull Grigory away, but the old servant pushed him back. Beside himself with fury, Dmitri struck out, and hit Grigory with all his might. The old man fell like a log, and Dmitri, leaping over him, broke in the door. Smerdyakov remained pale and trembling at the other end of the room, huddling close to Fyodor Pavlovich.

"She's here!" shouted Dmitri. "I saw her turn towards the house just now, but I couldn't catch her. Where is she? Where is she?"

That shout, "She's here!" produced an indescribable effect on Fyodor Pavlovich. All his fright left him.

"Hold him! Hold him!" he cried, and dashed after Dmitri. Meanwhile Grigory had got up from the floor, but still seemed stunned. Ivan and Alyosha ran after their father. In the third room something was heard to fall on the floor with a ringing crash: it was a large glass vase — not an expensive one — on a marble pedestal which Dmitri had brushed against as he ran past it.

"At him!" shouted the old man. "Help!"

Ivan and Alyosha caught the old man and were forcibly bringing him back.

"Why do you run after him? He'll murder you outright," Ivan cried wrathfully at his father.

"Ivan! Alyosha! She must be here. Grushenka's here. He said he saw her himself, running."

He was choking. He was not expecting

Grushenka at the time, and the sudden news that she was there overwhelmed him. He was trembling all over. He seemed frantic.

"But you've seen for yourself that she hasn't come," cried Ivan.

"But she may have come by that other entrance."

"You know that entrance is locked, and you have the key."

Dmitri suddenly reappeared in the drawing-room. He had, of course, found the other entrance locked, and the key actually was in Fyodor Pavlovich's pocket. The windows of all the rooms were closed, too, so that Grushenka could not have come in anywhere nor have run out anywhere.

"Hold him!" shrieked Fyodor Pavlovich, as soon as he saw him again. "He's been stealing money in my bedroom." And tearing himself from Ivan he rushed again at Dmitri. But Dmitri threw up both hands and suddenly clutched the old man by the two tufts of hair that remained on his temples, tugged at them, and flung him with a crash on the floor. He kicked him two or three times in the face with his heel. The old man moaned shrilly. Ivan, though not so strong as Dmitri, threw his arms round him, and with all his might pulled him away. Alyosha helped him with his slender strength, holding Dmitri in front.

"Madman! You've killed him!" cried Ivan.

"Serve him right!" shouted Dmitri breathlessly. "If I haven't killed him, I'll come again and kill him. You can't protect him!"

"Dmitri! Go away at once!" cried Alyosha commandingly.

"Alexey! You tell me. It's only you I can believe; was she here just now, or not? I saw her myself creeping this way by the fence from the lane. I shouted, she ran away."

"I swear she's not been here, and no one expected her."

"But I saw her. . . . So she must . . . I'll find out at once where she is. . . . Good-bye, Alexey! Not a word to Æsop about the money now. But go to Katerina Ivanovna at once and be sure to say, 'He sends his compliments to you!' Compliments, his compliments! Just compliments and farewell! Describe the scene to her."

Meanwhile Ivan and Grigory had lifted up the old man and seated him in an armchair. His face was covered with blood, but he was conscious and listened greedily to Dmitri's cries. He was still fancying that Grushenka really was somewhere in the house. Dmitri looked at him with hatred as he went out.

"I don't repent shedding your blood!" he cried. "Beware, old man, beware of your dream, for I have my dream, too. I curse you, and disown you altogether."

He ran out of the room.

"She's here. She must be here. Smerdyakov! Smerdyakov!" the old man wheezed, almost inaudibly, beckoning to him with his finger.

"No, she's not here, you old lunatic!" Ivan shouted at him angrily. "Here, he's fainting! Water! A towel! Hurry, Smerdyakov!"

Smerdyakov ran for water. At last they got the old man undressed, and put him to bed. They wrapped a wet towel round his head. Exhausted by the cognac, by his violent emotion, and the blows he had received, he shut his eyes and fell asleep as soon as his head touched the pillow. Ivan and Alyosha went back to the drawing-room. Smerdyakov removed the fragments of the broken vase, while Grigory stood by the table looking gloomily at the floor.

"Shouldn't you put a wet bandage on your head and go to bed, too?" Alyosha said to him.

THE MADNESS OF DMITRI

"We'll look after him. My brother gave you a terrible blow — on the head."

"He's insulted me!" Grigory articulated gloomily and distinctly.

"He's 'insulted' his father, not only you," observed Ivan with a forced smile.

"I used to wash him in his tub. He's insulted me," repeated Grigory.

"Damn it all, if I hadn't pulled him away perhaps he'd have murdered him. It wouldn't take much to do for Æsop, would it?" whispered Ivan to Alyosha.

"God forbid!" cried Alyosha.

"Why should He forbid?" Ivan went on in the same whisper, with a malignant grimace. "One reptile will devour the other. And serve them both right, too."

Alyosha shuddered.

"Of course I won't allow the murder to take place any more than I did just now. Stay here, Alyosha, I'll go for a turn in the yard. My head's begun to ache."

Alyosha went to his father's bedroom and sat by his bedside behind the screen for about an hour. The old man suddenly opened his eyes and gazed for a long while at Alyosha, evidently remembering and thinking. All at once his face betrayed extraordinary excitement. "Alyosha," he whispered apprehensively, "where's Ivan?"

"In the yard. He's got a headache. He's on the watch."

"Give me that looking-glass. It stands over there. Give it me."

Alyosha gave him a little round folding looking-glass which stood on the chest of drawers. The old man looked at himself in it; his nose was considerably swollen, and on the left side of his forehead there was a rather large crimson bruise.

"What does Ivan say? Alyosha, my dear, my only son, I'm afraid of Ivan. I'm more afraid of Ivan than of the other. You're the only one I'm not afraid of. . . ."

"Don't be afraid of Ivan either. He is angry, but he'll defend you."

"Alyosha, and what of the other? He's run to Grushenka. My angel, tell me the truth, was she here just now or not?"

"No one has seen her. It was a mistake. She has not been here."

"You know Mitya wants to marry her, to marry her."

"She won't marry him."

"She won't. She won't. She won't. She won't on any account!"

The old man fairly fluttered with joy, as though nothing more comforting could have been said to him. In his delight he seized Alyosha's hand and pressed it warmly to his heart. Tears positively glittered in his eyes.

"That image of the Mother of God of which I was telling you just now," he said. "Take it home and keep it for yourself. And I give you permission to go back to the monastery. . . . I was joking this morning, don't be angry with me. My head aches, Alyosha. . . . Alyosha, comfort my heart. Be an angel and tell me the truth!"

"You're still asking whether she has been here or not?" Alyosha said sorrowfully.

"No, no, no. I believe you. I'll tell you what it is: you go to Grushenka yourself, or see her somehow; make haste and ask her; see for yourself, which she means to choose, him or me? Eh? What? Can you, or can't you?"

"If I see her I'll ask her," Alyosha muttered, embarrassed.

"No, she won't tell you," the old man interrupted, "she's a minx. She'll begin kissing you and say that it's you she wants. She's a deceitful, shameless hussy. You mustn't go to her, you mustn't!"

"No, father, and it wouldn't be suitable, it wouldn't be right at all."

"Where was he sending you just now? He shouted 'Go' as he ran away."

"To Katerina Ivanovna."

"For money? To ask her for money?"

"No. Not for money."

"He's no money; not a bit. I'll settle down for the night, and think things over, and you can go. Perhaps you'll meet her. . . . Only be sure to come to me to-morrow in the morning. Be sure to. I have a word to say to you to-morrow. Will you come?"

"Yes."

"When you come, pretend you've come of your own accord to ask after me. Don't tell any one I told you to. Don't say a word to Ivan."

"Very well."

"Good-bye, my angel. You stood up for me, just now. I shall never forget it. I've a word to say to you to-morrow—but I must think about it."

"And how do you feel now?"

"I shall get up to-morrow and go out, perfectly well, perfectly well!"

Crossing the yard, Alyosha found Ivan sitting on the bench at the gateway. He was sitting writing something in pencil in his notebook. Alyosha told Ivan that their father had waked up, was conscious, and had let him go back to sleep at the monastery.

"Alyosha, I should be very glad to meet you to-morrow morning," said Ivan cordially, standing up. His cordiality was a complete surprise to Alyosha.

"I shall be at the Hohlakovs' to-morrow,"
answered Alyosha, "I may be at Katerina Ivanovna's, too, if I don't find her now."

"But you're going to her now, anyway? For that 'compliments and farewell,'" said Ivan, smiling. Alyosha was disconcerted.

"I think I quite understand his exclamations just now, and part of what went before. Dmitri has asked you to go to her and say that he—well, in fact—takes his leave of her?"

"Brother, how will all this horror end between father and Dmitri?" exclaimed Alyosha.

"One can't tell for certain. Perhaps in nothing: it may all fizzle out. That woman is a beast. In any case we must keep the old man indoors and not let Dmitri into the house."

"Brother, let me ask one thing more: has any man a right to look at other men and decide who is worthy to live and who isn't?"

"Why bring in the question of worth? The matter is most often decided in men's hearts on other grounds much more natural. And as for rights—who has not the right to wish?"

"Not for another man's death?"

"What even if for another man's death? Why lie to oneself, since all men live so and perhaps cannot help living so. Are you referring to what I said just now—that one reptile will devour the other? In that case let me ask you, do you think me, like Dmitri, capable of shedding Æsop's blood, murdering him?"

"What are you saying, Ivan? Such an idea never crossed my mind. I don't think Dmitri is capable of it, either."

"Thanks, if only for that," smiled Ivan. "Be sure, I should always defend him. But in my wishes I reserve myself full latitude in this case. Good-bye till to-morrow. Don't condemn me, and don't look on me as a villain," he added with a smile.

They shook hands warmly as they had never done before. Alyosha felt that his brother had taken the first step towards him, and that he had certainly done this with some definite purpose.

## CHAPTER X
### BOTH TOGETHER

ALYOSHA left his father's house feeling even more broken and dejected in spirit than when he had entered it. His mind, too, seemed crushed and scattered, as it were, while he felt that he was afraid to put together the disjointed fragments and form a general idea from all the agonising and conflicting experiences of the day. He felt something bordering upon despair, which he had never known till then. Towering like a mountain above all the rest stood the fatal insoluble question: How would things end between his father and his brother Dmitri with this terrible woman? Now he had himself been a witness of it, he had been present and seen them face to face. Yet only his brother Dmitri could be made unhappy, terribly, completely unhappy: there was trouble awaiting him. It appeared, too, that there were other people concerned, far more so than Alyosha could have supposed before. There was something positively mysterious in it, too. Ivan had made a step towards him, which was what Alyosha had long been desiring. Yet now he felt for some reason that he was frightened by this advance. And these women? Strange to say, that morning he had set out for Katerina Ivanovna's in the greatest embarrassment; now he felt nothing of the kind. On the contrary, he was hastening there as though expecting to find guidance from her. Yet to give her this message was obviously more difficult than before. The matter of the three thousand was decided irrevocably, and Dmitri, feeling himself dishonoured and losing his last hope, might sink to any depth. He had, moreover, told him to describe to Katerina Ivanovna the scene which had just taken place with his father.

It was by now seven o'clock, and it was getting dark as Alyosha entered the very spacious and comfortable house on Bolshaya Street occupied by Katerina Ivanovna. Alyosha knew that she lived with two aunts. One of them, a silent woman, was that aunt of her half-sister Agafya Ivanovna who had looked after her in her father's house when she came from boarding-school. The other aunt was a Moscow lady of style and consequence, though in straitened circumstances. It was said that they both gave way in everything to Katerina Ivanovna, and that she kept them with her only for the sake of the proprieties. Katerina Ivanovna herself heeded no one but her benefactress, the general's widow, who had been kept by illness in Moscow, and to whom she was obliged to write twice a week a full account of all her doings.

When Alyosha entered the hall and asked the maid who opened the door to announce him, it was evident that they were already aware of his arrival. Possibly he had been noticed from the window. At least, Alyosha heard a noise, caught the sound of flying footsteps and rustling skirts. Two or three women perhaps had run out of the room.

Alyosha thought it strange that his arrival should cause such excitement. But he was conducted to the drawing-room at once. It was a large room, elegantly and amply furnished, not at all in provincial style. There were many sofas, lounges, settees, big and little tables. There were pictures on the walls, vases and lamps on the tables, masses of flowers, and even an aquarium by the window. It was twilight and rather dark. Alyosha made out a silk mantle thrown down on the sofa, where people had evidently just been sitting; and on a table in front of the sofa were two unfinished cups of chocolate, biscuits, a crystal dish with blue raisins, and another with sweetmeats. Alyosha saw that he had interrupted visitors, and frowned. But at that instant the portière was raised, and with rapid, hurrying footsteps Katerina Ivanovna came in, holding out both hands to Alyosha with a radiant smile of delight. At the same instant a servant brought in two lighted candles and set them on the table.

"Thank God! At last you have come, too! I've been simply praying for you all day! Sit down."

Alyosha had been struck by Katerina Ivanovna's beauty when, three weeks before, Dmitri had first brought him, at Katerina Ivanovna's special request, to be introduced to her. There had been no conversation between them at that interview, however. Supposing Alyosha to be very shy, Katerina Ivanovna had talked all the time to Dmitri to spare him. Alyosha had been silent, but he had seen a great deal very clearly. He was struck by the imperiousness, proud ease, and self-confidence of the haughty girl. And all that was certain, Alyosha felt that he was not exaggerating it. He thought her great glowing black eyes were very fine, especially with her pale, even rather sallow, longish face. But in those eyes and in the lines of her exquisite lips there was something with which his brother might well be passionately in love, but which perhaps could not be loved for long. He expressed this thought almost plainly to Dmitri when, after

the visit, his brother besought and insisted that he should not conceal the impressions his betrothed made on him.

"You'll be happy with her, but perhaps — not tranquilly happy."

"Quite so, brother. Such people remain always the same. They don't yield to fate. So you think I shan't love her for ever."

"No; perhaps you will love her for ever. But perhaps you won't always be happy with her."

Alyosha had given his opinion at the time, blushing, and angry with himself for having yielded to his brother's entreaties and put such "foolish" ideas into words. For his opinion had struck him as awfully foolish immediately after he had uttered it. He felt ashamed, too, of having given so confident an opinion about a woman. It was with the more amazement that he felt now, at the first glance at Katerina Ivanovna as she ran in to him, that he had perhaps been utterly mistaken. This time her face was beaming with unfeigned good-natured kindliness, and direct warm-hearted sincerity. The "pride and haughtiness," which had struck Alyosha so much before, were betrayed now only in a frank, generous energy and a sort of bright strong faith in herself. Alyosha realised at the first glance, at the first word, that all the tragedy of her position in relation to the man she loved so dearly was no secret to her; that she perhaps already knew everything, positively everything. And yet, in spite of that, there was such brightness in her face, such faith in the future. Alyosha felt at once that he had gravely wronged her in his thoughts. He was conquered and captivated immediately. Besides all this, he noticed at her first words that she was in great excitement, an excitement perhaps quite exceptional and almost approaching ecstasy. "I was so eager to see you, because I can learn from you the whole truth — from you and no one else."

"I have come," muttered Alyosha confusedly, "I — he sent me."

"Ah, he sent you! I foresaw that. Now I know everything — everything!" cried Katerina Ivanovna, her eyes flashing. "Wait a moment, Alexey Fyodorovich, I'll tell you why I've been so longing to see you. You see, I know perhaps far more than you do yourself, and I don't need any news from you. I'll tell you what I want from you. I want to know your own last impression of him. I want you to tell me most directly, plainly, coarsely even (oh, as coarsely as you like!), what you thought of him just now and of his position after your meeting with him to-day. That will perhaps be better than if I had a personal explanation with him, as he does not want to come to me. Do you understand what I want from you? Now, tell me simply, tell me every word of the message he sent you with (I knew he would send you)."

"He told me to give you his compliments — and to say that he would never come again — but to give you his compliments."

"His compliments? Was that what he said — his own expression?"

"Yes."

"Accidentally perhaps he made a mistake in the word, perhaps he did not use the right word?"

"No; he told me precisely to repeat that word. He begged me two or three times not to forget to say so."

Katerina Ivanovna flushed hotly.

"Help me now, Alexey Fyodorovich. Now I really need your help. I'll tell you what I think, and you must simply say whether it's right or not. Listen! If he had sent me his compliments in passing, without insisting on your repeating the words, without emphasising them, that would be the end of everything! But if he particularly insisted on those words, if he particularly told you not to forget to repeat them to me, then perhaps he was in excitement, beside himself. He had made his decision and was frightened by it. He wasn't walking away from me with a resolute step, but leaping headlong. The emphasis on that phrase may have been simply bravado."

"Yes, yes!" cried Alyosha warmly. "I believe that is it."

"And, if so, he's not altogether lost. He's only in despair, but I can still save him. Wait! Did he not tell you anything about money — about three thousand roubles?"

"He did speak about it, and it's that more than anything that's crushing him. He said he had lost his honour and that nothing mattered now," Alyosha answered warmly, feeling a rush of hope in his heart and believing that there really might be a way of escape and salvation for his brother. "But do you know about the money?" he added, and suddenly broke off.

"I've known of it a long time; I telegraphed to Moscow to inquire, and heard long ago that the money had not arrived. He hadn't sent the money, but I said nothing. Last week I learnt that he was still in need of money. My only object in all this was that he should know to whom to return, and who was his true friend. No, he doesn't wish to believe that I am his truest friend; he won't know me, and looks on me merely as a woman. I've been tormented all week, trying to think how to prevent him from being ashamed to face me because he spent that three thousand. That is, let him feel ashamed of himself, let him be ashamed before other people, but not before me. He can tell God everything without shame. Why is it he still does not understand how much I am ready to bear for his sake? Why, why doesn't he know me? How dare he not know me after all that has happened? I want to save him for ever. Let him forget me as his betrothed. And here he fears that he is dishonoured in my eyes. Why, he wasn't afraid to be open with you, Alexey Fyodorovich. How is it that I don't deserve the same?"

The last words she uttered in tears. Tears gushed from her eyes.

"I must tell you," Alyosha began, his voice trembling, too, "what happened just now between him and my father."

And he described the whole scene, how Dmitri had sent him to get the money, how he had broken in, knocked his father down, and after that had again specially and emphatically begged him to take his compliments and farewells.

"He went to that woman," Alyosha added softly.

"And do you suppose that I can't put up with that woman? Does he think I can't? But he won't marry her," she suddenly laughed nervously. "Could such a passion last for ever in a Karamazov? It's passion, not love. He won't marry her because she won't marry him." Again Katerina Ivanovna laughed strangely.

"He may marry her," said Alyosha mournfully, looking down.

"He won't marry her, I tell you. That girl is an angel. Do you know that? Do you know that?" Katerina Ivanovna exclaimed suddenly with extraordinary heat. "She is one of the most fantastic of fantastic creatures. I

know how bewitching she is, but I know, too, that she is kind, firm, and noble. Why do you look at me like that, Alexey Fyodorovich? Perhaps you are wondering at my words, perhaps you don't believe me? Agrafena Alexandrovna, my angel!" she cried suddenly to some one, peeping into the next room, "come in to us. This is a friend. This is Alyosha. He knows all about our affairs. Show yourself to him."

"I've only been waiting behind the curtain for you to call me," said a soft, one might even say sugary, feminine voice.

The portière was raised and Grushenka herself, smiling and beaming, came up to the table. A violent revulsion passed over Alyosha. He fixed his eyes on her and could not take them off. Here she was, that awful woman, the "beast," as Ivan had called her half an hour before. And yet one would have thought the creature standing before him most simple and ordinary, a good-natured, kind woman, handsome certainly, but so like other handsome ordinary women! It is true she was very, very good-looking with that Russian beauty so passionately loved by many men. She was a rather tall woman, though a little shorter than Katerina Ivanovna, who was exceptionally tall. She had a full figure, and moved softly, noiselessly, as it were, her movements having a peculiar soft and cloying quality, like her voice. She moved, not like Katerina Ivanovna, with a vigorous, bold step, but silently. Her feet made absolutely no sound on the floor. She sank softly into an armchair, softly rustling her sumptuous black silk dress, and delicately wrapping her milk-white neck and broad shoulders in a costly black cashmere shawl. She was twenty-two years old, and her face looked exactly that age. She was very white in the face, with a pale pink tint on her cheeks. Her face might be said to be too broad, and the lower jaw was set a trifle forward. Her upper lip was thin, but the slightly prominent lower lip was at least twice as full, and looked slightly swollen, as it were. But her magnificent, abundant dark brown hair, her fine brown eyebrows and charming grey-blue eyes with their long lashes, would have made the most indifferent person, meeting her casually in a crowd in the street, stop at the sight of her face and remember it long after. What struck Alyosha most in that face was its expression of childlike good-nature. There was a childlike look in her eyes, a look of childish delight. She came up to the table, beaming with delight and seeming to expect something with childish, impatient, and confiding curiosity. The light in her eyes gladdened the soul — Alyosha felt that. There was something else in her which he could not understand, or would not have been able to define, and which yet perhaps unconsciously affected him. It was that softness, that voluptuousness of her bodily movements, that cat-like noiselessness. Yet it was a vigorous, ample body. Under the shawl could be guessed full broad shoulders, a high, still quite girlish bosom. Her figure suggested the lines of the Venus of Milo, though already in somewhat exaggerated proportions. That could be divined. Connoisseurs of Russian beauty could have foretold with certainty, looking at Grushenka, that this fresh, still youthful, beauty would lose its perfection when she reached thirty, would "spread"; that the face would become puffy, and that wrinkles would very soon appear upon her forehead and round the eyes; the complexion would grow coarse and red perhaps — in fact, that it was a momentary beauty, the fleeting beauty which is so often met with in Russian women. Alyosha, of course, did not think of this; but though he was fascinated, yet he wondered with an unpleasant sensation, and as it were regretfully, why she drawled in that way and could not speak naturally. She did so evidently feeling there was a charm in the exaggerated, honeyed modulation of the syllables. It was, of course, only a bad, underbred habit that showed lack of education and a false idea of good manners. And yet this intonation and manner of speaking impressed Alyosha as almost incredibly incongruous with the childishly simple and happy expression of her face, the soft, babyish radiance in her eyes. Katerina Ivanovna at once made her sit down in an armchair facing Alyosha, and ecstatically kissed her several times on her smiling lips. She seemed quite in love with her.

"This is the first time we've met, Alexey Fyodorovich," she said rapturously. "I wanted to know her, to see her. I wanted to go to her, but I'd no sooner expressed the wish than she came to me. I knew we should settle everything together — everything. My heart told me so — I was begged not to take the step, but I foresaw it would be a way out of the difficulty, and I was not mistaken. Grushenka has explained everything to me, told me all she means to do. She flew here like an angel of goodness and brought us peace and joy."

"You did not disdain me, sweet, excellent young lady," drawled Grushenka in her sing-song voice, still with the same charming smile of delight.

"Don't dare to speak to me like that, you sorceress, you witch! Disdain you! Here I must kiss your lower lip once more. It looks as though it were swollen, and now it will be more so, and more and more. Look how she laughs, Alexey Fyodorovich! It does one's heart good to see the angel."

Alyosha flushed, and faint, imperceptible shivers ran through him.

"You make so much of me, dear young lady, and perhaps I am not at all worthy of your kindness."

"Not worthy! She's not worthy of it!" Katerina Ivanovna cried again with the same heat. "You know, Alexey Fyodorovich, we're fanciful, we're self-willed, but proudest of the proud in our little heart. We're noble, we're generous, Alexey Fyodorovich, let me tell you. We have only been unfortunate. We were too ready to make every sacrifice for an unworthy, perhaps, or fickle man. There was one man — one, an officer too, we loved him, we sacrificed everything to him. That was long ago, five years ago, and he has forgotten us, he has married. Now he is a widower, he has written, he is coming here, and, do you know, we've loved him, none but him, all this time, and we've loved him all our life! He will come, and Grushenka will be happy again. For the last five years she's been wretched. But who can reproach her, who can boast of her favour? Only that bedridden old merchant, but he is more like her father, her friend, her protector. He found her then in despair, in agony, deserted by the man she loved. She was ready to drown herself then, but the old merchant saved her — saved her!"

"You defend me very kindly, dear young lady. You are in a great hurry about everything," Grushenka drawled again.

"Defend you! Is it for me to defend you? Should I dare to defend you? Grushenka, angel, give me your hand. Look at that charm-ing soft little hand, Alexey Fyodorovich! Look at it! It has brought me happiness and has lifted me up, and I'm going to kiss it, outside and inside, here, here, here!"

And three times she kissed the certainly charming, though rather plump, hand of Grushenka in a sort of rapture. She held out her hand with a charming, musical, nervous little laugh, watched the "sweet young lady," and obviously liked having her hand kissed.

"Perhaps there's rather too much rapture," thought Alyosha. He blushed. His heart was peculiarly uneasy the whole time.

"You won't make me blush, dear young lady, kissing my hand like this before Alexey Fyodorovich."

"Do you think I meant to make you blush?" said Katerina Ivanovna, somewhat surprised. "Ah, my dear, how little you understand me!"

"Yes, and you, too, perhaps quite misunderstand me, dear young lady. Maybe I'm not so good as I seem to you. I've a bad heart; I will have my own way. I fascinated poor Dmitri Fyodorovich that day simply for fun."

"But now you'll save him. You've given me your word. You'll explain it all to him. You'll break it to him that you have long loved another man, who is now offering you his hand."

"Oh, no! I didn't give you my word to do that. It was you kept talking about that. I didn't give you my word."

"Then I didn't quite understand you," said Katerina Ivanovna slowly, turning a little pale. "You promised . . . ."

"Oh, no, angel lady, I've promised nothing," Grushenka interrupted softly and evenly, still with the same gay and simple expression. "You see at once, dear young lady,

KATERINA KISSES GRUSHENKA'S HAND

what a wilful wretch I am compared with you. I do what I feel like doing. I may have made you some promise just now. But now again I'm thinking: I may take to Mitya again. I liked him very much once — liked him for almost a whole hour. Now maybe I shall go and tell him to stay with me from this day forward. You see, I'm so changeable."

"Just now you said — something quite different," Katerina Ivanovna whispered faintly.

"Ah, just now! But, you know, I'm such a soft-hearted, silly creature. Only think what he's gone through on my account! What if when I go home I feel sorry for him? What then?"

"I never expected ——"

"Ah, young lady, how good and generous you are compared with me! Now perhaps you won't care for a silly creature like me, now you know my character. Give me your sweet little hand, angelic lady," she said tenderly, and with a sort of reverence took Katerina Ivanovna's hand.

"Here, dear young lady, I'll take your hand and kiss it as you did mine. You kissed mine three times, but I ought to kiss yours three hundred times to be even with you. Well, but let that pass. And then it shall be as God wills. Perhaps I shall be your slave entirely and want to do your bidding like a slave. Let it be as God wills, without any agreements or promises. What a sweet hand — what a sweet hand you have! You sweet young lady, you incredible beauty!"

She slowly raised the hand to her lips, with the strange object indeed of "being even" with her in kisses.

Katerina Ivanovna did not take her hand away. She listened with timid hope to the last words, though Grushenka's promise to do her bidding like a slave was very strangely expressed. She looked intently into her eyes; she still saw in those eyes the same simple-hearted, confiding expression, the same serene gaiety.

"She's perhaps too naïve," thought Katerina Ivanovna, with a gleam of hope.

Grushenka meanwhile seemed enthusiastic over the "sweet hand." She raised it slowly to her lips. But as it reached her lips, she suddenly held it there for two or three moments, as though reconsidering something.

"Do you know, angel lady," she suddenly drawled in an even more soft and sugary voice, "do you know, after all, I think I won't kiss your hand?" And she laughed a little merry laugh.

"As you please. What's the matter with you?" said Katerina Ivanovna, starting suddenly.

"So that you may be left to remember that you kissed my hand, but I didn't kiss yours."

There was a sudden flash in her eyes. She looked with awful intentness at Katerina Ivanovna.

"Insolent creature!" cried Katerina Ivanovna, as though suddenly grasping something. She flushed all over and leapt up from her seat.

Grushenka too got up, but without haste.

"So I shall tell Mitya how you kissed my hand, but I didn't kiss yours at all. And how he will laugh!"

"Vile slut! Out with you!"

"Ah, for shame, young lady! Ah, for shame! That's unbecoming, dear young lady, a word like that from you."

"Out with you! You're a creature for sale!" screamed Katerina Ivanovna. Every feature was working now in her utterly distorted face.

"For sale indeed! You used to visit gentlemen in the dusk for money once; you brought your beauty for sale. You see, I know."

Katerina Ivanovna shrieked, and would have rushed at her, but Alyosha held her with all his strength.

"Not a step, not a word! Don't speak, don't answer her. She'll go away — she'll go at once."

At that instant Katerina Ivanovna's two aunts ran in at her cry, and with them a maidservant. All hurried to her.

"I will go away," said Grushenka, taking up her mantle from the sofa. "Alyosha, darling, see me home!"

"Go away — go away, make haste!" cried Alyosha, clasping his hands imploringly.

"Dear little Alyosha, see me home! I've got a pretty little story to tell you on the way. I got up this scene for your benefit, Alyosha. See me home, darling, you'll be glad of it afterwards."

Alyosha turned away, wringing his hands. Grushenka ran out of the house, laughing musically.

Katerina Ivanovna went into a fit of hysterics. She sobbed, and was shaken with convulsions. Every one fussed round her.

"I warned you," said the elder of her aunts. "I tried to prevent your doing this. You're too impulsive. How could you do such a thing? You don't know these creatures, and they say she's worse than any of them. You are too self-willed."

"She's a tigress!" yelled Katerina Ivanovna. "Why did you hold me, Alexey Fyodorovich? I'd have beaten her — beaten her!"

She could not control herself before Alyosha; perhaps, indeed, she did not care to.

"She ought to be flogged in public on a scaffold!"

Alyosha withdrew towards the door.

"But, my God!" cried Katerina Ivanovna, striking her hands together. "He! He! He could be so dishonourable, so inhuman! Why, he told that creature what happened on that fatal, accursed day! 'You brought your beauty for sale, dear young lady.' She knows it! Your brother's a scoundrel, Alexey Fyodorovich."

Alyosha wanted to say something, but he couldn't find a word. His heart ached.

"Go away, Alexey Fyodorovich! It's shameful, it's awful for me! To-morrow, I beg you on my knees, come to-morrow. Don't condemn me. Forgive me. I don't know what I shall do with myself now!"

Alyosha walked out into the street reeling. He could have wept as she did. Suddenly he was overtaken by the maid.

"The young lady forgot to give you this letter from Madame Hohlakov; it's been left with us since dinner-time." Alyosha took the little pink envelope mechanically and put it, almost unconsciously, into his pocket.

## CHAPTER XI
### ANOTHER REPUTATION RUINED

It was not much more than three-quarters of a mile from the town to the monastery. Alyosha walked quickly along the road, at that hour deserted. It was almost night, and too dark to see anything clearly at thirty paces ahead. Half-way there his road was crossed by another. A figure came into sight under a solitary willow at the cross-roads. As soon as Alyosha reached the cross-roads the figure tore from its place and rushed at him, shouting savagely: "Your money or your life!"

"So it's you, Mitya," cried Alyosha, in surprise, violently startled however.

"Ha, ha, ha! You didn't expect me? I wondered where to wait for you. Near her house? There are three roads leading from it, and I might have missed you. At last I thought of waiting here, for you had to pass here, there's no other way to the monastery. Come, tell me the truth. Crush me like a beetle. But what's the matter?"

"Nothing, brother — it's the fright you gave me. Oh, Dmitri! A while ago — that blood!" (Alyosha began to cry; he had been on the verge of tears for a long time, and now something seemed to snap in his soul.) "You almost killed father — cursed him — and now — here — you're playing practical jokes — 'Your money or your life!' "

"Well, what of that? It's not proper — is that it? Not suitable in my position?"

"No — I only ——"

"Stop. Look at the night. You see what a dark night, what clouds, what a wind has risen. I hid here under the willow waiting for you. And as God's above, I suddenly thought, why go on in misery any longer, what is there to wait for? Here I have a willow, a handkerchief, a shirt, I can twist them into a rope in a minute, and braces besides, and why go on burdening the earth, dishonouring it with my vile presence. And then I heard you coming — Heavens, it was as though something flew down to me suddenly. So there is a man, then, whom I love. Here he is, that man, my dear little brother, whom I love more than any one in the world, the only one I love in the world. And I loved you so much, so much at that moment that I thought, 'I'll fall on his neck at once.' Then a stupid idea struck me: 'I'll joke with him, I'll scare him.' I shouted, like a fool,

'Your money!' Forgive my foolery — it was only nonsense, and there's nothing unseemly in my soul. . . . Damn it all, tell me what's happened. What did she say? Strike me, crush me, don't spare me! Was she furious?"

"No, not that. . . . There was nothing like that, Mitya. There — I found them both there."

"Both? Whom?"

"Grushenka at Katerina Ivanovna's."

Dmitri was struck dumb.

"Impossible!" he cried. "You're raving! Grushenka with her?"

Alyosha described all that had happened from the moment he went in to Katerina Ivanovna's. He was ten minutes telling his story. He can't be said to have told it fluently and consecutively, but he seemed to make it clear, not omitting any word or action of significance, and vividly describing, often in one word, his own sensations. Dmitri listened in silence, gazing at him with a terrible fixed stare, but it was clear to Alyosha that he understood it all, and had grasped every point. But as the story went on, his face became not merely gloomy, but menacing. He scowled, he clenched his teeth, and his fixed stare became still more rigid, more concentrated, more terrible, when suddenly, with incredible rapidity, his wrathful, savage face changed, his tightly compressed lips parted, and Dmitri Fyodorovich broke into uncontrolled, spontaneous laughter. He literally shook with laughter. For a long time he could not speak.

"So she wouldn't kiss her hand! So she didn't kiss it; so she ran away!" he kept exclaiming with hysterical rapture; insolent rapture it might have been called, if it had not been so spontaneous. "So the other one called her a tigress! And a tigress she is! So she ought to be flogged on a scaffold? Yes, yes, so she ought. That's just what I think; she ought to have been long ago. It's like this, brother, let her be punished, but I must recover first. I understand the queen of impudence. That's her all over! You saw her all over in that hand-kissing, the she-devil! She's the queen of all the infernal women you can imagine in the world! She's magnificent in her own line! So she ran home? I'll go — ah — I'll run to her! Alyosha, don't blame me, I agree that strangling is too good for her."

"But Katerina Ivanovna!" exclaimed Alyosha sorrowfully.

"I see her, too! I see right through her, as I've never done before! It's like a discovery of the four continents of the world, that is, of the five! What a thing to do! That's just like Katya, who was not afraid to face a coarse, unmannerly officer and risk a deadly insult on a generous impulse to save her father! But the pride, the recklessness, the defiance of fate, the unbounded defiance! You say that aunt tried to stop her? That aunt, you know, is an overbearing woman, herself. She's the sister of the general's widow in Moscow, and even more stuck-up than she. But her husband was caught stealing government money. He lost everything, his estate and all, and the proud wife had to lower her colours, and hasn't raised them since. So she tried to hold Katya back, but she wouldn't listen to her! She thinks she can overcome everything, that everything will give way before her. She thought she could bewitch Grushenka if she liked, and she believed it herself; she plays a part to herself, and whose fault is it? Do you think she kissed Grushenka's hand first, on purpose, with a sly design? No, she really, really fell in love with Grushenka, that's to

say, not with Grushenka, but with her own dream, her own delusion — because it was *her* dream, *her* delusion! Alyosha, darling, how did you escape from them, those women? Did you pick up your cassock and run? Ha, ha!"

"Brother, you don't seem to have noticed how you've insulted Katerina Ivanovna by telling Grushenka about that day. And she flung it in her face just now that she had gone to gentlemen in secret to sell her beauty! Brother, what could be worse than that insult?" What worried Alyosha more than anything was that, incredible as it seemed, his brother appeared pleased at Katerina Ivanovna's humiliation.

"Bah!" Dmitri frowned fiercely, and struck his forehead with his palm. He only now realised it, though Alyosha had just told him of the insult, and Katerina Ivanovna's cry: "Your brother is a scoundrel!"

"Yes, perhaps, I really did tell Grushenka about that 'fatal day,' as Katya calls it. Yes, I did tell her, I remember! It was that time at Mokroye. I was drunk, the gipsies were singing. . . . But I was sobbing. I was sobbing then, kneeling and praying to Katya's image, and Grushenka understood it. She understood it all then. I remember, she cried herself. . . . Damn it all! But it was bound to turn out this way. Then she cried, but now 'thrust the dagger into the heart'! That's how women are."

He looked down and sank into thought.

"Yes, I am a scoundrel, a thorough scoundrel!" he said suddenly, in a gloomy voice. "It doesn't matter whether I cried or not, I'm a scoundrel! Tell her I accept the name, if that's any comfort. Come, that's enough. Good-bye. It's no use talking! It's not amusing. You go your way and I mine. And I don't want to see you again until perhaps the very last moment. Good-bye, Alexey!" He warmly pressed Alyosha's hand, and still looking down, without raising his head, as though tearing himself away, turned rapidly towards the town.

Alyosha looked after him, unable to believe he would go away so abruptly.

"Wait, Alexey, one more confession to you alone!" cried Dmitri, suddenly turning back. "Look at me. Look at me well. You see here, here — there's terrible disgrace in store for me." (As he said "here," Dmitri struck his chest with his fist with a strange air, as though the dishonour lay precisely on his chest, and was hidden in some spot there, in a pocket, perhaps, or hanging round his neck.) "You know me now, a scoundrel, an avowed scoundrel, but let me tell you that I've never done anything before and never shall again, anything that can compare in baseness with the dishonour which I bear now at this very minute on my breast, here, here, which will come to pass, though I'm perfectly free to stop it. I can stop it or carry it through, note that. Well, let me tell you, I shall carry it through. I shan't stop it. I told you everything just now, but I didn't tell you this, because even I had not brass enough for it. I can still stop; if I do, I can give back the full half of my lost honour to-morrow. But I shan't pull up. I shall carry out my base plan, and you can bear witness that I told you so beforehand. Darkness and ruin! No need to explain. You'll find out in due time. The filthy back-alley and the she-devil. Good-bye. Don't pray for me, I'm not worth it. And there's no need, no need at all. . . . I don't need it! Away!"

And he suddenly retreated, this time finally. Alyosha went towards the monastery. "What? I shall never see him again! What

is he saying?" he wondered wildly. "Why, I shall certainly see him to-morrow. I shall look him up. I shall make a point of it. What does he mean?"

He went round the monastery, and crossing the pine-wood went straight to the hermitage. The door was opened to him, though no one was admitted at that hour. There was a tremor in his heart as he went into Father Zosima's cell.

Why, why, had he gone forth? Why had his elder sent him into the world? Here was peace. Here was holiness. But there was confusion, there was darkness in which one lost one's way and went astray at once. . . .

In the cell he found the novice Porfiry and Father Païssy, who came every hour to inquire after Father Zosima. Alyosha learnt with alarm that he was getting worse and worse. Even his usual evening discourse with the brothers could not take place that day. As a rule every evening after service the monks flocked into Father Zosima's cell, and all confessed aloud their sins of the day, their sinful thoughts and temptations; even their disputes, if there had been any. Some confessed kneeling. The elder absolved, reconciled, exhorted, imposed penance, blessed, and dismissed them. It was against this general "confession" that the opponents of "elders" protested, maintaining that it was a profanation of the sacrament of confession, almost a sacrilege, though this was quite a different thing. They even represented to the diocesan authorities that such confessions attained no good object, but actually to a large extent led to sin and temptation. Many of the brothers disliked going to the elder, and went against their own will because every one went, and for fear they should be accused of pride and rebellious ideas. People said that some of the monks agreed beforehand, saying, "I'll confess I lost my temper with you this morning, and you confirm it," simply in order to have something to say. Alyosha knew that this actually happened sometimes. He knew, too, that there were among the monks some who deeply resented the fact that letters from relations were habitually taken to the elder, to be opened and read by him before those to whom they were addressed.

It was assumed, of course, that all this was done freely, and in good faith, by way of voluntary submission and salutary edification. But, in fact, there was sometimes no little insincerity, and much that was false and strained in this practice. Yet the older and more experienced of the monks adhered to their opinion, arguing that "for those who have come within these walls sincerely seeking salvation, such obedience and sacrifice will certainly be salutary and of great benefit; those, on the other hand, who find it irksome, and murmur against it, are no true monks, and have made a mistake in entering the monastery — their proper place is in the world. Even in church one cannot be safe from sin and the devil. So it was no good being too lenient."

"He is weaker, a drowsiness has come over him," Father Païssy whispered to Alyosha, as he blessed him. "It's difficult to rouse him. And he must not be roused. He waked up for five minutes, sent his blessing to the brothers, and begged their prayers for him at night. He intends to take the sacrament again in the morning. He remembered you, Alexey. He asked whether you had gone away, and was told that you were in the town. 'I blessed him for that work,' he said, 'his place is there, not here, for awhile.' Those were his words about

you. He remembered you lovingly, with anxiety; do you understand how he honoured you? But how is it that he has decided that you shall spend some time in the world? He must have foreseen something in your destiny! Understand, Alexey, that if you return to the world, it must be to do the duty laid upon you by your elder, and not for frivolous vanity and worldly pleasures."

Father Païssy went out. Alyosha had no doubt that Father Zosima was dying, though he might live another day or two. Alyosha firmly and ardently resolved that in spite of his promises to his father, the Hohlakovs, and Katerina Ivanovna, he would not leave the monastery next day, but would remain with his elder to the end. His heart glowed with love, and he reproached himself bitterly for having been able for one instant to forget him whom he had left in the monastery on his death-bed, and whom he honoured above every one in the world. He went into Father Zosima's bedroom, knelt down, and bowed to the ground before the elder, who slept quietly without stirring, with regular, hardly audible breathing and a peaceful face.

Alyosha returned to the other room, where Father Zosima had received his guests in the morning. Taking off his boots, he lay down on the hard, narrow, leathern sofa, which he had long used as a bed, bringing nothing but a pillow. The mattress, about which his father had shouted to him that morning, he had long forgotten to place there. He took off his cassock, which he used as a covering. But before going to bed, he fell on his knees and prayed a long time. In his fervent prayer he did not beseech God to lighten his darkness but only thirsted for the joyous emotion which always visited his soul after the praise and adoration of which his evening prayer usually consisted. That joy always brought him light untroubled sleep. As he was praying, he suddenly felt in his pocket the little pink note the servant had handed him as he left Katerina Ivanovna's. He was disturbed, but finished his prayer. Then, after some hesitation, he opened the envelope. In it was a note to him, signed by Lise, the young daughter of Madame Hohlakov, who had laughed at him before the elder in the morning.

"Alexey Fyodorovich," she wrote, "I am writing to you without any one's knowledge, even mamma's, and I know how wrong it is. But I cannot live without telling you the feeling that has sprung up in my heart, and this no one but we two must know for a time. But how am I to say what I want so much to tell you? Paper, they say, does not blush, but I assure you it's not true and that it's blushing just as I am now, all over. Dear Alyosha, I love you, I've loved you from my childhood on, since our Moscow days, when you were very different from what you are now, and I shall love you all my life. My heart has chosen you, to unite our lives, and pass them together till our old age. Of course, on condition that you will leave the monastery. As for our age, we will wait for the time fixed by the law. By that time I shall certainly be quite strong, I shall be walking and dancing. There can be no doubt of that.

"You see how I've thought of everything. There's only one thing I can't imagine: what you'll think of me when you read this? I'm always laughing and being naughty. I made you angry this morning, but I assure you before I took up my pen, I prayed before the Image of the Mother of God, and now I'm praying, and almost crying.

"My secret is in your hands. When you come to-morrow, I don't know how I shall look at you. Ah, Alexey Fyodorovich, what if I can't restrain myself like a silly and laugh when I look at you as I did to-day? You'll think I'm a nasty girl making fun of you, and you won't believe my letter. And so I beg you, dear one, if you've any pity for me, when you come to-morrow, don't look me straight in the face, for if I meet your eyes, it will be sure to make me laugh, especially as you'll be in that long gown. I feel cold all over when I think of it, so when you come, don't look at me at all for a time, look at mamma or at the window. . . .

"Here I've written you a love-letter. Oh, God, what have I done? Alyosha, don't despise me, and if I've done something very horrid and wounded you, forgive me. Now the secret of my reputation, ruined perhaps for ever, is in your hands.

"I shall certainly cry to-day. Good-bye till our meeting, our *awful* meeting. LISE.

"P.S. Alyosha! You must, must, must come! LISE."

Alyosha read the note in amazement, read it through twice, thought a little, and suddenly laughed a soft, sweet laugh. He started. That laugh seemed to him sinful. But a minute later he laughed again just as softly and happily. He slowly replaced the note in the envelope, crossed himself and lay down. The agitation in his heart passed at once. "God have mercy upon all of them, have all these unhappy and turbulent souls in Thy keeping, and set them in the right path. All ways are Thine. Save them according to Thy wisdom. Thou art love. Thou wilt send joy to all!" Alyosha murmured, crossing himself, and falling into peaceful sleep.

PART
II

# BOOK IV

## LACERATIONS

### CHAPTER I
#### FATHER FERAPONT

ALYOSHA was roused early, before daybreak. Father Zosima woke up feeling very weak, though he wanted to get out of bed and sit up in a chair. His mind was quite clear; his face looked very tired, yet serene and almost joyful. It wore an expression of gaiety, kindness, and cordiality. "May be I shall not live through the day," he said to Alyosha. Then he desired to confess and take the sacrament at once. His confessor was always Father Païssy. After the communion, came the service of extreme unction. The monks assembled and the cell was gradually filled up by the inmates of the hermitage. Meantime it grew light. People began coming from the monastery, too. After the service was over the elder desired to take leave of every one, and kissed them all. As the cell was so small the earlier visitors withdrew to make room for others. Alyosha stood beside the elder, who was seated again in his armchair. He talked and preached as much as he could. Though his voice was weak, it was fairly steady.

"I've been teaching you so many years, and therefore I've been talking aloud so long, that I've got into the habit of talking, and so much so that it's almost more difficult for me to hold my tongue than to talk, even now, in spite of my weakness, dear fathers and brethren," he jested, looking with emotion at the group crowding round him.

Alyosha remembered afterwards something of what he said to them. But though he spoke out distinctly and his voice was fairly steady, his speech was somewhat disconnected. He spoke of many things, he seemed anxious before the moment of death to say everything he had not said in his life, and not simply for the sake of edifying them, but as though thirsting to share with all men and all creation his joy and ecstasy, and once more in his life to open his whole heart.

"Love one another, fathers," said the elder, as far as Alyosha could remember afterwards. "Love God's people. Because we have come here and shut ourselves within these walls, we are no holier than those who are outside, but on the contrary, from the very fact of coming here, each of us has confessed to himself that he is worse than the laity, than all men on earth. . . . And the longer the monk lives in his seclusion, the more keenly he must recognise that. Else he would have had no reason to come here. When he realises that he is not only worse than others, but that he is responsible to all men for all and everything, for all human sins, communal and individual, only then the aim of our seclusion is attained. For know, dear ones, that every one of us is undoubtedly responsible for everything and

123

shares the guilt of all men on earth, not merely through the general universal guilt, but each one is personally responsible for all mankind and every individual man. This knowledge is the crown of the monastic way of life and of every man on earth. For monks are not a special sort of men, but only what all men on earth ought to be. Only then our heart would grow soft with infinite, universal, unquenchable love. Then every one of you will have the power to win over the whole world by love and to wash away the sins of the world with your tears. . . . Each of you keep watch over your heart and confess your sins to yourself unceasingly. Be not afraid of your sins, even when perceiving them, if only there be penitence, but make no conditions with God. Again I say, Be not proud. Be proud neither before the little nor before the great. Hate not those who reject you, who disgrace you, who abuse and slander you. Hate not the atheists, the teachers of evil, the materialists — and I mean not only the good ones — for there are many good ones among them, especially in our day — hate not even the wicked ones. Remember them in your prayers thus: Save, O Lord, all those who have none to pray for them, save all those who will not pray. And add: it is not in pride that I make this prayer, O Lord, for I am more abominable than all men. . . . Love God's people, let not strangers ravish the flock, for if you slumber in your slothfulness and squeamish pride, or worse still, in covetousness, they will come from all sides and ravish your flock. Expound the Gospel to the people unceasingly . . . be not extortionate. . . . Do not love gold and silver, do not hoard them. . . . Have faith. Cling to the banner and raise it on high."

But the elder spoke more disconnectedly than Alyosha reported his words afterwards. Sometimes he broke off altogether, as though to take breath and recover his strength, but he was in a sort of ecstasy. They heard him with emotion, though many wondered at his words and found them obscure. . . . Afterwards all these words were remembered.

When Alyosha happened for a moment to leave the cell, he was struck by the general excitement and suspense that swayed the monks who were crowding about it. Some were alarmed, others were solemn, but all were expecting that some great miracle would happen immediately after the elder's disease. Their expectation was, in a sense, almost frivolous, but even the most austere of the monks were affected by it. The most austere of all was the countenance of Father Païssy.

Alyosha had absented himself from the cell only because he had been mysteriously summoned by a monk to see Rakitin, who had arrived from town with a singular letter for him from Madame Hohlakov. In it she informed Alyosha of a curious and very appropriate incident. It appeared that among the women who had come on the previous day to receive Father Zosima's blessing there had been an old woman from the town, a sergeant's widow, called Prohorovna. She had inquired whether she might pray for the rest of the soul of her son, Vasenka, who had gone to Irkutsk, and had sent her no news for over a year. To which Father Zosima had answered sternly, forbidding her to do so, and saying that to pray for the living as though they were dead was a kind of sorcery. He afterwards forgave her on account of her ignorance, and added "as though reading the book of the future" (this was Madame Hohlakov's expression) words of comfort: "that her son Vassya was certainly alive and he would either come himself very shortly or send a letter, and that she was to go home and wait for him." And "would you believe it," exclaimed Madame Hohlakov enthusiastically, "the prophecy has been fulfilled literally indeed, and more than that." Scarcely had the old woman reached home when they gave her a letter from Siberia which had been awaiting her. But that was not all; in the letter written on the road from Ekaterinburg, Vassya informed his mother that he was returning to Russia with an official, and that three weeks after her receiving the letter he hoped "to embrace his mother."

Madame Hohlakov warmly entreated Alyosha to report this new "miracle of prediction" to the Superior and all the brotherhood. "All, all, ought to know of it!" she concluded. The letter had been written in haste, the excitement of the writer was apparent in every line of it. But Alyosha had no need to tell the monks, for all knew of it already. Rakitin had commissioned the monk who brought his message "to inform most respectfully his reverence Father Païssy, that he, Rakitin, must speak with him on a matter of such gravity that he dare not defer it for a moment, and humbly begs forgiveness for his presumption." As the monk had given the message to Father Païssy before delivering the note to Alyosha, the latter found after reading it that there was nothing left for him to do but to hand it to Father Païssy in confirmation of the story.

And even that austere and cautious man, though he frowned as he read the news of the "miracle," could not completely restrain some inner emotion. His eyes flashed, and a grave and solemn smile came to his lips. "We shall see greater things!" broke from him.

"We shall see greater things, greater things yet!" the monks around repeated.

But Father Païssy, frowning again, begged all of them, at least for a time, not to speak of the matter "till it be more fully confirmed, seeing there is so much credulity among the worldlings, and indeed this might well have chanced naturally," he added, prudently, as it were to satisfy his conscience, though scarcely believing his own disavowal, a fact his listeners very clearly perceived.

Within the hour the "miracle" was of course known to the whole monastery, and to many outsiders who had come for the mass. No one seemed more impressed by it than the monk who had come the day before from St. Sylvester, from the little monastery of Obdorsk in the far North. It was he who had been standing near Madame Hohlakov the previous day and had asked Father Zosima with great earnestness, referring to the "healing" of the lady's daughter, "How can you presume to do such things?"

He was now somewhat puzzled and did not know what to believe. The evening before he had visited Father Ferapont in his cell apart, behind the apiary, and had been greatly impressed and overawed by the visit. This Father Ferapont was that aged monk so devout in fasting and observing silence, who has been mentioned already as antagonistic to Father Zosima and the whole institution of "elders," which he regarded as a pernicious and frivolous innovation. He was a very formidable opponent, in spite of the fact that because of his practice of silence he scarcely spoke a word to any one. What made him formidable was that a number of monks fully shared his feeling, and many of the visitors looked upon him as a great saint and ascetic, although they had no doubt that he was a fool in Christ. But it was just this that attracted them.

Father Ferapont never went to see the elder. Though he lived in the hermitage, they did not insist on his keeping its regulations, and this, too, because he behaved as though he were out of his mind. He was seventy-five or more, and he lived in a corner beyond the apiary in an old decaying wooden cell which had been built long ago for another great ascetic, Father Iona, who had lived to be a hundred and five, and of whose saintly doings many curious stories were still current in the monastery and the neighbourhood.

Father Ferapont had succeeded in getting himself installed in this same solitary cell seven years previously. It was simply a peasant hut, though it looked like a chapel, for it contained an extraordinary number of ikons with lamps perpetually burning before them — which had been brought as offerings. It was as though Father Ferapont had been appointed to look after them and keep the lamps burning. It was said (and indeed it was true) that he ate only two pounds of bread in three days. The beekeeper, who lived close by the apiary, used to bring him the bread every three days, and even to this man who waited upon him Father Ferapont rarely uttered a word. The four pounds of bread, together with the sacrament bread, regularly sent him on Sundays after the late mass by the Father Superior, made up his weekly ration. The water in his jug was changed every day. He rarely appeared at mass. Visitors who came to do him homage saw him sometimes kneeling all day long at prayer without looking round. If he addressed them, he was brief, abrupt, strange, and almost always rude. On very

rare occasions, however, he would strike up a conversation with visitors, but for the most part he would utter some one strange saying which was a complete riddle, and no entreaties would induce him to pronounce a word in explanation. He was not a priest, but a simple monk. There was a strange rumour, chiefly current, however, among the most ignorant, that Father Ferapont had communication with heavenly spirits and conversed only with them, and so was silent with men.

The monk from Obdorsk, having been directed to the apiary by the beekeeper, who was also a very silent and surly monk, went to the corner where Father Ferapont's cell stood. "Maybe he will speak as you are a stranger and maybe you'll get nothing out of him," the beekeeper had warned him. The monk, as he related afterwards, approached with the utmost awe. It was rather late in the evening. Father Ferapont was sitting at the door of his cell on a low bench. A huge old elm was lightly rustling overhead. There was an evening freshness in the air. The monk from Obdorsk bowed down before the saint and asked his blessing.

"Do you want me to bow down to you, monk?" said Father Ferapont. "Rise!"

The monk got up.

"Blessing, be blessed! Sit beside me. Whence do you come?"

What most struck the poor monk was the fact that in spite of his strict fasting and great age, Father Ferapont still looked a vigorous old man. He was tall, held himself erect, and had a thin, but fresh and healthy face. There was no doubt he still had considerable strength. He was of athletic build. In spite of his great age he was not even quite grey, and still had very thick hair and a full beard, both

FATHER FERAPONT

of which had once been black. His eyes were grey, large and luminous, but strikingly prominent. He spoke with a broad accent. He was dressed in a peasant's long reddish coat of coarse convict cloth (as it used to be called) and had a stout rope round his waist. His throat and chest were bare. Beneath his coat, his shirt of the coarsest linen showed almost black with dirt, not having been changed for months.

They said that he wore irons weighing thirty pounds under his coat. His stockingless feet were thrust into old slippers almost dropping to pieces.

"From the little Obdorsk monastery, from St. Sylvester," the monk answered humbly, whilst his keen and inquisitive, but rather frightened little eyes kept watch on the hermit.

"I have been at your Sylvester's. I used to stay there. Is Sylvester well?"

The monk hesitated.

"You are a senseless lot! How do you keep the fasts?"

"Our dietary is according to the ancient conventual rules. During Lent there are no meals provided Mondays, Wednesdays, and Fridays. On Tuesday and Thursday we have white bread, stewed fruit with honey, wild berries, or salt cabbage and oatmeal stirabout. On Saturday white cabbage soup, noodles with peas, kasha, all with hemp oil. On weekdays we have dried fish and kasha with the cabbage soup. From Monday till Saturday evening, six days in Holy Week, we have only bread and water and uncooked vegetables, and that sparingly; if possible we do not take food every day, just as in the first week in Lent. On Good Friday nothing is eaten. In the same way on Saturday of Holy Week we have to fast till three o'clock, and then take a little bread and water and drink a single cup of wine. On Holy Thursday we drink wine and have something cooked without oil or not cooked at all. Inasmuch as the Laodicean council lays down for Holy Thursday: 'It is unseemly to break the fast on the Holy Thursday and dishonour the whole of Lent!' This is how we keep the fast. But what is that compared with you, holy father," added the monk, growing more confident, "for all the year round, even at Easter, you take nothing but bread and water, and what we should eat in two days lasts you full seven. It's truly marvellous — your great abstinence."

"And mushrooms?" asked Father Ferapont, suddenly.

"Mushrooms?" repeated the surprised monk.

"Yes. I can give up their bread, not needing it at all, and go away into the forest and live there on the mushrooms or the berries, but they can't give up their bread here, wherefore they are in bondage to the devil. Nowadays the unclean deny that there is need of such fasting. Haughty and unclean is their judgment."

"Och, true," sighed the monk.

"And have you seen devils among them?" asked Ferapont.

"Among them? Among whom?" asked the monk timidly.

"I went to the Father Superior on Trinity Sunday last year, I haven't been since. I saw a devil sitting on one man's chest hiding under his cassock, only his horns poked out; another had one peeping out of his pocket with such sharp eyes, he was afraid of me; another settled in the unclean belly of one, another was hanging round a man's neck, and so he was carrying him about without seeing him."

"You — can see spirits?" the monk inquired.

"I tell you I can see, I can see through them. When I was coming out from the Superior's I saw one hiding from me behind the door, and a husky one, a yard and a half or more high, with a thick long grey tail, and the tip of his tail was in the crack of the door and I was quick and slammed the door, pinching his tail in it. He squealed and began to struggle, and I made the sign of the cross over him three times. And he croaked on the spot like a crushed spider. He must have rotted there in the corner and be stinking, but they don't see, they don't smell it. It's a year since I have been there. I reveal it to you, as you are a stranger."

"Your words are fearful! But, holy and blessed father," said the monk, growing bolder and bolder, "is it true, as they noise abroad even to distant lands about you, that you are in continual communication with the Holy Ghost?"

"He does fly down at times. It happens."

"How does he fly down? In what form?"

"As a bird."

"The Holy Ghost in the form of a Dove?"

"There's the Holy Ghost and there's the Holy Spirit. The Holy Spirit can appear as other birds — sometimes as a swallow, sometimes a goldfinch and sometimes as a bluetit."

"How do you know him from an ordinary tit?"

"He speaks."

"How does he speak, in what language?"

"Human language."

"And what does he tell you?"

"Why, to-day he told me that a fool would visit me and would ask unseemly questions. You want to know too much, monk."

"Fearful are your words, most holy and blessed father," the monk shook his head. But there was a doubtful look in his frightened little eyes.

"Do you see this tree?" asked Father Ferapont, after a pause.

"I do, blessed father."

"You think it's an elm, but to me it looks otherwise."

"How does it look?" inquired the monk, after a pause of vain expectation.

"It happens at night. You see those two branches? In the night it is Christ holding out His arms to me and seeking me with those arms, I see it clearly and tremble. Oh, terror, terror!"

"What is terrible about it, if it's Christ Himself?"

"Why, He'll seize me and carry me aloft."

"Alive?"

"In the spirit and glory of Elijah, haven't you heard? He will take me in His arms and bear me away."

Although after this talk the monk returned to the cell he was sharing with one of the brothers, in considerable perplexity of mind, he was undoubtedly drawn towards Father Ferapont rather than towards Father Zosima. The monk from Obdorsk stood for fasting, above all, and it was not strange that one who kept so rigid a fast as Father Ferapont should "see marvels." His words certainly seemed queer, but only the Lord knew what was hidden in those words, and were not worse words and acts usual with those who renounced their intellects for the sake of Christ? The pinching of the devil's tail he was ready and eager to believe, and not only in the figurative sense. Besides he had, before visiting the monastery, a strong prejudice against the institution of "elders," which he only knew of by hearsay and believed to be a pernicious innovation. Before he had been long at the monastery, he had detected the secret murmurings of some frivolous brothers who disliked the institution. He was, besides, a meddlesome, inquisitive man, who poked his nose into everything. This was why the news of the fresh "miracle" performed by Father Zosima reduced him to extreme perplexity. Alyosha remembered afterwards how their inquisitive guest from Obdorsk had been continually flitting to and fro from one group to another, listening and asking questions among the monks who were crowding within and without the elder's cell. But he did not pay much attention to him at the time, and only recollected it afterwards.

He had no thought to spare for it indeed, for when Father Zosima, feeling tired again, had gone back to bed, he thought of Alyosha as he was closing his eyes, and sent for him. Alyosha ran at once. There was no one else in the cell but Father Païssy, Father Iosif, and Porfiry, a novice. The elder, opening his weary eyes and looking intently at Alyosha, asked him suddenly:

"Are your people expecting you, my son?"

Alyosha hesitated.

"Haven't they need of you? Didn't you promise some one yesterday to see them to-day?"

"I did promise—to my father—my brothers—others, too."

"You see. Go without fail. Don't grieve. Be sure I shall not die without your being by to hear my last word. To you I will say that word, my son, it will be my legacy to you. To you, dear son, because you love me. But now go to keep your promise."

Alyosha immediately obeyed, though it was hard to go. But the promise that he should hear his last word on earth, and above all that it would be bequeathed to him, Alyosha, sent a thrill of rapture through his soul. He made haste that he might finish what he had to do in the town and return quickly. Father Païssy, too, uttered some words of exhortation which moved and surprised him greatly. He spoke as they left the cell together.

"Remember, young man, constantly," Father Païssy began, without preface, "that the science of this world, which has become a great power, has, especially in the last century, analysed everything divine handed down to us in the holy books. After this cruel analysis, the learned of this world have nothing left of all that was sacred of old. But they have only analysed the parts and overlooked the whole, and indeed their blindness is astounding. Yet the whole still stands steadfast before their eyes, and the gates of hell shall not prevail against it. Has it not lasted nineteen centuries, is it not still a living, a moving power in the individual soul and among the masses of the people? It dwells as unshakably as before in the souls of the very atheists, who have destroyed everything! For even those who have renounced Christianity and rebel against it, in their inmost being still follow the Christian ideal, for hitherto neither their subtlety nor the ardour of their hearts has been able to create a higher image of man and of virtue than the image manifested by Christ of old. When it has been attempted, the result has been only grotesque. Remember this especially, young man, since you are being sent into the world by your departing elder. Maybe, remembering this great day, you will not forget my words, uttered from the heart for your guidance, seeing you are young, and the temp-

·tations of the world are great and beyond your strength to endure. Well, now go, my orphan."

With these words Father Païssy blessed him. As Alyosha left the monastery and thought them over, he suddenly realised that he had met a new and unexpected friend, a warmly loving teacher, in this austere monk who had hitherto treated him sternly. It was as though Father Zosima had bequeathed him to him at his death, and "perhaps that's just what had passed between them," Alyosha thought suddenly. The philosophic reflections he had just heard so unexpectedly testified to the ardour of Father Païssy's heart. He was in haste to arm the boy's mind for battle with temptation and to guard the young soul left in his charge with the strongest defence he could imagine.

## CHAPTER II
### AT HIS FATHER'S

FIRST of all, Alyosha went to his father. As he approached the house he recalled that his father had insisted the day before that he should come without his brother Ivan seeing him. "Why so?" Alyosha wondered suddenly. "Even if my father has something to say to me alone, why should I go in unseen? Most likely in his excitement yesterday he meant to say something different," he decided. Yet he was very glad when Marfa Ignatyevna, who opened the garden gate to him (Grigory, it appeared, was ill in bed in the lodge), told him in answer to his question that Ivan Fyodorovich had gone out two hours ago.

"And my father?"

"He is up, taking his coffee," Marfa answered somewhat drily.

Alyosha went in. The old man was sitting alone at the table, wearing slippers and an old dressing-gown. He was amusing himself by looking through some accounts, rather inattentively however. He was quite alone in the house, for Smerdyakov, too, had gone out, marketing. Though he had got up early and was trying to put a bold face on it, he looked tired and weak. His forehead, upon which huge purple bruises had come out during the night, was bandaged with a red handkerchief; his nose had swollen terribly in the night, and some smaller bruises covered it in patches, giving his whole face a peculiarly spiteful and irritable look. The old man was aware of this, and turned a hostile glance on Alyosha as he came in.

"The coffee is cold," he cried harshly; "I won't offer you any. I've ordered nothing but a lenten fish soup to-day, and I don't invite any one to share it. Why have you come?"

"To find out how you are," said Alyosha.

"Yes. Besides, I told you to come yesterday. It's all of no consequence. You need not have troubled. But I knew you'd drag yourself here directly."

He said this with the most hostile feeling. At the same time he got up and looked anxiously in the looking-glass (perhaps for the fortieth time that morning) at his nose. He began, too, adjusting the red handkerchief on his forehead more becomingly.

"Red's better. It's just like the hospital in a white one," he observed sententiously. "Well, how are things over there? How is your elder?"

"He is very ill; he may die to-day," answered Alyosha. But his father had not listened, and had forgotten his own question at once.

"Ivan's gone out," he said suddenly. "He

is doing his utmost to carry off Mitya's fiancée. That's what he is staying here for," he added maliciously, and, twisting his mouth, looked at Alyosha.

"Surely he did not tell you so?" asked Alyosha.

"Yes, he did, long ago. Would you believe it, he told me three weeks ago? You don't suppose he, too, came to murder me, do you? He must have had some object in coming."

"What do you mean? Why do you say such things?" said Alyosha, troubled.

"He doesn't ask for money, it's true, but yet he won't get a groat from me. I intend living as long as possible, you may as well know, my dear Alexey Fyodorovich, and so I need every copeck, and the longer I live, the more I shall need it," he continued, pacing from one corner of the room to the other, keeping his hands in the pockets of his loose greasy dressing-gown, which was made of yellow cotton material. "Now I am still a man, I am only fifty-five, but I want to remain something of a man for another twenty years yet. As I get older, you know, I'll become disgusting. The wenches won't come to me of their own accord, so I shall need my money. So I am saving up more and more, simply for myself, my dear son Alexey Fyodorovich. You may as well know. For I mean to wallow in my filth to the end, let me tell you. For filth is sweet; all abuse it, but all men live in it, only others do it on the sly, and I openly. And so all the other dirty ones fall upon me for being so simple. And your paradise, Alexey Fyodorovich, is not to my taste, let me tell you that; and it's not the proper place for a gentleman, your paradise, even if it exists. I believe that I fall asleep and don't wake up again, and that's all. You can pray for my soul if you

like. And if you don't want to, don't, damn you! That's my philosophy. Ivan talked well here yesterday, though we were all drunk. Ivan is a conceited coxcomb, but he has no particular learning . . . nor education either. He sits silent and smiles at one without speaking —that's what pulls him through."

Alyosha listened to him in silence.

"Why won't he talk to me? If he does speak, he gives himself airs. Your Ivan is a scoundrel! And I'll marry Grushenka in a minute if I want to. For if you've money, Alexey Fyodorovich, you have only to want a thing and you can have it. That's what Ivan is afraid of, he is on the watch to prevent me getting married and that's why he is egging on Mitya to marry Grushenka himself. He hopes to keep me from Grushenka by that (as though I should leave him my money if I don't marry her!). Besides if Mitya marries Grushenka, Ivan will carry off his rich fiancée, that's what he's reckoning on! He is a scoundrel, your Ivan!"

"How cross you are. It's because of yesterday; you had better lie down," said Alyosha.

"There! you say that," the old man observed suddenly, as though it had struck him for the first time, "and I am not angry with you. But if Ivan said it, I should be angry with him. It is only with you I have good moments, otherwise you know I am an ill-natured man."

"You are not an ill-natured man, but a warped one," said Alyosha with a smile.

"Listen. I meant this morning to get that ruffian Mitya locked up and even now I don't know what I shall decide about it. Of course in these fashionable days fathers and mothers are looked upon as a prejudice, but even now the law does not allow you to drag your old father about by the hair, to kick him in the face with your heels in his own house, and brag of murdering him outright — all in the presence of witnesses. If I liked, I could nab him and have him locked up at once for what he did yesterday."

"Then you don't mean to lodge a complaint?"

"Ivan has dissuaded me. I shouldn't care about Ivan, but there's another thing."

And bending down to Alyosha, he went on in a confidential half-whisper.

"If I send the ruffian to prison, she'll hear of it and run to see him at once. But if she hears that he has beaten me, a weak old man, within an inch of my life, she may give him up and come to me. . . . For that's her way, everything by contraries. I know her through and through! Won't you have a drop of cognac? Take some cold coffee and I'll pour a quarter of a glass into it, it's delicious, my boy."

"No, thank you. I'll take that roll with me if I may," said Alyosha, and taking a three-copeck French roll he put it in the pocket of his cassock. "And you'd better not have cognac, either," he suggested apprehensively, looking into the old man's face.

"You are quite right, it irritates my nerves instead of soothing them. Only one little glass. I'll get it out of the cupboard."

He unlocked the cupboard, poured out a glass, drank it, then locked the cupboard and put the key back in his pocket.

"That's enough. One glass won't kill me."

"You see you are in a better humour now," said Alyosha, smiling.

"Um! I love you even without the cognac, but with scoundrels I am a scoundrel. Ivan is not going to Chermashnya — why is that? He is bent on spying, he wants to know how much I give Grushenka if she comes. They are all scoundrels! But I don't recognise Ivan, I don't know him at all. Where does he come from? He is not one of us in soul. As though I'd leave him anything! I shan't leave a will at all, you may as well know. And I'll crush Mitya like a beetle. I squash black beetles at night with my slipper; they squelch when you tread on them. And your Mitya will squelch, too. *Your* Mitya, for you love him. Yes, you love him and I am not afraid of your loving him. But if Ivan loved him I should be afraid for myself at his loving him. But Ivan loves nobody. Ivan is not one of us. People like Ivan are not our sort, my boy. They are like a cloud of dust. When the wind blows, the dust will be gone. . . . I had a silly idea in my head when I told you to come to-day; I wanted to find out from you about Mitya. If I were to hand him over a thousand or maybe two now, would the beggarly wretch agree to take himself off altogether for five years or, better still, thirty-five, and without Grushenka, and give her up once for all, eh?"

"I — I'll ask him," muttered Alyosha. "If you would give him three thousand, perhaps he ——"

"That's nonsense! You needn't ask him now, no need! I've changed my mind. It was a nonsensical idea of mine. I won't give him anything, not a penny, I want my money myself," cried the old man, waving his hand. "I'll crush him like a beetle without it. Don't say anything to him or else he will begin hoping. There's nothing for you to do here, you needn't stay. Is that fiancée of his, Katerina Ivanovna, whom he has kept so carefully hidden from me all this time, going to marry him or not? You went to see her yesterday, I believe?"

"Nothing will induce her to leave him."

"There you see how dearly these fine young ladies love a rake and a scoundrel. They are trash, I tell you, those pale young ladies, very different from . . . Ah, if I had his youth and the looks I had then (for I was better-looking than he at eight and twenty) I'd have been a conquering hero just as he is. He is a low cad! But he shan't have Grushenka, anyway, he shan't! I'll wipe the floor with him!"

His anger had returned with the last words.

"You can go. There's nothing for you to do here to-day," he snapped harshly.

Alyosha went up to say good-bye to him, and kissed him on the shoulder.

"What's that for?" the old man was a little surprised. "We shall see each other again, or do you think we shan't?"

"Not at all, I didn't mean anything."

"Nor did I, I did not mean anything," said the old man, looking at him. "Listen, listen," he shouted after him, "make haste and come again and I'll have a fish soup for you, a fine one, not like to-day. Be sure to come! Come to-morrow, do you hear, to-morrow!"

And as soon as Alyosha had gone out the door, he went to the cupboard again and gulped down another half-glass.

"That's enough!" he muttered, clearing his throat, and again he locked the cupboard and put the key in his pocket. Then he went into his bedroom, lay down on the bed, exhausted, and in one minute he was asleep.

## CHAPTER III
### A MEETING WITH SCHOOLBOYS

"Thank goodness he did not ask me about Grushenka," thought Alyosha, as he left his father's house and turned towards Madame Hohlakov's, "or I might have had to tell him of my meeting with Grushenka yesterday."

Alyosha felt painfully that since yesterday both combatants had renewed their energies, and that their hearts had grown hard again. "Father is spiteful and angry, he's made some plan and will stick to it. And what of Dmitri? He, too, will be harder than yesterday, he, too, must be spiteful and angry, and he, too, no doubt, has made some plan. Oh, I must succeed in finding him to-day, whatever happens."

But Alyosha had not long to meditate. An incident occurred on the road, which, though apparently of little consequence, made a great impression on him. Just after he had crossed the square and turned into an alley in order to reach Mihailovsky Street, which is divided by a small ditch from Bolshaya Street (our whole town is intersected by ditches), he saw a group of schoolboys between the ages of nine and twelve, at the bridge. They were going home from school, some with their bags on their shoulders, others with leather satchels slung across them, some in short jackets, others in little overcoats. Some even had those high boots with pleats round the ankles, such as little boys spoilt by rich fathers love to wear. The whole group was talking eagerly about something, apparently holding a council. Since his Moscow days Alyosha had never been able to pass children without taking notice of them, and although he was particularly fond of children of three or thereabouts, he liked schoolboys of ten and eleven, too. And so, anxious as he was to-day, he wanted at once to turn aside to talk to them. He looked into their excited rosy faces, and noticed at once that all the boys had stones in their hands. Beyond the ditch some thirty paces away, there was another schoolboy standing by a fence. He, too, had a satchel at his side. He was about ten years old, pale, delicate-looking, and with sparkling black eyes. He kept an attentive and anxious watch on the other six, obviously his schoolfellows with whom he had just come out of school, but with whom he evidently had a feud.

Alyosha went up and addressing a fair, curly-headed, rosy boy in a black jacket observed:

"When I had a satchel like yours, I always used to carry it on my left side, so as to have my right hand free, but you've got yours on your right side. So it will be awkward for you to get at it."

It was without premeditated artfulness that Alyosha began with this practical remark. But it is the only way for a grown-up person to get at once into confidential relations with a child, or still more with a group of children. One must begin in a serious businesslike way so as to be on a perfectly equal footing. Alyosha understood this by instinct.

"But he is left-handed," another, a fine healthy-looking boy of eleven, answered promptly. All the others stared at Alyosha.

"He even throws stones with his left hand," observed a third.

At that instant a stone flew into the group, but only just grazed the left-handed boy, though it was well and vigorously thrown by the boy standing on the other side of the ditch.

"Give it him, hit him back, Smurov," they all shouted. But Smurov, the left-handed boy, needed no telling, and at once revenged himself; he threw a stone, but it missed the boy and hit the ground. The boy on the other side of the ditch, the pocket of whose coat was visibly bulging with stones, flung another stone at the group; this time it flew straight at Alyosha

and hit him rather painfully on the shoulder.

"He aimed it at you, he meant it for you. You are Karamazov, Karamazov!" the boys shouted, laughing. "Come, let's all go for him at once, go!" and six stones flew at the boy. One struck the boy on the head and he fell down, but at once leapt up and began ferociously returning their fire. Both sides threw stones incessantly. Many of the group had their pockets full, too.

"What are you about! Aren't you ashamed? Six against one! Why, you'll kill him," cried Alyosha.

He ran forward and met the flying stones to screen the solitary boy. Three or four ceased throwing for a minute.

"He began first!" cried a boy in a red shirt in an angry childish voice. "He is a beast, he stabbed Krasotkin in class the other day with a penknife. It bled. Krasotkin wouldn't tell tales, but he must be thrashed."

"But what for? I suppose you tease him."

"There, he sent a stone at your back again, he knows you," cried the children. "It's you he is aiming at now, not us. Come, all of you, at him again, don't miss, Smurov!" and again a fire of stones, and a very vicious one, began. The boy on the other side of the ditch was hit in the chest; he screamed, began to cry, and ran away uphill towards Mihailovsky Street. They all shouted: "Aha, he is funking, he is running away. Bath-mop!"

"You don't know what a beast he is, Karamazov, killing is too good for him," said the boy in the jacket, with flashing eyes. He seemed to be the eldest.

"What's wrong with him?" asked Alyosha, "is he a tell-tale or what?"

The boys looked at one another as though derisively.

"Are you going that way, to Mihailovsky?" the same boy went on. "Catch up with him. . . . You see he's stopped again, he is waiting and looking at you."

"He is looking at you," the other boys chimed in.

"You ask him, if he likes a ragged bath-mop. Do you hear, ask him that!"

There was a general burst of laughter. Alyosha looked at them, and they at him.

"Don't go near him, he'll hurt you," cried Smurov in a warning voice.

"I shan't ask him about the bath-mop, for I expect you tease him with that question somehow. But I'll find out from him why you hate him so."

"Find out then, find out," cried the boys, laughing.

Alyosha crossed the bridge and walked uphill by the fence, straight towards the boy.

"You'd better look out," the boys called after him; "he won't be afraid of you. He will stab you in a minute, on the sly, as he did Krasotkin."

The boy waited for him without budging. Coming up to him, Alyosha saw facing him a child about nine years old. He was an undersized weakly boy with a thin long pale face, with large dark eyes that gazed at him vindictively. He was dressed in a rather shabby old overcoat, which he had monstrously outgrown. His bare arms stuck out of his sleeves. There was a large patch on the right knee of his trousers, and in his right boot just at the toe there was a big hole in the leather, carefully blackened with ink. Both the pockets of his overcoat were weighed down with stones. Alyosha stopped two steps in front of him, looking inquiringly at him. The boy, seeing at once from Alyosha's eyes that he wouldn't beat him, became less defiant, and addressed him first.

"I am alone, and there are six of them. I'll beat them all, alone!" he said suddenly, with flashing eyes.

"I think one of the stones must have hurt you badly," observed Alyosha.

"But I hit Smurov on the head!" cried the boy.

"They told me that you know me, and that you threw a stone at me on purpose," said Alyosha.

The boy looked darkly at him.

"I don't know you. Do you know me?" Alyosha continued.

"Let me alone!" the boy cried irritably; but he did not move, as though he were expecting something, and again there was a vindictive light in his eyes.

"Very well, I am going," said Alyosha; "only I don't know you and I don't tease you. They told me how they tease you, but I don't want to tease you. Good-bye!"

"Monk in silk trousers!" cried the boy, following Alyosha with the same vindictive and defiant expression, and he threw himself into an attitude of defence, feeling sure that now Alyosha would fall upon him; but Alyosha turned, looked at him, and walked away. He had not gone three steps before the biggest stone the boy had in his pocket hit him a painful blow in the back.

"So you'll hit a man from behind! They tell the truth, then, when they say that you attack on the sly," said Alyosha, turning round again. This time the boy threw a stone savagely right into Alyosha's face; but Alyosha just had time to guard himself, and the stone struck him on the elbow.

"Aren't you ashamed? What have I done to you?" he cried.

# THE BROTHERS KARAMAZOV

The boy waited in silent defiance, certain that now Alyosha would attack him. Seeing that even now he would not, his rage was like a little wild beast's; he flew at Alyosha himself, and before Alyosha had time to move, the spiteful child had seized his left hand with both of his and bitten his middle finger. He fixed his teeth in it and it was ten seconds before he let go. Alyosha cried out with pain and pulled his finger away with all his might. The child let go at last and retreated to his former distance. Alyosha's finger had been badly bitten to the bone, close to the nail; it began to bleed.

Alyosha took out his handkerchief and bound it tightly round his injured hand. He was a full minute bandaging it. The boy stood waiting all the time.

At last Alyosha raised his gentle eyes and looked at him.

"Very well," he said, "you see how badly you've bitten me. That's enough, isn't it? Now tell me, what have I done to you?"

The boy stared in amazement.

"Though I don't know you and it's the first time I've seen you," Alyosha went on with the same serenity, "yet I must have done something to you — you wouldn't have hurt me like this for nothing. So what have I done? How have I wronged you, tell me?"

Instead of answering, the boy broke into a loud tearful wail and ran away. Alyosha walked slowly after him towards Mihailovsky Street, and for a long time he saw the child running in the distance as fast as ever, not turning his head, and no doubt still keeping up his tearful wail. He made up his mind to find him out as soon as he had time, and to solve this mystery. Just now he had not the time.

## CHAPTER IV
### AT THE HOHLAKOVS'

ALYOSHA soon reached Madame Hohlakov's house, a handsome stone house of two storeys, one of the finest in our town. Though Madame Hohlakov spent most of her time in another province where she had an estate, or in Moscow, where she had a house of her own, yet she had a house in our town, too, inherited from her forefathers. The estate in our district was the largest of her three estates, yet she had been very little in our province before this time. She ran out to Alyosha in the hall.

"Did you get my letter about the new miracle?" She spoke rapidly and nervously.

"Yes."

"Did you show it to every one? He restored the son to his mother!"

"He will die to-day," said Alyosha.

"I have heard, I know, oh, how I long to talk to you, to you, or some one about all this. No, to you, to you! And how sorry I am I can't see him! The whole town is in excitement, they are all suspense. But now — do you know Katerina Ivanovna is here now?"

"Ah, that's lucky," cried Alyosha. "Then I shall see her here. She told me yesterday to be sure to come and see her to-day."

"I know, I know all. I've heard exactly what happened yesterday — and the atrocious behaviour of that — creature. C'est tragique, and if I'd been in her place I don't know what I should have done. And your brother Dmitri Fyodorovich, what do you think of him? — my goodness! Alexey Fyodorovich, I am wandering, only fancy; your brother is in there with her, not that dreadful brother who was so shocking yesterday, but the other, Ivan Fyodorovich, he is sitting with her talking;

136

THE BOY WHO THREW THE STONE

# IV: LACERATIONS

they are having a serious conversation. If you could only imagine what's passing between them now — it's awful, I tell you, it's lacerating, it's like some incredible tale of horror. They are ruining themselves for no reason any one can see. They both recognize this and revel in it. I've been waiting for you! I've been thirsting for you! It's too much for me, that's the worst of it. I'll tell you all about it presently, but now I must speak of something else, the most important thing — I had quite forgotten what's most important. Tell me, why has Lise been in hysterics? As soon as she heard you were here, she threw a fit!"

"*Maman*, it's you who are hysterical now, not I." Lise's voice chirped through a tiny crack of the door leading into an inner room. Her voice sounded as though she wanted to laugh, but was doing her utmost to control it. Alyosha at once noticed the crack, and no doubt Lise was peeping through it, but that he could not see.

"And no wonder, Lise, no wonder . . . your caprices will make me hysterical, too. But she is so ill, Alexey Fyodorovich, she has been so ill all night, feverish and moaning! I could hardly wait for the morning and for Herzenstube to come. He says that he can make nothing of it, that we must wait. Herzenstube always comes and says that he can make nothing of it. As soon as you approached the house, she screamed, went into hysterics, and insisted on being wheeled back into her old room here."

"Mamma, I didn't know he had come. It wasn't on his account I wanted to be wheeled into this room."

"That's not true, Lise, Yulia ran to tell you that Alexey Fyodorovich was coming. She was on the look-out for you."

"My darling mamma, it's not at all clever of you. But if you want to make up for it and say something very clever, dear mamma, you'd better tell our honoured visitor, Alexey Fyodorovich, that he has shown his want of wit by venturing to come to us after what happened yesterday and although every one is laughing at him."

"Lise, you go too far. I declare I shall have to be severe. Who laughs at him? I am so glad he has come, I need him, I can't do without him. Oh, Alexey Fyodorovich, I am exceedingly unhappy!"

"But what's the matter with you, mamma, darling?"

"Ah, your caprices, Lise, your fidgetiness, your illness, that awful night of fever, that awful everlasting Herzenstube, everlasting, everlasting, that's the worst of it! Everything, in fact, everything. . . . Even that miracle, too! Oh, how it has upset me, how it has struck me, that miracle, dear Alexey Fyodorovich! And that tragedy in the drawing-room there, it's more than I can bear, I warn you. I can't bear it. A comedy, perhaps, not a tragedy. Tell me, will Father Zosima live till to-morrow, will he? Oh, my God! What is happening to me? Every minute I close my eyes and see that it's all nonsense, all nonsense."

"I should be very grateful," Alyosha interrupted suddenly, "if you could give me a clean rag to bind up my finger with. I have hurt it, and it's very painful."

Alyosha unbound his bitten finger. The handkerchief was soaked with blood. Madame Hohlakov screamed and shut her eyes.

"Good heavens, what a wound, how awful!"

But as soon as Lise saw Alyosha's finger through the crack, she flung the door open.

"Come, come here," she cried imperiously. "No nonsense now! Good heavens, why did you stand there saying nothing about it all this time? He might have bled to death, mamma! How did you do it? Water, water! You must wash it first of all, simply hold it in cold water to stop the pain, and keep it there, keep it there. . . . Make haste, mamma, some water in a slop basin. But do make haste," she finished nervously. She was quite frightened at the sight of Alyosha's wound.

"Shouldn't we send for Herzenstube?" cried Madame Hohlakov.

"Mamma, you'll be the death of me. Your Herzenstube will come and say that he can make nothing of it! Water, water! Mamma, for goodness' sake go yourself and hurry Yulia, she is such a slowcoach and never can come quickly! Make haste, mamma, or I shall die."

"Why, it's a trifle," cried Alyosha, frightened by this alarm.

Yulia ran in with water and Alyosha put his finger in it.

"Some lint, mamma, for mercy's sake, bring some lint and that muddy caustic lotion for cuts, what's it called? We've got some, we have. You know where the bottle is, mamma; it's in your bedroom in the right-hand cupboard, there's a big bottle of it there with the lint."

"I'll bring everything in a minute, Lise, only don't scream and don't fuss. You see how bravely Alexey Fyodorovich bears it. Where did you get such a dreadful wound, Alexey Fyodorovich?"

Madame Hohlakov hastened away. This was all Lise was waiting for.

"First of all, answer the question, where did you get hurt like this?" she asked Alyosha quickly. "And then I'll talk to you about something quite different. Well?"

Instinctively feeling that the time of her mother's absence was precious to her, Alyosha hastened to tell her of his enigmatic meeting with the schoolboys in the fewest words possible. Lise struck her hands together at his story.

"How can you, and in that dress too, get mixed up with schoolboys!" she cried angrily, as though she had rights over him. "You are nothing but a boy yourself if you can do that, a little boy! But you must find out for me about that horrid boy and tell me all about it, for there's some mystery in it. Now for the second thing, but first a question: can you, Alexey Fyodorovich, in spite of the pain, talk about the merest trifles, but talk sensibly?"

"Of course, and I don't feel much pain now."

"That's because your finger is in the water. It must be changed directly for it will get warm in a minute. Yulia, bring some ice from the cellar and another basin of water. Now she is gone, I can speak; will you give me the letter I sent you yesterday, dear Alexey Fyodorovich — be quick for mamma will be back in a minute and I don't want ——"

"I haven't got the letter."

"That's not true, you have. I knew you would say that. You've got it in that pocket. I've been regretting that foolish joke all night. Give me back the letter at once, give it me."

"I've left it at home."

"But you can't consider me as a child, a little girl, after that silly joke! I beg your pardon for that silliness, but you must bring me the letter, if you really haven't got it — bring it to-day, you must, you must."

"To-day I can't possibly, for I am going

back to the monastery and I shan't come and see you for the next two days — three or four perhaps — for Father Zosima ———"

"Four days, what nonsense! Listen. Did you laugh at me very much?"

"I didn't laugh a bit."

"Why not?"

"Because I believed all you said."

"You are insulting me!"

"Not at all. As soon as I read it, I thought that all that would come to pass, for as soon as Father Zosima dies, I am to leave the monastery. Then I shall go back and finish my studies, and when you reach the legal age we will be married. I shall love you. Though I haven't had time to think about it, I believe I couldn't find a better wife than you, and Father Zosima tells me I must marry."

"But I am a cripple, wheeled about in a chair," laughed Lise, flushing crimson.

"I'll wheel you about myself, but I'm sure you'll get well by then."

"But you are mad," said Lise, nervously, "to turn a joke into all this nonsense! Here's mamma, very conveniently, perhaps. Mamma, you are always late, how can you be so long! And here's Yulia with the ice!"

"Oh, Lise, don't scream, above all things don't scream. That scream drives me . . . How can I help it when you stuck the lint in another place. I've been hunting and hunting — I do believe you did it on purpose."

"But I couldn't tell that he would come with a bad finger, or else perhaps I might have done it on purpose. Angel mamma, you begin to say really witty things."

"Never mind my being witty, but I must say you show nice feeling for Alexey Fyodorovich's sufferings! Oh, my dear Alexey Fyodorovich, what's killing me is no one thing in particular, not Herzenstube, but everything together, that's what is too much for me."

"That's enough, mamma, enough about Herzenstube," Lise laughed gaily. "Hurry up with the lint and the lotion, mamma. That's simply Goulard water, Alexey Fyodorovich, I remember the name now, but it's a splendid lotion. Would you believe it, mamma, on the way here he had a fight with the boys in the street, and it was a boy bit his finger; isn't he a child, a child himself? Is he fit to be married after that? For only fancy, he wants to be married, mamma. Just think of him married, isn't it funny, isn't it awful?"

And Lise kept laughing her thin hysterical giggle, looking slyly at Alyosha.

"But why married, Lise? What makes you talk of such a thing? It's quite out of place — and perhaps the boy was rabid."

"Why, mamma! As though there were rabid boys!"

"Why not, Lise, as though I had said something stupid! Your boy might have been bitten by a mad dog and he would become mad and bite any one near him. How well she has bandaged it, Alexey Fyodorovich. I couldn't have done it. Do you still feel the pain?"

"It's nothing much now."

"You don't feel afraid of water?" asked Lise.

"Come, that's enough, Lise, perhaps I really was rather too quick talking of the boy being rabid, and you pounced upon it at once. Katerina Ivanovna has only just heard that you are here, Alexey Fyodorovich, she simply rushed at me, she's dying to see you, dying!"

"Ach, mamma, go to them yourself. He can't go just now, he is in too much pain."

"Not at all, I can go quite well," said Alyosha.

"What! You are going away? Is that what you say?"

"Well, when I've seen them, I'll come back here and we can talk as much as you like. But I should like to see Katerina Ivanovna at once, for I am very anxious to be back at the monastery as soon as I can."

"Mamma, take him away quickly. Alexey Fyodorovich, don't trouble to come and see me afterwards, but go straight back to your monastery — and a good riddance. I want to sleep, I didn't sleep all night."

"Ah, Lise, you are only making fun, but how I wish you would sleep!" cried Madame Hohlakov.

"I don't know what I've done. . . . I'll stay another three minutes, five if you like," muttered Alyosha.

"Even five! Do take him away quickly, mamma, he is a monster."

"Lise, you are crazy. Let us go, Alexey Fyodorovich, she is too capricious to-day. I am afraid to cross her. Oh, the trouble one has with nervous girls! Perhaps she really will be able to sleep after seeing you. How quickly you have made her sleepy, and how fortunate it is."

"Ah, mamma, how sweetly you talk. I must kiss you for it, mamma."

"And I kiss you, too, Lise. Listen, Alexey Fyodorovich," Madame Hohlakov began mysteriously and importantly, speaking in a rapid whisper. "I don't want to suggest anything, I don't want to lift the veil, you will see for yourself what's going on. It's appalling. It's the most fantastic farce. She loves your brother Ivan, and she is doing her utmost to persuade herself she loves your brother Dmitri. It's appalling! I'll go in with you, and if they don't turn me out, I'll stay to the end."

# CHAPTER V
### LACERATION IN THE DRAWING-ROOM

BUT in the drawing-room the conversation was already over. Katerina Ivanovna was greatly excited, though she looked resolute. At the moment Alyosha and Madame Hohlakov entered, Ivan Fyodorovich stood up to take leave. His face was rather pale, and Alyosha looked at him anxiously. The fact is, that at that moment a doubt, a harassing enigma, which had for some time haunted Alyosha, was being cleared up for him. During the preceding month it had been several times suggested to him that his brother Ivan was in love with Katerina Ivanovna, and, what was more, that he meant "to snatch her away" from Dmitri. Until quite lately the idea had seemed monstrous to Alyosha, though it worried him extremely. He loved both his brothers, and dreaded such rivalry between them. Meantime, Dmitri had said outright on the previous day that he was glad that Ivan was his rival, and that it was a great assistance to him, Dmitri. In what way would it help him? Would it enable him to marry Grushenka? But that Alyosha considered the worst thing possible. Besides all this, Alyosha had implicitly believed till the evening before that Katerina Ivanovna had a steadfast and passionate love for Dmitri; but he had only believed it till the evening before. He had fancied, too, that she was incapable of loving a man like Ivan, and that she did love Dmitri, and loved him just as he was, in spite of the monstrosity of such a passion.

But during yesterday's scene with Grushenka another idea had vaguely suggested itself to him. The word "lacerating," which Madame Hohlakov had just uttered, almost made him start, because half waking up towards daybreak that night he had cried out, "Laceration, laceration," probably in response to a dream of his. He had been dreaming all night of the previous day's scene at Katerina Ivanovna's. And now Alyosha was struck by Madame Hohlakov's blunt and persistent assertion that Katerina Ivanovna was in love with Ivan, and was only deceiving herself through some sort of pose, from "self-laceration," and was torturing herself with her pretended love for Dmitri out of some fancied sense of duty. "Yes," he thought, "perhaps the whole truth lies in those words." But in that case what was Ivan's position? Alyosha felt instinctively that a character like Katerina Ivanovna's must dominate, and she could only dominate some one like Dmitri, and never a man like Ivan. For Dmitri might at last submit to her domination "and be happy" (which was what Alyosha would have desired), but Ivan — no, Ivan could not submit to her, and such submission would not give him happiness. That was the notion that for some reason Alyosha had formed in his mind about Ivan. And now all these doubts and reflections flitted through his mind as he entered the drawing-room. Another idea, too, suddenly and irresistibly took hold of him: "What if she loved neither of them — neither Ivan nor Dmitri?"

I must note that Alyosha felt as it were ashamed of his own thoughts and had reproached himself when they kept recurring to him during the last month. "What do I know about love and women and how can I decide such questions?" he thought self-reproachfully, after each such thought or conjecture. And yet it was impossible not to think about it. He felt instinctively that this rivalry was

of immense importance in his brothers' lives and that a great deal depended upon it.

"One reptile will devour the other," Ivan had pronounced the day before, speaking in anger of his father and Dmitri. So Ivan looked upon Dmitri as a reptile, and perhaps had long done so. Was it perhaps since he had known Katerina Ivanovna? That phrase had, of course, escaped Ivan unawares yesterday, but that only made it more important. If he felt like that, what chance was there of peace? Were there not, on the contrary, new grounds for hatred and hostility in their family? And with which of them was Alyosha to sympathise? And what was he to wish for each of them? He loved them both, but what could he desire for each in the midst of such terrible conflicts? He might go quite astray in this maze, and Alyosha's heart could not endure uncertainty, because his love was always of an active character. He was incapable of passive love. If he loved any one, he set to work at once to help him. And to do so he must know what he was aiming at; he must know for certain what was best for each, and having ascertained this it was natural for him to help them both.

But instead of a definite aim, he found nothing but uncertainty and perplexity on all sides. "It was lacerating," as was said just now. But what could he understand even in this "laceration"? He did not understand the first word in this perplexing maze.

Seeing Alyosha, Katerina Ivanovna said quickly and joyfully to Ivan, who had already got up to go: "One minute! Stay another minute! I want to hear the opinion of this person here whom I trust absolutely. Don't go away," she added, addressing Madame Hohlakov. She made Alyosha sit down beside her, and Madame Hohlakov sat opposite, beside Ivan.

"You are all my friends here, all I have in the world, my dear friends," she began ardently, in a voice which quivered with tears of genuine suffering, and again Alyosha's heart turned to her at once. "You, Alexey Fyodorovich, were a witness yesterday of that terrible scene, and saw how I acted. You did not see it, Ivan Fyodorovich, he did. What he thought of me yesterday I don't know. I only know one thing, that if it were repeated to-day, this minute, I should have the same feelings again as yesterday — have the same feelings, speak the same words, make the same gestures. You remember my actions, Alexey Fyodorovich; you checked me in one of them . . . (as she said that, she flushed and her eyes gleamed). I must tell you that I can't get reconciled to anything. Listen, Alexey Fyodorovich. I don't even know whether I still love *him*. I feel *pity* for him, and that is a poor sign of love. If I loved him, if I still loved him, perhaps I shouldn't pity him now, but should hate him."

Her voice quivered, and tears glittered on her eyelashes. Alyosha shuddered inwardly. "That girl is truthful and sincere," he thought, "and she does not love Dmitri any more."

"That's true, that's true," cried Madame.

"Wait, dear. I haven't told you the chief, the final decision I came to during the night. I feel that perhaps my decision is a terrible one — for me, but I foresee that nothing will induce me to change it — nothing. It will be so all my life. My dear, kind, ever-faithful and generous adviser, the one friend I have in the world, Ivan Fyodorovich, with his deep insight into the heart, approves and commends my decision. He knows it."

"Yes, I approve of it," Ivan assented, in a subdued but firm voice.

"But I should like Alyosha, too (Ah! Alexey Fyodorovich, forgive my calling you simply Alyosha), I should like Alexey Fyodorovich, too, to tell me before my two friends whether I am right. I feel instinctively that you, Alyosha, my dear brother (for you are a dear brother to me)," she said again ecstatically, taking his cold hand in her hot one, "I foresee that your decision, your approval, will bring me peace, in spite of all my sufferings, for, after your words, I shall be calm and submit — I feel that."

"I don't know what you are asking me," said Alyosha, flushing. "I only know that I love you and at this moment wish for your happiness more than my own! . . . But I know nothing about such affairs," something impelled him to add hurriedly.

"In such affairs, Alexey Fyodorovich, in such affairs, the chief thing is honour and duty and something higher — I don't know what — but higher perhaps even than duty. I am conscious of this irresistible feeling in my heart, and it compels me irresistibly. But it may all be put in two words. I've already decided, even if he marries that — creature (she began solemnly), whom I never, never can forgive, *even then I will not abandon him.* Henceforward I will never, never abandon him!" she cried, torn by a sort of pale, forced ecstasy. "Not that I would tag after him continually, get in his way and worry him. Oh, no! I will go away to another town — wherever you please — but I will watch over him all my life — I will watch over him all my life untiringly. When he becomes unhappy with that woman, and that is bound to happen quite soon, let him come to me and he will find

142

a friend, a sister. . . . Only a sister, of course, and so for ever; but he will learn at least that that sister is really his sister, who loves him and has sacrificed all her life to him. I will gain my point. I will insist on his finally getting to know me and confiding entirely in me, without reserve," she cried, in a sort of frenzy. "I will be his god, to whom he will pray — and that, at least, he owes me for his treachery and for what I suffered yesterday through him. And let him see that all my life I will be true to him and the promise I gave him, in spite of his being untrue and betraying me. I will — I will become nothing but a means for his happiness, or — how shall I say? — an instrument, a machine for his happiness, and this all my life, all my life, and he will see this all his life! That's my decision. Ivan Fyodorovich fully approves of me."

She was breathless. She had perhaps intended to express her thought in a more dignified, graceful, and natural way, but it was expressed too hastily and crudely. Her manner was full of youthful impulsiveness, it betrayed that she was still smarting from yesterday's insult, and that her pride craved satisfaction. She felt this herself. Her face suddenly darkened, an unpleasant look came into her eyes. Alyosha at once saw it and felt a pang of sympathy. His brother Ivan made it worse by putting in:

"I've only expressed my own view. Coming from any one else," he said, "this would have been affected and overstrained, but from you — no. Any other woman would have been wrong, but you are right. I don't know how to explain it, but I see that you are absolutely sincere and, therefore, you are right."

"But that's only for the moment. And what does this moment mean? Nothing but yester-day's insult." Madame Hohlakov obviously had not intended to interfere, but she could not refrain from this very just comment.

"Quite so, quite so," cried Ivan, with peculiar eagerness, obviously annoyed at being interrupted, "in any one else this moment would be due only to yesterday's impression and would be only a moment. But with Katerina Ivanovna's character, that moment will last all her life. What for any one else would be only a promise is for her an everlasting, burdensome, grim, perhaps, but unremitting duty. And she will be sustained by the sense of having fulfilled this duty. Your life, Katerina Ivanovna, will henceforth be spent in painful contemplation of your own feelings, your own heroism, and your own sorrow; but in the end that suffering will be softened and your life will turn into sweet contemplation of a bold and proud design which has been carried out. Yes, proud it certainly is, and desperate in any case, but a triumph for you. And the consciousness of it will in the end be a source of complete satisfaction and will reconcile you to everything else."

This was unmistakably said with some malice and obviously with intention; even perhaps with no desire to conceal that he spoke ironically and mockingly.

"Oh, dear, how wrong it all is!" Madame Hohlakov cried again.

"Alexey Fyodorovich, you speak. I want dreadfully to know what you will say!" cried Katerina Ivanovna, and suddenly burst into tears. Alyosha got up from the sofa.

"It's nothing, nothing!" she went on through her tears. "I'm upset, I didn't sleep last night. But by the side of two such friends as you and your brother I still feel strong — for I know — you two will never desert me."

"Unluckily I may be obliged to return to Moscow — to-morrow — and to leave you for a long time — And, unluckily, it's unavoidable," Ivan said suddenly.

"To-morrow — to Moscow!" her face was suddenly contorted; "but — but, dear me, how fortunate," she cried in a voice suddenly changed. In one instant there was no trace left of her tears. She underwent an instantaneous transformation, which amazed Alyosha. Instead of a poor, insulted girl, weeping in a sort of emotional "laceration," he saw a woman completely self-possessed and even exceedingly pleased, as though something agreeable had just happened.

"Oh, not fortunate that I am losing you, of course not," she corrected herself suddenly, with the charming smile of a woman of the world. "Such a friend as you are could not suppose that. I am only too unhappy at losing you." She rushed impulsively at Ivan, and seizing both his hands, pressed them ardently. "But what is fortunate is that in Moscow you will be able to see auntie and Agafya and to tell them all the horror of my present position. You can speak with complete openness to Agafya, but spare dear auntie. You will know how to do that. You can't think how wretched I was yesterday and this morning, wondering how I could write them that dreadful letter — for one can never tell such things in a letter. . . . Now it will be easy for me to write, for you will see them and explain everything. Oh, how glad I am! But I am only glad of that, believe me. Of course, no one can take your place. . . . I will run at once to write the letter," she finished suddenly, and took a step as though to leave the room.

"And what about Alyosha and his opinion, which you were so desperately anxious to hear?" cried Madame Hohlakov. There was a sarcastic, angry note in her voice.

"I had not forgotten that," cried Katerina Ivanovna, coming to a sudden standstill, "and why are you so antagonistic at such a moment?" she added, with warm and bitter reproachfulness. "What I said, I repeat. I must have his opinion. More than that, I must have his decision! As he says, so it shall be. You see how anxious I am for your words, Alexey Fyodorovich. . . . But what's the matter?"

"I couldn't have believed it. I can't understand it!" Alyosha cried suddenly in distress.

"What? what?"

"He is going to Moscow, and you cry out that you are glad. You said that on purpose! And you begin explaining that you are not glad of that but sorry to be — losing a friend. But that was acting, too — you were playing a part — as in a theatre!"

"In a theatre? What? What do you mean?" exclaimed Katerina Ivanovna, profoundly astonished, flushing crimson, and frowning.

"Though you assure him you are sorry to lose a friend in him, you persist in telling him to his face that it's fortunate he is going," said Alyosha breathlessly. He was standing at the table and did not sit down.

"What are you talking about? I don't understand . . ."

"I don't understand myself. . . . It's like a sudden illumination . . . I know I am not saying it properly, but I'll say it all the same," Alyosha went on in the same shaking and broken voice. "What I see is that perhaps you don't love Dmitri at all . . . and never have, from the beginning. . . . And Dmitri, too, has never loved you . . . . and only esteems you. . . . I really don't know how I dare to say all this, but somebody must tell the truth . . . for nobody here wishes to tell the truth."

"What truth?" cried Katerina Ivanovna, and there was an hysterical note in her voice.

"I'll tell you," Alyosha went on with desperate haste, as though he were leaping headlong from a house-top. "Call Dmitri; I will fetch him — and let him come here and take your hand and take Ivan's and join your hands. For you're torturing Ivan, simply because you love him — and torturing him, because you love Dmitri through 'self-laceration' — with an unreal love — because you've persuaded yourself to."

Alyosha broke off and was silent.

"You . . . you . . . you are a little religious idiot — that's what you are!" Katerina Ivanovna snapped. Her face was white and her lips were contorted with anger.

Ivan suddenly laughed and got up. His hat was in his hand.

"You are mistaken, my good Alyosha," he said, with an expression Alyosha had never seen in his face before — an expression of youthful sincerity and strong, irresistibly frank feeling. "Katerina Ivanovna has never cared for me! She has known all the time that I cared for her — though I never said a word of my love to her — she knew, but she didn't care for me. I have never been her friend either, not for one moment; she is too proud to need my friendship. She kept me at her side as a means of revenge. She revenged herself through me and on me for all the insults which she has been continually receiving from Dmitri ever since their first meeting. For even that first meeting has rankled in her heart as an insult — that's what her heart is like! All the time I did nothing but listen to her speak of her love for him. I am going now; but, believe me, Katerina Ivanovna, you really love only him. And the more he insults you, the more you love him — that's your 'laceration.' You love him just as he is; you love him for insulting you. If he reformed, you'd give him up at once and cease to love him. But you need him so as to contemplate continually your heroic fidelity and to reproach him for infidelity. And it all comes from your pride. Oh, there's a great deal of humiliation and self-abasement about it, but it all comes from pride. . . . I am too young and I've loved you too much. I know that I ought not to say this, that it would be more dignified on my part simply to leave you, and it would be less offensive for you. But I am going far away, and shall never come back. . . . It is for ever. I don't want to sit beside a 'laceration.' . . . But I don't know how to speak now. I've said everything. . . . Good-bye, Katerina Ivanovna; you can't be angry with me, for I am a hundred times more severely punished than you, if only by the fact that I shall never see you again. Good-bye! I don't want your hand. You have tortured me too deliberately for me to be able to forgive you at this moment. I shall forgive you later, but now I don't want your hand. 'Den Dank, Dame, begehr ich nicht,' " he added, with a crooked smile, showing, however, that he had read Schiller, and read him, indeed, till he knew him by heart — which Alyosha would never have believed. He went out of the room without saying good-bye even to his hostess, Madame Hohlakov. Alyosha struck his hands together.

"Ivan!" he cried desperately after him. "Come back, Ivan! No, nothing will induce him to come back now!" he cried again, with sorrowful understanding; "but it's my fault, my fault. I began it! Ivan spoke angrily, wrongly. Unjustly and angrily. He must come back here, come back," Alyosha kept exclaiming frantically.

Katerina Ivanovna went suddenly into the next room.

"You have done no harm. You behaved beautifully, like an angel," Madame Hohlakov whispered rapidly and ecstatically to Alyosha. "I will do my utmost to prevent Ivan Fyodorovich from going."

Her face beamed with delight, to the great distress of Alyosha, but Katerina Ivanovna suddenly returned. She had two hundred-rouble notes in her hand.

"I have a great favour to ask of you, Alexey Fyodorovich," she began, addressing Alyosha with an apparently calm and even voice, as though nothing had happened. "A week — yes, I think it was a week ago — Dmitri Fyodorovich was guilty of a hasty and unjust action — a very ugly action. There is a low tavern here and in it he met that discharged officer, that captain, whom your father used to employ in some business. Dmitri Fyodorovich somehow lost his temper with this captain, seized him by the beard and dragged him out into the street and along it for some distance, in that insulting fashion. And I am told that his son, a boy, still a child, who is at school here, saw it and ran beside them crying and begging for his father, appealing to every one to defend him, but every one laughed. You must forgive me, Alexey Fyodorovich, I cannot think without indignation of that disgraceful action of *his* . . . one of those actions of which only Dmitri Fyodorovich would be capable in his anger . . . and his passions! I can't speak of it even. . . . I can't find words. I've made inquiries about his vic-

tim, and find he is a very poor man. His name is Snegiryov. He did something wrong in the army and was discharged. I can't tell you what. And now he has sunk into terrible destitution, with his family — a miserable family of sick children, and, I believe, an insane wife. He has been living here a long time; he used to work as a copying clerk, but now he is getting nothing. I thought if you . . . that is I thought . . . I don't know. I am so confused. You see, I wanted to ask you, my dear Alexey Fyodorovich, to go to him, to find some excuse to go to them — I mean to that captain — oh, goodness, how badly I explain it! — and delicately, carefully, as only you know how to (Alyosha blushed), manage to give him this assistance, these two hundred roubles. He will be sure to take it. . . . I mean, persuade him to take it. . . . Or, rather, what do I mean? You see it's not by way of compensation to prevent him from taking proceedings (for I believe he meant to), but simply a token of sympathy, of a desire to assist him, from me, Dmitri Fyodorovich's betrothed, not from himself. . . . But you know. . . . I would go myself, but you'll know how to do it ever so much better. He lives in Ozyornaya Street, in the house of a woman called Kalmikov. . . . For God's sake, Alexey Fyodorovich, do it for me, and now . . . now I am rather . . . tired. Good-bye!"

She turned so quickly and disappeared behind the portière that Alyosha had not time to utter a word, though he wanted to speak. He longed to beg her pardon, to blame himself, to say something, for his heart was full and he could not bear to go out of the room without doing so. But Madame Hohlakov took him by the hand and drew him along with her. In the hall she stopped him again as before.

146

"She is proud, she is struggling with herself; but kind, charming, generous," she exclaimed, in a half-whisper. "Oh, how I love her, especially sometimes, and how glad I am again of everything! Dear Alexey Fyodorovich, you didn't know, but I must tell you, that we all, all — both her aunts, I and all of us, Lise, even — have been hoping and praying for nothing for the last month but that she may give up your favourite Dmitri, who takes no notice of her and does not care for her, and marry Ivan Fyodorovich — such an excellent and cultivated young man, who loves her more than anything in the world. We are in a regular plot to bring it about, and I am even staying on here perhaps on that account."

"But she has been crying — she has been wounded again," cried Alyosha.

"Never trust a woman's tears, Alexey Fyodorovich. I am never for the women in such cases. I am always on the side of the men."

"Mamma, you are spoiling and ruining him," Lise's thin voice cried from behind the door.

"No, it was all my fault. I am horribly to blame," Alyosha repeated unconsoled, hiding his face in his hands in an agony of remorse for his indiscretion.

"Quite the contrary; you behaved like an angel, like an angel. I am ready to say so a thousand times over."

"Mamma, how has he behaved like an angel?" Lise's voice was heard again.

"I somehow fancied all at once," Alyosha went on as though he had not heard Lise, "that she loved Ivan, and so I said that stupid thing. . . . What will happen now?"

"To whom, to whom?" cried Lise. "Mamma, you really want to be the death of me. I ask you and you don't answer."

At the moment the maid ran in.

"Katerina Ivanovna is ill. . . . She is crying, struggling . . . in hysterics."

"What is the matter?" cried Lise, in a tone of real anxiety. "Mamma, I shall be having hysterics, and not she!"

"Lise, for mercy's sake, don't scream, don't kill me. At your age one can't know everything that grown-up people know. I'll come and tell you everything you ought to know. Oh, mercy on us! I am coming, I am coming. . . . Hysterics is a good sign, Alexey Fyodorovich; it's an excellent thing that she is hysterical. That's just as it ought to be. In such cases I am always against the woman, against all these feminine tears and hysterics. Run and say, Yulia, that I'll fly to her. As for Ivan Fyodorovich's going away like that, it's her own fault. But he won't go away. Lise, for mercy's sake, don't scream! Oh, yes; you are not screaming. It's I am screaming. Forgive your mamma; but I am delighted, delighted, delighted! Did you notice, Alexey Fyodorovich, how young, how young Ivan Fyodorovich was just now when he went out, when he said all that and went out? I thought he was so learned, such a *savant*, and all of a sudden he behaved so warmly, openly, and youthfully, with such youthful inexperience, and it was all so fine, like you. . . . And the way he repeated that German verse, it was just like you! But I must fly, I must fly! Alexey Fyodorovich, make haste to carry out her commission, and then make haste back. Lise, do you want anything now? For mercy's sake, don't keep Alexey Fyodorovich a minute. He will come back to you at once."

Madame Hohlakov at last ran off. Before leaving, Alyosha would have opened the door to see Lise.

THE BROTHERS KARAMAZOV

"On no account," cried Lise. "On no account now. Speak through the door. How have you come to be an angel? That's the only thing I want to know."

"For an awful piece of stupidity, Lise! Good-bye!"

"Don't dare to go away like that!" Lise was beginning.

"Lise, I have a real sorrow! I'll be back directly, but I have a great, great sorrow!"

And he ran out of the room.

## CHAPTER VI
### LACERATION IN THE COTTAGE

HE was really grieved in a way he had seldom been before. He had rushed in like a fool, and meddled in what? In a love-affair. "But what do I know about it? What can I tell about such things?" he repeated to himself for the hundredth time, flushing crimson. "Oh, being ashamed would be nothing; shame is but the punishment I deserve. The trouble is I shall certainly have caused more unhappiness. . . . And Father Zosima sent me to reconcile and unite. Is this the way to bring people together?" Then he suddenly remembered how he had tried to join their hands, and he felt fearfully ashamed again. "Though I acted quite sincerely, I must be more sensible in the future," he concluded suddenly, and did not even smile at his conclusion.

Katerina Ivanovna's commission took him to Ozyornaya Street, and his brother Dmitri lived close by, in a lane. Alyosha decided to go to him in any case before going to the captain, though he had a presentiment that he would not find his brother. He suspected that he would intentionally keep out of his way now, but he must find him anyhow. Time was passing: the thought of his dying elder had not left Alyosha for one minute from the time he set off from the monastery.

There was one point which interested him particularly about Katerina Ivanovna's commission: when she had mentioned the captain's son, the little schoolboy who had run beside his father crying, the idea had at once struck Alyosha that this must be the schoolboy who had bitten his finger when he, Alyosha, asked him what he had done to hurt him. Now Alyosha felt practically certain of this, though he could not have said why. Thinking of another subject was a relief, and he resolved to think no more about the "mischief" he had done, and not to torture himself with remorse, but to do what he had to do, let come what would. At that thought he was completely comforted. Turning to the street where Dmitri lodged, he felt hungry, and taking out of his pocket the roll he had brought from his father's, he ate it. It made him feel stronger.

Dmitri was not at home. The people of the house, an old cabinet-maker, his son, and his old wife, looked with positive suspicion at Alyosha. "He hasn't slept here for the last three nights. Maybe he has gone away," the old man said in answer to Alyosha's persistent inquiries. Alyosha saw that he was answering in accordance with instructions. When he asked whether he were not at Grushenka's or in hiding at Foma's (Alyosha spoke so freely on purpose), all three looked at him in alarm. "They are fond of him, they are doing their best for him," thought Alyosha. "That's good."

At last he found the house in Ozyornaya Street. It was a decrepit little house, leaning to one side, with three windows looking into the street, and with a muddy yard, in the middle of which stood a solitary cow. He crossed the yard and found the door opening into the passage. On the left of the passage lived the old woman of the house with her old daughter. Both seemed to be deaf. In answer to his repeatèd inquiry for the captain, one of them at last understood that he was asking for their lodgers, and pointed to a door across the passage. The captain's lodging turned out to be a simple cottage room. Alyosha had his hand on the iron latch to open the door, when he was struck by the strange hush within. Yet he knew from Katerina Ivanovna's words that the man had a family. "Either they are all asleep or perhaps they have heard me coming and are waiting for me to open the door. I'd better knock first," and he knocked. An answer came, but not at once, after an interval of perhaps ten seconds.

"Who's there?" shouted some one in a loud and very angry voice.

Then Alyosha opened the door and crossed the threshold. He found himself in a regular peasant's room. Though it was large, it was cumbered up with domestic belongings of all sorts, and there were several people in it. On the left was a large Russian stove. From the stove to the window on the left a rope was strung across the room, and there were rags hanging on it. There was a bedstead against the wall on each side, right and left, covered with knitted quilts. On the one on the left was a pyramid of four print-covered pillows, each smaller than the one beneath. On the other there was only one very small pillow. The opposite corner was screened off by a curtain or a sheet hung on a string. Behind this curtain could be seen a bed made up on a bench and a chair. The rough square table of plain wood had been moved against the middle window. The three windows, which consisted each of four tiny greenish mouldy panes, gave lit-

tle light, and were close shut, so that the room was not very light and rather stuffy. On the table was a frying-pan with the remains of some fried eggs, a half-eaten piece of bread, and a small bottle with a few drops of vodka.

A woman of genteel appearance, wearing a cotton gown, was sitting on a chair by the bed on the left. Her face was thin and yellow, and her sunken cheeks betrayed at the first glance that she was ill. But what struck Alyosha most was the expression in the poor woman's eyes — a look of surprised inquiry and yet of haughty pride. And while he was talking to her husband, her big brown eyes moved from one speaker to the other with the same haughty and questioning expression. Beside her at the window stood a young girl, rather plain, with scanty reddish hair, poorly but very neatly dressed. She looked disdainfully at Alyosha as he came in. Beside the other bed was sitting another female figure. She was a very pathetic creature, a young girl of about twenty, but hunchbacked and crippled, "with withered legs," as Alyosha was told afterwards. Her crutches stood in the corner close by. The strikingly beautiful and gentle eyes of this poor girl looked with mild serenity at Alyosha. A man of forty-five was sitting at the table, finishing the fried eggs. He was spare, small, and weakly built. He had reddish hair and a scanty light-coloured beard, very much like a ragged bath-mop (this comparison and the phrase "bath-mop" flashed at once into Alyosha's mind for some reason, he remembered it afterwards). It was obviously this gentleman who had shouted to him, as there was no other man in the room. But when Alyosha went in, he leapt up from the bench on which he was sitting, and, hastily wiping his mouth with a ragged napkin, darted up to Alyosha.

"It's a monk come to beg for the monastery. A nice place to come to!" the girl standing in the corner on the left said aloud. The man spun round towards her instantly and answered her in an excited and breaking voice.

"No, Varvara, you are wrong. Allow me to ask, sir," he turned again to Alyosha, "what has brought you to — our retreat?"

Alyosha looked attentively at him. It was the first time he had seen him. There was something angular, flurried, and irritable about him. Though he had obviously just been drinking, he was not drunk. There was extraordinary impudence in his expression, and yet, strange to say, at the same time there was obvious cowardice. He looked like a man who had long been kept in subjection and had submitted to it, and now had suddenly turned and was trying to assert himself. Or, better still, like a man who wants dreadfully to hit you but is horribly afraid you will hit him. In his words and in the intonation of his shrill voice there was a sort of crazy humour, at times spiteful and at times cringing, and continually shifting from one tone to another. The question about "our retreat" he had asked as it were quivering all over, rolling his eyes, and skipping up so close to Alyosha that he instinctively drew back a step. He was dressed in a very shabby dark cotton coat, patched and spotted. He wore checked trousers of an extremely light colour, long out of fashion, and of very thin material. They were so crumpled and so short that he looked as though he had grown out of them like a boy.

"I am Alexey Karamazov," Alyosha began in reply.

"I quite understand that, sir," the gentleman snapped out at once to assure him that he knew who he was already. "I am Captain Sne-giryov, sir, but I am still desirous to know precisely what has led you ——"

"Oh, I've come for nothing special. I wanted to have a word with you — if only you allow me."

"In that case, here is a chair, sir; kindly take a seat, sir. That's what they used to say in the old comedies, 'kindly take a seat,'" and with a rapid gesture he seized an empty chair (it was a rough wooden chair, not upholstered) and set it for him almost in the middle of the room; then, taking another similar chair for himself, he sat down facing Alyosha, so close to him that their knees almost touched.

"Nikolay Ilyich Snegiryov, sir, formerly a captain in the Russian infantry, put to shame for his vices, but still a captain. Though I don't talk like one now; it's in the last half of my life that I've learnt to say 'sir.' It's a word you use when you've come down in the world."

"That's very true," smiled Alyosha. "But is it used involuntarily or on purpose?"

"As God's above, it's involuntary, and I usen't to use it! I didn't use the word 'sir' all my life, but as soon as I sank into the depths I began to say 'sir.' It's the work of a higher power. I see you are interested in contemporary questions, but how can I have excited your curiosity, living as I do in surroundings impossible for the exercise of hospitality?"

"I've come — about that business."

"About what business?" the captain interrupted impatiently.

"About your meeting with my brother Dmitri Fyodorovich," Alyosha blurted out awkwardly.

"What meeting, sir? You don't mean that meeting? About my 'bath-mop,' then?" He moved closer so that his knees positively knocked against Alyosha.

His lips were strangely compressed to a thread.

"What mop?" muttered Alyosha.

"He is come to complain of me, father!" cried a voice familiar to Alyosha — the voice of the schoolboy — from behind the curtain. "I bit his finger just now." The curtain jerked back, and Alyosha saw his assailant lying on a little bed made up on the bench and the chair in the corner under the ikons. The boy lay covered by his coat and an old wadded quilt. He was evidently unwell, and, judging by his glittering eyes, he was in a fever. He looked at Alyosha without fear, as though he felt he was at home and could not be touched.

"What! Did he bite your finger?" The captain jumped up from his chair. "Was it your finger he bit?"

"Yes. He was throwing stones at schoolboys who were stoning him. There were six of them against him alone. I went up to him, and he threw a stone at me and then another at my head. I asked him what I had done to him. And then he rushed at me and bit my finger badly, I don't know why."

"I'll thrash him, sir, at once — this minute!" The captain jumped up from his seat.

"But I am not complaining at all, I am simply telling you. . . . I don't want him to be thrashed. Besides, he seems to be ill."

"And do you suppose I'd thrash him? That I'd take my Ilusha and thrash him before you for your satisfaction? Would you like it done at once, sir?" said the captain, suddenly turning to Alyosha, as though he were going to attack him. "I am sorry about your finger, sir; but instead of thrashing Ilusha, would you like me to chop off my four fingers with this knife here before your eyes to satisfy your just wrath? I should think four fingers would be enough to satisfy your thirst for vengeance. You won't ask for the fifth one, too?" He stopped short with a catch in his throat. Every feature in his face was twitching and working; he looked extremely defiant. He was in a sort of frenzy.

"I think I understand it all now," said Alyosha gently and sorrowfully, still keeping his seat. "So your boy is a good boy, he loves his father, and he attacked me as the brother of your assailant. . . . Now I understand it," he repeated thoughtfully. "But my brother Dmitri Fyodorovich regrets his action, I know that, and if only it is possible for him to come to you, or better still, to meet you in that same place, he will ask your forgiveness before every one — if you wish it."

"After pulling out my beard, you mean, he will ask my forgiveness? And he thinks that will be a satisfactory finish, doesn't he?"

"Oh, no! On the contrary, he will do anything you like and in any way you like."

"So if I were to ask his Excellency to go down on his knees before me in that very tavern — 'The Metropolis' it's called — or in the market-place, he would do it?"

"Yes, he would even go down on his knees."

"You've pierced me to the heart, sir. Touched me to tears and pierced me to the heart, sir. I am only too sensible of your brother's generosity. Allow me to introduce my family, my two daughters and my son — my litter. If I die, who will care for them, sir, and while I live who but they will care for a wretch like me? That's a great thing the Lord has ordained for every man of my sort, sir. For there must be some one able to love even a man like me."

"Ah, that's perfectly true!" exclaimed Alyosha.

"Oh, do leave off playing the buffoon! Some fool comes in, and you put us to shame!" cried the girl by the window, suddenly turning to her father with a scornful and contemptuous air.

"Wait a little, Varvara! Permit me to sustain my tone," cried her father, speaking peremptorily but looking at her quite approvingly. "That's her character," he said, addressing Alyosha again.

*And in all nature there was naught*
*Whereon he let his blessing fall . . .*

or rather in the feminine: whereon she let her blessing fall. But now let me present you to my spouse, Arina Petrovna. She is crippled, sir, she is forty-three; she can move, but very little, sir. She is of humble origin. Arina Petrovna, compose your countenance. This is Alexey Fyodorovich Karamazov. Get up, Alexey Fyodorovich." He took him by the hand and with unexpected force pulled him up. "You must stand up to be introduced to a lady. It's not the Karamazov, mamma, who . . . h'm . . . et cetera, but his brother, radiant with modest virtues. Come, Arina Petrovna, come, mamma, first your hand to be kissed."

And he kissed his wife's hand respectfully and even tenderly. The girl at the window turned her back indignantly on the scene; an expression of extraordinary cordiality came over the haughtily inquiring face of the woman.

"Good morning! Sit down, Mr. Chernomazov," she said.

"Karamazov, mamma, Karamazov (we are of humble origin)," he whispered again.

"Well, Karamazov, or whatever it is, but I always think of Chernomazov. . . . Sit down.

Why has he pulled you up? He calls me crippled but I am not, only my legs are swollen like barrels, and I am shrivelled up myself. Once I used to be so fat, but now it's as though I had swallowed a needle."

"We are of humble origin, sir," the captain muttered again.

"Oh, father, father!" the hunchback girl, who had till then been silent on her chair, said suddenly, and she hid her eyes in her handkerchief.

"Clown!" blurted out the girl at the window.

"Have you heard our news?" said the mother, pointing at her daughters. "It's like clouds blowing over; the clouds pass and we have music again. When we were with the army, we used to have many such guests. I don't mean to make any comparisons, young man; every one to his taste. The deacon's wife used to come then and say, 'Alexander Alexandrovich is a man of the noblest heart, but Nastasya Petrovna,' she would say, 'is a child of hell.' 'Well,' I said, 'that's a matter of taste; but you are a small one, but a skunk.' 'And you want keeping in your place,' says she. 'You black sword,' said I, 'who asked you to teach me?' 'But my breath,' says she, 'is clean, and yours is unclean.' 'You ask all the officers whether my breath is unclean,' and ever since then I had it in my mind. Not long ago I was sitting here as I am now, when I saw that very general come in who came here at Easter, and I asked him: 'Your Excellency,' said I, 'could a noble lady let in fresh air?' 'Yes,' he answered; 'you ought to open a window or open the door, for the air is not fresh here.' And they all go on like that! And what is my breath to them? The dead smell worse still! 'I won't spoil the air,' said I, 'I'll order shoes and go away.' My darlings, don't reproach your own mother! Nikolay Ilyich, how is it I can't please you? There's only Ilusha who comes home from school and loves me. Yesterday he brought me an apple. Forgive your own mother — forgive a poor lonely creature! Why has my breath become unpleasant to you?" And the poor mad woman broke into sobs, and tears streamed down her cheeks. The captain rushed up to her.

"Mamma, mamma, my dear, give over! You are not lonely. Every one loves you, every one adores you." He began kissing both her hands again and tenderly stroking her face; taking the napkin, he began wiping away her tears. Alyosha fancied that he, too, had tears in his eyes. "There, you see, you hear?" he turned with a sort of fury to Alyosha, pointing to the poor imbecile.

"I see and hear," muttered Alyosha.

"Father, father, how can you — with him! Let him alone!" cried the boy, sitting up in his bed and gazing at his father with glowing eyes.

"Do give over clowning, stop your silly antics which never lead to anything!" shouted Varvara, stamping her foot with passion.

"Your anger is quite just this time, Varvara, and I'll make haste to satisfy you. Come, put on your cap, Alexey Fyodorovich, and I'll put on mine. We will go out. I have a word to say to you in earnest, but not within these walls. This girl sitting here is my daughter Nina; I forgot to introduce her to you. She is a heavenly angel incarnate . . . who has flown down to us mortals . . . if you can understand."

"There he is shaking all over, as though he were in convulsions!" Varvara went on indignantly.

"And she there stamping her foot at me and calling me a clown just now, she is a heavenly angel incarnate, too, and she has good reason to call me so. Come along, Alexey Fyodorovich, we must make an end."

And, snatching Alyosha's hand, he drew him out of the room into the street.

## CHAPTER VII
### AND IN THE OPEN AIR

"THE air is fresh, but in my mansion it is not so in any sense of the word. Let us walk slowly, sir. I should like very much to engage your interest, sir."

"I, too, have something important to say to you," observed Alyosha, "only I don't know how to begin."

"To be sure you must have business with me. You would never have looked in upon me without some object. Unless you come simply to complain of the boy, and that's hardly likely. And, by the way, sir, about the boy: I could not explain to you in there, but here I will describe that scene to you. You see, sir, my mop was thicker a week ago — I mean my beard. That's the nickname they have given my beard, the schoolboys most of all, sir. Well, your brother Dmitri Fyodorovich was pulling me by the beard — he dragged me out of the tavern into the square; at that moment the boys were coming out of school, and with them Ilusha. As soon as he saw me in such a state, sir, he rushed up to me. 'Papa,' he cried, 'papa!' He caught hold of me, hugged me, tried to pull me away, crying to my assailant, 'Let go, let go, it's my father, forgive him!' — yes, he actually cried, 'forgive him.' He clutched at that hand, that very hand, sir, with his little hands and kissed it, sir. . . . I remember his little face at that moment, I haven't forgotten it, sir, and I never shall!''

"I swear," cried Alyosha, "that my brother will express his most deep and sincere regret, even if he has to go down on his knees in that same square. . . . I'll make him or he is no brother of mine!"

"Aha, then it's only your idea! And it does not come directly from him but simply from the generosity of your own ardent heart. You should have said so, sir. No, in that case allow me to finish telling you of your brother's highly chivalrous, soldierly high-mindedness, for he did give expression to it at the time, sir. He left off dragging me by the beard and released me: 'You are an officer,' he said, 'and I am an officer, if you can find a decent man to be your second, send me your challenge. I will give you satisfaction, though you are a scoundrel.' That's what he said, sir. A chivalrous spirit indeed! I retired with Ilusha, and that scene is a family record imprinted for ever on Ilusha's soul, sir. No, it's not for us to claim the privileges of the gentry, sir. Judge for yourself. You've just been in our mansion, what did you see there? Three ladies, one a cripple and weak-minded, another a cripple and hunchback, and the third not crippled but far too clever. She is a student, dying to get back to Petersburg, to work for the emancipation of the Russian woman on the banks of the Neva. I won't speak of Ilusha, sir, he is only nine. He is alone in the world, for if I die, what will become of all of them, I simply ask you that, sir. And if I challenge him and he kills me on the spot, what then? What will become of them all? And worse still, if he doesn't kill me but only cripples me: I couldn't work, but I should still be a mouth to feed. Who would feed it, sir, and who would feed them all? Must I take Ilusha from school and send

him to beg in the streets? That's what it means for me to challenge him to a duel, sir. It's silly talk and nothing else."

"He will beg your forgiveness, he will bow down at your feet in the middle of the square," cried Alyosha again, with glowing eyes.

"I did think of prosecuting him," the captain went on, "but look in our code, sir, could I get much compensation for a personal injury? And then Agrafena Alexandrovna* sent for me and shouted at me: 'Don't dare to dream of it! If you proceed against him, I'll publish it to all the world that he beat you for your dishonesty, and then you will be prosecuted.' I call God to witness whose was the dishonesty and on whose instructions I acted, I, a mere pawn — wasn't it by her own and Fyodor Pavlovich's? 'And what's more,' she went on, 'I'll dismiss you for good and you'll never earn another penny from me. I'll speak to my merchant, too (that's what she calls her old man), and he, too, will chase you out!' And if he dismisses me, how can I earn anything? Those two are all I have to look to, for your father has not only given over employing me, for another reason, but he means to make use of papers I've signed to drag me to court. And so I kept quiet, and you have seen my family, sir. But now let me ask you: did Ilusha bite your finger badly? I didn't like to go into it in our mansion before him."

"Yes, very badly, and he was greatly irritated. He was avenging you on me as a Karamazov, I see that now. But if only you had seen how he was throwing stones at his schoolfellows! It's very dangerous. They might kill him. They are children and stupid. A stone may be thrown and break somebody's head."

"That's just what has happened. He has

* Grushenka.

been bruised by a stone to-day, sir. Not on the head but on the chest, just above the heart. He came home crying and groaning and now he is ill."

"And you know he attacks them first. He is bitter against them on your account. They say he stabbed a boy called Krasotkin with a penknife not long ago."

"I've heard about that, too, it's dangerous, sir. Krasotkin is an official here, we may hear more about it."

"I would advise you," Alyosha went on warmly, "not to send him to school at all for a time till he is calmer . . . and his anger has subsided."

"Anger!" the captain repeated, "anger indeed, sir. In a small creature, a mighty anger. You don't know all, sir. Let me tell you more. Since that incident all the boys have been teasing him about the 'bath-mop.' Schoolboys are a merciless crew; individually they are angels, but together, especially at school, they are often merciless. They began to tease him and a gallant spirit arose in Ilusha. An ordinary boy, a weak son, would have submitted, would have felt ashamed of his father, sir, but he stood up for his father against them all. For his father and for truth and justice, sir. For what he suffered when he kissed your brother's hand and cried to him, 'forgive father, forgive him' — that only God knows — and I, sir. For our children — not your children, but ours — the children of the poor gentlemen looked down upon by every one — know what justice means, sir, even at nine years old. How should the rich know? They don't explore such depths once in their lives. But at that moment in the square when he kissed his hand, at that moment my Ilusha had grasped all that justice means. That truth

entered into him and crushed him for ever, sir," the captain said hotly again with a sort of frenzy, and he struck his right fist against his left palm as though he wanted to show how "the truth" had crushed Ilusha. "That very day, sir, he fell ill with fever and was delirious all night. All that day he hardly said a word to me, but I noticed he kept watching me from the corner, though he turned to the window and pretended to be learning his lessons. But I could see his mind was not on his lessons. Next day I got drunk to forget my troubles, sinful man that I am, sir, and I don't remember much, sir. Mamma began crying, too — I am very fond of mamma — well, I spent my last penny drowning my troubles. Don't despise me for that, sir, in Russia men who drink are the best. The best men amongst us are the greatest drunkards. I lay down and I don't remember about Ilusha, though all that day the boys had been jeering at him at school. 'Bath-mop,' they shouted, 'your father was pulled out of the tavern by his ragged mop, you ran by and begged forgiveness.'

"On the third day when he came back from school, I saw he looked pale and wretched. 'What is it?' I asked. He wouldn't answer. Well, there's no talking in our mansion without mamma and the girls taking part in it. What's more, the girls had heard about it the very first day. Varvara had begun snarling. 'You fools and buffoons, can you ever do anything sensible?' 'Quite so,' I said, 'can we ever do anything sensible?' for the time I turned it off like that. So in the evening I took the boy out for a walk, sir, for you must know we go for a walk every evening, always the same way, along which we are going now — from our gate to that great stone which lies alone in the road under the hurdle, which marks the

155

beginning of the town pasture. A beautiful and lonely spot, sir. Ilusha and I walked along hand in hand as usual. He has a little hand, his fingers are thin and cold — he has trouble with his chest, you know. 'Father,' says he, 'father!' 'Well?' say I. I saw his eyes flashing. 'Father, what he did to you then!' 'It can't be helped, Ilusha,' I say. 'Don't make up with him, father, don't make up with him! At school they say that he has paid you ten roubles for it.' 'No, Ilusha,' say I, 'I would not take money from him for anything.' Then he began trembling all over, took my hand in both his and kissed it again. 'Father,' he says, 'father, challenge him to a duel, at school they say you are a coward and won't challenge him, and that you'll accept ten roubles from him.' 'I can't challenge him to a duel, Ilusha,' I answered. And I told him briefly what I've just told you. He listened. 'Father,' he said, 'anyway don't make up with him. When I grow up I'll call him out myself and kill him.' His eyes flashed and burned. Well, of course I am his father, and I had to tell him what's right: 'It's a sin to kill,' I said, 'even in a duel.' 'Father,' he said, 'when I grow up, I'll knock him down, knock the sword out of his hand with my own sword, I'll fall on him, wave my sword over him and say: "I could kill you, but I forgive you, so there!"' You see what the workings of his little mind have been during these two days; he must have been planning that vengeance all day, and raving about it at night.

"But he began to come home from school badly beaten, I found out about it the day before yesterday, and you are right, I won't send him to that school any more, sir. I heard that he was standing up alone against all the class and defying them all, that his heart was full of resentment, of bitterness — I was alarmed about him. We went for a walk again. 'Father,' he asked, 'are the rich people stronger than any one else on earth?' 'Yes, Ilusha,' I said, 'there are no people on earth stronger than the rich.' 'Father,' he said, 'I will get rich, I will become an officer and conquer everybody. The Tsar will reward me, I will come back here and then no one will dare . . .' Then he was silent and his lips still kept trembling. 'Father,' he said, 'what a horrid town this is.' 'Yes, Ilusha,' I said, 'it isn't a very nice town.' 'Father, let us move into another town, a nice one,' he said, 'where people don't know about us.' 'We will move, we will, Ilusha,' said I, 'only I must save up for it.' I was glad to be able to turn his mind from painful thoughts, and we began to dream of how we would move to another town, how we would buy a horse and cart. 'We will put mamma and your sisters inside, we will cover them up and we'll walk, you shall have a lift now and then, and I'll walk beside, for we must spare our horse, we can't all ride. That's how we'll go.' He was enchanted at that, most of all at the thought of having a horse and driving him. For of course a Russian boy is born with the idea of a horse. We chatted a long while. Thank God, I thought, I have diverted his mind and comforted him.

"That was the day before yesterday, in the evening, but last night everything was changed. He had gone to school in the morning, he came back depressed, terribly depressed. In the evening I took him by the hand and we went for a walk; he would not talk. There was a wind blowing and no sun, and a feeling of autumn; twilight was coming on. We walked along, both of us depressed. 'Well, my boy,' said I, 'how about our setting off on our travels?' I thought I might bring him back

"AND IN THE OPEN AIR"

to our talk of the day before. He didn't answer, but I felt his fingers trembling in my hand. Ah, I thought, it's a bad job; there's something new. We had reached the stone where we are now. I sat down on the stone. And in the air there were lots of kites flapping and whirling. There were as many as thirty in sight. Of course, it's just the season for the kites. 'Look, Ilusha,' said I, 'it's time we got out our last year's kite again. I'll mend it, where have you put it away?' My boy made no answer. He looked away and turned sideways to me. And then a gust of wind blew up the sand. He suddenly fell on me, threw both his little arms round my neck and held me tight. You know, when children are silent and proud, and try to keep back their tears when they are in great trouble and suddenly break down, their tears flow in streams. With those warm streams of tears, he suddenly wetted my face. He sobbed and shook as though he were in convulsions, and squeezed up against me as I sat on the stone. 'Father,' he kept crying, 'dear father, how he insulted you!' And I sobbed, too. We sat shaking in each other's arms. 'Ilusha,' I said to him, 'Ilusha darling.' No one saw us then. God alone saw us, I hope he will record it to my credit, sir. You must thank your brother, Alexey Fyodorovich. No, sir, I won't thrash my boy for your satisfaction."

He had gone back to his original tone of resentful buffoonery. Alyosha felt, though, that he trusted him, and that if there had been some one else in his, Alyosha's, place, the man would not have spoken so openly and would not have told what he had just told. This encouraged Alyosha, whose heart was trembling with inward tears.

"Ah, how I would like to make friends with your boy!" he cried. "If you could arrange it ——"

"Certainly, sir," muttered the captain.

"But now listen to something quite different!" Alyosha went on. "I have a message for you. That same brother of mine, Dmitri, has insulted his betrothed, too, a noble-hearted girl of whom you have probably heard. I have a right to tell you of her wrong; I ought to do so, in fact, for hearing of the insult done to you and learning all about your unfortunate position, she commissioned me at once — just now — to bring you this help from her — but only from her alone, not from Dmitri, who has abandoned her. Nor from me, his brother, nor from any one else, but from her, only from her! She entreats you to accept her help. . . . You have both been insulted by the same man. She thought of you only when she had just received a similar insult from him — similar in its cruelty, I mean. She comes like a sister to help a brother in misfortune. . . . She told me to persuade you to take these two hundred roubles from her, as from a sister, knowing that you are in such need. No one will know of it, it can give rise to no unjust slander. There are the two hundred roubles, and I swear you must take them unless — unless all men are to be enemies on earth! But there are brothers even on earth. . . . You have a generous heart . . . you must see that, you must," and Alyosha held out two new rainbow-coloured hundred-rouble notes.

They were both standing at the time by the great stone close to the fence, and there was no one near. The notes seemed to produce a tremendous impression on the captain. He started, but at first only from astonishment. Such an outcome of their conversation was the last thing he had expected. Nothing could have been further from his dreams than help from any one — and such a sum!

He took the notes, and for a minute he was almost unable to answer, quite a new expression came into his face.

"That for me? So much money — two hundred roubles! Good heavens! Why, I haven't seen so much money for the last four years! Mercy on us! And she says she is a sister . . . And is that the truth?"

"I swear that all I told you is the truth," cried Alyosha.

The captain flushed red.

"Listen, my dear, listen. If I take it, I shan't be behaving like a scoundrel? In your eyes, Alexey Fyodorovich, I shan't be a scoundrel? No, Alexey Fyodorovich, listen, listen," he said hurriedly, touching Alyosha with both his hands. "You are persuading me to take it, saying that it's a sister sends it, but inwardly, in your heart won't you feel contempt for me if I take it, eh?"

"No, no, on my salvation I swear I shan't! And no one will ever know but me — I, you, and she, and one other lady, her great friend."

"Never mind the lady! Listen, Alexey Fyodorovich, at a moment like this you must listen, for you can't understand what these two hundred roubles mean to me now." The poor fellow went on rising gradually into a sort of incoherent, almost wild enthusiasm. He was thrown off his balance and talked extremely fast, as though afraid he would not be allowed to say all he had to say.

"Besides it's being honestly acquired from a 'sister,' so highly respected and revered, do you know that now I can look after mamma and Nina, my hunchback angel daughter? Dr. Herzenstube came to me in the kindness of his heart and was examining them both for a whole hour. 'I can make nothing of it,' said he, but he prescribed a mineral water which is to be had at a chemist's here. He said it would be sure to do her good, and he ordered foot-baths, too, with some medicine in them. The mineral water costs thirty copecks, and she'd need to drink forty bottles perhaps; so I took the prescription and laid it on the shelf under the ikons, and there it lies. And he ordered hot baths for Nina with something dissolved in them, morning and evening. But how can we carry out such a cure in our mansion, without servants, without help, without a tub, and without water? Nina is rheumatic all over, I don't think I told you that. All her right side aches at night, she is in agony, and, would you believe it, the angel bears it without groaning for fear of waking us. We eat what we can get, and she'll only take the leavings, what you'd scarcely give to a dog. 'I am not worth it, I am taking it from you, I am a burden on you,' that's what her angel eyes try to express. We wait on her, but she doesn't like it. 'I am a useless cripple, no good to any one.' As though she were not worth it, when she is the salvation of all of us with her angelic sweetness. Without her, without her gentle word it would be hell among us! She softens even Varvara. And don't judge Varvara harshly either, she is an angel, too; she, too, has suffered wrong. She came to us for the summer, and she brought sixteen roubles she had earned by lessons and saved up, to go back with to Petersburg in September, that is now. But we took her money and ate it up, so now she has nothing to go back with. Though indeed she couldn't go back, for she has to work for us like a slave. She is like an overdriven horse with all of us on her back. She waits on us all, mends and washes, sweeps the floor, puts mamma to bed. And mamma is capricious and tearful and insane! And now I can get a servant with this money, you understand, Alexey Fyodorovich, I can get medicines for the dear creatures, I can send my student to Petersburg, I can buy beef, I can feed them properly. Good Lord, but it's a dream!"

Alyosha was delighted that he had brought him such happiness and that the poor fellow had consented to be made happy.

"Wait, Alexey Fyodorovich, wait," the captain began to talk with frenzied rapidity carried away by a new daydream. "Do you know that Ilusha and I will perhaps really carry out our dream. We will buy a horse and cart, a black horse, he insists on its being black, and we will set off as we pretended the other day. I have an old friend, a lawyer in K. province, and I heard through a trustworthy man that if I were to go he'd give me a place as clerk in his office, so, who knows, maybe he would. So I'd just put mamma and Nina in the cart, and Ilusha could drive, and I'd walk, I'd walk. . . . Why, if I only succeed in getting one debt paid that's owing me, I should have perhaps enough for that, too!"

"There would be enough!" cried Alyosha. "Katerina Ivanovna will send you as much more as you need, and you know I have money, too; take what you want, as you would from a brother, from a friend, you can give it back later. . . . (You'll get rich, you'll get rich!) And you know you couldn't have a better idea than to move to another province! It would be the saving of you, especially of your boy — and you ought to go quickly, before the winter, before the cold. You must write to us when you are there, and we will always be brothers. . . . No, it's not a dream!"

Alyosha was about to hug him, he was so

pleased. But glancing at him he stopped short. The man was standing with his neck outstretched and his lips protruding, with a pale and frenzied face. His lips were moving as though trying to articulate something; no sound came, but still his lips moved. It was uncanny.

"What is it?" asked Alyosha, startled.

"Alexey Fyodorovich . . . I . . . you," muttered the captain, faltering, looking at him with a strange, wild, fixed stare, and an air of desperate resolution. At the same time there was a sort of grin on his lips. "I, sir . . . you, sir . . . wouldn't you like me to show you a little trick I know?" he murmured, suddenly, in a firm rapid whisper, his voice no longer faltering.

"What trick?"

"A pretty trick, a bit of hocus-pocus," whispered the captain. His mouth was twisted on the left side, his left eye was screwed up. He still stared at Alyosha.

"What is the matter, what trick?" Alyosha cried, now thoroughly alarmed.

"Why, look," squealed the captain suddenly, and showing him the two notes which he had been holding by one corner between his thumb and forefinger during the conversation, he crumpled them up savagely and squeezed them tight in his right hand. "Do you see, do you see?" he shrieked, pale and infuriated. And suddenly flinging up his hand, he threw the crumpled notes on the sand. "Do you see?" he shrieked again, pointing to them. "Look there!"

And with wild fury he began trampling them under his heel, gasping and exclaiming as he did so: "Here's your money, sir! Here's your money, sir! Here's your money, sir! Here's your money, sir!"

Suddenly he darted back and drew himself up before Alyosha, and his whole figure expressed unutterable pride.

"Tell those who sent you that the bath-mop does not sell his honour," he cried, raising his arm in the air. Then he turned quickly and began to run; but he had not run five steps before he turned completely round and kissed his hand to Alyosha. He ran another five paces and then turned round for the last time. This time his face was not contorted with laughter, but quivering all over with tears. In a tearful, faltering, sobbing voice he cried:

"What should I say to my boy if I took money from you for our shame?"

And then he ran on without turning. Alyosha looked after him, inexpressibly grieved. Oh, he saw that till the very last moment the man had not known he would crumple up and fling away the notes. He did not turn back. Alyosha knew he would not. He would not follow him and call him back, he knew why. When he was out of sight, Alyosha picked up the two notes. They were very much crushed and crumpled, and had been pressed into the sand, but were uninjured and even rustled like new ones when Alyosha unfolded them and smoothed them out. After smoothing them out, he folded them up, put them in his pocket and went to Katerina Ivanovna to report on the success of her commission.

# BOOK V

# PRO AND CONTRA

## CHAPTER I
### THE ENGAGEMENT

MADAME HOHLAKOV was again the first to meet Alyosha. She was flustered; something important had happened. Katerina Ivanovna's hysterics had ended in a fainting fit, and then "a terrible, awful weakness had followed, she lay with her eyes turned up and was delirious. Now she was in a fever. They had sent for Herzenstube; they had sent for the aunts. The aunts were already here, but Herzenstube had not yet come. They were all sitting in her room, waiting. She was unconscious now, and what if it turned out to be brain fever!"

Madame Hohlakov looked gravely alarmed. "This is serious, serious," she added at every word, as though nothing that had happened to her before had been serious. Alyosha listened with distress, and began to describe his adventures, but she interrupted him at the first words. She had not time to listen. She begged him to sit with Lise and wait for her there.

"Lise," she whispered almost in his ear, "Lise has greatly surprised me just now, dear Alexey Fyodorovich. She touched me, too, and so my heart forgives her everything. Only fancy, as soon as you had gone, she began to be sincerely remorseful for having laughed at you to-day and yesterday, though she was not laughing at you, but only joking. But she was seriously sorry for it, almost ready to cry, so that I was quite surprised. She has never been really sorry for laughing at me, but has only made a joke of it. And you know she is laughing at me every minute. But this time she was in earnest. Now she is in earnest about everything. She thinks a great deal of your opinion, Alexey Fyodorovich, and don't take offence or be wounded by her if you can help it. For my part, I am always lenient towards her, for she's such a clever little thing — would you believe it? She said just now that you were a friend of her childhood, 'the greatest friend of her childhood' — just think of that — 'greatest friend' — and what about me? In that respect, she has very strong feelings and memories, and, what's more, she has these phrases, most unexpected words, which come out all of a sudden when you least expect them. She spoke lately about a pine-tree, for instance: there used to be a pine-tree in our garden in her early childhood. Very likely it's standing there still; so there's no need to speak in the past tense. Pine-trees are not like people, Alexey Fyodorovich, they don't change quickly. 'Mamma,' she said, 'I remember this pine-tree as in a dream,' only she said

something so original about it that I can't repeat it. Besides, I've forgotten it. Well, good-bye! I am so worried I feel I shall go out of my mind. Ah! Alexey Fyodorovich, I've been out of my mind twice in my life, and I was being treated for it. Go to Lise, cheer her up, as you always can so charmingly. Lise," she cried, going to her door, "here I've brought you Alexey Fyodorovich, whom you insulted so. He is not at all angry, I assure you; on the contrary, he is surprised that you could imagine it."

"*Merci, maman.* Come in, Alexey Fyodorovich."

Alyosha went in. Lise looked rather embarrassed, and at once flushed crimson. She was evidently ashamed of something, and, as people always do in such cases, she began immediately talking of other things, as though they alone were of absorbing interest to her at the moment.

"Mamma has just told me all about the two hundred roubles, Alexey Fyodorovich, and your taking them to that poor officer . . . and she told me the whole awful story of how he had been insulted . . . and you know, although mamma muddles things . . . she always rushes from one thing to another . . . I cried listening to it. Well, did you give him the money and how is that poor man getting on?"

"The fact is I didn't give it to him, and it's a long story," answered Alyosha, as though he, too, could think of nothing but his regret at having failed, yet Lise saw perfectly well that he, too, looked away, and that he, too, was trying to talk of other things.

Alyosha sat down at the table and began to tell his story, but at the first words he lost his embarrassment and gained Lise's complete attention as well. He spoke with deep feeling, under the influence of the strong impression he had just received, and he succeeded in telling his story well and circumstantially. In the old days in Moscow, when Lise was a child, he had been fond of coming to Lise and describing to her what had just happened to him, what he had read, or what he remembered of his childhood. Sometimes they had made day-dreams and woven whole romances together — generally cheerful and amusing ones. Now they both felt suddenly transported to the old days in Moscow, two years before. Lise was deeply touched by his story. Alyosha, mastered by his emotion, succeeded in bringing the image of Ilusha clearly before her. When he finished describing the scene in which the luckless man trampled on the money, Lise could not help striking her hands together and crying out:

"So you didn't give him the money! So you let him run away! Oh, dear, you ought to have run after him!"

"No, Lise; it's better I didn't run after him," said Alyosha, getting up from his chair and walking across the room with a careworn look.

"How so? How is it better? Now they are without food and they will perish."

"They will not perish, for the two hundred roubles will come to them yet. He'll take the money to-morrow. To-morrow he will be sure to take it," said Alyosha, pacing up and down, pondering. "You see, Lise," he went on, stopping suddenly before her, "I made one blunder, but that, even that, is all for the best."

"What blunder, and why is it for the best?"

"I'll tell you. He is a man of weak and cowardly character; he has suffered so much and is very good-natured. I keep wondering why he took offence so suddenly, and trampled on the notes, for I assure you, up to the last minute, he did not know that he was going to trample on the money. And I think now that there was a great deal to offend him . . . and it could not have been otherwise in his position. . . . To begin with, he was vexed at having shown himself so overjoyed by the money in my presence and not having concealed it from me. If he had been pleased, but not so much; if he had not shown it; if he had begun affecting scruples and making difficulties, as other people do when they take money, he might still have endured taking it. But he was too genuinely delighted, and that was mortifying. Ah, Lise, he is a good and truthful man — that's the worst of the whole business in such cases. All the while he talked his voice was so weak, so broken, he talked so fast, so fast, he kept tittering so, or else he was crying — yes, I am sure he was crying, he was in such transports — and he talked about his daughters — and about the position he could get in another town. . . . And when he had poured out his heart, he felt ashamed at having shown me his inmost soul like that. So he began to hate me at once. He is one of those awfully sensitive poor people. What had made him feel most ashamed was that he had given in too soon and accepted me as a friend, you see. At first he had almost flown at me and tried to intimidate me, but as soon as he saw the money he began embracing me; he kept touching me with his hands. This must have been how he came to feel so humiliated by it all, and then I made that blunder, a very grave one. I suddenly said to him that if he had not money enough to move to another town, we would give it to him, and, indeed, I myself would give him as much as he wanted out of my own money. That struck him all at once. Why, he thought, did I put myself forward to help him? You know, Lise, it's awfully hard for a man who has suffered insults, when other people look at him as though they were his benefactors. . . . I've heard that; Father Zosima told me so. I don't know how to put it, but I have often seen it myself. And I feel like that myself, too. And the worst of it was that though he did not know, up to the very last minute, that he would trample on the notes, he had a kind of presentiment of it, I am sure of that. That's just what made him so ecstatic, that he had that presentiment. . . . And though it's so dreadful, it's all for the best. In fact, I believe nothing better could have happened."

"Why, why could nothing better have happened?" cried Lise, looking with great surprise at Alyosha.

"Because if he had taken the money, an hour after getting home, he would be crying with mortification, that's just what would have happened. And most likely he would have come to me early to-morrow, and perhaps have flung the notes at me and trampled upon them as he did just now. But now he has gone home awfully proud and triumphant, though he knows he has 'ruined himself.' So now nothing could be easier than to make him accept the two hundred roubles by to-morrow, for he has already vindicated his honour, tossed away the money, and trampled it under foot. . . . He couldn't know when he did it that I should bring it to him again to-morrow, and yet he is in terrible need of that money. Though he is proud of himself now, yet even to-day he'll be thinking what a help he has lost. He will think of it more than ever at night, will dream of it, and by to-morrow

morning he may be ready to run to me to ask forgiveness. It's just then that I'll appear. 'Here, you are a proud man,' I shall say: 'you have proved it; but now take the money and forgive us!' And then he will take it!"

Alyosha was carried away with joy as he uttered the last words. "And then he will take it!" Lise clapped her hands.

"Ah, that's true! I understand that perfectly now. Ah, Alyosha, how do you know all this? So young and yet he knows what's in the heart. . . . I should never have worked it out."

"The great thing now is to persuade him that he is on an equal footing with us, in spite of his taking money from us," Alyosha went on in his excitement, "and not only on an equal, but even on a higher footing."

"On a higher footing is charming, Alexey Fyodorovich; but go on, go on!"

"You mean there isn't such an expression as 'on a higher footing'; but that doesn't matter because —— "

"Oh, no, of course it doesn't matter. Forgive me, Alyosha, dear. . . . You know, I scarcely respected you till now — that is, I respected you but on an equal footing; but now I shall begin to respect you on a higher footing. Don't be angry, dear, at my joking," she put in at once, with strong feeling. "I am ridiculous and small, but you, you! Listen, Alexey Fyodorovich. Isn't there in all our analysis — I mean your analysis . . . no, better call it ours — aren't we showing contempt for him, for that poor man — in analysing his soul like this, as it were, from above, eh? In deciding so certainly that he will take the money?"

"No, Lise, it's not contempt," Alyosha answered, as though he had prepared himself for the question. "I was thinking of that on the way here. How can it be contempt when we are all like him, when we are all just the same as he is. For you know we are just the same, no better. And if we were better, we should still have been just the same in his place. . . . I don't know about you, Lise, but I consider that I have a petty soul in many ways, and his soul is not petty; on the contrary, full of fine feeling. . . . No, Lise, I have no contempt for him. Do you know, Lise, my elder once said: one must take care of most people exactly as one would of children, and of some of them as one would of the sick in hospitals."

"Ah, Alexey Fyodorovich, dear, let us take care of people as we would of the sick!"

"Let us, Lise; I am ready. Though I am not really ready. I am sometimes very impatient and at other times I don't see things. It's different with you."

"Ah, I don't believe it! Alexey Fyodorovich, how happy I am."

"I am so glad you say so, Lise."

"Alexey Fyodorovich, you are wonderfully good, but you are sometimes a kind of pedant. . . . And yet you are not really a pedant at all. Go to the door, open it gently, and see whether mamma is eavesdropping," said Lise, in a nervous, hurried whisper.

Alyosha went, opened the door, and reported that no one was listening.

"Come here, Alexey Fyodorovich," Lise went on, flushing redder and redder. "Give me your hand — so. I have to make a great confession, I didn't write to you yesterday in jest, but in earnest," and she hid her eyes with her hand. It was evident that she was greatly ashamed of the confession.

Suddenly she snatched his hand and impulsively kissed it three times.

"Ah, Lise, what a fine thing!" cried Alyosha joyfully. "You know, I was perfectly sure you were in earnest."

"Sure? Upon my word!" She put aside his hand, but did not let go of it, blushing hotly, and laughing a little happy laugh. "I kiss his hand and he says, 'What a fine thing.'"

But her reproach was undeserved, Alyosha, too, was in great confusion.

"I should like to please you always, Lise, but I don't know how to do it," he muttered, blushing too.

"Alyosha, dear, you are cold and rude. Do you see? He has chosen me as his wife and is quite settled about it. He is sure that I wrote in earnest. What a thing to say! Why, that's impertinence — that's what it is."

"Why, was it wrong of me to feel sure?" Alyosha asked, laughing suddenly.

"Ah, Alyosha, on the contrary, it was altogether right," cried Lise, looking tenderly and happily at him.

Alyosha stood still, holding her hand in his. Suddenly he stooped down and kissed her on her lips.

"What's that you're doing? What is it?" cried Lise. Alyosha was terribly abashed.

"Oh, forgive me if I shouldn't. . . . Perhaps I'm awfully stupid. . . . You said I was cold, so I kissed you. . . . But I see it was stupid."

Lise laughed, and hid her face in her hands. "And in that costume!" she ejaculated in the midst of her mirth. But she suddenly ceased laughing and became serious, almost stern.

"Alyosha, we must put off kissing, because neither of us knows how, and we shall have a long time to wait," she ended suddenly. "Tell me rather why you who are so clever, so intellectual, so observant, choose a little idiot, an invalid like me? Ah, Alyosha, I am awfully happy for I don't deserve you a bit."

"You do, Lise. I shall be leaving the monastery altogether in a few days. If I go into the world, I must marry. I know that. *He* told me to marry, too. Whom could I marry better than you — and who would have me except you? I have been thinking it over. In the first place, you've known me from childhood on; and in the second place, you've a great many qualities I haven't. You have a more joyous soul than I; above all, you are more innocent than I am. I have been brought into contact with many, many things already. . . . Ah, you don't know, but I, too, am a Karamazov. What does it matter if you do laugh and make jokes, and at me, too? Go on laughing. I am so glad you do. You laugh like a little child, but in your heart you think like a martyr."

"Like a martyr? How?"

"Yes, Lise, your question just now: whether we weren't showing contempt for that poor man by dissecting his soul — that was the question of a sufferer. . . . You see, I don't know how to express it, but any one who thinks of such questions is capable of suffering. Sitting in your invalid chair you must have thought over many things already."

"Alyosha, give me your hand. Why are you taking it away?" murmered Lise in a failing voice, weak with happiness. "Listen, Alyosha. What will you wear when you come out of the monastery? What sort of suit? Don't laugh, don't be angry, it's very, very important to me."

"I haven't thought about the suit, Lise; but I'll wear whatever you like."

"I should like you to have a dark blue velvet coat, a white piqué waistcoat, and a soft grey felt hat. . . . Tell me, did you believe that I didn't care for you when I said I didn't mean what I wrote?"

"No, I didn't believe it."

"Oh, you intolerable person, you are incorrigible."

"You see, I knew that you — perhaps cared for me, but I pretended to believe that you didn't care for me to make it — easier for you."

"That makes it worse! Worse and better than all! Alyosha, I love you awfully. Just before you came this morning, I tried my fortune. I decided I would ask you for my letter, and if you brought it out calmly and gave it to me (as might have been expected from you) it would mean that you did not love me at all, that you felt nothing, and were simply a stupid worthless boy, and that I was ruined. But you left the letter at home and that cheered me. You left it behind on purpose, so as not to give it back, because you knew I would ask for it? That was it, wasn't it?"

"Ah, Lise, it was not so at all. The letter is with me now, and it was this morning, in this pocket. Here it is."

Alyosha pulled the letter out, laughing, and showed it to her at a distance.

"But I am not going to give it to you. Look at it from here."

"Why, then you told a lie? You, a monk, told a lie!"

"I told a lie if you like." Alyosha laughed, too. "I told a lie so as not to give you back the letter. It's very precious to me," he added suddenly, with strong feeling, and again he flushed. "It always will be, and I won't give it up to any one!"

Lise looked at him ecstatically. "Alyosha," she lisped again, "look at the door. Isn't mamma eavesdropping?"

"Very well, Lise, I'll look; but wouldn't it be better not to look? Why suspect your mother of such meanness?"

"What meanness? As for her spying on her daughter, it's her right, it's not meanness!" cried Lise, firing up. "You may be sure, Alexey Fyodorovich, that when I am a mother, if I have a daughter like myself I shall certainly spy on her!"

"Really, Lise? That's not right."

"Oh, my goodness! What has meanness to do with it? If it were ordinary drawing-room talk, and I were eavesdropping, it would be meanness, but when your own daughter is locked up with a young man . . . Listen, Alyosha, do you know I shall spy upon you as soon as we are married, and let me tell you I shall open all your letters and read them, so you may as well be prepared."

"Yes, of course, if that's what you mean —" muttered Alyosha, "only it's not right."

"Ah, what contempt! Alyosha, dear, let's not quarrel the very first day. I'd better tell you the whole truth. Of course, it's very wrong to eavesdrop, and, of course, I am not right and you are, only I shall eavesdrop all the same."

"Do, then; you won't find out anything," laughed Alyosha.

"And Alyosha, will you give in to me? We must decide that, too."

"I shall be delighted to, Lise, and certain to, only not in the most important things. Even if you don't agree with me, I shall do my duty in the most important things."

"That's right; but let me tell you I am ready to give in to you not only in the most important matters, but in everything. And I am ready to swear to do so now — in everything, and for all my life!" cried Lise fervently,

"and I'll do it gladly, gladly! What's more I'll swear never to spy on you, never once, never to read one of your letters. For you are right and I am not. And though I shall be awfully tempted to eavesdrop, I know that I won't do it since you consider it dishonourable. You are my Providence now. . . . Listen, Alexey Fyodorovich, why have you been so sad lately — both yesterday and to-day? I know you have a lot of anxiety and trouble, but I see you have some special grief besides, some secret one, perhaps?"

"Yes, Lise, I have a secret one, too," answered Alyosha sadly. "I see you love me, since you guessed that."

"What grief? What about? Can you tell me?" asked Lise with timid entreaty.

"I'll tell you later, Lise — afterwards," said Alyosha, confused. "Now you wouldn't understand it perhaps — and perhaps I couldn't explain it."

"I know your brothers and your father are worrying you, too?"

"Yes, my brothers, too," murmured Alyosha, pondering.

"I don't like your brother Ivan, Alyosha," said Lise suddenly.

He noticed this remark with some surprise, but did not answer it.

"My brothers are ruining themselves," he went on, "my father, too. And they are ruining others with them. It's 'the primitive Karamazov force,' as Father Païssy said the other day, an earthy, frenzied, uncouth force. Does the spirit of God move above that force? Even that I don't know. I only know that I, too, am a Karamazov. . . . I, a monk, a monk? Am I a monk, Lise? You said just now that I was."

"Yes, I did."

"And perhaps I don't even believe in God."

"You don't believe? What is the matter?" said Lise quietly and gently. But Alyosha did not answer. There was something too mysterious, too personal in these last words of his, perhaps obscure to himself, but yet torturing him.

"And now on top of it all, my friend is leaving, the best man in the world is quitting the earth! If you knew, Lise, how bound up in soul I am with him, how welded to him! And then I shall be left alone. . . . I shall come to you, Lise. . . . In the future we will be together."

"Yes, together, together! Henceforward we shall be always together, all our lives! Listen, kiss me, I allow you."

Alyosha kissed her.

"Well, now go. Christ be with you!" and she made the sign of the cross over him. "Hurry back to *him* while he is alive. I see I've kept you cruelly. I'll pray to-day for him and you. Alyosha, we shall be happy! Shall we be happy, shall we?"

"I believe we shall, Lise."

Alyosha thought it better not to go in to Madame Hohlakov and was going out of the house without saying good-bye to her. But no sooner had he opened the door than he found Madame Hohlakov standing before him. From the first word Alyosha guessed that she had been waiting on purpose to meet him.

"Alexey Fyodorovich, this is awful. This is all childish nonsense and ridiculous. I trust you won't dream . . . It's foolishness, nothing but foolishness!" she said, attacking him at once.

"Only don't tell her that," said Alyosha, "or she will be upset, and that's bad for her now."

"Sensible advice from a sensible young man. Am I to understand that you only agreed with her from compassion for her invalid state, because you didn't want to irritate her by contradiction?"

"Oh, no, not at all. I was quite serious in what I said," Alyosha declared stoutly.

"To be serious about it is impossible, unthinkable, and in the first place I shall never be at home to you again, and I shall take her away, you may be sure of that."

"But why?" asked Alyosha. "It's all so far off. We may have to wait another year and a half."

"Ah, Alexey Fyodorovich, that's true, of course, and you'll have time to quarrel and separate a thousand times in a year and a half. But I am so unhappy! Though it's such nonsense, it's a great blow to me. I feel like Famusov in the last scene of *Sorrow from Wit*. You are Chatsky and she is Sofya, and, only fancy, I've run down to meet you on the stairs, and in the play too the fatal scene takes place on the staircase. I heard it all; I almost dropped. So this is the explanation of her dreadful night and her hysterics of late! It means love to the daughter but death to the mother. I might as well be in my grave at once. And a more serious matter still, what is this letter she has written? Show it me at once, at once!"

"No, there's no need. Tell me, how is Katerina Ivanovna now? I must know."

"She is still delirious; she has not regained consciousness. Her aunts are here; but they do nothing but sigh and give themselves airs. Herzenstube came, and he was so alarmed that I didn't know what to do for him. I nearly sent for a doctor to look after him. He was driven home in my carriage. And on top of it all, you and this letter! It's true nothing can happen for a year and a half. In the name of all that's great and holy, in the name of your dying elder, show me that letter, Alexey Fyodorovich. I'm her mother. Hold it in your hand, if you like, and I will read it so."

"No, I won't show it to you. Even if she sanctioned it, I wouldn't. I am coming tomorrow, and if you like, we can talk over many things, but now good-bye!"

And Alyosha ran downstairs and into the street.

## CHAPTER II
### SMERDYAKOV WITH A GUITAR

HE had no time to lose indeed. Even while he was saying good-bye to Lise, the thought had struck him that he must at once attempt some stratagem to catch his brother Dmitri, who was evidently hiding from him. It was getting late, nearly three o'clock. Alyosha's whole soul turned to the monastery, to his dying saint, but the necessity of seeing Dmitri outweighed everything. The conviction that a great inevitable catastrophe was about to happen grew stronger in Alyosha's mind with every hour. What that catastrophe was, and what he wished to say at this moment to his brother, he could perhaps not have said definitely.

"Even if my benefactor must die without me, anyway I won't have to reproach myself all my life with the thought that I might have prevented something and did not, but passed by and hastened home. If I do this, I shall be following his great precept."

His plan was to catch his brother Dmitri unaware, namely, to climb over the fence, as he had the day before, get into the garden and take up his post in the summer-house. If Dmitri were not there, thought Alyosha, he would not announce himself to Foma or the women of the house, but would remain hidden in the summer-house, even if he had to wait there till evening. If, as before, Dmitri were lying in wait for Grushenka to come, he would be very likely to come to the summer-house. Alyosha did not, however, give much thought to the details of his plan, but resolved to act upon it, even if it meant not getting back to the monastery that day.

Everything happened without hindrance, he climbed over the hurdle almost at the same spot as the day before, and stole into the summer-house unseen. He did not want to be noticed. The women of the house and Foma, too, if he were there, might be loyal to his brother and obey his instructions, and so refuse to let Alyosha come into the garden, or might warn Dmitri that he was being sought and inquired for.

There was no one in the summer-house. Alyosha sat down and began to wait. He looked round the summer-house, which somehow struck him as a great deal more dilapidated than before. Though the day was just as fine as yesterday, it seemed a wretched little place this time. There was a circle on the green table, left no doubt from the glass of cognac spilt the day before. Foolish and irrelevant ideas strayed into his mind, as they always do in a time of tedious waiting. He wondered, for instance, why he had sat down precisely in the same place as the previous day, why not elsewhere. In the end he felt very depressed — depressed by suspense and uncertainty. But he had not sat there more than a quarter of an hour, when he suddenly heard the thrum of a guitar somewhere quite close. People were sitting, or had only just sat down, somewhere in the bushes not more than twenty paces away.

Alyosha suddenly recollected that on coming out of the summer-house the day before, he had caught a glimpse of an old low green garden-seat among the bushes on the left, by the fence. The newcomers must have seated themselves on it now.

Who were they?

A man's voice suddenly began singing in a sugary falsetto, accompanying himself on the guitar:

> "By impregnable ties
> I am bound to my dear.
> Oh, Lord, have mercy
> On her and on me!
> On her and on me!
> On her and on me!"

The voice ceased. It was a lackey's tenor and somehow a lackey's song. Another voice, a woman's, suddenly asked ingratiatingly and bashfully, as it were, though with a great deal of mincing affectation:

"Why haven't you been to see us for so long, Pavel Fyodorovich? Why do you always look down upon us?"

"Not at all," answered a man's voice politely, but with firm and emphatic dignity. It was clear that the man had the best of the situation, and that the woman was making advances.

"I believe the man must be Smerdyakov," thought Alyosha, "to judge by his voice. And the lady must be the daughter of the house here, who has come from Moscow, the one who wears the dress with a train and goes to Marfa for soup."

"I am awfully fond of verses of all kinds, if they rhyme," the woman's voice continued. "Why don't you go on?"

The man sang again:

> "What do I care for royal wealth
> If but my dear one be in health?
> Lord have mercy
> On her and on me!
> On her and on me!
> On her and on me!"

"It was even better last time," observed the woman's voice. "You sang 'If my darling be in health'; it sounded more tender. I suppose you've forgotten to-day."

"Verse is rubbish!" said Smerdyakov curtly.

"Oh, no! I am very fond of verse."

"So far as it's verse, it's fundamentally rubbish. Consider for yourself: who ever talks in rhyme? And if we were all to talk in rhyme, even if it were decreed by the authorities, we shouldn't say much, should we? Poetry is no good, Marya Kondratyevna."

"How clever you are! How is it you've gone so deep into everything?" The woman's voice was more and more ingratiating.

"I could have done better than that. I could have learnt more than that, if it had not been for my lot from my childhood up. I would have shot a man in a duel if he called me names because I am descended from a filthy beggar and have no father. And they used to throw it in my teeth in Moscow, too. It had reached them from here, thanks to Grigory Vasilyevich. Grigory Vasilyevich blames me for rebelling against my birth: 'You,' he says, 'came forth from her womb.' Call it 'womb' if you please, but I would have allowed them to kill me before I was born so that I might not have come into the world at all. They used to say in the market-place, and your mamma, too, with great lack of delicacy, set off telling me, that her hair was like a mat on her head, and that she was short of five foot by a wee bit. Why talk of a wee bit while she might have said 'a little bit,' like every one else? She wanted to make it sound pitiful, but that's a yokel's pity, a regular peasant's feeling. Can a Russian peasant have the refined feelings of an educated man? He can't be said to have feeling at all, in his ignorance. From my childhood up when I hear 'a wee bit,' I am ready to run riot. I hate all Russia, Marya Kondratyevna."

"If you'd been a cadet in the army, or a young hussar, you wouldn't have talked like that, but would have drawn your sabre to defend all Russia."

"I don't want to be a hussar, Marya Kondratyevna, and, what's more, I should like to abolish all soldiers."

"And when an enemy comes, who is going to defend us?"

"There's no need of defence. In 1812 there was a great invasion of Russia by Napoleon, first Emperor of the French, father of the present one, and it would have been a good thing if they had conquered us. A clever nation would have conquered a very stupid one and annexed it. We should have had quite a different order of things."

"Are they so much better in their country than we are? I wouldn't change a Russian dandy for three young Englishmen," observed Marya Kondratyevna tenderly, doubtless accompanying her words with a most languishing glance.

"That depends, ma'am, on what you idolise."

"But you are just like a foreigner yourself — just like a most refined foreigner. I tell you that, though it makes me blush."

"If you care to know, when it comes to debauchery, the foreigners and our own people are all alike. They are rascals, only there the scoundrel wears patent leather boots while here he is wretchedly poor and stinking and sees no harm in it. The Russian people want thrashing, as Fyodor Pavlovich said properly yesterday, though he is crazy, and all his children, too."

"You said yourself though, you had such respect for Ivan Fyodorovich."

"But he said I was a stinking lackey. The gentleman thinks that I might get out of hand. He is mistaken there. If I had a certain sum in my pocket, I would have left here long ago. Dmitri Fyodorovich is worse than any lackey in his behaviour, in his mind, and in his poverty. He doesn't know how to do anything, and yet he is respected by every one. I may be only a bouillon-maker, but with luck I could open a café restaurant in the Petrovka section of Moscow, for my cookery is something special, and there's no one in Moscow, except the foreigners, whose cookery is anything special. Dmitri Fyodorovich is a beggar, but if he were to challenge the son of the first count in the country, he'd fight him. Though in what way is he better than I am? For he is ever so much stupider than I am. Look at the money he has wasted to no purpose!"

"It must be lovely, a duel," Marya Kondratyevna observed suddenly.

"How so?"

"It must be so frightful and so brave, especially when young officers with pistols in their hands pop at one another for the sake of some lady. A perfect picture! Ah, if only girls were allowed to look on, I'd give anything to see one!"

"It's all very well when you are firing at some one, but when he is firing straight in your mug, you must feel pretty silly. You'd be glad to run away, Marya Kondratyevna."

"You don't mean you would run away?" But Smerdyakov did not deign to reply. After a moment's silence the guitar tinkled again, and he sang again in the same falsetto:

> *"Whatever you may say,*
> *I shall go far away.*
> *Life will be bright and gay*
> *In the city far away.*
> *I shall not grieve,*
> *I shall not grieve at all,*
> *I don't intend to grieve at all."*

Then something unexpected happened. Alyosha suddenly sneezed. They were silent. Alyosha got up and walked towards them. It was indeed Smerdyakov dressed up and wearing patent leather boots, his hair pomaded, and perhaps curled. The guitar lay on the garden-seat. His companion was the daughter of the house. She was wearing a light blue dress with a train two yards long. She was young and would not have been bad-looking, but that her face was so round and terribly freckled.

"Will my brother Dmitri soon be back?" asked Alyosha with as much composure as he could muster.

Smerdyakov got up slowly; Marya Kondratyevna rose, too.

"How am I to know about Dmitri Fyodorovich? It's not as if I were his keeper," answered Smerdyakov quietly, distinctly, and superciliously.

"But I simply asked whether you do know?" Alyosha explained.

"I know nothing of his whereabouts and don't want to."

"But my brother told me that you let him know all that goes on in the house, and prom-ised to let him know when Agrafena Alexandrovna comes."

Smerdyakov turned a deliberate, unmoved look upon him.

"And how did you get in this time, since the gate was bolted an hour ago?" he asked, looking at Alyosha.

"I came in from the lane, over the fence, and went straight to the summer-house. I hope you'll excuse me," he added, addressing Marya Kondratyevna. "I was in a hurry to find my brother."

"Ach, as though we could take it amiss in you!" drawled Marya Kondratyevna, flattered by Alyosha's apology. "For Dmitri Fyodorovich often goes to the summer-house in that way. We don't know he is here and he is sitting in the summer-house."

"I am very anxious to find him, or to learn from you where he is now. Believe me, it's on business of great importance to him."

"He never tells us," lisped Marya Kondratyevna.

"Though I used to come here as an acquaintance," Smerdyakov began again, "Dmitri Fyodorovich has pestered me in a merciless way even here by his incessant questions about the master. 'What news?' he'll ask. 'What's going on in there now? Who's coming and going?' and can't I tell him something more. Twice already he's threatened me with death."

"With death?" Alyosha exclaimed in surprise.

"Do you suppose he'd think much of that, sir, with his temper, which you had a chance of observing yourself yesterday? He says if I let Agrafena Alexandrovna in and she spends the night there, I'll be the first he'll kill. I am terribly afraid of him, sir, and if I were not even more afraid of what that might mean, I ought to let the police know. God only knows, sir, what he might not do!"

"Dmitri Fyodorovich said to him the other day, 'I'll pound you in a mortar!'" added Marya Kondratyevna.

"Oh, if it's pounding in a mortar, it may be only talk," observed Alyosha. "If I could meet him, I might speak to him about that, too."

"Well, the only thing I can tell you is this," said Smerdyakov, as though thinking better of it; "I come here as a neighbour, an old acquaintance, and why shouldn't I come? On the other hand, Ivan Fyodorovich sent me first thing this morning to your brother's lodging in Ozyornaya Street, without a letter, but with a message to Dmitri Fyodorovich to come and dine with him at the restaurant here, in the market-place. I went, but didn't find Dmitri Fyodorovich at home, though it was eight o'clock. 'He's been here, but he is gone for good,' those were the very words of his landlady. It's as though there was a conspiracy between them. Perhaps at this moment he is in the restaurant with Ivan Fyodorovich, for Ivan Fyodorovich has not been home to dinner and Fyodor Pavlovich dined alone an hour ago, and is now taking a nap. But I beg you, sir, most particularly not to speak of me and of what I have told you, for he'd kill me, sir, for nothing at all."

"Brother Ivan invited Dmitri to the restaurant to-day?" repeated Alyosha quickly.

"That is correct, sir."

"The 'Metropolis,' in the square?"

"The very same."

"That's quite likely," cried Alyosha, much excited. "Thank you, Smerdyakov; that's important. I'll go there at once."

"Don't betray me, sir," Smerdyakov called after him.

"Oh, no, I'll step into the tavern as though by chance. Don't be anxious."

"But wait a minute, I'll open the gate for you," cried Marya Kondratyevna.

"No; this is nearer, I'll climb the fence again."

The news threw Alyosha into great agitation. He ran to the tavern. It was improper for him to go into the tavern in his monastic dress, but he could inquire at the entrance for his brothers and call them out. But just as he reached the tavern, a window was flung open, and his brother Ivan called down to him from it.

"Alyosha, can't you come up here to me? I shall be awfully obliged."

"To be sure I can, only I don't quite know whether in this dress . . ."

"But I am in a private room. Come up the steps; I'll run down to meet you."

A minute later Alyosha was sitting beside his brother. Ivan was alone, dining.

## CHAPTER III
### THE BROTHERS GET ACQUAINTED

IVAN was not, however, in a private room. It was only a place by the window shut off by a screen, so that those sitting there could not be seen by other people in the room. It was the first room from the entrance with a buffet along the wall. Waiters were continually darting to and fro. The only customer in the room was an old retired military man drinking tea in a corner. But there was the usual bustle going on in the other rooms of the tavern; there were shouts for the waiters, the sound of popping corks, the click of billiard balls, the drone of the organ. Alyosha knew that Ivan did not usually visit this tavern and disliked taverns in general. So he must have come here, he reflected, simply to meet Dmitri by arrangement. Yet Dmitri was not there.

"Shall I order you fish soup or anything, you don't live on tea alone, I suppose," cried Ivan, apparently delighted at having got hold of Alyosha. For his own part, he had finished dinner and was taking tea.

"Let me have soup, and tea afterwards, I am hungry," said Alyosha gaily.

"And cherry jam? They have it here. You remember how you used to love cherry jam when you were little?"

"You remember that? Let me have jam, too, I like it still."

Ivan rang for the waiter and ordered soup, tea, and jam.

"I remember everything, Alyosha, I remember you till you were eleven, I was nearly fifteen. There's such a difference between fifteen and eleven that brothers are never companions at those ages. I don't know whether I was fond of you even. When I went away to Moscow for the first few years I never thought of you at all. Then, when you came to Moscow yourself, we only met once somewhere, I believe. And now I've been here more than three months, and so far we have scarcely said a word to each other. To-morrow I am going away, and I was just thinking as I sat here how I could see you to say good-bye and just then you passed."

"Were you very anxious to see me then?"

"Very, I want to get to know you once for all, and I want you to know me. And then to say good-bye. I believe it's always best to get to know people just before parting from them. I've noticed how you've been looking at me

these three months. There has been a continual look of expectation in your eyes, and I can't endure that. That's why I've kept away from you. But in the end I have learnt to respect you. The little man stands firm, I thought. Though I am laughing, I am serious. You do stand firm, don't you? I like people who are firm like that whatever it is they stand on, even if they are such little boys as you. Your expectant look ceased to annoy me, I grew fond of it in the end that expectant look. You seem to love me for some reason, Alyosha?"

"I do love you, Ivan. Dmitri says of you — Ivan is a tomb! I say of you, Ivan is a riddle. You are a riddle to me even now. But I come to understand something in you, and that only happened this morning."

"What's that?" laughed Ivan.

"You won't be angry?" Alyosha laughed, too.

"Well?"

"That you are just as young as other young men of three and twenty, that you are just a young, fresh, charming boy, unfledged in fact! Now, have I insulted you dreadfully?"

"On the contrary, I am struck by a coincidence," cried Ivan, warmly and good-humouredly. "Would you believe it that ever since that scene with her, I have thought of nothing else but what a green youth I am, and just as though you guessed that, you begin about it. Do you know I've been sitting here thinking to myself: that if I didn't believe in life, if I lost faith in the woman I love, lost faith in the order of things, were convinced in fact that everything is a disorderly, damnable, and perhaps devilish chaos, if I were struck by every horror of man's disillusionment — still I should want to live and, having once tasted of the cup, I would not turn away from it till I had drained it! At thirty, though, I shall be sure to drop the cup, even if I've not emptied it, and turn away — where I don't know. But till I am thirty, I know that my youth will triumph over everything — every disillusionment, every disgust with life. I've asked myself many times whether there is in the world any despair that would overcome this frantic and perhaps unseemly thirst for life in me, and I've come to the conclusion that there isn't, that is till I am thirty, and then I shall lose it of myself, I fancy. Some drivelling consumptive moralists—and poets especially—often call that thirst for life base. It's a feature of the Karamazovs, it's true, that thirst for life regardless of everything; you have it no doubt, too, but why is it base? The centripetal force on our planet is still fearfully strong, Alyosha. I have a longing for life, and I go on living even in spite of logic. Though I may not believe in the order of the universe, yet the sticky little leaves as they open in spring are precious to me. The blue sky is precious to me, sometimes a person is dear to me — you know, one loves people sometimes without knowing why. Some great deeds done by men are precious to me, though I've long ceased perhaps to have faith in them, yet from old habit one's heart honours them. Here they have brought the fish soup for you, eat it, and good health to you. It's first-rate soup, they know how to make it here. I want to go to Europe, Alyosha, I shall set off from here. And yet I know that I am only going to a graveyard, but it's a most precious graveyard, that's what it is! Precious are the dead that lie there, every stone over them speaks of such burning life gone by, of such passionate faith in their work, their truth, their struggle, and their science, that I know I shall fall on the ground and kiss those stones

and weep over them; though I'm convinced in my heart that it's long been nothing but a graveyard. And I shall not weep out of despair, but simply because I shall be happy in my tears, I shall get drunk on my own emotion. I love the sticky leaves of spring, the blue sky —. that's what it is. It's not a matter of intellect or logic, you love with your insides, with your belly. You love the first strength of your youth. Do you understand anything of my twaddle, Alyosha?" Ivan laughed suddenly.

"I understand too well, Ivan. One longs to love with one's insides, with one's belly. You said that so well and I am awfully glad that you have such a strong will to live," cried Alyosha. "I think every one should love life above every thing in the world."

"Love life more than the meaning of it?"

"Certainly, love it, regardless of logic as you say, it must be regardless of logic, and it's only then that one will understand the meaning of it, too. I have had this feeling a long time. Half your work is done, Ivan, you love life; now you've only to try to do the second half and you are saved."

"Here you are trying to save me, but perhaps I am not lost! And what does your second half mean?"

"Why, one has to raise up your dead, who perhaps have not died after all. Come, let me have tea. I am so glad of our talk, Ivan."

"I see you are in an exalted mood. I am awfully fond of such *professions de foi* from such — novices. You are a steadfast person, Alexey. Is it true that you mean to leave the monastery?"

"Yes, my elder sends me out into the world."

"We shall see each other then in the world.

We shall meet before I am thirty, when I shall begin to turn aside from the cup. Father doesn't want to turn aside from his cup till he is seventy, he dreams of hanging on till he's eighty in fact, so he says. He means it only too seriously, though he is a clown. He stands on his sensuality as on a rock — though, indeed, after we are thirty there may be nothing else to stand on. . . . But to hang on till seventy is nasty, better only until thirty; one might retain 'a shadow of nobility' by deceiving oneself. Have you seen Dmitri to-day?"

"No, but I saw Smerdyakov," and Alyosha rapidly, though minutely, described his meeting with Smerdyakov. Ivan began listening anxiously and even questioned him on some points.

"But he begged me not to tell Dmitri that he had told me about him," added Alyosha. Ivan frowned and grew thoughtful.

"Are you frowning on Smerdyakov's account?" asked Alyosha.

"Yes, on his account. Damn him, I certainly did want to see Dmitri, but now there's no need," said Ivan reluctantly.

"But are you really leaving so soon, brother?"

"Yes."

"What of Dmitri and father? how will it end?" asked Alyosha anxiously.

"You are always harping on it! What have I to do with it? Am I my brother Dmitri's keeper?" Ivan snapped irritably, but then he suddenly smiled bitterly. "Cain's answer about his murdered brother, wasn't it? Perhaps that's what you're thinking at this moment? Well, damn it all, I can't stay here to be their keeper, can I? I've finished what I had to do, and I am going. Do you imagine I am jealous of Dmitri, that I've been trying to steal his beautiful Katerina Ivanovna for the last three months? Nonsense, I had business of my own. I finished it. I am going. I finished it just now, you were witness."

"At Katerina Ivanovna's?"

"Yes, and I've released myself once for all. And after all, what have I to do with Dmitri? Dmitri doesn't come in. I had my own business to settle with Katerina Ivanovna. You know yourself, on the contrary, that Dmitri behaved as though there was an understanding between us. I didn't ask him to do it, but he solemnly handed her over to me and gave us his blessing. It's all too funny. Ah, Alyosha, if you only knew how light my heart is now! Would you believe it, I sat here eating my dinner and was nearly ordering champagne to celebrate my first hour of freedom. Phew! It's been going on nearly six months, and all at once I've thrown it off. I could never have guessed even yesterday, how easy it would be to put an end to it if I wanted."

"You are speaking of your love, Ivan?"

"Of my love, if you like. I fell in love with the young lady, the finishing-school miss, I worried myself over her and she tormented me. I hung around her . . . and all at once it's over! I spoke this morning with inspiration, but I went away and roared with laughter. Would you believe it? Yes, it's the truth."

"You seem very merry about it now," observed Alyosha, looking into his face, which had all at once really grown brighter.

"But how could I tell that I didn't care for her a bit! Ha-ha! It appears after all I didn't. And yet how she attracted me! How attractive she was just now when I made my speech! And do you know she attracts me awfully even now, yet how easy it is to leave her. Do you think I am putting it on?"

THE BROTHERS KARAMAZOV

"No, only perhaps it wasn't love."

"Alyosha," laughed Ivan, "don't get into discussions about love, it doesn't become you. How you rushed into the conversation this morning! I've forgotten to kiss you for it. . . . But how she tormented me! It certainly was sitting by a 'laceration.' Ah, she knew how I loved her! She loved me and not Dmitri," Ivan insisted gaily. "Her feeling for Dmitri was simply a self-laceration. All I told her then was perfectly true, but the worst of it is, it may take her fifteen or twenty years to find out that she doesn't care for Dmitri, and loves me whom she torments, and perhaps she may never find it out at all, in spite of to-day's lesson. Well, it's better so; I just up and went, for good. By the way, how is she now? What happened after I left?"

Alyosha told him she had been hysterical, and that she was now, he heard, unconscious and delirious.

"Isn't Madame Hohlakov laying it on?"

"I think not."

"I must find out. Nobody dies of hysterics though. Well, let it be hysterics. God gave woman hysterics out of kindness. I won't go there at all. Why push myself forward again?"

"But you told her that she had never cared for you."

"I did that on purpose. Alyosha, shall I call for some champagne? Let us drink to my freedom. Ah, if only you knew how glad I am!"

"No, brother, we had better not drink," said Alyosha suddenly. "Besides I feel somehow depressed."

"Yes, you've been depressed a long time, I've noticed it."

"Have you decided on going to-morrow morning then?"

"Morning? I didn't say I should go in the morning. . . . But perhaps it may be the morning. Would you believe it, I dined here to-day only to avoid dining with the old man, I loathe him so. I should have left long ago, just to get away from him. But why are you so worried about my going away? We've plenty of time before I go, a whole eternity of it!"

"If you are going away to-morrow, what do you mean by an eternity?"

"But what does it matter to us?" laughed Ivan, "we'll have time enough for our talk, for what brought us here. Why do you look so surprised? Answer: why have we met here? To talk of my love for Katerina Ivanovna, of the old man and Dmitri? of foreign travel? of the fatal position of Russia? of the Emperor Napoleon? Is that it?"

"No."

"Then you know what for. It's different for other people; but we in our green youth have to settle the eternal questions first of all. That's what we care about. Young Russia is talking about nothing but the eternal questions now. Just when the old folks are all taken up with practical questions. Why have you been looking at me in expectation for the last three months? To ask me: 'what do you believe, or don't you believe at all?' That's what your look has been meaning for these three months, hasn't it?"

"Perhaps so," smiled Alyosha. "You are not laughing at me, now, Ivan?"

"I, laughing! I don't want to hurt my little brother who has been watching me with such expectation for three months. Alyosha, look straight at me! Of course I am just such a little boy as you are, only not a novice. And what have Russian boys been doing up till now, some of them, I mean? In this stinking

176

tavern here, for instance, they meet and sit down in a corner. They've never met in their lives before and, when they go out of the tavern, they won't meet again for forty years. And what will they talk about during that momentary encounter in the tavern? Of the eternal questions, nothing else: is there a God, is there immortality? And those who do not believe in God will talk of socialism or anarchism, of the transformation of all humanity on a new pattern, which all comes to the same thing, they're the same questions turned inside out. And in our time numbers, numbers of the most original Russian boys do nothing but talk of the eternal questions! Isn't it so?"

"Yes, for real Russians the questions of God's existence and of immortality, or, as you say, the same questions turned inside out, come first and foremost, of course, and so they should," said Alyosha, still watching his brother with the same gentle and inquiring smile.

"Well, Alyosha, it's sometimes far from intelligent to be a Russian at all, but anything stupider than the way Russian boys spend their time nowadays one can hardly imagine. But there's one Russian boy called Alyosha I am awfully fond of."

"How nicely you put that in!" Alyosha laughed suddenly.

"Well, tell me where to begin, give your orders. The existence of God, eh?"

"Begin where you like, even from the wrong end. You declared yesterday at father's that there was no God." Alyosha looked searchingly at his brother.

"I said that yesterday at dinner on purpose to tease you and I saw how your eyes began to flash. But now I've no objection to talking things over with you, and I say so very seri-

ously. I want to be friends with you, Alyosha, for I have no friends and want to try it. Well, only fancy, perhaps I, too, accept God," laughed Ivan, "that's a surprise for you, isn't it?"

"Yes, of course, if you are not joking now."

"Joking? I was told at the elder's yesterday that I was joking. You know, dear boy, there was an old sinner in the eighteenth century who declared that, if there were no God, he would have to be invented. *S'il n'existait pas Dieu, il faudrait l'inventer.* And man has actually invented God. And what's strange, what would be marvellous, is not that God should really exist; the marvel is that such an idea, the idea of the necessity of God, could enter the head of such a savage, vicious beast as man. So holy it is, so touching, so wise, and so great a credit it does to man. As for me, I've long resolved not to wonder whether man created God or God man. And I won't go through all the axioms laid down by Russian boys on that subject, all derived from European hypotheses; for what's a hypothesis there, is an axiom with the Russian boy, and not only with the boys but with their teachers, too, for our Russian professors are often just the same boys themselves. And so I omit all the hypotheses. For what are we aiming at now? I am trying to explain as quickly as possible my essential nature, that is, what manner of man I am, what I believe in, and what I hope for, that's it, isn't it? And therefore I tell you that I accept God simply and directly. But you must note this: if God exists and if He really did create the earth, then, as we all know, He created it according to Euclidean geometry, and the human mind has the conception of only three dimensions in space. Yet there have been and still are geometricians and philosophers, and even some of the most distinguished, who doubt whether the whole universe, or to speak more widely the whole of being, was only created according to Euclid's geometry; they even dare to dream that two parallel lines, which according to Euclid can never meet on earth, may meet somewhere in infinity. I have come to the conclusion that, since I can't understand even that, I can't expect to understand about God. I acknowledge humbly that I have no faculty for settling such questions, I have a Euclidean earthly mind, and how could I solve problems that are not of this world? And I advise you never to think about it either, my dear Alyosha, especially about God, whether He exists or not. All such questions are utterly inappropriate to a mind created with a concept of only three dimensions. And so I accept God and am glad to, and what's more I accept His wisdom, His purpose — which are utterly beyond our ken; I believe in the underlying order and the meaning of life; I believe in the eternal harmony in which they say we shall one day be blended. I believe in the Word to Which the universe is striving, and Which Itself was 'with God,' and Which Itself is God and so on, and so on, to infinity. There are all sorts of phrases for it. I seem to be on the right path, don't I? Yet would you believe it, in the last account I don't accept this world of God's, and, although I know it exists, I don't admit it at all. It's not that I don't accept God, you must understand, it's the world created by Him, it's God's world that I don't and cannot accept. Let me make it plain. I believe like a child that suffering will be healed and made up for, that all the humiliating comedy of human contradictions will vanish like a pitiful mirage, like the despicable fabrication of the im-

potent and infinitely small Euclidean mind of man, finally, that in the cosmic *dénouement*, at the moment of eternal harmony, something so precious will come to pass that it will suffice for all hearts, for the assuagement of all indignation, for the redemption of all the crimes of humanity, of all the blood they've shed; that it will make it not only possible to forgive but to justify all that has happened to men — but though all that may come to pass, I don't accept it. I won't accept it. Even if parallel lines do meet and I see it myself, I shall see it and say that they've met, but still I won't accept it. That's what's at the root of me, Alyosha; that's my creed. I am in earnest in what I say. I began our talk as foolishly as I could on purpose, but I've led up to my confession, for that's all you want. You didn't want to hear about God, but only to know what the brother you love lives by. And so I've told you."

Ivan concluded his long tirade with marked and unexpected feeling.

"And why did you begin 'as foolishly as you could'?" asked Alyosha, looking dreamily at him.

"To begin with, for the sake of the Russian style. Russian conversations on such subjects are always carried on as foolishly as possible. And secondly, the more foolish, the nearer to the point. The more foolish one is, the clearer one is. Foolishness is short and artless, while intelligence wriggles and hides itself. Intelligence is a knave, but foolishness is honest and straight. I've led the conversation to my despair, and the more foolishly I have presented it, the better for me."

"Will you explain why you don't accept the world?" said Alyosha.

"To be sure I will, it's not a secret, that's

what I've been leading up to. Dear little brother, I don't want to corrupt you or to push you off your rock, perhaps I want to be healed by you." Ivan smiled suddenly quite like a little gentle child. Alyosha had never seen such a smile on his face before.

## CHAPTER IV
### REBELLION

"I MUST make you one confession," Ivan began. "I could never understand how one can love one's neighbours. It's just one's neighbours, to my mind, that one can't love, though one might love those far away. I once read somewhere of John the Merciful, a saint, that when a hungry, frozen beggar came to him, asking for warmth, he took him into his bed, held him in his arms, and began breathing into his mouth, which was putrid and loathsome from some dreadful disease. I am convinced that he did that out of 'self-laceration,' out of the self-laceration of hypocrisy, for the sake of a dutiful charity, as a self-imposed penance. For any one to love a man, he must be hidden, for as soon as he shows his face, love is gone."

"Father Zosima has talked of that more than once," observed Alyosha, "he, too, said that the face of a man often hinders many people not practised in love, from loving him. But yet there's a great deal of love in mankind, and almost Christlike love. I know that myself, Ivan."

"Well, I know nothing of it so far, and can't understand it, and the innumerable mass of mankind are with me there. The question is, whether that's due to men's bad qualities or whether it's inherent in their nature. To my thinking, Christlike love for men is a miracle impossible on earth. True, He was God. But we, we are not gods. Suppose I, for instance,

suffer intensely. Another can never know how much I suffer, because he is another and not I. And what's more, a man is rarely ready to admit another's suffering (as though it were a distinction). Why won't he admit it, do you think? Because I smell bad, because I have a stupid face, because I once trod on his foot. Besides there is suffering and suffering; degrading, humiliating suffering such as humbles me — hunger, for instance — my benefactor will perhaps allow me; but when you come to higher suffering — for an idea, for instance — he will very rarely admit that, perhaps because my face strikes him as not at all what he fancies a man should have who suffers for an idea. And so he deprives me instantly of his favour, and not at all because of an evil heart. Beggars, especially genteel beggars, ought never to show themselves, but to ask for charity through the newspapers. One can love one's neighbours in the abstract, and sometimes even at a distance, but at close quarters it's almost impossible. If it were as on the stage, in the ballet, where, if beggars come in, they wear silken rags and tattered lace and beg for alms dancing gracefully, then one might like looking at them. Like looking at them, but not love them. But enough of that. I simply wanted to show you my point of view. I meant to speak of the suffering of mankind generally, but we had better confine ourselves to the sufferings of children. That reduces the scope of my argument to a tenth of what it would be. Still we'd better keep just to the children, though it does weaken my case. But, in the first place, children can be loved even at close quarters, even when they are dirty, even when they are ugly (I fancy, though, children never are ugly). In the second place, I won't speak of grown-up people because, besides being disgusting and unworthy of love, they have a compensation — they've eaten the apple and know good and evil, and they have become 'like gods.' They go on eating it still. But the children haven't eaten of it, and are so far innocent. Are you fond of children, Alyosha? I know you are, and you will understand why I prefer to speak of them. If they, too, suffer horribly on earth, they suffer for their fathers' sins, they are punished for their fathers, who have eaten the apple; but that reasoning is of another world and is incomprehensible to the heart of man here on earth. The innocent must not suffer for another's sins, and especially such innocents! You may be surprised at me, Alyosha, but I am awfully fond of children, too. And observe, cruel people, the passionate, the carnal, the Karamazovs, are sometimes very fond of children. Children while they are quite little — up to seven, for instance — are so remote from grown-up people; they are different creatures, as it were, of a different species. I knew a criminal in prison who had, in the course of his career as a robber, murdered whole families, including several children. But when he was in prison, he had a strange affection for them. He spent all his time at his window, watching the children playing in the prison yard. He trained one little boy to come up to his window and made great friends with him. . . . You don't know why I am telling you all this, Alyosha? My head aches and I am sad."

"You speak with a strange air," observed Alyosha uneasily, "as though you were out of your mind, almost."

"By the way, a Bulgarian I met lately in Moscow," Ivan went on, seeming not to hear his brother's words, "told me about the crimes committed by Turks and Circassians in all parts of Bulgaria through fear of a general rising of the Slavs. They burn villages, murder, outrage women and children, they nail their prisoners by the ears to the fences, leave them so till morning, and in the morning they hang them — all sorts of things you can't imagine. People talk sometimes of bestial cruelty, but that's a great injustice and insult to the beasts; a beast can never be so cruel as a man, so artistically cruel. The tiger only tears and gnaws, that's all he can do. He would never think of nailing people by the ears overnight, even if he were able to do it. These Turks took a pleasure in torturing children, too; cutting the unborn child from the mother's womb, and tossing babies up in the air and catching them on the points of their bayonets before their mother's eyes. Doing it before the mother's eyes was what gave zest to the amusement. Here is another scene that I thought very interesting. Imagine a trembling mother with her baby in her arms, a circle of invading Turks around her. They've planned a diversion: they pet the baby, laugh to make it laugh. They succeed, the baby laughs. At that moment a Turk points a pistol four inches from the baby's face. The baby laughs with glee, holds out its little hands to the pistol, and suddenly the artist pulls the trigger in the baby's face and blows out its brains. Artistic, wasn't it? By the way, Turks are particularly fond of sweet things, they say."

"Brother, what are you driving at?" asked Alyosha.

"I think if the devil doesn't exist, but man has created him, he has created him in his own image and likeness."

"Just as he did God, then?" observed Alyosha.

"THAT'S REBELLION'

" 'It's wonderful how you can turn words,' as Polonius says in *Hamlet*," laughed Ivan. "You turn my words against me. Well, I am glad. Yours must be a fine God, if man created Him in his image and likeness. You asked just now what I was driving at. You see, I am a connoisseur and collector of certain facts, and, would you believe, I even copy anecdotes of a certain sort from newspapers and books, and I've already got a fine collection. The Turks, of course, have gone into it, but they are foreigners. I have specimens from home that are even better than the Turks. You know we prefer beating — rods and scourges — that's our national institution. Nailing ears is unthinkable for us, for we are, after all, Europeans. But the rod and the scourge we have always with us and they cannot be taken from us. Abroad now they scarcely do any beating. Manners are more humane, or laws have been passed, so that they don't dare to flog men now. But they make up for it in another way just as national as ours. And so national that it would be practically impossible among us, though I believe we are being inoculated with it, since the religious movement began in our aristocracy. I have a charming pamphlet, translated from the French, describing how, quite recently, five years ago, a murderer, Richard, was executed — a young man, I believe, of three and twenty, who repented and was converted to the Christian faith at the very scaffold. This Richard was an illegitimate child who at the age of six was donated by his parents to some shepherds on the Swiss mountains. They brought him up to work for them. He grew up like a little wild beast among them. The shepherds taught him nothing, and scarcely fed or clothed him, but sent him out at seven to herd the flock in cold and wet, and no one hesitated or scrupled to treat him so. Quite the contrary, they thought they had every right, for Richard had been given to them as a chattel, and they did not even see the necessity of feeding him. Richard himself testifies how in those years, like the Prodigal Son in the Gospel, he longed to eat of the mash given to the pigs, which were fattened for sale. But they wouldn't even give him that, and beat him when he stole from the pigs. And that was how he spent all his childhood and his youth, till he grew up and was strong enough to go away and be a thief. The savage began to earn his living as a day labourer in Geneva. He drank what he earned, he lived like a brute, and finished by killing and robbing an old man. He was caught, tried, and condemned to death. They are not sentimentalists there. And in prison he was immediately surrounded by pastors, members of Christian brotherhoods, philanthropic ladies, and the like. They taught him to read and write in prison, and expounded the Gospel to him. They exhorted him, worked upon him, drummed at him incessantly, till at last he solemnly confessed his crime. He was converted. He wrote to the court himself that he was a monster, but that in the end God had vouchsafed him light and sent him grace. All Geneva was in excitement about him — all philanthropic and religious Geneva. All the prominent and well-bred people of the town rush to the prison, kiss Richard and embrace him: 'You are our brother, you have been visited with grace.' And Richard does nothing but weep with emotion, 'Yes, I've been visited with grace! All my childhood and youth I was glad of pigs' food, but now even I have been visited with grace. I am dying in the Lord.' 'Yes, Richard, die in the Lord; you have shed blood and must die. Though it's not your fault that you knew not the Lord, when you coveted the pigs' food and were beaten for stealing it (which was very wrong of you, for stealing is forbidden); but you've shed blood and you must die.' And on the last day, Richard, perfectly limp, did nothing but cry and repeat every minute: 'This is my happiest day. I am going to the Lord.' 'Yes,' cry the pastors and the judges and the philanthropic ladies. 'This is the happiest day of your life, for you are going to the Lord!' They all walk or drive to the scaffold in procession behind the prison van. At the scaffold they call to Richard: 'Die, brother, die in the Lord, for even you have been visited with grace!' And so, covered with his brothers' kisses, Richard is dragged on to the scaffold, and led to the guillotine. And they chopped off his head in brotherly fashion, because he, too, had been visited with grace. Yes, that's characteristic. That pamphlet has been translated into Russian by some Russian philanthropists of aristocratic rank and evangelical aspirations, and has been distributed gratis for the enlightenment of the people. The case of Richard is interesting because it's national. Though to us it's absurd to cut off a man's head, because he has become our brother and has been visited with grace, yet we have our own speciality, which is all but worse. Our own historic immediate and dearest delight lies in torture by beating. There are lines in Nekrasov describing how a peasant lashes a horse across the eyes, 'the meek eyes.' Every one has seen it, it's a peculiarly Russian trait. He describes how a feeble little nag has foundered under too heavy a load and cannot move. The peasant beats it, beats it savagely, beats it at last not knowing what he is doing in the intoxication of cruelty, thrashes it mercilessly over and over again. 'You may be on your last legs, but you must pull, if you die for it.' The nag strains, and then he begins lashing the poor defenceless creature on its weeping, on its 'meek eyes.' The frantic beast tugs and draws the load, trembling all over, gasping for breath, moving sideways, with a sort of unnatural spasmodic leaping motion — it's awful in Nekrasov. But that's only a horse, and God has given us horses to beat. So the Tatars have taught us, and they left us the knout as a remembrance. But men, too, can be beaten. A well-educated, cultured gentleman and his wife beat their own child with a birch-rod, a girl of seven. I have an exact account of it. The papa was glad that the birch was covered with twigs. 'It stings more,' said he, and so he began to do in his own daughter. I know for a fact there are people who at every blow are worked up to sensuality, to literal sensuality, which increases progressively at every blow they inflict. They beat for a minute, for five minutes, for ten minutes, more rapidly and more savagely. The child screams. At last the child cannot scream, it gasps, 'Daddy! daddy!' By some diabolical unseemly chance the case was brought into court. A counsel is engaged. The Russian people have long called a barrister 'a conscience for hire.' The counsel protests in his client's defence. 'It's such a simple thing,' he says, 'an everyday domestic event. A father corrects his child. To our shame be it said, it is brought into court.' The jury, convinced by him, retire and bring in a favourable verdict. The public roars with delight that the torturer is acquitted. Ah, a pity I wasn't there! I would have proposed establishing a scholarship fund in the torturer's name! . . . Charming pictures.

"But I've still better things about children. I've collected a great, great deal about Russian children, Alyosha. There was a little girl of five who was hated by her father and mother, 'most worthy and respectable people, of good education and breeding.' You see, I must repeat again, it is a peculiar characteristic of many people, this love of torturing children, and children only. To all other types of humanity these torturers behave mildly and benevolently, like cultivated and humane Europeans; but they are very fond of tormenting children, even fond of children themselves in that sense. It's just their defencelessness that tempts the tormentor, just the angelic confidence of the child who has no refuge and no appeal, that sets his vile blood on fire. In every man, of course, a beast lies hidden — the beast of rage, the beast of lust roused by the screams of the tortured victim, the beast of unchained lawlessness, the beast of diseases that follow on vice — gout, kidney disease, and so on.

"This poor child of five was subjected to every possible torture by those cultivated parents. They beat her, thrashed her, kicked her for no reason till her body was one bruise. Then, they went to greater refinements of cruelty — shut her up all night in the cold and frost in a privy, and because she didn't ask to be taken up at night (as though a child of five sleeping its angelic, sound sleep could be trained to wake and ask), they smeared her face with excrement and forced her to eat it, and it was her mother, her mother did this. And that mother could sleep, hearing the groans of the poor child locked up in that vile place at night! A little creature, who can't even understand what's done to her, in the dark and cold of that vile place, beats her little aching breast with her tiny fist and weeps her bloody meek unresentful tears begging dear, kind God to protect her! Do you understand this rot, friend and brother, you God-fearing and humble novice? Do you understand why this infamy is necessary and why it has come about? Without it, I am told, man could not have existed on earth, for he could not have known good and evil. But why know that devilish good and evil when it costs so much? Why, the whole world of knowledge is not worth that child's tears! I say nothing of the sufferings of grown-up people, they have eaten the apple, damn them, and the devil take them all! But these little ones! I am making you suffer, Alyosha, you are not yourself. I'll leave off if you like."

"Never mind. I, too, want to suffer," muttered Alyosha.

"One picture, only one more, because it's so curious, so characteristic, and I have only just read it in some collection of Russian antiquities. I've forgotten the name. I must look it up. It was in the darkest days of serfdom at the beginning of the century, and long live the Liberator of the People! There was in those days a general with high connections, and a very wealthy landowner, one of those men — somewhat rare, I believe, by then — who, retiring from the service to a life of leisure, were convinced that they had earned absolute power over the lives of their subjects. There were such men then. So our general, settled on his property to which his two thousand souls were attached, lives in pomp, and lords it over his poor neighbours as though they were dependents and clowns. He has kennels of hundreds of hounds and nearly a hundred whips — all mounted, and in uniform. One day a serf boy, a little child of eight, threw a stone in play and hurt the paw of the general's favourite hound. 'Why is my favourite dog lame?' He is told that the boy threw a stone that hurt the dog's paw. 'So you did it.' The general looked the child up and down. 'Take him.' He was taken — taken from his mother and kept shut up all night. Early that morning the general comes out on horseback, with the hounds, his dependents, whips, and huntsmen, all mounted, in full hunting parade, around him. The servants are summoned for their edification, and in front of them all stands the mother of the child. The child is brought from the lock-up. It's a gloomy, cold, foggy autumn day, a capital day for hunting. The general orders the child to be undressed; the child is stripped naked. He shivers, numb with terror, not daring to peep. . . . 'Make him run,' commands the general. 'Run! run!' shout the outriders. The boy runs. . . . 'At him!' yells the general, and he sets the whole pack of hounds on the child. The hounds catch him, and tear him to pieces before his mother's eyes! . . . I believe the general was afterwards declared incapable of administering his estates. Well — what did he deserve? To be shot? To be shot for the satisfaction of our moral feelings? Speak, Alyosha!"

"To be shot," murmured Alyosha, lifting his eyes to Ivan with a pale, twisted smile.

"Bravo!" cried Ivan, delighted. "If even you say so . . . You're a pretty monk! So there is a little devil sitting in your heart, Alyosha Karamazov!"

"What I said was absurd, but —— "

"That's just the point, that 'but'!" cried Ivan. "Let me tell you, novice, that the absurd is only too necessary on earth. The world stands on absurdities, and perhaps nothing would have come to pass in it without them. We know what we know!"

"What do you know?"

"I understand nothing," Ivan went on, as though in delirium. "I don't want to understand anything now. I want to stick to the fact. I made up my mind long ago not to understand. If I try to understand anything, I shall be false to the fact and I have determined to stick to the fact."

"Why are you trying me?" Alyosha cried, with sudden distress. "Will you say what you mean at last?"

"Of course, I will; that's what I've been leading up to. You are dear to me, I don't want to let you go, and I won't give you up to your Zosima."

Ivan for a minute was silent, all at once his face became very sad.

"Listen! I confined myself to children only to make my case clearer. Of the other human tears with which the earth is soaked from its crust to its centre, I will say nothing. I have narrowed my subject on purpose. I am a bug, and I recognise in all humility that I cannot understand why the world is arranged as it is. Men are themselves to blame, I suppose; they were given paradise, they wanted freedom, and stole fire from heaven, though they knew they would become unhappy, so there is no need to pity them. All that my pitiful, earthly, Euclidean understanding tells me is that there is suffering and that there are none guilty; that cause follows effect, simply and directly; that everything flows and finds its level — but that's only Euclidean nonsense, I know that, and I can't consent to live by it! What comfort is it to me that there are none guilty and that cause follows effect simply and directly, and that I know it — I must have retribution, or I will destroy myself. And not retribution in some remote infinite time and space, but here on earth, and that I see it myself. I have believed in it. I want to see it myself, and if I am dead by then, let them raise me from the dead, for if it all happens without me, it will be too great an outrage. Surely I haven't suffered, simply that I, my crimes and my sufferings, may manure the soil for future harmony for somebody else. I want to see with my own eyes the hind lie down with the lion and the victim rise up and embrace his murderer. I want to be there when every one suddenly learns what it has all been for. All the religions of the world are built on this longing, and I am a believer. But then there are the children, and what am I to do about them? That's a question I can't answer. For the hundredth time I repeat, there are numbers of questions, but I've taken only the children, because in their case what I mean is so unanswerably clear. Listen! If all must suffer to pay for the eternal harmony, what have children to do with it, tell me, please? It's beyond all comprehension why they should suffer, and why they should pay for the harmony. Why should they, too, furnish material to enrich the soil for the harmony of the future? I understand solidarity in sin among men. I understand solidarity in retribution, too; but there can be no such solidarity with children. And if it is really true that they must share responsibility for all their fathers' crimes, such a truth is not of this world and is beyond my comprehension. Some jester will say, perhaps, that the child would have grown up and have sinned, but you see he didn't grow up, he was torn to pieces by the dogs, when he was eight years old. Oh, Alyosha, I am not blaspheming! I understand, of course, how the universe will

be shaken to its core, when everything in heaven and earth blends in one hymn of praise and everything that lives and has lived cries aloud: 'Thou art just, O Lord, for Thy ways are revealed.' When the mother embraces the fiend who threw her child to the dogs, and all three cry aloud with tears, 'Thou art just, O Lord!' then, of course, the crown of knowledge will be reached and all will be made clear. But what pulls me up here is that I can't accept that harmony. And while I am on earth, I make haste to take my own measures. You see, Alyosha, perhaps it really may happen that if I live to that moment, or rise again to see it, I, too, perhaps, may cry aloud with the rest, looking at the mother embracing the child's torturer, 'Thou art just, O Lord!' but I don't want to cry aloud then. While there is still time, I hasten to protect myself, and so I renounce the higher harmony altogether. It's not worth the tears of that one tortured child who beat itself on the breast with its little fist and prayed in its stinking outhouse, with its unexpiated tears to 'dear, kind God'! It's not worth it, because those tears are unatoned for. They must be atoned for, or there can be no harmony. But how? How are you going to atone for them? Is it possible? By their being avenged? But what do I care for avenging them? What do I care for a hell for oppressors? What good can hell do, since those children have already been tortured? And what becomes of harmony, if there is hell? I want to forgive. I want to embrace. I don't want more suffering. And if the sufferings of children go to swell the sum of sufferings which was necessary to pay for truth, then I assert in advance that the truth is not worth such a price. I don't want the mother to embrace the oppressor who threw her son to the dogs! She dare not forgive him! Let her forgive him for herself, if she will, let her forgive the torturer for the immeasurable suffering of her mother's heart. But the sufferings of her tortured child she has no right to forgive; she dare not forgive the torturer, even if the child were to forgive him! And if that is so, if they dare not forgive, what becomes of the harmony? Is there in the whole world a being who would have the right to forgive and could forgive? I don't want harmony. Out of love for humanity I don't want it. I would rather be left with the unavenged suffering. I would rather remain with my unavenged suffering and unassuaged indignation, *even if I were wrong*. Besides, too high a price is asked for harmony; it's beyond our means to pay so much for admission. And so I hasten to give back my ticket, and if I am an honest man I am bound to give it back as soon as possible. And that I am doing. It's not God that I don't accept, Alyosha, only I most respectfully return Him the ticket."

"That's rebellion," said Alyosha gently, looking down.

"Rebellion? I am sorry you call it that," said Ivan earnestly. "One can hardly live by rebellion, and I want to live. Tell me yourself, I challenge you — answer. Imagine that you are erecting the edifice of human destiny with the object of making men happy at last, giving them peace and rest at last, but that to this end it was essential and inevitable to torture to death only one tiny creature — that baby beating its breast with its fist, for instance — and to found that edifice on its unavenged tears, would you consent to be the architect on those conditions? Tell me, and do not lie."

"No, I wouldn't consent," said Alyosha softly.

"And can you admit the idea that men, for whom you are building it, would agree to accept a happiness based upon the unexpiated blood of a little victim? And accepting it would remain happy for ever?"

"No, I can't admit it. Brother," said Alyosha suddenly, with flashing eyes, "you said just now, is there a being in the whole world who would have the right to forgive and could forgive? But there is a Being and He can forgive everything, all and for all, because He gave His innocent blood for all and everything.

"You have forgotten Him, and on Him is built the edifice, and it is to Him they will cry aloud, 'Thou art just, O Lord, for Thy ways are revealed!'"

"Ah! the One without sin and His blood! No, I have not forgotten Him; on the contrary, I've been wondering all the time how it was you did not bring Him in before, for usually in argument those like you put Him in the foreground.

"Do you know, Alyosha — don't laugh! I made up a poem once, about a year ago. If you can waste another ten minutes on me, I'll tell it to you."

"You wrote a poem?"

"Oh, no, I didn't write it," laughed Ivan, "and I've never written two lines of poetry in my life. But I made up this poem and I remembered it. I was carried away when I made it up. You will be my first reader — that is, listener. Why should an author forego even one listener?" smiled Ivan. "Shall I tell it to you?"

"I am all attention," said Alyosha.

"My poem is called 'The Grand Inquisitor'; it's an absurd thing, but I want to tell it to you."

## CHAPTER V
### THE GRAND INQUISITOR

"Even this must have a preface—that is, a literary preface," laughed Ivan, "and what kind of *littérateur* am I? You see, the action takes place in the sixteenth century, and at that time, as you probably learnt at school, it was customary in poetry to bring down heavenly powers on earth. Not to speak of Dante, in France, court clerks, as well as the monks in the monasteries, used to give regular performances in which the Madonna, the saints, the angels, Christ, and God Himself were brought on the stage. In those days it was done in all simplicity. In Victor Hugo's 'Notre Dame de Paris' an edifying and gratuitous spectacle was provided for the people in the Hôtel de Ville of Paris in the reign of Louis XI in honour of the birth of the dauphin. It was called *Le bon jugement de la très sainte et gracieuse Vierge Marie*, and she appears in person on the stage and pronounces her *bon jugement*. Similar plays, chiefly from the Old Testament, were occasionally performed in Moscow, too, up to the time of Peter the Great. But besides dramatic spectacles there were current in the world all sorts of tales and songs, in which the holy angels and all the powers of heaven took part when required. In our monasteries the monks busied themselves in translating, copying, and even composing such poems—and as far back as the time of the Tatars. There is, for instance, one monastic poem (of course, from the Greek), 'The Wanderings of Our Lady through Hell,' with descriptions as bold as Dante's. Our Lady visits hell, and the Archangel Michael guides her through the torments. She sees the sinners and their tortures.

There is there among others one very entertaining set of sinners in a burning lake; some of them sink so deep in the lake that they can't swim out, and 'these God forgets'—an expression of extraordinary depth and force. And so Our Lady, overcome and weeping, falls before the throne of God and begs for mercy for all in hell—for all she has seen there, indiscriminately. Her conversation with God is immensely interesting. She beseeches Him, she will not desist, and when God points to the hands and feet of her Son, nailed to the Cross, and asks, 'How can I forgive His tormentors?' she bids all the saints, all the martyrs, all the angels and archangels to kneel down with her and pray for mercy on all without distinction. It ends by her winning from God a respite from suffering every year from Good Friday till Trinity day, and the sinners at once raise a cry of gratitude from hell, chanting, 'Thou art just, O Lord, in this judgment.' Well, my poem would have been of the same sort if it had appeared at that time. In my poem He comes on the scene, but He says nothing, only appears and passes on. Fifteen centuries have passed since He promised to come in His glory, fifteen centuries since His prophet wrote, 'Behold, I come quickly'; 'Of that day and that hour knoweth no man, neither the Son, but the Father,' as He Himself said on earth. But humanity awaits him with the same faith and with the same emotion. Oh, with greater faith, for it is fifteen centuries since man has ceased to see signs from Heaven.

*Believe but what the heart doth say*
*No signs from Heaven come to-day.*

There was nothing left but faith in what the heart doth say. It is true there were many miracles in those days. There were saints who performed miraculous cures; some holy people, according to their 'Lives,' were visited by the Queen of Heaven herself. But the devil does not slumber, and doubts were already arising among men regarding the truth of these miracles. And just then there appeared in the north, in Germany, a terrible new heresy. 'A great star like unto a torch' (that is, a church) 'fell upon the fountains of the waters and they were made bitter.' These heretics began blasphemously denying miracles. But those who remained faithful were all the more ardent in their faith. Humanity poured out its tears to Him as before, awaited His coming, loved Him, hoped for Him, yearned to suffer and die for Him as before. And so many ages mankind had prayed with faith and fervour, 'O Lord our God, hasten Thy coming,' so many ages called upon Him, that in His infinite mercy He conceived the desire to descend to His worshippers. Before that day He had come down, He had visited some holy men, martyrs and hermits, as is written in their 'Lives.' Among us, Tyutchev, with absolute faith in the truth of his words, bore witness that

> *Bearing the Cross, in slavish dress*
> *Weary and worn, the Heavenly King*
> *Our mother, Russia, came to bless,*
> *And through our land went wandering.*

And that certainly was so, I assure you.

"And behold, He desired to appear, if only for a moment, to the people, to the tortured, suffering people, sunk in foul iniquity, but loving Him like children. My story is laid in Spain, in Seville, in the most terrible time of the Inquisition, when fires were lighted every day to the glory of God, and 'in mag-

nificent *autos-da-fé* the wicked heretics were burnt.' Oh, of course, this was not the coming in which He will appear according to His promise at the end of time in all His heavenly glory, and which will be sudden 'as lightning flashing from east to west.' No, He desired to visit His children only for a moment, and just there where the flames were crackling round the heretics. In His infinite mercy He walks once more among men in that human shape in which He walked among men for three years fifteen centuries ago. He descends upon the 'torrid plazas' of the southern town in which on the day before almost a hundred heretics had, *ad majorem gloriam Dei*, been burnt by monseigneur, the Grand Inquisitor, in a magnificent *auto-da-fé*, in the presence of the king, the court, the knights, the cardinals, the most charming ladies of the court, and the whole population of Seville.

"He came softly, unobserved, and yet, strange to say, every one recognised Him. That might be one of the best passages in the poem. I mean, why they recognised Him. The people are irresistibly drawn to Him, they surround Him, they flock about Him, follow Him. He moves silently in their midst with a gentle smile of infinite compassion. The sun of love burns in His heart, light and power shine from His eyes, and their radiance, shed on the people, stirs their hearts with responsive love. He stretches out His hands to them, blesses them, and a healing virtue comes from contact with Him, even with His garments. An old man in the crowd, blind since childhood, cries out, 'O Lord, heal me and I shall see Thee!' and, as it were, scales fall from his eyes and the blind man sees Him. The crowd weeps and kisses the earth under His feet. Children throw flowers before Him, sing, and cry hosannah.

'It is He — it is He!' all repeat. 'It must be He, it can be no one but He!' He stops at the steps of the Seville cathedral at the moment when the weeping mourners are bringing in a little open white coffin. In it lies a child of seven, the only daughter of a prominent citizen. The dead child lies covered with flowers. 'He will raise your child,' people in the crowd shout to the weeping mother. The priest, coming to meet the coffin, looks perplexed, and frowns, but the mother of the dead child throws herself at His feet with a wail. 'If it be Thou, raise my child!' she cries, stretching out her hands to Him. The procession halts, the coffin is laid on the steps at His feet. He looks with compassion, and His lips once more softly pronounce, *'Talitha cumi!'* — 'and the damsel rose up.'

"The little girl sits up in the coffin and looks round, smiling with wide-open wondering eyes, holding a bunch of white roses they had put in her hand.

"There are cries, sobs, confusion among the people, and at that moment the monseigneur himself, the Grand Inquisitor, passes by the cathedral. He is an old man, almost ninety, tall and erect, with a withered face and sunken eyes, in which there is still a gleam of light. He is not dressed in the gorgeous pontifical robes, which he had flaunted before the people the previous day, when the enemies of the Roman Church were being burned — no, at this moment he is wearing his coarse, old, monk's cassock. At a distance behind him come his gloomy assistants and his slaves and the 'sacred guard.' He stops at the sight of the crowd and watches it from a distance. He had seen everything; he had seen them set the coffin down at His feet, seen the child rise up. His face darkens. He knits his thick grey brows and his eyes gleam with a sinister fire. He holds out his finger and bids the guards take Him. And such is his power, so completely are the people cowed into submission and trembling obedience to him, that the crowd immediately makes way for the guards, and in the midst of deathlike silence they lay hands on Him and lead Him away. The crowd instantly bows down to the earth, like one man, before the old Inquisitor. He blesses the people in silence and passes on. The guards lead their Prisoner to the close, gloomy, vaulted prison in the ancient palace of the Holy Inquisition and shut Him in it. The day passes and is followed by the black, hot, 'breathless' night of Seville. The air is 'fragrant with laurel and lemon.' In the pitch darkness the iron door of the prison is suddenly opened and the Grand Inquisitor himself comes in with a lantern in his hand. He is alone; the door is closed at once behind him. He stands in the doorway and for a minute or two gazes into His face. At last he goes up slowly, sets the lantern on the table and speaks.

" 'Is it Thou? Thou?' but receiving no answer, he adds at once. 'Don't answer, be silent. What canst Thou say, indeed? I know too well what Thou wouldst say. And Thou hast no right to add anything to what Thou didst say of old. Why, then, art Thou come to hinder us? For Thou hast come to hinder us, and Thou knowest that. But dost Thou know what will be to-morrow? I know not who Thou art and care not to know whether it is Thou or only a semblance of Thee, but to-morrow I shall condemn Thee and burn Thee at the stake as the worst of heretics. And the very people who have to-day kissed Thy feet, to-morrow at the faintest sign from me will rush to heap up the embers of Thy fire. Knowest

Thou that? Yes, maybe Thou knowest it,' he added with thoughtful penetration, never for a moment taking his eyes off the Prisoner."

"I don't quite understand, Ivan. What does it mean?" Alyosha, who had been listening in silence, said with a smile. "Is it simply a wild fantasy, or a mistake on the part of the old man — some impossible *qui pro quo?*"

"Take it as the last," said Ivan, laughing, "if you are so corrupted by modern realism and can't stand anything fantastic. If you like it to be a case of mistaken identity, let it be so. It is true," he went on, laughing, "the old man was ninety, and he may well have gone crazy over his set idea. He might have been struck by the appearance of the Prisoner. It might, in fact, be simply his ravings,.the delusion of an old man of ninety, over-excited by the *auto-da-fé* of a hundred heretics the day before. But does it matter to us after all whether it was a mistake of identity or a wild fantasy? All that matters is that the old man should speak out, should speak openly of what he has thought in silence for ninety years."

"And the Prisoner, too, is silent? Does He look at him and not say a word?"

"That's inevitable in any case." Ivan laughed again. "The old man has told Him He hasn't the right to add anything to what He has said of old. One may say it is the most fundamental feature of Roman Catholicism, in my opinion at least. 'All has been transmitted by Thee to the Pope,' they say, 'and all, therefore, is now in the Pope's hands, and there is no need for Thee to come now at all. Thou must not meddle for the time, at least.' That's how they speak and write too — the Jesuits, at any rate. I have read it myself in the works of their theologians. 'Hast Thou the right to reveal to us one of the mysteries of that world from which Thou hast come?' my old man asks Him, and answers the question for Him. 'No, Thou hast not; that Thou mayest not add to what has been said of old, and mayest not take from men the freedom which Thou didst uphold when Thou wast on earth. Whatsoever Thou revealest anew will encroach on men's freedom of faith; for it will be manifest as a miracle, and the freedom of their faith was dearer to Thee than anything in those days fifteen hundred years ago. Didst Thou not often say then, "I would make you free"? But now Thou hast seen these "free" men,' the old man adds suddenly, with pensive irony. 'Yes, we've paid dearly for it,' he goes on, looking sternly at Him, 'but at last we have completed that work in Thy name. For fifteen centuries we have been wrestling with Thy freedom, but now it is ended and over for good. Dost Thou not believe that it's over for good? Thou lookest meekly at me and deignest not even to be wroth with me. But let me tell Thee that now, to-day, people are more convinced than ever that they have perfect freedom, yet they have brought their freedom to us and laid it humbly at our feet. But that has been our doing. Was this what Thou didst desire? Was this Thy freedom?'"

"I don't understand again," Alyosha broke in. "Is he ironical, is he jesting?"

"Not a bit of it! He claims it as a merit for himself and his Church that at last they have vanquished freedom and have done so to make men happy. 'For now' (he is speaking of the Inquisition, of course) 'for the first time it has become possible to think of the happiness of men. Man was created a rebel; and how can rebels be happy? Thou wast warned,' he says to Him. 'Thou hast had no lack of signs and warnings, but Thou didst not listen to those

THE GRAND INQUISITOR

warnings; Thou didst reject the only way by which men might be made happy. But, fortunately, departing, Thou didst hand on the work to us. Thou hast promised, Thou hast established by Thy word, Thou hast given to us the right to bind and to unbind, and now, of course, Thou canst not think of taking it away. Why, then, hast Thou come to hinder us?' "

"And what's the meaning of 'no lack of signs and warnings'?" asked Alyosha.

"Why, that's the chief part of what the old man must say.

" 'The wise and dread spirit, the spirit of self-destruction and non-existence,' the old man goes on, 'the great spirit talked with Thee in the wilderness, and we are told in the books that he "tempted" Thee. Is that so? And could anything truer be said than what he revealed to Thee in three questions and what Thou didst reject, and what in the books is called "the temptation"? And yet if there has ever been on earth a real stupendous miracle, it took place on that day, on the day of the three temptations. The statement of those three questions was itself the miracle. If it were possible to imagine simply for the sake of argument that those three questions of the dread spirit had perished utterly from the books, and that we had to restore them and to invent them anew, in order to restore them to the books, and to do so had gathered together all the wise men of the earth — rulers, chief priests, learned men, philosophers, poets — and had set them the task of inventing three questions, such as would not only fit the occasion, but express in three words, three human phrases, the whole future history of the world and of humanity — dost Thou believe that all the combined wisdom of the earth could have invented anything in depth and force equal to the three questions which were actually put to Thee then by the wise and mighty spirit in the wilderness? From those questions alone, from the miracle of their statement, we can see that we have here to do not with the fleeting human intelligence, but with the absolute and eternal. For in those three questions the whole subsequent history of mankind is, as it were, brought together into one whole, and foretold, and in them are united all the unsolved historical contradictions of human nature. At the time it could not be so clear, since the future was unknown; but now that fifteen hundred years have passed, we see that everything in those three questions was so justly divined and foretold, and has been so truly fulfilled, that nothing can be added to them or taken from them.

" 'Judge Thyself who was right — Thou or he who questioned Thee then? Remember the first question; its meaning, though not its letter, was this: "Thou wouldst go into the world, and art going with empty hands, with some promise of freedom which men in their simplicity and their native unruliness cannot even understand, which they fear and dread — for nothing has ever been more insupportable for man and human society than freedom. But seest Thou these stones in this parched and barren wilderness? Turn them into bread, and mankind will run after Thee like a flock of sheep, grateful and obedient, though for ever trembling, lest Thou withdraw Thy hand and deny them Thy bread." But Thou didst not will to deprive man of freedom and didst reject the offer, thinking, what is that freedom worth, if obedience is bought with bread? Thou didst reply that man lives not by bread alone. But dost Thou know that for the sake of that earthly bread the spirit of the earth will rise up against Thee and will strive with Thee and overcome Thee and all will follow him, crying, "Who is like unto this beast? He has given us fire from heaven!" Dost Thou know that ages will pass, and humanity will proclaim by the lips of their sages and men of science that there is no crime, and therefore no sin; there is only hunger? "Feed men, and then ask of them virtue!" that's what they'll write on the banner, which they will raise against Thee, and with which Thy temple will be destroyed. Where Thy temple stood will rise a new building; the terrible tower of Babel will be built again, and though, like the one of old, it will not be finished, yet Thou mightest have prevented that new tower and have cut short the sufferings of men by a thousand years; for they will come back to us after a thousand years of agony with their tower. They will seek us again, hidden underground in the catacombs, for we shall be again persecuted and tortured. They will find us and cry to us, "Feed us, for those who have promised us fire from heaven haven't given it!" And then we shall finish building their tower, for he will finish the building who will feed them. And we alone shall feed them in Thy name, declaring falsely that it is in Thy name. Oh, never, never can they feed themselves without us! No science will give them bread so long as they remain free. In the end they will lay their freedom at our feet, and say to us, "Make us your slaves, but feed us." They will understand themselves, at last, that freedom and bread enough for all are inconceivable together, for never, never will they be able to share between them! They will be convinced, too, that they can never be free, for they are weak, vicious, worthless, and rebellious. Thou didst promise them the bread of Heaven, but, I repeat again, can it compare with earthly bread in the eyes of the weak, ever sinful and ignoble race of man? And if for the sake of the bread of Heaven thousands and tens of thousands shall follow Thee, what is to become of the millions and tens of thousands of millions of creatures who will not have the strength to forego the earthly bread for the sake of the heavenly? Or dost Thou care only for the tens of thousands of the great and strong, while the millions, numerous as the sands of the sea, who are weak but love Thee, must exist only to serve as raw material for the great and strong? No, we cherish the weak, too. They are sinful and rebellious, but in the end they, too, will become obedient. They will marvel at us and look on us as gods, because we are ready to endure the freedom which they have found so dreadful and to rule over them — so awful will they find it in the end to be free. But we shall tell them that we obey Thee and rule in Thy name. We shall deceive them again, for we will not let Thee come to us again. That deception will be our suffering, for we shall be forced to lie.

" 'This is the meaning of the first question in the wilderness, and this is what Thou hast rejected in the name of that freedom which Thou hast exalted above everything. Yet in this question lay hid the great mystery of this world. Choosing "bread," Thou wouldst have satisfied the universal and everlasting craving of each man and of humanity as a whole — to find some one to bow down to. Having remained free, man strives for nothing so incessantly and so painfully as to find some one to bow down to. But man seeks to bow down to what is established beyond dispute, so that all men would agree at once to bow down to it. For these pitiful creatures are concerned not only to find what one or the other can bow down to, but to find something that all would believe in and bow down to; and it is essential that they all do it *together*. This craving for *community* of worship is the chief torment of every man individually and of all humanity from the beginning of time. For the sake of common worship they've slain each other with the sword. They have set up gods and challenged one another, "Put away your gods and come and worship ours, or we will kill you and your gods!" And so it will be to the end of the world, even when gods disappear from the earth; they will fall down before idols just the same. Thou didst know, Thou couldst not but have known, this fundamental secret of human nature, but Thou didst reject the one infallible banner which was offered Thee to make all men bow down to Thee alone — the banner of earthly bread; and Thou hast rejected it for the sake of freedom and the bread of Heaven. Behold what Thou didst further. And all again in the name of freedom! I tell Thee that man is tormented by no greater anxiety than to find some one quickly to whom he can hand over that gift of freedom with which the ill-fated creature is born. But only he will take possession of their freedom who can appease their conscience. In bread there was offered Thee an infallible token; give bread, and man will worship thee, for nothing is more certain than bread. But if some one else, apart from Thee, will gain possession of his conscience — oh! then he will cast away Thy bread and follow after him who has ensnared his conscience. In that Thou wast right. For the secret of man's being is not only to live but to have something to live for. Without a stable conception of the object of life, man would not consent to go on living, and would rather destroy himself than remain on earth, though he had bread in abundance. That is true. But what happened? Instead of taking men's freedom from them, Thou didst make it greater than ever! Didst Thou forget that man prefers peace, and even death, to freedom of choice in the knowledge of good and evil? Nothing is more seductive for man than his freedom of conscience, but nothing is more painful. And behold, instead of furnishing a firm foundation for setting the conscience of man at rest for ever, Thou didst choose all that is extraordinary, vague, and conjectural; Thou didst choose what was utterly beyond the strength of men, acting as though Thou didst not love them at all — Thou who didst come to give Thy life for them! Instead of taking possession of men's freedom, Thou didst increase it, and burdened the spiritual kingdom of mankind with its sufferings for ever. Thou didst desire man's free love, that he should follow Thee freely, enticed and captivated by Thee. In place of the firm ancient law, man must hereafter with free heart decide for himself what is good and what is evil, having only Thy image before him as his guide. But did it not occur to Thee that he would at last question and indeed reject even Thy image and Thy truth, if he were weighed down with such a fearful burden as freedom of choice? They will cry aloud at last that the truth is not in Thee, for they could not have been left in greater confusion and suffering than Thou hast caused, laying upon them so many cares and insoluble problems.

" 'So that, in truth, Thou didst Thyself lay the foundation for the destruction of Thy kingdom, and no one is more to blame for it.

And yet was that what was offered Thee? There are three powers on earth, three powers alone, able to conquer and to hold captive for ever the conscience of these impotent rebels for their happiness — those powers are miracle, mystery, and authority. Thou hast rejected all three and hast set the example for doing so. When the wise and dread spirit set Thee on the pinnacle of the temple and said to Thee, "If Thou wouldst know whether Thou art the Son of God, cast Thyself down from hence, for it is written: the angels shall bear him up lest haply he dash his foot against a stone, and Thou shalt know then whether Thou art the Son of God and shalt prove then how great is Thy faith in Thy Father." But Thou didst refuse and wouldst not cast Thyself down. Oh! of course, Thou didst proudly and splendidly, like God; but the weak, unruly race of men, are they gods? Oh, Thou didst know then that in taking one step, in making one movement to cast Thyself down, Thou wouldst be tempting God and wouldst have lost all Thy faith in Him, and wouldst have been dashed to pieces against that earth which Thou didst come to save. And the wise spirit that tempted Thee would have rejoiced. But I ask again, are there many like Thee? And couldst Thou believe for one moment that men, too, could face such a temptation? Is the nature of men such, that they can reject miracle, and at the great moments of life, the moments of their deepest, most agonising spiritual difficulties, cling only to the free verdict of the heart? Oh, Thou didst know that Thy deed would be recorded in the books, would be handed down to remote times and reach the utmost ends of the earth, and Thou didst hope that man, following Thee, would cling to God without needing a miracle. But Thou didst not know that when man rejects miracle he rejects God, too; for man seeks not so much God as miracles. And as man cannot bear to be without the miracle, he will create new miracles of his own for himself, and will worship deeds of sorcery and witchcraft, though he might be a hundred times over a rebel, a heretic, and an atheist. Thou didst not come down from the Cross when they shouted to Thee, mocking and reviling Thee, "Come down from the cross and we will believe that Thou art He." Thou didst not come down, for again Thou wouldst not enslave man by a miracle, and didst crave faith given freely, not based on miracle. Thou didst crave free love and not the base raptures of the slave before the might that has overawed him for ever. But Thou didst think too highly of men therein, for they are slaves, of course, though rebellious by nature. Look round and judge; fifteen centuries have passed, look upon them. Whom hast Thou raised up to Thyself? I swear, man is weaker and baser by nature than Thou hast believed him! Can he, can he do what Thou didst? By showing him so much respect, Thou didst, as it were, cease to compassionate him, for Thou didst ask far too much from him — Thou who hast loved him more than Thyself! Respecting him less, Thou wouldst have asked less of him. That would have been more like love, for his burden would have been lighter. He is weak and vile. What though he is everywhere now rebelling against our power, and proud of his rebellion? It is the pride of a child and a school-boy. They are little children rioting and barring out the teacher at school. But their childish delight will end; it will cost them dear. They will cast down temples and drench the earth with blood. But they will see at last, the foolish children, that, though they are rebels, they are impotent rebels, unable to keep up their own rebellion. Bathed in their foolish tears, they will recognise at last that He who created them rebels must have meant to mock at them. They will say this in despair, and their utterance will be a blasphemy which will make them more unhappy still, for man's nature cannot bear blasphemy, and in the end always avenges it on itself. And so unrest, confusion, and unhappiness — that is the present lot of men after Thou didst suffer so much for their freedom! Thy great prophet tells in vision and in allegory, that he saw all those who took part in the first resurrection and that there were of each tribe twelve thousand. But if there were so many of them, they must have been not men but gods. They had borne Thy cross, they had endured scores of years in the barren, hungry wilderness, living upon locusts and roots — and Thou mayest indeed point with pride at those children of freedom, of free love, of free and splendid sacrifice in Thy name. But remember that they were only some thousands; and what of the rest? And how are the other weak ones to blame, because they could not endure what the strong have endured? How is the weak soul to blame that it is unable to receive such terrible gifts? Canst Thou have simply come to the elect and for the elect? But if so, it is a mystery and we cannot understand it. And if it is a mystery, we, too, have a right to preach a mystery, and to teach them that it's not the free judgment of their hearts, not love that matters, but a mystery which they must follow blindly, even against their conscience. So we have done. We have corrected Thy work and have founded it upon *miracle*, *mystery*, and *authority*. And men rejoiced that they were again led like

sheep, and that the terrible gift that had brought them such suffering was, at last, lifted from their hearts. Were we right teaching them this? Speak! Did we not love mankind, so meekly acknowledging their feebleness, lovingly lightening their burden, and permitting their weak nature even sin with our sanction? Why hast Thou come now to hinder us? And why dost Thou look silently and searchingly at me with Thy meek eyes? Show anger. I don't want Thy love, for I love Thee not. And what use is it for me to hide anything from Thee? Don't I know to Whom I am speaking? All that I can say is known to Thee already, I read it in Thy eyes. And is it for me to conceal from Thee our secret? Perhaps it is Thy will to hear it from my lips. Listen, then. We are not with Thee, but with *him* — that is our secret. It's a long time — eight centuries — since we have been not with Thee but with *him*. Just eight centuries ago, we took from him what Thou didst reject with scorn, that last gift he offered Thee, showing Thee all the kingdoms of the earth. We took from him Rome and the sword of Cæsar, and proclaimed ourselves sole rulers of the earth, though hitherto we have not been able to bring our work to full completion. But whose fault is that? Oh, the work is only beginning, but it has begun. We have long to wait for completion and the earth has yet much to suffer, but we shall triumph and shall be Cæsars, and then we shall plan the universal happiness of man. But Thou mightest have taken even then the sword of Cæsar. Why didst Thou reject that last gift? Hadst Thou accepted that last counsel of the mighty spirit, Thou wouldst have accomplished all that man seeks on earth — that is, some one to bow down to, some one to hand his conscience to, and some means of uniting all in one unanimous and harmonious ant-heap, for the craving for universal unity is the third and last anguish of men. Mankind as a whole has always striven to organise a universal state. There have been many great nations with great histories, but the more highly they were developed the more unhappy they were, for they felt more acutely than other people the craving for world-wide union. The great conquerors, Timours and Genghis-Khans, whirled like hurricanes over the face of the earth striving to conquer the universe, but even they, though unconsciously, expressed the same great craving of mankind for universal unity. Hadst Thou taken the world and Cæsar's purple, Thou wouldst have founded the universal state and have given universal peace. For who can rule men if not he who holds their conscience and their bread in his hands. We have taken the sword of Cæsar, and in taking it, of course, have rejected Thee and followed *him*. Oh, there will yet be ages of the confusion of free thought, ages of their science and cannibalism. For having begun to build their tower of Babel without us, they will end, of course, with cannibalism. But then the beast will crawl to us and lick our feet and spatter them with tears of blood. And we shall sit upon the beast and raise the cup, and on it will be written, "Mystery." But then, and only then, the reign of peace and happiness will come for men. Thou art proud of Thine elect, but Thou hast only the elect, while we shall give rest to all. And besides, how many of those elect, those mighty ones who could become elect, have grown weary waiting for Thee, and have carried and will carry the powers of their spirit and the ardour of their heart to the other camp, and will end by raising their *free* banner against Thee.

Thou didst Thyself lift up that banner. But with us all will be happy and will neither rebel nor destroy one another any more as under Thy freedom. Oh, we shall persuade them that they will become free only when they renounce their freedom in our favour and submit to us. And shall we be right or shall we be lying? They will be convinced that we are right, for they will remember the horrors of slavery and confusion to which Thy freedom brought them. Freedom, free thought and science, will lead them into such straits and will bring them face to face with such marvels and insoluble mysteries, that some of them, the fierce and rebellious, will destroy themselves, others, rebellious but weak, will destroy one another, while the rest, weak and unhappy, will crawl fawning to our feet and cry to us: "Yes, you were right, you alone possess His mystery, and we come back to you: save us from ourselves!"

" 'Receiving bread from us, they will see clearly that we take the bread made by their hands from them, to give it to them, without any miracle. They will see that we do not change the stones to bread, but in truth they will be more thankful for taking it from our hands than for the bread itself! For they will remember only too well that in old days, without our help, even the bread they made turned to stones in their hands, while since they have come back to us, the very stones have turned to bread in their hands. Too, too well will they know the value of complete submission! And until men know that, they will be unhappy. Who is most to blame for their not knowing it? Speak! Who scattered the flock and sent it astray on unknown paths? But the flock will come together again and will submit once more, and then it will be for all time.

Then we shall give them the quiet humble happiness of weak creatures such as they are by nature. Oh, we shall persuade them at last not to be proud, for Thou didst lift them up and thereby taught them pride. We shall show them that they are weak, that they are only pitiful children, but that childlike happiness is the sweetest of all. They will become timid and will look to us and huddle close to us in fear, as chicks to the hen. They will marvel at us and will be awe-stricken before us, and will be proud of our being so powerful and clever that we have been able to subdue such a turbulent flock of thousands of millions. They will tremble impotently before our wrath, their minds will grow timid, they will become as tearful as women and children, but they will be just as ready at a sign from us to pass to laughter and rejoicing, to happy mirth and childish song. Yes, we shall set them to work, but in their leisure hours we shall make their life like a child's game, with children's songs and innocent dances. Oh, we shall allow them even sin, they are weak and helpless, and they will love us like children because we allow them to sin. We shall tell them that every sin will be expiated, if it is committed with our permission, that we allow them to sin because we love them, and the punishment for these sins we take upon ourselves. And we shall take it upon ourselves, and they will adore us as their saviours who have taken on themselves their sins before God. And they will have no secrets from us. We shall allow or forbid them to live with their wives and mistresses, to have or not to have children — according to whether they have been obedient or disobedient — and they will submit to us gladly and cheerfully. The most painful secrets of their conscience, all, all they will bring to us, and

we shall absolve all. And they will be glad to accept our absolution, for it will save them from the great anxiety and terrible agony they endure at present in making a free decision for themselves. And all will be happy, all the millions of creatures except the hundred thousand who rule over them. For only we, we who guard the mystery, shall be unhappy. There will be thousands of millions of happy babes, and a hundred thousand sufferers who have taken upon themselves the curse of the knowledge of good and evil. Peacefully they will die, peacefully they will expire in Thy name, and beyond the grave they will find nothing but death. But we shall keep the secret, and for their happiness we shall allure them with the reward of heaven and eternity. For if there were anything in the other world, it certainly would not be for such as they. It is prophesied that Thou wilt come again victorious, Thou wilt come with Thy chosen, the proud and strong, but we will say that they have only saved themselves, but we have saved all. We are told that the harlot who sits upon the beast, and holds in her hands *mystery*, shall be put to shame, that the weak will rise up again, and will rend her royal purple and will strip naked her loathsome body. But I will then stand up and point out to Thee the thousand millions of happy babes who knew no sin. And we who have taken their sins upon us for the sake of their happiness will stand up before Thee and say: "Judge us if Thou canst and darest." Know that I fear Thee not. Know that I, too, have been in the wilderness, I, too, have lived on roots and locusts, I, too, prized the freedom with which Thou hast blessed men, and I, too, was striving to stand among Thy elect, among the strong and powerful, thirsting "to complete the number." But I awakened and would not serve madness. I turned back and joined the ranks of those *who have corrected Thy work.* I left the proud and went back to the humble, for the happiness of the humble. What I say to Thee will come to pass, and our Kingdom will be built. I repeat, to-morrow Thou shalt see that obedient flock who at a sign from me will hasten to heap up the hot embers about the pile on which I shall burn Thee for coming to hinder us. For if there ever was one who more than all others deserved our fires, it is Thou. To-morrow I shall burn Thee. *Dixi.'* "

Ivan stopped. He was carried away as he talked and spoke with excitement; when he had finished, he suddenly smiled.

Alyosha, who had listened in silence, towards the end was greatly moved and seemed several times on the point of interrupting, but restrained himself. Now his words came with a rush.

"But . . . that's absurd!" he cried, flushing. "Your poem is in praise of Jesus, it does not blame Him — as you meant it to do. And who will believe you about freedom? Is that the way to understand it? That's not the idea of it in the Orthodox Church. . . . That's Rome, and not even the whole of Rome, it's false — those are the worst of the Catholics, the Inquisitors, the Jesuits! . . . And there could not be such a fantastic creature as your Inquisitor. What are these sins of mankind they take on themselves? Who are these keepers of the mystery who have taken some curse upon themselves for the happiness of mankind? When have they ever been seen? We know the Jesuits, they are spoken ill of, but are they really what you describe? They are not that at all, not at all. . . . They are simply the Romish army of the future uni-

versal earthly kingdom, with the Pontiff of Rome for Emperor . . . that's their ideal, but there's no sort of mystery or lofty melancholy about it. . . . It's simple lust for power, for filthy earthly goods, for domination — something like a universal serfdom with them as masters — that's all they stand for. They don't even believe in God perhaps. Your suffering Inquisitor is a mere fantasy."

"Stop, stop," laughed Ivan, "how hot you are! A fantasy you say, let it be so! Of course it's a fantasy. But allow me to say: do you really think that the Roman Catholic movement of the last centuries is actually nothing but the lust for power, for filthy goods? Is that what Father Païssy teaches you?"

"No, no, on the contrary, Father Païssy did once say something rather like what you said . . . but of course it's not that, not that at all," Alyosha hastily corrected himself.

"A precious admission, in spite of your 'not that at all.' I ask you why your Jesuits and Inquisitors have united simply for vile material gain? Why can there not be among them one martyr oppressed by great sorrow and loving humanity? You see, only suppose that there was one such man among all those who desire nothing but filthy material goods — if there's only one like my old Inquisitor, who had himself eaten roots in the desert and made frenzied efforts to subdue his flesh to make himself free and perfect. But yet all his life he loved humanity, and suddenly his eyes were opened, and he saw that it is no great moral blessedness to attain perfection and freedom, if at the same time one gains the conviction that millions of God's creatures have remained a mockery, that they will never be capable of using their freedom, that these poor rebels can never turn into giants to complete the tower, that it was not for such geese that the great idealist dreamt his dream of harmony. Seeing all that he turned back and joined — the clever people. Surely that could have happened?"

"Joined whom, what clever people?" cried Alyosha, almost in a frenzy. "They have no such great cleverness and no mysteries and secrets. . . . Perhaps nothing but atheism, that's all their secret. Your Inquisitor does not believe in God, that's his whole secret!"

"What if it is so! At last you have guessed it. It's perfectly true, it's true that that's the whole secret, but isn't that suffering, at least for a man like that, who has wasted his whole life in the desert and yet could not shake off his incurable love of humanity? In his declining days he reaches the clear conviction that nothing but what the great dread spirit advised could make any tolerable sort of life for the feeble, unruly, 'incomplete, experimental creatures fashioned in jest.' And so, convinced of this, he sees that he must follow the counsel of the wise spirit, the dread spirit of death and destruction, and therefore accept falsehood and deception, and lead men consciously to death and destruction, and yet deceive them all the way so that they may not notice where they are being led, that the poor blind creatures may at least on the way think themselves happy. And note, the deception is in the name of Him in Whose ideal the old man had so fervently believed all his life long. Isn't that a misfortune? And if only one such found himself at the head of the whole army 'filled with the lust for power only for the sake of filthy goods' — would not one such be enough to make a tragedy? More than that, one such standing at the head is enough to create the actual leading idea of the Roman Church with all its armies and Jesuits, its highest idea. I tell you frankly that I firmly believe that there has always been such a man among those who stood at the head of the movement. Who knows, there may have been some such even among the Roman Popes. Who knows, perhaps the spirit of that accursed old man who loves mankind so obstinately in his own way is to be found even now in a whole multitude of such old men, existing not by chance but by agreement, as a secret league formed long ago for the guarding of the mystery, to keep it from the weak and the unhappy, so as to make them happy. No doubt it is so, and so it must be indeed. I fancy that even among the Masons there's something of the same mystery at the bottom, and that that's why the Catholics so detest the Masons as their rivals breaking up the unity of the idea, while it is so essential that there should be one flock and one shepherd. . . . But from the way I defend my idea I might be an author impatient of your criticism. Enough of it."

"You are perhaps a Mason yourself!" broke suddenly from Alyosha. "You don't believe in God," he added, speaking this time very sorrowfully. He fancied besides that his brother was looking at him ironically. "How does your poem end?" he asked, suddenly looking down. "Or was it the end?"

"I meant to end it like this. When the Inquisitor ceased speaking he waited some time for his Prisoner to answer him. The Prisoner's silence weighs down upon him. He saw that the Prisoner had listened intently all the time, looking gently in his eyes and evidently not wishing to reply. The old man longs for Him to say something, however bitter and terrible. But He suddenly approaches the old man in silence and gently kisses him on his bloodless aged lips. That is his whole answer. The old man shudders. The corners of his lips tremble. He goes to the door, opens it, and says to Him: 'Go, and come no more . . . come not at all, never, never!' And he lets Him out into the dark streets of the town. The Prisoner goes away."

"And the old man?"

"The kiss burns in his heart, but the old man adheres to his idea."

"And you with him, you too?" cried Alyosha mournfully.

Ivan laughed.

"Why, it's all nonsense, Alyosha. It's only a silly poem by a silly student, who could never write two lines of verse. Why do you take it so seriously? Surely you don't suppose I am going straight off to the Jesuits, to join the men who are correcting His work? Good Lord, it's no business of mine. I told you, all I want is to live on till I'm thirty, and then . . . dash the cup to the ground!"

"But the little sticky leaves, and the precious graves, and the blue sky, and the woman you love! How will you live, how will you love them?" Alyosha cried sorrowfully. "With such a hell in your heart and your head, how can you? No, that's just what you are going away for, to join them . . . if not, you will kill yourself, you can't endure it!"

"There is a strength to endure everything," Ivan said with a cold smile.

"What strength?"

"The strength of the Karamazovs — the strength of the Karamazov baseness."

"To sink into debauchery, to stifle your soul with corruption, yes?"

"Possibly even that . . . only perhaps till I am thirty I shall escape it, and then . . ."

"How will you escape it? By what means will you escape it? That's impossible with your ideas."

"In the Karamazov way, again."

"'Everything is permitted,' you mean? Everything is permitted, is that it?"

Ivan scowled, and all at once turned strangely pale.

"Ah, you've caught up yesterday's phrase, which so offended Miüsov — and which Dmitri pounced upon so naïvely and paraphrased!" he smiled queerly. "Yes, if you like, 'everything is lawful' since the word has been said. I won't deny it. And Mitya's version isn't bad."

Alyosha looked at him in silence.

"I thought that going away from here I have you at least," Ivan said suddenly, with unexpected feeling; "but now I see that there is no place for me even in your heart, my dear hermit. The formula, 'everything is permitted,' I won't renounce — will you renounce me for that, yes?"

Alyosha got up, went to him and gently kissed him on the lips.

"That's plagiarism," cried Ivan, highly delighted. "You stole that from my poem. Thank you though. Get up, Alyosha, it's time we were going, both of us."

They went out, but stopped when they reached the entrance of the restaurant.

"Listen, Alyosha," Ivan began in a resolute voice, "if I am really able to care for the sticky little leaves I shall only love them, remembering you. It's enough for me that you are somewhere here, and I shan't lose my desire for life yet. Is that enough for you? Take it as a declaration of love if you like. And now you go to the right and I to the left. And it's enough, do you hear, enough. I mean even if I don't go away to-morrow (I think I certainly shall go) and we meet again, don't say a word more on these subjects. I beg that particularly. And about Dmitri, too, I ask you specially never speak to me again," he added, with sudden irritation; "it's all done with, it has all been said over and over again, hasn't it? And I'll make you one promise in return for it. When, at thirty, I am ready to 'dash the cup to the ground,' wherever I may be I'll come to have one more talk with you, even though it were from America, you may be sure of that. I'll come on purpose. It will be very interesting to have a look at you, to see what you'll be by that time. It's rather a solemn promise, you see. And we really may be parting for seven years or ten. Come, go now to your Pater Seraphicus, he is dying. If he dies without you, you will be angry with me for having kept you. Good-bye, kiss me once more; that's right, now go."

Ivan turned suddenly and went his way without looking back. It was just as Dmitri had left Alyosha the day before, though the parting had been very different. The strange thought flashed like an arrow through Alyosha's mind in the distress and dejection of that moment. He waited a little, looking after his brother. He suddenly noticed that Ivan swayed as he walked and that his right shoulder looked lower than his left. He had never noticed it before. But all at once he turned, too, and almost ran to the monastery. It was nearly dark, and he felt almost frightened; something new was growing up in him for which he could not account. The wind had risen again as on the previous evening, and the ancient pines murmured gloomily about him when he entered the hermitage copse. He almost ran. "Pater Seraphicus — he got that name from somewhere — where from?" Al-

yosha wondered. "Ivan, poor Ivan, and when shall I see you again? . . . Here is the hermitage. Yes, yes, that he is, Pater Seraphicus, he will save me — from him and for ever!"

Several times afterwards he wondered how on leaving Ivan he could so completely forget his brother Dmitri, though he had that morning, only a few hours before, so firmly resolved to find him and not to give up the hunt for him, even should he be unable to return to the monastery that night.

## CHAPTER VI
### FOR AWHILE A FAR FROM CLEAR ONE

IVAN, on parting from Alyosha, went home to Fyodor Pavlovich's house. But, strange to say, he was overcome by insufferable depression, which grew greater at every step he took towards the house. There was nothing strange in his being depressed; what was strange was that Ivan could not have said what the cause of it was. He had often been depressed before, and there was nothing surprising in his feeling so at such a moment, when he had broken off with everything that had brought him here, and was preparing that day to make a new start and enter upon a new, unknown path. He would again be as solitary as ever, and though he had great hopes, and great — too great — expectations from life, he could not have given any definite account of his hopes, his expectations, or even his desires.

Yet at that moment, though the apprehension of the new and unknown was certainly in his heart, what worried him was something quite different. "Is it loathing for my father's house?" he wondered. "Quite likely; I am so sick of it; and though it's the last time I shall cross its hateful threshold, still I loathe it. . . . No, it's not that either. Is it the parting with Alyosha and the conversation I had with him? For so many years I've been silent with the whole world and not deigned to speak, and all of a sudden I reel off a rigmarole like that." It certainly might have been the youthful vexation of youthful inexperience and vanity — vexation at having failed to express himself, especially before such a being as Alyosha, upon whom he had certainly been reckoning in his heart. No doubt that came in, that vexation, it must have indeed; but yet that was not it, that was not it either. "I feel sick with depression and yet I can't tell what I want. Better not think, perhaps."

Ivan tried "not to think," but that, too, was no use. What made his depression so vexatious and irritating was that it had a kind of casual, external character — he felt that. Some person or thing seemed to be standing out somewhere, just as something will sometimes obtrude itself upon the eye, and though one may be so busy with work or conversation that for a long time one does not notice it, yet it irritates and almost torments one till at last one realises, and removes the offending object, often quite a trifling and ridiculous one — some article left about in the wrong place, a handkerchief on the floor, a book not replaced on the shelf, and so on.

At last, feeling very cross and ill-humoured, Ivan arrived home, and suddenly, about fifteen paces from the garden gate, he guessed what was fretting and worrying him.

On a bench in the gateway the valet Smerdyakov was sitting, enjoying the coolness of the evening, and at the first glance at him Ivan knew that the valet Smerdyakov was on his mind, and that it was this man that his soul loathed. It all dawned upon him suddenly and became clear. A while ago, when Alyosha

had been telling him of his meeting with Smerdyakov, he had felt a sudden twinge of gloom and loathing, which had immediately stirred responsive anger in his heart. Afterwards, as he talked, Smerdyakov had been forgotten for the time being; but still he had remained in his mind, and as soon as Ivan parted from Alyosha and was walking home alone, the forgotten sensation began to obtrude itself again. "Is it possible that this contemptible wretch can worry me so much?" he wondered, with insufferable irritation.

Indeed, Ivan had come of late to feel an intense dislike for the man, especially during the last few days. He had even begun to notice in himself a growing feeling that was almost one of hatred for the creature. Perhaps this hatred was accentuated by the fact that when Ivan first came to the neighbourhood he had felt quite differently. Then he had taken a marked interest in Smerdyakov, and had even thought him very original. He had encouraged him to talk, although he had always wondered at a certain incoherence in the man, or rather intellectual restlessness in him, and could not understand what it was that so continually and insistently worked upon the brain of "the contemplative." They discussed philosophical questions and even how there could have been light on the first day when the sun, moon, and stars were created only on the fourth day, and how that should be interpreted. But Ivan soon saw that, though the sun, moon, and stars might be an interesting subject, yet that it was quite secondary to Smerdyakov, and that he was looking for something altogether different. In one way and another, he began to betray a boundless vanity, and a wounded vanity, at that. Ivan disliked this very much. That was how his aversion arose. Later on, there had been trouble in the house. Grushenka had come on the scene, and there had been the scandals with his brother Dmitri — they discussed that, too. But though Smerdyakov always talked of that with great excitement, it was impossible to discover what his own desire in the matter was. There was, in fact, something surprising in the illogical and incoherent character of some of his desires, which came out involuntarily, yet always remained vague. Smerdyakov was always inquisitive, asking certain indirect but obviously premeditated questions, but what his object was he did not explain, and usually at the most important moment he would break off and relapse into silence or change the subject. But what finally irritated Ivan most and roused his disgust was the peculiar, revolting familiarity which Smerdyakov began to show more and more markedly. Not that he forgot himself and was rude; on the contrary, he always spoke very respectfully, yet he had obviously begun to consider — goodness knows why! — that there was some sort of understanding between him and Ivan Fyodorovich. He always spoke in a tone that suggested that those two had some kind of compact, some secret between them, that had at some time been expressed on both sides, known only to them and beyond the comprehension of those around them. But for a long while Ivan did not recognise the real cause of his growing disgust and he had only lately realised what was at the root of it.

With a feeling of disgust and irritation he tried to pass in at the gate without speaking to or looking at Smerdyakov. But Smerdyakov rose from the bench, and from that action alone Ivan knew instantly that he wanted to talk to him on a particular subject. Ivan looked at him and stopped, and the fact that he did stop, instead of passing by, as he had meant to the minute before, drove him to fury. With anger and repulsion he looked at Smerdyakov's sickly eunuch's face, with the little curls combed over the temples and a tuft of hair above the brow. His left eye, slightly screwed up, winked as though to say, "Where are you going? You won't pass by; you see that we two clever people have something to say to each other."

Ivan shook. "Get away, you blackguard; what kind of companion am I for you, you fool!" was on the tip of his tongue, but to his profound astonishment he heard himself say something entirely different: "Is my father still asleep, or has he waked?"

He asked the question softly and meekly, to his own surprise, and at once, again to his own surprise, sat down on the bench. For an instant he felt almost frightened; he remembered it afterwards. Smerdyakov stood facing him, his hands behind his back, looking at him with assurance and almost with severity.

"Still asleep, sir," he articulated deliberately. ("You were the first to speak, not I," he seemed to say.) "I am surprised at you, sir," he added, after a pause, dropping his eyes affectedly, setting his right foot forward, and playing with the tip of his polished boot.

"Why are you surprised at me?" Ivan asked abruptly and sternly, doing his utmost to restrain himself, and suddenly realising, with disgust, that he was feeling intense curiosity and would not, on any account, go away without satisfying it.

"Why don't you go to Chermashnya, sir?" Smerdyakov suddenly raised his eyes and smiled familiarly. "Why I smile you must understand of yourself, if you are a clever man," his screwed-up left eye seemed to say.

"Why should I go to Chermashnya?" Ivan Fyodorovich asked in surprise.

Smerdyakov was silent again.

"Fyodor Pavlovich himself has so earnestly begged you to, sir," he said at last, slowly and apparently attaching no significance to his answer. "I put you off with a minor reason," he seemed to suggest, "simply to say something."

"Damn you! Say outright what you want!" Ivan cried angrily at last, passing from meekness to violence.

Smerdyakov drew his right foot up to his left, pulled himself up, but went on looking at him with the same serenity and the same little smile.

"Substantially nothing — but just by way of conversation."

Another silence followed. They did not speak for nearly a minute. Ivan knew that he ought to get up and show anger, and Smerdyakov stood before him and seemed to be waiting as though to see whether he would be angry or not. So at least it seemed to Ivan. At last he moved to get up. Smerdyakov seemed to seize the moment.

"I'm in an awful position, Ivan Fyodorovich. I don't know how to help myself," he said all at once resolutely and distinctly, and at his last word he sighed. Ivan Fyodorovich sat down again.

"They are both utterly unhinged, they are no better than little children, sir," Smerdyakov went on. "I am speaking of your parent and your brother Dmitri Fyodorovich, sir. Here Fyodor Pavlovich will get up directly and begin worrying me every minute, 'Has she come? Why hasn't she come?' and so on up till midnight and even after midnight. And if Agrafena Alexandrovna doesn't come (for very likely she does not mean to come at all), then he will be at me again to-morrow morning, 'Why hasn't she come? When will she come?' — as though I were to blame for it. On the other side it's no better, sir. As soon as it gets dark, or even before, your brother will appear hereabouts with a gun in his hands: 'Look out, you rogue, you bouillon-maker. If you miss her and don't let me know she's come — I'll kill you before any one.' When the night's over, in the morning, he, too, like Fyodor Pavlovich, begins worrying me to death. 'Why hasn't she come? Will she come soon?' And he, too, thinks I am to blame because his lady hasn't come. And every day and every hour they get angrier and angrier, so that I sometimes think, sir, I shall take my own life in fright. I can't depend upon them, sir."

"And why did you stick your nose in? Why did you begin to spy for Dmitri Fyodorovich?" said Ivan irritably.

"How could I help it? Though, indeed, I haven't meddled at all, if you want to know the truth of the matter. I kept quiet from the very beginning, not daring to argue; but he appointed me to be his personal servant. He has had only one thing to say since: 'I'll kill you, you scoundrel, if you miss her.' I feel certain, sir, that I shall have a long fit to-morrow."

"What do you mean by 'a long fit'?"

"A long fit, lasting a long time — several hours, or perhaps a day or two. Once it went on for three days. I fell from the garret that time. The convulsions ceased and then began again, and for three days I couldn't come back to my senses. Fyodor Pavlovich sent for Her-

THE CRAZY OLD MAN

zenstube, the doctor here, and he put ice on my head and tried another remedy, too. . . . I might have died, sir."

"But they say one can't tell with epilepsy when a fit is coming. What makes you say you will have one to-morrow?" Ivan inquired, with a peculiar, irritable curiosity.

"That's just so. You can't tell beforehand."

"Besides you fell from the garret then."

"I climb up to the garret every day. I might fall from the garret again to-morrow. And, if not, I might fall down the cellar steps. I have to go into the cellar every day, too."

Ivan took a long look at him.

"You are talking nonsense, I see, and I don't quite understand you," he said softly, but with a sort of menace. "Do you mean to pretend to be ill for three days, beginning to-morrow, eh?"

Smerdyakov, who was looking at the ground again, and playing with the toe of his right foot, set the foot down, moved the left one forward, raised his head and, grinning, articulated:

"If I were able to play such a trick, that is, pretend to have a fit — and it would not be difficult for a man accustomed to them — I should have a perfect right to use such a means to save myself from death. For even if Agrafena Alexandrovna comes to see his father while I am ill in bed, Dmitri Fyodorovich, sir, can't blame a sick man for not telling him. He'd be ashamed to."

"Hang it all!" Ivan cried, his face working with anger. "Why are you always in such a funk over your life? All my brother Dmitri's threats are only hasty words and mean nothing. He won't kill you; it's not you he'll kill!"

"He'd kill me first of all, like a fly. But even more than that, I am afraid I shall be taken for an accomplice of his when he does something absurd to his father."

"Why should you be taken for an accomplice?"

"They'll think I am an accomplice, because I let him know the signals as a great secret."

"What signals? Whom did you tell?"

"I'm bound to admit the fact," Smerdyakov drawled with pedantic composure, "that Fyodor Pavlovich and I have a secret together in this business. As you know yourself (if only you do know it) he has for several days past locked himself in as soon as night or even evening comes on. Of late you've been going upstairs to your room early every evening, and yesterday you did not go out at all, and so perhaps you don't know how carefully he has begun to lock himself in at night, and even if Grigory Vasilyevich himself comes to the door he won't open to him till he hears his voice. But Grigory Vasilyevich does not come, sir, because I wait upon him alone in his rooms now. That's the arrangement he made himself ever since this to-do with Agrafena Alexandrovna began. But at night, by his orders, I go away to the lodge, so that I don't get to sleep till midnight, sir, but am on the watch, getting up and walking about the yard, waiting for Agrafena Alexandrovna to come, sir. For the last few days he's been perfectly frantic expecting her. What he argues is, she is afraid of him, that is, of Dmitri Fyodorovich (Mitya, as he calls him), 'and so,' says he, 'she'll come the back-way, late at night, to me. You look out for her,' says he, 'till midnight and later; and if she does come, you run up and knock at my door or at the window opening on the garden. Knock at first twice, rather slowly, and then three times more quickly, then,' says he, 'I shall understand at once that she has come, and will open the door to you quietly.' Another signal he gave me in case anything unexpected happens. At first, two knocks, and then, after an interval, another much louder. Then he will understand that something has happened suddenly and that I must see him, and he will open to me so that I can go and speak to him. That's all in case Agrafena Alexandrovna can't come herself, but sends a message. Besides, Dmitri Fyodorovich might come, too, so I must let him know he is near. Your father is awfully afraid of Dmitri Fyodorovich, so that even if Agrafena Alexandrovna had come and were locked in with him, and Dmitri Fyodorovich were to turn up anywhere near at the time, I should be bound to let him know at once, knocking three times. So that the first signal of five knocks means Agrafena Alexandrovna has come, while the second signal of three knocks means 'something important to tell you.' Your father has rehearsed them with me several times and explained them to me. And as in the whole universe no one knows of these signals but myself and your father, sir, he'd open the door without the slightest hesitation and without calling out (he is awfully afraid of calling out aloud). Well, those signals have now become known to Dmitri Fyodorovich, too."

"How are they known? Did you tell him? How dared you tell him?"

"It was out of fear I did it, sir. How could I dare to keep it back from him, sir? Dmitri Fyodorovich kept persisting every day, 'You are deceiving me, you are hiding something from me! I'll break both your legs for you.' So I told him those secret signals that he might see my slavish devotion, and might be satisfied that I was not deceiving him, but was telling him all I could."

"If you think that he'll make use of those signals and try to get in, don't let him in."

"But if I should be laid up with a fit, how can I prevent him coming in then, even if I dared to hold him back, knowing how desperate he is?"

"Hang it! How can you be so sure you are going to have a fit, confound you? Are you laughing at me?"

"How could I dare laugh at you? — and I am in no laughing humour with this fear on me. I feel I am going to have a fit. I have a presentiment. Fright alone will bring it on."

"Confound it! If you are laid up, Grigory will be on the watch. Let Grigory know beforehand; he will be sure not to let him in."

"I should never dare to tell Grigory Vasilyevich about the signals without orders from my master. And as for Grigory Vasilyevich hearing him and not admitting him, he has been ill ever since yesterday, and Marfa Ignatyevna intends to give him medicine to-morrow. They've just arranged it. It's a very curious remedy they have. Marfa Ignatyevna knows of a decoction and always keeps it on hand. It's a strong thing made from some herb. She has the secret of it, and she gives it to Grigory Vasilyevich about three times a year when his lumbago's so bad he is almost paralysed by it. Then she takes a towel, sir, wets it with the stuff, and rubs his whole back for half an hour till it's quite red and swollen, and what's left in the bottle she gives him to drink with a special prayer; but not quite all, for on such occasions she leaves some for herself, and drinks it herself. And as they never take strong drink, I assure you, sir, they both drop asleep at once and sleep soundly a very long time. And when Grigory Vasilyevich wakes up, sir, he is perfectly well after it, but Marfa Ignatyevna always has a headache from it. So, if Marfa Ignatyevna carries out her intention to-morrow, sir, they won't hear anything and won't hinder Dmitri Fyodorovich. They'll be asleep, sir."

"What a rigmarole! And it all seems to happen at once, as though it were planned. You'll have a fit and they'll both be dead to the world," cried Ivan. "But aren't you per-haps trying to arrange it this way?" broke from him suddenly, and he frowned threaten-ingly.

"How could I, sir? . . . And why should I, when it all depends on Dmitri Fyodorovich and his designs? . . . If he means to do any-thing, he'll do it, sir; but if not, surely I shan't be the one to thrust him upon his father."

"And why should he go to father, especially on the sly, if, as you say yourself, Agrafena Alexandrovna won't come at all?" Ivan went on, turning white with anger. "You say that yourself, and all the while I've been here, I've felt sure it was all the old man's fancy, and the slut won't come to him. Why should Dmitri break in on him if she doesn't come? Speak, I want to know what you are thinking!"

"You know yourself why he'll come. What does it matter what I think? He will come simply because he is in a rage or suspicious on account of my illness perhaps, and he'll dash in, as he did yesterday through impatience to search the rooms, to see whether she hasn't slipped in on the sly. He is perfectly well aware, too, that Fyodor Pavlovich has a big envelope with three thousand roubles in it, tied up with ribbon and sealed with three seals. On it is written in his own hand, 'To my angel Grushenka, if she will wish to come,' to which he added three days later, 'and for

my little chick.' That is what it is, sir."

"Nonsense!" cried Ivan, almost beside him-self. "Dmitri isn't the one to commit robbery and kill his father while he's at it. He might have killed him yesterday on account of Gru-shenka, like the frantic, savage fool he is, but he won't steal."

"He is in great need of money just now — very great need, Ivan Fyodorovich. You don't know how badly he needs it, sir," Smerdya-kov explained, with perfect composure and re-markable distinctness. "Besides, he looks on that three thousand as his own. He said so to me himself, sir. 'My father still owes me just three thousand,' he said. And besides that, consider, Ivan Fyodorovich, this other point: it's as good as certain, so to say, that Agrafena Alexandrovna will force him, if only she cares to, to marry her — the master himself, I mean, Fyodor Pavlovich — if only she cares to, and of course she may care to, sir. I was only talking when I said that she wouldn't come, but maybe she's looking for more than that — I mean, to be mistress here. I know myself that Samsonov, her merchant, was laughing with her about it, telling her quite openly that it would not be at all a foolish thing to do. And she's got plenty of sense, sir. She wouldn't marry a beggar like Dmitri Fyo-dorovich, not she, sir. So, taking that into con-sideration, Ivan Fyodorovich, reflect that then neither Dmitri Fyodorovich nor yourself and your brother, Alexey Fyodorovich, would get anything after the master's death, not a rouble, for Agrafena Alexandrovna would marry him simply to get hold of it all, all the money there is. But if your father were to die now, there'd surely be some forty thousand for each one of you, even for Dmitri Fyodoro-vich whom the master hates so, for he's made no will. . . . Dmitri Fyodorovich knows all that very well." A sort of shudder passed over Ivan's face. He suddenly flushed.

"Then why on earth," he suddenly interrupted Smerdyakov, "do you advise me to go to Chermashnya? What did you mean by that? If I go away, you see what will happen here." Ivan drew his breath with difficulty.

"Precisely so, sir," said Smerdyakov, softly and reasonably, watching Ivan intently.

"What do you mean by 'precisely so'?" Ivan questioned him, with a menacing light in his eyes, restraining himself with difficulty.

"I spoke because I felt sorry for you. If I were you I should simply throw it all up . . . rather than have anything to do with such a mess," answered Smerdyakov, with the most candid air, looking at Ivan's flashing eyes. They were both silent.

"You seem to be a confounded idiot, and what's more . . . an awful scoundrel, too." Ivan rose suddenly from the bench. He was about to pass straight through the gate, but he stopped short and turned to Smerdyakov. Something strange happened. Ivan, in a sudden paroxysm, bit his lip, clenched his fists, and, in another minute, would have flung himself on Smerdyakov. The latter, anyway, noticed it at the same moment, started, and shrank back. But the moment passed without mischief to Smerdyakov, and Ivan turned in silence, as it seemed in perplexity, to the gate.

"I am going away to Moscow to-morrow, if you care to know — early to-morrow morning. That's all!" he suddenly said aloud angrily, and wondered himself afterwards what need there was to say this then to Smerdyakov.

"That's the best thing you can do, sir," he responded, as though he had expected to hear it; "except that you may be disturbed in Mos-

cow by a telegram, sir, if anything should happen here."

Ivan stopped again, and again turned quickly to Smerdyakov. But a change had passed over him, too. All his familiarity and carelessness had completely disappeared. His face expressed attention and expectation, intense but timid and cringing.

"Haven't you something more to say — something to add?" could be read in the intent gaze he fixed on Ivan.

"And couldn't I be sent for from Chermashnya, too — in case anything happened?" Ivan shouted suddenly, for some unknown reason raising his voice.

"From Chermashnya, too . . . you could be sent for, sir," Smerdyakov muttered, almost in a whisper, looking disconcerted, but gazing intently into Ivan's eyes.

"Only Moscow is further and Chermashnya is nearer. Is it to save my fare, or to save my going so far out of my way, that you insist on Chermashnya?"

"Precisely so, sir . . ." muttered Smerdyakov, with a breaking voice. He looked at Ivan with a revolting smile, and again made ready to draw back. But to his astonishment Ivan broke into a laugh, and went through the gate still laughing. Any one who had seen his face at that moment would have known that he was not laughing from lightness of heart, and he could not have explained himself what he was feeling at that instant. His movements had the involuntary character of convulsions.

# CHAPTER VII
## "A CLEVER MAN IS WORTH TALKING TO"

His speech, too, had the same impulsive character. Meeting Fyodor Pavlovich in the drawing-room directly he entered, he suddenly shouted to him, waving his hands, "I am going upstairs to my room, not in to you. Good-bye!" and passed by, trying not even to look at his father. Very possibly the old man was too hateful to him at that moment; but such an unceremonious display of hostility was a surprise even to Fyodor Pavlovich. And the old man evidently wanted to tell him something at once and had come to meet him in the drawing-room on purpose. Receiving this amiable greeting, he stood still in silence and with an ironical air watched his son going upstairs, till he passed out of sight.

"What's the matter with him?" he promptly asked Smerdyakov, who had followed Ivan.

"Angry about something, sir. Who can tell?" the valet muttered evasively.

"Confound him! Let him be angry then. Bring in the samovar, and get along with you. Look sharp! No news?"

Then followed a series of questions such as Smerdyakov had just complained of to Ivan, all relating to his expected visitor, and these questions we will omit. Half an hour later the house was locked, and the crazy old man paced alone through the rooms in excited expectation of hearing every minute the five knocks agreed upon. Now and then he peered out into the darkness, seeing nothing.

It was very late, but Ivan was still awake and reflecting. He went to bed late that night, about two o'clock. But we will not trouble to give an account of his thoughts, and this is not the time to look into that soul — its turn will come. And even if one tried, it would be very hard to give an account of them, for there were no thoughts in his brain, but something very vague, and, above all, intense excitement. He felt himself that he had lost his bearings. He

was fretted, too, by all sorts of strange and almost surprising desires; for instance, after midnight he suddenly had an intense irresistible inclination to go down, open the door, go to the lodge and beat up Smerdyakov. But if he had been asked why, he could not have given any exact reason, except perhaps that he loathed the valet as one who had insulted him more gravely than any one in the world. On the other hand, he was more than once that night overcome by a sort of inexplicable humiliating fear, which, he felt, positively paralysed his physical powers. His head ached and he was dizzy. A feeling of hatred was rankling in his heart, as though he meant to avenge himself on some one. He even hated Alyosha, recalling the conversation he had just had with him. At moments he hated himself intensely. Of Katerina Ivanovna he almost forgot to think, and wondered greatly at this afterwards, especially as he remembered perfectly that when he had protested so valiantly to Katerina Ivanovna that he would go away next day to Moscow, something had whispered in his heart, "That's nonsense, you are not going, and it won't be so easy to tear yourself away as you are now so boastfully pretending."

Remembering that night long afterwards, Ivan recalled with peculiar repulsion how he would suddenly get up from the sofa and stealthily, as though he were afraid of being watched, open the door, go out on the staircase and listen to Fyodor Pavlovich stirring down below, listen a long while — some five minutes at a stretch — with a sort of strange curiosity, holding his breath while his heart throbbed. And why he did all this, why he was listening, he could not have said. That "action" all his life afterwards he called "infamous," and at the bottom of his heart, he thought of it as the basest action of his life. For Fyodor Pavlovich himself he felt no hatred in those moments, but was simply intensely curious to know how he was walking down there below and what he must be doing now. He wondered and imagined how he must be peeping out of the dark windows and stopping in the middle of the room, listening, listening — for some one to knock. Ivan went out onto the stairs twice to listen like this.

About two o'clock when everything was quiet, and even Fyodor Pavlovich had gone to bed, Ivan, too, had got into bed, firmly resolved to fall asleep at once, as he felt fearfully exhausted. And he did fall asleep at once, and slept soundly without dreams, but waked early, at seven o'clock, when it was broad daylight. Opening his eyes, he was surprised to feel himself extraordinarily vigorous. He jumped up at once and dressed quickly; then pulled out his trunk and began packing hastily. His linen had come back from the laundress the previous morning. Ivan positively smiled at the thought that everything was helping his sudden departure. And his departure certainly was sudden. Though Ivan had said the day before (to Katerina Ivanovna, to Alyosha, and to Smerdyakov) that he was leaving next day, yet he remembered that he had had no thought of departure when he went to bed, or, at least, had not thought for a moment that his first act in the morning would be to pack his trunk. At last his trunk and bag were ready. It was about nine o'clock when Marfa Ignatyevna came in with her usual inquiry, "Where will you take your tea, sir, in your own room or downstairs?" Ivan Fyodorovich went downstairs. He looked almost cheerful, but there was about him, about

his words and gestures, something hurried and scattered. Greeting his father affably, and even inquiring specially after his health, though he did not wait to hear his answer to the end, he announced that he was starting off in an hour to return to Moscow for good, and begged him to send for the horses. His father heard this announcement with no sign of surprise, and forgot in an unmannerly way to show regret at his departure. Instead of doing so, he flew into a great flutter at the recollection of some important business of his own.

"What a fellow you are! Not to tell me yesterday! Never mind; we'll manage it all the same. Do me a great service, my dear boy. Stop at Chermashnya on the way. It only means turning to the left from the station at Volovya, only another twelve versts, and there is Chermashnya."

"I'm sorry, I can't. It's eighty versts to the railway and the train starts for Moscow at seven o'clock to-night. I can only just catch it."

"You'll catch it to-morrow or the day after, but to-day turn off to Chermashnya. It won't put you out much to humour your father! If my affairs hadn't kept me here, I would have run over myself long ago, for I've some urgent and important business there. But here I . . . it's not the time for me to go now. . . . You see, I've two pieces of woodland there, one at Begichevo and one at Dyachkino. The Maslovs, father and son, will give eight thousand for the timber. But last year I just missed a purchaser who would have given twelve. There's no getting any one about here to buy it. The Maslovs have it all in their fist. One has to take what they'll give, for no one here dare bid against them. The priest at Ilyinskoe wrote to me last Thursday that a merchant called Gorstkin, a man I know, had turned up. What makes him valuable is that he is not from these parts, so he is not afraid of the Maslovs. He says he will give me eleven thousand for the copse. Do you hear? But he'll only be here, the priest writes, for a week altogether, so you must go at once and come to terms with him."

"Well, you write to the priest; he'll make the bargain."

"He can't do it. He has no eye for business. He is a perfect treasure, I'd give him twenty thousand to keep for me without a receipt; but he has no eye for business, he is a perfect child, a crow could cheat him. And yet he is a learned man, would you believe it? This Gorstkin looks like a peasant, he wears a blue kaftan, but he is a thorough scamp. That's the common complaint. He is a liar, that's what. Sometimes he tells such lies that you wonder why he is doing it. He told me the year before last that his wife was dead and that he had married again, and would you believe it, there was not a word of truth in it? His wife never died at all, she is alive to this day and gives him a beating twice a week. So what you have to find out is whether he is lying or speaking the truth, when he says he wants to buy it and would give eleven thousand."

"I shall be no use in such a business. I have no eye either."

"Stop, wait a bit! You will be of use, for I will tell you the signs by which you can judge about Gorstkin. I've done business with him a long time. You see, you must watch his beard; he has a nasty, thin, red beard. If his beard shakes when he talks and he gets cross, it's all right, he means what he says, he wants to do business. But if he strokes his beard with

his left hand and grins — he is trying to cheat you. Don't watch his eyes, you won't find out anything from his eyes, he is a deep one, a scamp — but watch his beard! I'll give you a note and you show it to him. He's called Gorstkin, though his real name is Lyagavy;* but don't call him so, he will be offended. If you come to an understanding with him, and see it's all right, write here at once. You need only write: 'He's not lying.' Stand out for eleven thousand; one thousand you can knock off, but not more. Just think! there's a difference between eight thousand and eleven thousand. It's as good as finding three thousand; it's not so easy to get a purchaser, and I'm in desperate need of money. Only let me know it's serious, and I'll run over and fix it up. I'll snatch the time somehow. But what's the good of my galloping over, if it's all a notion of the priest's? Come, will you go?"

"Oh, I can't spare the time. You must excuse me."

"Come, you might oblige your father. I shan't forget it. You've no heart, any of you — that's what it is! What's a day or two to you? Where are you going now — to Venice? Your Venice will keep another two days. I would have sent Alyosha, but what use is Alyosha in a thing like that? I send you just because you are a clever fellow. Do you suppose I don't see that? You know nothing about timber, but you've got an eye. All that is wanted is to see whether the man is in earnest. I tell you, watch his beard — if his beard shakes, you know he is in earnest."

"You force me to go to that damned Chermashnya yourself, then?" cried Ivan, with a malignant smile.

Fyodor Pavlovich did not catch, or would

* *i.e.*, setter dog.

not catch, the malignancy, but he caught the smile.

"Then you'll go, you'll go? I'll scribble the note for you at once."

"I don't know whether I shall go. I don't know. I'll decide on the way."

"Nonsense! Decide at once. My dear fellow, decide! If you settle the matter, write me a line; give it to the priest and he'll send it on to me at once. And I won't delay you longer than that. You can go to Venice. The priest will give you horses back to Volovya station."

The old man was simply in transports. He wrote the note, and sent for the horses. A light lunch was brought in, with cognac. When Fyodor Pavlovich was pleased, he usually became expansive, but this time he seemed to restrain himself. Of Dmitri, for instance, he did not say a word. He was quite unmoved by the parting, and seemed, in fact, at a loss for something to say. Ivan noticed this particularly. "He must be bored with me," he thought. Only when seeing his son off on the steps, the old man began fussing a bit, and was evidently ready to go through the ceremony of kissing. But Ivan made haste to hold out his hand, obviously avoiding the kisses. His father saw it at once, and instantly pulled himself up.

"Well, God bless you, God bless you!" he repeated from the steps. "You'll come again some time or other? Mind you do come. I shall always be glad. Well, Christ be with you!"

Ivan got into the carriage.

"Good-bye, Ivan! Don't be too hard on me!" the father called for the last time.

The whole household came out to take leave — Smerdyakov, Marfa, and Grigory. Ivan gave them ten roubles each. When he had seated himself in the carriage, Smerdyakov jumped up to arrange the rug. "You see . . . I am going to Chermashnya," broke suddenly from Ivan.

Again, as on the day before, the words seemed to drop of themselves, and he laughed, too, a peculiar, nervous laugh. He remembered it long after.

"It's a true saying then, that 'a clever man is worth talking to,'" answered Smerdyakov firmly, looking significantly at Ivan.

The carriage rolled away. Nothing was clear in the traveller's soul, but he looked eagerly around him at the fields, at the hills, at the trees, at a flock of geese flying high overhead in the bright sky. And all of a sudden he felt very happy. He tried to talk to the driver, and he felt intensely interested in an answer the peasant made him; but a minute later he realised that he was not hearing anything, and that he had not really even taken in the peasant's answer. He was silent, and it was pleasant even so. The air was fresh, pure and cool, the sky bright. The images of Alyosha and Katerina Ivanovna floated into his mind. But he smiled softly, blew gently on the friendly phantoms, and they flew away. "Their time will come," he thought. They reached the station quickly, changed horses, and galloped to Volovya. "Why is it worth while talking to a clever man? What did he mean by that?" The thought seemed suddenly to choke off his breath. "And why did I report to him that I was going to Chermashnya?" They reached Volovya station. Ivan got out of the carriage, and the drivers stood round him bargaining over the journey of twelve versts to Chermashnya. He told them to harness the horses. He went into the station, looked round, glanced at the station-master's wife, and suddenly went out again.

THE SCREAM OF THE EPILEPTIC

"I won't go to Chermashnya. Am I too late to reach the railway by seven, brothers?"

"We shall just do it. Shall we hitch up?"

"At once. Will any one of you be going to town to-morrow?"

"To be sure. Mitri here will."

"Can you do me a service, Mitri? Go to my father's, to Fyodor Pavlovich Karamazov, and tell him I haven't gone to Chermashnya. Can you?"

"Of course I can. I've known Fyodor Pavlovich a long time."

"And here's something for you, for I dare say he won't give you anything," said Ivan, laughing gaily.

"You may depend on it he won't." Mitri laughed, too. "Thank you, sir. I'll be sure to do it."

At seven o'clock Ivan got into the train and set off for Moscow. "Away with the past. I've done with the old world for ever, and may I have no news, no echo, from it. To a new life, new places, and no looking back!" But instead of delight his soul was filled with such gloom, and his heart ached with such anguish, as he had never known in his life before. He spent the night in thought. The train flew on, and only at daybreak, when he was approaching Moscow, he suddenly roused himself from his meditation.

"I am a scoundrel," he whispered to himself.

Meanwhile, Fyodor Pavlovich, having seen his son off, remained well satisfied. For two hours afterwards he felt almost happy, and sat sipping cognac. But suddenly something happened which was very annoying and unpleasant for every one in the house, and completely upset Fyodor Pavlovich's equanimity at once. Smerdyakov went to the cellar for something and fell down from the top of the steps. Fortunately, Marfa Ignatyevna was in the yard and heard him in time. She did not see the fall, but heard his scream — the strange, peculiar scream, long familiar to her — the scream of the epileptic falling in a fit. It was impossible to tell whether the fit had come on him at the moment he was descending the steps, so that he must have fallen while unconscious, or whether it was the fall and the shock that had caused the fit in Smerdyakov, who was known to be an epileptic. He was found at the bottom of the cellar steps, writhing in convulsions and foaming at the mouth. It was thought at first that he must have broken something — an arm or a leg — and hurt himself, but "God had preserved him," as Marfa Ignatyevna expressed it — nothing of the kind had happened. But it was difficult to get him out of the cellar. They asked the neighbours to help and managed it somehow. Fyodor Pavlovich himself was present at the whole ceremony. He helped, evidently alarmed and upset. The sick man did not, however, regain consciousness; the convulsions ceased for a time, but then began again, and every one concluded that the same thing would happen as had happened a year before, when he accidentally fell from the garret. They remembered that ice had been put on his head then. There was still ice in the cellar, and Marfa Ignatyevna had some brought up. In the evening, Fyodor Pavlovich sent for Dr. Herzenstube, who arrived at once. He was a most estimable old man, and the most careful and conscientious doctor in the province. After careful examination, he concluded that the fit was a very violent one and might have serious consequences; that meanwhile he, Herzenstube, did not fully understand it, but that by to-morrow morning, if the present remedies were unavailing, he would venture to try something else. The patient was taken to the lodge, to a room next to Grigory's and Marfa Ignatyevna's.

After that Fyodor Pavlovich had to put up with one misfortune after another. Marfa Ignatyevna cooked the dinner, and the soup, compared with Smerdyakov's, was no "better than dish water," and the fowl was so dried up that it was impossible to chew it. To her master's bitter, though deserved, reproaches, Marfa Ignatyevna replied that the fowl was a very old one to begin with, and that she had never been trained as a cook. In the evening there was another trouble in store for Fyodor Pavlovich; he was informed that Grigory, who had not been well for the last three days, was completely laid up by his lumbago. Fyodor Pavlovich finished his tea as early as possible and locked himself up alone in the house. He was in terrible excitement and suspense. That evening he reckoned on Grushenka's coming almost as a certainty. He had received from Smerdyakov that morning an assurance "that she had promised to come without fail." The irrepressible old man's heart throbbed with excitement; he paced up and down his empty rooms listening. He had to be on the alert. Dmitri might be on the watch for her somewhere, and when she knocked on the window (Smerdyakov had informed him two days before that he had told her where and how to knock) the door must be opened at once. She must not be a second in the passage, for fear — God forbid! — that she might be frightened and run away.

Fyodor Pavlovich had much to think of, but never had his heart bathed in sweeter hopes. This time he could say almost certainly that she would come!

214

# BOOK VI
# THE RUSSIAN MONK

## CHAPTER I
### FATHER ZOSIMA AND HIS VISITORS

WHEN with an anxious and aching heart Alyosha went into his elder's cell, he stood still almost astonished. Instead of a sick man at his last gasp, perhaps unconscious, as he had feared to find him, he suddenly saw him sitting up in his chair and, though weak and exhausted, his face was bright and cheerful, he was surrounded by visitors and engaged in a quiet and joyful conversation with them. But he had only got up from his bed a quarter of an hour before Alyosha's arrival; his visitors had gathered together in his cell earlier, waiting for him to wake, having received a most confident assurance from Father Païssy that "the teacher would get up, and, as he had himself promised in the morning, converse once more with those dear to his heart." This promise and indeed every word of the dying elder's Father Païssy believed implicitly. If he had seen him unconscious, if he had seen him breathe his last, and yet had his promise that he would rise up and take leave of him, he would not have credited perhaps his very death, but would still have expected the dead man to recover and fulfil his promise. In the morning as he lay down to sleep, Father Zosima had told him positively: "I shall not die ere I have delighted in another conversation with all of you, beloved of my heart. I shall look once more on your dear faces and pour out my heart to you once again." The monks, who had gathered for what was probably to be their last conversation with Father Zosima, had all been his devoted friends for many years. There were four of them: Father Iosif and Father Païssy, Father Mihail, the abbot of the hermitage, a man not very old and far from learned. He was of humble origin, of strong will and steadfast faith, of austere appearance, but of deep tenderness, though he seemed to conceal it as though he were almost ashamed of it. The fourth, Father Anfim, was a very old and humble little monk of the poorest peasant class. He was almost illiterate, and very quiet, scarcely speaking to any one. He was the humblest of the humble, and looked as though he had been permanently frightened by something great and dreadful beyond the scope of his intelligence. Father Zosima had a great affection for this, as it were, quaking man, and always treated him with marked respect, though perhaps there was no one he had known to whom he had said less, in spite of the fact that he had spent years wandering about holy Russia with him. That was very long ago, forty years before, when Father Zosima first began his life as a monk in a poor, little known monastery at Kostroma, and when, shortly after, he had accompanied Father Anfim on his pilgrimage to collect alms for their poor monastery.

The whole company was in the elder's bedroom which, as we mentioned before, was very small, so that there was scarcely room for the four of them (in addition to Porfiry, the novice, who was on his feet) to sit round Father Zosima on chairs brought from the living-room. It was already beginning to get dark, the room was lighted up by the lamps and wax tapers before the ikons.

Seeing Alyosha standing embarrassed in the doorway, Father Zosima smiled at him joyfully and held out his hand.

"Welcome, my quiet one, welcome, my dear, here you are, too. I knew you would come."

Alyosha went up to him, bowed down before him to the ground and wept. Something surged up from his heart, his soul was quivering, he wanted to sob.

"Come, don't mourn me yet," Father Zosima smiled, laying his right hand on his head. "You see I am sitting up talking; maybe I shall live another twenty years yet, as that dear good woman from Vyshegorye, with her little Lizaveta in her arms, wished me yesterday. God bless the mother and the little girl Lizaveta," he crossed himself. "Porfiry, did you take her offering where I told you?"

He meant the sixty copecks brought him the day before by his jolly admirer, to be given "to some one poorer than me." Such offerings, always of money gained by personal toil, are made by way of penance voluntarily undertaken. The elder had sent Porfiry the evening before to a widow, whose house had been burnt down lately, and who after the fire had gone with her children begging alms. Porfiry hastened to reply that he had given the money, as he had been instructed, "from an unknown benefactress."

"Get up, my dear boy," the elder went on, addressing Alyosha. "Let me look at you. Have you been home and seen your brother?" It seemed strange to Alyosha that he asked so confidently and precisely, about one of his brothers only — but which one? Then perhaps he had sent him out both yesterday and to-day for the sake of that brother. "I have seen one of my brothers," answered Alyosha.

"I mean the elder one, to whom I bowed down."

"I only saw him yesterday and could not find him to-day," said Alyosha.

"Make haste to find him, go again to-morrow and make haste, leave everything and make haste. Perhaps you may still have time to prevent something terrible. I bowed down yesterday to the great suffering in store for him." He was suddenly silent and seemed to be pondering. The words were strange. Father Iosif, who had witnessed the scene yesterday, exchanged glances with Father Païssy. Alyosha could not resist asking a question.

"Father and teacher," he began with extreme emotion, "your words are too obscure. . . . What is this suffering in store for him?"

"Do not be curious. I seemed to see something terrible yesterday . . . as though his whole future were expressed in his eyes. A look came into his eyes — so that my heart was instantly stricken with horror at what that man is preparing for himself. Once or twice in my life I've seen such a look in a man's face . . . reflecting as it were his future fate, and that fate, alas, came to pass. I sent you to him, Alexey, for I thought your brotherly countenance would help him. But everything and all our destinies are from the Lord. 'Except a corn of wheat fall into the ground and die, it abideth alone; but if it die, it bringeth forth much fruit.' Remember that. You, Alexey, I've many times silently blessed for your countenance, know that," added the elder with a gentle smile. "This is what I think of you, you will go forth from these walls, but will live like a monk in the world. You will have many antagonists, but your very foes will love you. Life will bring you many misfortunes, but it is precisely in them you will find your happiness, and you will bless life and will make others bless it — which is what matters most. Well, that is what you are like. Fathers and teachers," he addressed his friends with a tender smile, "I have never till to-day told even him why the countenance of this youth is so dear to me. Now I will tell you. His countenance has been as it were a remembrance and a prophecy for me. At the dawn of my life when I was a child I had an elder brother who died before my eyes at seventeen. And later on in the course of my life I gradually became convinced that that brother had been for a guidance and a sign from on high for me. For had he not come into my life, I should never perhaps, so I fancy at least, have become a monk and entered on this precious path. He appeared first to me in my childhood, and here at the end of my journey he seems to have come to me over again. It is marvellous, fathers and teachers, that Alexey, who bears him some, though not great, resemblance in features, has seemed to me so like him spiritually, that many times I have taken him for that youth, my brother, mysteriously come back to me at the end of my journey, as a reminder and an inspiration. So that I positively marvelled at my having so strange a fancy. Do you hear this, Porfiry?" He turned to the novice who waited on him. "Many times I've seen in your face as it were a look of mortification because I love Alexey more than you. Now you know why that was so, but I love you, too, know that, and many times I grieved at your mortification. I should like to tell you, dear friends, of that youth, my brother, for there has been no presence in my life more precious, more prophetic and touching. My heart is full of emotion, and I look at my whole life at this moment as though living through it again."

Here I must observe that this last talk of Father Zosima with the friends who visited him on the last day of his life has been partly preserved in writing. Alexey Fyodorovich Karamazov wrote it down for remembrance, a short time after the elder's death. But whether this was only the conversation that took place then, or whether in his memoir he added parts of former conversations with his teacher, I cannot determine. In his account, Father Zosima's talk goes on without interruption, as though he told his life to his friends in the form of a story, though there is no doubt, from other accounts of it, that the conversation that evening was general. Though the visitors did not interrupt Father Zosima much, yet they, too, talked, perhaps even told something themselves. Besides, Father Zosima could not have carried on an uninterrupted narrative, for he was sometimes gasping for breath, his voice failed him, and he even lay down to rest on his bed, though he did not fall asleep and his visitors did not leave their seats.

Once or twice the conversation was interrupted by Father Païssy's reading the Gospel. It is worthy of note, too, that no one of them supposed that he would die that night, for on that last evening of his life after his deep sleep during the day he seemed suddenly to have found new strength, which kept him up through this long conversation with his friends. It was like a last effort of love which was the source of incredible animation; only for a little time, however, for his life was cut short immediately. . . . But of that later. I will only state that I have preferred to confine myself to the account written down by Alexey Fyodorovich Karamazov, without going into the details of the conversation. It will be shorter and not so fatiguing, though of course, as I must repeat, Alyosha took a great deal from previous conversations, combining the parts into a whole.

## CHAPTER II
### NOTES ON THE LIFE OF THE ELDER ZOSIMA, PRIEST AND MONK, WHO DIED IN THE LORD; COUCHED IN HIS OWN WORDS, AND COMPILED BY ALEXEY FYODOROVICH KARAMAZOV

*BIOGRAPHICAL INFORMATION*

(a) *Concerning the youth who was the elder Zosima's brother*

BELOVED fathers and teachers, I was born in a distant northern province, in the town of V. My father was a gentleman by birth, but of no great consequence or rank. He died when I was only two years old, and I don't remember him at all. He left my mother a small framehouse, and a fortune, not large, but sufficient to keep her and her children in comfort. There were two of us, my elder brother Markel and I. He was eight years older than I was, with a hasty irritable temper, but kind-hearted and never ironical. He was remarkably silent, especially at home with me, his mother, and the servants. He did well at school, but did not get on with his schoolfellows, though he never quarrelled, at least so my mother has told me. Six months before his death, when he was past seventeen, he made friends with a political exile who had been banished from Moscow to our town for freethinking, and led a solitary existence there. The exile was a man of learning who had gained distinction in philosophy at the university. Something made him take a fancy to Markel, and he made him welcome. The young man would spend whole evenings with him during that winter, till the exile was summoned to Petersburg to take up his post again at his own request, as he had powerful friends.

It was the beginning of Lent, and Markel would not fast, he was rude and laughed at it. "That's all silly twaddle and there is no God," he said, horrifying my mother, the servants, and me, too. For though I was only nine, I, too, was aghast at hearing such words. We had four servants, all serfs, bought in the name of a landowner of our acquaintance. I remember my mother selling one of the four, the cook Afimya, who was lame and elderly, for sixty paper roubles, and hiring a free servant to take her place.

Well, in the sixth week in Lent, my brother, who was never strong and had a tendency to consumption, was taken ill. He was tall but thin and delicate-looking, and with very pleasing features. I suppose he caught cold, anyway the doctor who came soon whispered to my mother that it was galloping consumption, that he would not live through the spring. My mother began weeping, and careful not to

alarm my brother, she entreated him to go to church, to confess and take the sacrament, as he was still able to move about. This made him angry, and he said something profane about the church. He grew thoughtful, however; he guessed at once that he was seriously ill, and that that was why his mother was begging him to confess and take the sacrament while he still had his strength. He had been aware, indeed, for a long time past, that he was far from well, and had a year before coolly observed at dinner to our mother and me, "I shan't be with you long, I may not live another year," which seemed now like a prophecy.

Three days passed and Holy Week had come. And on Tuesday morning my brother began going to church. "I am doing this simply for your sake, mother, to please and comfort you," he said. My mother wept with joy and grief, "his end must be near," she thought, "if there's such a change in him." But he was not able to go to church long, he took to his bed, so he had to confess and take the sacrament at home.

It was a late Easter, and the days were bright, clear, and fragrant. I remember he used to cough all night and sleep badly, but in the morning he dressed and tried to sit up in an armchair. That's how I remember him, sitting there, sweet and gentle, smiling, his face bright and joyous, in spite of his illness. A marvellous change came over him, his spirit seemed transformed. The old nurse would come in and say, "Let me light the lamp before the holy image, my dear." Formerly he would not have allowed it and would have blown it out.

"Light it, light it, dear, I was a monster to have prevented you doing it. You are praying when you light the lamp, and I pray rejoicing at you. So we are praying to the same God."

Those words seemed strange to us, and mother would go to her room and weep, but when she went in to him she wiped her eyes and looked cheerful. "Mother, don't cry, darling," he would say, "I've long to live yet, long to rejoice with you, and life is glad and joyful."

"Ah, dear boy, how can you talk of joy when you lie feverish at night, coughing as though your chest were being torn to pieces."

"Don't cry, mother," he would answer, "life is paradise, and we are all in paradise, but we won't see it; if we would, we should have heaven on earth the next day."

Every one wondered at his words, he spoke so strangely and firmly; we were all touched and wept. Friends came to see us. "Dear ones," he would say to them, "what have I done that you should love me so, how can you love any one like me, and how was it I did not know, I did not appreciate it before?"

When the servants came in to him he would say continually, "Dear, kind people, why are you doing so much for me, do I deserve to be waited on? If it were God's will for me to live, I would wait on you, for all men should wait on one another."

Mother shook her head as she listened. "My darling, it's your illness makes you talk like that."

"Mother, my joy," he would say, "there must be servants and masters, but if so I will be the servant of my servants, the same as they are to me. And another thing, mother, every one of us is guilty towards all men, of all sins, and I more than any."

Mother positively smiled at that, smiled through her tears. "Why, how could you be guilty towards all, more than anybody else?

There are robbers and murderers, but what sin have you committed yet, that you blame yourself more than all?"

"Mother, my darling little life," he said (he had begun using such strange caressing words at that time), "my darling little life, my joy, believe me, every one is really responsible to all men for all and everything. I don't know how to explain it to you, but I feel it is so, painfully even. And how is it we went on living before, getting angry and not understanding anything?"

So he would get up every day, more and more sweet and joyous and full of love. When the doctor, an old German called Eisenschmidt, came: "Well, doctor, have I another day in this world?" he would ask, joking.

"You'll live many days yet," the doctor would answer, "and months and years, too."

"Months and years!" he would exclaim. "Why reckon the days? One day is enough for a man to know all happiness. My dear ones, why do we quarrel, try to outshine each other and bear grudges against each other? Let's go straight into the garden, walk and play there, love, appreciate, and kiss each other, and bless our life."

"Your son cannot last long," the doctor told my mother, as she accompanied him to the door. "The disease is affecting his mind."

The windows of his room looked out into the garden, and our garden was a shady one, with old trees in it which were coming into bud. The first birds of spring were flitting in the branches, chirruping and singing at his windows. And looking at them and admiring them, he began suddenly begging their forgiveness, too, "Birds of heaven, happy birds, forgive me, for I have sinned against you, too." That none of us could understand at the time, but he shed tears of joy. "Yes," he said, "there was God's glory all about me; birds, trees, meadows, sky, I alone lived in shame and dishonoured it all and did not notice the beauty and glory."

"You take too many sins on yourself," mother used to say, weeping.

"Mother, darling, it's for joy, not for grief I am crying. Though I can't explain it to you, I myself like to feel guilty towards them, for I don't know how to love them enough. If I have sinned against every one, yet all forgive me, too, and that's heaven. Am I not in heaven now?"

And there was a great deal more I don't remember. I remember I once went into his room when there was no one else there. It was a bright evening, the sun was setting, and the whole room was lighted up with oblique sun-rays. He beckoned me, and I went up to him. He put his hands on my shoulders and looked into my face tenderly, lovingly; he said nothing for a minute, only looked at me like that.

"Well," he said, "run and play now, live for me, too."

I went out then and ran to play. And many times in my life afterwards I remembered even with tears how he told me to live for him, too. There were many other marvellous and beautiful sayings of his, though we did not understand them at the time. He died the third week after Easter. He was fully conscious though he could not talk; up to his last hour he did not change. He looked happy, his eyes beamed and sought us, he smiled at us, beckoned us. There was a great deal of talk even in the town about his end. I was impressed by all this at the time, but not too much so, though I cried a great deal at his funeral. I was young then, a child, but a lasting impression, a secret

feeling about it all, remained in my heart, ready to rise up and respond when the time came. So indeed it happened.

(*b*) *Concerning the Holy Scriptures in the life of Father Zosima*

I was left alone with my mother. Her friends began advising her to send me to Petersburg as other parents did. "You have only one son now," they said, "and have a fair income, and you will perhaps be depriving him of a brilliant career if you keep him here." They suggested that mother send me to Petersburg to the Cadet Corps, that I might afterwards enter the Imperial Guard. My mother hesitated for a long time; it was awful to part with her only child, but she made up her mind to do it at last, though not without many tears, believing she was acting for my happiness. She took me to Petersburg and put me into the Cadet Corps, and I never saw her again. For she, too, died three years afterwards. She spent those three years mourning and grieving for both of us.

From the house of my childhood I have brought nothing but precious memories, for there are no memories more precious than those of early childhood in one's first home. And that is almost always so if there is any love and harmony in the family at all. Indeed, precious memories may remain even of a bad home, if only the heart knows how to find what is precious. With my memories of home I count, too, my memories of the Bible, which, child as I was, in my parents' house, I was very eager to know. I had a book of sacred history then with excellent pictures, called "A Hundred and Four Sacred Stories from the Old and New Testament," and I learnt to read from it. I have it lying on my shelf now, I keep it as a precious memento of the past. But even before I learnt to read, I remember first being visited by a kind of spiritual feeling when I was only eight years old. My mother took me alone to mass (I don't remember where my brother was at the time) on the Monday before Easter. It was a clear day, and recalling it now, it is as though I see before me the incense as it rose from the censer and softly floated upwards in rising waves, and, overhead in the cupola, melted in the rays of the sunlight that streamed in at the little window. I was stirred by the sight, and for the first time in my life I consciously received the seed of God's word into my soul. A youth came out into the middle of the church carrying a large book, so large that at the time I fancied he could scarcely carry it. He laid it on the lectern, opened it, and began reading, and suddenly for the first time I understood something read in the church of God. In the land of Uz, there lived a man, righteous and God-fearing, and he had great wealth, so many camels, so many sheep and asses, and his children feasted, and he loved them very much and prayed for them. "It may be that my sons have sinned in their feasting." And behold, the devil came before the Lord together with the sons of God, and said to the Lord that he had gone up and down the earth and under the earth. "And hast thou considered my servant Job?" God asked of him. And God boasted to the devil, pointing to his great and holy servant. And the devil laughed at God's words. "Give him over to me and Thou wilt see that Thy servant will murmur against Thee and curse Thy name." And God gave up the just man He so loved, to the devil. And the devil smote his children and his cattle and scattered his wealth, all of a sudden like a thunderbolt from heaven. And Job rent his

mantle and fell down upon the ground and cried aloud, "Naked came I out of my mother's womb, and naked shall I return into the earth; the Lord gave and the Lord hath taken away. Blessed be the name of the Lord for ever and ever."

Fathers and teachers, forgive my tears now, for all my childhood rises up again before me, and I breathe now as I breathed then, with the breast of a little child of eight, and I feel as I did then, awe and wonder and gladness. The camels at that time caught my imagination, and Satan, who talked like that with God, and God who gave His servant up to destruction, and His servant crying out: "Blessed be Thy name although Thou dost punish me," and then the soft and sweet singing in the church: "Let my prayer rise up before Thee," and again incense from the priest's censer and the kneeling and the prayer. Ever since then — only yesterday I took it up — I've never been able to read that sacred tale without tears. And how much that is great, mysterious and unfathomable there is in it! Afterwards I heard the words of mockers and blasphemers, proud words, "How could God give up the most loved of His saints for the diversion of the devil, take from him his children, smite him with sore boils so that he cleansed the corruption from his sores with a potsherd — and for no object except to boast to the devil! 'See what My saint can suffer for My sake.'" But the greatness of it lies just in the fact that it is a mystery — that the transient earthly show and the eternal verity touch here. In the face of the earthly truth, the eternal truth is enacted. The Creator, just as on the first days of creation He ended each day with praise: "that is good that I have created," looks upon Job and again boasts of His creation. And Job praising the Lord, serves not only Him but all His creation for generations and generations, and for ever and ever, since for that he was ordained. Good heavens, what a book it is, and what lessons there are in it! What a book the Bible is, what a miracle, what strength is given with it to man. It is like a mould cast of the world and man and human nature, everything is named there, and indicated for all time. And what mysteries are solved and revealed; God raises Job again, gives him wealth again. Many years pass by, and he has other children and loves them. But how could he love those new ones when those first children are no more, when he has lost them? Remembering them, how could he be fully happy with those new ones, however dear to him the new ones might be? But he could, he could. It's the great mystery of human life that old grief passes gradually into quiet tender joy. The mild serenity of age takes the place of the riotous blood of youth. I bless the rising sun each day, and, as before, my heart sings to it, but now I love even more its setting, its long slanting rays and the soft tender gentle memories that come with them, the dear images from the whole of my long blessed life — and over all the Divine Truth, softening, reconciling, forgiving! My life is ending, I know that well, but every day that is left me I feel how my earthly life touches a new, infinite, unknown, but imminent life, the presentiment of which sets my soul quivering with rapture, my mind glowing and my heart weeping with joy.

Friends and teachers, I have heard more than once, and of late one may hear it more often, that the priests, and above all the village priests, are complaining on all sides of their miserable income and their humiliating lot. They plainly state, even in print — I've read it myself — that they are unable to teach the Scriptures to the people because of the smallness of their means, and if Lutherans and heretics come and lead the flock astray, they show no resistance because they have so little to live upon. May the Lord increase the sustenance that is so precious to them, for their complaint is just, too. But of a truth I say, if any one is to blame in the matter, half the fault is ours. For he may be short of time, he may say truly that he is oppressed all the time with chores and duties, but still it's not all the time, even he has an hour a week to remember God. And he does not work the whole year round. Let him gather round him once a week, some hour in the evening, if only the children at first — the fathers will hear of it and they, too, will begin to come. There's no need to build mansions for this, let him take them into his own cottage. They won't spoil his cottage, they would be there only one hour. Let him open that book and begin reading it without grand words or superciliousness, without condescension to them, but gently and kindly, being glad that he is reading to them and that they are listening with attention, loving the words himself, only stopping from time to time to explain words that are not understood by the peasants. Don't be anxious, they will understand everything, the orthodox heart will understand all! Let him read them about Abraham and Sarah, about Isaac and Rebecca, of how Jacob went to Laban and wrestled with the Lord in his dream and said, "This place is holy" — and he will impress the devout mind of the plain man. Let him read, especially to the children, how the brothers sold Joseph, the tender boy, the dreamer and prophet, into bondage, and told their father that a wild beast had devoured him, and showed him his blood-stained clothes. Let him read them how the brothers afterwards journeyed into Egypt for corn, and Joseph, already a great courtier, unrecognised by them, tormented them, accused them, kept his brother Benjamin, and all through love: "I love you, and loving you I torment you." For he remembered all his life how they had sold him to the merchants there in the burning desert by the well, and how, wringing his hands, he had wept and besought his brothers not to sell him as a slave into a strange land. And how, seeing them again after many years, he loved them beyond measure, but he harassed and tormented them out of love. He left them at last not able to bear the suffering of his heart, flung himself on his bed and wept. Then, wiping his tears away, he went out to them joyful and told them, "Brothers, I am your brother Joseph!" Let him read them further how happy old Jacob was on learning that his darling boy was still alive, and how he journeyed to Egypt leaving his native land, and died in a strange country, uttering in his testament the great prophecy that had lain mysteriously hidden in his meek and timid heart all his life, to the effect that from his offspring, from Judah, would come the great hope of the world, its Messiah and Saviour.

Fathers and teachers, forgive me and don't be angry, because like a little child I've been babbling of what you have known for a long time, and can teach me a hundred times more skilfully. I only speak from rapture, and forgive my tears, for I love the Bible. Let him too weep, the priest of God, and be sure that the hearts of his listeners will throb in response. Only a little tiny seed is needed — drop it into the heart of the peasant and it won't die, it will live in his soul all his life, it will be hidden in the midst of his darkness and sin, like a bright spot, like a great reminder. And there's no need of much teaching or explanation, he will understand it all simply. Do you suppose that the peasants don't understand? Try reading them the touching story of the fair Esther and the haughty Vashti; or the miraculous story of Jonah in the whale. Don't forget either the parables of Our Lord, choose especially from the Gospel of St. Luke (that is what I did) and then from the Acts of the Apostles the conversion of Saul (that you mustn't leave out on any account), and from the "Lives of the Saints," for instance, the life of Alexey, the man of God and, greatest among the great, the joyful martyr, the seer of God and Christ-bearer, Mother Mary of Egypt — and you will pierce their hearts with these simple tales. Give one hour a week to it in spite of your poverty, only one little hour. And you will see for yourself that our people are gracious and grateful, and will repay you a hundredfold. Mindful of the kindness of their priest and the moving words they have heard from him, they will of their own accord help him in his fields and in his house, and will treat him with more respect than before — so that it will even increase his worldly well-being, too. The thing is so simple that sometimes one is even afraid to put it into words, for fear of being laughed at, and yet how true it is! One who does not believe in God will not believe in God's people. He who believes in God's people will see His Holiness, even though he had not believed in it till then. Only the people and their future spiritual power will convert our atheists, who have torn themselves away from their native soil.

And what good is Christ's word, unless we set an example? The masses are lost without the word of God, for their souls are athirst for the Word and for all that is beautiful.

In my youth, long ago, nearly forty years ago, I travelled all over Russia with Father Anfim, collecting alms for our monastery, and once we were benighted on the bank of a great navigable river and stayed with some fishermen there. And we were joined by a fine peasant lad, of about eighteen; he had to hurry off to work next morning, to tow a merchant's barge up the river. I noticed him looking straight before him with clear and loving eyes. It was a bright, warm, still July night, a cool mist rose from the broad river, we could hear the plash of a fish, the birds were still, all was hushed and beautiful, everything praying to God. Only we two were not sleeping, the lad and I, and we fell to talking of the beauty of this world of God's and of its great mystery. Every blade of grass, every insect, ant, and golden bee, all so marvellously know their path, though they have not intelligence, they bear witness to the mystery of God and continually accomplish it themselves. I saw the dear lad's heart was aflame. He told me that he loved the forest and the forest birds. He was a bird-catcher, knew the note of each of them, could call each bird. "I know nothing better than to be in the forest," said he, "though all things are good."

"Truly," I answered him, "all things are good and fair, because all is truth. Look," said I, "at the horse, that great beast that is so near to man; or the lowly, pensive ox, which feeds him and works for him; look at their faces, what meekness, what devotion to man, who often beats them mercilessly. What gentleness, what confidence and what beauty in its countenance! It's touching to know that there's no sin in them, for all, all except man, are sinless, and Christ has been with them before us."

"Why," asked the boy, "is Christ with them, too?"

"It cannot but be so," said I, "since the Word is for all. All creation and all creatures, every leaf is striving towards the Word, singing glory to God, crying to Christ, unwittingly accomplishing this by the mystery of their sinless life. Yonder," said I, "in the forest wanders the dread bear, fierce and menacing, and yet innocent in it. And I told him how once a bear came to a great saint who was saving his soul in a tiny cell in the wood. And the great saint felt tenderness towards him, went up to him without fear and gave him a piece of bread. "Go along," said he, "Christ be with you," and the savage beast walked away meekly and obediently, having done no harm. And the lad was touched to hear that the bear had walked away without hurting the saint, and that Christ was with him, too. "Ah," said he, "how good that is, how good and beautiful is all God's work!" He sat musing softly and sweetly. I saw he understood. And he slept beside me a light and sinless sleep. May God bless youth! And I prayed for him as I went to sleep. Lord, send peace and light to Thy people!

(c) *Recollections of Father Zosima's youth before he became a monk. The duel*

I spent a long time, almost eight years, in the Cadet Corps at Petersburg, and in the novelty of my surroundings there many of my childish impressions grew dimmer, though I forgot nothing. I picked up so many new habits and opinions that I was transformed into a cruel, absurd, almost savage creature. A surface polish of courtesy and society manners I did acquire, together with the French language, but we all, myself included, looked upon the soldiers in our service as the merest cattle. I was perhaps worse than the rest in that respect, for I was so much more impressionable than my companions. By the time we left the school as officers, we were ready to shed our blood for the honour of the regiment, but no one of us had any knowledge of the real meaning of honour, and if any one had come to know it, he would have been the first to ridicule it. Drunkenness, debauchery, and devilry were what we almost prided ourselves on. I don't say that we were bad by nature, all these young men were good fellows, but they behaved badly, and I worst of all. The main thing was that I found myself with money, and so I flung myself into a life of pleasure, and plunged into it headlong with all the recklessness of youth.

I was then fond of reading, yet, strange to say, the Bible was the one book I never opened at that time, though I always carried it about with me, and I was never separated from it; in very truth I was saving that book "for the day and the hour, for the month and the year," though I knew it not.

I had been in the service about four years when I chanced to be in the town of K., where our regiment was stationed at the time. The local society was varied, well-to-do, hospitable, and fond of entertainments. I met with a cordial reception everywhere, as I was of a lively temperament and was known to be well off, which always goes a long way in the world. And then a circumstance happened which was the beginning of it all.

I formed an attachment to a beautiful and intelligent young lady of serene nature and lofty character, the daughter of highly respected people. They were well-to-do people of influence and position. They always gave me a cordial and friendly reception. Well, I fancied that the young lady looked on me with favour and my heart was aflame at such an idea. Later on I saw and fully realised that I was perhaps not so passionately in love with her at all, but only respected her mind and lofty character, which I could not indeed have helped doing. I was prevented, however, from making her an offer at the time by my selfishness; I was loth to part with the allurements of my free and licentious bachelor life in the heyday of my youth, and with money in my pockets. I did drop some hint as to my feelings, however, though I put off taking any decisive step for a time. Then, all of a sudden, we were ordered off to another district.

On my return two months later, I found the young lady already married to a rich neighbouring landowner, a very amiable man, still young though older than I was, connected with the best Petersburg society, which I was not, and of excellent education, which I also lacked. I was so overwhelmed at this unexpected circumstance that my mind was positively clouded. The worst of it all was that, as I learnt then, the young landowner had been a long while betrothed to her, and I had met him indeed many times in her house, but blinded by my conceit I had noticed nothing. And this particularly mortified me; almost everybody had known all about it, while I knew nothing. I was filled with sudden irrepressible fury. With flushed face I began recalling how often I had been on the point of declaring my love to her, and as she had not attempted to stop me or to warn me, she must, I concluded, have been laughing at me all the time. Later on, of course, I reflected and remembered that she had been very far from laughing at me; on the contrary, she used to turn off any love-making on my part with a jest and begin talking of other subjects; but at that moment I was incapable of reflecting and was all eagerness for revenge. I remember with surprise that my wrath and revengeful feelings were extremely repugnant to my own nature, for being of an easy temper, I found it difficult to be angry with any one for long, and so I had to work myself up artificially and became at last revolting and absurd.

I bided my time and succeeded in insulting my "rival" at a large gathering on a perfectly extraneous pretext, jeering at his opinion upon an important public event — it was in the year 1826* — and my jibe was, so people said, clever and effective. Then I forced him to ask for an explanation, and behaved so rudely that he accepted my challenge in spite of the vast difference between us, as I was younger, a person of no consequence, and of inferior rank. I learnt afterwards for a fact that it was from a jealous feeling on his side also that he accepted my challenge; he had been rather jealous of me on his wife's account before their marriage; he fancied now that if he submitted to be insulted by me and refused to accept my challenge, and if she heard of it, she might begin to despise him and waver in her love for him. I soon found a second in a comrade, an ensign of our regiment. In those days though duels were severely punished, yet duelling was a kind of fashion among the officers — so strong and deeply rooted will a brutal prejudice sometimes be.

It was the end of June, and our meeting was

* The public event referred to was probably the conspiracy of December, 1825, in which many distinguished men were involved. *Translator's note.*

to take place at seven o'clock in the morning the next day on the outskirts of the town — and then something happened that in very truth was the turning-point of my life. In the evening, returning home in a savage and brutal humour, I flew into a rage with my orderly Afanasy, and gave him two blows in the face with all my might, so that it bled. He had not been long in my service and I had struck him before, but never with such ferocious cruelty. And, believe me, though it's forty years ago, I recall it now with shame and pain. I went to bed and slept for about three hours; when I waked the day was breaking. I got up — I did not want to sleep any more — I went to the window — opened it, it looked out upon the garden; I saw the sun rising; it was warm and beautiful, the birds were trilling.

What's the meaning of it, I thought, why do I feel in my heart something vile and shameful, as it were? Is it because I am going to shed blood? No, I thought, I feel it's not that. Can it be that I am afraid of death, afraid of being killed? No, that's not it, that's not it at all. . . . And all at once I knew what it was: it was because I had struck Afanasy the evening before! It all rose before my mind, it all was, as it were, repeated over again; he stood before me and I was striking him straight on the face and he was holding his arms stiffly down, his head erect, his eyes fixed upon me as though on parade. He flinched at every blow and did not even dare to raise his hands to protect himself. That is what a man has been brought to, and that was a man beating a fellow creature! What a crime! It was as though a sharp needle had pierced me right through. I stood as if I were struck dumb, while the sun was shining, the leaves were sparkling and rejoicing and the birds were praising God. . . . I hid my face in my hands, fell on my bed and broke into a storm of tears. And then I remembered my brother Markel and what he said on his deathbed to his servants: "My dear ones, why do you wait on me, why do you love me, am I worth your waiting on me?"

Yes, am I worth it? flashed through my mind. After all, what am I worth, that another man, a fellow creature, made in the likeness and image of God, should serve me? For the first time in my life this question forced itself upon me. He had said, "Mother, my darling little life, in truth we are each responsible to all for all, it's only that men don't know this. If they knew it, the world would be a paradise at once."

"God, can that too be false?" I thought as I wept; "in truth perhaps, I am more than all others responsible for all, a greater sinner than all men in the world." And all at once the whole truth in its full light appeared to me: what was I going to do? I was about to kill a good, intelligent, high-minded man, who had done me no wrong, and thus deprive his wife of happiness for ever, and torture and kill her, too. I lay thus in my bed with my face in the pillow, heedless how the time was passing. Suddenly my second, the ensign, came in with the pistols to fetch me.

"Ah," said he, "it's a good thing you are up already, it's time we were off, come along!"

I did not know what to do and flung myself this way and that undecided; we went out to the carriage, however.

"Wait here a minute," I said to him. "I'll be back directly, I have forgotten my purse."

And I ran back alone, straight to Afanasy's cubicle. "Afanasy," I said, "I struck you twice on the face yesterday. Forgive me," I begged.

He started as though he were frightened, and looked at me; and I saw that it was not enough, and on the spot, in my full regalia, I dropped at his feet and bowed my head to the ground. "Forgive me," I said.

Then he was completely aghast.

"Your honour . . . sir, what are you doing? Am I worth it?"

And he burst out crying as I had done before, hid his face in his hands, turned to the window and shook all over with his sobs. I flew out to my comrade and jumped into the carriage.

"Ready," I cried. "Have you ever seen a conqueror?" I asked him. "Here is one before you." I was in ecstasy, laughing and talking all the way, I don't remember what I said.

He looked at me. "Well, brother, you are a plucky fellow, you'll keep up the honour of the uniform, I can see."

So we reached the place and found them there, waiting for us. We were placed twelve paces apart; he had the first shot. I stood gaily, looking him full in the face; I did not twitch an eyelash, I looked lovingly at him, for I knew what I would do. His shot just grazed my cheek and ear.

"Thank God," I cried, "no man has been killed," and I seized my pistol, turned back and flung it far away into the wood. "That's the place for you," I cried.

I turned to my adversary.

"Forgive me, young fool that I am, sir," I said, "for my unprovoked insult to you and for forcing you to fire at me. I am ten times worse than you and more, may be. Tell that to the person whom you hold dearest in the world." I had no sooner said this than they all three shouted at me.

"Upon my word," cried my adversary, annoyed, "if you did not want to fight, why did you bother me?"

"Yesterday I was a fool, to-day I know better," I answered him gaily.

"As to yesterday, I believe you, but as for to-day, it is difficult to agree with your opinion," said he.

"Bravo," I cried, clapping my hands. "I agree with you there, too. I have deserved it!"

"Will you shoot, sir, or not?"

"No, I won't," I said, "if you like, fire at me again, but it would be better for you not to fire."

The seconds, especially mine, were shouting, too: "Can you disgrace the regiment like this, facing your antagonist and begging his forgiveness! If I'd only known this!"

I stood facing them all, not laughing now.

"Gentlemen," I said, "is it really so wonderful in these days to find a man who can repent of his stupidity and publicly confess his wrongdoing?"

"But not at the barrier," cried my second.

"That's what's so strange," I said. "For I ought to have owned my fault as soon as I got here, before he had fired a shot, before leading him into a great and deadly sin; but we have made our life so grotesque, that to act in that way would have been almost impossible, for only after I have faced his shot at the distance of twelve paces could my words have any significance for him, and if I had spoken before, he would have said, 'He is a coward, the sight of the pistols frightened him, no use listening to him.' Gentlemen," I cried suddenly, speaking straight from my heart, "look around you at the gifts of God, the clear sky, the pure air, the tender grass, the birds; nature is beautiful and sinless, and we, only

we, are godless and foolish, and we don't understand that life is paradise, for we have only to understand that and it will at once be fulfilled in all its beauty, we shall embrace each other and weep."

I would have said more but I could not; my breath failed me with the sweetness and youthful gladness of it, and there was such bliss in my heart as I had never known before in my life.

"All this is sensible and edifying," said my antagonist, "and in any case you are an odd fellow."

"You may laugh," I said to him, laughing too, "but afterwards you will approve of me."

"Oh, I am ready to approve of you now," said he; "I will give you my hand, for I believe you are genuinely sincere."

"No," I said, "not now, later on when I have grown worthier and deserve your esteem, then give me your hand and you will do well."

We went home, my second upbraiding me all the way, while I kissed him. All my comrades heard of the affair at once and gathered together to pass judgment on me the same day.

"He has disgraced the uniform," they said; "let him tender his resignation."

Some stood up for me: "He faced the shot," they said.

"Yes, but he was afraid of the other shots and begged forgiveness at the barrier."

"If he had been afraid of shots, he would have fired his own pistol first before asking forgiveness, while instead he flung it loaded into the forest. No, there's something else in this, something original."

I enjoyed listening to and looking at them. "My dear friends and comrades," said I, "don't worry about my resigning my commission, for I have done so already. I have sent in my papers this morning and as soon as I get my discharge I shall go into a monastery —it's with that object I am leaving the regiment." When I had said this every one of them burst out laughing.

"You should have told us of that first, that explains everything, we can't try a monk."

They laughed and could not stop themselves, and not scornfully, but kindly and merrily. They all felt friendly to me at once, even those who had been sternest in their censure, and all the following month, until my discharge came, they could not make enough of me. "Ah, you monk," they would say. And every one said something kind to me, they began trying to dissuade me, even to pity me: "What are you doing to yourself?" "No," they would say, "he is a brave fellow, he faced the bullet and could have fired his own pistol, too, but he had a dream the night before that he should become a monk, that's why he did it."

Local society took it the same way. Till then I had been kindly received, but had not been the object of special attention, and now all took notice of me at once and extended invitations to me; they laughed at me, but they loved me. I may mention that although everybody talked openly of our duel, the authorities took no notice of it, because my antagonist was a near relation of our general, and as there had been no bloodshed and no serious consequences, and as I resigned my commission, they took it as a joke. And I began then to speak aloud and fearlessly, regardless of their laughter, for it was always kindly and not spiteful laughter. These conversations took place mostly in the evening, in the company of ladies; women particularly liked listening to me then and they made the men listen.

"But how can I possibly be responsible for all?" every one would laugh in my face. "Can I, for instance, be responsible for you?"

"You may well not know it," I would answer, "since the whole world has long been following a different road and since we consider the veriest lies as truth and demand the same lies from others. Here I have for once in my life acted sincerely and, well, you all look upon me as a saintly fool. Though you have come to love me, yet, you all laugh at me."

"But how can we help loving you?" said my hostess, laughing. The room was full of people. All of a sudden I saw arise the very young lady on whose account the duel had been fought and whom only lately I had intended to ask to be my wife. I had not noticed her coming into the room. She got up, came to me and held out her hand.

"Allow me to tell you," she said, "that I am the first who does not laugh at you, but on the contrary I thank you, with tears, and wish to say that I respect you for your action then."

Her husband, too, came up and then they all approached me and almost kissed me. My heart was filled with joy, but my attention was particularly attracted by a middle-aged man who came up to me with the others. I knew him by name already, but had never made his acquaintance nor exchanged a word with him till that evening.

## (d) The mysterious visitor

He had long been an official in the town; he was wealthy, in a prominent position, respected by all, and had a reputation for benevolence. He subscribed considerable sums to the almshouse and the orphan asylum; he performed many acts of charity, too, in secret, a fact which became known only after his death. He was a man of about fifty, almost stern in appearance and not much given to conversation. He had been married about ten years and his wife, who was still young, had borne him three children. Well, I was sitting alone in my room the following evening, when my door suddenly opened and this gentleman walked in.

I must mention, by the way, that I was no longer living in my former quarters. As soon as I resigned my commission, I took rooms with an old lady, the widow of a government clerk. My landlady's servant waited upon me, for I had moved into her rooms simply because on my return from the duel I had sent Afanasy back to the regiment, as I felt ashamed to look him in the face after my last interview with him. So prone is the man of the world to be ashamed of any righteous action.

"I have listened to you," said my visitor, "with great interest when you were speaking in different houses the last few days, and I wanted at last to make your acquaintance personally so as to talk to you more fully. Can you, dear sir, grant me this favour?"

"I can, with the greatest pleasure, and I shall consider it a signal honour." I said this, though I felt almost dismayed, so greatly was I impressed from the first moment by the appearance of this man. For though other people had listened to me with interest and attention, no one had come to me before with such a serious, stern, and concentrated expression. And now he had come to see me in my own rooms. He sat down.

"You are, I see, a man of great strength of character," he said; "as you have dared to serve the truth, even when by doing so you risked incurring the contempt of all."

"Your praise is, perhaps, excessive."

"No, it's not excessive," he answered; "believe me, such a course of action is far more difficult than you think. It is that which has impressed me, and it is only on that account that I have come to you," he continued. "Tell me, please, that is if you are not annoyed by my perhaps unseemly curiosity, what were your exact sensations, if you can recall them, at the moment when you made up your mind to ask forgiveness at the duel. Do not think my question frivolous; on the contrary, in asking the question I have a secret motive of my own, which I will perhaps explain to you later on, if it is God's will that we should become more intimately acquainted."

All the while he was speaking, I was looking him straight in the face and I felt all at once a complete trust in him and great curiosity on my side also, for I felt that he was carrying some secret in his soul.

"You ask what were my exact sensations at the moment when I asked my opponent's forgiveness," I answered; "but I had better tell you from the beginning what I have not yet told any one else." And I described all that had passed between Afanasy and me, and how I had bowed down to the ground before him. "From that you can see for yourself," I concluded, "that at the time of the duel it was easier for me, for I had made a beginning already at home, and when once I had started on that road, to go further along it was far from being difficult, but became a source of joy and happiness."

I liked the way he looked at me as he listened. "All that," he said, "is exceedingly interesting, I will come to see you again and again."

And from that time forth he came to see me nearly every evening. And we should have become greater friends, if only he had talked of himself, too. But about himself he scarcely ever said a word, though he continued to question me about myself. In spite of that I became very fond of him and spoke with perfect frankness to him about all my feelings; for, thought I, what need have I to know his secrets, since I can see without that that he is a righteous man. Moreover, though he is such a serious man and my senior, he comes to see a youngster like me and doesn't look down on me. And I learnt many useful things from him, for he was a man of lofty mind.

"That life is paradise," he said to me suddenly, "I have been thinking for a long time"; and all at once he added, "indeed, I think of nothing else." He looked at me and smiled. "I am more convinced of it than you are, I will tell you later why."

I listened to him and thought that he evidently wanted to confide something to me.

"Paradise," he went on, "lies hidden within all of us — here it lies hidden in me now, and if I desire it, it will become a reality for me tomorrow and remain with me the rest of my life." I looked at him; he was speaking with great emotion and looking mysteriously at me, as if he were questioning me.

"And that each of us is responsible for all men and all things, apart from his own sins, you were quite right in thinking that, and it is wonderful how you could suddenly comprehend this thought in all its fulness. And in very truth, as soon as men understand this thought, the Kingdom of Heaven will be theirs, not in fancy, but in reality."

"And when," I cried out to him bitterly, "when will that come to pass? and will it ever come to pass? Is it not simply a dream of ours?"

"Look, already you don't believe it," he said. "You preach it and don't believe it yourself. Believe me, this dream, as you call it, will come true, without doubt; it will come true, but not now, for every process has its law. It's a matter of the soul, a psychological thing. To make the world over anew, men must turn into another path psychologically. Until you have become, in actual fact, a brother to every one, brotherhood will not come to pass. No sort of science, no kind of self-interest, will ever enable men to share their property and their rights with equal consideration for all. Every one will think his share too small and they will be always envying, complaining, and destroying one another. You ask when it will come to pass; it will come to pass, but first the period of human *isolation* must be concluded."

"What do you mean by isolation?" I asked him.

"Why, the isolation that prevails everywhere, above all in our age — it has not fully developed, it has not reached its limit yet. For nowadays every one strives to keep his individuality as distinct as possible, wishes to secure the greatest possible fulness of life for himself; but meantime all his efforts result not in fulness of life but in utter self-destruction, for instead of self-realisation he arrives at complete isolation. For in our age all mankind has split up into units, each withdraws into his own hole; each one holds aloof, hides himself and hides what he has, from the rest, and he ends by repelling others and being repelled by them. He heaps up riches in solitude and thinks, 'How strong I am now and how secure,' and in his folly he does not understand that the more he heaps up, the more he sinks into self-destructive impotence. For he is accustomed to rely upon himself alone and to cut himself off from the whole; he has trained his soul not to believe in the help of others, in men and in humanity, and only trembles for fear he should lose his money and the rights that he has won for himself. Everywhere in these days men have ceased to understand that the true security is to be found in social solidarity rather than in isolated individual effort. But this dreadful isolation must inevitably come to an end, and all will suddenly understand how unnaturally they are separated from one another. It will be the spirit of the time, and people will marvel that they have sat so long in darkness and did not see the light. And then the sign of the Son of Man will be seen in the heavens. . . . But, until then, we must guard the banner, and from time to time a man must set an example, even if it's only an isolated case, and so draw men's souls out of their solitude, and spur them to some act of brotherly communion, though it may be at the risk of appearing a saintly fool, and this to the end that the great idea may not die."

It was in such stirring and fervent talk that we spent our evenings, one after another. I gave up society and visited my friends much less frequently. Besides, my vogue was somewhat over. I say this, not in blame, for they still loved me and treated me good-humouredly, but there's no denying that fashion is a great power in society. I began to regard my mysterious visitor with deep admiration, for besides enjoying his intelligence, I began to perceive that he was brooding over some plan in his heart, and was preparing himself perhaps for a great deed. Perhaps he liked my not showing curiosity about his secret, not seeking to discover it by direct question nor by hints. But I noticed at last that he was himself fretted by the desire to open his heart to

me. This had become quite evident, indeed, about a month after he first began to visit me. "Do you know," he said to me once, "that people are very curious about us in the town and wonder why I come to see you so often. But let them wonder, for *soon all will be explained*."

Sometimes an extraordinary agitation would come over him, and almost always on such occasions he would get up and go away. Sometimes he would fix a long piercing look upon me, and I thought "He will say something directly now." But he would suddenly change the subject and speak of something ordinary and familiar. He often complained of headache, too.

One day, quite unexpectedly indeed, after he had been talking with great fervour a long time, I saw him suddenly turn pale, and his face worked convulsively, while he stared persistently at me.

"What's the matter?" I said; "do you feel ill?" — he had just been complaining of headache.

"I . . . do you know . . . I killed a human being."

He said this and smiled with a face as white as chalk. "Why is it he is smiling?" The thought flashed through my mind before I realised anything else. I, too, turned pale.

"What are you saying?" I cried.

"You see," he said, with a pale smile, "how much it has cost me to say the first word. Now I have said it, I feel I've taken the first step and shall go on."

For a long while I could not believe him, and I did not believe him at that time, but only after he had been to see me three days running and told me about it in detail. I thought he was mad, but ended by being convinced, to my great grief and amazement. His crime was a great and terrible one.

Fourteen years before, he had murdered the widow of a landowner, a wealthy and handsome young woman who had a house in our town. He had fallen passionately in love with her, declared himself and tried to persuade her to marry him. But she had already given her heart to another, a military man of noble birth and high rank in the service, who was at that time away at the front, and whom she expected to return soon. She refused his offer and asked him to stop calling on her. After he had ceased to visit her, he took advantage of his knowledge of the house to enter at night through the garden by the roof, with extreme boldness at the risk of being discovered. But as often happens, crimes committed with extraordinary audacity are the ones to be carried out successfully.

Entering the garret through the dormer window, he went down the ladder, knowing that the door at the bottom of it was sometimes, through the negligence of the servants, left unlocked. He hoped to find it so, and so it was. He made his way in the dark to her bedroom, where a light was burning before an ikon. As though on purpose, both her maids had gone off to a birthday-party in the neighbourhood, without asking leave. The other servants slept in the servants' quarters and in the kitchen on the ground-floor. His passion flamed up at the sight of her asleep, and then vindictive, jealous anger took possession of his heart, and like a drunken man, beside himself, he thrust a knife into her heart, so that she did not even cry out. Then with devilish and criminal cunning he contrived that suspicion should fall on the servants. He did not disdain to take her purse, to open her chest with keys

which he drew from under her pillow, and to take some things from it, doing it all as it might have been done by an ignorant servant, that is, he left valuable papers and took only money, carried off some of the larger gold things, but left smaller articles that were ten times as valuable. He took with him, too, some things for himself as remembrances, but of that later. Having done this awful deed, he returned by the way he had come.

Neither the next day, when the alarm was raised, nor at any time after in his life, did any one dream of suspecting that he was the criminal. No one indeed knew of his love for her, for he was always reserved and uncommunicative and had no friend to whom he would have opened his heart. He was looked upon simply as an acquaintance, and not a very intimate one, of the murdered woman, all the more so since he had not even visited her during the fortnight before the murder. A serf of hers called Pyotr was at once suspected, and every circumstance confirmed the suspicion. The man knew — indeed his mistress had not concealed the fact — that having to send one of her serfs as a recruit she had decided to send him, as he had no family and, furthermore, his conduct was unsatisfactory. People had heard him angrily threatening to murder her when he was drunk in a pot-house. Two days before her death, he had run away, staying no one knew where in the town. The day after the murder, he was found on the road leading out of the town, dead drunk, with a knife in his pocket and his right hand happened to be stained with blood. He declared that his nose had been bleeding, but no one believed him. The maids confessed that they had gone to a party and that the street-door had been left open till they returned. And a number of similar details came to light, throwing suspicion on the innocent servant.

They arrested him, and he was tried for the murder; but a week after the arrest, the prisoner fell sick of a fever and died unconscious in the hospital. There the matter ended and was left to the will of God, while the judges and the authorities and every one in the town remained convinced that the crime had been committed by no one but the servant who had died in the hospital. And after that the punishment began for the real criminal.

My mysterious visitor, now my friend, told me that at first he was not in the least troubled by pangs of conscience. He was miserable a long time, but not for that reason; only from regret that he had killed the woman he loved, that she was no more, that in killing her he had killed his love, while the fire of passion was still in his veins. But of the innocent blood he had shed, of the murder of a fellow creature, he scarcely thought. The thought that his victim might have become the wife of another man was insupportable to him, and so, for a long time, he was convinced in his conscience that he could not have acted otherwise.

At first he was worried at the arrest of the servant, but his illness and death soon set his mind at rest, for the man's death was apparently (so he reflected at the time) not owing to his arrest or his fright, but to a chill he had taken on the day he ran away, when he had lain all night dead drunk on the damp ground. The theft of the money and other things troubled him little, for he argued that the theft had not been committed for gain but to avert suspicion. The sum stolen was small, and he shortly afterwards subscribed the whole of it, and much more, towards the funds for maintaining an almshouse in the town. He

did this on purpose to set his conscience at rest about the theft, and it's a remarkable fact that for a long time he really was at peace — he told me this himself. He entered then upon a career of great activity in the service, volunteered for a difficult and laborious task, which occupied him two years, and being a man of strong will almost forgot the past. Whenever he recalled it, he tried not to think of it at all. He became active in philanthropy, too, founded and helped maintain many institutions in the town, did a good deal in the two capitals, and in both Moscow and Petersburg was elected a member of charitable societies.

At last, however, he began brooding over the past, and the strain of it was too much for him. Then he was attracted by a fine and intelligent girl and soon after married her, hoping that marriage would dispel his loneliness and depression, and that by entering on a new life and scrupulously doing his duty towards his wife and children, he would escape from old memories altogether. But the very opposite of what he expected happened. He began, even in the first month of his marriage, to be continually fretted by the thought, "My wife loves me — but what if she knew?" When she became pregnant with their first child, and told him of it, he was troubled: "I am giving life, but I have taken life." Children came. "How dare I love them, teach and educate them, how can I talk to them of virtue? I have shed blood." They were splendid children, he longed to caress them; "and I can't look at their innocent candid faces, I am unworthy."

At last he began to be bitterly and ominously haunted by the blood of his murdered victim, by the young life he had destroyed, by the blood that cried out for vengeance. He had begun to have terrifying dreams. But, being a

234

man of fortitude, he bore his suffering a long time, thinking: "I shall expiate everything by this secret agony of mine." But that hope, too, was vain; the longer it went on, the more intense was his suffering.

He was respected in society for his active benevolence, though every one feared him because of his stern and gloomy character. But the more he was respected, the more intolerable it was for him. He confessed to me that he had had thoughts of killing himself. But he began to be haunted by another idea — an idea which he had at first regarded as impossible and insane, but at last it got such a hold on his heart that he could not shake it off. He dreamed of rising up, going out and confessing in the face of all men that he had committed murder. For three years this dream had pursued him, haunting him in different forms. At last he believed with his whole heart that if he confessed his crime, he would cure his soul and would be at peace for ever. But this belief filled his heart with terror, for how could he carry it out? And then suddenly came my duel. "With your example before me, I have now made up my mind."

I looked at him.

"Is it possible," I cried, striking my hands together, "that such a trivial incident should move you to such a resolution?"

"My resolution took three years to mature," he answered, "and your act only gave the last touch to it. Looking at you, I reproached myself and envied you." He said this to me almost sullenly.

"But you won't be believed," I observed; "fourteen years have elapsed."

"I have proofs, great proofs. I shall submit them." Then I cried and kissed him.

"Tell me one thing, one thing," he said (as though it all depended upon me), "my wife, my children! My wife may die of grief, and though my children won't lose their rank and property, they'll be a convict's children, and for ever! And what a memory, what a memory of me I shall leave in their hearts!"

I said nothing.

"And to part from them, to leave them for ever? It's for ever, you know, for ever!"

I sat still and repeated a silent prayer. I got up at last, I felt afraid.

"Well?" He looked at me.

"Go!" said I, "confess. Everything passes, only the truth remains. Your children will understand, when they grow up, the nobility of your great resolution."

He left me that time as though he had made up his mind. Yet for more than a fortnight afterwards, he came to me every evening, still preparing himself, still unable to bring himself to the point. He made my heart ache. One day he would come in a determined mood and say fervently:

"I know it will be heaven for me, heaven, the moment I confess. Fourteen years I've been in hell. I want to suffer. I will accept my suffering and begin to live. You can travel to the end of the world on lies, but they won't carry you back again. Now I dare not love my neighbour nor even my own children. Good God, my children will understand, perhaps, what my suffering was and will not condemn me! God is not in might but in truth."

"All will understand your high deed," I said to him, "if not at once, they will understand later; for you have served truth, the higher truth, not of this earth."

And he would go away seeming comforted, but next day he would come again, bitter, pale, sarcastic.

"Every time I come to you, you look at me so inquisitively, as though to say, 'He has still not confessed!' Wait a bit, don't despise me too much. It's not such an easy thing to do, as you would think. Perhaps I shall not do it at all. You won't go and inform against me then, will you?"

And far from looking at him with indiscreet curiosity, I was afraid to look at him at all. I was quite ill with it all, and my heart was full of tears. I could not sleep at night.

"I have just come from my wife," he went on. "Do you understand what the word 'wife' means? When I went out, the children called to me, 'Good-bye, father, make haste back to read "The Children's Magazine" with us.' No, you don't understand that! No one grows wise through another man's woe."

His eyes were glittering, his lips were twitching. Suddenly he struck the table with his fist so that everything on it danced — it was the first time he had done such a thing, he was such a mild man.

"But need I?" he exclaimed, "must I? No one has been condemned, no one has been sent to Siberia in my place, the man died of fever. And I've been punished by my sufferings for the blood I shed. And I shan't be believed, they won't believe my proofs. Need I confess, need I? I am ready to go on suffering all my life for the blood I have shed, if only my wife and children may be spared. Will it be just to ruin them with me? Aren't we making a mistake? What is right in this case? And will people recognise it, will they appreciate it, will they respect it?"

"Good Lord!" I thought to myself, "he is thinking of other people's respect at such a moment!" And I felt so sorry for him then, that I believe I would have shared his fate if it could have comforted him. I saw he was beside himself. I was aghast, realising with my heart as well as my mind what such a resolution meant.

"Decide my fate!" he exclaimed again.

"Go and confess," I whispered to him. My voice failed me, but I whispered it firmly. I took up the New Testament from the table, the Russian translation, and showed him the Gospel of St. John, ch. xii. verse 24:

"Verily, verily, I say unto you, except a corn of wheat fall into the ground and die, it abideth alone: but if it die, it bringeth forth much fruit." I had just been reading that verse when he came in. He read it.

"That's true," he said, but he smiled bitterly. "It's terrible the things you find in those books," he said, after a pause. "It's easy enough to thrust them upon one. And who wrote them? Can they have been written by men?"

"The Holy Ghost wrote them," said I.

"It's easy for you to prate." He smiled again, this time almost with hatred.

I took the book again, opened it in another place and showed him the Epistle to the Hebrews, ch. x. verse 31. He read:

"It is a fearful thing to fall into the hands of the living God."

He read it and simply flung down the book. He was trembling all over.

"A terrible text," he said. "There's no denying you've picked out fitting ones." He rose from the chair. "Well!" he said, "good-bye, perhaps I shan't come again . . . we shall meet in heaven. So I have been for fourteen years 'in the hands of the living God,' that's how one must think of those fourteen years. To-morrow I will beseech those hands to let me go." I wanted to take him in my arms and kiss him, but I did not dare — his face was contorted and sombre. He went away.

"Good God," I thought, "what has he gone to face!" I fell on my knees before the ikon and wept for him before the Holy Mother of God, our swift defender and helper. I was half an hour praying in tears, and it was late, about midnight. Suddenly I saw the door open and he came in again. I was surprised.

"Where have you been?" I asked him.

"I think," he said, "I've forgotten something . . . my handkerchief, I think. . . . Well, even if I've not forgotten anything, let me stay a little."

He sat down. I stood over him.

"You sit down, too," said he.

I sat down. We sat still for two minutes; he looked intently at me and suddenly smiled — I remember that — then he got up, embraced me warmly and kissed me.

"Remember," he said, "how I came to you a second time. Do you hear, remember it!"

And he went out.

"To-morrow," I thought.

And so it was. I did not know that evening that the next day was his birthday. I had not been out for the last few days so I had no chance of hearing it from any one. On that day he always had a great gathering, every one in the town went to it. It was the same this time. After dinner he walked into the middle of the room, with a paper in his hand — a formal declaration to his superior, who was present. This declaration he read aloud to the whole assembly. It contained a full account of the crime, with every detail.

"I cut myself off from men as a monster. God has visited me," he said in conclusion. "I want to suffer for my sin!"

Then he brought out and laid on the table all the things he had been keeping for fourteen years, that he thought would prove his crime, the jewels belonging to the murdered woman which he had stolen to divert suspicion, a cross and a locket taken from her neck with a portrait of her betrothed in the locket, her note-book and two letters; one from her betrothed, telling her that he would soon be with her, and her unfinished answer left on the table to be sent off next day. He had carried off these two letters — what for? Why had he kept them for fourteen years afterwards instead of destroying them as evidence against him?

And this is what happened: every one was amazed and horrified, every one refused to believe it and thought that he was deranged, though all listened with intense curiosity. A few days later it was fully decided and agreed upon in every house that the unhappy man had lost his mind. The legal authorities could not refuse to take up the case, but they, too, dropped it. Though the trinkets and letters made them ponder, they decided that even if they did turn out to be authentic, no final conviction could be obtained on the basis of this evidence alone. Besides, she might have given him those things for safe-keeping as a friend. I heard afterwards, however, that the genuineness of the things was proved by the friends and relations of the murdered woman, and that there was no doubt about them. Yet nothing was destined to come of it, after all.

Five days later, all had heard that he was ill and that his life was in danger. The nature of his illness I can't explain, they said it was an affection of the heart. But it became known that the doctors had been induced by his wife to investigate his mental condition also, and had come to the conclusion that it was a case of insanity. I betrayed nothing, though people ran to question me. But when I wanted to visit him, I was for a long while forbidden to do so, above all by his wife.

"It's you who have caused his illness," she said to me; "he was always gloomy, but for the last year people noticed that he was peculiarly excited and did strange things, and now you have been the ruin of him. Your preaching has brought him to this; for the last month he was always with you."

Indeed, not only his wife but the whole town were down upon me and blamed me. "It's all your doing," they said. I was silent and indeed rejoiced at heart, for I saw plainly God's mercy to the man who had turned against himself and punished himself. I could not believe in his insanity.

They let me see him at last, he insisted upon saying good-bye to me. I went in to him and saw at once that not only his days, but his hours were numbered. He was weak, yellow, his hands trembled, he gasped for breath, but his face was full of tender and happy feeling.

"It is done!" he said. "I've long been yearning to see you, why didn't you come?"

I did not tell him that they would not let me see him.

"God has had pity on me and is calling me to Himself. I know I am dying, but I feel joy and peace for the first time after so many years. There was heaven in my heart from the moment I had done what I had to do. Now I dare to love my children and to kiss them. Neither my wife nor the judges, nor any one has believed it. My children will never believe it either. I see in that God's mercy to them. I shall die, and my name will be without a stain for them. And now I feel God near, my heart rejoices as in heaven. . . . I have done my duty."

He could not speak, he gasped for breath, he pressed my hand warmly, looking fervently at me. We did not talk long, his wife kept peeping in at us. But he had time to whisper to me:

"Do you remember how I came back to you that second time, at midnight? I told you to remember it. You know what I came back for? I came to kill you!"

I started.

"I went out from you then into the darkness, I wandered about the streets, struggling with myself. And suddenly I hated you so that I could hardly bear it. Now, I thought, he is all that binds me, and he is my judge. I can't refuse to face my punishment to-morrow, for he knows all. It was not that I was afraid you would betray me (I never even thought of that) but I thought, 'How can I look him in the face if I don't confess?' And if you had been at the other end of the earth, but alive, it would have been all the same, the thought was unendurable that you were alive knowing everything and condemning me. I hated you as though you were the cause, as though you were to blame for everything. I came back to you then, remembering that you had a dagger lying on your table. I sat down and asked you to sit down, and for a whole minute I pondered. If I had killed you, I should have been ruined by that murder even if I had not confessed the other. But I didn't think that at all, and I didn't want to think of it at that moment. I only hated you and longed to revenge myself on you for everything. But the Lord vanquished the devil in my heart. But let me tell you, you were never nearer death."

A week later he died. The whole town followed him to the grave. The chief priest made a speech full of feeling. All lamented the terrible illness that had cut short his days. But all the town was up in arms against me after the funeral, and people even forbade me the house. Some, at first a few and afterwards more, began indeed to believe in the truth of his story, and they visited me and questioned me with great interest and eagerness, for man loves to see the downfall and disgrace of the righteous.

But I held my tongue, and very shortly after, I left the town, and five months later by God's grace I entered upon the safe and blessed path, praising the unseen finger which had guided me so clearly to it. But I remember in my prayer to this day the servant of God, Mihail, who suffered so greatly.

## CHAPTER III
### FROM THE CONVERSATIONS
### AND EXHORTATIONS OF FATHER ZOSIMA
*(e) Concerning the Russian monk and his possible significance*

FATHERS and teachers, what is a monk? In the cultivated world the word is nowadays pronounced by some people with a jeer, and by others it is used as a term of abuse, and this contempt for the monk is growing. It is true, alas, it is true, that there are many idlers, gluttons, lechers, and insolent beggars among monks. Men of the world point to these: "You are idlers, useless members of society, you live on the labour of others, you are shameless beggars."

And yet how many there are among the monks who are meek and humble, and who yearn for solitude and fervent prayer in peace. These are less noticed, or passed over in silence. And how surprised men would be if I were to say that from these meek monks, who yearn for solitary prayer, the salvation of Russia will come perhaps once more. For they are in truth prepared in peace and quiet "for the day and the hour, the month and the year." Meanwhile, in their solitude, they keep the image of Christ fair and undefiled, in the purity of God's truth, from the times of the Fathers of old, the Apostles and the martyrs. And when the time comes they will show it to the tottering truth of the world. That is a great thought. That star will shine forth out of the East.

That is my view of the monk, and is it false? is it too haughty? Look at the worldly and all who set themselves up above the people of God, has not God's image and His truth been distorted in them? They have science; but in science there is nothing but what is subject to the senses. The spiritual world, the higher part of man's being, is rejected altogether, banished with a sort of triumph, even with hatred. The world has proclaimed freedom, especially of late, but what do we see in this freedom of theirs? Nothing but slavery and self-destruction! For the world says: "You have wants and so satisfy them, for you have the same rights as the most rich and powerful. Don't be afraid of satisfying them and even multiply your wants." That is the modern doctrine of the world. In that they see freedom. And what follows from this right of multiplication of wants? In the rich, isolation and spiritual suicide; in the poor, envy and murder; for they have been given rights, but have not been shown the means of satisfying their wants. It is maintained that the world is becoming more and more united, more and more bound together in brotherly community, as it overcomes distance and transmits thoughts through the air.

Alas, put no faith in such a way of uniting

men. Interpreting freedom as the multiplication and rapid satisfaction of desires, men distort their own nature, for they thus engender in themselves many senseless and foolish desires and habits and most absurd fancies. They live only for mutual envy, for the lusts of the flesh and ostentation. To have dinners, visits, carriages, rank, and slaves to wait on one is looked upon as a necessity, for which life, honour, and human feeling are sacrificed, and men even commit suicide if they are unable to satisfy this craving. We see the same thing among those who are not rich, while the poor drown their unsatisfied wants and their envy in drink. But soon they will drink blood instead of wine, they are being led on to it. I ask you is such a man free? I knew one "champion of ideas" who told me himself that, when he was deprived of tobacco in prison, he was made so wretched by the privation that he almost went and betrayed his cause for the sake of getting tobacco again! And such a man says, "I am fighting in the cause of humanity."

How can such a one fight, what is he fit for? He is capable perhaps of some rash action, but he has no endurance. And it's no wonder that instead of gaining freedom they have sunk into slavery, and instead of serving the cause of brotherly love and the union of men have fallen, on the contrary, into disunion and isolation, as my mysterious visitor and teacher said to me in my youth. And therefore the idea of the service of humanity, of brotherly love and the solidarity of mankind, is more and more dying out in the world, and indeed this idea is sometimes treated with derision. For how can a man shake off his habits, whither shall this slave go, if he is so habituated to satisfying the innumerable wants which he has himself invented? He is isolated, and what concern has he with the rest of humanity? They have managed to accumulate a greater number of things, but the joy in the world has grown less.

The monastic way is very different. Obedience, fasting, and prayer are laughed at, yet only through them lies the way to real, true freedom. I cut off my superfluous and unnecessary wants, I subdue my proud and wanton will and chastise it with obedience, and with God's help I attain freedom of spirit and therewith spiritual joy. Which of the two is more capable of conceiving a great idea and serving it — the rich man in his isolation or the man who has freed himself from the tyranny of material things and habits? The monk is reproached for his solitude, "You have secluded yourself within the walls of the monastery for your own salvation, and have forgotten the brotherly service of humanity!" But we shall see which will be most zealous in the cause of brotherly love. For it is not we, but they, who are in isolation, though they don't see that. Even in the olden days, leaders of the people came from among us, and why should they not again? The same meek and humble ascetics will rise up and go out to work for the great cause. From the people comes the salvation of Russia. And the Russian monastery has always been on the side of the people. We are isolated only if the people are isolated. The people believe as we do, and an unbelieving reformer will never do anything in Russia, even if he is sincere in heart and a genius. Remember that! The people will meet the atheist and overcome him, and Russia will be one and orthodox. Take care of the peasant and guard his heart. Educate him quietly. That's your duty as monks, for this is a God-bearing people.

*(f) Of masters and servants, and of whether it is possible for them to be brothers in the spirit*

Of course, I don't deny that there is sin in the people, too. And the fire of corruption is spreading visibly, hourly, working from above downwards. The spirit of isolation is coming upon the people, too. Exploiters and oppressors are rising up. Already the merchant grows more and more eager for honours, and strives to show himself cultured though he has not a trace of culture, and to this end meanly despises his old traditions, and is even ashamed of the faith of his fathers. He visits princes, though he is only a peasant, spoiled. The people are rotting with drunkenness and cannot shake off the habit. And what cruelty to their wives, to their children even! All because of drunkenness! I've seen in the factories children nine years old, frail, rickety, bent, and already depraved. The stuffy work-room, the din of machinery, work all day long, the vile language and the drink, the drink — is that what a little child's heart needs? He needs sunshine, childish play, good examples all about him, and at least a little love. There must be no more of this, monks, no more torturing of children, rise up and preach that, make haste, make haste!

But God will save Russia, for though the masses are corrupted and cannot renounce their filthy sin, yet they know it is cursed by God and that they do wrong in sinning. So that our people still believe in righteousness, have faith in God and weep tears of devotion.

It is different with the upper classes. They, following science, want to base a just social order on reason alone, without the help of Christ, as before, and they have already proclaimed that there is no crime, that there is no sin. And that's consistent, for if you have no God, what is the meaning of crime? In Europe the people are already rising up against the rich with violence, and the leaders of the masses are everywhere leading them to bloodshed, and teaching them that their wrath is righteous. But their "wrath is accursed, for it is cruel." But God will save Russia as He has saved her many times. Salvation will come from the people, from their faith and their meekness.

Fathers and teachers, watch over the people's faith and this is not a vain dream. I've been struck all my life by the dignity, the true and seemly dignity, of our great people. I've seen it myself, I can testify to it, I've seen it and marvelled at it, I've seen it in spite of the degraded sins and poverty-stricken appearance of our peasantry. They are not servile, and even after two centuries of serfdom, they are free in manner and bearing, yet without insolence, and not revengeful and not envious. "You are rich and noble, you are clever and talented, well, be so, God bless you. I honour you, but I know that I, too, am a man. By the very fact that I honour you without envy I prove my dignity as a man."

In truth if they don't say this (for they don't know how to say this yet) that is how they act. I have seen it myself, I have experienced it myself, and, would you believe it, the poorer our Russian peasant is, the more noticeable is his seemliness and dignity, for the rich exploiters among them are for the most part corrupted already, and much of that is due to our carelessness and indifference. But God will save His people, for Russia is great in her humility. I dream of seeing, and seem to see clearly already, our future. It will come to pass that even the most corrupt of our rich will end by being ashamed of his riches before the poor, and the poor, seeing his humility, will understand and give way before him, will respond joyfully and kindly to his seemly shame. Believe me that it will end in that; things are moving in that direction. Equality is to be found only in the spiritual dignity of man, and that will only be understood among us. If we were brothers, there would be fraternity, but before that, they will never agree about the division of wealth.

We preserve the image of Christ, and it will shine forth like a precious diamond to the whole world. So be it, so be it!

Fathers and teachers, I had a touching experience once. In my wanderings I met in the city of K. my old orderly, Afanasy. It was eight years since I had parted from him. He chanced to see me in the market-place, recognised me, ran up to me, and how delighted he was, he simply rushed at me: "Master, father, is it you? is it really you I see?" He took me home with him.

He was no longer in the army, he was married and already had two little children. He and his wife earned their living as costermongers in the market-place. His room was poor, but bright and clean.

He made me sit down, set the samovar, sent for his wife, as though my appearance were a festival for them. He brought me his children; "Bless them, father."

"Is it for me to bless them, I say, I am only a simple, humble monk. I will pray to God for them. And for you, Afanasy Pavlovich, I have prayed every day since that day, for it all began with you," said I. And I explained that to him as well as I could. And what do you think? The man kept gazing at me and could not believe that I, his former master, an officer, was now before him in such a guise and garb; it made him weep.

"Why are you weeping?" said I, "better rejoice over me, dear friend, whom I can never forget, for my path is a glad and joyful one."

He did not say much, but kept sighing and shaking his head over me tenderly.

"What has become of your fortune?"

"I gave it to the monastery," I answered; "we live in common."

After tea I began saying good-bye, and suddenly he brought out half a rouble as an offering to the monastery, and another half-rouble I saw him thrusting hurriedly into my hand: "That's for you in your wanderings, it may be of use to you, father."

I took his half-rouble, bowed to him and his wife, and went out rejoicing. And on my way I thought: "Here we are both now, he at home and I on the road, sighing and shaking our heads, no doubt, and yet smiling joyfully in the gladness of our hearts, remembering how God brought about our meeting."

I have never seen him again since then. I had been his master and he my servant, but now when we kissed each other, lovingly and with spiritual emotion, a great human bond sprang up between us. I have thought a great deal about that, and now what I think is this: is it so inconceivable that that grand and simple-hearted unity might in due time become universal among the Russian people? I believe that it will come to pass and that the time is at hand.

And of servants I will add this, in former days when I was young I was often angry with servants: "the cook had served something too hot, the orderly had not brushed my clothes properly." But what enlightened me then was a thought of my dear brother's, which I had heard from him in childhood: "Am I worth it, that another should serve me and be ordered about by me because of his poverty and ignorance?" And I wondered at the time that such simple and self-evident ideas should be so slow to occur to our minds.

It is impossible that there should be no servants in the world, but act so that your servant may be freer in spirit than if he were not a servant. And why cannot I be a servant to my servant, and even let him see it, and that without any pride on my part or any mistrust on his? Why should not my servant be like my own kindred, so that I may take him into my family and rejoice in doing so? Even now this can be done, but it will lead to the magnificent union of men in the future, when a man will not seek servants for himself, or desire to turn his fellow creatures into servants as he does now, but, on the contrary, will long with his whole heart to be the servant of all, as the Gospel teaches.

And can it be a dream, that in the end man will find his joy only in deeds of enlightenment and mercy, and not in cruel pleasures as now, in gluttony, fornication, ostentation, boasting, and envious vying of one with the other? I firmly believe that it is not, and that the time is at hand. People laugh and ask: "When will that time come, and does it look as though it were coming?" I believe that with Christ's help we shall accomplish this great task. And how many ideas there have been on earth in the history of man which were unthinkable ten years before they appeared! Yet when their destined hour arrived, they came forth and spread over the whole earth. So it will be with us, and our people will shine forth in the world, and all men will say:

"The stone which the builders rejected has become the corner-stone of the building."

And we may ask the scornful themselves: if our hope is a dream, when will you build up your edifice and order things justly by your intellect alone, without Christ? If they declare that it is they who are advancing towards union, only the most simple-hearted among them believe it, so that one may positively marvel at such simplicity. Of a truth, their dreams are more fantastic than ours. They aim at a just order, but, having rejected Christ, they will end by flooding the earth with blood, for blood cries out for blood, and he that taketh the sword shall perish with the sword. And if it were not for Christ's promise, they would slaughter one another down to the last two men on earth. And those two last men would not be able to restrain each other in their pride, and the one would slay the other and then himself. And that would come to pass, were it not for the promise of Christ that for the sake of the humble and meek the time shall be shortened.

While I was still wearing an officer's uniform after my duel, I talked about servants in society, and I remember every one was amazed at me: "What!" they asked, "are we to make our servants sit down on the sofa and offer them tea?" And I answered them: "Why not, sometimes at least." Every one laughed. Their question was frivolous and my answer was not clear; but I believe there was some truth in it.

(g) *Of prayer, of love, and of contact with other worlds*

Young man, be not forgetful of prayer. Every time you pray, if your prayer is sincere, there will be new feeling and new meaning in it, which will give you fresh courage, and you will understand that prayer is an education.

Remember, too, every day, and whenever you can, repeat to yourself, "Lord, have mercy on all who have appeared before Thee to-day." For every hour and every moment thousands of men leave life on this earth, and their souls appear before the Lord. And how many of them depart in solitude, unknown, sad, dejected, because no one mourns for them or even knows whether they have lived or not. And behold, from the other end of the earth perhaps, your prayer for their rest will rise up to God though you knew them not nor they you. How touching it must be to a soul standing in dread before the Lord to feel at that instant that, for him, too, there is one to pray, that there is a fellow creature left on earth to love him, too. And God will look on you both more graciously, for if you have had so much pity on him, how much more will He have pity Who is infinitely more loving and merciful than you. And He will forgive him for your sake.

Brothers, have no fear of men's sin. Love a man even in his sin, for that is the semblance of Divine Love and is the highest love on earth. Love all God's creation, the whole and every grain of sand in it. Love every leaf, every ray of God's light. Love the animals, love the plants, love everything. If you love everything, you will perceive the divine mystery in things. Once you perceive it, you will begin to comprehend it better every day. And you will come at last to love the whole world with an all-embracing universal love. Love the animals: God has given them the rudiments of thought and unclouded joy. Do not trouble it, don't harass them, don't deprive them of their happiness, don't work against God's intent. Man, do not consider yourself superior to the animals; they are without sin, and you, with your greatness, defile the earth by your appearance on it, and leave the traces of your foulness after you — alas, it is true of almost every one of us! Love children especially, for they, too, are sinless, like the angels; they live to soften and purify our hearts and as it were to guide us. Woe to him who offends a child! Father Anfim taught me to love children. The kind, silent man used often on our wanderings to spend the farthings given us on sweets and cakes for the children. He could not pass by a child without emotion, that was the nature of the man.

At some thoughts one stands perplexed, especially at the sight of men's sin, and wonders whether one should use force or humble love. Always decide to use humble love. If you resolve on that once for all, you may subdue the whole world. Loving humility is a mighty force, the strongest of all things and there is nothing else like it.

Every day and every hour, every minute, walk round yourself and watch yourself, and see that your image be seemly. You pass by a little child, you pass by, spiteful, with ugly words, with wrathful heart; you may not have noticed the child, but he has seen you, and your image, unseemly and impious, may remain in his defenceless heart. You don't know it, but you may have sown an evil seed in him and it may grow, and all because you were not careful before the child, because you did not foster in yourself a circumspect, actively benevolent love. Brothers, love is a teacher; but one must know how to acquire it, for it is hard to acquire, it is dearly bought, it is won slowly by long labour. For we must love not only occasionally, for a moment, but for all time. Every one can love occasionally, even the wicked can.

My brother used to ask the birds to forgive him; that sounds senseless, but it is right; for all is like the ocean, all things flow and touch each other; a disturbance in one place is felt at the other end of the world. It may be folly to beg forgiveness of the birds, but birds would be happier at your side — a little happier, anyway — and children and all animals, if you yourself were nobler than you are now. It's all like an ocean, I tell you. Then you would pray to the birds, too, consumed by an all-embracing love, in a sort of transport, and pray that they will forgive you your sin. Prize this ecstasy, however senseless it may seem to men.

My friends, pray to God for gladness. Be merry as children, as the birds of heaven. And let not the sin of men confound you in your doings. Fear not that it will erase your work and hinder its being accomplished. Do not say, "Sin is mighty, wickedness is mighty, evil environment is mighty, and we are lonely and helpless, evil environment will overwhelm us and hinder our good work from being done." Fly from that dejection, children! There is only one means of salvation, then take yourself in hand and make yourself responsible for all men's sins; that is the truth, you know, friends, for as soon as you sincerely make yourself responsible for everything and for all men, you will see at once that it is really so, and that you are to blame for every one and for all things. But throwing your own indolence and impotence on others you will end by sharing the pride of Satan and murmuring against God.

Of the pride of Satan what I think is this: it is hard for us on earth to comprehend it, and therefore it is so easy to fall into error and to share it, even imagining that we are doing something great and splendid. Indeed many of the strongest feelings and movements of our nature we on earth still cannot comprehend. Do not let this tempt you, and think not that it may serve as a justification to you for anything. For the Eternal Judge will hold you responsible for what you can comprehend and not for what you cannot. You will know that yourself hereafter, for you will behold all things truly then and will not dispute them. On earth, indeed, we are as it were astray, and if it were not for the precious image of Christ before us, we should perish and be altogether lost, as was the human race before the flood. Much on earth is hidden from us, but to make up for that we have been given a precious sense of our living bond with the other world, with the higher heavenly world, and the roots of our thoughts and feelings are not here but in other worlds. That is why the philosophers say that we cannot apprehend the essence of things on earth.

God took seeds from other worlds and sowed them on this earth, and planted a garden, and everything came up that could come up, but what He grew lives and is alive only through the feeling of its contact with other mysterious worlds. If that feeling grows weak or is destroyed in you, the heavenly growth will die away in you. Then you will be indifferent to life and even grow to hate it. That's what I think.

## (h) Can a man judge his fellow creatures? Concerning faith to the end

Remember particularly that you cannot be a judge of any one. For no one on earth can judge a criminal, until he recognises that he is just such a criminal as the man standing before him, and that he perhaps is more than all men to blame for that crime. When he understands that, he will be able to be a judge. Though outwardly that is absurd, it is true. For if I had been righteous myself, perhaps there would have been no criminal standing before me. If you can take upon yourself the crime of the criminal your heart is judging, take it at once, suffer for him yourself, and let him go without reproach. And even if the law itself sets you up as his judge, act in the same spirit so far as possible, for he will go away and condemn himself more bitterly than you have done. But if, after your kiss, he goes away unmoved, mocking at you, do not let that be a stumbling-block to you either. It shows his time has not yet come, but it will come in due course. And if it come not, no matter; if not he, then another in his place will understand and suffer, and judge and condemn himself, and the truth will be fulfilled. Believe that, believe it without doubt; for in that lies all the hope and faith of the saints.

Work without ceasing. If you remember in the night as you go to sleep, "I have not done what I ought to have done," rise up at once and do it. If the people around you are spiteful and callous and will not hear you, fall down before them and beg their forgiveness; for in truth you are to blame for their not wanting to heed you. And if you cannot speak to them in their bitterness, serve them in silence and in humility, never losing hope. If all men abandon you and even drive you away by force, then when you are left alone fall on the earth and kiss it, water it with your tears and it will bring forth fruit even though no one has seen or heard you in your loneliness. Believe to the end, even if all men went astray and you were left the only faithful one; bring your offering even then and praise God though you be the

only one remaining. And if two of you are gathered together — then there is a whole world, a world of living love. Embrace each other tenderly and praise God, for if only in you two His truth has been fulfilled.

If you sin yourself and grieve even unto death for your sins or for your sudden sin, then rejoice for others, rejoice for the righteous man, rejoice that if you have sinned, he is righteous and has not sinned.

If the evil doing of men moves you to indignation and overwhelming distress, even to a desire for vengeance on the evil-doers, shun above all things that feeling. Go at once and seek suffering for yourself, as though you were yourself guilty of that wrong. Accept that suffering and bear it and your heart will find comfort, and you will understand that you, too, are guilty, for you might have been a light to the evil-doers, even as the one man sinless, and you were not a light to them. If you had been a light, you would have lightened the path for others, too, and the evil-doer might perhaps have been saved by your light from his sin. And even though you were a light, but you see that men were not saved by it, hold firm and doubt not the power of the heavenly light. Believe that if they were not saved now, they will be saved hereafter. And if they are not saved hereafter, then their sons will be saved, for your light will not die even when you are dead. The righteous man passes, but his light remains. Men are always saved after the death of the deliverer. Men reject their prophets and slay them, but they love their martyrs and honour those whom they have slain. You are working for the whole, you are acting for the future. Seek no reward, for great is your reward on this earth: the spiritual joy which is vouchsafed only to the righteous man. Fear not the great nor the mighty, but be wise and ever serene. Know the measure, know the times, study that. When you are left alone, pray. Love to throw yourself on the earth and kiss it. Kiss the earth and love it with an unceasing, consuming love. Love all men, love everything. Seek that rapture and ecstasy. Water the earth with the tears of your joy and love those tears. Don't be ashamed of that ecstasy, prize it, for it is a gift of God and a great one; it is not given to many but only to the elect.

## (i) Of hell and hell-fire: a mystic reflection

Fathers and teachers, I ponder "What is hell?" I maintain that it is the suffering of being no longer able to love. Once in infinite existence, immeasurable in time and space, a spiritual creature was given, on his coming to earth, the power of saying to itself, "I am and I love."

Once, only once, there was given him a moment of active *living* love and for that was earthly life given him, and with it times and seasons. And what happened? — That fortunate creature rejected the priceless gift, prized it and loved it not, scorned it and remained callous. Such a one, having left the earth, sees Abraham's bosom and talks with Abraham as we are told in the parable of the rich man and Lazarus, and beholds paradise and can go up to the Lord. But that is just his torment, to rise up to the Lord without ever having loved, to be brought close to those who have loved when he has despised their love. For he sees clearly and says to himself, "Now I have understanding and though I now thirst to love, there will be nothing great, no sacrifice in my love, for my earthly life is over, and Abraham will not come even with a drop of living water (that

is the gift of earthly, active life) to cool the fiery thirst of spiritual love which burns in me now, though I disdained it on earth; there is no more life for me and time will be no more! Even though I would gladly give my life for others, it can never be, for that life is passed which can be sacrificed for love, and now there is a gulf fixed between that life and this existence."

They talk of hell-fire in the material sense. I don't go into that mystery and I dread it. But I think if there were fire in the material sense, they would be glad of it, for, I imagine, that in material agony their still greater spiritual agony would be forgotten for a moment. Moreover, that spiritual agony cannot be taken from them, for that suffering is not external but within them. And if it could be taken from them, I think it would be bitterer still for the unhappy creatures. For even if the righteous in paradise forgave them, beholding their torments, and called them up to heaven in their infinite love, they would only multiply their torments, for they would arouse in them still more keenly a flaming thirst for responsive, active, and grateful love which is now impossible. In the timidity of my heart I imagine, however, that the very recognition of this impossibility would serve at last to console them. For accepting the love of the righteous together with the impossibility of repaying it, by this submissiveness and the effect of this humility, they will attain at last, as it were, to a certain semblance of that active love which they scorned on earth, to something like its outward expression. . . . I regret, friends and brothers, that I cannot express this clearly. But woe to those who have destroyed themselves on earth, woe to the suicides! I believe that there can be none more miserable than they. They tell us that it is a sin to pray for them and outwardly the Church, as it were, rejects them, but in my secret heart I believe that we may pray even for them. Love can never be an offence to Christ. For such as those I have prayed inwardly all my life, I confess it, fathers and teachers, and even now I pray for them every day.

Oh, there are some who remain proud and fierce even in hell, in spite of their certain knowledge and contemplation of the absolute truth; there are some terrible ones who have given themselves over to Satan and his proud spirit entirely. For such, hell is voluntary and unappeasable; they are tortured by their own choice. For they have cursed themselves, cursing God and life. They live upon their vindictive pride like a starving man in the desert sucking blood out of his own body. But they are never satisfied, and they refuse forgiveness, they curse God Who summons them. They cannot behold the living God without hatred, and they demand that there be no God of life, that God should destroy Himself and His own creation. And they will burn in the fire of their own wrath for ever and yearn for death and annihilation. But they will not attain to death. . . .

Here Alexey Fyodorovich Karamazov's manuscript ends. I repeat, it is incomplete and fragmentary. Biographical details, for instance, cover only the elder's earliest youth. His exhortations and opinions have been assembled to form a whole, although they were evidently uttered at different times and on different occasions. His utterances during the last few hours have not been kept separate from the rest, but their general character can be gathered from what we have in this manuscript.

The elder's death came in the end quite unexpectedly. For although those who were gathered about him that last evening realised fully that his death was approaching, yet it was difficult to imagine that it would come so suddenly. On the contrary, his friends, as I observed already, seeing him that night apparently so cheerful and talkative, were convinced that there was at least a temporary change for the better in his condition. Even five minutes before his death, they said afterwards wonderingly, it was impossible to foresee it. He seemed suddenly to feel an acute pain in his chest, he turned pale and pressed his hands to his heart. All rose from their seats and hastened to him. But though suffering, he still looked at them with a smile, sank slowly from his chair on to his knees, then bowed his face to the ground, stretched out his arms and as though in joyful ecstasy, praying and kissing the earth (as he had himself taught), quietly and joyfully gave up his soul to God.

The news of his death spread at once through the hermitage and reached the monastery. The nearest friends of the deceased and those whose position made it their duty began to lay out the body according to the ancient ritual, and all the monks gathered together in the church. And before dawn the news of the death reached the town. By morning all the town was talking of the event, and crowds were flocking from the town to the monastery. But of this we shall speak in the next book; I will only add here that before a day had passed something happened so unexpected, so strange, upsetting, and bewildering in its effect on the monks and the townspeople, that after all these years the most vivid memory of that agitating day is still preserved in our town.

PART
III

PART

III

# BOOK VII

## ALYOSHA

### CHAPTER I
#### THE BREATH OF CORRUPTION

THE body of the deceased monk, Father Zosima, was prepared for burial according to the established ritual. As is known, the bodies of dead monks and hermits are not washed. In the words of the Church Manual: "If any one of the monks depart to the Lord, the monk designated (that is, whose office it is) shall wipe the body with warm water, making first the sign of the cross with a sponge on the forehead of the deceased, on the breast, on the hands and feet and on the knees, and naught more." All this was done by Father Païssy, who then clothed the deceased in his monastic garb and wrapped him in his cloak, which was, according to custom, somewhat slit to allow of its being folded about him in the form of a cross.

On his head he put a hood with an eight-cornered cross. The hood was left open and the dead man's face was covered with black cloth. In his hands was put an ikon of the Saviour. Towards morning he was put in the coffin which had been made ready long before. It was decided to leave the coffin all day in the cell, in the larger room in which the elder used to receive his visitors and fellow monks. As the deceased was a priest and monk, the Gospel, not the Psalter, had to be read over his body by ordained monks and deacons. The reading was begun by Father Iosif immediately after the requiem service. Father Païssy desired to read the Gospel later on all day and all night over his dead friend, but for the present he, as well as the Father Superior of the hermitage, was very busy and worried, for something extraordinary, an unheard of, even "unseemly" excitement and impatient expectation began to be apparent in the monks, and in the visitors arriving from the monastery hostelries, and the crowds of people flocking from the town. And as time went on, this grew more and more marked. Both the Superior and Father Païssy did their utmost to calm the general bustle and agitation.

When it was full daylight, some people began bringing their sick, in most cases children, with them from the town — as though they had been waiting expressly for this moment to do so, evidently persuaded that the dead elder's remains had a power of healing, which would be immediately made manifest in accordance with their faith. It was only then apparent how unquestionably every one in our town had accepted Father Zosima during his lifetime as a great saint. And those who came were far from being all of the humbler classes.

This intense expectation on the part of the

believers, displayed with such haste, so nakedly, even impatiently and almost demandingly, appeared to Father Païssy as a snare. Though he had long foreseen something of the sort, the actual manifestation of the feeling was beyond anything he had looked for. When he came across any of the monks who displayed this excitement, Father Païssy began to reprove them. "Such immediate expectation of something extraordinary," he said, "shows a levity, possible to worldly people but unseemly in us."

But little attention was paid him and Father Païssy noticed this with uneasiness. Yet he himself (if the whole truth must be told), secretly, at the bottom of his heart, cherished almost the same hopes and could not but be aware of it, though he was indignant at the too eager expectation around him, and saw in it light-mindedness and vanity. Nevertheless, it was particularly unpleasant to him to meet certain persons, whose presence seemed to him to bode ill. In the crowd that filled the dead man's cell he noticed with inward aversion (for which he immediately reproached himself) the presence of Rakitin and of the monk from Obdorsk, who was still staying in the monastery. Of both of them Father Païssy felt for some reason suddenly suspicious — though, indeed, he might well have felt the same about others.

The monk from Obdorsk was conspicuous as the most fussy in the excited crowd. He was to be seen everywhere; everywhere he was asking questions, everywhere he was listening, on all sides he was whispering with a peculiar, mysterious air. His expression showed the greatest impatience and even a sort of irritation because what he expected was so long in coming. As for Rakitin, he, as appeared later,

had come so early to the hermitage at the special request of Madame Hohlakov. As soon as that good-hearted but weak-minded woman, who could not herself have been admitted to the hermitage, waked and heard of the death of Father Zosima, she was overtaken with such intense curiosity that she promptly despatched Rakitin to the hermitage, with instructions to keep a careful look-out and report to her by letter every half-hour or so *"everything that takes place."* She regarded Rakitin as a most religious and devout young man. He was particularly clever in getting round people and assuming whatever part he thought most to their taste, if he detected the slightest advantage to himself in doing so.

It was a bright, clear day and many of the visitors were thronging about the tombs, which were particularly numerous round the church and scattered here and there about the hermitage. As he walked round the hermitage, Father Païssy suddenly remembered Alyosha and that he had not seen him for some time, not since the night before. And he had no sooner thought of him than he at once noticed him in the most remote corner of the hermitage garden, sitting on the tombstone of a monk who had been famous long ago for his saintliness. He sat with his back to the hermitage and his face to the wall, and seemed to be hiding behind the tombstone. Going up to him, Father Païssy saw that he was weeping quietly but bitterly, with his face hidden in his hands, and that his whole frame was shaking with sobs. Father Païssy stood over him for a little.

"Enough, dear son, enough, dear," he pronounced with feeling at last. "Why do you weep? Rejoice and weep not. Don't you know that this is the greatest of his days? Think only where he is now, at this moment!"

ALYOSHA AMONG THE TOMBS

Alyosha glanced at him, uncovering his face, which was swollen with crying like a child's, but turned away at once without uttering a word and hid his face in his hands again.

"May be it is well," said Father Païssy thoughtfully; "weep if you must, Christ has sent you those tears."

"Your touching tears are but a relief to your spirit and will serve to gladden your dear heart," he added to himself, walking away from Alyosha, and thinking lovingly of him. He moved away quickly, however, for he felt that he, too, might weep looking at him.

Meanwhile the time was passing; the monastery services and the requiems for the dead followed in their due course. Father Païssy again took Father Iosif's place by the coffin and began reading the Gospel. But before three o'clock in the afternoon there occurred that to which I alluded at the end of the last book, a thing so unexpected by all of us and so contrary to the general hope that, I repeat, a detailed account of this matter is remembered to this day in our town and all the surrounding neighborhood. I may add here, for myself personally, that it is almost repulsive to me to recall that event which caused such frivolous agitation and was such a stumbling-block to many, though in reality it was the most natural and trivial matter. I should, of course, have omitted all mention of it in my story, if it had not exerted a very strong influence on the heart and soul of the chief, *though future*, hero of my story, Alyosha, forming a crisis and turning-point, as it were, in his spiritual development, giving a shock to his intellect, which finally strengthened it for the rest of his life and gave it a definite aim.

And so, to return to our story. When before dawn they laid Father Zosima's body in the coffin and brought it into the front room, the question of opening the windows was raised among those who were around the coffin. But this suggestion made casually by some one was unanswered and almost unnoticed. Some of those present may perhaps have inwardly noticed it, only to reflect that the anticipation of decay and corruption from the body of such a saint was an actual absurdity, meriting compassion (if not a smile) for the lack of faith and the frivolity it implied. For they expected something quite different.

And, behold, soon after midday something began, which was at first only noted in silence by those who came in and out and each of whom was evidently afraid to communicate the thought vaguely in his mind. But by three o'clock the thing had become so clear and unmistakable that the news swiftly reached all the monks and visitors in the hermitage, promptly penetrated to the monastery, throwing all the monks into amazement, and finally, in the shortest possible time, spread to the town, exciting every one in it, believers and unbelievers alike. The unbelievers rejoiced, and as for the believers, some of them rejoiced even more than the unbelievers, for "men love the downfall and disgrace of the righteous," as the deceased elder had said in one of his exhortations.

The fact is that the breath of corruption began to come from the coffin, growing gradually more marked, and by three o'clock it was quite unmistakable. In all the past history of our monastery, no such scandal could be recalled, and in no other circumstances could such a scandal have been possible, as showed itself in unseemly disorder immediately after this discovery among the very monks themselves. Afterwards, even many years afterwards, some sensible monks, when they recalled that day, were amazed and horrified that the scandal could have reached such proportions. For in the past, monks of very holy life had died, God-fearing old men, whose saintliness was acknowledged by all, yet from their humble coffins, too, the breath of corruption had come, naturally, as from all dead bodies, but that had caused no scandal nor even the slightest excitement. Of course there had been, in former times, saints in the monastery whose memory was carefully preserved and whose relics, according to tradition, showed no signs of corruption. This fact was regarded by the monks as touching and mysterious, and the tradition of it was cherished as something seemly and miraculous, and as a promise, by God's grace, of still greater glory from their tombs in the future.

One such, whose memory was particularly cherished, was Father Job, who had died half a century earlier, at the great age of a hundred and five. He had been a celebrated ascetic, rigid in fasting and silence, and his tomb was pointed out to all visitors on their arrival with peculiar respect and mysterious hints of great hopes connected with it. (That was the very tomb on which Father Païssy had found Alyosha sitting in the morning.) Another memory cherished in the monastery was that of the famous Father Varsonofy, only recently deceased, who had preceded Father Zosima as elder, and who during his lifetime was revered as a saintly fool by all the pilgrims to the monastery. There was a tradition that both of these had lain in their coffins as though alive, that they had shown no signs of corruption when they were buried and that there had been a holy light in their countenances when they were in their coffins. And some people even insisted that a sweet fragrance came from their bodies.

Yet, in spite of these edifying precedents, it would be difficult to explain the direct cause of the frivolity, absurdity, and malice that were manifested beside the coffin of Father Zosima. It is my private opinion that several different causes were simultaneously at work, one of which was the deeply rooted hostility to the institution of elders as a pernicious innovation, an antipathy hidden deep in the hearts of many of the monks. Even more powerful was jealousy of the dead man's saintliness, so firmly established during his lifetime that it was almost a forbidden thing to question it. For though the late elder had won over many hearts, more by love than by miracles, and had gathered round him a whole world of loving adherents, none the less, in fact, rather the more on that account, he had awakened jealousy and so had come to have bitter enemies, secret and open, not only in the monastery but even among the laity. He did no one any harm, but "Why do they think him so saintly?" And that question alone gradually repeated gave rise at last to an intense, insatiable hatred of him. That I believe was why many people were extremely delighted at the smell of corruption which came so quickly, for not a day had passed since his death. At the same time there were some among those who had been hitherto reverently devoted to the elder, who were almost mortified and personally affronted by this incident. This is the way in which it all happened.

As soon as signs of decomposition had begun to appear, the whole aspect of the monks betrayed their secret motives in entering the cell. They went in, stayed a little while, and hastened out to confirm the news to the crowd of other monks waiting outside. Some of the latter shook their heads mournfully, but others did not even care to conceal the delight which gleamed unmistakably in their malicious eyes. And now no one reproached them for it, no one raised his voice in protest, which was strange, for the majority of the monks had been devoted to the dead elder. But it seemed as though God had in this case let the minority get the upper hand for a time.

Visitors from outside, particularly of the educated class, soon went into the cell, too, with the same spying intent. Of the peasantry few went into the cell, though there were crowds of them at the gates of the hermitage. After three o'clock the rush of worldly visitors was greatly increased and this was no doubt owing to the scandalous news. People were attracted who would not otherwise have come on that day and had not intended to come, and among them were some personages of high rank. But external decorum was still preserved and Father Païssy, with a stern face, continued firmly and distinctly reading aloud the Gospel, apparently not noticing what was taking place around him, though he had, in fact, observed something unusual long before. But at last the murmurs, first subdued but gradually louder and more confident, reached even him. "It shows God's judgment is not as man's," Father Païssy heard suddenly. The first to give utterance to this sentiment was a layman, an elderly official from the town, known to be a man of great piety. But he only repeated aloud what the monks had long been whispering to each other. They had long before formulated this damning conclusion, and the worst of it was that a sort of triumphant satisfaction at that conclusion became more and more apparent every moment. Soon even external decorum began to be violated and presently all almost seemed to feel they had a sort of right to violate it.

"And for what reason can *this* have happened," some of the monks said, at first with a show of regret; "he had a small frame and his flesh was dried up on his bones, why the breath?" "It must be a sign from heaven," others hastened to add, and this opinion was adopted at once without protest. For it was pointed out, too, that if the decomposition had been natural, as in the case of every dead sinner, it would have been apparent later, after a lapse of at least twenty-four hours, but this premature corruption "was in excess of nature," and so the finger of God was evident. It was meant for a sign. This conclusion seemed irresistible.

Gentle Father Iosif, the librarian, a great favourite of the dead man's, tried to reply to some of those who spoke evil that "this is not held everywhere alike," and that the incorruptibility of the bodies of the just was not a dogma of the Orthodox Church, but only an opinion, and that even in the most Orthodox regions, at Athos for instance, they were not greatly confounded by the smell of corruption, and there the chief sign of the glorification of the saved was not bodily incorruptibility, but the colour of the bones when the bodies had lain many years in the earth and had decayed in it. "And if the bones are yellow as wax, that is the great sign that the Lord has glorified the deceased saint; if they are not yellow but black, it shows that God has not deemed him worthy of such glory — that is the belief at Athos, a saintly place, where the Orthodox faith has been preserved from of old, unbroken and in the greatest purity," said Father Iosif in conclusion. But the meek father's words had little effect and even provoked a mocking retort. "That's all pedantry and innovation, no use listening to it," the monks decided. "We stick to the old doctrine; there are all sorts of innovations nowadays, are we to follow them all?" added others. "We have had as many holy fathers as they had. There they are subjects of the Turk, they have forgotten everything. Orthodoxy among them has long been impure, and they have no bells even," the greatest scoffers added.

Father Iosif walked away grieving the more since he had put forward his own opinion with little confidence as though scarcely believing in it himself. He foresaw with distress that something very unseemly was beginning and that arrant disobedience was raising its head. Little by little, all the sensible monks were reduced to silence like Father Iosif. And so it came to pass that all who loved the deceased elder and had accepted with devout obedience the institution of elders were all at once terribly cast down and glanced timidly in one another's faces when they met. Those who were hostile to the institution, as an innovation, held up their heads proudly. "There was no smell of corruption from the late elder Varsonofy, but a sweet fragrance," they recalled maliciously. "But he earned that glory not because he was an elder, but because he was a holy man."

And this was followed by a shower of criticism and even blame of Father Zosima. "His teaching was false; he taught that life is a great joy and not a vale of tears," said some of the more unreasonable. "He followed the fashionable belief, he did not recognise material fire in hell," others, still more unreason-

able, added. "He was not strict in fasting, allowed himself sweet things, ate cherry jam with his tea, ladies used to send it to him. Is it right for a monk of strict rule to drink tea?" could be heard among some of the envious. "He sat in pride," the most malicious declared vindictively; "he considered himself a saint and he took it as his due when people knelt before him." "He abused the sacrament of confession," the fiercest opponents of the institution of elders added in a malicious whisper. And among these were some of the oldest monks, strictest in their devotion, genuine ascetics, who had kept silent during the life of the deceased elder, but now suddenly unsealed their lips. And this was terrible, for their words had great influence on young monks who were not yet firm in their convictions. The monk from Obdorsk heard all this attentively, heaving deep sighs and nodding his head. "Yes, clearly Father Ferapont was right in his judgment yesterday," he thought to himself, and at that moment Father Ferapont himself made his appearance, as though on purpose to increase the confusion.

I have mentioned already that he rarely left his wooden cell close by the apiary. He was seldom seen even at church and this was forgiven him on the ground of his being a saintly fool, and he was not held to rules that were binding on all the rest. But if the whole truth is to be told, he was granted these privileges out of necessity, as it were. For it would have been disgraceful to insist on burdening with the common regulations so great an ascetic, who prayed day and night (he even dropped asleep on his knees). If they had insisted, the monks would have said, "He is holier than all of us and he follows a rule harder than ours. And if he does not go to church, it's because he knows when he ought to; he has his own rule." It was to avoid the chance of such murmur and scandal that Father Ferapont was left in peace.

As every one was aware, Father Ferapont particularly disliked Father Zosima. And now the news had reached him in his hut that "God's judgment is not the same as man's," and that something had happened which was "in excess of nature." It may well be supposed that among the first to run to him with the news was the monk from Obdorsk, who had visited him the evening before and left his cell terror-stricken.

I have mentioned above, that though Father Païssy, standing firm and immovable reading the Gospel over the coffin, could not hear nor see what was passing outside the cell, he gauged most of it correctly in his heart, for he knew the men surrounding him, well. He was not confused, but awaited what would come next without fear, watching with a penetrating eye for the outcome of the general excitement which was already present to his mind.

Suddenly an extraordinary uproar in the passage in open defiance of decorum burst on his ears. The door was flung open and Father Ferapont appeared in the doorway. Behind him there could be seen a crowd of monks, together with many people from the town. They did not, however, enter the cell, but stood at the bottom of the steps, waiting to see what Father Ferapont would say and do. For they felt with a certain awe, in spite of their audacity, that he had not come for nothing. Standing in the doorway, Father Ferapont raised his arms, and under his right arm the keen inquisitive little eyes of the monk from Obdorsk peeped out. He alone, in his intense curiosity, could not resist running up the steps after Father Ferapont. The others, on the contrary, pressed further back in sudden alarm when the door was noisily flung open. Holding his hands aloft, Father Ferapont suddenly roared:

"I will cast thee out!" and, turning about, he began at once making the sign of the cross over each of the four walls and four corners of the cell in succession. All who accompanied Father Ferapont immediately understood his action. For they knew he always did this wherever he went, and that he would not sit down or say a word till he had driven out the evil spirits. "Satan, go hence! Satan, go hence!" he repeated at each sign of the cross. "I will cast thee out," he roared again.

He was wearing his coarse gown girt with a rope. His bare chest, covered with grey hair, could be seen under his hempen shirt. His feet were bare. As soon as he began waving his arms, the cruel irons he wore under his gown could be heard clanking.

Father Païssy paused in his reading, stepped forward and stood before him waiting.

"What have you come for, worthy father? Why do you offend against good order? Why do you stir up the humble flock?" he said at last, looking sternly at him.

"What have you come for? Why are you asking? What is your faith?" shouted Father Ferapont, acting like the saintly fool that he was. "I've come here to drive out your guests, the filthy devils. I've come to see how many have gathered here while I have been away. I want to sweep them out with a birch broom."

"You cast out the evil spirit, but perhaps you are serving him yourself," Father Païssy went on fearlessly. "And who can say of himself 'I am holy.' Can you, father?"

257

"I am unclean, not holy. I would not sit in an armchair and would not have them bow down to me as an idol," thundered Father Ferapont. "Nowadays folk destroy the true faith. The dead man, your saint," he turned to the crowd, pointing with his finger to the coffin, "did not believe in devils. He gave medicine to keep off the devils. And so they have become as common as spiders in the corners. And now he is stinking himself. In that we see a great sign from God."

The incident he referred to was this. One of the monks was haunted in his dreams and, later on, while awake, by visions of evil spirits. When in the utmost terror he confided this to Father Zosima, the elder had advised continual prayer and rigid fasting. But when that was of no use, he advised him, while persisting in prayer and fasting, to take a certain medicine.

Many persons were scandalised at the time and wagged their heads as they talked it over — and most of all Father Ferapont, to whom some of the censorious had hastened to report this "extraordinary" counsel on the part of the elder.

"Go hence, father!" said Father Païssy, in a commanding voice, "it's not for man to judge, but for God. Perhaps we see here a 'sign' which neither you, nor I, nor any one of us is able to comprehend. Go, father, and do not stir up the flock!" he repeated insistently.

"He did not keep the fasts according to the rule and therefore the sign has come. That is clear and it's a sin to hide it." The fanatic, carried away by a zeal that outstripped his reason, would not be quieted. "He was seduced by sweetmeats, ladies brought them to him in their pockets, he sipped tea, he worshipped his belly, filling it with sweet things

and his mind with haughty thoughts. . . . And for this he is put to shame. . . ."

"You speak frivolously, father." Father Païssy, too, raised his voice. "I admire your fasting and severities, but you speak lightly like some frivolous youth, fickle and childish. Go hence, father, I command you!" Father Païssy thundered in conclusion.

"I will go," said Father Ferapont, seeming somewhat taken aback, but still as bitter. "You learned men! You are so clever you look down upon my humbleness. I came hither with little learning and here I have forgotten what I did know, the Lord God himself has preserved me, little as I am, from your subtlety."

Father Païssy stood over him, waiting resolutely. Father Ferapont paused and, suddenly leaning his cheek on his hand despondently, pronounced in a sing-song voice, looking at the coffin of the deceased elder:

"To-morrow they will sing over him 'Our Helper and Defender' — a splendid anthem — and over me when I croak all they'll sing will be 'What earthly joy' — a little canticle,"* he added with tearful regret. "They are proud and puffed up, this is an empty place!" he shouted suddenly like a madman, and with a wave of his hand he turned sharply and quickly descended the steps. The crowd awaiting him below wavered; some followed him at once and some lingered, for the cell was still open, and Father Païssy, following Father Ferapont on to the steps, stood watching him. But the excited old fanatic was not completely silenced. Walking twenty steps

* When a monk's body is carried out from the cell to the church and from the church to the graveyard, the canticle "What earthly joy" is sung. If the deceased was a priest as well as a monk the canticle "Our Helper and Defender" is sung instead.

"SATAN, GO HENCE!"

away, he suddenly turned towards the setting sun, raised both his arms and, as though some one had cut him down, fell to the ground with a loud shout.

"My Lord has conquered! Christ has conquered the setting sun!" he shouted frantically, stretching up his hands to the sun, and falling face downwards on the ground, he sobbed like a little child, shaken by his tears and spreading out his arms on the ground. Then all rushed up to him; there were exclamations and sympathetic sobs . . . a kind of frenzy seemed to take possession of them all.

"This is the one who is a saint! This is the one who is a holy man!" some cried aloud, losing their fear. "This is he who should be an elder," others added maliciously.

"He wouldn't be an elder . . . he would refuse . . . he wouldn't foster the cursed innovation . . . he wouldn't imitate their foolery," other voices chimed in at once. And it is hard to say how far they might have gone, but at that moment the bell rang summoning them to service. All began crossing themselves at once. Father Ferapont, too, got up and crossing himself went back to his cell without looking round, still uttering exclamations which were utterly incoherent. A few followed him, but the greater number dispersed, hastening to service. Father Païssy let Father Iosif read in his place and went down. The frantic outcries of bigots could not shake him, but his heart was suddenly filled with sadness and began to ache strangely. He stood still and suddenly asked himself, "Why am I sad even to dejection?" and immediately grasped with surprise that his sudden sadness was due to a very small and special cause. In the crowd thronging the entrance to the cell he had noticed Alyosha and he remembered that he had felt at once a pang at heart on seeing him. "Can that boy mean so much to me now?" he asked himself, wondering.

At that moment Alyosha passed him, hurrying away, but not in the direction of the church. Their eyes met. Alyosha quickly turned away his eyes and dropped them to the ground, and from the boy's look alone Father Païssy guessed what a great change was taking place in him at that moment.

"Have you, too, fallen into temptation?" cried Father Païssy. "Can you be with those of little faith?" he added mournfully.

Alyosha stood still and gazed vaguely at Father Païssy, but quickly turned his eyes away again and again looked at the ground. He stood sideways and did not turn his face to Father Païssy, who watched him attentively.

"Where are you hastening? The bell calls to service," he said again, but again Alyosha made no answer. "Are you leaving the hermitage? What, without asking leave, without asking a blessing?"

Alyosha suddenly gave a wry smile, cast a strange, very strange, look at the father to whom his former guide, the former sovereign of his heart and mind, his beloved elder, had confided him as he lay dying. And suddenly, still without speaking, waved his hand, as though not caring even to be respectful, and with rapid steps walked towards the gates away from the hermitage.

"You will come back again!" murmured Father Païssy, looking after him with sorrowful surprise.

## CHAPTER II

### THE PSYCHOLOGICAL MOMENT

FATHER PAÏSSY, of course, was not wrong when he decided that his "dear boy" would come back again. Perhaps indeed, to some extent, he had a penetrating insight into the true meaning of Alyosha's spiritual condition. Yet I must frankly own that it would be very difficult for me to give a clear account of that strange, vague moment in the life of my young and dearly beloved hero. To Father Païssy's sorrowful question, "are you, too, with those of little faith?" I could of course confidently answer for Alyosha, no, he is not with those of little faith. Quite the contrary. Indeed, all his distress was due precisely to the fact that he was of great faith. But still the distress was there and was so agonising that even long afterwards Alyosha thought of that sorrowful day as one of the bitterest and most fateful days of his life. If the question is asked: "Could all his grief and disturbance have been due only to the fact that his elder's body had shown signs of premature decomposition instead of at once working miraculous cures?" I must answer without beating about the bush, "Yes, it certainly was." I would only beg the reader not to be in too great a hurry to laugh at my young hero's pure heart. I am far from intending to apologise for him or to justify his innocent faith on the ground of his youth, or the little progress he had made in his studies, or any such reason. I must declare, on the contrary, that I have genuine respect for the qualities of his heart. No doubt a youth whose heart received impressions cautiously, whose love was lukewarm, and whose mind, though keen, was too prudent for his age and so worthless, such a young man might, I admit, have

avoided what happened to my hero. But in some cases it is really more creditable to be carried away by an emotion, however unreasonable, which springs from a great love, than to resist such an emotion. And this is even truer of youth, for a young man who is always sensible is suspect and is of little worth — that's my opinion!

"But," sensible people will exclaim perhaps, "every young man cannot be swayed by such a superstition and your hero is no model for others." To this I reply again, yes! my hero had faith, a faith holy and steadfast, but still I am not going to apologise for him.

You see, though I declared above, and perhaps too hastily, that I would not make explanations, apologise, and justify my hero, I see that some explanation is necessary for the understanding of the rest of my story. Let me say then, it was not a question of miracles. There was no frivolous and impatient expectation of miracles in his mind. And Alyosha needed no miracles at the time, for the triumph of his convictions, for the triumph of some preconceived idea — oh, no, not at all — what he saw above all was a countenance — the countenance of his beloved elder, the countenance of that holy man whom he revered with such adoration. The fact is that all the love that lay concealed in his pure young heart for every one and everything had, for the past year, been concentrated — and perhaps wrongly so — on one being, his beloved elder. It is true that being had for so long been accepted by him as his unquestioned ideal, that all his young strength and yearning could not but turn towards that ideal, even to the forgetting at the moment of "every one and everything." He remembered afterwards how, on that terrible day, he had entirely forgotten his brother Dmitri, about whom he had been so anxious and troubled the day before; he had forgotten, too, to take the two hundred roubles to Ilusha's father, though he had so heartily intended to do so the preceding evening. But again it was not miracles he needed but only "the higher justice" which had been in his belief outraged by the blow that had so suddenly and cruelly wounded his heart. And what does it signify that this "justice" looked for by Alyosha inevitably took the shape of miracles to be wrought immediately by the remains of his adored mentor? Why, every one in the monastery cherished the same thought and the same hope, even those whose intellects Alyosha revered, Father Païssy himself, for instance. And so Alyosha, untroubled by doubts, clothed his dreams, too, in the same form as all the rest. And a whole year of life in the monastery had formed the habit of this expectation in his heart. But it was justice, justice, he thirsted for, not simply miracles.

And now the man who should, he believed, have been exalted above every one in the whole world, that man, instead of receiving the glory that was his due, was suddenly cast down and dishonoured! What for? Who had judged him? Who could have decreed this? Those were the questions that wrung his inexperienced and virginal heart. He could not endure without a sense of insult, without bitter resentment even, that the most righteous of the righteous should have been exposed to the jeering and spiteful mockery of the frivolous crowd so inferior to him. Even had there been no miracles, had there been nothing marvellous to justify his hopes, why this indignity, why this disgrace, why this premature decay, "in excess of nature," as the spiteful monks said? Why this "sign from heaven," which they so triumphantly acclaimed in company with Father Ferapont, and why did they believe they had won the right to acclaim it? Where is the finger of Providence? Why did Providence hide its face "at the most critical moment" (so Alyosha thought), as though voluntarily submitting to the blind, dumb, pitiless laws of nature?

That was why Alyosha's heart was bleeding, and, of course, as I have said already, the sting of it all was that the man he loved above everything on earth should be put to shame and disgraced! This murmuring may have been frivolous and unreasonable in my hero, but I repeat again for the third time — and am prepared to admit that it might be difficult to defend my feeling — I am glad that my hero showed himself not too reasonable at that moment, for any man of sense will always come back to reason in time, but, if love does not gain the upper hand in a boy's heart at such an exceptional moment, when will it? I will not, however, omit to mention something strange, which came for a time to the surface of Alyosha's mind at this fateful and subversive moment. This new something was the harassing impression left by the conversation with Ivan, which now persistently haunted Alyosha's mind. At this moment it haunted him. Oh, it was not that something of the fundamental, elemental, so to speak, faith of his soul had been shaken. He loved his God and believed in Him steadfastly, though he was suddenly murmuring against Him. Yet a vague but tormenting and evil impression left by his conversation with Ivan the day before, suddenly revived again now in his soul and seemed forcing its way to the surface of his consciousness.

It had begun to get dusk when Rakitin, crossing the pine copse from the hermitage to the monastery, suddenly noticed Alyosha, lying face downwards on the ground under a tree, motionless and apparently asleep. He went up and called him by his name.

"You here, Alexey? Can you have . . ." he began wondering but broke off. He had meant to say, "Can you have come to this?"

Alyosha did not look at him, but from a slight movement Rakitin at once saw that he heard and understood him.

"What's the matter?" he went on; but the surprise in his face gradually passed into a smile that became more and more ironical.

"I say, I've been looking for you for the last two hours. You suddenly disappeared. What are you about? What foolery is this? You might just look at me. . . ."

Alyosha raised his head, sat up and leaned his back against the tree. He was not crying, but there was a look of suffering and irritability in his face. He did not look at Rakitin, however, but looked away to one side of him.

"Do you know your face is quite changed? There's none of your famous meekness to be seen in it. Are you angry with some one? Have you been ill-treated?"

"Let me alone," said Alyosha suddenly, with a weary gesture of his hand, still looking away from him.

"Oho! So that's how we are feeling! So you can shout at people like other mortals. This is a come-down for an angel. I say, Alyosha, you have amazed me, do you hear? I mean it. It's long since I've been surprised at anything here. Still, I always took you for an educated man . . ." Alyosha at last looked at him, but absently, as it were, as though scarcely understanding what he said.

"Can you really be so upset simply because your old man has begun to stink? You don't mean to say you seriously believed that he was going to turn out miracles?" exclaimed Rakitin, genuinely surprised again.

"I believed, I believe, I want to believe, and I will believe, what more do you want?" cried Alyosha irritably.

"Nothing at all, darling. Damn it all, why, no schoolboy of thirteen believes in that now. But there . . . So now you are in a temper with your God, you are rebelling against Him; promotion has been withheld, the order of merit hasn't been bestowed! Eh, you are a set!"

Alyosha gazed a long while with his eyes half closed at Rakitin, and there was a sudden gleam in his eyes . . . but not of anger with Rakitin.

"I am not rebelling against my God; I simply 'don't accept His world.'" Alyosha suddenly smiled a crooked smile.

"How do you mean, you don't accept the world?" Rakitin thought a moment over his answer. "What idiocy is this?"

Alyosha did not answer.

"Come, enough nonsense, now to business. Have you had anything to eat to-day?"

"I don't remember. . . . I think I have."

"You need a bite, to judge by your looks. It makes one's heart ache to look at you. You didn't sleep all night either, I hear, you had a meeting in there. And then all this bobbery afterwards. Most likely you've had nothing to chew but a mouthful of holy bread. I've got some sausage in my pocket; I've brought it from the town in case of need, only you won't eat sausage. . . ."

"Give me some."

"I say! You are going it! Why, it's a regular mutiny, with barricades! Well, my boy, we must make the most of it. Come to my place. . . . I shouldn't mind a drop of vodka myself, I am tired to death. Vodka is going too far for you, I suppose . . . or would you like some?"

"Give me some vodka, too."

"Hullo! You amaze me, brother!" Rakitin looked at him in astonishment. "Well, one way or another, vodka or sausage, this is a jolly fine chance and mustn't be missed. Come along."

Alyosha got up in silence and followed Rakitin.

"If your little brother Ivan could see this — wouldn't he be surprised! By the way, your brother Ivan set off for Moscow this morning, did you know?"

"Yes," answered Alyosha listlessly, and suddenly the image of his brother Dmitri rose before his mind. But only for a minute, and though it reminded him of something that must not be put off for a moment, some duty, some terrible obligation, even that reminder made no impression on him, did not reach his heart and instantly faded out of his mind and was forgotten. But, a long while afterwards, Alyosha remembered this.

"Your brother Ivan declared once that I was a 'liberal booby with no talents whatever.' Once you, too, could not resist letting me know I was 'dishonourable.' Well! I should like to see what your talents and sense of honour will do for you now." This phrase Rakitin finished to himself in a whisper.

"Pooh! Listen!" he said aloud, "let's take the path clear of the monastery straight to the town. H'm! I ought to go to Madame Hohlakov's by the way. Only fancy, I've written to tell her everything that happened, and would

you believe it, she answered me instantly in pencil (the lady has a passion for writing notes) that 'she would never have expected *such conduct* from such an estimable elder as Father Zosima.' That was her very word: 'conduct.' She, too, is angry. Eh, you are a set! Stay!" he cried suddenly again. He stopped abruptly and taking Alyosha by the shoulder made him stop, too.

"Do you know, Alyosha" — he peeped inquisitively into his eyes, absorbed in a sudden new thought which had dawned on him, and though he was laughing outwardly he was evidently afraid to utter that new idea aloud, so difficult he still found it to believe in the strange and unexpected mood in which he now saw Alyosha. "Alyosha, do you know where we had better go now?" he brought out at last timidly, and pleadingly.

"I don't care . . . where you like."

"Let's go to Grushenka, eh? Will you come?" pronounced Rakitin at last, trembling with timid suspense.

"Let's go to Grushenka," Alyosha answered calmly, at once, and this prompt and calm agreement was such a surprise to Rakitin that he almost jumped back.

"Well! I say!" he cried in amazement, but seizing Alyosha firmly by the arm he led him along the path, still dreading that he would change his mind.

They walked along in silence, Rakitin was positively afraid to talk.

"And how glad she will be, how delighted," he muttered, but lapsed into silence again. And indeed it was not to please Grushenka that he was taking Alyosha to her. He was a practical person and never undertook anything without a prospect of gain for himself. His object in this case was two-fold, first a revengeful desire to see "the disgrace of the righteous," and Alyosha's fall "from saintliness to sin," over which he was already gloating in his imagination, and in the second place he had in view a certain material gain for himself, of which more will be said later.

"Well, this is the psychological moment," he thought to himself with spiteful glee, "and we shall catch it by the collar, for it's just what we want."

## CHAPTER III
### AN ONION

GRUSHENKA lived in the busiest part of the town, near the cathedral square, renting a wooden lodge close by the house of her landlady, the widow of a merchant by the name of Morozov. The house was a large stone building of two storeys, old and of a very unprepossessing appearance. The widow, an old woman, led a secluded life there with her two unmarried nieces, who were elderly spinsters. She had no need to let her lodge, but every one knew that she had taken in Grushenka as a lodger, four years before, solely to please her kinsman, the merchant Samsonov, who was publicly known to be the girl's protector. It was said that the jealous old man's object in placing his "favourite" with the widow Morozov was that the old woman should keep a sharp eye on her new lodger's conduct. But this sharp eye soon proved to be unnecessary, and in the end the widow Morozov seldom met Grushenka and did not worry her by looking after her in any way. It is true that four years had passed since the old man had brought the slim, delicate, shy, timid, dreamy, and sad girl of eighteen from the chief town of the province, and much water had flowed under the bridges since then. Little was known of the girl's history in the town and that little was vague. Nothing more had been learnt more recently, even after many people had become interested in the great beauty that Agrafena Alexandrovna had meanwhile become. There were rumours that at seventeen she had been deceived by some one, some sort of officer, and immediately afterwards abandoned by him. The officer had gone away and afterwards married, while Grushenka had been left in destitution and disgrace. It was said, however, that though Grushenka had been actually saved from destitution by the old man, Samsonov, she came of a respectable family belonging to the clergy, that she was the daughter of a supernumerary deacon or something of the sort.

And now after four years the sensitive, injured, and pathetic little orphan had become a plump, rosy beauty of the Russian type, a woman of bold and determined character, proud and insolent. She had a good head for business, was acquisitive, saving, and careful, and by fair means or foul had succeeded, it was said, in amassing a little fortune of her own. There was only one point on which all were agreed. Grushenka was not easy of access, and except her aged protector there had not been one man who could boast of her favours during those four years. It was a positive fact, for there had been a good many, especially during the last two years, who had attempted to obtain those favours. But all their efforts had been in vain and some of these suitors had been forced to beat an undignified and even comic retreat, owing to the firm and ironical resistance they met from the strong-willed young person. It was known, too, that the young person had, especially of late, been engaging in what is called "business," and that she had shown marked abilities in that direction, so that many people called her a regular Jewess. It was not that she lent money at interest, but it was known, for instance, that she had for some time past, in partnership with old Karamazov, actually invested in the purchase of bad debts for a trifle, a tenth of their nominal value, and afterwards had made out of them ten times what they were worth.

The old widower Samsonov, a man of large fortune, was stingy and merciless. He tyrannised over his grown-up sons, but, for the last year, during which he had been ill and lost the use of his swollen legs, he had fallen greatly under the influence of his protégée, whom he had at first kept strictly and on short rations, "on lenten fare" as the wits said at the time. But Grushenka had succeeded in emancipating herself, while she established in him a boundless belief in her fidelity. The old man, now long since dead, had had a large business in his day and was also a noteworthy character, miserly and hard as flint. Though Grushenka's hold upon him was so strong that he could not live without her (it had been so especially for the last two years), he did not settle any considerable fortune on her and would not have been moved to do so, even if she had threatened to leave him. But he had presented her with a small sum, and even that was a surprise to every one when it became known.

"You are a wench with brains," he said to her, when he gave her eight thousand roubles, "and you must look after yourself, but let me tell you that except your yearly allowance as before, you'll get nothing more from me to the day of my death, and I'll leave you nothing in my will either."

And he kept his word; he died and left everything to his sons, whom, with their wives and children, he had treated all his life as servants. Grushenka was not even mentioned in his will. All this became known afterwards. He did, however, offer Grushenka advice as to how to manage her affairs, and put business in her way.

When Fyodor Pavlovich, who first came into contact with Grushenka over a matter of business, ended to his own surprise by falling madly in love with her, old Samsonov, gravely ill as he was, was immensely amused. It is remarkable that throughout their whole acquaintance Grushenka was absolutely and spontaneously open with the old man, and he seems to have been the only person in the world with whom she was on such terms. Of late, when Dmitri, too, had come on the scene with his love, the old man left off laughing. On the contrary, he once gave Grushenka a stern and earnest piece of advice.

"If you have to choose between the two, father and son, you'd better choose the old man, if only you make sure the old scoundrel will marry you and settle some money on you beforehand. But don't get mixed up with the captain, no good will come of that."

These were the very words of the old sensualist, who felt already that his death was not far off and who actually died five months later.

I will note, too, in passing, that although many in our town knew of the grotesque and monstrous rivalry of the Karamazovs, father and son, the object of which was Grushenka, scarcely any one understood what really underlay her attitude to both of them. Even Grushenka's two servants (after the catastrophe of which we will speak later) testified in court that she received Dmitri Fyodorovich simply out of fear because "he threatened to murder her." These servants were an old cook, something of an invalid and almost deaf, who came from Grushenka's old home, and her grand-daughter, a smart young girl of twenty, who performed the duties of a maid. Grushenka lived very economically and her surroundings were anything but luxurious. Her lodge consisted of three rooms containing mahogany furniture in the fashion of 1820, belonging to her landlady.

It was quite dark when Rakitin and Alyosha entered her rooms, yet they were not lighted up. Grushenka was lying down in her drawing-room on the big, hard, clumsy sofa with a mahogany back. The sofa was covered with shabby and ragged leather. Under her head she had two white down pillows taken from her bed. She was lying stretched out motionless on her back with her hands behind her head. She was dressed as though expecting some one, in a black silk dress, with a dainty lace fichu on her head, which was very becoming. Over her shoulders was thrown a lace shawl pinned with a massive gold brooch. She certainly was expecting some one. She lay as though impatient and weary, her face rather pale and her lips and eyes hot, restlessly tapping the arm of the sofa with the tip of her right foot. The appearance of Rakitin and Alyosha caused a slight excitement. From the hall they could hear Grushenka leap up from the sofa and cry out in a frightened voice, "Who's there?" But the maid met the visitors and at once called back to her mistress.

"It's not he, it's nothing, only other visitors."

"What can be the matter?" muttered Rakitin, leading Alyosha into the drawing-room. Grushenka was standing by the sofa as though still alarmed. A thick coil of her dark brown hair escaped from its lace covering and fell on her right shoulder, but she did not notice it and did not put it back till she had scrutinised her visitors and recognised them.

"Ah, it's you, Rakitin? You quite frightened me. Whom have you brought? Who is this with you? Good heavens, you have brought him!" she exclaimed, recognising Alyosha.

"Do send for candles!" said Rakitin, with the free-and-easy air of a most intimate friend, who is privileged to give orders in the house.

"Candles . . . of course, candles. . . . Fenya, fetch him a candle. . . . Well, you have chosen a moment to bring him!" she exclaimed again, nodding towards Alyosha, and turning to the looking-glass she began quickly fastening up her hair with both hands. She seemed annoyed.

"Have I displeased you?" asked Rakitin, instantly almost offended.

"You frightened me, Rakitin, that's what it is." Grushenka turned with a smile to Alyosha. "Don't be afraid of me, my dear Alyosha, you can't think how glad I am to see you, my unexpected visitor. But you frightened me, Rakitin, I thought it was Mitya breaking in. You see, I deceived him just now, I made him promise to believe me but I told him a lie. I told him that I was going to spend the evening with my old man Kuzma Kuzmich, and should be there till late counting money. I always spend one whole evening a week with him making up his accounts. We lock ourselves in and he counts on the abacus while I sit and put things down in the book. I am the only person he trusts. Mitya believes that I am there, but I came back and have been sitting locked in here, expecting some news. How was it Fenya let you in? Fenya, Fenya, run out to the gate, open it and find out whether the captain is to be seen! Perhaps he is hiding and spying, I am dreadfully frightened."

"There's no one there, Agrafena Alexandrovna, I've just looked out; I keep running to peep through the crack, I am in fear and trembling myself."

"Are the shutters fastened, Fenya? And we must draw the curtains — that's better!" She drew the heavy curtains herself. "He'd rush in at once if he saw a light. I am afraid of your brother Mitya to-day, Alyosha."

Grushenka spoke aloud, and, though she was alarmed, she seemed to be elated over something.

"Why are you so afraid of Mitya to-day?" inquired Rakitin. "I should have thought you were not timid with him, he dances to your piping."

"I tell you, I am expecting news, priceless news, so I don't want Mitya at all now. And he didn't believe, I feel he didn't, that I would stay at Kuzma Kuzmich's. He must be in ambush now, in the back of his father's garden, watching for me. And if he's there, he won't come here, so much the better! But I really have been to Kuzma Kuzmich's, Mitya escorted me there. I told him I should stay there till midnight, and I asked him to be sure to come at midnight to fetch me home. He went away and I sat ten minutes with Kuzma Kuzmich and came back here again. Ugh, I was afraid, I ran for fear of meeting him."

"And why are you so dressed up? What a curious cap you've got on!"

"How curious you are yourself, Rakitin! I tell you, I am expecting a message. If the message comes, I shall fly, I shall gallop away and you will see no more of me. That's why I am dressed up, so as to be ready."

"And where are you flying to?"

"If you know too much, you'll get old too soon."

"Upon my word! You are all aflutter . . . I've never seen you like this before. You are dressed up as if you were going to a ball." Rakitin looked her up and down.

"Much you know about balls."

"And do you know much about them?"

"I have seen a ball. The year before last, Kuzma Kuzmich's son was married and I looked on from the gallery. Do you suppose I want to be talking to you, Rakitin, while a prince like this is standing here? Such a visitor! Alyosha, my dear boy, I look at you and can't believe my eyes. Good heavens, can you have come here to see me! To tell you the truth I never had a thought of seeing you and I didn't dream that you would ever come and see me. Though this is not the proper moment now, I am awfully glad to see you. Sit down on the sofa, here, that's right, my bright young moon. I really can't take it in even now. . . . Eh, Rakitin, if only you had brought him yesterday or the day before! But I am glad as it is! Perhaps it's better he has come now, at such a moment, and not the day before yesterday."

She gaily sat down beside Alyosha on the sofa, looking at him with positive delight. And she really was glad, she was not lying when she said so. Her eyes glowed, her lips laughed, but it was a good-natured merry laugh. Alyosha had not expected to see such a kind expression in her face. . . . He had hardly met her till the day before, he had formed an alarming idea of her, and had been horribly distressed the day before by the spiteful and treacherous trick she had played on Katerina Ivanovna. He was greatly surprised to find her now altogether different from what he had expected. And, crushed as he was by his own sorrow, his eyes involuntarily rested on her with attention. Her whole manner seemed changed for the better since yesterday, there was scarcely any trace of that mawkish sweetness in her speech, of that voluptuous softness in her movements. Everything was simple and good-natured, her gestures were rapid, direct, confiding, but she was greatly excited.

"Dear me, how everything comes together to-day," she chattered on again. "And why I am so glad to see you, Alyosha, I couldn't say myself! If you asked me, I couldn't tell you."

"Come, don't you know why you're glad?" said Rakitin, grinning. "You used to be always pestering me to bring him, you'd some object, I suppose."

"I had a different object once, but now that's over, this is not the moment. I say, I want to serve you something nice. I am good-natured now. You sit down, too, Rakitin, why are you standing? You've sat down already? There's no fear of Rakitin's forgetting to look after himself. Look, Alyosha, he's sitting there opposite us, so offended that I didn't ask him to sit down before you. Ugh, Rakitin is such a one to take offence!" laughed Grushenka. "Don't be angry, Rakitin, I'm kind to-day. Why are you so depressed, Alyosha, are you afraid of me?" She peeped into his eyes with merry mockery.

"He's sad. There's been no promotion," boomed Rakitin.

"What promotion?"

"His elder started to smell."

"What? You are talking some nonsense, you want to say something nasty. Be quiet, you stupid! Will you let me sit on your knee, Alyosha, like this?" She suddenly skipped forward and jumped, laughing, on his knee, like a nestling kitten, placing her right arm tenderly around his neck. "I'll cheer you up, my pious boy. Yes, really, will you let me sit on your knee, you won't be angry? If you tell me, I'll hop off."

Alyosha did not speak. He sat afraid to stir, he heard her words, "If you tell me, I'll hop off," but he did not answer, it was as though he couldn't move. But there was nothing in his heart such as Rakitin, for instance, watching him from his corner with a leer, might have expected or fancied. The great grief in his heart swallowed up every sensation that might have been aroused in him, and, if only he could have thought clearly at that moment, he would have realised that he had now the strongest armour to protect him from every snare and temptation. Yet in spite of the confusion of his spiritual condition and the sorrow that overwhelmed him, he could not help wondering at a new and strange sensation that was rising in his heart. This woman, this "dreadful" woman, had no terror for him now, none of that terror that had stirred in his soul at any passing thought of woman. On the contrary, this woman, dreaded above all women, sitting now on his knee, holding him in her arms, aroused in him now a quite different, unexpected, peculiar feeling, a feeling of the intensest and purest interest without a trace of fear, of his former terror. That was what instinctively surprised him.

"You've talked nonsense enough," cried Rakitin, "you'd much better serve us some champagne. You owe it me, you know!"

"Yes, I really do. Do you know, Alyosha, I promised him champagne on top of everything, if he'd bring you? I'll have some, too! Fenya, Fenya, bring us the bottle Mitya left! Look sharp! Though I am so stingy, I'll stand a bottle, not for you, Rakitin, you're a toadstool, but he is a lord! And though my heart is full of something very different, so be it, I'll drink with you. I long for some dissipation."

"But what is this 'moment' you're talking about? And what is this news, may I ask, or is it a secret?" Rakitin put in inquisitively, doing his best to pretend not to notice the snubs that were being continually aimed at him.

"Ah, it's not a secret, and you know it, too," Grushenka said, in a voice suddenly anxious, turning her head towards Rakitin, and drawing a little away from Alyosha, though she still sat on his knee with her arm round his neck. "My officer is coming, Rakitin, my officer is coming."

"I heard he was coming, but is he so near?"

"He is at Mokroye now, he'll send a message from there, so he wrote, I got a letter from him to-day. I am expecting the message every minute."

"You don't say so! Why at Mokroye?"

"That's a long story, I've told you enough."

"Mitya'll be up to something now — I say! Does he know or doesn't he?"

"He know! Of course he doesn't. If he knew, there would be murder. But I am not afraid of that now, I am not afraid of his knife. Be quiet, Rakitin, don't remind me of Dmitri Fyodorovich, he has bruised my heart. And I don't want to think of that at this moment. I can think of Alyosha here, I can look at Alyosha . . . smile at me, darling, cheer up, smile at my foolishness, at my pleasure. . . .

Ah, he's smiling, he's smiling! How kindly he looks at me! And you know, Alyosha, I've been thinking all this time you were angry with me, because of the day before yesterday, because of that young lady. I was a cur, that's the truth. . . . But it's a good thing it happened so. It was a horrid thing, but a good thing, too." Grushenka smiled pensively and a little cruel line showed in her smile. "Mitya told me that she screamed out that I 'ought to be flogged.' I did insult her dreadfully. She sent for me, she wanted to make a conquest of me, to win me over with her chocolate. . . . No, it's a good thing it did end like that." She smiled again. "But I am still afraid of your being angry."

"Yes, that's really true," Rakitin put in suddenly with genuine surprise. "Alyosha, she is really afraid of a chicken like you."

"He is a chicken to you, Rakitin . . . because you've no conscience, that's what it is! You see, I love him with all my soul, that's how it is! Alyosha, do you believe I love you with all my soul?"

"Ah, you shameless woman! She is making you a declaration, Alexey!"

"Well, what of it, I love him!"

"And what about your officer? And the priceless message from Mokroye?"

"That is quite different."

"That's a woman's way of looking at it!"

"Don't you make me angry, Rakitin." Grushenka caught him up hotly. "This is quite different. I love Alyosha in a different way. It's true, Alyosha, I had sly designs on you before. For I am a horrid, violent creature. But at other times I've looked upon you, Alyosha, as my conscience. I've kept thinking 'how any one like that must despise a nasty thing like me.' I thought that the day before yesterday, as I ran home from the young lady's. I have thought of you a long time in that way, Alyosha, and Mitya knows, I've talked to him about it. Mitya understands. Would you believe it, I sometimes look at you and feel ashamed, utterly ashamed of myself. . . . And how, and since when, I began to think about you like that, I can't say, I don't remember. . . ."

Fenya came in and put a tray with an uncorked bottle and three glasses of champagne on the table.

"Here's the champagne!" cried Rakitin. "You're excited, Agrafena Alexandrovna, and not yourself. When you've had a glass of champagne, you'll be ready to dance. Eh, they can't even do that properly," he added, looking at the bottle. "The old woman's poured it out in the kitchen and the bottle's been brought in warm and without a cork. Well, let me have some, anyway."

He went up to the table, took a glass, emptied it at one gulp and poured himself out another.

"One doesn't often stumble upon champagne," he said, licking his lips. "Now, Alyosha, take a glass, show what you can do! What shall we drink to? The gates of paradise? Take a glass, Grushenka, you drink to the gates of paradise, too."

"What gates of paradise?"

She took a glass, Alyosha took his, tasted it and put it back.

"No, I'd better not," he smiled gently.

"And you bragged!" cried Rakitin.

"Well, if so, I won't either," chimed in Grushenka, "I really don't want any. You can drink the whole bottle alone, Rakitin. If Alyosha has some, I will."

"What calf-like sentimentality!" said Ra-

kitin tauntingly, "and she's sitting on his knee, too! He's got something to grieve over, but what's the matter with you? He was rebelling against his God and was ready to eat sausage . . ."

"How so?"

"His elder died to-day, Father Zosima, the saint."

"So Father Zosima is dead," cried Grushenka. "Good God, I did not know!" She crossed herself devoutly. "Goodness, what have I been doing, sitting on his knee like this at such a time!" She started up as though in dismay, instantly slipped off his knee and sat down on the sofa.

Alyosha bent a long wondering look upon her and a light seemed to dawn in his face.

"Rakitin," he said suddenly, in a firm and loud voice, "don't taunt me with having rebelled against God. I don't want to feel angry with you, so you must be kinder, too. I've lost a treasure such as you have never had, and you cannot judge me now. You had much better look at her — do you see how she spared me? I came here to find a wicked soul — I felt drawn to evil because I was base and evil myself, and I've found a true sister, I have found a treasure — a loving heart. She spared me just now. . . . Agrafena Alexandrovna, I am speaking of you. You've restored my soul just now."

Alyosha's lips were quivering and he caught his breath.

"She has saved you, it seems," laughed Rakitin spitefully. "And she meant to swallow you, do you realise that?"

"Stay, Rakitin." Grushenka jumped up. "Hush, both of you. Now I'll tell you all about it. Hush, Alyosha, your words make me ashamed, for I am bad and not good — that's

"DRINK TO THE GATES OF PARADISE"

what I am. And you hush, Rakitin, because you are telling lies. I had the low idea of trying to swallow him, but now you are lying, now it's all different. And don't let me hear anything more from you, Rakitin."

All this Grushenka said with extreme emotion.

"They are both crazy," said Rakitin, looking at them with amazement. "I feel as though I were in a madhouse. They're both weakening so that they'll begin crying in a minute."

"I shall begin to cry, I shall," repeated Grushenka. "He called me his sister and I shall never forget that. Only let me tell you, Rakitin, though I am bad, I did give away an onion."

"An onion? Hang it all, you really are crazy."

Rakitin wondered at their exaltation. He was aggrieved and annoyed, though he might have reflected that each of them was just passing through a spiritual crisis such as does not come often in a lifetime. But though Rakitin was very sensitive about everything that concerned himself, he was very obtuse as regards the feelings and sensations of others — partly because of his youth and inexperience, partly because of his intense egoism.

"You see, Alyosha," Grushenka turned to him with a nervous laugh, "I was boasting when I told Rakitin I had given away an onion, but it's not to boast I tell you about it. It's only a story, but it's a nice story. I heard it when I was a child from Matryona, my cook, who is still with me. It's like this. 'Once upon a time there was a peasant woman and a very wicked woman she was. And she died and did not leave a single good deed behind. The devils caught her and plunged her into a lake of fire. So her guardian angel stood and wondered what good deed of hers he could remember to tell to God; he did remember one and said to God: "She once pulled up an onion in her garden," said he, "and gave it to a beggar woman." And God answered: "You take that onion then, hold it out to her in the lake, and let her take hold of it. And if you can pull her out of the lake, let her come to Paradise, but if the onion breaks, then the woman must stay where she is." The angel ran to the woman and held out the onion to her. "Come," said he, "catch hold and I'll pull you out." And he began cautiously pulling her out. He had nearly pulled her out, when the other sinners in the lake, seeing how she was being drawn out, began catching hold of her so as to be pulled out with her. But she was a very wicked woman and she began kicking them. "I'm to be pulled out, not you. It's my onion, not yours." As soon as she said that, the onion broke. And the woman fell into the lake and she is burning there to this day. So the angel wept and went away.' So that's the story, Alyosha; I know it by heart, for I am that wicked woman myself. I boasted to Rakitin that I had given away an onion, but to you I'll say: 'I've done nothing but give away one onion all my life, that's the only good deed I've done.' So don't praise me, Alyosha, don't think me good, I am bad, I am a wicked woman and you make me ashamed if you praise me. Eh, I must confess everything. Listen, Alyosha. I was so anxious to get hold of you that I promised Rakitin twenty-five roubles if he would bring you to me. Stay, Rakitin, wait!" She went rapidly to the table, opened a drawer, pulled out a purse and took from it a twenty-five rouble note.

"What nonsense! What nonsense!" cried Rakitin, disconcerted.

"Take it, Rakitin, I owe it you, there's no fear of your refusing it, you asked for it yourself." And she threw the note to him.

"Likely I should refuse it," boomed Rakitin, obviously abashed, but carrying off his confusion with a swagger. "That will come in very handy; fools are made for wise men's profit."

"And now hold your tongue, Rakitin, what I am going to say now is not for your ears. Sit down in that corner and keep quiet. You don't like us, so hold your tongue."

"What should I like you for?" Rakitin snarled, not concealing his ill-humour. He put the twenty-five rouble note in his pocket and he felt ashamed at Alyosha's seeing it. He had reckoned on receiving his payment later, without Alyosha's knowing of it, and now, feeling ashamed, he lost his temper. Till that moment he had thought it discreet not to contradict Grushenka too flatly in spite of her snubbing, since he had something to get out of her. But now he, too, was angry:

"One loves people for some reason, but what have either of you done for me?"

"You should love people without a reason, as Alyosha does."

"How does he love you? How has he shown it, that you make such a fuss about it?"

Grushenka was standing in the middle of the room; she spoke with heat and there were hysterical notes in her voice.

"Hush, Rakitin, you know nothing about us! And don't dare to speak to me like that again. How dare you be so familiar! Sit in that corner and be quiet, as though you were my footman! And now, Alyosha, I'll tell you the whole truth, that you may see what a hussy I am! I am not talking to Rakitin, but to you. I wanted to ruin you, Alyosha, that's the holy

truth; I quite meant to. I wanted to so much, that I bribed Rakitin to bring you. And why did I want to do such a thing? You knew nothing about it, Alyosha, you turned away from me, if you passed me, you dropped your eyes. And I've looked at you a hundred times before to-day, I began asking every one about you. Your face haunted my heart. 'He despises me,' I thought, 'he won't even look at me.' And I felt it so much at last that I wondered at myself for being so scared of a boy. I'll swallow him whole and laugh. I was full of spite and anger. Would you believe it, nobody here dares talk or think of coming to Agrafena Alexandrovna with any evil purpose. The old man is the only one I have anything to do with, I was bound and sold to him, Satan married us, but there has been no one else. But looking at you, I decided, I'll swallow him and laugh. You see what a spiteful cur I am, and you called me your sister! And now that man who wronged me has come; I sit here waiting for a message from him. And do you know what that man has been to me? Five years ago, when Kuzma brought me here, I used to shut myself up, that no one might have sight or sound of me. I was a silly slip of a girl; I used to sit here sobbing, I used to lie awake all night, thinking: 'Where is he now, the man who wronged me? He is laughing at me with another woman, most likely. If only I could see him, if I could meet him again, I'd pay him out, I'd pay him out!' At night I used to lie sobbing into my pillow in the dark, and I used to brood over it, I used to tear my heart on purpose and gloat over my anger. 'I'll pay him out, I'll pay him out!' That's what I used to cry out in the dark. And when I suddenly thought that I should really do nothing to him, and that he was laughing at me then, or perhaps had utterly forgotten me, I would fling myself on the floor, melt into helpless tears, and lie there shaking till dawn. In the morning I would get up more spiteful than a dog, ready to tear the whole world to pieces. And then what do you think? I began saving money, I became hard-hearted, grew plump — grew wiser, would you say? No, no one in the whole world sees it, no one knows it, but when night comes on, I sometimes lie as I did five years ago, when I was a silly girl, grinding my teeth and crying all night, thinking: 'I'll pay him out, I'll pay him out!' Do you hear? Well, then, now you understand me. A month ago a letter came to me — he was coming, he was a widower, he wanted to see me. It took my breath away, then I suddenly thought: 'If he comes and whistles to call me, I shall creep back to him like a beaten dog.' I couldn't believe myself. Am I so abject? Shall I run to him or not? And I've been in such a rage with myself all this month that I am worse than I was five years ago. Do you see now, Alyosha, what a violent, savage creature I am? I have shown you the whole truth! I played with Mitya to keep me from running to that other. Hush, Rakitin, it's not for you to judge me, I am not speaking to you. Before you came in, I was lying here waiting, brooding, deciding my whole future life, and you can never know what was in my heart. Yes, Alyosha, tell your young lady not to be angry with me for what happened the day before yesterday. . . . Nobody in the whole world knows what I am going through now, and no one ever can know. . . . For perhaps I shall take a knife with me to-day, I can't make up my mind . . ."

And at this "pathetic" phrase Grushenka broke down, hid her face in her hands, flung herself on the sofa pillows, and sobbed like a child. Alyosha got up and went to Rakitin.

"Misha," he said, "don't be angry. She wounded you, but don't be angry. You heard what she said just now? You mustn't ask too much of human endurance, one must be more merciful."

Alyosha said this at the instinctive prompting of his heart. He felt obliged to speak and he turned to Rakitin. If Rakitin had not been there, he would have spoken to the air. But Rakitin looked at him ironically and Alyosha stopped short.

"You were so primed up with your elder's teaching the other night that now you have to shoot it off at me, Alexey, man of God!" said Rakitin, with a smile of hatred.

"Don't laugh, Rakitin, don't grin, don't talk of the dead — he was better than any one on earth!" cried Alyosha, with tears in his voice. "I didn't get up to speak to you as a judge but as the lowest of the judged. What am I beside her? I came here seeking my ruin, and said to myself, 'What does it matter?' and that because of cowardice, but she, after five years in torment, as soon as any one says a word from the heart to her — she forgives everything, she forgets everything, and cries. The man who has wronged her has come back, he sends for her and she forgives him everything, and hastens joyfully to meet him and she won't take a knife with her. She won't! No, I am not like that. I don't know whether you are, Misha, but I am not like that. It's a lesson to me. . . . She loves better than we. . . . Have you heard her speak before of what she has just told us? No, you haven't; if you had, you'd have understood her long ago . . . and the person insulted the day before yesterday must forgive her, too! She will, when she knows . . . and she shall know. . . . This soul is not yet at peace with itself, one must spare it . . . there may be a treasure in that soul. . . ."

Alyosha stopped, because he was breathless. In spite of his ill-humour Rakitin looked at him with astonishment. He had never expected such a tirade from the gentle Alyosha.

"What an advocate she has found! Are you in love with her? Agrafena Alexandrovna, our monk's really in love with you, you've made a conquest!" he cried, with an insolent laugh.

Grushenka lifted her head from the pillow and looked at Alyosha with a tender smile shining on her face, which suddenly appeared swollen with tears.

"Let him alone, Alyosha, my cherub, you see the sort he is, he is not a person for you to speak to. Mihail Osipovich," she turned to Rakitin, "I meant to beg your pardon for being rude to you, but now I don't want to. Alyosha, come to me, sit down here." She beckoned to him with a happy smile. "That's right, sit here. Tell me," she took him by the hand and peeped into his face, smiling, "tell me, do I love that man or not? the man who wronged me, do I love him or not? Before you came, I lay here in the dark, asking my heart whether I loved him. Decide for me, Alyosha, the time has come, it shall be as you say. Am I to forgive him or not?"

"But you have forgiven him already," said Alyosha, smiling.

"Yes, I really have forgiven him," Grushenka murmured thoughtfully. "What a vile heart! To my vile heart!" She snatched up a glass from the table, emptied it at a gulp, lifted it in the air and flung it on the floor. The glass broke with a crash. A little cruel line came into her smile.

"Perhaps I haven't forgiven him, though," she said, with a sort of menace in her voice, and she dropped her eyes to the ground as though she were talking to herself. "Perhaps my heart is only getting ready to forgive. I shall yet struggle with my heart. You see, Alyosha, I've grown to love my tears awfully in these five years. . . . Perhaps I love only my resentment, not him. . . ."

"Well, I shouldn't care to be in his skin," hissed Rakitin.

"Well, you won't be, Rakitin, you'll never be in his skin. You shall black my shoes, Rakitin, that's the kind of work I'll make you do. You'll never get one like me . . . and he won't either, perhaps. . . ."

"Won't he? Then why are you dressed up like that?" said Rakitin, with a venomous sneer.

"Don't taunt me with dressing up, Rakitin, you don't know all that is in my heart! If I choose to tear off my finery, I'll tear it off at once, this minute," she cried in a resonant voice. "You don't know what that finery is for, Rakitin! Perhaps I shall come before him and say: 'Have you ever seen me look like this before?' He left me a thin, consumptive cry-baby of seventeen. I'll sit with him, fascinate him and work him up. 'Do you see what I am like now?' I'll say to him; 'well, and that's enough for you, my dear sir, there's many a slip twixt the cup and the lip!' That may be what the finery is for, Rakitin." Grushenka finished with a malicious laugh. "I'm violent and savage, Alyosha, I'll tear off my finery, I'll destroy my beauty, I'll scorch my face, slash it with a knife, and turn beggar. If I choose, I won't go anywhere now to see any one. If I choose, I'll send Kuzma back all he has ever given me, and all his money, to-morrow, and I'll go out charing for the rest of my life. You

CANA OF GALILEE

think I wouldn't do it, Rakitin, that I would not dare to do it? I would, I would, I could do it directly, only don't exasperate me . . . and I'll send him about his business, I'll snap my fingers in his face, he shan't have me!"

She screamed the last words hysterically, but broke down again, hid her face in her hands, buried it in the pillow and shook with sobs.

Rakitin got up.

"It's time we were off," he said, "it's late, we shall be shut out of the monastery."

Grushenka leapt up from her place.

"Surely you don't want to go, Alyosha!" she cried, in mournful surprise. "What are you doing to me? You've shaken me, tortured me, and now you'll leave me to face this night alone!"

"He can hardly spend the night with you! Though if he wants to, let him! I'll go alone," Rakitin joked sneeringly.

"Hush, evil soul!" Grushenka cried savagely at him; "you never said such words to me as he has come to say."

"What has he said to you, after all?" muttered Rakitin irritably.

"I can't say, I don't know. I don't know what he said to me, it went straight to my heart; he has wrung my heart. . . . He is the first, the only one who has pitied me, that's what it is. Why did you not come before, you angel?" She fell on her knees before him as though in a sudden frenzy. "I've been waiting all my life for some one like you, I knew that some one like you would come and forgive me. I believed that, nasty as I am, some one would really love me, not only with a shameful love!"

"What have I done to you?" answered Alyosha, bending over her with a tender smile, and gently taking her by the hands; "I only gave you an onion, nothing but a tiny little onion, that was all!"

He was moved to tears himself as he said it. At that moment there was a sudden noise in the passage, some one came into the hall. Grushenka jumped up, seeming greatly alarmed. Fenya ran noisily into the room.

"Mistress, mistress darling, a messenger has galloped up," she cried, breathless and joyful. "A carriage from Mokroye for you, Timofey the driver, with a troika, they are just putting in fresh horses. . . . A letter, here's the letter, mistress."

A letter was in her hand and she waved it in the air all the while she talked. Grushenka snatched the letter from her and carried it to the candle. It was only a note, a few lines. She read it in one instant.

"He has sent for me," she cried, her face white and distorted, with a sickly smile; "he whistles! Crawl back, little dog!"

But only for one instant she stood as though hesitating; suddenly the blood rushed to her head and sent a glow to her cheeks.

"I'm going," she cried; "five years of my life! Good-bye! Good-bye, Alyosha, my fate is sealed. Go, go, leave me, all of you, don't let me see you again! Grushenka is flying to a new life. . . . Don't you remember evil against me either, Rakitin. I may be going to my death! Ugh! I feel as though I were drunk!"

She suddenly left them and ran into her bedroom.

"Well, she has no thoughts for us now!" grumbled Rakitin. "Let's go, or we may hear that female shriek again. I am sick of all these tears and screams."

Alyosha mechanically let himself be led

275

out. In the yard stood a covered carriage. Horses were being taken out of the shafts, men were running to and fro with a lantern. Three fresh horses were being led in at the open gate. But when Alyosha and Rakitin reached the bottom of the steps, Grushenka's bedroom window was suddenly opened and she called in a ringing voice after Alyosha:

"Alyosha, give my greetings to your brother Mitya and tell him not to remember evil against me, though I have brought him misery. And tell him, too, in my words: 'Grushenka has fallen to a scoundrel, and not to you, noble heart.' And add, too, that Grushenka loved him only one hour, only one short hour she loved him — so let him remember that hour all his life — say, 'Grushenka tells you to!'"

She ended in a voice full of sobs. The window was shut with a slam.

"H'm, h'm!" growled Rakitin, laughing, "she murders your brother Mitya and then tells him to remember it all his life! What carnality!"

Alyosha made no reply, he seemed not to have heard. He walked fast beside Rakitin as though in a terrible hurry. He was lost in thought and moved mechanically. Rakitin felt a sudden twinge as though he had been touched on an open wound. He had expected something quite different by bringing Grushenka and Alyosha together. Something very different from what he had hoped for had happened.

"He is a Pole, that officer of hers," he began again, restraining himself; "and indeed he is not an officer at all now. He served in the customs in Siberia, somewhere on the Chinese frontier, some puny little beggar of a Pole, I expect. Lost his job, they say. He's heard now that Grushenka's saved a little money, so he's

turned up again — that's the explanation of the mystery."

Again Alyosha seemed not to hear. Rakitin could not control himself.

"Well, so you've converted the Magdalene?" he laughed spitefully. "You have turned the harlot into the path of virtue? Driven out the seven devils, eh? So that's where those long-expected miracles of ours have come to pass!"

"Hush, Rakitin," Alyosha answered, with an aching heart.

"So you despise me now for those twenty-five roubles? I've sold my friend, you think. But you are not Christ, you know, and I am not Judas."

"Oh, Rakitin, I assure you I'd forgotten about it," cried Alyosha, "you have reminded me of it yourself. . . ."

But this was the last straw for Rakitin.

"Damnation take you all and each of you!" he yelled suddenly; "why the devil did I have anything to do with you? I don't want to know you from now on. Take yourself off, there's your road!"

And he turned abruptly into another street, leaving Alyosha alone in the dark. Alyosha passed out of the town and walked across the fields to the monastery.

## CHAPTER IV
### CANA OF GALILEE

IT was very late, according to monastery ideas, when Alyosha returned to the hermitage; the door-keeper let him in by a special entrance. It had struck nine o'clock — the hour of rest and repose after a day of such agitation for all. Alyosha timidly opened the door and went into the elder's cell where his coffin was now standing. There was no one in the cell but

Father Païssy, reading the Gospel in solitude over the coffin, and the young novice Porfiry, who, exhausted by the previous night's conversation and the exciting incidents of the day, was sleeping the sound sleep of youth on the floor of the other room. Though Father Païssy heard Alyosha come in, he did not even look in his direction. Alyosha turned from the door to the right-hand corner, fell on his knees and began to pray.

His soul was overflowing, but with mingled feelings; no single sensation stood out distinctly; on the contrary, one drove out another in a slow, continual rotation, as it were. But the moment was sweet to his heart and, strange to say, Alyosha was not surprised at it. Again he saw that coffin before him, the hidden dead figure so precious to him, but tearful, poignant grief no longer gnawed at his soul as it had in the morning. As soon as he came in, he fell down before the coffin as before a holy shrine, but joy, joy was glowing in his mind and in his heart. The one window of the cell was open, the air was fresh and cool. "So the smell must have become stronger, if they opened the window," thought Alyosha. But even this thought of the breath of corruption, which had seemed to him so dreadful and disgraceful a few hours before, no longer made him feel miserable or indignant. He began quietly praying, but he soon felt that he was praying almost mechanically. Fragments of thought floated through his soul, flashed like stars and went out again at once, to be succeeded by others. But yet there was reigning in his soul a sense of the wholeness of things — something steadfast and comforting — and he was aware of it himself. Sometimes he began praying ardently, he longed to pour out his thankfulness and love. . . .

But having begun to pray, he passed suddenly to something else, and sank into thought, forgetting both the prayer and what had interrupted it.

He began listening to what Father Païssy was reading, but in his great exhaustion he gradually began to doze.

"*And the third day there was a marriage in Cana of Galilee,*" read Father Païssy. "*And the mother of Jesus was there: And both Jesus was called, and his disciples, to the marriage.*"

"Marriage? What's that . . . marriage . . ." whirled through Alyosha's mind. "There is happiness for her, too. . . . She has gone to the feast. . . . No, she has not taken the knife. . . . That was only a pathetic phrase. . . . Well . . . pathetic phrases should be forgiven, they must be. Pathetic phrases comfort the heart. . . . Without them, sorrow would be too heavy for men to bear. Rakitin turned into the lane. As long as Rakitin broods over his wrongs, he will always turn into the lane. . . . But the high road . . . The high road is wide and straight and bright as crystal, and the sun is at the end of it. . . . Ah! . . . What's being read?" . . .

"*And when they wanted wine, the mother of Jesus saith unto him, They have no wine . . .*" Alyosha heard.

"Ah, yes, I had missed that, and I didn't want to miss it, I love that passage: it's Cana of Galilee, the first miracle. . . . Ah, that miracle! Ah, that sweet miracle! It was not men's grief, but their joy that Christ visited, He worked His first miracle to help men's gladness. . . . 'He who loves men loves their joy, too.' . . . The deceased was always repeating that, it was one of his leading ideas. . . . 'There's no living without joy,' Mitya says. . . . Yes, Mitya. . . . 'Everything that is true and good is always full of forgiveness,' *he* used to say that, too." . . .

"*Jesus saith unto her, Woman, what have I to do with thee? Mine hour is not yet come.*"

"*His mother saith unto the servants, Whatsoever he saith unto you, do it.*" . . .

"Do it. . . . Joy, the joy of some poor, very poor, people. . . . Of course they were poor, since they hadn't wine enough even at a wedding. . . . Historians write that, in those days, the people living about the Lake of Genesareth were the poorest that can possibly be imagined . . . and another great heart, that other great being, His mother, knew that He had come not only to make His great terrible sacrifice. She knew that His heart was open even to the simple, artless merry-making of some obscure, simple people, who had warmly bidden Him to their poor wedding. 'Mine hour is not yet to come,' He said, with a soft smile (He must have smiled gently to her). And indeed was it to make wine abundant at poor weddings He had come down to earth? And yet He went and did as she asked Him. . . . Ah, he is reading again." . . .

"*Jesus saith unto them, Fill the waterpots with water. And they filled them up to the brim. And he saith unto them, Draw out now, and bear unto the governor of the feast. And they bare it.*

*When the ruler of the feast had tasted the water that was made wine, and knew not whence it was: (but the servants which drew the water knew;) the governor of the feast called the bridegroom,*

*And saith unto him, Every man at the beginning doth set forth good wine; and when men have well drunk, then that which is worse; but thou hast kept the good wine until now.*"

"But what's this, what's this? Why is the room growing wider? . . . Ah, yes. . . . It's the marriage, the wedding . . . yes, of course. Here are the guests, here are the young couple sitting, and the merry crowd and . . . Where is the wise governor of the feast? But who is this? Who? Again the walls are receding. . . . Who is getting up there from the great table? What! . . . He here, too? But he's in the coffin . . . but he's here, too. He has stood up, he sees me, he is coming here. . . . Lord! . . ."

Yes, he came up to him, to him, he, the little, thin old man, with tiny wrinkles on his face, joyful and laughing softly. There was no coffin now, and he was in the same dress as he had worn yesterday sitting with them, when the visitors had gathered about him. His face was open, his eyes were shining. How was this, then, he, too, had been called to the feast. He, too, at the marriage of Cana in Galilee. . . .

"Yes, my dear, I am called, too, called and bidden," he heard a soft voice saying over him. "Why have you hidden yourself here, out of sight? You come and join us, too."

It was his voice, the voice of Father Zosima. And it must be he, since he called him!

The elder raised Alyosha by the hand and he rose from his knees.

"We are making merry," the little, thin old man went on. "We are drinking the new wine, the wine of new, great joy; do you see how many guests there are? Here are the bride and bridegroom, here is the wise governor of the feast, he is tasting the new wine. Why do you wonder at me? I gave an onion to a beggar, so I, too, am here. And many here have given only an onion each — only one little onion. . . . What are all our deeds? And you, my gentle

278

THE MYSTERY OF EARTH

one, you, my meek boy, you, too, have known how to give a famished woman an onion to-day. Begin your work, dear one, begin it, gentle one! . . . Do you see our Sun, do you see Him?"

"I am afraid . . . I dare not look," whispered Alyosha.

"Do not fear Him. He is terrible in His majesty, awful in His grandeur, but infinitely merciful. He has made Himself like unto us out of love and rejoices with us. He is changing the water into wine that the joy of the guests may not be cut short. He is expecting new guests, He is calling new ones unceasingly for ever and ever. . . . There they are bringing new wine. Do you see they are bringing the vessels . . ."

Something glowed in Alyosha's heart, something filled it till it ached, tears of rapture gushed from his soul. . . .

He stretched out his hands, uttered a cry and awoke.

Again the coffin, the open window, and the soft, solemn, distinct reading of the Gospel. But Alyosha no longer listened to the reading. Strange, he had fallen asleep on his knees, but now he was on his feet, and suddenly, as though flung forward, with three firm rapid steps he went right up to the coffin. His shoulder brushed against Father Païssy without his noticing it. Father Païssy raised his eyes for an instant from his book, but looked away again at once, seeing that something strange had happened to the boy. Alyosha gazed for half a minute at the coffin, at the covered, motionless dead man that lay in the coffin, with the ikon on his breast and the peaked cap with the Orthodox cross on his head. He had only just been hearing his voice, and that voice was still ringing in his ears. He was listening, still expecting other words, but suddenly he turned sharply and went out of the cell.

He did not stop on the steps either, but went quickly down; his soul, overflowing with rapture, yearned for freedom, space, breadth. The vault of heaven, full of soft, shining stars, stretched vast and limitless above him. The Milky Way ran in a pale double stream from the zenith to the horizon. The fresh, motionless, still night enfolded the earth. The white towers and golden domes of the cathedral gleamed out against the sapphire sky. The gorgeous autumn flowers, in the beds round the house, were slumbering till morning. The silence of earth seemed to melt into the silence of the heavens. The mystery of earth touched the mystery of the stars. . . .

Alyosha stood, gazed, and suddenly fell upon the earth as though mowed down. He did not know why he embraced it. He could not have told why he longed so irresistibly to kiss it, to kiss it all. But he kissed it weeping, sobbing, and watering it with his tears, and vowed passionately to love it, to love it for ever and ever. "Water the earth with the tears of your joy and love those tears," echoed in his soul. What was he weeping over?

Oh! in his rapture he was weeping even over those stars, which were shining to him from the abyss of space, and "he was not ashamed of that ecstasy." There seemed to be threads from all those innumerable worlds of God, linking his soul to them, and it was trembling all over "in contact with other worlds." He longed to forgive every one and for everything, and to beg forgiveness. Oh, not for himself, but for all men, for all and for everything. "And others are praying for me, too," echoed again in his soul. But with every instant he felt clearly and, as it were, tangibly, that something firm and unshakable as that vault of heaven had entered into his soul. It was as though some idea had seized the sovereignty of his mind — and it was for all his life and for ever and ever. He had fallen on the earth a weak boy, but he rose up a resolute fighter, and he knew and felt it suddenly at the very moment of his ecstasy. And never,

never, all his life long, could Alyosha forget that minute.

"Some one visited my soul in that hour," he said afterwards, with firm faith in his words.

Three days later he left the monastery, which was in accordance, too, with the words of his elder, who had bidden him "sojourn in the world."

BOOK VIII

MITYA

## CHAPTER I

### KUZMA SAMSONOV

As for Dmitri, to whom Grushenka, flying away to a new life, had left her last greetings, bidding him remember the hour of her love for ever, he knew nothing of what had happened to her, and was at that moment also in a condition of feverish agitation and activity. For the last two days he had been in such an inconceivable state of mind that he

might easily have fallen ill with inflammation of the brain, as he said himself afterwards. Alyosha had not been able to find him the morning before, and Ivan had not succeeded in meeting him at the tavern on the same day. The people at his lodgings, by his orders, hid his traces.

He had spent those two days literally rushing in all directions, "struggling with his destiny and trying to save himself," as he expressed it himself afterwards, and for some hours he even made a dash out of the town on urgent business, terrible as it was to him to lose sight of Grushenka for a moment. All this became clear afterwards in detail, and was confirmed by documentary evidence; but for the present we will note only the most essential incidents of those two terrible days immediately preceding the awful catastrophe that broke so suddenly upon him.

Though Grushenka had, it is true, loved him for an hour, genuinely and sincerely, yet she tortured him sometimes cruelly and mercilessly. The worst of it was that he could never tell what she meant to do. To prevail upon her by force or kindness was also impossible: she would yield to nothing. She would only have become angry and turned away from him altogether, he knew that well already. He suspected, quite correctly, that she, too, was passing through an inward struggle, and was in a state of extraordinary indecision, that she was making up her mind to something, and was unable to determine upon it. And so, not without good reason, he divined, with a sinking heart, that at moments she must simply hate him and his passion. And so, perhaps, it was, but what was distressing Grushenka he did not understand. Properly speaking, for him, the whole tormenting question was expressed thus: "Either he, Mitya, or Fyodor Pavlovich."

Here, we must note, by the way, one established fact: he was firmly persuaded that Fyodor Pavlovich would offer, or perhaps had offered, Grushenka lawful wedlock, and did not for a moment believe that the old voluptuary hoped to get off by paying three thousand. Mitya had inferred this from his knowledge of Grushenka and her character. That was how it was that he could believe at times that all Grushenka's uneasiness rose from not knowing which of them to choose, which was most to her advantage.

Strange to say, during those days it never occurred to him to think of the approaching return of the "officer," that is, of the man who had been such a fatal influence in Grushenka's life, and whose arrival she was expecting with such emotion and dread. It is true that of late Grushenka had been very silent about it. Yet he was perfectly aware of a letter she had received a month ago from her former seducer, and had heard of it from her own lips. He partly knew, too, what the letter contained. In a moment of spite Grushenka had shown him that letter, but to her astonishment he attached hardly any consequence to it. It would be hard to say why this was so. Perhaps, weighed down by all the hideous horror of his struggle with his own father for this woman, he was incapable of imagining any danger more terrible, at any rate for the time. He simply did not believe in a suitor who suddenly turned up again after five years' absence, still less in his speedy arrival. Moreover, in the "officer's" first letter, which had been shown to Mitya, the possibility of his new rival's visit was very vaguely suggested. The letter was very vague, high-flown, and full of sentimentality. It must be noted that Grushenka had concealed from him the last lines of the letter, in which his return was spoken of more definitely. He had, besides, noticed at that moment, he remembered afterwards, a certain involuntary proud contempt for this missive from Siberia on Grushenka's face. Grushenka told him nothing of what had passed later between her and this rival; so that by degrees he had completely forgotten the officer's existence.

He felt that whatever might come later, whatever turn things might take, his final conflict with Fyodor Pavlovich was close upon him, and must be decided before anything else. With a sinking heart he was expecting every moment Grushenka's decision, always believing that it would come suddenly, on the impulse of the moment. All of a sudden she would say to him: "Take me, I'm yours for ever," and it would all be over. He would seize her and bear her away at once to the ends of the earth. Oh, then he would bear her away at once, as far, far away as possible; to the farthest end of Russia, if not of the earth, then he would marry her, and settle down with her incognito, so that no one would know anything about them, there, here, or anywhere. Then, oh, then, a new life would begin at once! Of this different, reformed, and "virtuous" life ("it must, it must be virtuous") he dreamed ecstatically and continually. He thirsted for this resurrection and renewal. The filthy morass, into which he had sunk of his own free will, was too revolting to him, and, like very many men in such cases, he put faith above all in change of place. If only it were not for these people, if only it were not for these circumstances, if only he could fly away from this accursed place — he would be altogether regenerated, would enter on a new path. That was what he believed in, and for that he was yearning.

But all this could only be in case of the first, the *happy* solution of the question. There was another possibility, a different and awful ending. Suddenly she might say to him: "Go away. I have just come to terms with Fyodor Pavlovich. I am going to marry him and don't want you" — and then . . . but then . . . But Mitya did not know what would happen

then. Up to the last hour he didn't know. That must be said to his credit. He had no definite intentions, had planned no crime. He was simply watching and spying in agony, while he prepared himself for the first, happy issue. He drove away any other idea, in fact. But here began a quite different anxiety, a new, extraneous, but yet fatal and insoluble difficulty presented itself.

If she were to say to him: "I'm yours; take me away," how could he take her away? Where had he the means, the money to do it? It was just at this time that all sources of revenue from Fyodor Pavlovich, doles which had gone on without interruption for so many years, ceased. Grushenka had money, of course, but with regard to this Mitya suddenly evinced extraordinary pride; he wanted to carry her away and begin the new life with her himself, at his own expense, not at hers. He could not conceive of taking her money, and the very idea caused him a pang of intense repulsion. I won't enlarge on this fact or analyze it here, but confine myself to remarking that this was the bent of his mind at the moment. All this may have arisen indirectly and unconsciously from the secret stings of his conscience for the money of Katerina Ivanovna that he had dishonestly appropriated. "I've behaved like a scoundrel before one of them, and I shall behave like a scoundrel again before the other directly," was his feeling then, as he explained afterwards: "and if Grushenka found out, she herself wouldn't care for such a scoundrel."

Where then was he to get the means, where was he to get the fateful money? Without it, all would be lost and nothing could be done, "and only because I hadn't the money. Oh, the shame of it!"

To anticipate things: he did, perhaps, know where to get the money, knew, perhaps, where it lay at that moment. I will say no more of this here, as it will all be clear later. But his chief trouble, I must explain, however obscurely, lay in the fact that to have that sum he knew of, to *have the right* to take it, he must first restore Katerina Ivanovna's three thousand — if not, "I'm a common pick-pocket, I'm a scoundrel, and I don't want to begin a new life as a scoundrel," Mitya decided. And so he made up his mind to move heaven and earth to return that three thousand to Katerina Ivanovna, and that *first of all*. The final stage of this decision, so to say, had been reached only during the last hours, that is, after his last interview with Alyosha, two days before, on the high road, on the evening when Grushenka had insulted Katerina Ivanovna, and Mitya, after hearing Alyosha's account of it, had admitted that he was a scoundrel, and told him to tell Katerina Ivanovna so, if it could be any comfort to her. After parting from his brother on that night, he had felt in his frenzy that it would be better "to murder and rob some one than fail to pay my debt to Katya. I'd rather every one thought me a robber and a murderer, I'd rather go to Siberia than that Katya should have the right to say that I deceived her and stole her money, and used her money to run away with Grushenka and begin a virtuous life! That I can't do!" So Mitya spoke, grinding his teeth, and he might well fancy at times that he would end by having inflammation of the brain. But meanwhile he went on struggling. . . .

Strange to say, though one would have supposed there was nothing left for him but despair — for what chance had he, with nothing in the world, to raise such a sum? — yet to the very end he persisted in hoping that he would get that three thousand, that the money would somehow come to him, of itself, as though it might drop from heaven. That is just how it is with people who, like Dmitri, have never had anything to do with money, except to squander what has come to them by inheritance without any effort of their own, and have no notion how money is obtained. A whirl of the most fantastic notions took possession of his brain immediately after he had parted with Alyosha two days before, and threw his thoughts into a tangle of confusion. This is how it was he pitched first on a perfectly wild enterprise. And perhaps to men of that kind in such circumstances the most impossible, fantastic schemes occur first, and seem most practical.

He suddenly determined to go to Samsonov, the merchant who was Grushenka's protector, and to propose a "scheme" to him, whereby he would obtain from him at once the whole of the sum required. Of the commercial value of his scheme he had not the slightest doubt, and was only uncertain how Samsonov would look upon his vagary, supposing he were to consider it from any but the commercial point of view. Though Mitya knew the merchant by sight, he was not acquainted with him and had never spoken a word to him. But for some unknown reason he had long entertained the conviction that the old reprobate, who was lying at death's door, would perhaps not at all object now to Grushenka's securing a respectable position, and marrying a "dependable" man. And he believed not only that he would not object, but that this was what he desired, and, if opportunity arose, that he would be ready to further matters. From some rumour, or perhaps from some stray word of Grushenka's, he had gathered further that the old man would perhaps prefer him to Fyodor Pavlovich for Grushenka.

Possibly many of the readers of my novel will feel that in reckoning on such assistance, and being ready to take his bride, so to speak, from the hands of her protector, Dmitri showed great coarseness and want of delicacy. I will only observe that Mitya looked upon Grushenka's past as something completely done with. He looked on that past with infinite pity and resolved with all the fervour of his passion that when once Grushenka told him she loved him and would marry him, it would mean the beginning of a new Grushenka and a new Dmitri, free from every vice. They would forgive one another and would begin their lives afresh. As for Kuzma Samsonov, Dmitri looked upon him as a man who had exercised a fateful influence in that remote past of Grushenka's, though she had never loved him, and who was now himself a thing of the past, completely done with, and, so to say, non-existent. Besides, Mitya hardly looked upon him as a man at all, for it was known to every one in the town that he was only the ruin of one, whose relations with Grushenka had changed their character and were now simply fatherly, and that this had been so for a long time.

In any case there was much simplicity on Mitya's part in all this, for, in spite of all his vices, he was a very simple-hearted man. It was an instance of this simplicity that Mitya was seriously persuaded that, being on the eve of his departure for the next world, old Kuzma must sincerely repent of his past relations with Grushenka, and that she had no more devoted friend and protector in the world than this, now harmless, old man.

After his conversation with Alyosha, at the cross-roads, he hardly slept all night, and, at ten o'clock next morning, he was at the house of Samsonov and telling the servant to announce him. It was a very spacious and gloomy old house, of two storeys, with a wing and outhouses. In the lower storey lived Samsonov's two married sons with their families, his aged sister, and one unmarried daughter. In the wing lived two of his clerks, one of whom also had a large family. Both the wing and the lower storey were overcrowded, but the old man kept the upper floor to himself, and would not even let the daughter live there with him, though she waited upon him, and in spite of her asthma was obliged at certain fixed hours, and at any time he might call her, to run upstairs to him from below.

This upper floor contained a number of large rooms kept purely for show, furnished in the old-fashioned merchant style, with long, monotonous rows of clumsy mahogany chairs along the walls, with crystal chandeliers in covers, and gloomy mirrors on the walls. All these rooms were entirely empty and unused, for the old man kept to one room, a small, remote bedroom, where he was waited upon by an old servant with a kerchief on her head, and by a lad, who used to sit on the bench in the passage. Owing to his swollen legs, the old man could hardly walk at all, and was only rarely lifted from his leather armchair, when the old woman, supporting him, led him up and down the room once or twice. He was morose and taciturn even with this old woman.

When he was informed of the arrival of the "captain," he at once refused to see him. But Mitya persisted and sent his name up again. Samsonov questioned the lad minutely: What he looked like? Whether he was drunk?

Was he rowdy? The answer he received was: that he was sober, but wouldn't go away. The old man again refused to see him. Then Mitya, who had foreseen this, and purposely brought pencil and paper with him, wrote clearly on the piece of paper the words: "On most important business closely concerning Agrafena Alexandrovna," and sent it up to the old man.

After thinking a little Samsonov told the lad to take the visitor to the drawing-room, and sent the old woman downstairs with a summons to his younger son to come upstairs to him at once. This younger son, a man over six foot and of exceptional physical strength, who was closely shaven and dressed in the European style, though his father still wore a kaftan and a beard, came at once and without comment. All the family trembled before the father. The old man had sent for this giant, not because he was afraid of the "captain" (he was by no means of a timorous temper), but in order to have a witness in case of any emergency. Supported by his son and the servant-lad, he waddled at last into the drawing-room. It may be assumed that he felt considerable curiosity. The drawing-room in which Mitya was awaiting him was a vast, dreary room that crushed the heart with ennui. It had a double row of windows, a gallery, marbled walls, and three immense chandeliers with crystal lustres in covers.

Mitya was sitting on a little chair at the entrance, awaiting his fate with nervous impatience. When the old man appeared at the opposite door, seventy feet away, Mitya jumped up at once, and with his long, military stride walked to meet him. Mitya was decently dressed, in a frock-coat, buttoned up, with a round hat and black gloves in his hands, just as he had been three days before at the

elder's, at the family meeting with his father and brothers. The old man waited for him, standing dignified and unbending, and Mitya felt at once that he had looked him through and through as he advanced. Mitya was greatly impressed, too, with Samsonov's immensely swollen face. His lower lip, which had always been thick, hung down now, looking like a bun. He bowed to his guest in dignified silence, motioned him to a low chair by the sofa, and, leaning on his son's arm, he began lowering himself on to the sofa opposite, groaning painfully, so that Mitya, seeing his painful exertions, immediately felt remorseful and sensitively conscious of his insignificance in the presence of the dignified person he had ventured to disturb.

"What is it you want of me, sir?" said the old man, deliberately, distinctly, severely, but courteously, when he was at last seated.

Mitya started, leapt up, but sat down again. Then he began at once speaking with loud, nervous haste, gesticulating, and in a positive frenzy. He was unmistakably a man driven into a corner, on the brink of ruin, catching at a straw, knowing that he was done for if this hope failed him.

Old Samsonov probably grasped all this in an instant, though his face remained cold and immovable as a statue's.

"Most honoured sir, Kuzma Kuzmich, you have no doubt heard, more than once, of my disputes with my father, Fyodor Pavlovich Karamazov, who robbed me of my inheritance from my mother . . . seeing the whole town is gossiping about it . . . for here every one's gossiping of what they shouldn't . . . and besides, it might have reached you through Grushenka . . . I beg your pardon, through Agrafena Alexandrovna . . . Agrafena Alexandrovna, the lady for whom I have the highest respect and esteem . . ."

So Mitya began, and broke down at the first sentence. We will not reproduce his speech word for word, but will only give a summary of it. Three months ago, he said, he had of express intention (Mitya purposely used these words instead of "intentionally") consulted a lawyer in the chief town of the province, "a distinguished lawyer, Kuzma Kuzmich, Pavel Pavlovich Korneplodov. You have perhaps heard of him? A man of vast intellect, the mind of a statesman . . . he knows you, too . . . spoke of you in the highest terms . . ." Mitya broke down again. But these breaks did not deter him. He leapt instantly over the gaps, and struggled on and on.

This Korneplodov, after questioning him minutely, and inspecting the documents he was able to bring him (Mitya alluded somewhat vaguely to these documents, and slurred over the subject with special haste) reported that they certainly might take proceedings concerning the village of Chermashnya, which ought, he said, to have come to him, Mitya, from his mother, and so checkmate the old villain, his father . . . "because every door was not closed and justice might still find a loophole." In fact, he might reckon on an additional sum of six or even seven thousand roubles from Fyodor Pavlovich, as Chermashnya was worth, at least, twenty-five thousand, he might say twenty-eight thousand, in fact, "thirty, thirty, Kuzma Kuzmich, and, would you believe it, I didn't get seventeen from that heartless man!" So he, Mitya, had thrown the business up, for the time, knowing nothing about the law, but on coming here was struck dumb by a cross-claim made upon him (here Mitya went adrift again, and again took a

flying leap forward), "so will not you, excellent and honoured Kuzma Kuzmich, be willing to take up all my claims against that unnatural monster, and pay me a sum down of only three thousand? . . . You see, you cannot, in any case, lose on it. On my honour, my honour, I swear that. Quite the contrary, you may make six or seven thousand instead of three. . . ." Above all, he wanted this concluded that very day.

"I'll do the business with you at a notary's, or whatever it is . . . in fact, I'm ready to do anything. . . . I'll hand over all the deeds . . . whatever you want, sign anything . . . and we could draw up the agreement at once . . . and if it were possible, if it were only possible, this very morning. . . . You could pay me that three thousand, for there isn't a capitalist in this town to compare with you, and so you would save me from . . . would save my poor head, in fact . . . for a good, I might say an honourable, action. . . . For I cherish the most honourable feelings for a certain person, whom you know well, and care for as a father. I would not have come, indeed, if it had not been as a father. And, indeed, it's a struggle of three in this business, for it's fate — that's a fearful thing, Kuzma Kuzmich! Realism, Kuzma Kuzmich, realism! And as you've dropped out long ago, it's a tug-of-war between two. I'm expressing it awkwardly, perhaps, but I'm not a literary man. You see, I'm on the one side, and that monster on the other. So you must choose. It's either I or the monster. It all lies in your hands — the fate of three lives, and the happiness of two. . . . Excuse me, I'm making a mess of it, but you understand. I see from your esteemed eyes that you understand . . . and if you don't understand, I've got to drown myself . . . there!"

OLD SAMSONOV

Mitya broke off his absurd speech with that "there!" and, jumping up from his seat, awaited the answer to his foolish proposal. At the last phrase he had suddenly become hopelessly aware that it had all fallen flat, above all, that he had been talking utter nonsense.

"How strange it is! On the way here it seemed all right, and now it's nothing but nonsense." The idea suddenly dawned on his despairing mind. All the while he had been talking, the old man sat motionless, watching him with an icy expression in his eyes. After keeping him for a moment in suspense, Kuzma Kuzmich pronounced at last, in the most positive and chilling tone:

"Excuse me, we don't handle such business."

Mitya suddenly felt his legs growing weak under him.

"What am I to do now, Kuzma Kuzmich?" he muttered, with a pale smile. "I suppose it's all up with me — what do you think?"

"Excuse me . . ."

Mitya remained standing, staring motionless. He suddenly noticed a movement in the old man's face. He started.

"You see, sir, business of that sort's not in our line," said the old man slowly. "There's the court, and the lawyers — it's a wretched affair. But if you like, there is a man here you might apply to."

"Good heavens! Who is it? You're my salvation, Kuzma Kuzmich," faltered Mitya.

"He doesn't live here, and he's not here just now. He is a peasant, he does business in timber. His name is Lyagavy. He's been haggling with Fyodor Pavlovich for the last year, over your copse at Chermashnya. They can't agree on the price, maybe you've heard? Now he's come back again and is staying with the priest at Ilyinskoe, about twelve versts from the Volovya station. He wrote to me, too, about the business of the copse asking my advice. Fyodor Pavlovich means to go and see him, himself. So if you were to get ahead of Fyodor Pavlovich and to make Lyagavy the offer you've made me, he might possibly . . ."

"A stroke of genius!" Mitya interrupted ecstatically. "He's the very man, it would just suit him. He's haggling with him for it, being asked too much, and here he would have all the documents entitling him to the property itself. Ha-ha-ha!"

And Mitya suddenly went off into his short, wooden laugh, startling Samsonov.

"How can I thank you, Kuzma Kuzmich?" cried Mitya effusively.

"Don't mention it," said Samsonov, inclining his head.

"But you don't know, you've saved me. Oh, it was a true presentiment brought me to you. . . . So now to this priest!"

"No need of thanks."

"I'll make haste and fly there. I'm afraid I've overtaxed your strength. I shall never forget it. It's a Russian says that, Kuzma Kuzmich, a R-r-russian!"

"To be sure!"

Mitya seized his hand to press it, but there was a malicious gleam in the old man's eye. Mitya drew back his hand, but at once blamed himself for his mistrustfulness.

"It's because he's tired," he thought.

"For her sake! For her sake, Kuzma Kuzmich! You understand that it's for her," he cried, his voice ringing through the room. He bowed, turned sharply round, and with the same long stride walked to the door without looking back. He was trembling with ecstasy.

"Everything was on the verge of ruin and

my guardian angel saved me," was the thought in his mind. And if such a businessman as Samsonov (a most worthy old man, and what dignity!) had suggested this course, then . . . then success was assured. He would fly off immediately. "I will be back before night, I shall be back at night and the thing is done. Could the old man have been laughing at me?" exclaimed Mitya, as he strode towards his lodging. He could, of course, imagine nothing, but that the advice was practical "from such a businessman" with an understanding of business, with an understanding of this Lyagavy (curious surname!) Or — the old man was laughing at him.

Alas! the second alternative was the correct one. Much later, after the catastrophe had occurred, old Samsonov himself confessed, laughing, that he had made a fool of the "captain." He was a cold, spiteful, and sarcastic man, liable to morbid antipathies. Whether the old man was worked on by the "captain's" excited face, or by the foolish conviction of the "rake and spendthrift," that he, Samsonov, could be taken in by such a cock-and-bull story as his scheme, or by jealousy over Grushenka, in whose name this "scapegrace" had rushed in on him with such a tale to get money — I can't tell. But, at the instant when Mitya stood before him, feeling his legs grow weak under him, and frantically exclaiming that he was ruined, at that moment the old man looked at him with intense spite, and resolved to make a laughing-stock of him. When Mitya had gone, Kuzma Kuzmich, white with rage, turned to his son and bade him see to it that that beggar never be admitted again, and never be allowed even into the yard, or else he'd . . .

He did not utter his threat. But even his son,

who often saw him enraged, trembled with fear. For a whole hour afterwards, the old man was shaking with anger, and by evening he was worse, and sent for the doctor.

## CHAPTER II

### LYAGAVY

So he must drive at full speed, and he had not the money for horses. He had forty copecks, and that was all, all that was left after so many years of prosperity! But he had at home an old silver watch which had long since ceased to go. He snatched it up and carried it to a Jewish watchmaker who had a shop in the market-place. The Jew gave him six roubles for it.

"And I didn't expect that," cried Mitya, ecstatically. (He was still in a state of ecstasy.) He seized his six roubles and ran home. At home he borrowed three roubles from the people of the house, who loved him so much that they were pleased to give it him, though it was all they had. Mitya in his excitement told them on the spot that his fate would be decided that day, and he described, in desperate haste, the whole scheme he had put before Samsonov, the latter's decision, his own hopes for the future, and so on. These people had been told many of their lodger's secrets before, and so looked upon him as a gentleman who was not at all proud, and almost one of themselves. Having thus collected nine roubles Mitya sent for posting-horses to take him to the Volovya station. This was how the fact came to be remembered and established that "at midday, on the day before the event, Mitya had not a farthing, and that he had sold his watch to get money and had borrowed three roubles from his landlord, all in the presence of witnesses."

I note this fact, later on it will be apparent why I do so.

Though he was radiant with the joyful anticipation that he would at last solve all his difficulties, yet, as he drew near Volovya station, he trembled at the thought of what Grushenka might be doing in his absence. What if she made up her mind to-day to go to Fyodor Pavlovich? This was why he had gone off without telling her and why he left orders with his landlady not to let out where he had gone, if any one came to inquire for him.

"I must, I must get back to-night," he repeated, as he was jolted along in the cart, "and I dare say I shall have to bring this Lyagavy back here . . . to draw up the deed." So mused Mitya, with a throbbing heart, but alas! his dreams were not fated to be carried out.

To begin with, he was late, taking a short cut from Volovya station which turned out to be eighteen versts instead of twelve. Secondly, he did not find the Ilyinskoe priest at home; he had gone off to a neighbouring village. While Mitya, setting off there with the same exhausted horses, was looking for him, it was almost dark.

The priest, a shy and amiable-looking little man, informed him at once that, though Lyagavy had been staying with him at first, he was now at Suhoy Posyolok, that he was staying the night in the forester's cottage, as he was buying timber there, too. At Mitya's urgent request that he would take him to Lyagavy at once, and by so doing "save him, so to speak," the priest agreed, after some demur, to conduct him to Suhoy Posyolok; his curiosity was obviously aroused. But, unluckily, he advised their going on foot, as it would not be "much over" a verst. Mitya, of course, agreed, and marched off with his yard-long strides, so that

the poor priest almost ran after him. He was a very cautious man, though not old.

Mitya at once began talking to him, too, of his plans, nervously and excitedly asking advice in regard to Lyagavy, and talked all the way. The priest listened attentively, but gave little advice. He turned off Mitya's questions with: "I don't know. Ah, I can't say. How can I tell?" and so on. When Mitya began to speak of his quarrel with his father over his inheritance, the priest was positively alarmed, as he was in some way dependent on Fyodor Pavlovich. He inquired, however, with surprise, why he called the peasant-trader Gorstkin, Lyagavy, and obligingly explained to Mitya that, though the man's name really was Lyagavy, he was never called so, as he would be grievously offended at the name, and that he must be sure to call him Gorstkin, "or you'll do nothing with him; he won't even listen to you," said the priest in conclusion.

Mitya was somewhat surprised for a moment, and explained that that was what Samsonov had called him. On hearing this fact, the priest immediately dropped the subject, though he would have done well to have expressed to Dmitri Fyodorovich his conjecture: wasn't there something wrong about Samsonov having sent him to that peasant, and calling him Lyagavy, and wasn't Samsonov trying to put him into a ridiculous position? But Mitya had no time to pause over such trifles. He hurried, striding along, and only when he reached Suhoy Posyolok he realised that they had walked not one verst, nor one and a half, but at least three. This annoyed him, but he controlled himself.

They went into the hut. The forester, who was the priest's acquaintance, occupied one half of the hut, and Gorstkin was lodging in the other, the better half on the other side of the passage. They went into that room and lighted a tallow candle. The hut was extremely overheated. On the table there was a samovar that had gone out, a tray with cups, an empty rum bottle, a bottle of vodka partly full, and some half eaten crusts of wheaten bread. The occupant himself lay stretched at full length on the bench, with his coat crushed up under his head for a pillow, snoring heavily. Mitya stood in perplexity.

"Of course I must wake him. My business is too important. I've come in such haste. I'm in a hurry to get back today," he said in great agitation. But the priest and the forester stood in silence, not giving their opinion. Mitya went up and began trying to wake him himself; he tried vigorously, but the sleeper did not wake.

"He's drunk," Mitya decided. "Good Lord! What am I to do? What am I to do?" And, terribly impatient, he began pulling him by the arms, by the legs, shaking his head, lifting him up and making him sit on the bench. Yet, after prolonged exertions, he could only succeed in getting the drunken man to utter absurd grunts, and violent, but inarticulate oaths.

"No, you'd better wait a little," the priest pronounced at last, "for he's obviously not in a fit state."

"He's been drinking the whole day," the forester chimed in.

"Good heavens!" cried Mitya. "If only you knew how important it is to me and how desperate I am!"

"No, you'd better wait till morning," the priest repeated.

"Till morning? Mercy! that's impossible!" And in his despair he was on the point of renewing his attempt to rouse the drunkard, but stopped short at once, realising the uselessness of his efforts. The priest said nothing, the sleepy forester looked gloomy.

"What terrible tragedies life contrives for people," said Mitya, in complete despair. The perspiration was streaming down his face. The priest seized the moment to put before him, very reasonably, that, even if he succeeded in wakening the man, he would still be drunk and incapable of conversation. "And your business is important," he said, "so you'd certainly better put it off till morning." With a gesture of despair Mitya agreed.

"Father, I will stay here with a light, and seize the favourable moment. As soon as he wakes I'll begin. I'll pay you for the light," he said to the forester, "for the night's lodging, too; you'll remember Dmitri Karamazov. Only, father, I don't know what we're to do with you. Where will you sleep?"

"No, I'm going home. I'll take his horse and get home," he said, indicating the forester. "And now I'll say good-bye. I wish you all success."

So it was settled. The priest rode off on the forester's horse, delighted to escape, though he shook his head uneasily, wondering whether he ought not, next day, inform his benefactor, Fyodor Pavlovich, of this curious incident, "or he may in an unlucky hour hear of it, be angry, and withdraw his favour."

The forester, scratching himself, went back to his room without a word, and Mitya sat on the bench to "seize the favourable moment," as he expressed it. Profound dejection clung to his soul like a heavy mist. A profound, intense dejection! He sat thinking, but could reach no conclusion. The candle burnt dimly, a cricket chirped; it became insufferably close in the overheated room. He suddenly pictured the garden, the path behind the garden, the door of his father's house mysteriously opening and Grushenka running in. He leapt up from the bench.

"It's a tragedy!" he said, grinding his teeth. Mechanically he went up to the sleeping man and looked in his face. He was a lean, middle-aged peasant, with a very long face, flaxen curls, and a long, thin, reddish beard, wearing a cotton shirt and a black waistcoat, from the pocket of which peeped the chain of a silver watch. Mitya looked at his face with intense hatred, and for some unknown reason his curly hair particularly irritated him.

What was insufferably humiliating was, that, after leaving things of such importance and making such sacrifices, he, Mitya, utterly worn out, should with business of such urgency be standing over this dolt on whom his whole fate depended, while he snored as though there were nothing the matter, as though he'd dropped from another planet.

"Oh, the irony of fate!" cried Mitya, and, quite losing his head, he fell again to rousing the tipsy peasant. He tried to rouse him with a sort of ferocity, pulled at him, pushed him, even beat him; but after five minutes of vain exertions, he returned to his bench in helpless despair, and sat down.

"Stupid! Stupid!" cried Mitya. "And how dishonourable it all is!" something made him add. His head began to ache horribly. "Should he fling it up and go away altogether?" he wondered. "No, wait till to-morrow now. I'll stay on purpose. What else did I come for? Besides, I've no means of going. How am I to get away from here now? Oh, the idiocy of it!"

But his head ached more and more. He sat without moving, dozed off and suddenly fell asleep as he sat. He seemed to have slept for two hours or more. He was waked up by his head aching so unbearably that he could have screamed. There was a hammering in his temples, and the top of his head ached. It was a long time before he could wake up fully and understand what had happened to him.

At last he realised that the room was full of charcoal fumes from the stove, and that he might die of suffocation. And the drunken peasant still lay snoring. The candle guttered and was about to go out. Mitya cried out, and ran staggering across the passage into the forester's room. The forester waked up at once, but hearing that the other room was full of fumes, to Mitya's surprise and annoyance, accepted the fact with strange unconcern, though he did go to see to it.

"But he's dead, he's dead! and . . . what shall I do then?" cried Mitya frantically.

They threw open the doors, opened a window and the chimney. Mitya brought a pail of water from the passage. First he wetted his own head, then, finding a rag of some sort, dipped it into the water, and put it on Lyagavy's head. The forester still treated the matter contemptuously, and when he opened the window said grumpily:

"It'll be all right, now."

He went back to sleep, leaving Mitya a lighted lantern. Mitya fussed about the drunken peasant for half an hour, wetting his head, and gravely resolved not to sleep all night. But he was so worn out that when he sat down for a moment to take breath, he closed his eyes, unconsciously stretched himself full length on the bench and slept like the dead.

It was dreadfully late when he waked. It

was somewhere about nine o'clock. The sun was shining brightly in the two little windows of the hut. The curly-headed peasant was sitting on the bench and had his coat on. He had another samovar and another bottle in front of him. Yesterday's bottle had already been finished, and the new one was more than half empty. Mitya jumped up and saw at once that the cursed peasant was drunk again, hopelessly and incurably. He stared at him for a moment with bulging eyes. The peasant was silently and slyly watching him, with insulting composure, and even a sort of contemptuous condescension, so Mitya fancied. He rushed up to him. "Excuse me, you see. . . . I . . . you've most likely heard from the forester here in the hut. I'm Lieutenant Dmitri Karamazov, the son of the old Karamazov whose copse you are buying."

"You're lying!" said the peasant, calmly and deliberately.

"I'm lying? You know Fyodor Pavlovich?"

"I don't know any of your Fyodor Pavloviches," said the peasant, speaking thickly.

"You're bargaining with him over the copse, the copse. Do wake up, and come to. Father Pavel of Ilyinskoe brought me here. You wrote to Samsonov, and he has sent me to you," Mitya gasped breathlessly.

"You're l — lying!" Lyagavy blurted out again. Mitya's legs went cold.

"For mercy's sake! It isn't a joke! You're drunk, perhaps. Yet you can speak and understand . . . or else . . . I understand nothing!"

"You're a house-painter!"

"For mercy's sake! I'm Karamazov, Dmitri Karamazov. I have an offer to make you, an advantageous offer . . . very advantageous offer, concerning the copse!"

The peasant stroked his beard importantly. "No, you've contracted for the job and turned out a scamp. You're a scoundrel!"

"I assure you you're mistaken," cried Mitya, wringing his hands in despair. The peasant still stroked his beard, and suddenly screwed up his eyes cunningly.

"No, you show me this: you tell me the law that allows roguery. D'you hear? You're a scoundrel! Do you understand that?"

Mitya stepped back gloomily, and suddenly "something seemed to hit him on the head," as he said afterwards. In an instant a light seemed to dawn in his mind, "a light was kindled and I grasped it all." He stood, stupefied, wondering how he, after all a man of intelligence, could have yielded to such folly, have been led into such an adventure, and have kept it up for almost twenty-four hours, fussing round this Lyagavy, wetting his head.

"Why, the man's drunk, dead drunk, and he'll go on drinking now for a week; what's the use of waiting here? And what if Samsonov sent me here on purpose? What if she . . . ? Oh, God, what have I done?"

The peasant sat watching him and grinning. Another time Mitya might have killed the fool in a fury, but now he felt as weak as a child. He went quietly to the bench, took up his overcoat, put it on without a word, and went out of the hut. He did not find the forester in the next room; there was no one there. He took fifty copecks in small change out of his pocket and put them on the table for his night's lodging, the candle, and the trouble he had given. Coming out of the hut he saw nothing but forest all round. He walked at hazard, not knowing which way to turn out of the hut, to the right or to the left. Hurrying there the evening before with the priest, he had not noticed the road. He had no revengeful feeling in his heart for anybody, not even for Samsonov. He strode along a narrow forest path, aimless, dazed, without heeding where he was going. A child could have knocked him down, so weak was he in body and soul. He got out of the forest somehow, however, and a vista of fields, bare after the harvest, stretched as far as the eye could see.

"What despair! What death all round!" he repeated, striding on and on.

He was saved by meeting an old merchant who was being driven across country in a hired trap. When he overtook him, Mitya asked the way, and it turned out that the old merchant, too, was going to Volovya. After some discussion Mitya got into the trap. Three hours later they arrived. At Volovya, Mitya at once ordered posting-horses to drive to the town, and suddenly realised that he was appallingly hungry. While the horses were being harnessed, an omelette was prepared for him. He ate it all in an instant, ate a huge hunk of bread, ate a sausage, and swallowed three glasses of vodka. After eating, his spirits and his heart grew lighter. He flew towards the town, urged on the driver, and suddenly made a new and "unalterable" plan to procure that "accursed money" before evening. "And to think, only to think that a man's life should be ruined for the sake of that paltry three thousand!" he cried, contemptuously. "I'll settle it to-day." And if it had not been for the thought of Grushenka and of what might have happened to her, which never left him, he would perhaps have become quite cheerful again. . . . But the thought of her was stabbing him to the heart every moment, like a sharp knife. At last they arrived, and Mitya at once ran to Grushenka.

## CHAPTER III
### GOLD-MINES

THIS was the visit of Mitya of which Grushenka had spoken to Rakitin with such fear. She was just then expecting the "message," and was much relieved that Mitya had not been to see her that day or the day before. She hoped that, please God, he wouldn't come till she had gone, and he suddenly burst in on her. The rest we know already. To get him off her hands she suggested at once that he should walk with her to Samsonov's, where she said she absolutely must go "to count money," and when Mitya accompanied her at once, she said good-bye to him at the gate, making him promise to come at twelve o'clock to take her home again. Mitya, too, was delighted at this arrangement. If she was sitting at Samsonov's she could not be going to Fyodor Pavlovich's, "if only she's not lying," he added at once. But he thought she was not lying from what he saw.

He was that sort of jealous man who, in the absence of the beloved woman, at once invents all sorts of awful fancies of what may be happening to her, and how she may be betraying him, but, when shaken, heartbroken, convinced of her faithlessness, he runs back to her, at the first glance at her face, her gay, laughing, affectionate face, he revives at once, lays aside all suspicion and with joyful shame upbraids himself for his jealousy.

After leaving Grushenka at the gate he rushed home. Oh, he had so much still to do that night! But a load had been lifted from his heart, anyway.

"Now I must only make haste and find out from Smerdyakov whether anything happened there last night, whether, by any chance, she went to Fyodor Pavlovich; ough!" floated through his mind.

Before he had time to reach his lodging, jealousy had surged up again in his restless heart.

Jealousy! "Othello is not jealous, he is trustful," observed Pushkin. And that remark alone is enough to show the deep insight of our great poet. Othello's soul is shattered and his whole outlook clouded simply because *his ideal is destroyed*. But Othello will not hide, spy, peep. He is trustful. On the contrary, he has to be led up, pushed on, excited with great difficulty before he can entertain the idea of deceit. The truly jealous man is not like that. It is impossible to picture to oneself the shame and moral degradation to which the jealous man can descend without a qualm of conscience. And yet it's not as though the jealous were all vulgar and base souls. On the contrary, a man of lofty feelings, whose love is pure and full of self-sacrifice, may yet hide under tables, bribe the vilest people, and be familiar with the lowest ignominy of spying and eavesdropping.

Othello was incapable of reconciling himself to faithlessness — not incapable of forgiving it, but of reconciling himself to it — though his soul was as innocent and free from malice as a babe's. It is not so with the really jealous man. It is hard to imagine what some jealous men can get accustomed and reconciled to, and what they can forgive! The jealous are the readiest of all to forgive, and all women know it. The jealous man can forgive extraordinarily quickly (though, of course, after a violent scene), and he is able to forgive infidelity almost conclusively proved, the very kisses and embraces he has seen, if only he can somehow be convinced that it has all been "for the last time," and that his rival will vanish from that day forward, will depart to the ends of the earth, or that he himself will carry her away somewhere, where that dreaded rival will not get near her. Of course the reconciliation is only for an hour. For, even if the rival did disappear next day, he would invent another one and would be jealous of him. And one might wonder what there was in a love that had to be so watched over, what a love could be worth that needed such strenuous guarding. But that the jealous will never understand. And yet among them are men of noble hearts. It is remarkable, too, that those very men of noble hearts, standing hidden in some cupboard, listening and spying, never feel the stings of conscience at that moment, anyway, though they understand clearly enough with their "noble hearts" the shameful depths to which they have voluntarily sunk.

At the sight of Grushenka, Mitya's jealousy vanished, and for an instant he became trustful and generous, and positively despised himself for his evil feelings. But that only meant that, in his love for that woman, there was an element of something far higher than he himself imagined, that it was not only a sensual passion, not only the "curve of her body," of which he had talked to Alyosha. But, as soon as Grushenka vanished, Mitya began to suspect her of all the low cunning of faithlessness, and he felt no sting of conscience at it.

And so jealousy surged up in him again. He had, in any case, to make haste. The first thing to be done was to get hold of at least a small, temporary loan of money. The nine roubles had almost all gone on his expedition. And, as we all know, one can't take a step without money. But he had thought over in the carriage where he could get a loan. He had a brace

VIII: MITYA

of fine duelling pistols in a case, which he had not pawned till then because he prized them above all his possessions.

In the "Metropolis" tavern he had some time since made acquaintance with a young official and had learnt that this very opulent bachelor was passionately fond of weapons. He used to buy pistols, revolvers, daggers, hang them on his wall and show them to acquaintances. He prided himself on them, and was quite a specialist on the mechanism of the revolver. Mitya, without stopping to think, went straight to him, and offered to pawn his pistols to him for ten roubles. The official, delighted, began trying to persuade him to sell them outright. But Mitya would not consent, so the young man gave him ten roubles, protesting that nothing would induce him to take interest. They parted friends.

Mitya was in haste; he rushed towards Fyodor Pavlovich's by the back way, to his arbour, to get hold of Smerdyakov as soon as possible. In this way the fact was established that three or four hours before a certain event, of which I shall speak later on, Mitya had not a farthing, and pawned for ten roubles a possession he valued, though, three hours later, he was in possession of thousands. . . . But I am anticipating. From Marya Kondratyevna (the woman living near Fyodor Pavlovich's) he learnt the very disturbing fact of Smerdyakov's illness. He heard the story of his fall in the cellar, his fit, the doctor's visit, Fyodor Pavlovich's anxiety; he heard with interest, too, that his brother Ivan had set off that morning for Moscow.

"Then he must have driven through Volovya before me," thought Dmitri, but he was terribly distressed about Smerdyakov. "What will happen now? Who'll keep watch for me? Who'll bring me word?" he thought. He began greedily questioning the women whether they had seen anything the evening before. They quite understood what he was trying to find out, and completely reassured him. No one had been there. Ivan Fyodorovich had spent the night there; everything had been in perfect order. Mitya grew thoughtful. He would certainly have to keep watch to-night, but where? Here or at Samsonov's gate? He decided that he must be on the look-out both here and there, and meanwhile . . . meanwhile . . . The difficulty was that he had to carry out the new plan that he had made on the journey back. He was sure of its success, but he must not delay acting upon it. Mitya resolved to sacrifice an hour to it: "In an hour I shall know everything, I shall settle everything, and then, then, first of all to Samsonov's. I'll inquire whether Grushenka's there and instantly be back here again, stay till eleven, and then to Samsonov's again to bring her home." This was what he decided.

He flew home, washed, combed his hair, brushed his clothes, dressed, and went to Madame Hohlakov's. Alas! he had built his hopes on her. He had resolved to borrow three thousand from that lady. And what was more, he felt suddenly convinced that she would not refuse to lend it to him. It may be wondered why, if he felt so certain, he had not gone to her at first, one of his own sort, so to speak, instead of to Samsonov, a man he did not know, who was not of his own class, and to whom he hardly knew how to speak.

But the fact was that he had never known Madame Hohlakov well, and had seen nothing of her for the last month, and that he knew she could not endure him. She had detested him from the first because he was engaged to

295

Katerina Ivanovna, while she had, for some reason, suddenly conceived the desire that Katerina Ivanovna should throw him over, and marry the "charming, chivalrously refined Ivan, who had such excellent manners." Mitya's manners she detested. Mitya positively laughed at her, and had once said about her that she was just as lively and at her ease as she was uncultivated. But that morning in the carriage a brilliant idea had struck him: "If she is so anxious I should not marry Katerina Ivanovna" (and he knew she was positively hysterical upon the subject) "why should she refuse me now that three thousand, just to enable me to leave Katya and get away from her for ever. These spoilt fine ladies, if they set their hearts on anything, will spare no expense to satisfy their caprice. Besides, she's so rich," Mitya argued.

As for his "plan," it was just the same as before; it consisted of the offer of his rights to Chermashnya — but not with a commercial object, as it had been with Samsonov, not trying to allure the lady with the possibility of making a profit of six or seven thousand — but simply as a security for the debt. As he worked out this new idea, Mitya was enchanted with it, but so it always was with him in all his undertakings, in all his sudden decisions. He gave himself up to every new idea with passion. Yet, when he mounted the steps of Madame Hohlakov's house he felt a shiver of fear run down his spine. At that moment he saw fully, as a mathematical certainty, that this was his last hope, that if this broke down, nothing else was left him in the world but to "rob and murder some one for the three thousand." It was half-past seven when he rang the bell.

At first fortune seemed to smile upon him.

As soon as he was announced he was received with extraordinary rapidity. "As though she were waiting for me," thought Mitya, and as soon as he had been led to the drawing-room, the lady of the house herself ran in, and declared at once that she was expecting him.

"I was expecting you! I was expecting you! Though I'd no reason to suppose you would come to see me, as you will admit yourself. Yet, I did expect you. You may marvel at my instinct, Dmitri Fyodorovich, but I was convinced all the morning that you would come."

"That is certainly wonderful, madam," observed Mitya, sitting down awkwardly, "but I have come to you on a matter of great importance. . . . On a matter of supreme importance for me that is, madam . . . for me alone . . . and I hasten . . ."

"I know you've come on most important business, Dmitri Fyodorovich; it's not a case of presentiment, no reactionary harking back to the miraculous (have you heard about Father Zosima?). This is a case of mathematics: you couldn't help coming, after all that has passed with Katerina Ivanovna; you couldn't, you couldn't, that's a mathematical certainty."

"The realism of actual life, madam, that's what it is. But allow me to explain . . ."

"Realism indeed, Dmitri Fyodorovich. I'm all for realism now. I've had a lesson as regards miracles. You've heard that Father Zosima is dead?"

"No, madam, it's the first time I've heard of it." Mitya was a little surprised. The image of Alyosha rose to his mind.

"Last night, and only imagine . . ."

"Madam," said Mitya, "I can imagine nothing except that I'm in a desperate position, and that if you don't help me, everything will go to the dogs, and I first of all. Excuse me for the triviality of the expression, but I'm in a fever . . ."

"I know, I know that you're in a fever. You could hardly fail to be, and whatever you may say to me, I know beforehand. I have long been thinking over your destiny, Dmitri Fyodorovich, I am watching over it and studying it. . . . Oh, believe me, I'm an experienced doctor of the soul, Dmitri Fyodorovich."

"Madam, if you are an experienced doctor, I'm certainly an experienced patient," said Mitya, with an effort to be polite, "and I feel that if you are watching over my destiny in this way, you will come to my help in my ruin, and so allow me at last to explain to you the plan with which I have ventured to come to you . . . and what I am hoping of you. . . . I have come, madam . . ."

"Don't explain it. It's of secondary importance. But as for help, you're not the first I have helped, Dmitri Fyodorovich. You have most likely heard of my cousin, Madame Belmesov. Her husband was perishing, was 'going to the dogs,' as you characteristically express it, Dmitri Fyodorovich. I recommended him to take to horse-breeding, and now he's flourishing. Have you any idea of horse-breeding, Dmitri Fyodorovich?"

"Not the faintest, madam; ah, madam, not the faintest!" cried Mitya, in nervous impatience, positively starting from his seat. "I simply implore you, madam, to listen to me. Only give me two minutes of free speech that I may just explain everything to you, the whole plan with which I have come. Besides I am short of time. I'm in a fearful hurry," Mitya cried hysterically, feeling that she was just going to begin talking again, and hoping to cut her short. "I have come in despair . . .

in the last gasp of despair, to beg you to lend me the sum of three thousand, a loan, but on safe, most safe security, madam, with the surest guarantees! Only allow me to explain . . ."

"You must tell me all that afterwards, afterwards!" Madame Hohlakov in her turn motioned him to be silent, "and whatever you may tell me, I know it all beforehand; I've told you so already. You ask for a certain sum, you need three thousand, but I can give you more, immeasurably more, I will save you, Dmitri Fyodorovich, but you must listen to me."

Mitya started from his seat again.

"Madam, will you really be so good!" he cried, with strong feeling. "Good God, you've saved me! You have saved a man from a violent death, from a bullet. . . . My eternal gratitude . . ."

"I will give you more, infinitely more than three thousand!" cried Madame Hohlakov, looking with a radiant smile at Mitya's ecstasy.

"Infinitely? But I don't need so much. I only need that fatal three thousand, and on my part I can give security for that sum with infinite gratitude, and I propose a plan which . . ."

"Enough, Dmitri Fyodorovich, it's said and done." Madame Hohlakov cut him short, with the modest triumph of a benefactress: "I have promised to save you, and I will save you. I will save you as I did Belmesov. What do you think of gold-mines, Dmitri Fyodorovich?"

"Gold-mines, madam? I have never thought anything about them."

"But I have thought of them for you. Thought of them over and over again. I have been watching you for the last month. I've watched you a hundred times as you've walked past, saying to myself: that's a man of energy who ought to be at the gold-mines. I've studied your gait and come to the conclusion: that's a man who would find gold."

"From my gait, madam?" said Mitya, smiling.

"Yes, from your gait. You surely don't deny that character can be told from the gait, Dmitri Fyodorovich? The natural sciences support the idea. Oh, I'm a realist now. After all this business with Father Zosima, which has so upset me, from this very day I'm a perfect realist and I want to devote myself to practical activities. I'm cured. 'Enough!' as Turgenev says."

"But, madam, the three thousand you so generously promised to lend me . . ."

"It is yours, Dmitri Fyodorovich," Madame Hohlakov cut in at once. "The money is as good as in your pocket, not three thousand, but three million, Dmitri Fyodorovich, in less than no time. I'll make you a present of the idea: you shall find gold-mines, make millions, return and become a leading citizen, and wake us up and lead us to better things. Are we to leave it all to the Jews? You will erect buildings and start enterprises of all sorts. You will help the poor, and they will bless you. This is the age of railways, Dmitri Fyodorovich. You'll become famous and indispensable to the Department of Finance, which is so badly off at present. The depreciation of the rouble keeps me awake at night, Dmitri Fyodorovich; people don't know that side of me . . ."

"Madam, madam!" Dmitri interrupted with an uneasy presentiment. "I shall indeed, perhaps, follow your advice, your wise advice, madam. . . . I shall perhaps set off . . . to the gold-mines. . . . I'll come and see you again about it . . . many times, indeed . . . but now, that three thousand you so generously . . . oh, that would set me free, and if you could to-day . . . you see, I haven't a minute, a minute to lose to-day . . ."

"Enough, Dmitri Fyodorovich, enough!" Madame Hohlakov interrupted emphatically. "The question is, will you go to the gold-mines or not; have you quite made up your mind? Answer yes or no."

"I will go, madam, afterwards. . . . I'll go where you like . . . but now . . ."

"Wait!" cried Madame Hohlakov. And jumping up and running to a handsome bureau with numerous little drawers, she began pulling out one drawer after another, looking for something with desperate haste.

"The three thousand," thought Mitya, his heart almost stopping, "and at the instant . . . without any papers or formalities . . . that's doing things in gentlemanly style! She's a splendid woman, if only she didn't talk so much!"

"Here!" cried Madame Hohlakov, running back joyfully to Mitya, "here is what I was looking for!"

It was a tiny silver ikon on a cord, such as is sometimes worn next the skin with a cross.

"This is from Kiev, Dmitri Fyodorovich," she went on reverently, "from the relics of Varvara, the Great Martyr. Let me put it on your neck myself, and with it dedicate you to a new life, to a new career."

And she actually put the cord around his neck, and began arranging it. In extreme embarrassment, Mitya bent down and helped her, and at last he got it under his neck-tie and collar and next to his chest.

"Now you can set off," Madame Hohlakov pronounced, sitting down triumphantly in her place again.

"Madam, I am so touched. I don't know how to thank you, indeed . . . for such kindness, but . . . If only you knew how precious time is to me. . . . That sum of money, for which I shall be indebted to your generosity. . . . Oh, madam, since you are so kind, so touchingly generous to me," Mitya exclaimed impulsively, "then let me reveal to you . . . though, of course, you've known it a long time . . . that I love somebody here. . . . I have been false to Katya . . . Katerina Ivanovna I should say. . . . Oh, I've behaved inhumanly, dishonourably to her, but I fell in love here with another woman . . . a woman whom you, madam, perhaps, despise, for you know everything already, but whom I cannot leave on any account, and therefore that three thousand now . . ."

"Leave everything, Dmitri Fyodorovich," Madame Hohlakov interrupted in the most decisive tone. "Leave everything, especially women. Gold-mines are your goal, and there's no place for women there. Afterwards, when you come back rich and famous, you will find the companion of your heart in the highest society. That will be a modern girl, with education and without prejudices. By that time the budding woman question will have ripened, and the new woman will have appeared."

"Madam, that's not the point, not at all. . . ." Mitya clasped his hands in entreaty.

"Yes, it is, Dmitri Fyodorovich, just what you need; the very thing you're yearning for, though you don't realise it yourself. I am not at all opposed to the present woman's movement, Dmitri Fyodorovich. The development of woman, and even the political emancipation of woman in the near future — that's my ideal. I've a daughter myself, Dmitri Fyodorovich, people don't know that side of me. I wrote a letter to the author, Shchedrin, on that subject. He has taught me so much, so much about the vocation of woman. So last year I sent him an anonymous letter of two lines: 'I kiss and embrace you, my author, for the modern woman. Persevere.' And I signed myself, 'a Mother.' I thought of signing myself 'a contemporary Mother,' and hesitated, but I stuck to the simple 'Mother'; there's more moral beauty in that, Dmitri Fyodorovich. And the word 'contemporary' might have reminded him of 'The Contemporary' — a painful recollection owing to the censorship. . . . Good heavens, what is the matter with you?"

"Madam!" cried Mitya, jumping up at last, clasping his hands before her in helpless entreaty. "You will make me weep if you delay what you have so generously . . ."

"Oh, do weep, Dmitri Fyodorovich, do weep! That's a noble feeling . . . such a path lies open before you! Tears will ease your heart, and later on you will return rejoicing. You will hasten to me from Siberia on purpose to share your joy with me . . ."

"But allow me, too!" Mitya shouted suddenly. "For the last time I entreat you, tell me, can I have the sum you promised me to-day, if not, when may I come for it?"

"What sum, Dmitri Fyodorovich?"

"The three thousand you promised me . . . that you so generously . . ."

"Three thousand? Roubles? Oh, no, I haven't got three thousand," Madame Hohlakov announced with serene amazement. Mitya was stupefied.

"Why, you said just now . . . you said . . . you said it was as good as in my pocket."

"Oh, no, you misunderstood me, Dmitri Fyodorovich. In that case you misunderstood me. I was talking of the gold-mines. It's true I promised you more, infinitely more than three thousand, I remember it all now, but I was referring to the gold-mines."

"But the money? The three thousand?" Mitya exclaimed, awkwardly.

"Oh, if you meant money, I haven't any. I haven't a penny, now, Dmitri Fyodorovich. I'm in the midst of a fight with my steward, and I've just borrowed five hundred roubles from Miüsov, myself. No, no, I've no money. And, do you know, Dmitri Fyodorovich, if I had, I wouldn't give it to you. In the first place I never lend money. Lending money means losing friends. And I wouldn't give it to you particularly. I wouldn't give it you, because I like you and want to save you, for all you need is the gold-mines, the gold-mines, the gold-mines!"

"Oh, the devil!" roared Mitya, and with all his might brought his fist down on the table.

"Aie! Aie!" cried Madame Hohlakov, alarmed and she flew to the other end of the drawing-room.

Mitya spat, and strode rapidly out of the room, out of the house, into the street, into the darkness! He walked like one demented, beating himself on the breast, on the spot where he had struck himself two days previously, before Alyosha, the last time he saw him in the dark, on the road. What those blows upon his breast signified, *on that spot*, and what he meant by it — that was, for the time, a secret which was known to no one in the world, and had not been told even to Alyosha. But that secret meant for him more than disgrace; it meant ruin, suicide. So he had determined, if he did not get hold of the three thousand that would pay his debt to Katerina Ivanovna, and so remove from his breast, from *that spot on his breast*, the shame he carried upon it, that weighed on his conscience. All this will be fully explained to the reader later on, but now that his last hope had vanished, this man, so strong in appearance, burst out crying like a little child a few steps from the Hohlakovs' house. He walked on, and not knowing what he was doing, wiped away his tears with his fist. In this way he reached the square, and suddenly became aware that he had stumbled against something. He heard a piercing wail from an old woman whom he had almost knocked down.

"Good Lord, you've nearly killed me! Why don't you look where you're going, scapegrace?"

"Why, it's you!" cried Mitya, recognising the old woman in the dark. It was the old servant who waited on Samsonov, whom Mitya had particularly noticed the day before.

"And who are you, my good sir?" said the old woman in quite a different voice. "I don't know you in the dark."

"You live at Kuzma Kuzmich's. You're the servant there?"

"Just so, sir, I was only running out to Prohorich's . . . But I don't know you now."

"Tell me, my good woman, is Agrafena Alexandrovna there now?" said Mitya, beside himself with suspense. "I saw her to the house some time ago."

"She has been there, sir. She stayed a little while, and went off again."

"What? Went away?" cried Mitya. "When did she go?"

"Why, as soon as she came. She only stayed a minute. She only told Kuzma Kuzmich a tale that made him laugh, and then she ran away."

"You're lying, damn you!" roared Mitya.

"Aie! Aie!" shrieked the old woman, but Mitya had vanished.

He ran with all his might to the house where Grushenka lived. When he reached it, Grushenka had already left for Mokroye; she had not been gone for more than a quarter of an hour.

Fenya was sitting in the kitchen with her grandmother, the old cook, Matryona, when the "captain" ran in. Fenya uttered a piercing shriek on seeing him.

"You scream?" roared Mitya, "where is she?"

But without giving the terror-stricken Fenya time to utter a word, he fell all of a heap at her feet.

"Fenya, for the sake of our Lord Christ, tell me, where is she?"

"My sweet one, I don't know anything. Dmitri Fyodorovich, darling, I don't know anything. You may kill me but I don't know anything." Fenya swore and protested. "You went out with her yourself not long ago . . ."

"She came back!"

"Darling, she didn't. I swear by God she didn't come back."

"You're lying!" shouted Mitya. "From your fright I know where she is."

He dashed out. Fenya in her fright was glad she had got off so easily. But she knew very well that it was only that he was in such haste, or she might not have fared so well. But as he ran, he surprised both Fenya and old Matryona by an unexpected action. On the table stood a brass mortar, with a pestle in it, a small brass pestle, not much more than six inches long. Mitya had already opened the door with one hand when, with the other, he snatched up the pestle, thrust it in his side pocket, and was gone.

"Oh, Lord! He's going to murder some one!" cried Fenya, striking her hands together.

## CHAPTER IV
### IN THE DARK

WHERE was he running? "Where could she be except at Fyodor Pavlovich's? She must have run straight to him from Samsonov's, that was clear now. The whole intrigue, the whole deception was evident." . . . It all rushed whirling through his mind. He did not run to Marya Kondratyevna's. "There was no need to go there . . . not the slightest need . . . he must raise no alarm . . . they would run and tell directly. . . . Marya Kondratyevna was clearly in the plot, Smerdyakov, too, he, too, all had been bought over!"

He formed another plan of action: taking the long way, he ran round Fyodor Pavlovich's house, crossing the lane, running down Dmitrovsky Street, then over the little bridge, and so came straight to the deserted alley at the back, which was empty and uninhabited, with on one side the hurdle fence of a neighbour's kitchen-garden, on the other the strong high fence that ran all round Fyodor Pavlovich's garden. Here he chose a spot, apparently the very place where, according to the tradition he knew, Lizaveta had once climbed over the fence: "If she could climb over it," the thought, God knows why, occurred to him, "surely I can." He did in fact jump up, and instantly contrived to catch hold of the top of the fence. Then he vigorously pulled himself up and sat astride it. Close by, in the garden, stood the bath-house, but from the fence he could see the lighted windows of the house, too.

"Yes, the old man's bedroom is lighted up. She's there!" and he leapt from the fence into the garden. Though he knew Grigory was ill and very likely Smerdyakov, too, and that there was no one to hear him, he instinctively hid himself, stood still, and began to listen. But there was dead silence on all sides and, as though of design, complete stillness, not the slightest breath of wind.

"And only silence whispered there," the line for some reason rose to his mind. "If only no one heard me jump over the fence! I think not." Standing still for a minute, he walked softly across the grass in the garden, avoiding the trees and shrubs. He walked slowly, creeping stealthily at every step, listening to his own footsteps. It took him five minutes to reach the lighted window. He remembered that just under the window there were several thick and high bushes of elder and guelder-rose. The door from the house into the garden, on the left-hand side, was locked; he had carefully looked purposely to see, in passing. At last he reached the bushes and hid behind them. He held his breath. "I must wait now," he thought, "to reassure them, in case they heard my footsteps and are listening . . . if only I don't cough or sneeze."

He waited two minutes. His heart was beating violently, and, at moments, he was almost suffocated. "No, this throbbing of my heart won't stop," he thought. "I can't wait any longer." He was standing behind a bush in the shadow. The light of the window fell on the front part of the bush.

"How red the guelder-rose berries are!" he murmured, not knowing why. Softly and noiselessly, step by step, he approached the window, and raised himself on tiptoe. All Fyodor Pavlovich's bedroom lay open before him. It was not a large room, and was divided in two parts by a red screen, "Chinese," as Fyodor Pavlovich used to call it. The word "Chinese" flashed into Mitya's mind, "and behind the screen is Grushenka," thought Mitya. He began watching Fyodor Pavlovich, who was wearing his new striped-silk dressing-gown, which Mitya had never seen, and a silk cord with tassels round the waist. A clean, dandified shirt of fine linen with gold studs peeped out under the collar of the dressing-gown. On his head Fyodor Pavlovich had the same red bandage which Alyosha had seen.

"He has got himself up," thought Mitya.

His father was standing near the window, apparently lost in thought. Suddenly he jerked up his head, listened a moment, and, hearing nothing, went up to the table, poured out half a glass of brandy from a decanter, and drank it off. Then he breathed deeply, again stood still a moment, walked carelessly up to the looking-glass on the wall, with his right hand raised the red bandage on his forehead a little, and began examining his bruises and wounds, which had not yet disappeared.

"He's alone," thought Mitya, "in all probability he's alone."

Fyodor Pavlovich moved away from the looking-glass, turned suddenly to the window and looked out. Mitya instantly slipped away into the shadow.

"She may be there behind the screen. Perhaps she's asleep by now," he thought, with a pang at his heart. Fyodor Pavlovich moved away from the window. "He's looking for her out of the window, so she's not there. Why should he peer out into the dark? He's wild

AN OCCURRENCE IN THE DARK

with impatience." . . . Mitya slipped back at once, and fell to gazing in at the window again. The old man was sitting down at the table, apparently disappointed. At last he put his elbow on the table, and laid his right cheek against his hand.

Mitya watched him eagerly.

"He's alone, he's alone!" he repeated again. "If she were here, his face would be different."

Strange to say, a queer, irrational vexation rose up in his heart that she was not here. "It's not that she's not here," he explained to himself, immediately, "but that I can't tell for certain whether she is or not." Mitya remembered afterwards that his mind was, at that moment, exceptionally clear, that he took in everything to the slightest detail, and missed no point. But a feeling of misery, the misery of uncertainty and indecision, was growing in his heart with every instant. "Is she here or not?" The angry doubt filled his heart, and suddenly, making up his mind, he put out his hand and softly knocked on the window frame. He knocked the signal the old man had agreed upon with Smerdyakov, twice slowly and then three times more quickly, the signal that meant "Grushenka has come!"

The old man started, jerked up his head, and, jumping up quickly, ran to the window. Mitya slipped away into the shadow. Fyodor Pavlovich opened the window and thrust his whole head out.

"Grushenka, is it you? Is it you?" he said, in a sort of trembling half-whisper. "Where are you, my angel, where are you?" He was fearfully agitated and breathless.

"He's alone," Mitya decided.

"Where are you?" cried the old man again; and he thrust his head out farther, thrust it out to the shoulders, gazing in all directions, right

and left. "Come here, I've a little present for you. Come, I'll show you . . ."

"He means the package with the three thousand," thought Mitya.

"But where are you? Are you at the door? I'll open it directly."

And the old man almost climbed out of the window, peering out to the right, where there was a door into the garden, trying to see into the darkness. In another second he would certainly have run out to open the door without waiting for Grushenka's answer.

Mitya looked at him from the side without stirring. The old man's profile that he loathed so, his pendant Adam's apple, his hooked nose, his lips that smiled in greedy expectation, were all brightly lighted up by the slanting lamp-light falling on the left from the room. A dreadful fury of hatred suddenly surged up in Mitya's heart. "There he was, his rival, the man who had tormented him, who had ruined his life!" It was a rush of that sudden, furious, vengeful anger of which he had spoken to Alyosha, as though foreseeing it, four days ago in the arbour, when, in answer to Alyosha's question, "How can you say you'll kill our father?" he had said, "I don't know, I don't know. Perhaps I shall not kill him, perhaps I shall. I'm afraid he'll suddenly be so loathsome to me at that moment. I hate his Adam's apple, his nose, his eyes, his shameless grin. I feel a personal loathing. That's what I'm afraid of, that's what may be too much for me." . . . This personal loathing was growing unendurable. Mitya was beside himself, he suddenly pulled the brass pestle out of his pocket. . . .

"God was watching over me then," Mitya himself said afterwards. At that very moment Grigory waked up on his bed of sickness. Earlier in the evening he had undergone the treatment which Smerdyakov had described to Ivan Fyodorovich. He had rubbed himself all over with vodka mixed with a secret very strong decoction, had drunk what was left of the mixture while his wife repeated a "certain prayer" over him, after which he had gone to bed. Marfa Ignatyevna had quaffed of the stuff, too, and, being unused to strong drink, slept like the dead beside her spouse.

But Grigory waked up in the night, quite suddenly, and, after a moment's reflection, though he immediately felt a sharp pain in his back, he sat up in bed. Then he deliberated again, got up and dressed hurriedly. Perhaps his conscience was uneasy at the thought of sleeping while the house was unguarded "in such perilous times." Smerdyakov, exhausted by his fit, lay motionless in the next room. Marfa Ignatyevna did not stir. "The stuff's been too much for the woman," Grigory thought, glancing at her, and, groaning, he went out on the steps. No doubt he only intended to look out from the steps, for he was hardly able to walk, the pain in his back and his right leg was intolerable. But he suddenly remembered that he had not locked the little gate into the garden that evening. He was the most punctual and precise of men, a man who adhered to an unchangeable routine, and habits that lasted for years. Limping and writhing with pain, he went down the steps and towards the garden. Yes, the gate stood wide open. Mechanically he stepped into the garden. Perhaps he fancied something, perhaps caught some sound, and, glancing to the left, he saw his master's window open. No one was looking out of it then.

"What's it open for? It's not summer now," thought Grigory, and suddenly, at that very instant, he caught a glimpse of something extraordinary before him in the garden. Forty paces in front of him a man seemed to be running in the dark, a shadow was moving very fast.

"Good Lord!" cried Grigory, beside himself, and forgetting the pain in his back, he hurried to intercept the running figure. He took a short cut, evidently he knew the garden better than the stranger; the flying figure went towards the bath-house, ran behind it, and rushed to the garden fence. Grigory followed, not losing sight of him, and ran, forgetting everything. He reached the fence at the very moment the man was climbing over it. Grigory cried out, beside himself, pounced on him, and clutched his leg in his two hands.

Yes, his foreboding had not deceived him. He recognised him, it was he, the "monster," the "parricide."

"Parricide!" the old man shouted so that the whole neighbourhood could hear, but he had not time to shout again, he fell at once, as though struck by lightning.

Mitya jumped back into the garden and bent over the fallen man. In Mitya's hands was a brass pestle, and he flung it mechanically into the grass. The pestle fell two paces from Grigory, not in the grass but on the path, in a most conspicuous place. For some seconds he examined the prostrate figure before him. The old man's head was all bloody. Mitya put out his hand and began feeling it. He remembered afterwards clearly that he had been awfully anxious to make sure whether he had broken the old man's skull, or simply stunned him with the pestle. But the blood was flowing horribly, and in a moment Mitya's trembling fingers were drenched with the hot stream. He remembered taking out of his pocket the clean white handkerchief with which he had provided himself for his visit to Madame Hohlakov, and putting it to the old man's head, senselessly trying to wipe the blood from his face and temples. But the handkerchief was instantly soaked with blood.

"Good heavens! what am I doing it for?" thought Mitya, suddenly pulling himself together. "If I have broken his skull, how can I find out now? And what difference does it make now?" he added, hopelessly. "If I've killed him, I've killed him . . . you've come to grief, old man, so there you must lie!" he said aloud. And suddenly, turning to the fence, he vaulted over it into the lane and fell to running — the handkerchief soaked with blood he held, crushed up, in his right fist, and, as he ran, he thrust it into the back pocket of his coat.

He ran headlong, and the few passers-by who met him in the dark, in the streets, remembered afterwards that they had met a man running that night. He flew back again to the widow Morozov's house.

Immediately after he had left it, that evening, Fenya had rushed to the chief porter, Nazar Ivanovich, and besought him, for Christ's sake, "not to let the captain in again to-day or to-morrow." Nazar Ivanovich promised, but went upstairs to his mistress who had suddenly sent for him, and meeting his nephew, a boy of twenty, who had recently come from the country, on the way up, told him to take his place, but forgot to mention the "captain." Mitya, running up to the gate, knocked. The lad instantly recognised him, for Mitya had more than once tipped him. Opening the gate at once, he let him in, and hastened to inform him with a good-humoured smile that "Agrafena Alexandrovna is not at home now, you know."

"Where is she then, Prohor?" asked Mitya, stopping short.

"She set off this evening, some two hours ago, with Timofey, to Mokroye."

"What for?" cried Mitya.

"That I can't say. To see some officer. Some one invited her and horses were sent to fetch her."

Mitya left him, and ran like a madman to Fenya.

## CHAPTER V
### A SUDDEN RESOLUTION

SHE was sitting in the kitchen with her grandmother; they were both just going to bed. Relying on Nazar Ivanovich, they had not locked themselves in. Mitya ran in, pounced on Fenya and seized her by the throat.

"Speak at once! Where is she? With whom is she now at Mokroye?" he roared, beside himself.

Both the women squealed.

"Aie! I'll tell you. Aie, Dmitri Fyodorovich, darling, I'll tell you everything directly, I won't hide anything," gabbled Fenya, frightened to death; "she's gone to Mokroye, to her officer."

"What officer?" roared Mitya.

"To her officer, the same one she used to know, the one who threw her over five years ago," cackled Fenya, as fast as she could speak.

Mitya withdrew the hands with which he was squeezing her throat. He stood facing her, pale as death, unable to utter a word, but his eyes showed that he realised it all, all, from the first word, and guessed the whole situation. Poor Fenya was not in a condition at that moment to observe whether he understood or not. She remained sitting on the trunk as she had been when he ran into the room, trembling all over, holding her hands out before her as though trying to defend herself. She seemed to have grown rigid in that position. Her wide-open, scared eyes were fixed immovably upon him. And to make matters worse, both his hands were smeared with blood. On the way, as he ran, he must have touched his forehead with them, wiping off the perspiration, so that on his forehead and his right cheek were red patches of smeared blood. Fenya was on the verge of hysterics. The old cook had jumped up and was staring at him like a mad-woman, almost unconscious with terror.

Mitya stood for a moment, then mechanically sank onto a chair next to Fenya. He was sitting, not so much sunk in thought as terror-stricken, so to speak, benumbed. Yet everything was clear as day: that officer, he knew about him, he knew everything perfectly, he had known it from Grushenka herself, had known that a letter had come from him a month before. So that for a month, for a whole month this had been going on in secret from him, till the very arrival of this new man, and he had never thought of him! But how could he, how could he not have thought of him? Why was it he had forgotten this officer, like that, forgotten him as soon as he heard of him? That was the question that faced him like some monstrous thing. And he looked at this monstrous thing with fear, growing cold with fear.

But suddenly, as gently and meekly as a gentle and affectionate child, he began speaking to Fenya as though he had utterly forgotten how he had scared and hurt her just now. He fell to questioning Fenya with an extreme

preciseness, astonishing in his position, and though the girl looked wildly at his blood-stained hands, she, too, with wonderful readiness and haste, answered every question as though eager to put the whole truth and nothing but the truth before him. Little by little, even with a sort of enjoyment, she began explaining every detail, not wanting to torment him, but, as it were, eager to be of the utmost service to him. She described the whole of that day, in great detail, the visit of Rakitin and Alyosha, how she, Fenya, had been on the watch, how the mistress had set off, and how she had called out of the window to Alyosha to give him, Mitya, her greetings, and to tell him "to remember for ever how she had loved him for an hour."

Hearing of the message, Mitya suddenly smiled, and there was a flush of colour on his pale cheeks. At the same moment Fenya said to him, not a bit afraid now to be inquisitive:

"Look at your hands, Dmitri Fyodorovich. They're all over blood!"

"Yes," answered Mitya mechanically. He looked absent-mindedly at his hands and at once forgot them and Fenya's question.

He sank into silence again. Twenty minutes had passed since he had run in. His first horror was over, but evidently some new fixed determination had taken possession of him. He suddenly stood up, smiling dreamily.

"What has happened to you, sir?" said Fenya, pointing to his hands again. She spoke compassionately, as though she felt very near to him now in his grief. Mitya looked at his hands again.

"That's blood, Fenya," he said, looking at her with a strange expression. "That's human blood, and, my God! why was it shed? But . . . Fenya . . . there's a fence here" (he

306

FYODOR PAVLOVICH EXAMINES HIS BRUISES

looked at her as though setting her a riddle), "a high fence, and terrible to look at. But, at dawn to-morrow, 'when the sun soars,' Mitya will leap over that fence. . . . You don't understand what fence, Fenya, and, never mind. . . . You'll hear to-morrow and understand everything . . . and now, good-bye. I won't stand in her way. I'll step aside, I know how to step aside. Live, my joy. . . . You loved me for an hour, so remember Mityenka Karamazov for ever. . . . She always used to call me Mityenka, do you remember?"

And with those words he walked suddenly out of the kitchen. Fenya was almost more frightened at this sudden departure than she had been when he ran in and attacked her.

Just ten minutes later Dmitri went in to Pyotr Ilyich Perhotin, the young official with whom he had pawned his pistols. It was by now half-past eight, and Pyotr Ilyich had finished his evening tea, and had just put his coat on again to go to the "Metropolis" to have a game of billiards. Mitya caught him coming out.

Seeing him with his face all smeared with blood, the young man uttered a cry of surprise.

"Good heavens! What is the matter?"

"I've come for my pistols," said Mitya, "and brought you the money. And thanks very much. I'm in a hurry, Pyotr Ilyich, please make haste."

Pyotr Ilyich's surprise increased; he suddenly caught sight of a bundle of bank-notes in Mitya's hand, and what was more, he had walked in holding the notes as no one walks in and no one carries money: he had them in his right hand, and held them outstretched as if to show them. Perhotin's servant, a young boy, who met Mitya in the passage, said afterwards that he walked into the passage in the same way, with the money in his outstretched hand, so he must have been carrying it like that even in the street. They were all rainbow-coloured hundred-rouble notes, and the fingers holding them were covered with blood.

When Pyotr Ilyich was questioned later on as to the sum of money, he said that it was difficult to judge at a glance, but that it might have been two thousand, or perhaps three, but it was a big "fat" bundle. "Dmitri Fyodorovich," so he testified afterwards, "seemed unlike himself, too; not drunk, but in a kind of ecstasy, as it were, absent-minded, but at the same time, as it were, absorbed, as though pondering and searching for something and unable to come to a decision. He was in great haste, answered abruptly and very strangely, and at moments seemed not at all dejected but quite cheerful."

"But what *is* the matter with you? What's wrong?" cried Pyotr Ilyich, looking wildly at his guest. "How is it that you're all covered with blood? Have you had a fall? Look at yourself!"

He took him by the elbow and led him to the glass.

Seeing his blood-stained face, Mitya started and scowled wrathfully.

"Damnation! That's the last straw," he muttered angrily, hurriedly changing the notes from his right hand to his left, and impulsively jerked the handkerchief out of his pocket. But the handkerchief turned out to be soaked with blood, too (it was the handkerchief he had used to wipe Grigory's head and face). There was scarcely a white spot on it, and it had not merely begun to dry, but had stiffened into a crumpled ball and could not be unfolded. Mitya threw it angrily on the floor. "Oh, damn it!" he said. "Haven't you a rag of some sort . . . to wipe my face?"

"So you're only stained, not wounded? You'd better wash," said Pyotr Ilyich. "Here's a wash-stand. I'll pour you out some water."

"A wash-stand? That's all right . . . but where am I to put this?"

With the strangest perplexity he indicated his bundle of hundred-rouble notes, looking inquiringly at Pyotr Ilyich as though it were for him to decide what he, Mitya, was to do with his own money.

"In your pocket, or on the table here. They won't be lost."

"In my pocket? Yes, in my pocket. All right. . . . But, I say, that's all nonsense," he cried, as though suddenly coming out of his absorption. "Look here, let's first settle that business of the pistols. Give them back to me. Here's your money . . . because I am in great need of them . . . and I haven't a minute, a minute to spare."

And taking the topmost note from the bundle, he held it out to Pyotr Ilyich.

"But I shan't have change enough. Haven't you less?"

"No," said Mitya, looking again at the bundle, and as though not trusting his own words he fingered two or three of the topmost ones.

"No, they're all alike," he added, and again he looked inquiringly at Pyotr Ilyich.

"How have you grown so rich?" the latter asked. "Wait, I'll send my boy to Plotnikovs', they close late — to see if they won't change it. Here, Misha!" he called into the passage.

"To Plotnikovs' shop — first rate!" cried Mitya, as though struck by an idea. "Misha," he turned to the boy as he came in, "look here,

run to Plotnikovs' and tell them that Dmitri Fyodorovich sends his greetings, and will be there directly. . . . But listen, listen, tell them to have champagne, three dozen bottles ready before I come, and packed as it was to take to Mokroye. I took four dozen with me then," he added (suddenly addressing Pyotr Ilyich); "they know all about it, don't you trouble, Misha," he turned again to the boy. "Stay, listen; tell them to put in cheese, Strasburg pies, smoked fish, ham, caviare, and everything, everything they've got, up to a hundred roubles, or a hundred and twenty as before. . . . But wait: don't let them forget dessert, sweets, pears, watermelons, two or three or four — no, one melon's enough, and chocolate, candy, toffee, fondants; in fact, everything I took to Mokroye before, three hundred roubles' worth with champagne . . . let it be just the same again. And remember, Misha, if you are called Misha . . . His name is Misha, isn't it?" He turned to Pyotr Ilyich again.

"Wait a minute," Pyotr Ilyich intervened, listening and watching him uneasily, "you'd better go yourself and tell them. He'll muddle it."

"He will, I see he will! Eh, Misha! Why, I was going to kiss you for the commission. . . . If you don't make a mistake, there's ten roubles for you, run along, make haste. . . . Champagne's the chief thing, let them roll out champagne. And cognac, too, and red and white wine, and all I had then. . . . They know what I had then."

"But listen!" Pyotr Ilyich interrupted with some impatience. "I say, let him simply run and change the money and tell them not to close, and you go and tell them. . . . Give him your note. Be off, Misha! Shake a leg!"

Pyotr Ilyich seemed to hurry Misha off on

purpose, because the boy remained standing with his mouth and eyes wide open, apparently understanding little of Mitya's orders, gazing up with amazement and terror at his blood-stained face and the trembling blood-stained fingers that held the notes.

"Well, now come and wash," said Pyotr Ilyich sternly. "Put the money on the table or else in your pocket. . . . That's right, come along. But take off your coat."

And beginning to help him off with his coat, he cried out again:

"Look, your coat's covered with blood, too!"

"That . . . it's not the coat. It's only a little here on the sleeve. . . . And that's only here where the handkerchief lay. It must have soaked through. I must have sat on the handkerchief at Fenya's, and the blood's come through," Mitya explained at once with astonishing trustfulness. Pyotr Ilyich listened, frowning.

"Well, you must have been up to something; you must have had a fight with some one," he muttered.

They began to wash. Pyotr Ilyich held the jug and poured out the water. Mitya, in desperate haste, scarcely soaped his hands (they were trembling, and Pyotr Ilyich remembered it afterwards). But the young official insisted on his soaping them thoroughly and rubbing them more. He seemed to dominate Mitya, and more so as time passed. It may be noted in passing that he was a young man of far from timid character.

"Look, you haven't got your nails clean. Now rub your face; here, on your temples, by your ear. . . . Will you go in that shirt? Where are you going? Look, the whole cuff of your right sleeve is covered with blood."

"Yes, it's all bloody," observed Mitya, looking at the cuff of his shirt.

"Then change your shirt."

"I haven't time. You see I'll . . . ." Mitya went on in the same confiding way, drying his face and hands on the towel, and putting on his coat. "I'll turn it up at the wrist. It won't be seen under the coat. . . . You see!"

"Tell me now, what game have you been up to? Have you been fighting with some one? In the tavern again, as before? Have you been beating that captain again?" Pyotr Ilyich asked him reproachfully. "Whom did you beat up now . . . or kill, perhaps?"

"Nonsense!" said Mitya.

"How 'nonsense'?"

"Don't worry," said Mitya, and he suddenly grinned. "I crushed an old woman in the market-place just now."

"Crushed? An old woman?"

"An old man!" cried Mitya, looking Pyotr Ilyich straight in the face, laughing, and shouting at him as though he were deaf.

"Confound it! An old woman, an old man. . . . Have you killed some one?"

"We made it up. We had a row — and made it up. In a place I know of. We parted friends. A fool. . . . He's forgiven me. . . . He's sure to have forgiven me by now . . . if he had got up, he wouldn't have forgiven me" — Mitya suddenly winked — "only, damn him, you know, I say, Pyotr Ilyich, damn him! Don't worry about him! I don't want to just now!" Mitya snapped out, resolutely.

"Whatever do you want to go picking quarrels with every one for? . . . Just as you did with that captain over some trifle. . . . You've been fighting and now you're rushing off on a spree — that's you all over! Three dozen champagne — what do you want all that for?"

"Bravo! Now give me the pistols. Upon my honour I've no time now. I should like to have a chat with you, my dear boy, but I haven't the time. And there's no need, it's too late for talking. Where's my money? Where have I put it?" he cried, thrusting his hands into his pockets.

"You put it on the table . . . yourself. . . . Here it is. Had you forgotten? Money's like dirt or water to you, it seems. Here are your pistols. It's an odd thing, at six o'clock you pledged them for ten roubles, and now you've got thousands. Two or three I should say."

"Three, you bet," laughed Mitya, stuffing the notes into the side pockets of his trousers.

"You'll lose it like that. Have you found a gold-mine?"

"The mines? The gold-mines?" Mitya shouted at the top of his voice and went off in a roar of laughter. "Would you like to go to the mines, Perhotin? There's a lady here who'll stump up three thousand for you, if only you'll go. She did it for me, she's so awfully fond of gold-mines. Do you know Madame Hohlakov?"

"I don't know her, but I've heard of her and seen her. Did she really give you three thousand? Did she really hand them over to you?" said Pyotr Ilyich, eyeing him dubiously.

"As soon as the sun soars to-morrow, as soon as Phœbus, ever young, soars upwards, praising and glorifying God, you go to her, this Madame Hohlakov, and ask her whether she did stump up that three thousand or not. Try and find out."

"I don't know on what terms you are . . . since you say it so positively, I suppose she did

give it to you. You've got the money in your hand, but instead of going to Siberia you're spending it all. . . . Where are you really off to now, eh?"

"To Mokroye."

"To Mokroye? But it's night!"

"Once the lad had all, now the lad has naught," cried Mitya suddenly.

"How 'naught'? You say that with all those thousands!"

"I'm not talking about thousands. Damn thousands! I'm talking of the female character:

*Credulous is woman's heart,*
*Mutable and full of vices;*

I agree with Ulysses. That's what he says."

"I don't understand you!"

"Am I drunk?"

"Not drunk, but worse."

"I'm drunk in spirit, Pyotr Ilyich, drunk in spirit! But that's enough!"

"What are you doing, loading the pistol?"

"I'm loading the pistol."

Unfastening the pistol-case, Mitya actually opened the powder horn, and carefully placed and rammed in the charge. Then he took the bullet and, before inserting it, held it in two fingers in front of the candle.

"Why are you looking at the bullet?" asked Pyotr Ilyich, watching him with uneasy curiosity.

"Oh, a fancy. Why, if you meant to put that bullet in your brain, would you look at it when you charged the pistol, or not?"

"Why look at it?"

"It will go into my brain, so it's interesting to look and see what it's like. But that's foolishness, a moment's foolishness. Now that's done," he added, putting in the bullet and ramming it in with tow. "Pyotr Ilyich, my dear fellow, that's nonsense, all nonsense, and if only you knew what nonsense! Give me a little piece of paper now."

"Here's some paper."

"No, a smooth, clean piece, writing paper. That's right."

And taking a pen from the table, Mitya rapidly wrote two lines, folded the paper twice, and thrust it into his waistcoat pocket. He put the pistols in the case, locked it up, and took it in his hands. Then he looked at Pyotr Ilyich with a slow, thoughtful smile.

"Now, let's go," he said.

"Where are we going? No, wait a minute. . . . Are you thinking of putting that bullet in your brain, perhaps?" Pyotr Ilyich asked uneasily.

"The bullet is nonsense! I want to live. I love life! You may be sure of that. I love golden-haired Phœbus and his hot light. . . . Dear Pyotr Ilyich, do you know how to step aside?"

"What do you mean by 'stepping aside'?"

"Making way. Making way for a dear creature, and for one I hate. And to let the one I hate become dear — that's what making way means! And to say to them: God bless you, go your way, pass on, while I . . ."

"While you?"

"That's enough, let's go."

"Upon my word. I'll tell some one to prevent your going there," said Pyotr Ilyich, looking at him. "What are you going to Mokroye for, now?"

"There's a woman there, a woman. That's enough for you, Pyotr Ilyich. Finished."

"Listen, though you're such a savage I've always liked you. . . . I feel anxious."

"Thanks, old fellow. I'm a savage you say.

Savages, savages! That's what I am always saying. Savages! Why, here's Misha! I was forgetting him."

Misha ran in, post haste, with a handful of notes in change, and reported that every one was in a bustle at the Plotnikovs'; "They're carrying down the bottles, and the fish, and the tea; it will all be ready directly." Mitya seized ten roubles and handed it to Pyotr Ilyich, then tossed another ten-rouble note to Misha.

"Don't dare to do such a thing!" cried Pyotr Ilyich. "I won't have it in my house, it's a bad, demoralising habit. Put your money away. Here, put it here, why waste it? It would come in handy to-morrow, and I dare say you'll be coming to me to borrow ten roubles again. Why do you keep putting the notes in your side pocket? Ah, you'll lose them!"

"I say, my dear fellow, let's go to Mokroye together."

"What should I go for?"

"I say, let's open a bottle at once, and drink to life! I want to drink, and especially to drink with you. I've never drunk with you, have I?"

"Very well, we can go to the 'Metropolis.' I was just going there."

"I haven't time for that. Let's drink at the Plotnikovs', in the back room. Shall I set you a riddle?"

"Go ahead."

Mitya took the piece of paper out of his waistcoat pocket, unfolded it and showed it. In a large, distinct hand was written:

"I punish myself for my whole life, my whole life I punish!"

"I certainly will speak to some one. I'll go at once," said Pyotr Ilyich, after reading.

"You won't have time, darling, come and have a drink. March!"

Plotnikovs' shop was at the corner of the street, next door but one to Pyotr Ilyich's. It was the largest grocery shop in our town, and by no means a bad one, owned by rich merchants. They kept everything that could be got in a Petersburg shop, delicacies of all sorts, wines "bottled by the brothers Eliseyev," fruits, cigars, tea, coffee, sugar, and so on. There were three shop-assistants and two errand boys always employed. Though our part of the country had grown poorer, the landowners had gone away, and trade had got worse, yet the grocery stores flourished as before, every year increasing in prosperity; there were plenty of purchasers for their goods.

They were awaiting Mitya with impatience in the shop. They had vivid recollections of how he had bought, three or four weeks ago, wine and provisions of all sorts to the value of several hundred roubles, paid for in cash (they would never have let him have anything on credit, of course). They remembered that then, as now, he had had a bundle of hundred-rouble notes in his hand, and had scattered them at random, without bargaining, without reflecting, or caring to reflect, what use so much wine and so many provisions would be to him. The story was told all over the town that, driving off then with Grushenka to Mokroye, he had "spent three thousand in one night and the following day, and had come back from the spree without a penny, in his birthday-suit." He had picked up a whole troop of gipsies (encamped in our neighbourhood at the time), who for two days got money without stint out of him while he was drunk, and drank no end of expensive wine. People used to tell, laughing at Mitya, how he had given champagne to grimy-handed peasants, and feasted the village

women and girls on sweets and Strasburg pies. Though to laugh at Mitya to his face was rather a risky proceeding, there was much laughter behind his back, especially in the tavern, at his own ingenuous public avowal that all he had got out of Grushenka by this "escapade" was "permission to kiss her foot, and that was the utmost she had allowed him."

By the time Mitya and Pyotr Ilyich reached the shop, they found a carriage with three horses harnessed abreast with bells, and with Andrey, the driver, ready waiting for Mitya at the entrance. In the shop they had almost entirely finished packing one box of provisions, and were only waiting for Mitya's arrival to nail it down and put it in the troika. Pyotr Ilyich was astounded.

"Where did this troika come from in such a hurry?" he asked Mitya.

"I met Andrey as I ran to you, and told him to drive straight here to the shop. There's no time to lose. Last time I drove with Timofey, but Timofey now has gone on before me with an enchantress. Shall we be very late, Andrey?"

"They'll only get there an hour before us, at most, not even that maybe. I helped Timofey get ready. I know how he'll go. Their pace is nothing like ours, Dmitri Fyodorovich. How could it be? They won't get there an hour earlier!" Andrey, a lanky, red-haired, middle-aged driver, wearing a full-skirted coat, and with a kaftan on his arm, replied.

"A fifty roubles tip if we're only an hour behind them."

"I guarantee an hour, Dmitri Fyodorovich. Ech, they won't be half an hour ahead of us, let alone an hour."

Though Mitya bustled about seeing after

things, he gave his orders strangely, as it were disconnectedly, and inconsecutively. He began a sentence and forgot the end of it. Pyotr Ilyich found himself obliged to come to the rescue.

"Four hundred roubles' worth, not less than four hundred roubles' worth, just as it was then," commanded Mitya. "Four dozen champagne, not a bottle less."

"What do you want with so much? What's it for? Wait!" cried Pyotr Ilyich. "What's this box? What's in it? Surely there isn't four hundred roubles' worth here?"

The officious shopmen began explaining with oily politeness that the first box contained only half a dozen bottles of champagne, and only "the most indispensable articles" such as savouries, sweets, toffee, etc. But the main part of the provisions ordered would be packed and sent off, as on the previous occasion, in a special cart, also with three horses, travelling at full speed, so that it would arrive not more than an hour later than Dmitri Fyodorovich himself.

"Not more than an hour! Not more than an hour! And put in more toffee and fondants. The girls there are so fond of them," Mitya insisted hotly.

"The fondants are all right. But what do you want with four dozen of champagne? One would be enough," said Pyotr Ilyich, almost angry. He began bargaining, asking for an itemised bill, and refused to be satisfied. But he only succeeded in saving a hundred roubles. In the end it was agreed that only three hundred roubles' worth should be delivered.

"Well, you may go to the devil!" cried Pyotr Ilyich, on second thoughts. "What's it to do with me? Throw away your money, since it's cost you nothing."

"This way, my pinch-penny, this way, don't be angry." Mitya drew him into a room at the back of the shop. "They'll give us a bottle here directly. We'll taste it. Ech, Pyotr Ilyich, come along with me, for you're a nice fellow, the sort I like."

Mitya sat down on a wicker chair, before a little table, covered with the dirtiest napkin. Pyotr Ilyich sat down opposite, and the champagne soon appeared, and oysters were suggested to the gentlemen. "First-class oysters, the last lot in."

"Hang the oysters. I don't eat them. And we don't need anything," cried Pyotr Ilyich, almost angrily.

"There's no time for oysters," said Mitya. "And I have no appetite. Do you know, friend," he said suddenly, with feeling, "I never have liked all this disorder."

"Who does like it? Three dozen of champagne for peasants, upon my word, that's enough to make any one explode!"

"That's not what I mean. I'm talking of a higher order. There's no order in me, no higher order. But . . . that's all over. There's no need to grieve about it. It's too late, damn it! My whole life has been disorder, and one must set it in order. Is that a pun, eh?"

"You're raving, not making puns!"

> *"Glory be to God in heaven,*
> *Glory be to God in me . . .*

"That verse came from my heart once, it's not a verse, but a tear. . . . I made it up myself . . . not while I was pulling the captain's beard though. . . ."

"Why do you bring him in all of a sudden?"

"Why do I bring him in? Foolery! All things come to an end; all things are made equal. That's the long and the short of it."

"You know, I keep thinking of your pistols."

"That's all foolery, too! Drink, and don't be fanciful. I love life. I've loved life too much, shamefully much. Enough! To life, dear boy, let's drink to life, I propose a toast to life. Why am I pleased with myself? I'm a scoundrel, but I'm pleased with myself. And yet I'm tortured by the thought that I'm a scoundrel, but I'm pleased with myself. I bless creation. I'm ready right now to bless God and His creation, but . . . . it is necessary to destroy one vile insect so that it should not crawl and spoil life for others. . . . Let us drink to life, dear brother. What can be more precious than life? Nothing! To life, and to a queen of queens!"

"Let's drink to life and to your queen, too, if you like."

They drank a glass each. Although Mitya was excited and expansive, yet he was melancholy, too. It was as though some heavy, overwhelming anxiety were weighing upon him.

"Misha . . . . here's your Misha come! Misha, come here, my boy, drink this glass to Phœbus, the golden-haired, of to-morrow . . . ."

"What are you giving it to him for?" cried Pyotr Ilyich irritably.

"Please let me! I want to!"

"E — ech!"

Misha emptied the glass, bowed, and ran out.

"He'll remember it longer," Mitya remarked. "Woman I love, woman! What is woman? The queen of the earth! My heart is sad, sad, Pyotr Ilyich. Do you remember Hamlet? 'I am sad, so sad, good Horatio! Alas, poor Yorick!' Perhaps that's me, Yo-

rick? Yes, I'm Yorick now, and a skull afterwards."

Pyotr Ilyich listened in silence. Mitya, too, was silent for a while.

"What dog's that you've got here?" he suddenly asked the shopman, absent-mindedly, noticing a pretty little lap-dog with dark eyes, sitting in the corner.

"It belongs to Varvara Alexyevna, the mistress," answered the clerk. "She brought it and left it here. It must be taken back to her."

"I saw one like it . . . in the regiment . . ." murmured Mitya dreamily, "only that one had its hind leg broken. . . . By the way, Pyotr Ilyich, I wanted to ask you: have you ever stolen anything in your life?"

"What a question!"

"Oh, I didn't mean anything. From somebody's pocket, you know. I don't mean government money, every one steals that, and no doubt you do, too. . . ."

"You go to the devil."

"I'm talking of other people's money. Stealing straight out of a pocket? Out of a purse, eh?"

"I stole twenty copecks from my mother when I was nine years old. I took it off the table on the sly, and held it tight in my hand."

"Well, and what happened?"

"Oh, nothing. I kept it three days, then I felt ashamed, confessed, and gave it back."

"And what then?"

"Naturally I was whipped. But why do you ask? Have you stolen something?"

"I have," said Mitya, winking slyly.

"What have you stolen?" asked Pyotr Ilyich inquisitively.

"I stole twenty copecks from my mother when I was nine years old, and gave it back three days after."

As he said this Mitya suddenly got up.

"Dmitri Fyodorovich, won't you come now?" called Andrey from the door of the shop.

"Are you ready? We'll come!" Mitya started. " 'And now one final tale' and . . . A glass of vodka for Andrey before we start. And a glass of cognac, too. That box" (the one with the pistols) "put under my seat. Good-bye, Pyotr Ilyich, don't remember evil against me."

"But you're coming back to-morrow?"

"Of course."

"Will you settle the little bill now?" cried the clerk, springing forward.

"Oh, yes, the bill. Of course."

He pulled the bundle of notes out of his pocket again, picked out three hundred roubles, threw them on the counter, and ran hurriedly out of the shop. Every one followed him out, bowing and wishing him good luck. Andrey, clearing his throat after the brandy he had just swallowed, jumped up on the box. But Mitya was only just taking his seat when suddenly, to his surprise, he saw Fenya before him. She ran up panting, clasped her hands before him with a cry, and plumped down at his feet.

"Darling master, Dmitri Fyodorovich, don't harm my mistress. And it was I told you all about it. . . . And don't murder him, he came first, he's hers! He'll marry Agrafena Alexandrovna now. That's why he's come back from Siberia. Dmitri Fyodorovich, dear, don't take a fellow creature's life!"

"Tut-tut-tut! That's it, is it? So you're off there to make trouble!" muttered Pyotr Ilyich. "Now, it's all clear, as clear as daylight. Dmitri Fyodorovich, give me your pistols at once if you mean to behave like a man,"

he shouted aloud to Mitya. "Do you hear, Dmitri?"

"The pistols? Wait a bit, brother, I'll throw them into the pool on the road," answered Mitya. "Fenya, get up, don't lie there before me. Mitya won't do for any one, the silly fool won't do for any one again. But I say, Fenya," he shouted, after having taken his seat. "I insulted you just now, so forgive me and have pity on me, forgive the scoundrel. . . . But it doesn't matter if you don't. It's all the same now. Now then, Andrey, look alive, go full speed!"

Andrey whipped up the horses, and the bell tinkled.

"Farewell, Pyotr Ilyich! 'For you I shed my final tear!' . . ."

"He's not drunk, but he babbles like a lunatic," Pyotr Ilyich thought as he watched him go. He had half a mind to stay and see the cart packed with the remaining wines and provisions, knowing that Mitya would be deceived and defrauded. But, suddenly feeling vexed with himself, he turned away with a curse and went to the tavern to play billiards.

"He's a fool, though he's a good fellow," he muttered as he went. "I've heard of that officer, Grushenka's former flame. Well, if he has turned up . . . Ech, those pistols! Damn it all! I'm not his nurse! Let them do what they like! Besides, it'll all come to nothing. They're a set of brawlers, that's all. They'll drink and fight, fight and make friends again. They are not men who do anything real. What does he mean by 'I'm stepping aside, I'm punishing myself'? It'll come to nothing! He's shouted such stuff a thousand times, drunk, in the taverns. But now he's not drunk. 'Drunk in spirit' — they're fond of fine phrases, the scoundrels. Am I his nurse? He must have been fighting, his face was all over blood. With whom? I shall find out at the 'Metropolis.' And his handkerchief was soaked in blood. . . . It's still lying on my floor. . . . Hang it!"

He reached the tavern in a bad humour and at once got up a game. The game cheered him. He played a second game, and suddenly began telling one of his partners that Dmitri Karamazov had come in for some cash again — something like three thousand roubles, he had seen it himself, and had gone to Mokroye again to spend it with Grushenka. . . . This news roused singular interest in his listeners. They all spoke of it, not laughing, but with a strange gravity. They left off playing.

"Three thousand? But where can he have got three thousand?"

Questions were asked. The story of Madame Hohlakov's present was received skeptically.

"Hasn't he robbed his old father, that's the question?"

"Three thousand! There's something odd about it."

"He boasted aloud that he would kill his father; we all heard him, here. And it was three thousand he talked about . . ."

Pyotr Ilyich listened. All at once he became short and dry in his answers. He said not a word about the blood on Mitya's face and hands, though he had meant to speak of it at first.

They began a third game, and by degrees the talk about Mitya died away. But by the end of the third game, Pyotr Ilyich felt no more desire for billiards; he laid down the cue, and without having supper as he had intended, he walked out of the tavern. When he reached the market-place he stood still in perplexity, wondering at himself. He realised that what he wanted was to go to Fyodor Pavlovich's and find out if anything had happened there, "On account of some stupid nonsense — as it's sure to turn out — am I going to wake up the household and make a scandal? Faugh! damn it, is it my business to look after them?"

In a very bad humour he went straight home, and suddenly remembered Fenya. "Damn it all! I ought to have questioned her just now," he thought with vexation, "I should have heard everything." And the desire to speak to her, and so find out, became so pressing and importunate that when he was half-way home he turned abruptly and went towards the house where Grushenka lodged. Going up to the gate he knocked. The sound of the knock in the silence of the night suddenly sobered and annoyed him, as it were. And no one answered him; every one in the house was asleep.

"And I shall be making a scandal here, too!" he thought, with a feeling of positive distress. But instead of going away altogether, he fell to knocking again with all his might, filling the street with clamour. "No, but I will knock them up, I will!" he muttered at each knock, fuming at himself, but at the same time he redoubled his knocks on the gate.

## CHAPTER VI
### "I, MYSELF, AM COMING"

BUT Dmitri Fyodorovich was speeding along the road. It was a little more than twenty versts to Mokroye, but Andrey's three horses galloped at such a pace that the distance might be covered in an hour and a quarter. The swift motion suddenly refreshed Mitya, as it were. The air was fresh and cool, there were big stars

316

shining in the sky. It was the very night, and perhaps the very hour, in which Alyosha fell on the earth, and rapturously swore to love it for ever and ever.

All was confusion, extreme confusion, in Mitya's soul, but although many things were harassing his soul, at that moment his whole being was straining irrepressibly towards her, his queen, to whom he was flying in order to look upon her for the last time. One thing I can say for certain; his heart was not angered for an instant. I shall perhaps not be believed when I say that this jealous lover felt not the slightest jealousy of this new man, this new rival, the "officer," who seemed to have sprung out of the earth. If any other had appeared on the scene, he would have been jealous at once, and would perhaps have stained his fierce hands with blood again. But as he flew through the night, he felt no jealous hate, no hostility even, towards the man who had been her first lover. . . . It is true he had not yet seen him. "There is no room for dispute here: it is her right and his; this was her first love whom, after five years, she has not forgotten; so all these five years she loved him only, and I, how do I come in? What rights have I? Step aside, Mitya, and make way! Why fret anyhow? Now everything is over even apart from the officer — even if he had not appeared, everything would be over. . . ."

These words would roughly have expressed his feelings, if he had been capable of reasoning. But he could no longer reason at that moment. His present determination had arisen without reasoning. At Fenya's first words, he had become aware of it, and adopted his plan in a flash, with all its consequences. And yet, in spite of his resolution, there was confusion in his soul, an agonising confusion: his resolu-

tion did not give him peace. There was so much behind that tortured him. And it seemed strange to him, at moments, to think that he had written his own sentence of death with pen and paper: "I punish myself," and the paper was lying there in his pocket, ready; the pistol was loaded; he had already resolved how, next morning, he would meet the first warm ray of "golden-haired Phœbus."

And yet he could not be quit of the past, of all that he had left behind and that tortured him. He felt that miserably, and the thought of it filled his heart with despair. There was one moment when he felt an impulse to stop Andrey, to jump out of the cart, to pull out his loaded pistol, and to make an end of everything without waiting for the dawn. But that moment flew by like a spark. The horses galloped on, "devouring space," and as he drew near his goal, again the thought of her, of her alone, took more and more complete possession of his spirit, chasing away the fearful images that had been haunting it. Oh, how he longed to look upon her, if only for a moment, if only from a distance!

"She's now with *him*," he thought, "now I shall see what she looks like with him, her first love, and that's all I want." Never had this woman, who was such a fateful influence in his life, aroused such love in his breast, such a novel and hitherto unexperienced feeling, surprising even to himself, a feeling tender to the point of adoration, of self-effacement before her! "And I will efface myself!" he said, in a rush of almost hysterical ecstasy.

They had been galloping nearly an hour. Mitya was silent, and though Andrey was, as a rule, a talkative peasant, he did not utter a word, either. He seemed afraid to talk, he only whipped up smartly his three lean, but mettlesome, bay horses. Suddenly Mitya cried out in horrible anxiety:

"Andrey! What if they're asleep?"

This thought fell upon him like a blow. It had not occurred to him before.

"It may well be that they've gone to bed, by now, Dmitri Fyodorovich."

Mitya frowned as though in pain. Yes, indeed . . . he was rushing there . . . with such feelings . . . while they were asleep . . . she was asleep, perhaps, there, too. . . . An evil feeling surged up in his heart.

"Drive on, Andrey! Whip them up! Look alive!" he cried, beside himself.

"But maybe they haven't gone to bed!" Andrey went on after a pause. "Timofey said there were a lot of them there . . ."

"At the station?"

"Not at the posting-station, but at Plastunov's, at the inn, where they furnish horses, too."

"I know. So you say there are a lot of them? How's that? Who are they?" cried Mitya, greatly dismayed at this unexpected news.

"Well, Timofey was saying they're all gentlefolk. Two from our town — who they are I can't say — and there are two others, strangers, maybe more besides. I didn't ask particularly. They've set to playing cards, so Timofey said."

"Cards?"

"So, maybe they're not in bed if they're at cards. It's most likely not more than eleven."

"Quicker, Andrey! Quicker!" Mitya cried again, nervously.

"May I ask you something, sir?" said Andrey, after a pause. "Only I'm afraid of angering you, sir."

"What is it?"

"Why, Fenya threw herself at your feet just now, and begged you not to harm her mistress, and some one else, too . . . so you see, sir . . . It's I am taking you there . . . forgive me, sir, it's my conscience . . . maybe it's stupid of me to speak of it . . ."

Mitya suddenly seized him by the shoulders from behind. "Are you a driver? A driver?" he asked frantically.

"Yes, sir . . ."

"Then you know that one has to make way. What would you say to a driver who wouldn't make way for any one, but would just drive on and crush people? No, a driver mustn't run over people. One can't run over a man. One can't spoil people's lives. And if you have spoilt a life — punish yourself. . . . If only you've spoilt, if only you've ruined any one's life — punish yourself and go away."

These phrases broke from Mitya almost hysterically. Though Andrey was surprised at him, he kept up the conversation.

"That's right, Dmitri Fyodorovich, you're quite right, one mustn't crush or torment a man, or any kind of creature, for every creature is created by God. Take a horse, for instance, some folks, even among us drivers, dash ahead, any which way. Nothing will restrain them, they just push ahead."

"To hell?" Mitya interrupted, and went off into his abrupt, short laugh. "Andrey, simple soul," he seized him by the shoulders again, "tell me, will Dmitri Fyodorovich Karamazov go to hell, or not?"

"I don't know, my dear, it depends on you, for you are . . . You see, sir, when the Son of God was nailed on the Cross and died, He went straight down to hell from the Cross, and set free all sinners that were in agony. And Hell groaned, because it looked as though no more sinners would get there. And God said to

DMITRI ON THE ROAD

Hell, then, 'Don't groan, Hell, for you shall have all the mighty of the earth, the rulers, the chief judges, and the rich men, and shall be filled up as you have been in all the ages till I come again.' Those were His very words . . ."

"A folk legend! Capital! Whip up the left, Andrey!"

"So you see, sir, who it is hell's for," said Andrey, whipping up the left horse, "but you're like a little child . . . that's how we look on you . . . and though you're hasty-tempered, sir, yet God will forgive you for your kind heart."

"And you, do you forgive me, Andrey?"

"What should I forgive you for, sir? You've never done me any harm."

"No, for every one, for every one, you here alone, on the road, will you forgive me for every one? Speak, simple peasant heart!"

"Oh, sir! I feel afraid of driving you, your talk is so strange."

But Mitya did not hear. He was praying frantically and muttering fiercely to himself.

"Lord, receive me, in all my lawlessness, and do not judge me. Let me pass without Thy judgment . . . do not judge me, for I have condemned myself, do not judge me, for I love Thee, O Lord. I am vile, but I love Thee. If Thou sendest me to hell, I shall love Thee there, and from there I shall cry out that I love Thee for ever and ever. . . . But let me love to the end. . . . Here and now for just five hours . . . till the first burning beam of Thy day . . . for I love the queen of my soul . . . I love her and I cannot help loving her. Thou seest my whole heart. . . . I shall gallop up, I shall fall before her and say, 'You are right to pass on and leave me. Farewell, and forget your victim . . . never fret yourself about me!' "

"Mokroye!" cried Andrey, pointing ahead with his whip.

Through the pale darkness of the night loomed a solid black mass of buildings, scattered over a vast area. The village of Mokroye numbered two thousand inhabitants, but at that hour all were asleep, and only here and there a few lights still twinkled in the dark.

"Drive on, Andrey, I come!" Mitya exclaimed feverishly.

"They're not asleep," said Andrey again, pointing with his whip to the Plastunovs' inn, which was at the entrance to the village. The six windows, looking on the street, were all brightly lighted up.

"They're not asleep," Mitya repeated joyously. "Quicker, Andrey! Gallop! Drive up with a dash! Set the bells ringing! Let all know that I have come. I'm coming! I, myself, am coming!" Mitya exclaimed frantically.

Andrey lashed his exhausted team into a gallop, drove noisily and pulled up his steaming, panting horses at the high flight of steps.

Mitya jumped out of the cart just as the innkeeper, on his way to bed, peeped out from the steps, curious to see who had arrived.

"Trifon Borisovich, is that you?"

The innkeeper bent down, looked intently, ran down the steps, and rushed up to the guest with obsequious delight.

"Dmitri Fyodorovich, your honour! Is it you we're seeing again?"

Trifon Borisovich was a thick-set, robust peasant, of middle height, with a rather fat face. His expression was severe and uncompromising, especially with the peasants of Mokroye, but he had the power of assuming the most obsequious countenance when he had an inkling that it was to his interest. He dressed in Russian style, with a shirt buttoning down on one side, and a full-skirted coat. He had saved a good sum of money, but was for ever dreaming of bettering himself. More than half the peasants were in his clutches, every one in the neighbourhood was in debt to him. From the neighbouring landowners he bought and rented lands which were worked by the peasants, in payment of debts which they could never shake off. He was a widower, with four grown-up daughters. One of them was already a widow and lived in his house with her two children, his grandchildren, and worked for him like a charwoman. Another of his daughters was married to a petty official and in one of the rooms of the inn on the wall could be seen, among the family pictures, a miniature photograph of this official in uniform with epaulettes. The two younger daughters used to wear fashionable blue or green dresses, fitting tight at the back, and with trains a yard long, on Church holidays or when they went to pay visits. But the next morning they would get up at dawn, as usual, sweep out the rooms with a birch broom, empty the slops, and clean up after lodgers.

In spite of the thousands of roubles he had saved, Trifon Borisovich was very fond of emptying the pockets of a drunken guest, and, remembering that not a month ago he had, in twenty-four hours, made two if not three hundred roubles out of Dmitri, when he had come on his escapade with Grushenka, he met him now with eager welcome, scenting his prey by the very manner in which Mitya drove up to the steps.

"Dmitri Fyodorovich, dear sir, is it you we have with us again?"

"Hold on, Trifon Borisovich," began Mitya, "first and foremost, where is she?"

"Agrafena Alexandrovna?" The innkeeper understood at once, looking sharply into Mitya's face. "She, too, is here . . ."

"With whom? With whom?"

"Some strangers. One is an official, a Pole, to judge from his speech. He sent the horses for her from here; and there's another with him, a friend of his, or a fellow traveller, there's no telling. They're dressed like civilians."

"Well, are they on a spree? Have they money?"

"Spree, indeed! Small fry, Dmitri Fyodorovich."

"Small fry? And who are the others?"

"They're two gentlemen from the town. . . . They were returning from Cherny, and are putting up here. One's quite a young gentleman, a relative of Mr. Miüsov, he must be, but I've forgotten his name . . . and I expect you know the other, too, a gentleman called Maximov. He's been on a pilgrimage, so he says, to the monastery in the town. He's travelling with this young relation of Mr. Miüsov."

"Is that all?"

"Yes."

"Wait, listen, Trifon Borisovich. Tell me the chief thing: What of her? How is she?"

"Oh, she's only just come. She's sitting with them."

"Is she cheerful? Is she laughing?"

"No, I think she's not laughing much. She seems quite bored. She was combing the young gentleman's hair."

"The Pole's — the officer's?"

"He's not young, and he's not an officer, either. Not his hair, sir. It's the young gentleman that's Mr. Miüsov's relation . . . I forget his name."

"Kalganov?"

"That's it, Kalganov!"

"All right. I'll see for myself. Are they playing cards?"

"They have been playing, but they've left off. They've been drinking tea, the official called for liqueurs."

"Wait, Trifon Borisovich, wait, my good soul, I'll see for myself. Now answer one more question: are the gipsies here?"

"You can't have the gipsies now, Dmitri Fyodorovich. The authorities have chased them off. But we've Jews that play the cymbals and the fiddle in the village, so one might send for them. They'd come."

"Send for them. By all means send for them!" cried Mitya. "And you can get the girls together as you did then, Marya especially, Stepanida, too, and Arina. Two hundred roubles for a chorus!"

"Oh, for a sum like that I can rouse the whole village, though by now they're snoring. But are the peasants here worth such kindness, Dmitri Fyodorovich, or the girls either? To spend a sum like that on clodhoppers! What's the good of giving a peasant a cigarette to smoke, the stinking ruffian! And the girls are all lousy. Besides, I'll get my daughters up for nothing, let alone a sum like that. They've only just gone to bed, I'll kick them awake and set them singing for you. You gave the peasants champagne to drink the other day, e-ech!"

For all his pretended compassion for Mitya, Trifon Borisovich had hidden half a dozen bottles of champagne on the last occasion, and had picked up a hundred-rouble note under the table, and kept it in his fist. "Trifon Borisovich, I sent more than one thousand flying last time I was here. Do you remember?"

"You did send it flying. I remember very well. You must have left three thousand behind you."

"Well, I've come to do the same again, do you see?"

And he pulled out his roll of notes, and held them up before the innkeeper's nose.

"Now, listen and remember. In an hour's time the wine will arrive, savouries, pies, and sweets — bring them all up at once. That box Andrey has got is to be brought up at once, too. Open it, and serve champagne immediately. And the girls, we must have the girls, Marya especially."

He turned to the carriage and pulled the box of pistols out from under the seat.

"Here, Andrey, let's settle. Here's fifteen roubles for the drive, and fifty as a tip . . . for your readiness, for your love. . . . Remember Karamazov!"

"I'm afraid, sir," faltered Andrey. "Give me five roubles extra, but more I won't take. Trifon Borisovich, bear witness. Forgive my foolish words . . ."

"What are you afraid of?" asked Mitya, looking up and down. "Well, go to the devil, if that's it!" he cried, flinging him five roubles. "Now, Trifon Borisovich, take me up quietly and let me first get a look at them, so that they don't see me. Where are they? In the blue room?"

Trifon Borisovich looked apprehensively at Mitya, but at once obediently did his bidding. Leading him into the passage, he went himself into the first large room, adjoining that in which the visitors were sitting, and took the light away. Then he stealthily led Mitya in, and put him in a corner in the dark, whence he could freely watch the company without being seen. But Mitya did not look long, and, indeed, he could not see them, he saw her, his heart throbbed violently, and everything swam before his eyes.

She was sitting sideways at the table in an armchair, and beside her, on the sofa, was the pretty youth, Kalganov. She was holding his hand and seemed to be laughing, while he, seeming vexed and not looking at her, was saying something in a loud voice to Maximov, who sat on the other side of the table, facing Grushenka. Maximov was laughing violently at something. On the sofa sat *he*, and on a chair by the sofa there was another stranger. The one on the sofa was lolling backwards, smoking a pipe, and Mitya had an impression of a stoutish broad-faced short little man, who was apparently angry about something. His friend, the other stranger, struck Mitya as extraordinarily tall, but he could make out nothing more. He caught his breath. He could not bear it for a minute, he put the pistol-case on a chest, and with a throbbing heart, feeling cold all over, he walked straight into the blue room to face the company.

"Aie!" shrieked Grushenka, the first to notice him.

## CHAPTER VII
### THE FIRST AND RIGHTFUL LOVER

WITH his long, rapid strides, Mitya walked up close to the table.

"Gentlemen," he said in a loud voice, almost shouting, yet stammering over every word, "I . . . I'm all right! Don't be afraid!" he exclaimed, "I — there's nothing the matter," he turned suddenly to Grushenka, who had shrunk back in her chair in the direction of Kalganov, and clasped his hand tightly. "I . . . I'm travelling, too. I'm here till morning. Gentlemen, as a traveller . . . may I

stay with you till morning? Only till morning, for the last time, in this same room?"

His last phrases were addressed to the fat little man, with the pipe, sitting on the sofa. The latter removed his pipe from his lips with dignity and observed severely:

"*Panie*, this is our private room. There are other rooms available."

"Why, it's you, Dmitri Fyodorovich! What do you mean?" answered Kalganov suddenly. "Sit down with us. How are you?"

"Delighted to see you, dear . . . and precious fellow, I always thought a lot of you," Mitya responded, joyfully and eagerly, at once holding out his hand across the table.

"Aie! How hard you squeeze! You've quite broken my fingers," laughed Kalganov.

"He always squeezes like that, always," Grushenka put in gaily, with a timid smile, seeming suddenly convinced by Mitya's expression that he was not going to make a scene. She was watching him with intense curiosity and still some uneasiness. She was impressed by something about him, and indeed the last thing she expected of him was that he would come in and speak like this at such a moment.

"Good evening," Maximov ventured blandly, on the left. Mitya rushed up to him, too.

"Good evening. You're here, too! How glad I am to find you here, too! Gentlemen, gentlemen, I . . ." (He addressed the Polish gentleman with the pipe again, evidently taking him for the most important person present.) "I flew here. . . . I wanted to spend my last day, my last hour in this room, in this very room . . . where I, too, adored . . . my queen. . . . Forgive me, *panie*," he cried wildly, "I flew here and made a vow. . . . Oh, don't be afraid, it's my last night! Let's drink to our good understanding. They'll serve the wine at once. . . . I brought this with me." (He suddenly pulled out his bundle of notes.) "Allow me, *panie!* I want music, noise, thunder, like last time. . . . But the worm, the useless worm, will crawl away, and there'll be no more of him! I will celebrate my day of joy on my last night!"

He nearly choked. There was so much, so much he wanted to say, but queer exclamations were all that came from his lips. The Pole gazed fixedly at him, at the bundle of notes in his hand; looked at Grushenka, and was obviously perplexed.

"If my queen will permit . . ." he began.

"What does he mean?" interrupted Grushenka. "I can't help laughing at you, the way you talk. Sit down, Mitya, what are you saying? Don't frighten us, please. You won't frighten us, will you? If you won't, I am glad to see you . . ."

"I, I frighten you?" cried Mitya, flinging up his hands. "Oh, pass me by, go your way, I won't hinder you! . . ."

And suddenly he surprised them all, and no doubt himself as well, by flinging himself on a chair and bursting into tears; he turned his head to the opposite wall, while his arms clasped the back of the chair tight, as though embracing it.

"Come, come, what a fellow you are!" cried Grushenka reproachfully. "That's just how he acted when he came to see me — he would begin talking, and I couldn't make out what he meant. He cried like that once before, and now he's crying again! For shame! Why are you crying? *As though you had anything to cry for!*" she added enigmatically, emphasising each word with a kind of irritability.

"I . . . I'm not crying. . . . Well, good evening!" He instantly turned round in his chair, and suddenly laughed, not his abrupt, wooden laugh, but a long, quivering, inaudible nervous laugh.

"Well, there you are again. . . . Come, cheer up, cheer up!" Grushenka said to him persuasively. "I'm very glad you've come, very glad, Mitya, do you hear, I'm very glad? I want him to stay here with us," she said peremptorily, addressing the whole company, though her words were obviously meant for the man sitting on the sofa. "I wish it, I wish it! And if he goes away I shall go, too!" she added with flashing eyes.

"What my queen commands is law!" pronounced the Pole, gallantly kissing Grushenka's hand. "I beg you, *panie*, to join our company," he added politely, addressing Mitya.

Mitya jumped up with the obvious intention of delivering another tirade, but the words did not come.

"Let's have a drink, *panie*," he blurted out instead of making a speech. Every one laughed.

"Good heavens! I thought he was going to make another speech!" Grushenka exclaimed nervously. "Do you hear, Mitya," she went on insistently, "don't jump up any more; and as for the champagne you've brought, that's fine. I want some myself, and I can't bear liqueurs. And best of all, you've come yourself. We were fearfully dull here. . . . You're on a spree again, I suppose? But put your money in your pocket. Where did you get such a lot?"

Mitya had been, all this time, holding in his hand the crumpled bundle of notes on which the eyes of all, especially the Poles, were fixed. In confusion he thrust them hurriedly into his pocket. He flushed. At that moment the innkeeper brought in an uncorked bottle of champagne, and glasses on a tray. Mitya snatched up the bottle, but he was so bewildered that he did not know what to do with it. Kalganov took it from him and poured out the champagne.

"Another! Another bottle!" Mitya cried to the innkeeper, and, forgetting to clink glasses with the Pole whom he had so solemnly invited to drink to their good understanding, he drank off his glass without waiting for any one else. His whole countenance suddenly changed. The solemn and tragic expression with which he had entered vanished completely, and a look of something childlike came into his face. He seemed to have become suddenly gentle and subdued. He looked shyly and happily at every one, with a continual nervous little laugh, and the grateful expression of a dog who has done wrong, been punished, and forgiven. He seemed to have forgotten everything, and was looking round at every one with a childlike smile of delight. He looked at Grushenka, laughing continually, and bringing his chair close up to hers. By degrees he had gained some idea of the two Poles, though he had formed no definite conception of them yet.

The Pole on the sofa struck him by his dignified demeanour and his Polish accent; and, above all, by his pipe. "Well, what of it? It's a good thing he's smoking a pipe," he reflected. The Pole's puffy face, the face of a man almost forty, with its tiny nose and two very thin, pointed, waxed, and saucy moustaches, had not so far roused any questions in Mitya's mind. He was not even particularly struck by the Pole's wretched little wig made in Siberia, with love-locks foolishly combed forward over the temples. "I suppose it's all right since

he wears a wig," he went on, musing blissfully. The other, younger Pole, who was staring insolently and defiantly at the company and listening to the conversation with silent contempt, still only impressed Mitya by his great height, which was in striking contrast to that of the Pole on the sofa. "If he stood up he'd be six foot three." The thought flitted through Mitya's mind. It occurred to him, too, that this Pole must be the friend of the other, a "bodyguard," as it were, and no doubt the little Pole with the pipe was lording it over the big Pole. But this all seemed to Mitya perfectly right and unquestionable. In the little dog all feeling of rivalry had vanished.

Grushenka's mood and the enigmatic tone of some of her words he completely failed to grasp. All he understood, with thrilling heart, was that she was kind to him, that she had forgiven him, and made him sit by her. He was beside himself with delight, watching her sip her glass of champagne. The silence of the company seemed somehow to strike him, however, and he looked round at every one with expectant eyes.

"Why are we sitting here though, gentlemen? Why don't you begin doing something?" his smiling eyes seemed to ask.

"He keeps talking nonsense, and we were all laughing," Kalganov began suddenly, as though divining his thought, and pointing to Maximov. Mitya immediately stared at Kalganov and then at Maximov.

"He's talking nonsense?" — he laughed his short, wooden laugh, seeming suddenly delighted at something — "ha, ha!"

"Yes. Would you believe it, he will have it that all our cavalry officers in the twenties married Polish women. That's awful rot, isn't it?"

THE FIRST, THE RIGHTFUL LOVER

"Polish women?" repeated Mitya, perfectly ecstatic.

Kalganov was well aware of Mitya's attitude to Grushenka, and he guessed about the Pole, too, but that did not so much interest him, perhaps did not interest him at all; what he was interested in was Maximov. He had come here with Maximov by chance, and he met the Poles here at the inn for the first time in his life. Grushenka he had known before, and had once been with some one to see her; but she had not taken to him. But here she looked at him very affectionately: before Mitya's arrival, she had petted him, but he seemed somehow to be unmoved by it. He was a young man, not over twenty, dressed like a dandy, with a very charming fair-skinned face, and splendid thick, fair hair. From his fair face looked out beautiful pale blue eyes, with an intelligent and sometimes even deep expression, beyond his age indeed, although the young man sometimes looked and talked quite like a child, and was not at all embarrassed by it, even when he was aware of it himself. As a rule he was very wilful, even capricious, though always friendly. Sometimes there was something fixed and obstinate in his expression. He would look at you and listen, seeming all the while to be persistently dreaming about something else. Often he was listless and lazy, at other times he would grow excited, sometimes, apparently, over the most trivial matters.

"Only imagine, I've been taking him about with me for the last four days," he went on, indolently drawling his words, quite naturally though, without the slightest affectation. "Ever since your brother, do you remember, pushed him out of the carriage and sent him flying. That made me take an interest in him

at the time, and I took him into the country, but he keeps talking such rot I'm ashamed to be with him. I'm taking him back."

"The gentleman has not seen Polish ladies, and says what is impossible," the Pole with the pipe observed to Maximov.

He spoke Russian fairly well, much better, anyway, than he pretended. If he used Russian words, he always distorted them in a Polish fashion.

"But I was married to a Polish lady myself," tittered Maximov.

"But did you serve in the cavalry? You were talking about the cavalry. Were you a cavalryman?" put in Kalganov at once.

"Was he a cavalryman indeed? Ha, ha!" cried Mitya, listening eagerly, and turning his inquiring eyes to each as he spoke, as though he expected to hear something wonderful from each.

"No, you see," Maximov turned to him, "what I mean is that those pretty Polish ladies . . . when they danced the mazurka with our Uhlans . . . when one of them dances a mazurka with an Uhlan she jumps on his knee like a kitten . . . a little white one . . . and the *pan*-father and *pan*-mother look on and allow it. . . . They allow it . . . and next day the Uhlan comes and offers her his hand. . . . That's how it is . . . offers her his hand, he — he!" Maximov ended, tittering.

"The gentleman is a *lajdak!*" The tall Pole on the chair growled suddenly and crossed one leg over the other. Mitya's eye was caught by his huge greased boot, with its thick, dirty sole. The dress of both the Poles looked rather greasy.

"Well, now it's *lajdak!* What's he scolding about?" said Grushenka, suddenly vexed.

"*Pani* Agrippina, what the gentleman saw

in Poland were peasant girls, and not ladies of good birth," the Pole with the pipe observed to Grushenka.

"You can reckon on that," the tall Pole snapped contemptuously.

"What next! Let him talk! People talk, why hinder them? It makes it cheerful," Grushenka said crossly.

"I'm not hindering them, *pani*," said the Pole in the wig, with a long look at Grushenka, and relapsing into dignified silence he sucked his pipe again.

"No, no. The Polish gentleman spoke the truth." Kalganov got excited again, as though it were a question of vast import. "He's never been in Poland, so how can he talk about it? I suppose you weren't married in Poland, were you?"

"No, in the Province of Smolensk. Only, an Uhlan had brought her to Russia before that, my future wife, with her mamma and her aunt, and another female relation with a grown-up son. He brought her straight from Poland and handed her over to me. He was a lieutenant in our regiment, a very nice young man. At first he meant to marry her himself. But he didn't marry her, because she turned out to be lame."

"So you married a lame woman?" cried Kalganov.

"Yes. They both deceived me a little bit at the time, and concealed it. I thought she was hopping; she kept hopping . . . I thought it was out of gaiety."

"So glad she was going to marry you!" yelled Kalganov, in a ringing, childish voice.

"Yes, so glad. But the reason turned out to be quite a different one. Afterwards, when we were married, after the wedding, that very evening, she confessed, and very touchingly asked forgiveness. 'I once jumped over a puddle when I was a child,' she said, 'and injured my leg.' He — he!"

Kalganov went off into the most childish laughter, almost falling on the sofa. Grushenka, too, laughed. Mitya was at the pinnacle of happiness.

"Do you know, that's the truth, he's not lying now," exclaimed Kalganov, turning to Mitya; "and do you know, he's been married twice; it's his first wife he's talking about. But his second wife, do you know, ran away, and is alive now."

"Is it possible?" said Mitya, turning quickly to Maximov with an expression of the utmost astonishment on his face.

"Yes. She did run away. I've had that unpleasant experience," Maximov modestly assented, "with a *monsieur*. And what was worse, she'd had all my little property transferred to her beforehand. 'You're an educated man,' she said to me. 'You can always earn your bread.' That's how she settled my business. A venerable bishop once said to me: 'One of your wives was lame, but the other was too light-footed.' He-he!"

"Listen, listen!" cried Kalganov, bubbling over, "if he's telling lies — and he often is — he's only doing it to amuse us all. That's not nasty, is it? You know, I sometimes like him. He's an awful scoundrel, but a natural scoundrel, eh? Don't you think so? Some people are scoundrels out of self-interest, but he's simply so by nature. Only fancy, he claims (he was arguing about it all the way yesterday) that in his 'Dead Souls' Gogol wrote about him. Do you remember, there's a landowner called Maximov in it, whom Nozdryov thrashed? He was tried, do you remember, 'for inflicting bodily injury with rods on the landowner Maximov in a drunken condition.' Would you believe it, he claims that he was that Maximov and that he was flogged! Now can it be so? Chitchikov made his journey, at the very latest, at the beginning of the twenties, so that the dates don't fit. He couldn't have been flogged then, he couldn't, could he?"

It was difficult to imagine what Kalganov was excited about, but his excitement was genuine.

Mitya fully shared his interest.

"Well, but if they did flog him!" he cried, laughing.

"It's not that they flogged me exactly, but what I mean is . . ." put in Maximov.

"What do you mean? Either they flogged you or they didn't."

"What o'clock is it, *panie?*" the Pole with the pipe asked his tall friend, with a bored expression. The other shrugged his shoulders in reply. Neither of them had a watch.

"Why not talk? Let the others talk, too. Must other people keep still because you're bored?" Grushenka flew at him with the evident intention of finding fault. Something seemed for the first time to flash through Mitya's mind. This time the Pole answered with unmistakable irritability.

"*Pani*, I didn't oppose it. I didn't say anything."

"All right then. Come, tell us your story," Grushenka cried to Maximov. "Why did you all stop talking?"

"There's nothing to tell, it's all so foolish," answered Maximov at once, with evident pleasure and some affectation. "Besides, all that's by way of allegory in Gogol, for he's made all the names have a meaning. Nozdryov was really called Nosov, and Kuvshini-

kov had quite a different name, he was called Shkvornev. Fenardi really was called Fenardi, only he wasn't an Italian but a Russian, Petrov, and Mamsel Fenardi was a pretty girl with her pretty little legs in tights, and she had a little short skirt with spangles, and she kept turning round and round, only not for four hours but for four minutes only, and she bewitched every one . . ."

"But what did they flog you for, what for?" cried Kalganov.

"For Piron, sir!" answered Maximov.

"What Piron?" cried Mitya.

"The famous French writer, Piron. We were all drinking then, a big party of us, in a tavern at that very fair. They'd invited me, and first of all I began reciting epigrams. 'Is that you, Boileau? What a funny get-up!' and Boileau answers that he's going to a masquerade, that is to the baths, he-he! And they took it personally, so I made haste to repeat another, very sarcastic, well known to all educated people:

*You're Sappho, I'm Phaon, I see!*
*But one grief is weighing on me:*
*You don't know your way to the sea!*

They were still more offended and began abusing me in the most unseemly way for it. And as ill-luck would have it, to set things right, I began telling a very cultivated anecdote about Piron, how he was not admitted to the French Academy, and to revenge himself wrote his own epitaph:

*Ci-gît Piron qui ne fut rien*
*Pas même académicien.*

They took and flogged me."

"But what for? What for?"

"For my education. People can flog a man

for anything," Maximov concluded, briefly and sententiously.

"Eh, that's enough! That's all nasty, I don't want to listen. I thought it would be amusing," Grushenka cut them short, suddenly.

Mitya started, and at once left off laughing. The tall Pole rose to his feet, and, with the haughty air of a man bored and out of his element, began pacing the room, from one end to the other, his hands behind his back.

"Ah, he can't sit still," said Grushenka, looking at him contemptuously. Mitya began to feel anxious. He noticed besides, that the Pole on the sofa was looking at him with an irritable expression.

"*Panie!*" cried Mitya, "let's drink! and the other *pan*, too! Let us drink."

In a flash he had pulled three glasses towards him, and filled them with champagne.

"To Poland, *panowie*, I drink to your Poland!" cried Mitya.

"I shall be delighted, *panie*," said the Pole on the sofa, with dignity and affable condescension, and he took his glass.

"And the other *pan*, what's his name? Drink, most illustrious, take your glass!" Mitya urged.

"*Pan* Wróblewski," put in the Pole on the sofa.

*Pan* Wróblewski came up to the table, swaying as he walked, and accepted the glass, standing.

"To Poland, *panowie!*" cried Mitya, raising his glass. "Hurrah!"

All three drank. Mitya seized the bottle and again poured out three glasses. "Now to Russia, *panowie*, and let us be brothers!"

"Pour out some for us," said Grushenka; "I'll drink to Russia, too!"

"So will I," said Kalganov.

"And I would, too . . . to Russia, the old grandmother!" tittered Maximov.

"All! All!" cried Mitya. "Trifon Borisovich, some more bottles!"

The other three bottles Mitya had brought with him were put on the table. Mitya filled the glasses.

"To Russia! Hurrah!" he shouted again. All drank the toast except the Poles, and Grushenka tossed off her whole glass at once. The Poles did not touch theirs.

"How's this, *panowie?*" cried Mitya, "won't you drink it?"

*Pan* Wróblewski took the glass, raised it, and said with a resonant voice:

"To Russia as she was before 1772."

"Come, that's better!" cried the other Pole, and they both emptied their glasses at once.

"You're fools, you *panowie*," broke suddenly from Mitya.

"*Panie!*" shouted both the Poles, menacingly, setting on Mitya like a couple of cocks. *Pan* Wróblewski was specially furious.

"Can one help loving one's own country?" he shouted.

"Be silent! Don't quarrel! I won't have any quarrelling!" cried Grushenka imperiously, and she stamped her foot on the floor. Her face glowed, her eyes were shining. The effects of the glass she had just drunk were apparent. Mitya was terribly alarmed.

"*Panowie*, forgive me! It was my fault, I'm sorry. Wróblewski, *panie* Wróblewski, I'm sorry."

"Hold your tongue, you, anyway! Sit down, you stupid!" Grushenka scolded with angry annoyance.

Every one sat down, all were silent, looking at one another.

"Gentlemen, I was the cause of it all," Mitya began again, unable to make anything. of Grushenka's words. "Come, why are we sitting here? What shall we do . . . to amuse ourselves again?"

"Ach, it's certainly anything but amusing!" Kalganov mumbled lazily.

"Let's play faro again, as we did just now," Maximov tittered suddenly.

"Faro? Splendid!" cried Mitya. "If only the *panowie* . . ."

"It's late, *panowie*," the Pole on the sofa responded, as it were unwillingly.

"That's true," assented *Pan* Wróblewski.

"Late? What do you mean by 'late'?" asked Grushenka.

"Late, *pani!* 'a late hour' I mean," the Pole on the sofa explained.

"It's always late with them. They never let you do anything!" Grushenka almost shrieked in her anger. "They're dull themselves, so they want others to be dull. Before you came, Mitya, they sat there silently and kept turning up their noses at me."

"My goddess!" cried the Pole on the sofa. "As you say, so be it! I see you're not well-disposed towards me, that's why I'm gloomy. I'm ready, *panie*," added he, addressing Mitya.

"Begin, *panie*," Mitya assented, pulling his notes out of his pocket, and laying two hundred-rouble notes on the table. "I want to lose a lot to you. Take your cards. Make the bank."

"The cards must come from the innkeeper, *panie*," said the little Pole, gravely and emphatically.

"That's much the best way," chimed in *Pan* Wróblewski.

"From the innkeeper? Very good, I under-stand, let's get them from him. Cards!" Mitya shouted to the innkeeper.

The landlord brought in a new, unopened pack, and informed Mitya that the girls were getting ready, and that the Jews with the cymbals would most likely be there soon; but that the cart with the provisions had not yet arrived. Mitya jumped up from the table and ran into the next room to give orders, but only three girls had arrived, and Marya was not there yet. And he did not know himself what orders to give and why he had run out. He only told them to take out of the box the presents for the girls, the sweets, the toffee, and the fondants. "And vodka for Andrey, vodka for Andrey!" he cried in haste. "I was rude to Andrey!"

Suddenly Maximov, who had followed him out, touched him on the shoulder.

"Give me five roubles," he whispered to Mitya. "I'll stake something at faro, too, he-he!"

"Capital! Splendid! Take ten, here!"

Again he took all the notes out of his pocket and picked out a ten-rouble one. "And if you lose that, come again, come again."

"Very well, sir," Maximov whispered joy-fully, and he ran back again. Mitya too, re-turned, apologising for having kept them waiting. The Poles had already sat down, and opened the pack. They looked much more ami-able, almost cordial. The Pole on the sofa had lighted another pipe and was preparing to deal. He wore an air of solemnity.

"To your places, gentlemen," cried *Pan* Wróblewski.

"No, I'm not going to play any more," ob-served Kalganov, "I've lost fifty roubles to them just now."

"The gentleman had no luck, perhaps he'll

be lucky this time," the Pole on the sofa observed, glancing in his direction.

"How much in the bank? To correspond?" asked Mitya.

"Quite so, *panie*, maybe a hundred, maybe two hundred, as much as you will stake."

"A million!" Mitya guffawed.

"The *Pan* Captain has heard of *Pan* Podwysocki, perhaps?"

"Which Podwysocki?"

"In Warsaw, Podwysocki on one occasion comes to a gaming-house, sees a thousand gold-pieces, and stakes against the bank. The banker says, '*Panie* Podwysocki, are you laying down the gold, or must we trust to your honour?' 'To my honour, *panie*,' says Podwysocki. 'So much the better.' The banker deals out the cards. Podwysocki wins and takes a thousand gold-pieces. 'Wait, *panie*,' says the banker, and pulling out the drawer gives him a million. 'Take it, *panie*, this is your winnings.' There was a million in the bank. 'I didn't know that,' says Podwysocki. '*Panie* Podwysocki,' said the banker, 'you pledged your honour and we pledged ours.' Podwysocki took the million."

"That's not true," said Kalganov.

"*Panie* Kalganov, among gentlemen one doesn't say such things."

"As if a Polish gambler would give up a million, just like that!" cried Mitya, but checked himself at once. "Forgive me, *panie*, it's my fault again, he would, he would give away a million, for the sake of honour, Polish honour. You see how I talk Polish, ha-ha! Here, I stake ten roubles, the knave leads."

"And I put a rouble on the queen, the queen of hearts, the pretty little *panienochka*, he-he!" laughed Maximov, pulling out his queen, and, as though trying to conceal it from every one, he moved right up and crossed himself hurriedly under the table. Mitya won. The rouble won, too.

"A corner!" cried Mitya.

"I'll bet another rouble, a 'single' stake," Maximov muttered gleefully, hugely delighted at having won a rouble.

"Lost!" shouted Mitya. "A 'double' on the seven!"

The seven, too, was trumped.

"Stop!" cried Kalganov suddenly.

"Double! Double!" Mitya doubled his stakes, and each time he doubled the stake, the card he doubled was trumped by the Poles. The rouble stakes kept winning.

"On the double!" shouted Mitya, furiously.

"You've lost two hundred, *panie*. Will you stake another two hundred?" the Pole on the sofa inquired.

"What? Lost two hundred already? Then another two hundred! All doubles!"

And pulling his money out of his pocket, Mitya was about to fling two hundred roubles on the queen, but Kalganov covered it with his hand.

"That's enough!" he shouted in his ringing voice.

"What's the matter?" Mitya stared at him.

"That's enough! I don't want you to play any more. Don't!"

"Why?"

"Because I don't. Hang it, come away. That's why. I won't let you go on playing."

Mitya gazed at him in astonishment.

"Give it up, Mitya. He may be right. You've lost a lot as it is," said Grushenka, with a curious note in her voice. Both the Poles rose from their seats with a deeply offended air.

"Are you joking, *panie?*" said the short man, looking severely at Kalganov.

"How dare you!" *Pan* Wróblewski, too, growled at Kalganov.

"Don't dare to shout like that," cried Grushenka. "Ah, you turkey-cocks!"

Mitya looked at each of them in turn. But something in Grushenka's face suddenly struck him, and at the same instant something new flashed into his mind — a strange new thought!

"*Pani* Agrippina," the little Pole began, crimson with anger, when Mitya suddenly went up to him and slapped him on the shoulder.

"Most illustrious, two words with you."

"What do you want?"

"In the next room, I've two words to say to you, something pleasant, very pleasant. You'll be glad to hear it."

The little *pan* was taken aback and looked apprehensively at Mitya. He agreed at once, however, on condition that *Pan* Wróblewski went with them.

"The body-guard? Let him come, and I want him, too. I must have him!" cried Mitya. "March, *panowie!*"

"Where are you going?" asked Grushenka anxiously.

"We'll be back in one moment," answered Mitya.

There was a sort of boldness, a sudden confidence shining in his eyes. His face had looked very different when he entered the room an hour before.

He led the Poles, not into the large room where the chorus of girls was assembling and the table was being laid, but into the bedroom on the right, where the trunks and chests were kept, and there were two large beds, with pyr-amids of cotton pillows on each. There was a lighted candle on a small deal table in the corner. The small man and Mitya sat down at this table, facing each other, while the huge Wróblewski stood beside them, his hands behind his back. The Poles looked severe but were obviously curious.

"What can I do for you, *panie?*" lisped the little Pole.

"Well, look here, *panie*, I won't keep you long. Here's money for you," he pulled out his notes. "Would you like three thousand? Take it and go your way."

The Pole gazed open-eyed at Mitya, with a searching look.

"Three thousand, *panie?*" He exchanged glances with Wróblewski.

"Three, *panowie*, three! Listen, *panie*, I see you're a sensible man. Take three thousand and go to the devil, and take Wróblewski with you — d'you hear? But, at once, this very minute, and for ever. You understand that, *panie*, for ever. Here's the door, you go out of it. What have you got there, an overcoat, a fur coat? I'll bring it out to you. They'll get the horses out directly, and then — good-bye, *panie!* Eh?"

Mitya awaited an answer with assurance. He had no doubts. An expression of extraordinary resolution passed over the Pole's face.

"And the money, *panie?*"

"The money, *panie?* Five hundred roubles I'll give you this moment for the journey, and as a first instalment, and two thousand five hundred to-morrow, in town — I swear on my honour, I'll get it, I'll get it at any cost!" cried Mitya.

The Poles exchanged glances again. The short man's face looked more forbidding.

"Seven hundred, seven hundred, not five

hundred, at once, this minute, cash down!" Mitya added, feeling that something was wrong. "What's the matter, *panie?* Don't you trust me? I can't give you the whole three thousand straight off. If I give it, you may come back to her to-morrow. . . . Besides, I haven't the three thousand with me. I've got it at home in town," faltered Mitya, his spirit sinking at every word he uttered. "Upon my word, the money's there, hidden."

In an instant an extraordinary sense of personal dignity showed itself in the little man's face.

"What next?" he asked ironically. "For shame!" and he spat on the floor. *Pan* Wróblewski spat, too.

"You do that, *panie*," said Mitya, recognising with despair that all was over, "because you hope to make more out of Grushenka? You're a couple of capons, that's what you are!"

"This is a mortal insult!" The little Pole turned as red as a lobster, and he went out of the room, briskly, as though unwilling to hear another word. Wróblewski swung out after him, and Mitya followed, embarrassed and crestfallen. He was afraid of Grushenka, afraid that the *pan* would at once raise an outcry. And so indeed he did. The Pole walked into the room and threw himself in a theatrical attitude before Grushenka.

"*Pani* Agrippina, I have received a mortal insult!" he exclaimed. But Grushenka suddenly lost all patience, as though they had touched her in the tenderest spot.

"Speak Russian! Speak Russian!" she cried, "not another word of Polish! You used to talk Russian. You can't have forgotten it in five years."

She was red with anger.

"*Pani* Agrippina . . ."

"My name's Agrafena, Grushenka, speak Russian or I won't listen!"

The Pole gasped with offended dignity, and quickly and pompously delivered himself in broken Russian:

"*Pani* Agrafena, I came here to forget the past and forgive it, to forget all that has happened till to-day . . ."

"Forgive? Came here to forgive me?" Grushenka cut him short, jumping up from her seat.

"Just so, *pani*, I'm not small-minded, I'm magnanimous. But I was astounded when I saw your lovers. *Pan* Mitya offered me three thousand, in the other room, to depart. I spat in the *pan's* face."

"What? He offered you money for me?" cried Grushenka, hysterically. "Is it true, Mitya? How did you dare? Am I for sale?"

"*Panie, panie!*" shouted Mitya, "she's pure and shining, and I have never been her lover! That's a lie . . ."

"How dare you defend me before him?" shrieked Grushenka. "It wasn't virtue kept me pure, and it wasn't that I was afraid of Kuzma, but that I might hold up my head when I met him, and tell him he's a scoundrel. And did he actually refuse the money?"

"He took it! He took it!" cried Mitya; "only he wanted to get the whole three thousand at once, and I could only give him seven hundred straight off."

"I see: he heard I had money, and came here to marry me!"

"*Pani* Agrippina!" cried the little Pole. "I'm — a knight, I'm — a nobleman, and not a *lajdak*. I came here to make you my wife and I find you a different woman, wilful and shameless."

"Oh, go back where you came from! I'll tell them to turn you out and you'll be turned out," cried Grushenka, furious. "I've been a fool, a fool, to have tortured myself all these five years! And it wasn't for his sake, it was my anger made me miserable. And this isn't he at all! Was he like this? It might be his father! Where did you get your wig from? He was a falcon, but this is a gander. He used to laugh and sing to me. . . . And I've been crying for five years, damned fool that I was, low, shameless creature!"

She sank back in her armchair and hid her face in her hands.

At that instant the chorus of Mokroye girls began singing in the room on the left — a rollicking dance song.

"A regular Sodom!" Wróblewski roared suddenly. "Innkeeper, send the shameless hussies away!"

The innkeeper, who had been for some time past inquisitively peeping in at the door, hearing shouts and guessing that his guests were quarrelling, at once entered the room.

"What are you shouting for? D'you want to split your throat?" he said, addressing Wróblewski, with surprising rudeness.

"You beast!" bellowed *Pan* Wróblewski.

"Beast? And what sort of cards were you playing with just now? I gave you a pack and you hid it. You played with marked cards! I could send you to Siberia for playing with marked cards, d'you know that, for it's just the same as forged bank-notes . . ."

And going up to the sofa he thrust his fingers between the sofa-back and the cushion, and pulled out an unopened pack of cards.

"Here's my pack unopened!"

He held it up and showed it to all in the room. "From where I stood I saw him slip my pack away, and put his in place of it — you're a cheat and not a gentleman!"

"And I twice saw the *pan* change a card!" cried Kalganov.

"How shameful! How shameful!" exclaimed Grushenka, striking her hands together, and blushing for genuine shame. "Good Lord, he's come to that!"

"I thought so, too!" said Mitya. But before he had uttered the words, Wróblewski, abashed and infuriated, shook his fist at Grushenka, shouting:

"You common harlot!"

Mitya flew at him at once, seized him in both hands, lifted him in the air, and in one instant had carried him into the room on the right, from which they had just come.

"I've laid him on the floor, there," he announced, returning at once, gasping with excitement. "He's struggling, the scoundrel! But he won't come back, no fear of that! . . ."

He closed one half of the folding doors, and holding the other ajar called out to the little Pole:

"Most illustrious, will you be pleased to follow him? I beg you."

"My dear Dmitri Fyodorovich," said Trifon Borisovich, "make them give you back the money you lost. It's as good as stolen from you."

"I don't want my fifty roubles back," Kalganov declared suddenly.

"I don't want my two hundred, either," cried Mitya, "I wouldn't take it for anything! Let him keep it as a consolation."

"Bravo, Mitya! You're a trump, Mitya!" cried Grushenka, and there was a note of fierce anger in the exclamation.

The little *pan*, crimson with fury, but still mindful of his dignity, was making for the door, but he stopped short and said suddenly, addressing Grushenka:

"*Pani*, if you want to come with me, come. If not, good-bye."

And swelling with indignation and importance he went to the door. This was a man of character: he had so good an opinion of himself that after all that had passed, he still expected that she would go with him. Mitya slammed the door after him.

"Lock it," said Kalganov. But the key clicked on the other side, they had locked themselves in.

"That's capital!" exclaimed Grushenka angrily and ruthlessly. "That's capital! Serve them right!"

## CHAPTER VIII
### DELIRIUM

WHAT followed was almost an orgy, a feast to which all were welcome. Grushenka was the first to call for wine.

"I want to drink. I want to be quite drunk, as we were before. Do you remember, Mitya, do you remember how we made friends here last time!"

Mitya himself was almost delirious, feeling that his happiness was at hand. But Grushenka was continually sending him away from her:

"Go and enjoy yourself. Tell them to dance, to make merry, 'let the stove and cottage dance'; as it was last time," she kept exclaiming. She was tremendously excited. And Mitya kept running out to give orders. The chorus had assembled in the next room. The room in which they had been sitting till that moment was too small, and was divided in two by cotton curtains, behind which was a huge bed with a puffy feather mattress and a pyramid of cotton pillows. In the four rooms for visitors there were beds. Grushenka settled herself just at the door. Mitya placed an easy-chair for her. She had sat in the same place to watch the dancing and singing "the time before," when they had made merry there the first time. The same girls had come again; the Jewish band with fiddles and zithers had come, too, and at last the long expected cart had arrived with the wines and provisions.

Mitya bustled about. Strangers, too, began coming into the room to look on, peasants and their women, who had been roused from sleep and attracted by the hopes of another marvellous entertainment such as they had enjoyed a month before. Mitya remembered their faces, greeting and embracing every one he knew. He uncorked bottles and poured out wine for every one who presented himself. Only the girls were very eager for the champagne. The men preferred rum, cognac, and, above all, hot punch. Mitya had chocolate made for all the girls, and ordered that three samovars should be kept boiling all night to provide tea and punch for all and sundry; every one could help himself.

In a word, disorder and absurdity reigned, but Mitya was in his native element, as it were, and the more absurd things grew, the higher his spirits rose. If a peasant had asked him for money at that moment, he would have pulled out his entire roll and proceeded to distribute the money right and left. This was probably why the innkeeper, Trifon Borisovich, kept hovering about Mitya to protect him. He seemed to have given up all idea of going to bed that night, though he drank little, only one glass of punch, and kept sharp watch over Mitya's interests after his own fashion. He intervened in the nick of time, tenderly and obsequiously persuading Mitya not to give "cigarettes and Rhine wine" and, God forbid, money, to the peasants as he had done before. He was very indignant, too, at the peasant girls drinking liqueur, and eating sweets.

"They're a lousy lot, Dmitri Fyodorovich," he said. "I'll give them a kick, every one of them, and I will order them to take it as an honour — that's all they're worth!"

Mitya remembered Andrey again, and ordered punch to be sent out to him. "I was rude to him just now," he repeated in a weak, melting voice. Kalganov did not want to drink, and at first did not care for the girls' singing; but after he had drunk a couple of glasses of champagne he became extraordinarily lively, strolling about the room, laughing and praising the music and the songs, admiring every one and everything. Maximov, blissfully drunk, never left his side. Grushenka, too, was beginning to get drunk. Pointing to Kalganov, she said to Mitya: "What a charming, what a wonderful boy he is!"

And Mitya, delighted, ran to kiss Kalganov and Maximov. Oh, he had high anticipations! She had said nothing yet, and seemed, indeed, purposely to refrain from speaking. But she looked at him from time to time with caressing and ardent eyes. At last she suddenly gripped his hand and drew him vigorously to her. She was sitting at the moment in the armchair by the door.

"How was it you came just now, eh? How you walked in! . . . I *was* frightened. So you wanted to give me up to him, did you? Did you really want to?"

"I didn't want to spoil your happiness!" Mitya faltered blissfully. But she did not need his answer.

"Well, go and enjoy yourself . . ." she sent him away once more. "Don't cry, I'll call you back again."

He would run away, and she listened to the singing and looked at the dancing, though her eyes followed him wherever he went. But in another quarter of an hour she would call him once more and again he would run back to her.

"Come, sit beside me, tell me, how did you hear about me, and my going off yesterday? From whom did you first hear it?"

And Mitya began telling her all about it, disconnectedly, incoherently, feverishly. He spoke strangely, often frowning, and stopping abruptly.

"What are you frowning at?" she asked.

"Nothing. . . . I left a sick man there. If only he got well, if only I knew that he was going to get well, I'd give ten years of my life for that right away!"

"Well, never mind him, if he's ill. So you meant to shoot yourself to-morrow! What a silly boy! What for? I like such reckless fellows as you," she lisped, with a rather halting tongue. "So you would go to any lengths for me, eh? Did you really mean to shoot yourself to-morrow, you stupid? No, wait a little. To-morrow I may have a little word to say to you. . . . I won't say it to-night, but to-morrow. You'd like it to be to-night? No, I don't want to to-night.. Come, go along now, go and amuse yourself."

Once, however, she called him, as it were, puzzled and uneasy.

"Why are you sad? I see you're sad. . . . Yes, I see it," she added, looking intently into his eyes. "Though you keep kissing the peasants and shouting, I see something. No, be merry. I'm merry; you be merry, too. . . . I love somebody here. Guess who it is. Ah, look,

335

my boy has fallen asleep, poor dear, he's drunk."

She meant Kalganov. He was, in fact, drunk, and had dropped asleep for a moment, sitting on the sofa. But he was not merely drowsy from drink; he felt suddenly dejected, or, as he said, "bored." He was intensely depressed by the girls' songs, which, as the drinking went on, gradually became coarse and more reckless. And the dances were as bad. Two girls dressed up as bears, and a lively girl, called Stepanida, with a stick in her hand, acted the part of showman, and began to "exhibit them."

"Look alive, Marya, or you'll get the stick!" she shouted.

The bears rolled on the ground at last in the most unseemly fashion, amid roars of laughter from the closely packed crowd of men and women.

"Well, let them! Let them!" said Grushenka sententiously, with a blissful expression on her face. "When they do get a day to enjoy themselves, why shouldn't folks be happy?"

Kalganov looked as though he had been besmirched with dirt.

"It's swinish, all this peasant foolery," he murmured, moving away; "these are spring games, they play them when they watch for the sun all through the summer night."

He particularly disliked one "new" song which they sang to a jaunty dance tune. It described how a gentleman came and tried his luck with the girls, to see whether they would love him:

*The master came to ask the girls:*
*Would they love him, would they not?*

But the girls could not love the master:

*He would beat me cruelly:*
*I can't feel love for such as he.*

Then a gipsy comes along and he, too, tries his luck:

*The gipsy came and asked the girls:*
*Would they love him, would they not?*

But they couldn't love the gipsy either:

*The gipsy will be thieving,*
*And me, I will be grieving.*

And many more men come to try their luck, among them a soldier:

*The soldier came and asked the girls:*
*Would they love him, would they not?*

But the soldier is rejected with contempt, in an unprintable couplet, which was sung with perfect frankness and produced a furore in the audience. The song ends with a merchant:

*The merchant came and asked the girls:*
*Would they love him, would they not?*

And it appears that he wins their love because:

*The merchant will be trading,*
*And me, I'll be parading.*

Kalganov was positively indignant:

"That song must have been made just yesterday," he said aloud. "Who writes such things for them? They might just as well have had a railway man or a Jew come to try his luck with the girls; they'd have carried all before them."

And, almost as though it were a personal affront, he declared, on the spot, that he was bored, sat down on the sofa and immediately

THE ORGY

fell asleep. His pretty little face grew rather pale, as it fell back on the sofa cushion.

"Look how pretty he is," said Grushenka, taking Mitya up to him. "I was combing his hair just now; his hair's like flax, and so thick . . ."

And, bending over him tenderly, she kissed his forehead. Kalganov instantly opened his eyes, looked at her, stood up, and with the most anxious air inquired where was Maximov?

"So that's who it is you want," Grushenka laughed. "Stay with me a minute. Mitya, run and find his Maximov."

Maximov, it appeared, could not tear himself away from the girls, only running away from time to time to pour himself out a glass of liqueur. He had drunk two cups of chocolate. His face was red, and his nose was crimson; his eyes were moist, and melting. He ran up and announced that he was going to dance the "*sabotière*."

"They taught me all those well-bred, aristocratic dances when I was little . . ."

"Go, go with him, Mitya, and I'll watch from here how he dances," said Grushenka.

"No, no, I'm coming to look on, too," exclaimed Kalganov, brushing aside in the most naïve way Grushenka's offer to sit with him. They all went to look on. Maximov actually danced his dance. But it roused no great admiration in any one but Mitya. It consisted of nothing but skipping and hopping, kicking up the heels, and at every skip Maximov slapped the upturned sole of his foot with his palm. Kalganov did not like it at all, but Mitya kissed the dancer.

"Well, thank you. You're tired perhaps? What are you looking for here? Would you like some sweets? A cigarette, perhaps?"

"A cigarette."

"Don't you want a drink?"

"I'll just have a liqueur. . . . Have you any chocolates?"

"Yes, there's a heap of them on the table there. Take one, you dear soul!"

"No, sir, I like one with vanilla . . . the old men's sort. He-he!"

"No, brother, we've none of that special sort."

"I say," the old man bent down to whisper in Mitya's ear. "That girl there, little Marya, he-he! How would it be if out of your kindness you were to help me make friends with her?"

"So that's what you're after! No, brother, that won't do!"

"I'd do no harm to any one," Maximov muttered disconsolately.

"Oh, all right, all right. They only come here to dance and sing, you know, brother. But damn it all, wait a bit! . . . Eat and drink and be merry, meanwhile. Don't you want money?"

"Later on perhaps," smiled Maximov.

"All right, all right. . . ."

Mitya's head was burning. He went outside to the wooden balcony which ran round the whole building on the inner side, overlooking the courtyard. The fresh air revived him. He stood alone in a dark corner, and suddenly clutched his head in both hands. His scattered thoughts suddenly came together; his sensations blended into a whole and threw a sudden light into his mind. A fearful and terrible light! "If I'm to shoot myself, when shall I, if not now?" passed through his mind. "Why not go for the pistols, bring them here, and here, in this dark, dirty corner, make an end?" Almost a minute he stood, undecided.

A few hours earlier, when he had been dashing here, he was pursued by disgrace, by the theft he had committed, and that blood, that blood! . . . But yet it was easier for him then. Then everything was over: he had lost her, given her up. She had perished as far as he was concerned; she had vanished — oh, then his death sentence had been easier for him; at least it had seemed necessary, inevitable, for what had he to stay on earth for?

But now? Was it the same as then? Now one phantom, one terror at least was at an end: that first, rightful lover, that fateful figure had vanished, leaving no trace. The terrible ghost had turned into something so small, so comic; it had been carried into the bedroom and locked in. It would never return. She was ashamed, and from her eyes he could see now whom she loved. Now to live, to live! . . . But he could not go on living, he could not; oh, damnation! "Oh, God! restore to life the man I knocked down at the fence! Let this fearful cup pass from me! Lord, Thou hast wrought miracles for such sinners as me! But what, what if the old man's alive? Oh, then the shame of the other disgrace I would wipe away. I would restore the stolen money. I'd give it back; I'd get it somehow. . . . No trace of that shame will remain except in my heart for ever! But no, no; oh, impossible cowardly dreams! Oh, damnation!"

Yet there was a ray of light and hope in his darkness. He jumped up and ran back to the room — to her, to her, his queen for ever! Was not one moment of her love worth all the rest of life, even in the agonies of disgrace? This wild question clutched at his heart. "To her, to her alone, to see her, to hear her, to think of nothing, to forget everything, if only for that night, for an hour, for a moment!" Just as he turned from the balcony into the passage, he came upon the innkeeper, Trifon Borisovich. He thought he looked gloomy and worried, and fancied he was looking for him.

"What is it, Trifon Borisovich, are you looking for me?"

"No, sir." The innkeeper seemed disconcerted. "Why should I be looking for you? And you . . . where have you been?"

"Why do you look so glum? You're not angry, are you? Wait a bit, you shall soon get to bed. . . . What's the time?"

"It'll be three o'clock. Past three, it must be."

"We'll leave off soon. We'll leave off."

"Don't mention it; it doesn't matter. Keep it up as long as you like . . ."

"What's the matter with him?" Mitya wondered for an instant, and he ran back to the room where the girls were dancing. But she was not there. She was not in the blue room either; there was no one but Kalganov asleep on the sofa. Mitya peeped behind the curtain — she was there. She was sitting in the corner, on a trunk. Bent forward, with her head and arms on the bed close by, she was crying bitterly, doing her utmost to stifle her sobs that she might not be heard. Seeing Mitya, she beckoned him to her, and when he ran to her, she grasped his hand tightly.

"Mitya, Mitya, I loved him, you know," she began in a whisper. "How I have loved him these five years, all that time! Did I love him or only my own anger? No, him, him! It's a lie that it was my anger I loved and not him. Mitya, I was only seventeen then; he was so kind to me, so merry; he used to sing to me. . . . Or so it seemed to a silly girl like me. . . . And now, O Lord, it's not the same man. Even his face is not the same; he's different altogether. I shouldn't have known him. I drove here with Timofey, and all the way I was thinking how I should meet him, what I should say to him, how we should look at one another. My soul was faint, and all of a sudden it was just as though he had emptied a pail of dirty water over me. He talked to me like a schoolmaster, all so grave and learned; he met me so solemnly that I was struck dumb. I couldn't get a word in. At first I thought he was ashamed to talk before his great big Pole. I sat staring at him and wondering why I couldn't say a word to him now. It must have been his wife that spoiled him; you know he threw me over to get married. She must have changed him like that. Mitya, how shameful it is! Oh, Mitya, I'm ashamed, I'm ashamed of my whole life. Let those five years be cursed, cursed, cursed!"

And again she burst into tears, but clung tight to Mitya's hand and did not let it go.

"Mitya darling, stay, don't go away. I want to say one word to you," she whispered, and suddenly raised her face to him. "Listen, tell me who it is I love? I love one man here. Who is that man? That's what you must tell me."

A smile lighted up her face that was swollen with weeping, and her eyes shone in the half darkness.

"A falcon flew in, and my heart sank within me. 'Fool! that's the man you love!' That was what my heart whispered to me at once. You came in and everything grew bright. What's he afraid of? I wondered. For you were frightened; you couldn't speak. It's not them he's afraid of — could you be frightened of any one? It's me he's afraid of, I thought, only me. So Fenya told you, you little stupid, how I called to Alyosha out of the window that I'd loved Mityenka for one hour, and that I was

going now to love . . . another. Mitya, Mitya, how could I be such a fool as to think I could love any one after you? Do you forgive me, Mitya? Do you forgive me or not? Do you love me? Do you love me?" She jumped up and held him with both hands on his shoulders. Mitya, dumb with rapture, gazed into her eyes, at her face, at her smile, and suddenly clasped her tightly in his arms and kissed her passionately.

"You will forgive me for having tormented you? It was through spite I tormented you all. It was for spite I drove the old man out of his mind. . . . Do you remember how you drank at my house one day and broke the wineglass? I remembered that and I broke a glass to-day and drank 'to my vile heart.' Mitya, my falcon, why don't you kiss me? He kissed me once, and now he draws back and looks and listens. Why listen to me? Kiss me, kiss me hard, that's right. If you love, well then love! I'll be your slave now, your slave for the rest of my life. It's sweet to be a slave. Kiss me! Beat me, torture me, injure me. . . . And I do deserve to suffer. Stay, wait, afterwards, I won't have that . . ." she suddenly thrust him away. "Go along, Mitya, I'll come and have some wine, I want to be drunk, I'm going to get drunk and dance; I must, I must!" She tore herself away from him and disappeared behind the curtain. Mitya followed like a drunken man.

"Yes, come what may — whatever may happen now, for one minute I'd give the whole world," he thought. Grushenka did, in fact, toss off a whole glass of champagne at one gulp, and became at once very tipsy. She sat down in the same chair as before, with a blissful smile on her face. Her cheeks were blazing, her lips were burning, her flashing eyes grew

339

filmy; there was the lure of passion in her eyes. Even Kalganov's heart was stung and he went up to her.

"Did you feel how I kissed you when you were asleep just now?" she said thickly. "I'm drunk now, that's what it is. . . . And aren't you drunk? And why isn't Mitya drinking? Why don't you drink, Mitya? I drank, and you don't drink . . ."

"I am drunk! I'm drunk as it is . . . drunk with you . . . and now I'll be drunk with wine, too."

He drank off another glass, and — he thought it strange himself — that glass made him completely drunk. He was suddenly drunk, although till that moment he had been quite sober, he remembered that. From that moment everything whirled about him, as though he were delirious. He walked, laughed, talked to everybody, without knowing what he was doing. Only one persistent burning sensation made itself felt continually, "like a red-hot coal in his heart," he said afterwards. He went up to her, sat beside her, gazed at her, listened to her. . . . She became very talkative, kept calling every one to her, and beckoned to different girls out of the chorus. When the girl came up, she either kissed her or made the sign of the cross over her. In another minute she might have cried. She was greatly amused by the "little old man," as she called Maximov. He ran up every minute to kiss her hands, "each little finger," and finally he danced another dance to an old song, which he sang himself. He danced with special ardour to the refrain:

*The little pig says — umph! umph! umph!*
*The little calf says — moo, moo, moo,*
*The little duck says — quack, quack, quack,*

*The little goose says — gabble, gabble, gabble.*
*The hen went strutting through the entry.*
*Cluck, cluck, cluck, cluck, cluck, she says,*
*Cluck, cluck, cluck, cluck, cluck, she says.*

"Give him something, Mitya," said Grushenka. "Give him a present, he's poor, you know. Ah, the poor, the insulted. . . . Do you know, Mitya, I shall go into a nunnery. No, I really shall one day. Alyosha said something to me to-day that I shall remember all my life. . . . Yes. . . . But to-night let us dance. To-morrow to the nunnery, but to-night we'll dance. I want to play to-night, good people, and what of it? God will forgive us. If I were God, I'd forgive every one: 'My dear sinners, from this day forth I forgive you.' I'm going to beg forgiveness: 'Forgive me, good people, a silly woman.' I'm a beast, that's what I am. But I want to pray. I gave a little onion. Wicked as I've been, I want to pray. Mitya, let them dance, don't stop them. Every one in the world is good. Every one — even the worst of them. The world's a nice place. Though we're bad the world's all right. We're good and bad, good and bad. . . . Come tell me, I've something to ask you; come here every one, and I'll ask you: Why am I so good? You know I am good. I'm very good. . . . Come, why am I so good?"

So Grushenka babbled on, getting more and more drunk. At last she announced that she was going to dance, too. She got up from her chair, staggering. "Mitya, don't give me any more wine — if I ask you, don't give it to me. Wine gives me no peace. Everything's going round, the stove, and everything. I want to dance. Let every one see how I dance . . . let them see how beautifully I dance . . ."

She really meant it. She pulled a white cambric handkerchief out of her pocket, and took it by one corner in her right hand, to wave it in the dance. Mitya ran to and fro, the girls were quiet, and got ready to break into a dancing song at the first signal. Maximov, hearing that Grushenka wanted to dance, squealed with delight, and ran skipping about in front of her, humming:

> *"With legs so slim and sides so trim*
> *And its little tail curled tight."*

But Grushenka waved her handkerchief at him and drove him away.

"Sh-h! Mitya, why don't they come? Let every one come . . . to look on. Call them in, too, the ones that were locked in. . . . Why did you lock them in? Tell them I'm going to dance. Let them look on, too. . . ."

Mitya walked with a drunken swagger to the locked door, and began knocking at the door with his fist.

"Hi, you . . . Podwysockis! Come, she's going to dance. She wants you."

"*Lajdak!*" one of the Poles shouted in reply.

"You're a sub-*lajdak* yourself! You're a little scoundrel, that's what you are."

"Leave off laughing at Poland," said Kalganov sententiously. He, too, was drunk.

"Be quiet, boy! If I call him a scoundrel, it doesn't mean that I called all Poland so. One *lajdak* doesn't make a Poland. Be quiet, my pretty boy, eat a sweetmeat."

"Ach, what fellows! As though they were not human beings. Why won't they make friends?" said Grushenka, and went forward to dance. The chorus broke into "Ah, my entry, my new entry!" Grushenka flung back her head, half opened her lips, smiled, waved her handkerchief, and suddenly, with a violent lurch, stood still in the middle of the room, looking bewildered.

"I'm weak . . ." she said in an exhausted voice. "Forgive me. . . . I'm weak, I can't. . . . I'm sorry." She bowed to the chorus, and then began bowing in all directions.

"I'm sorry. . . . Forgive me. . . ."

"The lady's been drinking. The pretty lady has been drinking," voices were heard saying.

"The lady's drunk too much," Maximov explained to the girls, giggling.

"Mitya, lead me away . . . take me," said Grushenka helplessly. Mitya pounced on her, snatched her up in his arms, and carried the precious burden through the curtains.

"Well, now I'll go," thought Kalganov, and walking out of the blue room, he closed the two halves of the door after him. But the orgy in the larger room went on and grew louder and louder. Mitya laid Grushenka on the bed and kissed her on the lips.

"Don't touch me . . ." she faltered, in an imploring voice. "Don't touch me, till I'm yours. . . . I've told you I'm yours, but don't touch me . . . spare me. . . . With them here, with them close, you mustn't. He's here. It's nasty here . . ."

"I'll obey you! I won't think of it . . . I worship you!" muttered Mitya. "Yes, it's nasty here, it's despicable."

And still holding her in his arms, he sank on his knees by the bedside.

"I know, though you're a brute, you're noble-hearted," Grushenka articulated with difficulty. "It must be honourable . . . it shall be honourable in the future . . . and let us be honest, let us be good, not brutes, but good . . . take me away, take me far away, do you hear? I don't want it to be here, but far, far away. . . ."

"Oh, yes, yes, it must be!" said Mitya, pressing her in his arms. "I'll take you and we'll fly away. . . . Oh, I'd give my whole life for one year only to know about that blood!"

"What blood?" asked Grushenka, bewildered.

"Nothing," muttered Mitya, through his teeth. "Grusha, you wanted to be honest, but I'm a thief. But I've stolen money from Katya. . . . Disgrace, a disgrace!"

"From Katya, from that young lady? No, you didn't steal it. Give it her back, take it from me. . . . Why make a fuss? Now everything of mine is yours. What does money matter? We shall waste it anyway. . . . Folks like us are bound to run through money. But we'd better go and work the land. I want to dig the earth with my own hands. We must work, do you hear? Alyosha said so. I won't be your mistress, I'll be faithful to you, I'll be your slave, I'll work for you. We'll go to the young lady and bow down to her together, so that she may forgive us, and then we'll go away. And if she won't forgive us, we'll go, anyway. Take her her money and love me. . . . Don't love her. . . . Don't love her any more. If you love her, I will strangle her. . . . I'll put out both her eyes with a needle . . ."

"I love you. I love only you. I'll love you in Siberia . . ."

"Why Siberia? Never mind, Siberia if you like. I don't care . . . we'll work . . . there's snow in Siberia. . . . I love driving in the snow . . . and there must be bells. . . . Do you hear, there's a bell ringing? Where is that bell ringing? There are people coming. . . . Now it's stopped."

She closed her eyes, exhausted, and suddenly fell asleep for an instant. There had in-deed been the sound of a bell in the distance, but the ringing had ceased. Mitya let his head sink on her breast. He did not notice that the bell had ceased ringing, nor did he notice that the songs had ceased, and that instead of singing and drunken clamour there was absolute stillness in the house. Grushenka opened her eyes.

"What's the matter? Was I asleep? Yes . . . a bell . . . I've been asleep and dreamt I was driving over the snow with bells, and I dozed. I was with some one I loved, with you. And far, far away. I was holding you and kissing you, nestling close to you. I was cold, and the snow glistened. . . . You know how the snow glistens at night when the moon shines. It was as though I was not on earth. I woke up, and my dear one is close to me. How sweet that is . . ."

"Close to you," murmured Mitya, kissing her dress, her bosom, her hands. And suddenly he had a strange fancy: it seemed to him that she was looking straight before her, not at him, not into his face, but over his head, with an intent, almost uncanny fixity. An expression of wonder, almost of alarm, came suddenly into her face.

"Mitya, who is that looking at us?" she whispered.

Mitya turned, and saw that some one had, in fact, parted the curtains and seemed to be watching them. And not one person alone, it seemed.

He jumped up and walked quickly to the intruder.

"Here, this way, kindly, come here," said a voice, speaking gently but firmly and peremptorily.

Mitya passed to the other side of the curtain and stood stock still. The room was filled

"I AM DRUNK WITH YOU"

with people, but not those who had been there before. An instantaneous shiver ran down his back, and he shuddered. He recognised all those people instantly. That tall, stout old man in the overcoat and the cap with a cockade — was the police captain, Mihail Makarovich. And that "consumptive-looking" trim dandy, "who always has such polished boots" — that was the assistant prosecutor. "He has a watch worth four hundred roubles; he showed it to me." And that small young man in spectacles . . . Mitya forgot his surname though he knew him, had seen him: he was the magistrate, the examining magistrate, from the "school of jurisprudence," who had only lately come to the town. And this man — the inspector of police, Mavriky Mavrikyevich, a man he knew well. And those fellows with the brass badges on, why are they here? And those other two . . . peasants. . . . And there at the door Kalganov with Trifon Borisovich. . . .

"Gentlemen! What's this for, gentlemen?" began Mitya, but suddenly, as though beside himself, not knowing what he was doing, he cried aloud, at the top of his voice:

"I un — der — stand!"

The young man in spectacles moved forward suddenly, and stepping up to Mitya, began with dignity, though hurriedly:

"We have to make . . . in brief, I beg you to come this way, this way to the sofa. . . . It is absolutely imperative for us to have a talk with you."

"The old man!" cried Mitya frantically.

"The old man and his blood! . . . I understand." And he sank, almost fell, on a chair close by, as though he had been mown down by a scythe.

"You understand? He understands it! Monster and parricide! Your father's blood cries out against you!" the old captain of police roared suddenly, stepping up to Mitya.

He was beside himself, crimson in the face and quivering all over.

"This is impossible!" cried the small young man. "Mihail Makarovich, Mihail Makarovich, this won't do! It won't do, sir! . . . Allow me to be the one to speak. I should never have expected such behaviour from you . . ."

"This is delirium, gentlemen, raving delirium," cried the captain of police; "look at him: drunk, at this time of night, in the company of a disreputable woman, with the blood of his father upon him. . . . It's delirium!"

"I beg you most earnestly, dear Mihail Makarovich, to restrain your feelings," the prosecutor said in a rapid whisper to the old police captain, "or I shall be forced to resort to . . ."

But the little lawyer did not allow him to finish. He turned to Mitya, and delivered himself in a loud, firm, dignified voice:

"Ex-Lieutenant Karamazov, it is my duty to inform you that you are charged with the murder of your father, Fyodor Pavlovich Karamazov, perpetrated this night . . ."

He said something more, and the prosecutor, too, put in a word, but though Mitya heard them he did not understand them. He stared at them all with wild eyes.

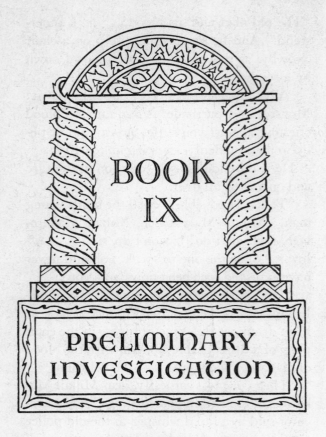

BOOK IX

PRELIMINARY INVESTIGATION

### CHAPTER I
#### THE BEGINNING OF PERHOTIN'S
#### OFFICIAL CAREER

PYOTR ILYICH PERHOTIN, whom we left knocking at the strong, locked gates of the widow Morozov's house, ended, of course, by making himself heard. Fenya, who was still excited by the fright she had had two hours before, and too much "upset" to go to bed, was almost frightened into hysterics on hearing the furious knocking at the gate. Though she had herself seen him drive away, she fancied that it must be Dmitri Fyodorovich knocking again, no one else could knock so rudely. She ran to the house-porter, who had already waked up and gone out to the gate, and began imploring him not to open it. But having ques-

tioned Pyotr Ilyich, and learnt that he wanted to see Fenya on very "important business," the man made up his mind at last to open. Pyotr Ilyich was admitted into Fenya's kitchen, but the girl begged him to allow the house-porter to be present, "because of her misgivings." He began questioning her and at once learnt the most vital fact, that is, that when Dmitri Fyodorovich had run out to look for Grushenka, he had snatched up a pestle from the mortar, and that when he returned, the pestle was not with him and his hands were bloody.

"And the blood was still dripping, dripping from them, dripping!" Fenya kept exclaiming. This horrible detail was simply the product of her disordered imagination. But Pyotr Ilyich had himself seen those hands stained with blood, although not "dripping," and had helped to wash them. Moreover, the question he had to decide was not how soon the blood had dried, but where Dmitri Fyodorovich had run with the pestle, or rather, whether it really was to Fyodor Pavlovich's, and how he could definitely deduce the fact. Pyotr Ilyich persisted in returning to this point, and though he found out nothing conclusive, yet he carried away a conviction that Dmitri Fyodorovich could have gone nowhere but to his father's house, and that therefore something must have happened there.

"And when he came back," Fenya added with excitement, "and I made a clean breast of it to him, then I began asking him: 'Why have you got blood on your hands, Dmitri Fyodorovich?' and he answered that that was human blood, and that he had just killed some one. He confessed it all to me, and suddenly ran off like a madman. I sat down and began thinking, where's he run off to now like a madman? He'll go to Mokroye, I thought, and kill my mistress there. I ran out to beg him not to kill her. I was running to his lodgings, but I looked at Plotnikov's shop, and saw him just setting off, and there was no blood on his hands then." (Fenya had noticed this and remembered it.) Fenya's old grandmother confirmed her evidence as far as she was able. After asking some further questions, Pyotr Ilyich left the house, even more upset and uneasy than he had been when he entered it.

It would seem that the most direct and the easiest thing for him to do would have been to go straight to Fyodor Pavlovich's, to find out whether anything had happened there, and if so, what; and only to go to the police captain, as Pyotr Ilyich firmly intended doing, when he had satisfied himself of the fact. But the night was dark, Fyodor Pavlovich's gates were strong, and he would have to knock again. His acquaintance with Fyodor Pavlovich was of the slightest, and what if, after he had aroused them, they opened to him, and nothing had happened, and Fyodor Pavlovich in his jeering way would go telling the story all over the town, how a stranger, Perhotin, the official, had broken in upon him at midnight to ask if any one had killed him. It would make a scandal. And scandal was what Pyotr Ilyich dreaded more than anything.

Yet the feeling that possessed him was so strong, that though he stamped his foot angrily and swore at himself, he set off again, not to Fyodor Pavlovich's, but to Madame Hohlakov's. He decided that if she denied having just given Dmitri Fyodorovich three thousand roubles, he would go straight to the police captain, but if she admitted having given him the money, he would go home and let the matter rest till next morning.

It is, of course, perfectly evident that there was even more likelihood of causing scandal by going at eleven o'clock at night to a fashionable lady, a complete stranger, and perhaps rousing her from her bed to ask her an amazing question, than by going to Fyodor Pavlovich. But that is just how it is, sometimes, especially in cases like the present one, with the decisions of the most precise and phlegmatic people. Pyotr Ilyich was by no means phlegmatic at that moment. He remembered all his life how an unconquerable uneasiness, which had gradually gained possession of him, had finally reached a point where it was actually painful and drove him on, against his will. Yet he kept cursing himself, of course, all the way for going to this lady, but "I will see it through, I will!" he repeated for the tenth time, grinding his teeth, and he carried out his intention.

It was exactly eleven o'clock when he entered Madame Hohlakov's house. He was admitted into the courtyard fairly quickly, but, in response to his inquiry whether the lady was resting or had not yet retired, the porter could give no answer, except that she was usually in bed by that time.

"Ask at the top of the stairs. If the lady wants to receive you, she'll receive you. If she won't, she won't."

Pyotr Ilyich went upstairs, but did not find things so easy here. The footman was unwilling to take in his name, but finally called a maid. Pyotr Ilyich politely but insistently begged her to inform her lady that a local official, called Perhotin, had called on particular business, and that, if it were not of the greatest importance, he would not have ventured to come. "Tell her in those words, in those words exactly," he asked the girl.

She went away. He remained waiting in the entry. Madame Hohlakov herself was already in her bedroom, though she had not yet retired. She had felt upset ever since Mitya's visit, and had a presentiment that she would not get through the night without the sick headache which always, with her, followed such excitement. She was surprised on hearing the announcement from the maid. She irritably declined to see him, however, though the unexpected visit at such an hour, of a "local official" who was a stranger, roused her feminine curiosity intensely. But this time Pyotr Ilyich was as obstinate as a mule. He begged the maid most earnestly to take another message in these very words:

"That he had come on business of the greatest importance, and that Madame Hohlakov might have cause to regret it later, if she refused to see him now."

"I plunged headlong," he described it afterwards.

The maid, gazing at him in amazement, went to take his message again. Madame Hohlakov was impressed. She thought a little, asked what he looked like, and learnt that he was "very well dressed, young, and so polite." We may note, parenthetically, that Pyotr Ilyich was a rather good-looking young man, and well aware of the fact. Madame Hohlakov made up her mind to see him. She was in her dressing-gown and slippers, but she flung a black shawl over her shoulders. The "official" was asked to walk into the drawing-room, the very room in which Mitya had been received shortly before. The lady came to meet her visitor, with a sternly inquiring countenance, and, without asking him to sit down, began at once with the question:

"What do you wish?"

"I have ventured to disturb you, madam, on a matter concerning our common acquaintance, Dmitri Fyodorovich Karamazov," Perhotin began.

But he had hardly uttered the name, when the lady's face showed signs of acute irritation. She almost shrieked, and interrupted him in a fury:

"How much longer am I to be tormented by that awful man?" she cried hysterically. "How dare you, sir, how could you venture to disturb a lady who is a stranger to you, in her own house at such an hour? . . . And to force yourself upon her to talk of a man who came here, to this very drawing-room, only three hours ago, to murder me, and went stamping out of the room, as no one would go out of a decent house. Let me tell you, sir, that I shall lodge a complaint against you, that I will not let it pass. Kindly leave me at once. . . . I am a mother. . . . I . . . I . . ."

"Murder! then he tried to murder you, too?"

"Why, has he killed somebody else?" Madame Hohlakov asked impulsively.

"If you would kindly listen, madam, for half a moment, I'll explain it all in a couple of words," answered Perhotin firmly. "At five o'clock this afternoon Dmitri Fyodorovich borrowed ten roubles from me, and I know for a fact that he had no money. Yet at nine o'clock, he came to see me with a bundle of hundred-rouble notes in his hand, about two or three thousand roubles in all. His hands and face were all covered with blood, and he looked like a madman. When I asked him where he had got so much money, he answered that he had just received it from you, that you had given him a sum of three thousand to go to the gold-mines . . ."

"YOU ARE CHARGED WITH THE MURDER OF YOUR FATHER"

Madame Hohlakov's face assumed an expression of intense and morbid excitement.

"Good God! He must have killed his old father!" she cried, striking her hands together. "I haven't given him any money at all, none whatsoever. Oh, run, run! . . . Don't say another word! Save the old man . . . run to his father . . . run!"

"Excuse me, madam, then you did not give him money? You remember distinctly that you did not give him any money?"

"No, I didn't, I didn't! I refused to give it him, for he could not appreciate it. He ran out in a fury, stamping. He rushed at me, but I slipped away. . . . And let me tell you, as I wish to hide nothing from you now, that he positively spat at me. Can you fancy that! But why are we standing? Ah, sit down. . . . Excuse me, I . . . or better run, run, you must run and save the poor old man from an awful death!"

"But if he has killed him already?"

"Ah, good heavens, yes! Then what are we to do now? What do you think we must do now?"

Meantime she had made Pyotr Ilyich sit down and sat down herself, facing him. Briefly, but rather clearly, Pyotr Ilyich told her the history of the affair, that part of it at least which he had himself witnessed. He described, too, his visit to Fenya, and told her about the pestle. All these details produced an overwhelming effect on the distracted lady, who kept uttering shrieks, and covering her face with her hands. . . .

"Would you believe it, I foresaw all this! I have that special faculty, whatever I imagine comes to pass. And how often I've looked at that awful man and always thought, that man will end by murdering me. And now it's hap-

pened . . . that is, if he hasn't murdered me, but only his own father, it's only because the finger of God preserved me, and what's more, he was ashamed to murder me because, on this very place, I put the holy ikon from the relics of the holy martyr, Saint Varvara, on his neck. . . . And to think how near I was to death at that minute, I went close up to him and he stretched out his neck to me! . . . Do you know, Pyotr Ilyich (I think you said your name was Pyotr Ilyich), I don't believe in miracles, but that ikon and this unmistakable miracle with me now — that shakes me, and I'm ready to believe in anything you like. Have you heard about Father Zosima? . . . But I don't know what I'm saying . . . and only fancy, with the ikon on his neck he spat at me. . . . He only spat, it's true, he didn't murder me and . . . he dashed away! But what shall we do, what must we do now? What do you think?"

Pyotr Ilyich got up, and announced that he was going straight to the police captain, to tell him all about it, and leave him to do what he thought fit.

"Oh, he's an excellent man, excellent! Mihail Makarovich, I know him. Of course, he's the person to go to. How practical you are, Pyotr Ilyich! How well it is that you've thought of everything! I should never have thought of it in your place!"

"Especially as I know the police captain very well, too," observed Pyotr Ilyich, who still continued to stand, and was obviously anxious to escape as quickly as possible from the impulsive lady, who would not let him say good-bye and go away.

"And be sure, be sure," she prattled on, "to come back and tell me what you see there, and what you find out . . . what comes to light

. . . how they'll try him . . . and what he's condemned to. . . . Tell me, we have no capital punishment, have we? But be sure to come, even if it's at three o'clock at night, at four, at half-past four. . . . Tell them to wake me, to wake me, to shake me, if I don't get up. . . . But, good heavens, I shan't sleep! But wait, hadn't I better come with you?"

"N-no. But if you would write three lines with your own hand, stating that you did not give Dmitri Fyodorovich money, it might, perhaps, be of use . . . in case it's needed. . . ."

"To be sure!" Madame Hohlakov skipped, delighted, to her bureau. "And you know I'm simply struck, amazed at your resourcefulness, your good sense in such affairs. Are you in the service here? I'm delighted to think that you're in the service here!"

And still speaking, she scribbled on half a sheet of note-paper the following lines:

"I've never in my life lent to that unhappy man, Dmitri Fyodorovich Karamazov (for, in spite of all, he is unhappy), three thousand roubles to-day. I've never given him money, never! That I swear by all that's holy!

"K. Hohlakov."

"Here's the note!" she turned quickly to Pyotr Ilyich. "Go, save him. It's a noble deed on your part!"

And she made the sign of the cross over him three times. She ran out to accompany him to the foyer.

"How grateful I am to you! You can't think how grateful I am to you for having come to me, first. How is it I haven't met you before? I shall feel flattered at seeing you at my house in the future. How delightful it is that you are in the service here! . . . Such pre-

cision! Such resourcefulness! . . . They must appreciate you, they must understand you. If there's anything I can do, believe me . . . oh, I love young people! I'm in love with young people! The younger generation are the one foundation of our suffering country. Her one hope. . . . Oh, go, go! . . ."

But Pyotr Ilyich had already run off or she would not have let him go so soon. Yet Madame Hohlakov had made a rather agreeable impression on him, which had somewhat softened his anxiety at being drawn into such an unpleasant affair. Tastes differ, as we all know. "She's by no means so elderly," he thought, feeling pleased, "on the contrary, I should have taken her for her daughter."

As for Madame Hohlakov, she was simply enchanted by the young man. "Such sense! such precision! in so young a man! in our day! and all that with such manners and appearance! They say the young people of to-day are no good for anything, but here's an example!" etc., etc. So she simply forgot this "dreadful affair," and it was only as she was getting into bed, that, suddenly recalling "how near death she had been," she exclaimed: "Ah, it is awful, awful!"

But she fell at once into a sound, sweet sleep.

I would not, however, have dwelt on such trivial and irrelevant details, if this eccentric meeting of the young official with the by no means elderly widow had not subsequently turned out to be the foundation of the whole career of that practical and precise young man. His story is remembered to this day with amazement in our town, and I shall perhaps have something to say about it, when I have finished my long tale of the Brothers Karamazov.

## CHAPTER II
### THE ALARM

OUR police captain, Mihail Makarovich Makarov, a retired lieutenant-colonel, with the rank of court councillor, was a widower and an excellent man. He had come to us only three years previously, but had won general esteem, chiefly because he "knew how to bring people together." He was never without visitors, and it would seem that he could not have got on without them. Some one or other was always dining with him; he never sat down to table without guests. He gave regular dinners, too, on all sorts of occasions, sometimes most surprising ones. Though the fare was not *recherché*, it was abundant. The fish pies were excellent, and the wine made up in quantity for what it lacked in quality.

The first room his guests entered was a well-fitted billiard-room, with pictures of English race-horses, in black frames, on the walls, an essential decoration, as we all know, for a bachelor's billiard-room. There was card-playing every evening at his house, if only at one table. But at frequent intervals, all the best society of our town, with the mammas and young ladies, assembled at his house to dance. Though Mihail Makarovich was a widower, he did not live alone. His widowed daughter lived with him, with her two unmarried daughters, grown-up girls, who had finished their education. They were of agreeable appearance and lively character, and though every one knew they would have no dowry, they attracted all the young men of fashion to their grandfather's house.

Mihail Makarovich was by no means very efficient in his work, though he performed his duties no worse than many others. To speak plainly, he was a rather uneducated man. His understanding of the limits of his administrative power could not always be relied upon. It was not so much that he failed to grasp certain reforms enacted during the present reign, as that he made conspicuous blunders in his interpretation of them. This was not from any special lack of intelligence, but from carelessness, for he was always in too great a hurry to go into the subject.

"I have the heart of a soldier rather than a civilian," he used to say of himself. He had not even formed a definite idea of the fundamental principles of the reforms connected with the emancipation of the serfs, and he added to his knowledge of it, so to speak, from year to year, involuntarily increasing his understanding by practice. And yet he was himself a landowner. Pyotr Ilyich knew for certain that he would meet some of Mihail Makarovich's visitors there that evening, but he didn't know which. As it happened, at that moment there were sitting in his house, over a game of whist, the prosecutor, and Varvinsky, our district doctor, a young man, who had only just come to us from Petersburg after graduating with high honours from the Academy of Medicine. Ippolit Kirillovich, the prosecutor (he was really the assistant prosecutor, but we always called him the prosecutor), was a rather peculiar man, of about five and thirty, inclined to be consumptive, and married to a fat and childless woman. He was vain and irritable, though he had a good intellect, and even a kind heart. It seemed that all that was wrong with him was that he had a better opinion of himself than his ability warranted. And that made him seem constantly uneasy. He had, moreover, certain higher, even artistic, leanings, towards psychology, for instance, a special study of the human heart, a special knowledge of the criminal and his crime. He cherished a grievance on this score, considering that he had been passed over in the service, and being firmly persuaded that in higher spheres he had not been properly appreciated, and had enemies. In gloomy moments he even threatened to give up his post, and practise as a barrister in criminal cases. The unexpected Karamazov case involving parricide shook him to the depths: "It was a case that might well be talked about all over Russia." But I am anticipating.

Nikolay Parfenovich Nelyudov, the young examining magistrate, who had come from Petersburg only two months before, was sitting in the next room with the young ladies. People talked about it afterwards and wondered that all these gentlemen, as though intentionally, should have been gathered together at the house of the executive authority on the evening of "the crime." Yet it was perfectly simple and happened quite naturally.

Ippolit Kirillovich's wife had had toothache for the last two days, and, naturally, he had to run off somewhere to escape from her groans. The doctor, from the very nature of his being, could not spend an evening except at cards. As for Nikolay Parfenovich Nelyudov, he had been intending for three days past to drop in that evening at Mihail Makarovich's, so to speak casually, so as slyly to startle the eldest granddaughter, Olga Mihailovna, by showing that he knew her secret, that he knew it was her birthday, and that she was trying to conceal it on purpose, so as not to be obliged to give a dance. He anticipated a great deal of merriment, many playful jests about her age, and her being afraid to reveal it, about his knowing her secret and telling everybody, and so on. The charming young man was a great adept at such teasing; the ladies called him "naughty," and he seemed to be delighted at the nickname. He was extremely well bred, however, of good family, education, and feelings, and, though leading a life of pleasure, his sallies were always innocent and in good taste. He was short and delicate looking. On his white, slender little fingers he always wore a number of big, glittering rings. When he was engaged in his official duties, he always became extraordinarily grave, as though realising his position and the sanctity of the obligations laid upon him. He had a special gift for nonplussing murderers and other criminals from among the common people during interrogation, and if he did not win their respect, he certainly succeeded in arousing their wonder.

Pyotr Ilyich was simply dumbfounded when he went into the police captain's. He saw instantly that every one knew. They had positively thrown down their cards, all were standing up and talking. Even Nikolay Parfenovich had left the young ladies and run in, looking strenuous and ready for action. Pyotr Ilyich was met with the astounding news that old Fyodor Pavlovich really had been murdered that evening in his own house, murdered and robbed. The news had only just reached them in the following manner:

Marfa Ignatyevna, the wife of old Grigory, who had been knocked senseless near the fence, was sleeping soundly in her bed and might well have slept till morning after the draught she had taken. But all of a sudden she waked up, no doubt roused by a fearful epileptic scream from Smerdyakov, who was lying in the next room unconscious. That scream always preceded his fits, and always terrified and upset Marfa Ignatyevna. She could never get accustomed to it. She jumped up and ran half-awake to Smerdyakov's room. But it was dark there, and she could only hear the invalid beginning to gasp and struggle. Then Marfa Ignatyevna herself screamed out and was going to call her husband, but suddenly realised that when she had got up he was not beside her in bed. She ran back to the bedstead and began groping with her hands, but the bed was really empty. Then he must have gone out — where? She ran to the steps and timidly called him. She got no answer, of course, but she caught the sound of groans far away in the garden in the darkness. She listened. The groans were repeated, and it was evident they came from the garden.

"Good Lord! Just as it was with Lizaveta Smerdyashchaya!" she thought distractedly. She went timidly down the steps and saw that the gate into the garden was open.

"He must be out there, poor dear," she thought. She went up to the gate and all at once she distinctly heard Grigory calling her by name, "Marfa! Marfa!" in a weak, moaning, dreadful voice.

"Lord, preserve us from harm!" Marfa Ignatyevna murmured, and ran towards the voice, and that was how she found Grigory. But she found him not by the fence where he had been knocked down, but about twenty paces off. It appeared later that he had crawled away on coming to himself, and probably had been a long time getting so far, losing consciousness several times. She noticed at once that he was covered with blood, and screamed at the top of her voice. Grigory was muttering incoherently: "He has murdered . . . murdered his father . . . Why scream, silly . . . run . . . fetch some one . . ."

But Marfa continued screaming, and seeing that her master's window was open and that there was a candle alight in the window, she ran there and began calling Fyodor Pavlovich. But peeping in at the window, she saw a fearful sight. Her master was lying on his back, motionless, on the floor. His light-coloured dressing-gown and white shirt were soaked with blood. The candle on the table brightly lighted up the blood and the motionless dead face of Fyodor Pavlovich. Terror-stricken, Marfa rushed away from the window, ran out of the garden, drew the bolt of the big gate, and ran headlong by the back way to the neighbour, Marya Kondratyevna. Both mother and daughter were asleep, but they were waked up by Marfa's desperate and persistent screaming and knocking at the shutter. Marfa, shrieking and screaming incoherently, managed to tell them the main fact, and to beg for assistance. It happened that Foma had come back from his wanderings and was spending the night with them. They got him up immediately and all three ran to the scene of the crime. On the way, Marya Kondratyevna remembered that at about eight o'clock she had heard a dreadful and piercing scream from their garden, and this was no doubt Grigory's scream, "Parricide!" uttered when he caught hold of Mitya's leg with his hands, Mitya then being astride the fence.

"Some one screamed out and then was silent," Marya Kondratyevna explained as she ran. Running to the place where Grigory lay, the two women with the help of Foma carried him to the lodge. They lighted a candle and saw that Smerdyakov was no better, that he was writhing in convulsions, his eyes fixed in a squint, and that foam was flowing from his lips. They moistened Grigory's forehead with water mixed with vinegar, and the water revived him at once. He asked immediately:

"Is the master murdered?"

Then Foma and both the women ran to the house and saw this time that not only the window, but also the door into the garden was wide open, though Fyodor Pavlovich had for the last week locked himself in every night and did not allow even Grigory to come in on any pretext. Seeing that door open, they were afraid to go in to Fyodor Pavlovich "for fear anything should happen afterwards." And when they returned to Grigory, the old man told them to go straight to the police captain. Marya Kondratyevna ran there and gave the alarm to the whole party at the police captain's. She arrived only five minutes before Pyotr Ilyich, so that his story came, not as his own surmise and theory, but as the direct confirmation, by a witness, of the theory held by all, as to the identity of the criminal (a theory he had at the bottom of his heart refused to believe till that moment).

It was resolved to act energetically. The deputy police inspector of the town was immediately commissioned to take four witnesses, and they entered Fyodor Pavlovich's house and there opened an inquiry on the spot, according to the regular forms, which I will not go into here. The district doctor, a zealous man, new to his work, almost insisted on accompanying the police captain, the prosecutor, and the examining magistrate.

I will note briefly that Fyodor Pavlovich was found to be quite dead, with his head broken. But by what? Most likely with the same weapon with which Grigory had been attacked later. And immediately that weapon was found, Grigory, to whom all possible medical assistance was at once given, described

in a weak and breaking voice how he had been knocked down. They began looking with a lantern by the fence and found the brass pestle dropped in a most conspicuous place on the garden path. There were no signs of disturbance in the room where Fyodor Pavlovich was lying. But by the bed, behind the screen, they picked up from the floor a big and thick envelope with the inscription: "A present of three thousand roubles for my angel Grushenka, if she will wish to come to me." And below had been added by Fyodor Pavlovich, "For my little chick." There were three big seals made with red sealing-wax on the envelope, but it had been torn open and was empty: the money had been removed. They found also on the floor a piece of narrow pink ribbon, with which the envelope had been tied up.

One piece of Pyotr Ilyich's evidence made a great impression on the prosecutor and the examining magistrate, namely, his idea that Dmitri Fyodorovich would shoot himself at daybreak, that he had resolved to do so, had spoken of it to Pyotr Ilyich, had taken the pistols, loaded them before him, written a note, put it in his pocket, etc., that when Pyotr Ilyich, though still unwilling to believe in it, had threatened to tell some one so as to prevent the suicide, Mitya had answered grinning: "You'll be too late." So they must make haste to Mokroye to catch the criminal, before he really did shoot himself.

"That's clear, that's clear!" repeated the prosecutor in great excitement. "That's just the way with mad fellows like that: 'I shall kill myself to-morrow, so I'll make merry before I die!'" The story of how he had bought the wine and provisions excited the prosecutor more than ever.

QUITE DEAD, WITH HIS HEAD BROKEN

"Do you remember the fellow that murdered a merchant called Olsufyev, gentlemen? He stole fifteen hundred, went at once to have his hair curled, and then, without even hiding the money, carrying it almost in his hand in the same way, he went off to the girls."

All were delayed, however, by the inquiry, the search, and the formalities, etc., in the house of Fyodor Pavlovich. It all took time and so, two hours before starting, they sent on ahead to Mokroye the officer of the rural police, Mavriky Mavrikyevich Shmertsov, who had arrived in the town the morning before to get his salary. He was instructed to avoid raising the alarm when he reached Mokroye, but to keep constant watch over the "criminal" till the arrival of the proper authorities, also to procure witnesses for the arrest, police constables, and so on. Mavriky Mavrikyevich did as he was told, preserving his incognito, and partly initiating only his old acquaintance, Trifon Borisovich, into the secret. He had spoken to him just before Mitya met the innkeeper on the balcony, looking for him in the dark, and noticed at once a change in Trifon Borisovich's face and voice. So neither Mitya nor any one else knew that he was being watched. The box with the pistols had been carried off by Trifon Borisovich and tucked away in a suitable place. Only after four o'clock, almost at sunrise, all the officials, the police captain, the prosecutor, the examining magistrate, drove up in two carriages, each drawn by three horses. The doctor remained at Fyodor Pavlovich's to make a post-mortem next day on the body. But he was particularly interested in the condition of the servant, Smerdyakov.

"Such violent and protracted epileptic fits, recurring continually for forty-eight hours, are rarely to be met with, and are of interest to science," he declared enthusiastically to his companions, and, as they left, they laughingly congratulated him on his find. The prosecutor and the examining magistrate distinctly remembered the doctor's saying that Smerdyakov could not outlive the night.

After these long, but, I think, necessary explanations, we return to that moment of our tale at which we broke off in the previous book.

## CHAPTER III
### THE SUFFERINGS OF A SOUL IN
### THE PLACE OF TORMENTS.
### THE FIRST ORDEAL

AND so Mitya sat looking wildly at the people round him, not understanding what was said to him. Suddenly he got up, flung up his hands and shouted aloud:

"I'm not guilty! I'm not guilty of that blood! I'm not guilty of my father's blood. . . . I meant to kill him. But I'm not guilty. Not I."

But he had hardly said this, before Grushenka rushed from behind the curtain and flung herself at the police captain's feet.

"It was my fault! Mine! My wickedness!" she cried, in a heart-rending voice, bathed in tears, stretching out her clasped hands towards them. "He did it through me. I tortured him and drove him to it. I tortured that poor old man that's dead, too, in my wickedness, and brought him to this! It's my fault, mine first, mine most, my fault!"

"Yes, you're the guilty one! You're the chief criminal! You're a fury! You're a loose woman! You're the most to blame!" shouted the police captain threatening her with his hand. But he was quickly and resolutely suppressed.

353

The prosecutor went so far as to restrain him with his arms.

"This is absolutely irregular, Mihail Makarovich!" he cried. "You are positively hindering the inquiry. . . . You're ruining the case . . ." he almost gasped.

"Take measures! Take measures!" cried Nikolay Parfenovich, fearfully excited, too, "otherwise it's absolutely impossible! . . ."

"Try us together!" Grushenka cried frantically, still kneeling. "Punish us together. I will go with him now, if it's to death!"

"Grusha, my life, my blood, my holy one!" Mitya fell on his knees beside her and held her tight in his arms. "Don't believe her," he cried, "she's not guilty of anything, of any blood, of anything!"

He remembered afterwards that he was forcibly dragged away from her by several men, and that she was led out, and that when he recovered himself he was sitting at the table. Beside him and behind him stood the men with metal badges. Facing him on the other side of the table sat Nikolay Parfenovich, the examining magistrate. He kept persuading him to drink a little water out of a glass that stood on the table.

"That will refresh you, that will calm you. Be calm, don't be frightened," he added, with extreme politeness. Mitya (he remembered it afterwards) became suddenly intensely interested in his big rings, one with an amethyst, and another with a transparent bright yellow stone, of great brilliance. And long afterwards he remembered with wonder how those rings had riveted his attention through all those terrible hours of interrogation, so that he was utterly unable to tear himself away from them and dismiss them, as things that had nothing to do with his position. On Mitya's left side, in the place where Maximov had been sitting at the beginning of the evening, the prosecutor was now seated, and on Mitya's right hand, where Grushenka had been, was a rosy-cheeked young man in a sort of shabby hunting jacket, with ink and paper before him. This was the secretary of the examining magistrate, who had brought him along. The police captain was now standing by the window at the other end of the room, beside Kalganov, who was sitting there.

"Have some water," said the examining magistrate softly, for the tenth time.

"I have had it, gentlemen, I have . . . but . . . come, gentlemen, crush me, punish me, decide my fate!" cried Mitya, staring with terribly fixed wide-open eyes at the investigating lawyer.

"So you positively declare that you are not guilty of the death of your father, Fyodor Pavlovich?" asked the examining magistrate softly but insistently.

"I am not guilty. I am guilty of the blood of another old man, but not of my father's. And I weep for it! I killed, I killed the old man and knocked him down. . . . But it's hard to have to answer for that murder with another, a terrible murder of which I am not guilty. . . . It's a terrible accusation, gentlemen, a knockdown blow. But who has killed my father, who has killed him? Who can have killed him if I didn't? It's miraculous, extraordinary, impossible."

"Yes, who can have killed him?" the examining magistrate was beginning, but Ippolit Kirillovich, the prosecutor, glancing at him, addressed Mitya.

"You need not worry yourself about the old servant, Grigory Vasilyevich. He is alive, he has recovered, and in spite of the terrible blows inflicted by you, according to his own and your statements, there seems no doubt that he will live, so the doctor says, at least."

"Alive? He's alive?" cried Mitya, striking his hands together. His face beamed. "Lord, I thank Thee for the miracle Thou hast wrought for me, a sinner and evil-doer. That's an answer to my prayer. I've been praying all night." And he crossed himself three times. He was almost choking.

"So from this Grigory we have received such important evidence concerning you, that . . ." The prosecutor would have continued, but Mitya suddenly jumped up from his chair.

"One minute, gentlemen, for God's sake, one minute; I will run to her ——"

"Excuse me, at this moment it's quite impossible," Nikolay Parfenovich almost shrieked. He, too, leapt to his feet. Mitya was seized by the men with the metal badges, but he sat down of his own accord. . . .

"Gentlemen, what a pity! I wanted to see her for one minute only; I wanted to tell her that it has been washed away, it has gone, that blood that was weighing on my heart all night, and that I am not a murderer now! Gentlemen, she is my betrothed!" he said ecstatically and reverently, looking round at them all. "Oh, thank you gentlemen! Oh, in one minute you have given me new life, new heart! . . . That old man used to carry me in his arms, gentlemen. He used to wash me in the tub when I was a baby three years old, abandoned by every one, he was like a father to me! . . ."

"And so you . . ." the examining magistrate began.

"Allow me, gentlemen, allow me one minute more," interposed Mitya, putting his elbows on the table and covering his face with his hands. "Let me have a moment to think, let me breathe, gentlemen. All this is horribly upsetting, horribly. A man is not a drum-head, gentlemen!"

"Take a little more water," murmured Nikolay Parfenovich.

Mitya took his hands from his face and laughed. His eyes were confident. He seemed completely transformed in a moment. His whole bearing was changed; he was once more the equal of these men, with all of whom he was acquainted, as though they had all met the day before, when nothing had happened, at some social gathering. We may note in passing that, on his first arrival, Mitya had been made very welcome at the police captain's, but later, during the last month especially, Mitya had hardly called at all, and when the police captain met him, in the street, for instance, Mitya noticed that he frowned and only bowed out of politeness. His acquaintance with the prosecutor was less intimate, though he sometimes paid his wife, a nervous and fanciful lady, visits of courtesy, without quite knowing why, and she always received him graciously and had, for some reason, taken an interest in him up to the last. He had not had time to get to know the examining magistrate, though he had met him and talked to him twice, each time about the fair sex.

"You're a most skilful examiner, I see, Nikolay Parfenovich," cried Mitya, laughing gaily, "but I can help you now. Oh, gentlemen, I feel like a new man, and don't be offended at my addressing you so simply and directly. I'm rather drunk, too, I'll tell you that frankly. I believe I've had the honour and pleasure of meeting you, Nikolay Parfenovich, at my kinsman Miusov's. Gentlemen, gentlemen, I don't pretend to be on equal terms with you. I understand, of course, in what character I am sitting before you. Oh, of course, there's a horrible suspicion . . . hanging over me . . . if Grigory has given evidence. . . . A horrible suspicion! It's awful, awful, I understand that! But to business, gentlemen, I am ready, and we will make an end of it in one moment; for, listen, listen, gentlemen! Since I know I'm innocent, we can put an end to it in a minute. Can't we? Can't we?"

Mitya spoke much and quickly, nervously and effusively, as though he positively took his listeners to be his best friends.

"So, for the present, we will write that you absolutely deny the charge brought against you," said Nikolay Parfenovich, impressively, and bending down to the secretary he dictated to him in an undertone what to write.

"Write it down? You want to write that down? Well, write it; I consent, I give my full consent, gentlemen, only . . . do you see . . . Stay, stay, write this. Of disorderly conduct he is guilty, of beating up a poor old man he is guilty. And there is something else at the bottom of my heart, of which I am guilty, too — but that you need not write down" (he turned suddenly to the secretary); "that's my personal life, gentlemen, that doesn't concern you, the bottom of my heart, that's to say. . . . But of the murder of my old father I'm not guilty. That's a wild idea. It's quite a wild idea! . . . I will prove it to you and you'll be convinced instantly. . . . You will laugh, gentlemen. You'll laugh yourself at your suspicion! . . ."

"Be calm, Dmitri Fyodorovich," said the examining magistrate, evidently trying to allay Mitya's excitement by his own composure. "Before we go on with our inquiry, I should like, if you will consent to answer, to hear you confirm the statement that you disliked your father, Fyodor Pavlovich, that you were involved in continual disputes with him. Here at least, a quarter of an hour ago, you exclaimed that you wanted to kill him: 'I didn't kill him,' you said, 'but I wanted to kill him'?"

"Did I say that? Ach, that may be so, gentlemen! Yes, unhappily, I did want to kill him . . . many times I wanted to . . . unhappily, unhappily!"

"You wanted to. Would you consent to explain what motives precisely led you to such a sentiment of hatred for the person of your parent?"

"What is there to explain, gentlemen?" Mitya shrugged his shoulders sullenly, looking down. "I have never concealed my feelings. All the town knows about it — every one knows in the tavern. Only lately I declared them in Father Zosima's cell at the monastery. . . . And the very same day, in the evening I beat my father. I nearly killed him, and I swore I'd come again and kill him, before witnesses. . . . Oh, a thousand witnesses! I've been shouting it aloud for the last month, any one can tell you that! . . . The fact stares you in the face, it speaks for itself, it cries aloud, but, feelings, gentlemen, feelings are another matter. You see, gentlemen" (Mitya frowned), "it seems to me that about feelings you've no right to question me. I know that you are invested with power, I quite understand that, but that's my affair, my private, intimate affair, yet . . . since I haven't concealed my feelings in the past . . . in the tavern, for instance, I've talked to every one, so . . . so I won't make a secret of it now. You see, I understand, gentlemen, that there is terrible evidence against me in this case. I told every one

356

THE FIRST ORDEAL

that I'd kill him, and now, all of a sudden, he's been killed. So it must have been I! Ha, ha! I can make allowances for you, gentlemen, I can quite make allowances. I'm struck all of a heap myself, for who can have murdered him, if not I? That's what it comes to, isn't it? If not I, who can it be, who? Gentlemen, I want to know, I insist on knowing!" he exclaimed suddenly. "Where was he murdered? How was he murdered? How, and with what? Tell me," he asked quickly, looking at the two magistrates.

"We found him in his study, lying on his back on the floor, with his head broken," said the prosecutor.

"That's horrible, gentlemen!" Mitya shuddered and, putting his elbows on the table, hid his face in his right hand.

"We will continue," interposed Nikolay Parfenovich. "So what was it that impelled you to this sentiment of hatred? You have asserted in public, I believe, that it was based upon jealousy?"

"Well, yes, jealousy. And not only jealousy."

"Disputes about money?"

"Yes, about money, too."

"There was a dispute about three thousand roubles, I think, which you claimed as part of your inheritance?"

"Three thousand! More, more," cried Mitya hotly; "more than six thousand, more than ten, perhaps. I told every one so, shouted it at them. But I made up my mind to let it go at three thousand. I was desperately in need of that three thousand . . . so the bundle of notes for three thousand that I knew he kept under his pillow, ready for Grushenka, I considered as simply stolen from me. Yes, gentlemen, I looked upon it as mine, as my own

property. . . ." The prosecutor looked significantly at the examining magistrate, and had time to wink at him on the sly.

"We will return to that subject later," said the examining magistrate promptly. "You will allow us to note that point and write it down; that you looked upon that money in the envelope as your own property?"

"Write it down, by all means. I know that's another fact that tells against me, but I'm not afraid of evidence and I give it against myself. Do you hear? Do you know, gentlemen, you take me for a different sort of man from what I am," he added, suddenly, gloomy and dejected. "You have to deal with a man of honour, a man of the highest honour; above all — don't lose sight of it — a man who's done a lot of nasty things, but has always been, and still is, honourable at bottom, in his inner being. I don't know how to express it. That's just what's made me wretched all my life, that I yearned to be honourable, that I was, so to say, a martyr to a sense of honour, seeking for it with a lantern, with the lantern of Diogenes, and yet all my life I've been doing filthy things like all of us, gentlemen . . . that is like me alone. That was a mistake, like me alone, me alone! . . . Gentlemen, my head aches. . . ." His brows contracted with pain. "You see, gentlemen, I couldn't bear the look of him, there was something in him ignoble, impudent, trampling on everything sacred, something sneering and irreverent, loathsome, loathsome. But now that he's dead, I feel differently."

"How do you mean?"

"I don't feel differently, but I wish I hadn't hated him so."

"You feel penitent?"

"No, not penitent, don't write that. I'm not much good myself, I'm not very beautiful, so I had no right to consider him repulsive. That's what I mean. Write that down, if you like."

Saying this Mitya became very mournful. He had grown more and more gloomy as the inquiry continued.

At that moment another unexpected scene followed. Though Grushenka had been removed, she had not been taken far away, only into the room next but one from the blue room, in which the examination was proceeding. It was a little room with one window, next beyond the large room in which they had danced and feasted so lavishly. She was sitting there with no one by her but Maximov, who was terribly bewildered, terribly scared, and clung to her side, as though for security. At their door stood one of the peasants with a metal badge on his breast. Grushenka was crying, and suddenly her grief was too much for her, she jumped up, flung up her arms, and with a loud wail of sorrow rushed out of the room to him, to her Mitya, and so unexpectedly that they had not time to stop her. Mitya, hearing her cry, trembled, jumped up, and with a yell rushed impetuously to meet her, not knowing what he was doing. But they were not allowed to come together, though they saw one another. He was seized by the arms. He struggled, and tried to tear himself away. It took three or four men to hold him. She was seized, too, and he saw her stretching out her arms to him, crying aloud as they carried her away. When the scene was over, he came to himself again, sitting in the same place as before, opposite the examining magistrate, and crying out to them:

"What do you want with her? Why do you torment her? She's innocent, innocent! . . ."

The magistrates tried to soothe him. About ten minutes passed like this. At last Mihail Makarovich, who had been absent, came hurriedly into the room, and said in a loud and excited voice to the prosecutor:

"She's been removed, she's downstairs. Will you allow me to say one word to this unhappy man, gentlemen? In your presence, gentlemen, in your presence."

"By all means, Mihail Makarovich," answered the examining magistrate. "In the present case we have nothing against it."

"Listen, Dmitri Fyodorovich, my dear fellow," began the police captain, and there was a look of warm, almost fatherly, compassion for the luckless man on his excited face. "I took your Agrafena Alexandrovna downstairs myself, and confided her to the care of the innkeeper's daughters, and that old fellow Maximov is with her all the time. And I soothed her, do you hear? I soothed and calmed her. I impressed on her that you have to clear yourself, so she mustn't hinder you, must not depress you, or you may lose your head and say the wrong thing in your evidence. In fact, I talked to her and she understood. She's a sensible girl, my boy, a good-hearted girl, she would have kissed my old hands, begging help for you. She sent me herself, to tell you not to worry about her. And I must go, my dear fellow, I must go and tell her that you are calm and comforted about her. And so you must be calm, do you understand? I was unfair to her; she is a Christian soul, gentlemen, yes, I tell you, she's a gentle soul, and not to blame for anything. So what am I to tell her, Dmitri Fyodorovich, will you sit quietly or not?"

The good-natured police captain said a great deal that was irregular, but Grushenka's suffering, a fellow creature's suffering, had touched his good-natured heart, and tears stood in his eyes. Mitya jumped up and rushed towards him.

"Forgive me, gentlemen, oh, allow me, allow me!" he cried. "You've the heart of an angel, an angel, Mihail Makarovich, I thank you for her. I will, I will be calm, cheerful, in fact. Tell her, in the measureless kindness of your heart, that I am cheerful, quite cheerful, that I shall be laughing in a minute, knowing that she has a guardian angel like you. I shall have done with all this directly, and as soon as I'm free, I'll be with her, she'll see, let her wait. Gentlemen," he said, turning to the two lawyers, "now I'll open my whole soul to you; I'll pour out everything. We'll finish this off directly, finish it off gaily. We shall laugh at it in the end, shan't we? But gentlemen, that woman is the queen of my heart. Oh, let me tell you that. That one thing I'll tell you now. . . . I see I'm with most honourable men. She is my light, she is my holy one, and if only you knew! Did you hear her cry, 'I'll go to death with you'? And what have I, a penniless beggar, done for her? Why such love for me? How can a clumsy, ugly brute like me, with my ugly face, deserve such love, that she is ready to go to exile with me? And how she fell down at your feet for my sake, just now! . . . and yet she's proud and has done nothing! How can I help adoring her, how can I help crying out and rushing to her as I did just now? Gentlemen, forgive me! But now, now I am comforted."

And he sank back in his chair and, covering his face with his hands, burst into tears. But they were happy tears. He recovered himself instantly. The old police captain seemed much pleased, and the lawyers also. They felt that the examination was passing into a new phase.

When the police captain went out, Mitya was positively gay.

"Now, gentlemen, I am at your disposal, entirely at your disposal. And if it were not for all these trivial details, we should understand one another in a minute. I'm at those details again. I'm at your disposal, gentlemen, but I declare that we must have mutual confidence, you in me and I in you, or there'll be no end to it. I speak in your interests. To business, gentlemen, to business, and don't rummage in my soul; don't vex it with trifles, but only ask me about facts and what matters, and I will satisfy you at once. And damn the details!" So spoke Mitya. The interrogation began again.

## CHAPTER IV
### THE SECOND ORDEAL

"You don't know how you encourage us, Dmitri Fyodorovich, by this readiness of yours," said Nikolay Parfenovich, with an animated air, and obvious satisfaction beaming in his very prominent, short-sighted, light grey eyes, from which he had removed his spectacles a moment before. "And you have made a very just remark about the mutual confidence, without which it is sometimes positively impossible to get on in cases of such importance, if the suspected party really hopes and desires to clear himself and is in a position to do so. We, on our side, will do everything in our power, and you can see for yourself how we are conducting the case. You approve, Ippolit Kirillovich?" He turned to the prosecutor.

"Oh, undoubtedly," replied the prosecutor. His tone was somewhat dry, compared with Nikolay Parfenovich's impulsiveness.

I will note once for all that Nikolay Parfenovich, who had but lately arrived among us, had from the first felt marked respect for Ippolit Kirillovich, our prosecutor, and had become almost his bosom friend. He was almost the only person who put implicit faith in the extraordinary talents as a psychologist and orator of our Ippolit Kirillovich, and who also fully believed that he had been slighted by his superiors. He had heard of him while he was still in Petersburg. On the other hand, young Nikolay Parfenovich was the only person in the whole world whom our "unappreciated" prosecutor genuinely liked. On their way to Mokroye they had time to come to an understanding about the present case. And now as they sat at the table, the sharp-witted junior caught and interpreted every indication on his senior colleague's face, every movement, half a word, a glance, a wink.

"Gentlemen, only let me tell my own story and don't interrupt me with trifles and I'll tell you everything in a jiffy," said Mitya excitedly.

"Excellent! Thank you. But before we proceed to listen to your communication, will you allow me to inquire as to another little fact of great interest to us. I mean the ten roubles you borrowed yesterday at about five o'clock on the security of your pistols, from your friend, Pyotr Ilyich Perhotin."

"I pawned them, gentlemen. I pawned them for ten roubles. What more? That's all about it. As soon as I got back to town I pawned them."

"You got back to town? Then had you been out of town?"

"Yes, I went a journey of forty versts into the country. Didn't you know?"

The prosecutor and Nikolay Parfenovich exchanged glances.

"Well, how would it be if you began your story with a systematic description of all you did yesterday, from the morning onwards? Allow us, for instance, to inquire why you were absent from the town, and just when you left and when you came back — all those facts."

"You should have asked me that from the beginning," cried Mitya, laughing aloud, "and, if you like, we won't begin from yesterday, but from the morning of the day before; then you'll understand how, why, and where I went. I went the day before yesterday, gentlemen, to a merchant of the town, called Samsonov, to borrow three thousand roubles from him on the best security. It was a pressing matter, gentlemen, it was a sudden necessity."

"Allow me to interrupt you," the prosecutor put in politely. "Why were you in such pressing need for just that sum, three thousand?"

"Oh, gentlemen, you needn't go into details, how, when, and why, and why just so much money, and not so much, and all that rigmarole. Why, it'll run to three volumes, and then you'll want an epilogue!"

Mitya said all this with the good-natured but impatient familiarity of a man who is anxious to tell the whole truth and is full of the best intentions.

"Gentlemen!" — he corrected himself hurriedly — "don't be vexed with me for my restiveness, I beg you again. Believe me once more, I feel the greatest respect for you and understand the true position of affairs. Don't think I'm drunk. I'm quite sober now. And, besides, even if I were drunk it would be no hindrance. It's with me, you know, like the saying: 'When he is sober, he is a fool; when he is drunk, he is a wise man.' Ha, ha! But I see, gentlemen, that for the time being it's not the proper thing for me to make jokes before you, till we've had our explanation, I mean. And I've my own dignity to keep up, too. I quite understand the difference for the moment. I come before you, after all, as a criminal, and so am far from being on an equal footing with you. And it's your business to watch me. I can't expect you to pat me on the head for what I did to Grigory, for one can't break old men's heads with impunity. I suppose you'll put me away on his account for six months, or a year perhaps, in a house of correction. I don't know what the punishment is — but it will be without loss of the rights of my rank, without loss of my rank, won't it, prosecutor? So you see, gentlemen, I understand the distinction between us. . . . But you must also admit that you could confuse God Himself with such questions. 'How did you step? Where did you step? When did you step? And on what did you step?' I shall get mixed up, if you go on like this, and you will put it all down against me, black on white. And what will that lead to? To nothing! And even if it's nonsense I'm talking now, let me finish, and you, gentlemen, being men of honour and education, forgive me! I'll finish by asking you, gentlemen, to drop that conventional method of questioning. I mean, beginning from some miserable trifle, how I got up, what I had for breakfast, how I spat, and where I spat, and so having distracted the attention of the criminal, suddenly stun him with an overwhelming question, 'Whom did you murder? Whom did you rob?' Ha, ha! That's your routine method, that's your rule, that's what all your cunning is based on. You can put peasants off their guard like that, but

not me. I know the tricks. I've been in the service, too. Ha, ha, ha! You're not angry, gentlemen? You forgive my impertinence?" he cried, looking at them with a good-nature that was almost surprising. "It's only Mitya Karamazov, you know, so you can overlook it. It would be inexcusable in a sensible man; but you can forgive it in Mitya. Ha, ha!"

Nikolay Parfenovich listened, and laughed, too. Though the prosecutor did not laugh, he kept his eyes fixed keenly on Mitya, as though anxious not to miss the least syllable, the slightest movement, the smallest twitch of any feature of his face.

"That's how we have treated you from the beginning," said Nikolay Parfenovich, still laughing. "We haven't tried to put you out by asking how you got up in the morning and what you had for breakfast. We began, indeed, with questions of the greatest importance."

"I understand. I saw it and appreciated it, and I appreciate still more your present kindness to me, an unprecedented kindness, worthy of the noblest souls. We three here are gentlemen, and let everything be on the footing of mutual confidence such as obtains among educated, well-bred people, who have the common bond of noble birth and honour. In any case, allow me to look upon you as my best friends at this moment of my life, at this moment when my honour is humbled. That's no offence to you, gentlemen, is it?"

"On the contrary. You've expressed all that so admirably, Dmitri Fyodorovich," Nikolay Parfenovich answered with dignified approbation.

"And enough of those trivial questions, gentlemen, all those tricky questions!" cried Mitya enthusiastically. "Or there is simply no knowing where we shall get to! Is there?"

"I will follow your sensible advice entirely," the prosecutor interposed, addressing Mitya. "But I don't withdraw my question, however. It is now vitally important for us to know exactly why you needed that sum, I mean precisely three thousand."

"Why I needed it? . . . Oh, for one thing and another. . . . Well, it was to pay a debt."

"A debt to whom?"

"That I absolutely refuse to answer, gentlemen. Not because I couldn't, or because I daren't or because I am afraid, for it's all a paltry matter and absolutely trifling, but — I won't, because it's a matter of principle: that's my private life, and I won't allow any intrusion into my private life. That's my principle. Your question has no bearing on the case, and whatever has nothing to do with the case is my private affair. I wanted to pay a debt. I wanted to pay a debt of honour, but to whom I won't say."

"Allow me to make a note of that," said the prosecutor.

"By all means. Write down that I won't say, that I won't. Write that I should think it dishonourable to say. Ech! you can write it; you've nothing else to do with your time."

"Allow me to caution you, sir, and to remind you once more, if you are unaware of it," the prosecutor began, with a peculiar and stern impressiveness, "that you have a perfect right not to answer the questions put to you now, and we, on our side, have no right to extort an answer from you, if you decline to give it for one reason or another. That is entirely a matter for your personal decision. But it is our duty, on the other hand, in such cases as the present, to explain and set before you the degree of injury you will be doing yourself by refusing to give this or that piece of evidence. After which I will beg you to continue."

"Gentlemen, I'm not angry . . . I . . ." Mitya muttered in a rather disconcerted tone. "Well, gentlemen, you see, that Samsonov to whom I went then . . ."

We will, of course, not reproduce his account of what is known to the reader already. Mitya was impatiently anxious not to omit the slightest detail. At the same time he was in a hurry to get it over. But as he gave his evidence it was written down, and therefore they had continually to pull him up. Mitya disliked this, but submitted; got angry, though still good-humouredly. He did, it is true, exclaim, from time to time, "Gentlemen, this would enrage God Himself!" Or, "Gentlemen, do you know that you're only irritating me to no purpose!"

But even though he exclaimed, he still preserved for a time his genially expansive mood. So he told them how Samsonov had made a fool of him two days before. (He had completely realised by now that he had been fooled.) The sale of his watch for six roubles to obtain money for the journey was something new to the lawyers. They were at once greatly interested, and even, to Mitya's immeasurable indignation, thought it necessary to write the fact down as a secondary confirmation of the circumstance that he had hardly a farthing in his pocket at the time. Little by little Mitya began to grow surly. Then, after describing his journey to see Lyagavy, the night spent in the stifling hut, and so on, he came to his return to the town. Here he began, without being particularly urged, to give a minute account of the agonies of jealousy he endured on Grushenka's account.

He was heard with silent attention. They

inquired particularly into the circumstance of his having established a look-out in Marya Kondratyevna's house at the back of Fyodor Pavlovich's garden to keep watch on Grushenka, and of Smerdyakov's bringing him information. They laid particular stress on this, and noted it down. Of his jealousy he spoke hotly and at length, and though inwardly ashamed at exposing his most intimate feelings, so to speak, to "public ignominy," he evidently overcame his shame in order to tell the truth.

The impersonal severity, with which the examining magistrate, and still more the prosecutor, stared at him as he told his story, disconcerted him at last considerably.

"That boy, Nikolay Parfenovich, to whom I was talking nonsense about women only a few days ago, and that sickly prosecutor are not worth my telling this to," he reflected mournfully. "It's ignominious. 'Be patient, humble, do not speak.' " He wound up his reflections with that line. But he pulled himself together to go on again. When he came to telling of his visit to Madame Hohlakov, he regained his spirits and even wished to tell a little anecdote of that lady which had nothing to do with the case. But the investigating lawyer stopped him, and civilly suggested that he should pass on to "more essential matters." At last, when he described his despair and told them how, when he left Madame Hohlakov's he thought that he'd "get three thousand if he had to murder some one to do it," they stopped him again and noted down that he had "meant to murder some one." Mitya let them write it without protest. At last he reached the point in his story when he learned that Grushenka had deceived him and had returned from Samsonov's as soon as he left her there, though she had said that she would stay with the old man till midnight.

"If I didn't kill Fenya then, gentlemen, it was only because I hadn't time," broke from him suddenly at that point in his story. That, too, was carefully written down. Mitya waited gloomily, and was beginning to tell how he ran into his father's garden when the examining magistrate suddenly stopped him, and opening the big portfolio that lay on the sofa beside him he brought out the brass pestle.

"Do you recognise this object?" he asked, showing it to Mitya.

"Oh, yes." He grinned gloomily. "Of course I recognise it. Let me have a look at it. . . . Damn it, never mind!"

"You have forgotten to mention it," observed the examining magistrate.

"Hang it all, I didn't mean to conceal it from you. Do you suppose I could have told my story without it? It simply escaped my memory."

"Be so good as to tell us precisely how you came to arm yourself with it."

"Certainly I will be so good, gentlemen."

And Mitya described how he took the pestle and ran.

"But what object had you in view in arming yourself with such a weapon?"

"What object? No object. I just picked it up and ran off."

"What for, if you had no object?"

Mitya was boiling with anger. He looked intently at "the boy" and smiled gloomily and viciously. He was feeling more and more ashamed at having told "such people" the story of his jealousy so sincerely and spontaneously.

"Bother the pestle!" broke from him suddenly.

"But still . . ."

"Oh, to keep off dogs. . . . Oh, because it was dark. . . . In case anything turned up."

"But have you ever on previous occasions taken a weapon with you when you went out, since you're afraid of the dark?"

"Ugh! damn it all, gentlemen! There's positively no talking to you!" cried Mitya, exasperated beyond endurance, and turning to the secretary, crimson with anger, he said quickly, with a note of fury in his voice:

"Write down at once . . . at once . . . 'that I snatched up the pestle to go and kill my father . . . Fyodor Pavlovich . . . by hitting him on the head with it!' Well, now are you satisfied, gentlemen? Are your minds relieved?" he said, glaring defiantly at the magistrates.

"We quite understand that you made that statement just now through exasperation with us and the questions we put to you, which you consider trivial, though they are, in fact, essential," the prosecutor remarked drily in reply.

"Well, upon my word, gentlemen! Yes, I took the pestle . . . What does one pick things up for at such moments? I don't know what for. I snatched it up and ran — that's all. Faugh, gentlemen, *passons*, or I declare I'll stop talking."

He put his elbows on the table and rested his head on his hands. He sat sideways to them and gazed at the wall, struggling against an evil feeling. He had, in fact, an intense inclination to get up and declare that he wouldn't say another word, "not if you hang me for it."

"You see, gentlemen," he said at last, with difficulty controlling himself, "you see. I listen to you and am haunted by a dream. . . . It's a dream I have sometimes, you know. . . .

I often dream it — it's always the same . . . that some one is chasing me, some one I'm awfully afraid of . . . that he's chasing me in the dark, in the night . . . tracking me, and I hide somewhere from him, behind a door or cupboard, hide in a degrading way, and the worst of it is, he always knows where I am, but he pretends not to know where I am on purpose, to prolong my agony, to enjoy my terror. . . . That's just what you're doing now. It's just like that!"

"Is that the sort of thing you dream about?" inquired the prosecutor.

"Yes, it is. Don't you want to write it down?" said Mitya, with a distorted smile.

"No; no need to write it down. But still you do have curious dreams."

"It's not a question of dreams now — this is realism, gentlemen, the realism of actual life! I'm a wolf and you're the hunters. Well, hunt him down!"

"You are wrong to make such comparisons . . ." began Nikolay Parfenovich, with extraordinary softness.

"No, I'm not wrong, gentlemen, not at all!" Mitya flared up again, though his outburst of wrath had obviously relieved his heart. He grew more good-humoured at every word. "You may not trust a criminal or a man on trial tortured by your questions, but an honourable man, the honourable impulses of the heart (I say that boldly!) — no! That you cannot disbelieve, you have no right indeed . . . but —

*Be silent, heart,*
*Be patient, humble, do not speak.*

Well, shall I go on?" he broke off gloomily.

"If you'll be so kind," answered Nikolay Parfenovich.

## CHAPTER V

### THE THIRD ORDEAL

THOUGH Mitya spoke sullenly, it was evident that he was trying more than ever not to forget or miss a single detail of his story. He told them how he had leapt over the fence into his father's garden; how he had gone up to the window; told them all that had passed at the window. Clearly, precisely, distinctly, he described the feelings that troubled him during those moments in the garden when he longed so terribly to know whether Grushenka was with his father or not. But, strange to say, both the lawyers listened now with a sort of awful reserve, looked coldly at him, asked few questions. Mitya could gather nothing from their faces.

"They're angry and offended," he thought. "Well, devil take them!"

When he told how he had made up his mind at last to make the "signal" to his father that Grushenka had come, so that he should open the window, the lawyers paid no attention to the word "signal," as though they entirely failed to grasp the meaning of the word in this connection: so much so, that Mitya noticed it. Coming at last to the moment when, seeing his father peering out of the window, his hatred flared up and he pulled the pestle out of his pocket, he suddenly, as though of design, stopped short. He sat gazing at the wall and was aware that their eyes were fixed upon him.

"Well?" said the examining magistrate. "You pulled out the weapon and . . . and what happened then?"

"Then? Why, then I murdered him . . . hit him on the head and cracked his skull. . . . I suppose that's your story. That's it!"

His eyes suddenly flashed. All his smoth-ered wrath suddenly flamed up with extraordinary violence in his soul.

"Our story?" repeated Nikolay Parfenovich. "Well — and yours?"

Mitya dropped his eyes and was silent a long time.

"My story, gentlemen? Well, it was like this," he began softly. "Whether it was some one's tears, or my mother prayed to God, or a good angel kissed me at that instant, I don't know. But the devil was conquered. I rushed from the window and ran to the fence. My father was alarmed and then, for the first time, he saw me, cried out, and sprang back from the window. I remember that very well. I ran across the garden to the fence . . . and it was there that Grigory reached me, when I was sitting on the fence."

At that point he raised his eyes at last and looked at his listeners. They seemed to be staring at him with perfectly unruffled attention. A sort of paroxysm of indignation seized on Mitya's soul.

"Why, you're laughing at me at this moment, gentlemen!" he broke off suddenly.

"What makes you think that?" observed Nikolay Parfenovich.

"You don't believe one word — that's why! I understand, of course, that I have come to the vital point. The old man's lying there now with his skull broken, while I — after dramatically describing how I wanted to kill him, and how I snatched up the pestle — I suddenly run away from the window. An epic! In verse! As though one could take a fellow's word for it. Ha, ha! You are making game of me, gentlemen!" And he swung round on his chair so that it creaked.

"And did you notice," asked the prosecutor suddenly, as though not observing Mitya's

365

excitement, "did you notice when you ran away from the window, whether the door into the garden, that is, the door at the other end of the wing, was open or not?"

"No, it was not open."

"It was not?"

"It was shut. And who could open it? Bah! the door. Wait a bit!" He seemed suddenly to bethink himself, and almost with a start:

"Why, did you find the door open?"

"Yes, it was open."

"Why, who could have opened it if you did not open it yourselves?" cried Mitya, tremendously astonished.

"The door stood open, and your father's murderer undoubtedly went in at that door, and, having accomplished the crime, went out again by the same door," the prosecutor pronounced deliberately, as though marking each word separately. "That is perfectly clear to us. The murder was apparently committed in the room and *not through the window;* that is absolutely certain from the examination that has been made, from the position of the body, and everything. There can be no doubt of that circumstance."

Mitya was absolutely dumbfounded.

"But that's utterly impossible!" he cried, completely at a loss. "I . . . I didn't go in. . . . I tell you positively, definitely, the door was shut the whole time I was in the garden, and when I ran out of the garden. I only stood at the window and saw him through the window. That's all, that's all. . . . I remember to the last minute. And if I didn't remember, it would be just the same. I know it, for no one knew the signals except Smerdyakov, and me, and the deceased. And he wouldn't have opened the door to any one in the world without the signals."

"Signals? What signals?" asked the prosecutor, with greedy, almost hysterical, curiosity. He instantly lost all trace of his reserve and dignity. He asked the question with a sort of cringing timidity. He scented an important fact of which he had known nothing, and was already filled with dread that Mitya might be unwilling to disclose it.

"So you didn't know!" Mitya winked at him with a malicious and mocking smile. "What if I won't tell you? From whom could you find out? No one knew about the signals except the deceased, myself, and Smerdyakov: that was all. Heaven knew, too, but it won't tell you. And the fact is a curious one. There's no knowing what you might build on it. Ha, ha! Take comfort, gentlemen, I'll reveal it. You've some foolish idea in your heads. You don't know the man you have to deal with! You have to do with a prisoner who gives evidence against himself, to his own damage! Yes, for I'm a man of honour and you — are not."

The prosecutor swallowed these pills without a murmur. He was trembling with impatience to learn the new fact. Fully and precisely, Mitya told them everything about the signals invented by Fyodor Pavlovich for Smerdyakov. He told them exactly what every tap on the window meant, tapped the signals on the table, and when Nikolay Parfenovich said that he supposed he, Mitya, had tapped the signal "Grushenka has come," when he tapped to his father, he answered precisely that he had tapped that signal, that "Grushenka had come."

"So now you can build up your tower," Mitya broke off, and again turned away from them contemptuously.

"So no one knew of the signals but your deceased parent, you, and the servant Smerdyakov? And no one else?" Nikolay Parfenovich inquired once more.

"Yes. The servant Smerdyakov, and heaven. Write down about heaven. That may be of use. Besides, you will need God yourselves."

And they had already, of course, begun writing it down. But while they wrote, the prosecutor said abruptly, as though suddenly stumbling on a new idea:

"But if Smerdyakov also knew of these signals and you absolutely deny the charge of having caused the death of your parent, was it not he, perhaps, who knocked the signal agreed upon, induced your father to open to him, and then . . . committed the crime?"

Mitya turned upon him a look of profound irony and intense hatred. His silent stare lasted so long that it made the prosecutor blink.

"You've caught the fox again," commented Mitya at last; "you've got the beast by the tail. Ha, ha! I see through you, Mr. Prosecutor. You thought, of course, that I should jump at that, catch at your prompting, and shout with all my might, 'Aie, it's Smerdyakov; he's the murderer.' Confess that's what you thought. Confess, and I'll go on."

But the prosecutor did not confess. He held his tongue and waited.

"You're mistaken. I'm not going to shout 'It's Smerdyakov,'" said Mitya.

"And you don't even suspect him?"

"Why, do you suspect him?"

"He was suspected, too."

Mitya fixed his eyes on the floor.

"Joking apart," he brought out gloomily. "Listen. From the very beginning, almost from the moment when I ran out to you from behind the curtain, I've had the thought of Smerdyakov in my mind. I've been sitting here, shouting that I'm innocent and thinking all the time 'Smerdyakov!' I can't get Smerdyakov out of my head. In fact, I, too, thought of Smerdyakov just now; but only for a second. Almost at once I thought, 'No, it's not Smerdyakov.' It's not his doing, gentlemen."

"In that case is there anybody else you suspect?" Nikolay Parfenovich inquired cautiously.

"I don't know any one it could be, whether it's the hand of heaven or of Satan, but . . . not Smerdyakov," Mitya snapped firmly.

"But what makes you affirm so confidently and emphatically that it's not he?"

"From my conviction — my impression. Because Smerdyakov is a man of the lowest sort and a coward. He's not a coward, he's the epitome of all the cowardice in the world walking on two legs. He was born of a chicken. When he talked to me, he was always trembling for fear I should kill him, though I never raised my hand against him. He fell at my feet and blubbered; he has kissed these very boots, literally, beseeching me 'not to frighten him.' Do you hear? 'Not to frighten him.' What a thing to say! Why, I gave him presents. He's a sickly chicken — epileptic, weak-minded — a boy of eight could thrash him. He has no character worth talking about. It's not Smerdyakov, gentlemen. Besides, he doesn't even care for money; he wouldn't take my presents. Besides, why should he murder the old man? Why, he's very likely his son, you know — his natural son. Do you know that?"

"We have heard that legend. But you are your father's son, too; yet you yourself told every one you wanted to murder him."

"That's a thrust! And a nasty, mean one, too! I'm not afraid! Oh, gentlemen, isn't it too base of you to say that to my face? It's base, because I told you that myself. I not only wanted to murder him, but I might have done it. And, what's more, I went out of my way to tell you of my own accord that I nearly murdered him. But, you see, I didn't murder him; you see, my guardian angel saved me — that's what you've not taken into account. And that's why it's so base of you. For I didn't kill him, I didn't kill him! Do you hear, Mr. Prosecutor, I did not kill."

He was almost choking. He had not been so agitated before during the whole interrogation.

"And what has he told you, gentlemen — Smerdyakov, I mean?" he added suddenly, after a pause. "May I ask that question?"

"You may ask any question," the prosecutor replied with frigid severity, "any question relating to the facts of the case, and we are, I repeat, bound to answer every inquiry you make. We found the servant Smerdyakov, concerning whom you inquire, lying unconscious in his bed, in an epileptic fit of extreme severity, that had recurred, possibly, ten times. The doctor who was with us told us, after seeing him, that he may possibly not outlive the night."

"Well, in that case, the devil must have killed father," broke suddenly from Mitya, as though until that moment he had been asking himself: "Was it Smerdyakov or not?"

"We will come back to this later," Nikolay Parfenovich decided. "Now, wouldn't you like to continue your statement?"

Mitya asked for a rest. His request was courteously granted. After resting, he went on with his story. But he was evidently depressed.

He was exhausted, mortified, and morally shaken. To make things worse, the prosecutor began to irritate him continually, as though intentionally, by attaching himself to "details." Scarcely had Mitya described how, sitting on the wall, he had struck Grigory on the head with the pestle, while the old man had hold of his left leg, and how he had then jumped down to look at him, when the prosecutor stopped him to ask him to describe in greater detail how he was sitting on the wall. Mitya was astonished.

"Oh, I was sitting like this, astride, one leg on one side and one on the other."

"And the pestle?"

"The pestle was in my hands."

"Not in your pocket? Do you remember that precisely? Was it a hard blow you gave him?"

"It must have been a violent one. But why do you ask?"

"Would you mind sitting on the chair just as you sat on the fence then and showing us just how you swung your arm, and in what direction?"

"Are you making fun of me?" asked Mitya, looking haughtily at the speaker; but the latter did not flinch.

Mitya turned convulsively, sat astride on his chair, and swung his arm.

"This was how I struck him! That's how I knocked him down! What more do you want?"

"Thank you. May I trouble you now to explain why you jumped down, with what object, and what you had in view?"

"Oh, hang it! . . . I jumped down to look at the man I'd hurt . . . I don't know what for!"

"Though you were so excited and were running away?"

"Yes, though I was excited and running away."

"You wanted to help him?"

"Help! . . . Yes, perhaps I did want to help him. . . . I don't remember."

"You don't remember? Then you were in a kind of daze?"

"Oh, no, not at all. I remember everything — every detail. I jumped down to look at him, and wiped his face with my handkerchief."

"We have seen your handkerchief. Did you hope to restore him to consciousness?"

"I don't know whether I hoped it. I simply wanted to make sure whether he was alive or not."

"Ah! You wanted to be sure? Well, what then?"

"I'm not a doctor. I couldn't decide. I ran away thinking I'd killed him. And now he's recovered."

"Excellent," commented the prosecutor. "Thank you. That's all I wanted. Kindly proceed."

Alas! it never entered Mitya's head to tell them, though he remembered it, that he had jumped down out of pity, and standing over the prostrate figure had even uttered some words of regret: "You've come to grief, old man — there's no help for it. Well, there you must lie."

The prosecutor could draw only one conclusion: that the man had jumped down "at such a moment and in such excitement simply with the object of ascertaining whether the *only* witness of his crime were alive or not; and that therefore what must have been the man's strength, coolness, decision, and shrewdness even at such a moment . . ." and so on. The prosecutor was satisfied: "I've provoked the nervous fellow by 'details' and he has said

more than he meant to." With painful effort Mitya went on. But this time he was pulled up immediately by Nikolay Parfenovich.

"How came you to run to the servant, Fedosya Markovna, with your hands so covered with blood, and, as it appears, your face, too?"

"Why, I didn't notice the blood at all at the time," answered Mitya.

"That's quite likely. That's how it happens." The prosecutor exchanged glances with Nikolay Parfenovich.

"I simply didn't notice. You're quite right there, prosecutor," Mitya assented suddenly.

Next came the account of Mitya's sudden determination to "step aside" and make way for their happiness. But he could not make up his mind to open up his heart to them as before, and tell them about "the queen of his soul." He disliked speaking of her before these chilly persons "who were nipping at him like bugs." And so in response to their reiterated questions he answered briefly and sharply:

"Well, I made up my mind to kill myself. What had I left to live for? That question stared me in the face. Her first, rightful lover had come back, the man who wronged her but who'd hurried back to offer his love, after five years, and atone for the wrong with marriage. . . . So I knew it was all over for me. . . . And behind me disgrace, and that blood — Grigory's. . . . What had I to live for? So I went to redeem the pistols I had pawned, in order to load them and put a bullet in my brain the next day."

"And a grand feast the night before?"

"Yes, a grand feast the night before. Damn it all, gentlemen! Hurry up and be done with it. I meant to shoot myself not far from here, beyond the village, and I'd planned to do it at five o'clock in the morning. And I had a note in my pocket already. I wrote it at Perhotin's when I loaded my pistols. Here's the note. Read it! It's not for you I tell it," he suddenly added with contempt. He took it from his waistcoat pocket and flung it on the table. The examiners read it with interest, and, as is usual, added it to the papers connected with the case.

"And you didn't even think of washing your hands at Perhotin's? You were not afraid then of arousing suspicion?"

"What suspicion? Suspicion or not, I should have galloped here just the same, and shot myself at five o'clock, and nothing could have been done. If it hadn't been for what's happened to my father, you would have known nothing about it, and wouldn't have come here. Oh, it's the devil's doing. It was the devil murdered father, it was through the devil that you found it out so soon. How did you manage to get here so quick? It's a marvel, a dream!"

"Mr. Perhotin informed us that when you came to him, you held in your hands . . . your blood-stained hands . . . your money . . . a great deal of money . . . a batch of hundred-rouble notes, and that his servant, a boy, saw it, too."

"That's true, gentlemen. I remember it was so."

"Now, there's one little point presents itself. Can you not inform us," Nikolay Parfenovich began, with extreme gentleness, "where you got so much money all of a sudden, when it appears from the facts, and by the reckoning of time, that you had not been home?" The prosecutor's brows contracted at the question being asked so plainly, but he did not interrupt Nikolay Parfenovich.

"No, I didn't go home," answered Mitya, apparently perfectly composed, but looking at the floor.

"Allow me then to repeat my question," Nikolay Parfenovich went on as though creeping along. "Where were you able to procure such a sum all at once, when, by your own confession, at five o'clock the same day you . . ."

"I was in want of ten roubles and pawned my pistols with Perhotin, and then went to Madame Hohlakov to borrow three thousand, which she wouldn't give me, and so on, and all the rest of it," Mitya interrupted sharply. "Yes, gentlemen, I was in want of it, and suddenly thousands turned up, eh? Do you know, gentlemen, you're both afraid now 'what if he won't tell us where he got it?' That's just what will happen. I'm not going to tell you, gentlemen. You've guessed right. You shall not know," Mitya suddenly pronounced, marking each word with extraordinary determination. The lawyers were silent for a moment.

"You must understand, Mr. Karamazov, that it is of vital importance for us to know," said Nikolay Parfenovich, softly and meekly.

"I understand; but still I won't tell you."

The prosecutor, too, intervened, and again reminded him that the prisoner was at liberty to refuse to answer questions, if he thought it to his interest, and so on. But in view of the damage he might do himself by his silence, especially in a case of such importance as . . .

"And so on, gentlemen, and so on. Enough! I've heard that rigmarole before," Mitya interrupted again. "I can see for myself how important it is, and that this is the vital point, and still I won't say."

"What is it to us? It's not our business, but it's yours. You are doing yourself harm," observed Nikolay Parfenovich very nervously.

"You see, gentlemen, joking apart" — Mitya lifted his eyes and looked firmly at them both — "I had an inkling from the first that we should come to loggerheads at this point. But at first when I began to give my evidence, it was all still far away and misty; it was all floating, and I was so simple that I began with the proposition of mutual confidence. Now I can see for myself that such confidence is out of the question, for in any case we were bound to come to this cursed stumbling-block. And now we've come to it! It's impossible and there's an end of it! But I don't blame you. You can't take my word for it. I understand that, of course."

He relapsed into gloomy silence.

"Couldn't you, without abandoning your resolution to be silent about the chief point, could you not, at the same time, give us some slight hint as to the nature of the motives which are strong enough to induce you to refuse to answer, at a point in the investigation which is so full of danger for you?"

Mitya smiled mournfully, almost dreamily.

"I'm much more good-natured than you think, gentlemen, and I'll tell you the reason why and give you that hint, though you don't deserve it. I refuse to speak, gentlemen, because the matter involves a disgrace for me. The answer to the question where I got the money involves me in a far greater disgrace than the murder and robbing of my father, if I had murdered and robbed him. That's why I can't speak. I can't because of the disgrace. What, gentlemen, are you going to write that down?"

"Yes, we'll write it down," lisped Nikolay Parfenovich.

"You ought not to write that down about 'disgrace.' I only told you that in the goodness of my heart. I needn't have told you. I made you a present of it, so to speak, and you pounce upon it at once. Oh, well, write — write what you like," he concluded, with scornful disgust. "I'm not afraid of you and I can still hold up my head before you."

"And can't you tell us the nature of that disgrace?" Nikolay Parfenovich hazarded.

The prosecutor frowned darkly.

"No, no, *c'est fini*, don't trouble yourselves. It's not worth while soiling one's hands. I have soiled myself enough through you as it is. You're not worth it — no one is . . . Enough, gentlemen. I'm not going on."

This was said too peremptorily. Nikolay Parfenovich did not insist further, but from Ippolit Kirillovich's eyes he saw that the latter had not given up hope.

"Can you not, at least, tell us what sum you had in your hands when you went into Mr. Perhotin's — that is, how many roubles exactly?"

"I can't tell you that, either."

"You spoke to Mr. Perhotin, I believe, of having received three thousand from Madame Hohlakov."

"Perhaps I did. Enough, gentlemen. I won't say how much I had."

"Will you be so good then as to tell us how you came here and what you have done since you arrived?"

"Oh! you might ask the people here about that. But I'll tell you if you like."

He proceeded to do so, but we will not repeat his story. He told it drily and rapidly. Of the raptures of his love he said nothing, but told them that he abandoned his determination to shoot himself, owing to "new factors in the case." He told the story without going

into motives or details. And this time the lawyers did not worry him much. It was obvious
that this was not of essential interest to them.

"We shall verify all that. We will come
back to it during the examination of the witnesses, which will, of course, take place in your
presence," said Nikolay Parfenovich in conclusion. "And now allow me to request you to
lay on the table everything in your possession,
especially all the money you still have about
you."

"My money, gentlemen? Certainly. I understand that that is necessary. I'm surprised,
indeed, that you haven't inquired about it
before. It's true I couldn't get away anywhere.
I'm sitting here where I can be seen. But here's
my money — count it — take it. That's all, I
think."

He took everything out of his pockets; even
the small change — two twenty-copeck pieces
— he pulled out of his waistcoat pocket. They
counted the money, which amounted to eight
hundred and thirty-six roubles, and forty copecks. "And is that all?" asked the examining
magistrate.

"Yes."

"You stated just now in your evidence that
you spent three hundred roubles at Plotnikovs'. You gave Perhotin ten, your driver
twenty, here you lost two hundred at cards,
then . . ."

Nikolay Parfenovich reckoned it all up.
Mitya helped him readily. They recollected
every farthing and included it in the reckoning. Nikolay Parfenovich hurriedly added up
the total. "With this eight hundred you must
have had about fifteen hundred at first?"

"I suppose so," snapped Mitya.

"How is it they all assert there was much
more?"

"Let them assert it."

"But you asserted it yourself."

"Yes, I did, too."

"We will compare all this with the evidence of other persons not yet examined.
Don't be anxious about your money. It will be
properly taken care of and be at your disposal
at the conclusion of . . . what is beginning
. . . if it appears, or, so to speak, is proved
that you have undisputed right to it. Well, and
now . . ."

Nikolay Parfenovich, suddenly got up, and
informed Mitya firmly that it was his duty
and obligation to conduct a minute and thorough search "of your clothes and everything
else . . ."

"By all means, gentlemen. I'll turn out all
my pockets, if you like."

And he did, in fact, begin turning out his
pockets.

"It will be necessary to take off your clothes,
too."

"What! Strip? Ugh! Damn it! Won't you
search me as I am? Can't you?"

"It's utterly impossible, Dmitri Fyodorovich. You must take off your clothes."

"As you like," Mitya submitted gloomily;
"only, please, not here, but behind the curtains. Who will search them?"

"Behind the curtains, of course."

Nikolay Parfenovich bent his head in assent. His small face wore an expression of
peculiar solemnity.

## CHAPTER VI
### THE PROSECUTOR CATCHES MITYA

SOMETHING utterly unexpected and amazing
to Mitya followed. He could never, even a
minute before, have conceived that any one
could treat him, Mitya Karamazov, like that.

What was worst of all, there was something humiliating in it, and on their side something "supercilious and contemptuous." It was nothing to take off his coat, but he was asked to undress further, or rather not asked but "commanded," he quite understood that. From pride and contempt he submitted without a word. Several peasants accompanied the lawyers and remained on the same side of the curtain. "To be ready if force is required," thought Mitya, "and perhaps for some other reason, too."

"Well, must I take off my shirt, too?" he asked sharply, but Nikolay Parfenovich did not answer. He was busily engaged with the prosecutor in examining the coat, the trousers, the waistcoat, and the cap; and it was evident that they were both much interested in the scrutiny. "They make no bones about it," thought Mitya, "they don't show the most elementary politeness."

"I ask you for the second time — need I take off my shirt or not?" he said, still more sharply and irritably.

"Don't trouble yourself. We will tell you what to do," Nikolay Parfenovich said, and there was something dictatorial about his voice, or so it seemed to Mitya.

Meantime a consultation was going on in undertones between the examining magistrate and the prosecutor. There turned out to be on the coat, especially on the left side at the back, huge patches of blood, dry, and still stiff. There were bloodstains on the trousers, too. Nikolay Parfenovich, moreover, in the presence of the peasant witnesses, passed his fingers along the collar, the cuffs, and all the seams of the coat and trousers, obviously looking for something — money, of course. He didn't even hide from Mitya his suspicion that

he was capable of sewing money up in his clothes.

"I am being treated not as an officer but as a thief," Mitya muttered to himself. They communicated their ideas to one another with amazing frankness. The secretary, for instance, who was also behind the curtain, fussing about and making himself useful, called Nikolay Parfenovich's attention to the cap, which they were also fingering.

"You remember Gridyenko, the copying-clerk," observed the secretary. "Last summer he received the wages of the whole office, and pretended to have lost the money when he was drunk. And where was it found? Why, in just such pipings in his cap. The hundred-rouble notes were screwed up in little rolls and sewed up in the piping."

Both the magistrates remembered Gridyenko's case perfectly, and so laid aside Mitya's cap, and decided that all his clothes must be more thoroughly examined later.

"Excuse me," cried Nikolay Parfenovich, suddenly, noticing that the right cuff of Mitya's shirt was turned in, and covered with blood, "excuse me, what's that, blood?"

"Yes," Mitya jerked out.

"That is, what blood . . . and why is the cuff turned in?"

Mitya told him how he had got the sleeve stained with blood looking after Grigory, and had turned it inside when he was washing his hands at Perhotin's.

"You must take off your shirt, too. That's very important as material evidence."

Mitya flushed red and flew into a rage.

"What, am I to stay naked?" he shouted.

"Don't disturb yourself. We will arrange something. And meanwhile take off your socks."

"You're not joking? Is that really necessary?" Mitya's eyes flashed.

"We are in no mood for joking," answered Nikolay Parfenovich sternly.

"Well, if I must . . ." muttered Mitya, and sitting down on the bed, he took off his socks. He felt unbearably awkward. All were clothed, while he was naked, and, strange to say, when he was undressed he felt somehow guilty in their presence, and was almost ready to believe himself that he was inferior to them, and that now they had a perfect right to despise him.

"When all are undressed, one is somehow not ashamed, but when one's the only one undressed and everybody is looking, it's disgraceful," he kept repeating to himself, again and again. "It's like a dream, I've sometimes dreamed of being in such degrading positions." It was a misery to him to take off his socks. They were very dirty, and so were his underclothes, and now everyone could see it. And what was worse, he disliked his feet. All his life he had thought both his big toes hideous. He particularly loathed the coarse, flat, crooked nail on the right one, and now they would all see it. Feeling intolerably ashamed made him, at once and intentionally, rougher. He pulled off his shirt, himself.

"Would you like to look anywhere else if you're not ashamed to?"

"No, there's no need to, at present."

"Well, am I to stay naked like this?" he added savagely.

"Yes, that can't be helped for the time. . . . Kindly sit down here for a while. You can wrap yourself in a quilt from the bed, and I . . . I'll see to all this."

All the things were shown to the witnesses. The report of the search was drawn up, and at last Nikolay Parfenovich went out, and the clothes were carried out after him. Ippolit Kirillovich went out, too. Mitya was left alone with the peasants, who stood in silence, never taking their eyes off him. Mitya wrapped himself up in the quilt. He felt cold. His bare feet stuck out, and he couldn't pull the quilt over so as to cover them. Nikolay Parfenovich seemed to be gone a long time, "an insufferable time." "He thinks of me as a puppy," thought Mitya, gnashing his teeth. "That rotten prosecutor has gone, too, contemptuous no doubt, it disgusts him to see me naked!"

Mitya imagined, however, that his clothes would be examined and returned to him. But what was his indignation when Nikolay Parfenovich came back with quite different clothes, brought in behind him by a peasant.

"Here are clothes for you," he observed airily, seeming well satisfied with the success of his mission. "Mr. Kalganov has kindly provided these for this unusual emergency, as well as a clean shirt. Luckily he had them all in his trunk. You can keep your own socks and underclothes." Mitya flew into a passion.

"I won't have other people's clothes!" he shouted menacingly, "give me my own!"

"It's impossible!"

"Give me my own. Damn Kalganov and his clothes, too!"

It was a long time before they could persuade him. But they succeeded somehow in quieting him down. They impressed upon him that his clothes, being stained with blood, must be "added to the other material evidence," and that they "had not even the right to let him have them now . . . taking into consideration the possible outcome of the case." Mitya at last understood this. He subsided into gloomy silence and hurriedly dressed himself. He merely observed, as he put them on, that the clothes were much better than his old ones, and that he disliked "gaining by the change." They were, besides, "shamefully narrow. Am I to be made to play the clown . . . for your amusement?"

They urged upon him again that he was exaggerating, that Kalganov was only a little taller, so that only the trousers might be a little too long. But the coat turned out to be really tight in the shoulders.

"Damn it all! I can hardly button it," Mitya grumbled. "Be so good as to tell Mr. Kalganov from me that I didn't ask for his clothes, and it's not my doing that they've dressed me up like a clown."

"He quite understands that, and is sorry . . . I mean, not sorry to lend you his clothes, but sorry about all this business," mumbled Nikolay Parfenovich.

"Confound his regrets! Well, where now, or am I to go on sitting here?"

He was asked to go back to the "other room." Mitya went in, scowling with anger, and trying to avoid looking at any one. Dressed in another man's clothes he felt himself disgraced, even in the eyes of the peasants, and of Trifon Borisovich, whose face appeared, for some reason, in the doorway, and vanished immediately. "He's come to look at me dressed up," thought Mitya. He sat down on the same chair as before. He had an absurd nightmarish feeling, as though he were out of his mind.

"Well, what now? Are you going to flog me? That's all that's left for you," he said, clenching his teeth and addressing the prosecutor. He would not turn to Nikolay Parfenovich, as though he disdained to speak to him.

"He looked too closely at my socks, and turned them inside out on purpose to show every one what dirty underclothes I wear — the scoundrel!"

"Well, now we must proceed to the examination of witnesses," observed Nikolay Parfenovich, as though in reply to Mitya's question.

"Yes," said the prosecutor thoughtfully, as though reflecting on something.

"We've done what we could in your interest, Dmitri Fyodorovich," Nikolay Parfenovich went on, "but having received from you such an uncompromising refusal to explain to us the source from which you obtained the money found upon you, we are, at the present moment . . ."

"What is the stone in your ring?" Mitya interrupted suddenly, as though awakening from a reverie. He pointed to one of the three rings adorning Nikolay Parfenovich's right hand.

"Ring?" repeated Nikolay Parfenovich with surprise.

"Yes, that one . . . on your middle finger, with the little veins in it, what stone is that?" Mitya persisted, like a peevish child.

"That's a smoky topaz," said Nikolay Parfenovich, smiling. "Would you like to look at it? I'll take it off . . ."

"No, no, don't take it off," cried Mitya furiously, suddenly waking up, and angry with himself. "Don't take it off . . . there's no need. . . . Damn it. . . . Gentlemen, you've sullied my soul! Can you suppose that I would conceal it from you, if I really had killed my father, that I would shuffle, lie, and hide myself? No, that's not like Dmitri Karamazov, that he couldn't bear, and if I were guilty, I swear I wouldn't have waited for your coming, or for the sunrise as I meant at first, but would have destroyed myself before this, without waiting for the dawn! I know that about myself now. I couldn't have learnt so much in twenty years as I've found out in this accursed night! . . . And should I have been like this on this night, and at this moment, sitting with you, could I have talked like this, could I have moved like this, could I have looked at you and at the world like this, if I had really been the murderer of my father, when the very thought of having accidentally killed Grigory gave me no peace all night — not from fear — oh, not simply from fear of your punishment! The digrace of it! And you want me to be open with such scoffers as you, who see nothing and believe in nothing, blind moles and scoffers, and to tell you another nasty thing I've done, another disgrace, even if that would save me from your accusation! No, better Siberia! The man who opened the door to my father and went in at that door, he killed him, he robbed him. Who was he — I'm racking my brains and can't think who. But I can tell you it was not Dmitri Karamazov, and that's all I can tell you, and that's enough, enough, leave me alone. . . . Exile me, execute me, but don't bother me any more. I'll say no more. Call your witnesses!"

Mitya uttered his sudden monologue as though he were determined to be absolutely silent for the future. The prosecutor watched him the whole time and only when he had ceased speaking, observed, as though it were the most ordinary thing, with the most frigid and composed air:

"Oh, about the open door of which you spoke just now, we may as well inform you, by the way, now, of a very interesting piece of evidence of the greatest importance both to

you and to us, that has been given us by Grigory, the old man you wounded. On his recovery, he clearly and emphatically stated, in reply to our questions, that when, on coming out to the steps, and hearing a noise in the garden, he made up his mind to go into it through the little gate which stood open, before he noticed you running, as you have told us already, in the dark from the open window where you saw your father, he, Grigory, glanced to the left, and, while noticing the open window, observed at the same time, much nearer to him, the door, standing wide open — that door which you have stated to have been shut the whole time you were in the garden. I will not conceal from you that Grigory himself confidently affirms and bears witness that you must have run from that door, though, of course, he did not see you do so with his own eyes, since he only noticed you first some distance away in the garden, running towards the fence."

Mitya had leapt up from his chair half-way through this speech.

"Nonsense!" he yelled, in a sudden frenzy, "it's a bare-faced lie. He couldn't have seen the door open because it was shut. He's lying!"

"I consider it my duty to repeat that he is firm in his statement. He does not waver. He adheres to it. We've questioned him several times."

"Precisely. I have questioned him several times," Nikolay Parfenovich confirmed warmly.

"It's false, false! It's either slander, or the hallucination of a madman," Mitya still shouted. "He's simply raving, from loss of blood, from the wound. He must have fancied it when he came to. . . . He's raving."

"Yes, but he noticed the open door, not

MITYA IS DISGRACED

when he came to after his injuries, but before that, as soon as he went into the garden from the lodge."

"But it's false, it's false! It can't be so! He's slandering me from spite. . . . He couldn't have seen it . . . I didn't run out of the door," gasped Mitya.

The prosecutor turned to Nikolay Parfenovich and said to him impressively:

"Confront him with it."

"Do you recognise this object?"

Nikolay Parfenovich laid upon the table a large and thick official envelope, on which three seals still remained intact. The envelope was empty, and slit open at one end. Mitya stared at it with open eyes.

"It . . . it must be that envelope of my father's, the envelope that contained the three thousand roubles . . . and if there's inscribed on it, allow me, 'for my little chick' . . . yes — three thousand!" he shouted, "do you see, three thousand, do you see?"

"Of course, we see. But we didn't find the money in it. It was empty, and lying on the floor by the bed, behind the screen."

For some seconds Mitya stood as though thunderstruck.

"Gentlemen, it's Smerdyakov!" he shouted suddenly, at the top of his voice. "It's he who's murdered him! He's robbed him! No one else knew where the old man hid the envelope. It's Smerdyakov, that's clear, now!"

"But you, too, knew of the envelope and that it was under the pillow."

"I never knew it. I've never seen it. This is the first time I've looked at it. I'd only heard of it from Smerdyakov. . . . He was the only one who knew where the old man kept it hidden, I didn't know . . ." Mitya was completely breathless.

"But you told us yourself that the envelope was under your deceased father's pillow. You especially stated that it was under the pillow, so you must have known it."

"We've got it written down," confirmed Nikolay Parfenovich.

"Nonsense! It's absurd! I'd no idea it was under the pillow. And perhaps it wasn't under the pillow at all. . . . It was just a chance guess that it was under the pillow. What does Smerdyakov say? Have you asked him where it was? What does Smerdyakov say? that's the chief point. . . . And I went out of my way to tell lies against myself. . . . I told you without thinking that it was under the pillow, and now you . . . Oh, you know how one says the wrong thing, without meaning it. No one knew but Smerdyakov, only Smerdyakov, and no one else. . . . He didn't even tell me where it was! But it's his doing, his doing; there's no doubt about it, he murdered him, that's as clear as daylight now," Mitya exclaimed more and more frantically, repeating himself incoherently, and growing more and more exasperated and excited. "You must understand that, and arrest him at once. . . . He must have killed him while I was running away and while Grigory was unconscious, that's clear now. . . . He gave the signal and father opened to him . . . for no one but he knew the signal, and without the signal father would never have opened the door. . . ."

"But you're again forgetting the circumstance," the prosecutor observed, still speaking with the same restraint, though with a note of triumph, "that there was no need to give the signal if the door already stood open when you were there, while you were in the garden . . ."

"The door, the door," muttered Mitya, and

he stared speechless at the prosecutor. He sank back helpless in his chair. All were silent.

"Yes, the door! . . . It's a nightmare! God is against me!" he exclaimed, staring before him in complete stupefaction.

"Come, you see," the prosecutor went on with dignity, "and you can judge for yourself, Dmitri Fyodorovich. On the one hand we have the evidence of the open door from which you ran out, a fact which overwhelms you and us. On the other side your incomprehensible, persistent, and, so to speak, obdurate silence with regard to the source from which you obtained the money which was so suddenly seen in your hands, when only three hours earlier, on your own showing, you pledged your pistols for the sake of ten roubles! In view of all these facts, judge for yourself. What are we to believe, and what can we depend upon? And don't accuse us of being 'frigid, cynical, scoffing people,' who are incapable of believing in the generous impulses of your heart. . . . Try to enter into our position . . ."

Mitya was indescribably agitated. He turned pale.

"Very well!" he exclaimed suddenly, "I will tell you my secret. I'll tell you where I got the money! . . . I'll reveal my shame, that I may not have to blame myself or you hereafter."

"And believe me, Dmitri Fyodorovich," put in Nikolay Parfenovich, in a voice of almost pathetic delight, "that every sincere and complete confession on your part at this moment may, later on, immensely alleviate your lot, and may, indeed, moreover . . ."

But the prosecutor gave him a slight shove under the table, and he checked himself in time. Mitya, it is true, had not heard him.

## CHAPTER VII
### MITYA'S GREAT SECRET. RECEIVED WITH HISSES

"GENTLEMEN," he began, still in the same agitation, "I want to make a full confession: that money was *my own*."

The magistrates' faces lengthened. That was not at all what they expected.

"How do you mean?" faltered Nikolay Parfenovich, "when at five o'clock on the same day, by your own confession . . ."

"Damn five o'clock on the same day and my own confession. That's got nothing to do with it now! That money was my own, my own, that is, stolen by me . . . not mine, I mean, but stolen by me, and it was fifteen hundred roubles, and I had it on me all the time, all the time . . ."

"But where did you get it?"

"I took it off my neck, gentlemen, off this very neck . . . it was here, round my neck, sewn up in a rag, and I'd had it round my neck a long time, it's a month since I put it round my neck . . . to my shame and disgrace!"

"And from whom did you . . . obtain it?"

"You mean, 'steal it'? Speak out plainly now. Yes, I consider that I practically stole it, but, if you prefer, I 'appropriated it.' I consider I stole it. And last night I stole it for good."

"Last night? But you said that it's a month since you . . . obtained it? . . ."

"Yes. But not from my father. Not from my father, don't be uneasy. I didn't steal it from my father, but from her. Let me tell you without interruption. It's hard to do, you know. You see, a month ago, I was sent for by Katerina Ivanovna Verhovtzev, formerly my betrothed. Do you know her?"

"Yes, of course."

"I know you know her. She's a noble creature, noblest of the noble. But she has hated me ever so long, oh, ever so long . . . and hated me with good reason, good reason!"

"Katerina Ivanovna!" the examining magistrate exclaimed with amazement. The prosecutor, too, stared.

"Oh, don't take her name in vain! I'm a scoundrel to bring her into it. Yes, I've seen that she hated me . . . a long while. . . . From the very first, even that evening at my lodging . . . but enough, enough. You're unworthy even to know of that. No need of that at all. . . . I need only tell you that she sent for me a month ago, gave me three thousand roubles to send off to her sister and another relation in Moscow (as though she couldn't have sent it off herself!), and I . . . it was just at that fatal moment in my life when I . . . Well, in fact, when I'd just come to love another, *her*, the present one, the one who's sitting down below now, Grushenka. I carried her off here to Mokroye then, and squandered here in two days half that damned three thousand, but the other half I kept on me. Well, I've kept that other half, that fifteen hundred, like a locket round my neck, but yesterday I opened it, and spent it. What's left of it, eight hundred roubles, is in your hands now, Nikolay Parfenovich. That's the change out of the fifteen hundred I had yesterday."

"Excuse me. How's that? Why, when you were here a month ago you spent three thousand, not fifteen hundred, everybody knows that."

"Who knows it? Who counted the money? Did I let any one count it?"

"Why, you told every one yourself that you'd spent exactly three thousand."

"It's true, I did. I told the whole town so, and the whole town said so. And here, at Mokroye, too, every one reckoned it was three thousand. Yet I didn't spend three thousand, but fifteen hundred. And the other fifteen hundred I sewed into a little bag. That's how it was, gentlemen. That's where I got that money yesterday. . . ."

"This is almost miraculous," murmured Nikolay Parfenovich.

"Allow me to inquire," observed the prosecutor at last, "have you informed any one whatever of this circumstance before, I mean that you had fifteen hundred left about you a month ago?"

"I told no one."

"That's strange. Do you mean absolutely no one?"

"Absolutely no one. No one and nobody."

"What was your reason for this reticence? What was your motive for making such a secret of it? To be more precise: You have told us at last your secret, in your words, so 'disgraceful,' though in reality — that is, of course, comparatively speaking — this action, that is, the appropriation of three thousand roubles belonging to some one else, and, of course, only for a time, is, in my view at least, only an act of the greatest recklessness and not so disgraceful, when one takes into consideration your character. . . . Even admitting that it was an action in the highest degree discreditable, still, discreditable is not 'disgraceful.' . . . Many people have already guessed, during this last month, about the three thousand of Katerina Ivanovna's that you have spent, and I had heard the legend myself, apart from your confession. . . . Mihail Makarovich, for instance, had heard it, too, so that indeed, it was scarcely a legend, but the gossip of the whole town. There are indications, too, if I am not mistaken, that you confessed this yourself to some one, I mean that the money was Katerina Ivanovna's, and so, it's extremely surprising to me that hitherto, that is, up to the present moment, you have made such an extraordinary secret of the fifteen hundred you say you put by, apparently connecting a feeling of positive horror with that secret. . . . It's not easy to believe that it could cost you such distress to confess such a secret. . . . You cried out, just now, that Siberia would be better than confessing it. . . ."

The prosecutor ceased speaking. He was provoked. He did not conceal his vexation, which was almost anger, and gave vent to all his accumulated spleen, without choosing words, disconnectedly and incoherently.

"It's not the fifteen hundred that's the disgrace, but that I put it apart from the rest of the three thousand," said Mitya firmly.

"Why?" smiled the prosecutor irritably. "What is there disgraceful, to your thinking, in your having set aside half of the three thousand you had discreditably, if you prefer, 'disgracefully,' appropriated? Your taking the three thousand is more important than what you did with it. And by the way, why did you do that — why did you set apart that half, for what purpose, for what object did you do it? Can you explain that to us?"

"Oh, gentlemen, the purpose is the whole point!" cried Mitya. "I put it aside because I was vile, that is, because I was calculating, and to be calculating in such a case is vile . . . and that vileness has lasted a whole month."

"It's incomprehensible."

"I am surprised at you. But I'll make it clearer. Perhaps it really is incomprehensible.

You see, attend to what I say. I appropriate three thousand entrusted to my honour, I spend it on a spree, say I spend it all, and next morning I appear before her and say, 'Katya, I've done wrong, I've squandered your three thousand,' well, is that right? No, it's not right — it's dishonest and mean, I'm a beast, with no more self-control than a beast, that's so, isn't it? But still I'm not a thief? Not a downright thief, you'll admit! I squandered it, but I didn't steal it. Now a second, rather more favourable alternative: follow me carefully, or I may get confused again — my head's going round — and so, for the second alternative: I squander here only fifteen hundred out of the three thousand, that is, only half. Next day I go and take that half to her: 'Katya, take this fifteen hundred from me, I'm a low beast, and an untrustworthy scoundrel, for I've squandered half the money, and I shall squander this, too, so keep me from temptation!' Well, what of that alternative? I should be a beast and a scoundrel, and whatever you like; but not a thief, not altogether a thief, for, if I were a thief, I should not have brought back what was left, but have kept that, too. She would see at once that since I brought back half, I should pay back what I'd squandered, that I should never give up trying to, that I should work to get it and pay it back. So in that case I should be a scoundrel, but not a thief, you may say what you like, not a thief!"

"I admit that there is a certain distinction," said the prosecutor, with a cold smile. "But it's strange that you see such a fateful difference."

"Yes, I see a fateful difference! Every man may be a scoundrel, and perhaps every man is a scoundrel, but not every one can be a thief, it takes an arch-scoundrel to be that. Oh, of course, I don't know how to make these fine distinctions . . . but a thief is lower than a scoundrel, that's my conviction. Listen, I carry the money about me a whole month, I may make up my mind to give it back to-morrow, and I'm a scoundrel no longer, but I cannot make up my mind, you see, though I'm making up my mind every day, and every day spurring myself on to do it, and yet for a whole month I can't bring myself to it, you see. Is that right to your thinking, is that right?"

"Certainly, that's not right, that I can quite understand, and that I don't dispute," answered the prosecutor with reserve. "And let us give up all discussions of these subtleties and distinctions, and, if you will be so kind, get back to the point. And the point is, that you have still not told us, although we've asked you, why, in the first place, you divided the money, squandering one half and hiding the other? For what purpose exactly did you hide it, what did you mean to do with that fifteen hundred? I insist upon that question, Dmitri Fyodorovich."

"Yes, of course!" cried Mitya, striking himself on the forehead; "forgive me, I'm tormenting you, and am not explaining the chief point, or you'd understand in a minute, for it's just the aim of it, the aim, that's the disgrace! You see, it all had to do with the old man, the deceased. He was always pestering Agrafena Alexandrovna, and I was jealous; I thought then that she was hesitating between me and him. So I kept thinking every day, suppose she were to make up her mind all of a sudden, suppose she were to leave off tormenting me, and were suddenly to say to me, 'I love you, not him; take me to the other end of the

world.' And I'd only forty copecks; how could I take her away, what could I do? Why, I'd be lost. You see, I didn't know her then, I didn't understand her, I thought she wanted money, and that she wouldn't forgive my poverty. And so I fiendishly counted out the half of that three thousand, sewed it up cold-bloodedly, calculating on it, sewed it up before I went on a spree, and after I had sewn it up, I went off to get drunk on the rest. Yes, that was base. Do you understand now?"

Both the magistrates laughed aloud.

"I should have called it sensible and moral on your part not to have squandered it all," chuckled Nikolay Parfenovich, "for after all what does it amount to?"

"Why, that I stole it, that's what it amounts to! Oh, God, you horrify me by your lack of understanding! All the time that I carried that fifteen hundred sewn up round my neck, every day and every hour I said to myself, 'You're a thief! you're a thief!' Yes, that's why I've been so savage all this month, that's why I fought in the tavern, that's why I attacked my father, it was because I felt I was a thief. I couldn't make up my mind, I didn't dare even to tell Alyosha, my brother, about that fifteen hundred: I felt I was such a scoundrel and such a pickpocket. But, do you know, while I carried it I said to myself at the same time every hour: 'No, Dmitri Fyodorovich, perhaps you are not a thief yet.' Why? Because I might go next day and hand over that fifteen hundred to Katya. And only yesterday I made up my mind to tear my amulet off my neck, on my way from Fenya's to Perhotin. I hadn't been able till that moment to bring myself to it. And as soon as I tore it off, at that very moment I became a downright thief, a thief and a dishonest man for the rest of my life. Why?

Because with that I destroyed, too, my dream of going to Katya and saying, 'I'm a scoundrel, but not a thief!' Do you understand now? Do you understand?"

"What was it made you decide to do it yesterday?" Nikolay Parfenovich interrupted.

"Why? It's absurd to ask. Because I had condemned myself to die at five o'clock this morning, here, at dawn. I thought it made no difference whether I died a thief or a man of honour. But I see it's not so, it turns out that it does make a difference. Believe me, gentlemen, what has tortured me most during this night has not been the thought that I'd killed the old servant, and that I was in danger of Siberia just when my love was being rewarded, and heaven was open to me again. Oh, that did torture me, but not so much; not so much as the accursed consciousness that I had torn that damned money off my breast at last and spent it, and had become a downright thief! Oh, gentlemen, I tell you again, with a bleeding heart, I have learnt a great deal this night. I have learnt that it's not only impossible to live a scoundrel, but impossible to die a scoundrel. . . . No, gentlemen, one must die honest . . ." Mitya was pale. His face had a haggard and exhausted look, in spite of his being intensely excited.

"I am beginning to understand you, Dmitri Fyodorovich," the prosecutor said slowly, in a soft and almost compassionate tone. "But all this, if you'll excuse my saying so, is a matter of nerves, in my opinion . . . your overwrought nerves, that's what it is. And why, for instance, should you not have saved yourself such misery for almost a month, by going and returning that fifteen hundred to the lady who had entrusted it to you? And why could you not have explained things to

her, and in view of your position, which you describe as being so awful, why could you not have had recourse to the plan which would so naturally have occurred to one's mind, that is, after honourably confessing your errors to her, why could you not have asked her to lend you the sum needed for your expenses, which, with her generous heart, she would certainly not have refused you in your distress, especially if it had been with some guarantee, or even on the security you offered to the merchant Samsonov, and to Madame Hohlakov. I suppose you still regard that security as of value?"

Mitya suddenly crimsoned.

"Surely you don't think me such an out and out scoundrel as that? You can't be speaking in earnest?" he said, with indignation, looking the prosecutor straight in the face, and seeming unable to believe his ears.

"I assure you I'm in earnest. . . . Why do you imagine I'm not serious?" It was the prosecutor's turn to be surprised.

"Oh, how base that would have been! Gentlemen, do you know, you are torturing me! Very well, I will tell you everything, if it must be so. I'll confess all my damnable vileness, but only in order to put you to shame, and you'll be surprised yourself at the depths of ignominy to which a medley of human passions can sink. You must know that I already had that plan myself, that plan you spoke of, just now, prosecutor! Yes, gentlemen, I, too, have had that thought in my mind all this accursed month, so that I was on the point of deciding to go to Katya — that's how mean I was. But to go to her, to tell her of my treachery, and for that very treachery, to carry out that treacherous act, for the expenses connected with it, to beg for money from her, Katya (to beg, do you hear, to beg), and straight from her to run away with the other, her rival, who hated her and had insulted her — to think of it! Why, you must have lost your mind, prosecutor!"

"I haven't lost my mind, but I did speak in haste, without thinking . . . of that feminine jealousy . . . if there could be jealousy in this case, as you assert . . . yes, perhaps there is something of the kind," said the prosecutor, smiling.

"But that would have been so infamous!" Mitya brought his fist down on the table fiercely. "That would have stunk beyond words! And do you know that she might have given me that money, yes, and she would have given it, too; she'd have been certain to give it, to be revenged on me, she'd have given it to satisfy her vengeance, to show her contempt for me, for hers is an infernal nature, too, and she's a woman of great wrath. I'd have taken the money, too, oh, I should have taken it; I should have taken it, and then, for the rest of my life . . . oh, God! Forgive me, gentlemen, I'm making such an outcry because I've had that thought in my mind so lately, only the day before yesterday, that night when I was having all that bother with Lyagavy, and afterwards yesterday, all day yesterday, I remember, till that happened . . ."

"Till what happened?" put in Nikolay Parfenovich inquisitively, but Mitya did not hear it.

"I have made you a dreadful confession," Mitya said gloomily in conclusion. "You must appreciate it, gentlemen, and what's more, you must feel it, for if not, if that leaves your souls untouched, then you've simply no respect for me, gentlemen, I tell you that, and I shall die of shame at having confessed it to men like you! Oh, I shall shoot myself! Yes,

I see, I see already that you don't believe me. What, you want to write that down, too?" he cried in fear.

"And what you said just now," said Nikolay Parfenovich, looking at him in surprise, "that is, that up to the last hour you were still planning to go to Katerina Ivanovna to beg that sum from her. . . . I assure you, that's a very important piece of evidence for us, Dmitri Fyodorovich, I mean for the whole case . . . and particularly for you, particularly important for you."

"Have mercy, gentlemen!" Mitya flung up his hands. "Don't write that, anyway; have some shame. Here I've torn my heart in half before you, and you seize the opportunity and dig your fingers into the torn parts of both halves. . . . Oh, my God!"

In despair he hid his face in his hands.

"Don't worry yourself so, Dmitri Fyodorovich," observed the prosecutor, "everything that is written down will be read over to you afterwards, and what you don't agree to we'll alter as you like. But now I'll ask you one little question for the third time. Has no one, absolutely no one, heard from you of that money you sewed up in the bag? That, I must tell you, is almost impossible to believe."

"No one, no one, I told you so before, or you've not understood anything! Let me alone!"

"Very well, this matter is bound to be explained, and there's plenty of time for it, but meantime, consider; we have perhaps a dozen witnesses that you yourself spread it abroad, and even shouted almost everywhere, about the three thousand you'd spent here; three thousand, not fifteen hundred. And now, too, when you got hold of the money you had yesterday, you gave many people to understand that you had brought three thousand with you."

"You've got not dozens, but hundreds of witnesses, two hundred witnesses, two hundred have heard it, thousands have heard it!" cried Mitya.

"Well, you see, all bear witness to it. And the word *all* means something."

"It means nothing. I told a lie, and every one began repeating it."

"But what need had you to 'tell a lie,' as you put it?"

"The devil knows. Out of bravado perhaps . . . just so . . . to show I'd squandered so much money. . . . To try and forget that money I had sewn up, perhaps . . . yes, that was why . . . damn it . . . how often will you ask me that question? Well, I told a fib, and that was the end of it, once I'd said it I didn't care to correct it. What does a man tell lies for sometimes?"

"That's very difficult to decide, Dmitri Fyodorovich, what makes a man tell lies," observed the prosecutor impressively. "Tell me, though, was that 'amulet,' as you call it, on your neck, a big thing?"

"No, not big."

"How big, for instance?"

"If you fold a hundred-rouble note in half, that would be the size."

"You'd better show us the remains of it. You must have them somewhere."

"Damnation, what nonsense! I don't know where they are."

"But excuse me: where and when did you take it off your neck? According to your own evidence you didn't go home."

"When I was going from Fenya's to Perhotin's, on the way I tore it off my neck and took out the money."

"In the dark?"

"What should I want a light for? I did it with a finger in one minute."

"Without scissors, in the street?"

"On the square I think it was. Why scissors? It was an old rag. It ripped in a minute."

"What did you do with it afterwards?"

"I dropped it there."

"Where was it, exactly?"

"On the square, somewhere on the square! The devil knows just where. What do you want to know for?"

"That's extremely important, Dmitri Fyodorovich. It would be material evidence in your favour. How is it you don't understand that? Who helped you to sew it up a month ago?"

"No one helped me. I did it myself."

"Can you sew?"

"A soldier has to know how to sew. It doesn't take any skill."

"Where did you get the material, that is, the rag in which you sewed the money?"

"Are you laughing at me?"

"Not at all. And we are in no mood for laughing, Dmitri Fyodorovich."

"I don't know where I got the rag from — somewhere I suppose."

"I should have thought that you would remember it."

"Upon my word, I don't remember. I might have torn a bit off my linen."

"That's very interesting. We might find in your lodgings to-morrow the shirt or whatever it is from which you tore the rag. What sort of rag was it, cloth or linen?"

"Goodness only knows what it was. Wait a bit. . . . I believe I didn't tear it off anything. It was a bit of calico. . . . I believe I sewed it up in a cap of my landlady's."

"In your landlady's cap?"

"Yes. I took it from her."

"How did you get it?"

"You see, I remember once taking a cap for a rag, perhaps to wipe my pen on. I took it without asking, because it was a worthless rag. I tore it up, and I took the notes and sewed them up in it. I believe it was in that very rag I sewed it. An old piece of calico, washed a thousand times."

"And you remember that for certain now?"

"I don't know whether for certain. I think it was in the cap. But what does it matter?"

"In that case your landlady might at least remember that she had lost the thing."

"No, she won't, she didn't miss it. It was an old rag, I tell you, not worth a groat."

"And where did you get the needle and thread?"

"I'll stop now. I won't say any more. Enough of it!" said Mitya, losing his temper at last.

"It's strange that you should have so completely forgotten where you threw the pieces in the square."

"Give orders for the square to be swept tomorrow, and perhaps you'll find it," said Mitya, sneering. "Enough, gentlemen, enough!" he decided, in an exhausted voice. "I see clearly you don't believe me! Not for a moment! It's my fault, not yours. I ought not to have been so ready. Why, why did I degrade myself by confessing my secret to you? It's a joke to you. I see that from your eyes. You led me on to it, prosecutor! Sing a hymn of triumph if you can. . . . Damn you, you torturers!"

He bent his head, and hid his face in his hands. The magistrates were silent. A minute later he raised his head and looked at them almost vacantly. His face now expressed complete, hopeless despair, and he sat mute and passive as though hardly conscious of what was happening. In the meantime they had to finish what they were about. They had immediately to begin examining the witnesses. It was by now eight o'clock in the morning. The candles had been extinguished long ago. Mihail Makarovich and Kalganov, who had been continually in and out of the room all the while the interrogation had been going on, had now both gone out again. The magistrates, too, looked very tired. It was a wretched morning, the whole sky was overcast, and the rain streamed down in bucketfuls. Mitya gazed blankly out the window.

"May I look out the window?" he asked Nikolay Parfenovich suddenly. "Oh, as much as you like," the latter replied.

Mitya got up and went to the window. The rain lashed against the little greenish panes of the window. He could see the muddy road just below the window, and farther away, in the rainy mist, a row of poor, black, dismal huts, looking even blacker and poorer in the rain. Mitya thought of "Phœbus the golden-haired," and how he had meant to shoot himself at his first ray. "Perhaps it would be even better on a morning like this," he thought with a smile, and suddenly, dropping his hands, he turned to his "torturers."

"Gentlemen," he cried, "I see that I am lost! But she? Tell me about her. I beseech you. Surely she need not be ruined with me? She's innocent, you know, she was out of her mind when she cried last night 'It's all my fault!' She's done nothing, nothing! I've been grieving over her all night as I sat with you. . . . Can't you, won't you tell me what you are going to do with her now?"

"You can set your mind quite at rest on that score, Dmitri Fyodorovich," the prosecutor answered at once, with visible alacrity. "We have, so far, no grounds for troubling the person in whom you are so interested. I trust that it may be the same in the later development of the case. . . . On the contrary, we'll do everything that lies in our power in that matter. Set your mind completely at rest."

"Gentlemen, I thank you. I knew that you were honest, just people in spite of everything. You've taken a load off my heart. . . . Well, what are we to do now? I'm ready."

"Well, we ought to make haste. We must pass to examining the witnesses without delay. That must be done in your presence and therefore . . . ."

"Shouldn't we have some tea first?" interposed Nikolay Parfenovich. "I think we've deserved it!"

They decided that if tea were ready downstairs (Mihail Makarovich had, no doubt, gone down to get some) they would have a glass and then "go on and on," putting off their proper breakfast until a more favourable opportunity. Tea really was ready below, and was soon brought up. Mitya at first refused the glass that Nikolay Parfenovich politely offered him, but afterwards he asked for it himself and drank it greedily. He looked surprisingly exhausted. It might have been supposed from his herculean strength that one night of carousing, even accompanied by the most violent emotions, could have had little effect on him. But he felt that he could hardly sit up, and from time to time all the objects about him seemed heaving and dancing before his eyes.

"A little more and I shall begin raving," he said to himself.

## CHAPTER VIII
### THE EVIDENCE
#### OF THE WITNESSES. THE BABE

THE examination of the witnesses began. But we will not continue our story in such detail as hitherto. And so we will omit to say how Nikolay Parfenovich impressed on every witness called that he must give his evidence in accordance with truth and conscience, and that he would afterwards have to repeat his evidence on oath, how every witness was called upon to sign his affidavit, and so on. We will only note that the point principally insisted upon in the examination was the question of the three thousand roubles, that is, was the sum spent here, at Mokroye, by Mitya on the first occasion, a month before, three thousand or fifteen hundred? And again had he spent three thousand or fifteen hundred the previous day? Alas, all the evidence, absolutely all, turned out to be against Mitya. There was not one deposition in his favour, and some witnesses introduced new, almost crushing facts, in contradiction of his, Mitya's, story.

The first witness examined was Trifon Borisovich. He was not in the least abashed as he stood before the magistrates. He had, on the contrary, an air of stern and severe indignation with the accused, which gave him an appearance of truthfulness and personal dignity. He spoke little, and with reserve, waited to be questioned, answered precisely and deliberately. Firmly and unhesitatingly he bore witness that the sum spent a month before could not have been less than three thousand, that all the peasants about here would testify that they had heard the sum of three thousand mentioned by Dmitri Fyodorovich himself. "What a lot of money he flung away on the gipsy girls alone. He wasted a thousand, I dare say, on them alone."

"I don't believe I gave them five hundred," was Mitya's gloomy comment on this. "It's a pity I didn't count the money at the time, but I was drunk . . ."

Mitya was sitting sideways with his back to the curtains. He listened gloomily, with a melancholy and exhausted air, as though he would say:

"Oh, say what you like. It makes no difference now."

"More than a thousand went to them, Dmitri Fyodorovich," retorted Trifon Borisovich firmly. "You flung it about at random and they picked it up. They were a rascally, thievish lot, horse-stealers, they've been driven away from here, or maybe they'd bear witness themselves how much they got from you. I saw the sum in your hands, myself — count it I didn't, you didn't let me, that's true enough — but by the look of it I should say it was far more than fifteen hundred . . . fifteen hundred, indeed! We've seen money, too. We can judge of amounts . . ."

As for the sum spent the day before, he asserted that Dmitri Fyodorovich had told him, as soon as he arrived, that he had brought three thousand with him.

"Come now, is that so, Trifon Borisovich?" replied Mitya. "Surely I didn't declare so positively that I'd brought three thousand?"

"You did say so, Dmitri Fyodorovich. You said it before Andrey. Andrey himself is still here. Send for him. And in the hall, when you were treating the chorus, you shouted straight out that you would leave your sixth thousand here — that is with what you spent before, we must understand. Stepan and Semyon heard it, and Pyotr Fomich Kalganov, too,

was standing beside you at the time. Maybe he'd remember it. . . ."

The evidence as to the "sixth" thousand made an extraordinary impression on the two magistrates. They were delighted with this new mode of reckoning, three and three made six, three thousand then and three now made six, that was clear.

They questioned all the peasants mentioned by Trifon Borisovich, Stepan and Semyon, the driver Andrey, and Kalganov. The peasants and the driver unhesitatingly confirmed Trifon Borisovich's evidence. They noted down, with particular care, Andrey's account of the conversation he had had with Mitya on the road: "'Where,' says he, 'am I, Dmitri Fyodorovich, going, to heaven or to hell, and shall I be forgiven in the next world or not?'"

The psychological Ippolit Kirillovich heard this with a subtle smile, and ended by recommending that these remarks as to where Dmitri Fyodorovich would go should be "included in the case."

Kalganov, when called, came in reluctantly, frowning and ill-humoured, and he spoke to the magistrates as though he had never met them before in his life, though they were acquaintances whom he had been meeting every day for a long time past. He began by saying that "he knew nothing about it and didn't want to." But it appeared that he had heard of the "sixth" thousand, and he admitted that he had been standing close by at the moment. So far as he could see he "didn't know" how much money Mitya had in his hands. He affirmed that the Poles had cheated at cards. In reply to reiterated questions he stated that, after the Poles had been turned out, Mitya's position with Agrafena Alexandrovna had certainly improved, and that she had said that she loved him. He spoke of Agrafena Alexandrovna with reserve and respect, as though she had been a lady of the best society, and did not once allow himself to call her Grushenka. In spite of the young man's obvious repugnance at giving evidence, Ippolit Kirillovich examined him at great length, and only from him learnt all the details of what made up Mitya's "love affair," so to say, on that night. Mitya did not once pull Kalganov up. At last they let the young man go, and he left the room with unconcealed indignation.

The Poles, too, were examined. Though they had gone to bed in their room, they had not slept all night, and on the arrival of the police officers they hastily dressed and got ready, realising that they would certainly be sent for. They gave their evidence with dignity, though not without some fear. The little Pole turned out to be a retired official of the twelfth class, who had served in Siberia as a veterinary surgeon. His name was Musialowicz. *Pan* Wróblewski turned out to be an unlicensed dentist. Although Nikolay Parfenovich asked them questions on their entering the room, they both addressed their answers to Mihail Makarovich, who was standing on one side, taking him in their ignorance for the most important person and in command, and addressed him at every word as "*Pan* Colonel." Only after several reproofs from Mihail Makarovich himself, they grasped that they had to address their answers only to Nikolay Parfenovich. It turned out that they could speak Russian quite correctly except for their pronunciation of some words. Of his relations with Grushenka, past and present, *Pan* Musialowicz spoke proudly and hotly, so that Mitya was roused at once and declared that he

would not allow the "scoundrel" to speak like that in his presence! *Pan* Musialowicz at once called attention to the word "scoundrel," and begged that it should be entered in the record. Mitya fumed with rage.

"He's a scoundrel! A scoundrel! You can put that down. And put down, too, that in spite of the record I still declare that he's a scoundrel!" he cried.

Though Nikolay Parfenovich did insert this in the record, he showed the most praiseworthy tact and management. After sternly reprimanding Mitya, he cut short all further inquiry into the romantic aspect of the case, and hastened to pass to what was essential. One piece of evidence given by the Poles roused special interest in the magistrates: that was how, in that very room, Mitya had tried to buy off *Pan* Musialowicz, and had offered him three thousand roubles to resign his claims, seven hundred roubles down, and the remaining two thousand three hundred "to be paid next day in the town." He had sworn at the time that he had not the whole sum with him at Mokroye, but that his money was in the town. Mitya observed hotly that he had not said that he would be sure to pay him the remainder next day in the town. But *Pan* Wróblewski confirmed the statement, and Mitya, after thinking for a moment, admitted, frowning, that it must have been as the Poles stated, that he had been excited at the time, and might indeed have said so.

The prosecutor positively pounced on this piece of evidence. It seemed to establish for the prosecution (and they did, in fact, base this deduction on it) that half, or a part of, the three thousand that had come into Mitya's hands might really have been left somewhere hidden in the town, or even, perhaps, somewhere here, in Mokroye. This would explain the circumstance, so baffling for the prosecution, that only eight hundred roubles were to be found in Mitya's hands. This circumstance had been the one piece of evidence which, insignificant as it was, had hitherto told, to some extent, in Mitya's favour. Now this one piece of evidence in his favour had broken down. In answer to the prosecutor's inquiry, where he would have got the remaining two thousand three hundred roubles, since he himself had denied having more than fifteen hundred, Mitya confidently replied that he had meant to offer the "little chap," not money, but a formal deed of conveyance of his rights to the village of Chermashnya, those rights which he had already offered to Samsonov and Madame Hohlakov.

The prosecutor positively smiled at the "innocence of this subterfuge."

"And you imagine he would have accepted such a deed as a substitute for two thousand three hundred roubles in cash?"

"He certainly would have accepted it," Mitya declared hotly. "Why, look here, he might have grabbed not two thousand, but four or six, for it. He would have put his lawyers, Poles and Jews, on to the job, and might have got, not three thousand, but the whole property out of the old man."

The evidence of *Pan* Musialowicz was, of course, entered into the record in the fullest detail. Then they let the Poles go. The incident of the cheating at cards was hardly touched upon. Nikolay Parfenovich was too well pleased with them, as it was, and did not want to worry them with trifles; moreover, it was nothing but a foolish, drunken quarrel over cards. There had been drinking and disorder enough, that night. . . . So the two

hundred roubles remained in the pockets of the Poles.

Then old Maximov was summoned. He came in timidly, approached with little steps, looking very dishevelled and sad. He had, all this time, taken refuge below with Grushenka, sitting silently beside her, and "now and then he'd begin blubbering over her and wiping his eyes with a blue-check handkerchief," as Mihail Makarovich described afterwards. So that she, herself, began trying to pacify and comfort him. The old man at once confessed that he had done wrong, that he had borrowed "ten roubles in my poverty," from Dmitri Fyodorovich, and that he was ready to refund it. To Nikolay Parfenovich's direct question, had he noticed how much money Dmitri Fyodorovich held in his hand, as he must have been able to see the sum better than any one when he took the note from him, Maximov, in the most positive manner, declared that there was twenty thousand.

"Have you ever seen as much as twenty thousand before, then?" inquired Nikolay Parfenovich, with a smile.

"To be sure I have, sir, not twenty, but seven, when my wife mortgaged my little property. She'd only let me look at it from a distance, boasting of it to me. It was a very thick bundle, sir, all rainbow-coloured notes. And Dmitri Fyodorovich's were all rainbow-coloured . . ."

He was soon dismissed. At last it was Grushenka's turn. The examiners were obviously apprehensive of the effect her appearance might have on Mitya, and Nikolay Parfenovich muttered a few words of admonition to him, but Mitya bowed his head in silence, giving him to understand "that he would not make a scene." Mihail Makarovich, himself, led Grushenka in. She entered with a stern and gloomy face, that looked almost composed, and sat down quietly on the chair offered her by Nikolay Parfenovich. She was very pale, she seemed to be cold, and wrapped herself closely in her magnificent black shawl. She was suffering from a slight feverish chill — the first symptom of the long illness which followed that night. Her grave air, her direct earnest look and quiet manner made a very favourable impression on every one. Nikolay Parfenovich was even somewhat "captivated." He admitted himself, when talking about it afterwards, that only then had he seen "how handsome the woman was," for, though he had seen her several times before, he had always looked upon her as something of a "provincial hetaira." "She has the manners of the best society," he said enthusiastically, gossiping about her in a circle of ladies. But this was received with positive indignation and he was immediately pronounced a "naughty man," to his great satisfaction.

As she entered the room, Grushenka only glanced for an instant at Mitya, who in his turn looked at her uneasily. But her appearance reassured him at once. After the first inevitable inquiries and admonitions, Nikolay Parfenovich asked her, hesitating a little, but preserving the most courteous manner, on what terms she was with the retired lieutenant, Dmitri Fyodorovich Karamazov. To this Grushenka firmly and quietly replied:

"He was an acquaintance. I have been receiving him this last month as an acquaintance." To further inquisitive questions she answered plainly and with complete frankness, that, though "at times" she had thought him attractive, she had not loved him, but that she had led him on, and his old father as well,

"out of nasty spite," that she had seen that Mitya was very jealous of Fyodor Pavlovich and every one else; but that had only amused her. She had never meant to go to Fyodor Pavlovich, she had simply been laughing at him. "I had no thoughts for either of them all this last month. I was expecting another man, who had wronged me. But I think," she said in conclusion, "that there's no need for you to inquire about that, nor for me to answer you, for that's my own affair."

Nikolay Parfenovich immediately acted upon this hint. He again dismissed the "romantic" points in the case and passed to the serious one, that is, to the question of most importance, concerning the three thousand roubles. Grushenka confirmed the statement that three thousand roubles had certainly been spent on the first carousal at Mokroye, and, though she had not counted the money herself, she had heard that it was three thousand from Dmitri Fyodorovich himself.

"Did he tell you that alone, or before some one else, or did you only hear him speak of it to others in your presence?" the prosecutor inquired immediately.

To which Grushenka replied that she had heard him say so before other people, and had heard him say so when they were alone.

"Did he say it to you alone once, or several times?" inquired the prosecutor, and learned that he had told Grushenka several times.

Ippolit Kirillovich was very well satisfied with this piece of evidence. Further examination elicited that Grushenka knew, too, where that money had come from, and that Dmitri Fyodorovich had got it from Katerina Ivanovna.

"And did you never, once, hear that the money spent a month ago was not three thousand, but less, and that Dmitri Fyodorovich had saved half that sum for his own use?"

"No, I never heard that," answered Grushenka. It transpired further that Mitya had, on the contrary, often told her during that month that he hadn't a copeck.

"He was always expecting to get some from his father," said Grushenka in conclusion.

"Did he never say before you . . . casually, or in a moment of irritation," Nikolay Parfenovich put in suddenly, "that he intended to make an attempt on his father's life?"

"Oh, he did say so," sighed Grushenka.

"Once or several times?"

"He mentioned it several times, always in anger."

"And did you believe he would do it?"

"No, I never believed it," she answered firmly. "I had faith in his noble heart."

"Gentlemen, allow me," cried Mitya suddenly, "allow me to say one word to Agrafena Alexandrovna, in your presence."

"You may speak," Nikolay Parfenovich assented.

"Agrafena Alexandrovna!" Mitya got up from his chair, "have faith in God and in me. I am not guilty of the blood of my father who was murdered yesterday!"

Having uttered these words, Mitya sat down again on his chair. Grushenka stood up and crossed herself devoutly before the ikon.

"Glory to Thee, O Lord," she said, in a voice thrilling with ardent emotion, and, still standing, she turned to Nikolay Parfenovich and added:

"What he has just said, that you must believe! I know him. He'll say anything as a joke or out of obstinacy, but he'll never deceive you against his conscience. He will tell the whole truth, you may believe it."

"Thanks, Agrafena Alexandrovna, you've given my heart comfort," Mitya responded in a quivering voice.

As to the money spent the previous night, she declared that she did not know what the sum was, but had heard him tell several people that he had three thousand with him. And to the question where he got the money, she said that he had told her that he had "stolen" it from Katerina Ivanovna, and that she had replied to that that he hadn't stolen it, and that he must pay the money back next day. On the prosecutor's asking her emphatically whether the money he said he had stolen from Katerina Ivanovna was what he had spent the previous night, or what he had squandered here a month ago, she declared that he meant the money spent a month ago, and that that was how she understood him.

Grushenka was at last released, and Nikolay Parfenovich informed her impulsively that she might at once return to the town and that if he could assist her in any way, with horses for example, or if she would care for an escort he . . . would be . . .

"I thank you sincerely," said Grushenka, bowing to him, "I'm going with this old gentleman, I am driving him back to town with me, and meanwhile, if you'll allow me, I'll wait below to hear what you decide about Dmitri Fyodorovich."

She went out. Mitya was calm, and even looked more cheerful, but only for a moment. He felt more and more overcome by a strange physical weakness. His eyes were closing with fatigue. The examination of the witnesses was, at last, over. They proceeded to a final revision of the testimony. Mitya got up, moved from his chair to the corner by the curtain, lay down on a large chest covered with a rug, and instantly fell asleep. He had a strange dream, utterly out of keeping with the place and the time.

He was driving somewhere in the steppes, where he had been stationed long ago, and a peasant was driving him in a cart with a pair of horses, over a muddy road. He was cold, it was early in November, and the snow was falling in big wet flakes, melting as soon as it touched the earth. And the peasant drove him smartly; he had a fair, long beard. He was not an old man, somewhere about fifty, and he had on a grey peasant's smock. Not far off was a village, he could see the black huts, and half the huts were burnt down, there were only the charred beams sticking up. And as they drove in, there were peasant women drawn up along the road, a lot of women, a whole row, all thin and wan, with their faces a sort of brownish colour, especially one at the edge, a tall, bony woman, who looked forty, but might have been only twenty, with a long thin face. And in her arms was a little baby crying. And her breasts seemed so dried up that there was not a drop of milk in them. And the child cried and cried, and held out its little bare arms, with its little fists blue from cold.

"Why are they crying? Why are they crying?" Mitya asked, as they dashed gaily by.

"It's the babe," answered the driver, "the babe weeping."

And Mitya was struck by his saying, in his peasant way, "the babe," and he liked the peasant's calling it a "babe." There seemed more pity in it.

"But why is it weeping?" Mitya persisted stupidly, "why are its little arms bare? Why don't they wrap it up?"

"The babe's cold, its little clothes are frozen and don't warm it."

"But why is it? Why?" Mitya still persisted foolishly.

"Why, they're poor people, burnt out. They've no bread. They're begging because they've been burnt out."

"No, no." Mitya, as it were, still did not understand. "Tell me why it is those poor mothers stand there? Why are people poor? Why is the babe poor? Why is the steppe barren? Why don't they hug each other and kiss? Why don't they sing songs of joy? Why are they so black with black misery? Why don't they feed the babe?"

And he felt that, though his questions were unreasonable and senseless, yet he wanted to ask just that, and he had to ask it in just that way. And he felt that a passion of pity, such as he had never known before, was rising in his heart, that he wanted to cry, that he wanted to do something for them all, so that the babe should weep no more, so that the dark-faced, withered mother should not weep, that no one should shed tears again from that moment, and he wanted to do it at once, at once, regardless of all obstacles, with true Karamazov recklessness.

"And I'm coming with you. I won't leave you now for the rest of my life, I'm coming with you," he heard close beside him Grushenka's tender voice, thrilling with emotion. And his heart glowed, and he struggled forward towards the light, and he longed to live, to live, to go on and on, towards the new, beckoning light, and to hasten, hasten, now, at once!

"What! Where?" he exclaimed, opening his eyes, and sitting up on the chest, as though he had revived from a swoon, he smiled serenely. Nikolay Parfenovich was standing over him, suggesting that he should hear the

THE PEASANT CALLED IT A "BABE"

testimony read aloud and sign it. Mitya guessed that he had been asleep an hour or more, but he did not listen to Nikolay Parfenovich. He was suddenly struck by the fact that there was a pillow under his head, which hadn't been there when he had leant back, exhausted, on the chest.

"Who put that pillow under my head? Who was so kind?" he cried, with a sort of ecstatic gratitude, and tears in his voice, as though some great kindness had been shown him.

He never found out who this kind man was, perhaps one of the peasant witnesses, or Nikolay Parfenovich's little secretary had compassionately thought to put a pillow under his head, but his whole soul was quivering with tears. He went to the table and said that he would sign whatever they liked.

"I've had a good dream, gentlemen," he said in a strange voice, with a new face, radiant with joy.

## CHAPTER IX
### THEY CARRY MITYA AWAY

WHEN the testimony had been signed, Nikolay Parfenovich turned solemnly to the prisoner and read him the "Commitment," setting forth that, in such a year, on such a day, in such a place, the examining magistrate of such-and-such a district court, having examined so-and-so (to wit, Mitya) accused of this and of that (all the charges were carefully itemized) and taking into consideration that the accused, pleading not guilty to the charges made against him, had brought forward nothing in his defence, while the witnesses, so-and-so and so-and-so, and the circumstances, such-and-such, testify against him, — the examining magistrate acting in accordance with

such-and-such articles of the Penal Code, and so on, has ruled that, in order to preclude such-and-such (Mitya) from all means of evading examination and trial, the said person be detained in such-and-such a prison, of which circumstance he hereby notifies the accused, and further, the examining magistrate delivers a copy of this same "Commitment" to the deputy prosecutor, and so on, and so on.

In brief, Mitya was informed that he was, from that moment, a prisoner, and that he would be driven at once to the town, and there locked up in a very unpleasant place. Mitya listened attentively, and only shrugged his shoulders.

"Well, gentlemen, I don't blame you. I'm ready. . . . I understand that there's nothing else for you to do."

Nikolay Parfenovich informed him gently that he would be escorted at once by the rural police officer, Mavriky Mavrikyevich, who happened to be on the spot. . . .

"Wait," Mitya interrupted suddenly, and impelled by uncontrollable feeling he said, addressing all in the room:

"Gentlemen, we're all cruel, we're all monsters, we all make men weep, and mothers, and babes at the breast, but of all, let it be settled here, now, of all I am the lowest reptile! Every day of my life, beating my breast, I swore to reform, and every day I did the same filthy things. I understand now that such men as I need a blow, a blow of fate to catch them as with a noose, and bind them by an external force. Never, never should I have risen of myself! But the thunderbolt has fallen. I accept the torture of accusation, and my public shame, I want to suffer and by suffering I shall be purified. Perhaps I shall be purified, gentlemen, eh? But listen, for the last time, I am not guilty of my father's blood. I accept my punishment, not because I killed him, but because I meant to kill him, and perhaps I really might have killed him. Still I mean to fight it out with you, I warn you of that. I'll fight it out with you to the end, and then God will decide. Good-bye, gentlemen, don't be vexed with me for having shouted at you during the examination. Oh, I was still such a fool then. . . . In another minute I shall be a prisoner, but now, for the last time, as a free man, Dmitri Karamazov offers you his hand. Saying good-bye to you, I say it to all men."

His voice quivered and he stretched out his hand, but Nikolay Parfenovich, who happened to stand nearest to him, with a sudden, almost nervous movement, hid his hands behind his back. Mitya instantly noticed this, and started. He let his outstretched hand drop at once.

"The preliminary inquiry is not yet over," Nikolay Parfenovich faltered, somewhat embarrassed. "We will continue it in the town, and I, for my part, of course, am ready to wish you all success . . . in your defence. . . . As a matter of fact, Dmitri Fyodorovich, I've always been disposed to regard you as, so to speak, more unfortunate than guilty. All of us here, if I may make bold to speak for all, are ready to recognise that you are, at bottom, a young man of honour, but, alas, one who has been carried away by certain passions to a somewhat excessive degree. . . ."

Nikolay Parfenovich's little figure was positively majestic by the time he had finished speaking. It struck Mitya that in another minute this "boy" would take his arm, lead him to another corner, and renew their conversation about "women." But many quite irrelevant and inappropriate thoughts sometimes occur

to a prisoner even when he is being led to execution.

"Gentlemen, you are good, you are humane, may I see *her* to say 'good-bye' for the last time?" asked Mitya.

"Certainly, but considering . . . in fact, now it's impossible except in the presence of . . . ."

"Oh, well, if it must be so, it must!"

Grushenka was brought in, but the farewell was brief and laconic, and did not at all satisfy Nikolay Parfenovich. Grushenka made a deep bow to Mitya.

"I have told you I am yours, and I will be yours. I will follow you for ever, wherever they may send you. Farewell, you who have been your own undoing, though you are guiltless."

Her lips quivered, tears flowed from her eyes.

"Forgive me, Grusha, for my love, for undoing you, too, with my love."

Mitya would have said something more, but he broke off and went out. He was at once surrounded by men who kept a constant watch on him. At the bottom of the steps to which he had driven up with such a dash the night before with Andrey's three horses, two carts stood in readiness. Mavriky Mavrikyevich, a sturdy, thick-set man with a flabby face, was annoyed about something, some sudden irregularity. He was shouting angrily. He asked Mitya to get into the cart with somewhat excessive surliness.

"When I stood him drinks in the tavern, the man had quite a different face," thought Mitya, as he got in. At the gates there was a crowd of people, peasants, women and drivers. Trifon Borisovich came down the steps, too. All stared at Mitya.

"Forgive me at parting, God's people!" Mitya shouted suddenly from the cart.

"Forgive us, too!" he heard two or three voices.

"Farewell to you, too, Trifon Borisovich!"

But Trifon Borisovich did not even turn round. He was, perhaps, too busy. He, too, was shouting and fussing about something. It appeared that everything was not yet ready in the second cart, in which two constables were to accompany Mavriky Mavrikyevich. The peasant who had been ordered to drive the second cart was pulling on his smock, stoutly maintaining that it was not his turn to go, but Akim's. But Akim was not to be seen. They ran to fetch him. The peasant persisted and besought them to wait.

"You see what our people are, Mavriky Mavrikyevich. They've no shame!" exclaimed Trifon Borisovich. "Akim gave you twenty-five copecks the day before yesterday. You've drunk it all and now you cry out. I'm simply surprised at how kind you are to our louts, Mavriky Mavrikyevich, that's all I can say."

"But what do we want a second troika for?" Mitya put in. "Let's start with the one, Mavriky Mavrikyevich. I won't be unruly, I won't run away from you, old fellow. What do we want an escort for?"

"I'll trouble you, sir, to learn how to speak to me if you've never been taught. I'm not 'old fellow' to you, and you can keep your advice for another time!" Mavriky Mavrikyevich snapped out savagely, as though glad to vent his wrath.

Mitya was reduced to silence. He flushed all over. A moment later he felt suddenly very cold. The rain had ceased, but the dull sky was still overcast, and a keen wind was blowing straight in his face. "I've taken a chill," thought Mitya, twitching his shoulders.

At last Mavriky Mavrikyevich, too, got into the cart, sat down heavily, and, as though without noticing it, squeezed Mitya into the corner. It is true that he was out of humour and greatly disliked the task that had been laid upon him.

"Good-bye, Trifon Borisovich!" Mitya shouted again, and felt himself that he had not called out this time from good-nature, but involuntarily, from resentment.

But Trifon Borisovich stood proudly, with both hands behind his back, and staring straight at Mitya with a stern and angry face, he made no reply.

"Good-bye, Dmitri Fyodorovich, good-bye!" he heard all at once the voice of Kalganov, who had suddenly darted out. Running up to the cart, he held out his hand to Mitya. He had no cap on.

Mitya had time to seize and press his hand.

"Good-bye, dear fellow! I shan't forget your magnanimity," he cried warmly.

But the cart moved and their hands parted. The bell began ringing and Mitya was driven off.

Kalganov ran back, sat down in a corner, bent his head, hid his face in his hands, and burst out crying.

For a long while he sat like that, crying as though he were a little boy instead of a young man of twenty. Oh, he believed almost without doubt in Mitya's guilt.

"What are people like? What can men be after this?" he exclaimed incoherently, in bitter despondency, almost despair. At that moment he had no desire to live.

"Is it worth it? Is it worth it?" exclaimed the boy in his grief.

PART
IV

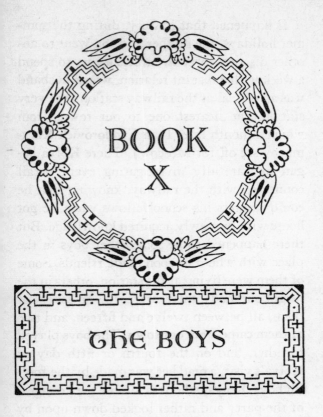

# BOOK X

## THE BOYS

### CHAPTER I
#### KOLYA KRASOTKIN

IT was the beginning of November. There had been a hard frost, eleven degrees below zero, with ice under foot, and only a little dry snow had fallen on the frozen ground during the night. A keen dry wind was lifting and blowing it along the dreary streets of our town, especially about the market-place. It was a dull morning, but the snow had ceased.

Not far from the market-place, close to the Plotnikov shop, there stands a small house, very neat both without and within. It belongs to Madame Krasotkin, the widow of a former provincial secretary, who has been dead for fourteen years. His widow, still a good-looking woman and in her thirties, is living in her neat little house on her private income. She

lives in respectable seclusion; she is of a soft but fairly cheerful disposition. She was about eighteen at the time of her husband's death; she had been married only a year and had just borne him a son. From the day of his death she devoted herself heart and soul to the bringing up of her darling boy Kolya. She loved him passionately all those fourteen years, though he had caused her far more suffering than happiness. She had been trembling and fainting with terror almost every day, afraid he would fall ill, would catch cold, do something naughty, climb on a chair and fall off it, and so on and so on. When Kolya began going to school, the mother devoted herself to studying all the subjects with him so as to help him, and go through his lessons with him. She hastened to make the acquaintance of the teachers and their wives, even made up to Kolya's schoolfellows, and fawned upon them in the hope of thus saving Kolya from being teased, laughed at, or beaten by them. She went so far that the boys actually began to mock at him on her account, and taunt him with being a "mamma's pet."

But the boy could stand up for himself. He was a daring boy, "tremendously strong," as was rumoured in his class, and soon proved to be the fact; he was agile, strong-willed, and of an audacious and enterprising temper. He was good at lessons, and there was a rumour in the school that he could beat the teacher, Dardanelov, himself at arithmetic and universal history. Though he looked down upon every one, and turned up his nose, he was a good comrade and not supercilious. He accepted his schoolfellows' respect as his due, but was friendly with them. Above all, he knew where to draw the line. He could restrain himself on occasion, and in his relations with the teachers he never overstepped that last forbidden limit beyond which a prank becomes an unpardonable breach of discipline. But he was as fond of mischief on every possible occasion as the smallest boy in the school, and not so much for the sake of mischief as for the sake of creating a sensation, inventing something, doing something effective and conspicuous. He was extremely vain. He knew how to make even his mother give in to him; he treated her almost despotically. She gave in to him, oh, she had begun giving in to him long ago. The one thought unendurable to her was that her boy did not love her enough. She was always fancying that Kolya was "unfeeling" towards her, and at times, dissolving into hysterical tears, she reproached him with coldness. The boy disliked this, and the more demonstrations of feeling were demanded of him the more he seemed intentionally to avoid them. Yet it was not intentional on his part but instinctive — it was his character. His mother was mistaken; he was very fond of her. He only disliked "sheepish sentimentality," as he expressed it in his schoolboy language.

There was a bookcase in the house containing a few books that had been his father's. Kolya was fond of reading, and had read several of them by himself. His mother did not mind that and only wondered sometimes at seeing the boy stand for hours by the bookcase poring over a book instead of going to play. And in that way Kolya read some things unsuitable for his age.

Though the boy, as a rule, knew where to draw the line in his mischief, he had of late begun to play pranks that caused his mother serious alarm. It is true there was nothing vicious, but a wild mad recklessness.

It happened that in July, during the summer holidays, the mother and son went to another district, forty-five miles away, to spend a week with a distant relation, whose husband was an official at the railway station (the very station, the nearest one to our town, from which a month later Ivan Fyodorovich Karamazov set off for Moscow). There Kolya began by carefully investigating every detail connected with the railway, knowing that he could impress his schoolfellows when he got home with his newly acquired knowledge. But there happened to be some other boys in the place with whom he soon made friends. Some of them were living at the station, others in the neighbourhood; there were six or seven of them, all between twelve and fifteen, and two of them came from our town. The boys played together, and on the fourth or fifth day of Kolya's visit, a mad bet was made by the foolish boys. Kolya, who was almost the youngest of the party and rather looked down upon by the others in consequence, was moved by vanity or by reckless bravado to bet them two roubles that he would lie down between the rails at night when the eleven o'clock train was due, and would lie there without moving while the train rolled over him at full speed. It is true they made a preliminary investigation, from which it appeared that it was possible to stretch out and lie so flat between the rails that the train could pass over without touching one, but to lie there was no joke! Kolya maintained stoutly that he would do it. At first they laughed at him, called him a little liar, a braggart, but that only egged him on. What piqued him most was that these boys of fifteen turned up their noses at him unbearably, and were at first disposed to treat him as "a small boy," not fit to associate with them, and that was an unendurable insult to him.

And so it was resolved to go in the evening to a point half a mile from the station, so that the train might have time to get up full speed after leaving the station. The boys assembled. It was a pitch-dark moonless night. At the appointed time, Kolya lay down between the rails. The five others who had taken the bet waited among the bushes below the embankment, their hearts beating with suspense, which was followed by alarm and remorse. At last they heard in the distance the rumble of the train leaving the station. Two red lights gleamed out of the darkness; the monster roared as it approached.

"Run, run off the tracks!" the boys cried to Kolya from the bushes, breathless with terror. But it was too late: the train dashed up and flew past. The boys rushed to Kolya. He lay without moving. They began pulling at him, lifting him up. He suddenly got up and walked off the embankment without a word. Then he explained that he had lain there as though he were unconscious to frighten them, but the fact was that he really had lost consciousness, as he confessed long after to his mother. In this way his reputation as "a desperate character," was established for ever. He returned home to the station as white as a sheet. Next day he had a slight attack of nervous fever, but he was in high spirits and well pleased with himself. The incident did not become known at once, but when they came back to the town it penetrated to the school and even reached the ears of the masters. But then Kolya's mother hastened to entreat the masters on her boy's behalf, and in the end Dardanelov, a respected and influential teacher, exerted himself in his favour, and the affair was hushed up.

Dardanelov was a middle-aged bachelor, who had been passionately in love with Madame Krasotkin for many years past, and had once already, about a year previously, ventured, faint with fear and the delicacy of his sentiments, to offer her most respectfully his hand in marriage. But she refused him point-blank, feeling that to accept him would be an act of treachery to her boy, though Dardanelov had reason for believing, to judge from certain mysterious symptoms, that he was not an object of aversion to the charming but too chaste and tender-hearted widow. Kolya's mad prank seemed to have broken the ice, and Dardanelov was rewarded for his intercession by an intimation of hope. The intimation, it is true, was a slight one, but then Dardanelov himself was such a paragon of purity and delicacy that it was enough for the time being to make him perfectly happy. He was fond of the boy, though he would have felt it beneath him to try and win him over, and was severe and strict with him in class. Kolya, too, kept him at a respectful distance. He learnt his lessons perfectly; he was second in his class, was reserved with Dardanelov, and the whole class firmly believed that Kolya was so good at universal history that he could "beat" even Dardanelov. Kolya did indeed ask him the question, "Who founded Troy?" to which Dardanelov had made a very vague reply, referring to the movements and migrations of races, to the remoteness of the period, to the mythical legends. But the question, "Who had founded Troy?" that is, what individuals, he could not answer, and even for some reason regarded the question as idle and frivolous. But the boys remained convinced that Dardanelov did not know who founded Troy. Kolya had read of the founders of Troy in

Smaragdov, whose history was among the books in his father's bookcase. In the end all the boys became interested in the question, who it was that had founded Troy, but Krasotkin would not tell his secret, and his reputation for knowledge remained unshaken.

After the incident on the railway a certain change came over Kolya's attitude to his mother. When Anna Fyodorovna (Madame Krasotkin) heard of her son's exploit, she almost went out of her mind with horror. She had such terrible attacks of hysterics, lasting with intervals for several days, that Kolya, seriously alarmed at last, promised on his honour that such pranks should never be repeated. He swore on his knees before the holy image, and swore by the memory of his father, at Madame Krasotkin's instance, and the "manly" Kolya burst into tears like a boy of six. And all that day the mother and son were constantly rushing into each other's arms sobbing. Next day Kolya woke up as "unfeeling" as before, but he had become more silent, more modest, sterner, and more thoughtful.

Six weeks later, it is true, he played another prank, which even brought his name to the ears of our justice of the peace, but it was a prank of quite another kind, amusing, foolish, and he did not, as it turned out, take the leading part in it, but was only implicated in it. But of this later. His mother still fretted and trembled, but the more uneasy she became, the greater were the hopes of Dardanelov. It must be noted that Kolya understood and divined what was in Dardanelov's heart and, of course, despised him profoundly for his "feelings"; he had in the past been so tactless as to show this contempt before his mother, hinting vaguely that he knew what Dardanelov was after. But from the time of

the railway incident his behaviour in this respect also was changed; he did not allow himself the remotest allusion to the subject and began to speak more respectfully of Dardanelov before his mother, which the sensitive woman at once appreciated with boundless gratitude. But at the slightest mention of Dardanelov by a visitor in Kolya's presence, she would flush as pink as a rose. At such moments Kolya would either stare out the window scowling, or would investigate the state of his boots, or would shout angrily for "Perezvon," the big, shaggy, mangy dog, which he had picked up a month before, brought home, and kept for some reason secretly indoors, not showing him to any of his schoolfellows. He bullied him frightfully, teaching him all sorts of tricks, so that the poor dog howled for him whenever he was absent at school, and when he came in, whined with delight, rushed about as if he were crazy, begged, lay down on the ground and played dead, and so on; in fact, showed all the tricks he had taught him, not at the word of command, but simply from the zeal of his ecstatic and grateful heart.

I have forgotten, by the way, to mention that Kolya Krasotkin was the boy stabbed with a penknife by the boy already known to the reader as the son of Captain Snegiryov. Ilusha had been defending his father when the schoolboys jeered at him, shouting the nickname "bath-mop."

## CHAPTER II
### CHILDREN

AND so on that frosty, windy day in November, Kolya Krasotkin was sitting at home. It was Sunday and there was no school. It had just struck eleven, and he particularly wanted to go out "on very urgent business," but he was left alone in charge of the house, for it so happened that all its elder occupants were absent owing to a sudden and singular event. Madame Krasotkin had let two little rooms, separated from the rest of the house by a passage, to a doctor's wife with her two small children. This lady was the same age as Anna Fyodorovna, and a great friend of hers. Her husband, the doctor, had taken his departure a year ago, going first to Orenburg and then to Tashkent, and for the last six months she had not heard a word from him. Had it not been for her friendship with Madame Krasotkin, which was some consolation to the forsaken lady, she would certainly have dissolved in tears completely. And now, to add to her misfortunes, Katerina, her only servant, was suddenly moved the evening before to announce, to her mistress's amazement, that she proposed to bring a child into the world by morning. How it was that no one had noticed the imminence of the event before seemed almost miraculous to every one. The astounded doctor's wife decided to move Katerina while there was still time to an establishment kept for such emergencies by a midwife in our town. As she set great store by her servant, she promptly carried out this plan, took her to the institution and remained there looking after her. Then, by morning, for some reason there arose the need of all the friendly sympathy and assistance of Madame Krasotkin herself. It was thought that on this occasion she might be able to appeal to some one and give aid and comfort.

So both the ladies were absent from home, while Madame Krasotkin's servant, Agafya, had gone to market, and Kolya was thus left for a time to protect and look after the "kids,"

that is, the son and daughter of the doctor's wife, who were left alone. Kolya was not afraid of taking care of the house, besides he had Perezvon, who had been ordered to lie flat, without moving, under the bench in the hall. Every time Kolya, walking to and fro through the rooms, came into the hall, the dog shook his head and gave two firm and wheedling taps on the floor with his tail, but alas! no summoning whistle was heard. Kolya looked sternly at the luckless dog, who relapsed again into obedient rigidity. The one thing that troubled Kolya was the "kids." He looked, of course, with the utmost scorn on Katerina's unexpected adventure, but he was very fond of the bereaved "kiddies," and had already taken them a picture book. Nastya, the elder, a girl of eight, could read, and Kostya, the boy, aged seven, was very fond of being read to by her. Krasotkin could, of course, have provided more diverting entertainment for them. He could have made them stand side by side and played soldiers with them, or sent them hiding all over the house. He had done so more than once before and was not above doing it, so much so that a report once spread at school that at home Krasotkin played horses with the little lodgers, prancing with his head on one side like a trace-horse. But Krasotkin haughtily parried this thrust, pointing out that to play horses with boys of one's own age, boys of thirteen, would certainly be disgraceful "at this date," but that he did it for the sake of the "kids" because he liked them, and no one had a right to call him to account for his feelings. The two "kids" adored him.

But on this occasion he was in no mood for games. He had very important business of his own before him, something almost mysterious.

Meanwhile time was passing and Agafya, with whom he could have left the children, would not come back from market. He had several times already crossed the passage, opened the door of the lodgers' apartment and looked anxiously at the "kids," who were sitting over the book, as he had bidden them. Every time he opened the door they grinned at him, hoping he would come in and would do something delightful and amusing. But Kolya was uneasy and did not go in.

At last it struck eleven and he made up his mind, once for all, that if that "damned" Agafya did not come back within ten minutes he would go out without waiting for her, making the "kids" "promise," of course, to be brave when he was away, not to be naughty, not to cry from fright. With this idea he put on his wadded winter overcoat with its sealskin collar, slung his satchel round his shoulder, and, regardless of his mother's constantly reiterated entreaties that he would always put on goloshes in such cold weather, he looked at them contemptuously as he crossed the hall and went out with only his boots on. Perezvon, seeing him in his outdoor clothes, began tapping vigorously on the floor with his tail. Nervously twitching all over, he even uttered a plaintive whine. But Kolya, seeing his dog's passionate excitement, decided that it was a breach of discipline, kept him for another minute under the bench, and only when he had opened the door into the passage he whistled for him. The dog leapt up like a mad creature and began bounding before him with rapture.

Having crossed the passage, Kolya opened the door to peep at the "kids." They were both sitting as before at the table, not reading but warmly disputing about something. The children often argued together about various exciting problems of life, and Nastya, being the elder, always got the best of it. If Kostya did not agree with her, he almost always appealed to Kolya Krasotkin, and his verdict was regarded as final by both of them. This time the "kids' " discussion rather interested Krasotkin, and he stood still in the passage to listen. The children saw he was listening and that made them argue with even greater heat.

"I shall never, never believe," Nastya prattled, "that midwives find babies among the cabbages in the kitchen garden. It's winter now and there are no cabbages, and so the midwife couldn't have taken Katerina a daughter."

"Phew!" Kolya whistled to himself.

"Or perhaps they do bring babies from somewhere, but only to those who are married."

Kostya stared at Nastya and listened, pondering profoundly.

"Nastya, how silly you are," he said at last, firmly and calmly. "How can Katerina have a baby when she isn't married?"

Nastya was exasperated.

"You know nothing about it," she snapped irritably. "Perhaps she has a husband, only he is in prison, so now she's got a baby."

"But is her husband in prison?" the matter-of-fact Kostya inquired gravely.

"Or, I tell you what," Nastya interrupted impulsively, completely rejecting and forgetting her first hypothesis. "She hasn't a husband, you are right there, but she wants to be married, and so she's been thinking of getting married, and thinking and thinking of it till now she's got it, that is, not a husband but a baby."

"Well, perhaps so," Kostya agreed, entirely vanquished. "But you didn't say so before. So how could I tell?"

"Well, young ones," said Kolya, stepping into the room. "You're a dangerous sort, I see."

"And Perezvon with you!" grinned Kostya, and began snapping his fingers and calling Perezvon.

"I am in trouble, kids," Krasotkin began solemnly, "and you must help me. Agafya must have broken a leg, since she has not turned up till now, that's certain. And I must go out. Will you let me go?"

The children looked anxiously at one another. Their smiling faces showed signs of uneasiness, but they did not yet fully grasp what was expected of them.

"You won't be naughty while I am gone? You won't climb on the cupboard and break your legs? You won't be frightened alone and cry?"

A look of profound despondency came into the children's faces.

"And I could show you something as a reward, a little copper cannon which can be fired with real gunpowder."

The children's faces instantly brightened. "Show us the cannon," said Kostya, beaming all over.

Krasotkin put his hand in his satchel, and pulling out a little brass cannon stood it on the table.

"Ah, you are bound to ask that! Look, it's on wheels." He rolled the toy along on the table. "And it can be fired off, too. It can be loaded with shot and fired off."

"And it could kill?"

"It would kill everybody; you've only got to aim it," and Krasotkin explained where the powder had to be put, where the shot should be rolled in, showed a tiny hole like a touch-hole, and told them that it kicked when it was fired.

The children listened with intense interest. What particularly struck their imagination was that the cannon kicked.

"And have you got any powder?" Nastya inquired.

"Yes."

"Show us the powder, too," she drawled with a smile of entreaty.

Krasotkin dived again into his satchel and pulled out a small flask containing a little real gunpowder. He had some shot, too, in a screw of paper. He even uncorked the flask and shook a little powder into the palm of his hand.

"One has to be careful there's no fire about, or it would blow up and kill us all," Krasotkin warned them to produce a sensation.

The children gazed at the powder with an awe-stricken fear that only intensified their enjoyment. But Kostya liked the shot better.

"And does the shot burn?" he inquired.

"No, it doesn't."

"Give me a little shot," he asked in an imploring voice.

"I'll give you a little shot; here, take it, but don't show it to your mother till I come back, or she'll be sure to think it's gunpowder, and will die of fright and give you a thrashing."

"Mother never does whip us," Nastya observed at once.

"I know, I only said it for the sake of the style. And don't you ever deceive your mother except just this once, until I come back. And so, kiddies, can I go out? You won't be frightened and cry when I'm gone?"

"We sha — all cry," drawled Kostya, on the verge of tears already.

"We shall cry, we shall be sure to cry," Nastya chimed in with timid haste.

"Oh, children, children, how fraught with peril are your years! There's no help for it, chicks, I shall have to stay with you. I don't know how long. And time is passing, time is passing, oogh!"

"Tell Perezvon to play dead!" Kostya begged.

"There's no help for it, we must have recourse to Perezvon. *Ici*, Perezvon." And Kolya began giving orders to the dog, who performed all his tricks.

He was a shaggy dog, of a very common size, with a coat of a sort of lilac-grey colour. He was blind in his right eye, and his left ear was torn. He whined and jumped, stood and walked on his hind legs, lay on his back with his paws in the air, and lay rigid as though he were dead. While this last performance was going on, the door opened and Agafya, Madame Krasotkin's servant, a stout pock-marked woman of forty, appeared on the threshold. She had come back from market and had a bag full of provisions in her hand. Holding up the bag of provisions in her left hand, she stood still to watch the dog. Though Kolya had been so anxious for her return, he did not cut short the performance, and after keeping Perezvon dead for the usual time, at last he whistled to him. The dog jumped up and began bounding about in his joy at having done his duty.

"Only think, a dog!" Agafya observed sententiously.

"Why are you late, female?" asked Krasotkin sternly.

"Female, indeed! Go on with you, you brat."

"Brat?"

"Yes, brat. What is it to you if I'm late; if I'm late, you may be sure I have good reason," muttered Agafya, busying herself about the stove, without a trace of anger or displeasure

in her voice. She seemed quite pleased, in fact, to enjoy a chat with her merry young master.

"Listen, you frivolous old woman," Krasotkin began, getting up from the sofa, "can you swear by all you hold sacred in the world and something else besides, that you will watch vigilantly over the kids in my absence? I am going out."

"And what should I swear for?" laughed Agafya. "I shall look after them without that."

"No, you must swear on the salvation of your soul. Else I shan't go."

"Well, don't then. What does it matter to me? It's cold out; stay home."

"Kids," Kolya turned to the children, "this woman will stay with you till I come back or till your mother comes, for she ought to have been back long ago. She will give you some lunch, too. You'll give them something, Agafya, won't you?"

"That I can do."

"Good-bye, chicks, I go with my heart at rest. And you, granny," he added gravely, in an undertone, as he passed Agafya, "I hope you'll spare their tender years and not tell them any of your old woman's nonsense about Katerina. *Ici*, Perezvon!"

"Get along with you!" retorted Agafya, really angry this time. "Ridiculous boy! You want a whipping for saying such things, that's what you want!"

## CHAPTER III
### THE SCHOOLBOY

BUT Kolya did not hear her. At last he could go out. As he went out at the gate he looked round him, shrugged up his little shoulders, and saying "It is freezing," went straight along the street and turned off to the right towards the market-place. When he reached the last house but one before the market-place he stopped at the gate, pulled a whistle out of his pocket, and whistled with all his might as though giving a signal. He had not to wait more than a minute before a rosy-cheeked boy of about eleven, wearing a warm, neat, and even stylish coat, darted out to meet him. This was Smurov, a boy in the preparatory class (two classes below Kolya Krasotkin), son of a well-to-do official. Apparently he was forbidden by his parents to associate with Krasotkin, who was well known to be a desperately naughty boy, so Smurov was obviously slipping out on the sly. He was — if the reader has not forgotten — one of the group of boys who two months before had thrown stones across the ditch at Ilusha. He was the one who had told Alyosha Karamazov about Ilusha.

"I've been waiting for you for the last hour, Krasotkin," said Smurov stolidly, and the boys strode towards the market-place.

"I am late," answered Krasotkin. "I was detained by circumstances. You won't be thrashed for coming with me?"

"Come, I say, I'm never thrashed! And you've got Perezvon with you?"

"Yes."

"You're taking him, too?"

"Yes."

"Ah! if it were only Zhuchka!"

"That's impossible. Zhuchka doesn't exist. Zhuchka is lost in the mists of obscurity."

"Ah! couldn't we do this?" Smurov suddenly stood still. "You see Ilusha says that Zhuchka was a shaggy, greyish, smoky-looking dog like Perezvon. Couldn't you tell him this is Zhuchka, and maybe he'll believe it?"

"Boy, shun a lie, that's one thing; even a white lie — that's another. Above all, I hope you've not told them anything about my coming."

"Heaven forbid! I know what I am about. But you won't comfort him with Perezvon," said Smurov, with a sigh. "You know his father, the captain, the 'bath-mop,' told us that he was going to bring him a real mastiff pup, with a black nose, to-day. He thinks that would comfort Ilusha; but I doubt it."

"And how is Ilusha?"

"Ah, he is low, very low! I believe he's in consumption: he is quite conscious, but his breathing! He doesn't breathe well. The other day he asked them to lead him round the room. They put on his boots for him and he tried to walk, but he couldn't. 'Ah, I told you before, papa,' he said, 'that those boots were no good. I could never walk comfortably in them.' He fancied it was the boots that made him stagger, but it was simply weakness, really. He won't live another week. Herzenstube is looking after him. Now they are rich again — they've got heaps of money."

"They are rogues."

"Who are rogues?"

"Doctors and the whole medical crew collectively, and also, of course, individually. I'm against medicine. It's a useless institution. However, I mean to go into all that. But what's that sentimentality you've got up there? The whole class seems to be there every day?"

"Not the whole class: it's only ten of our fellows who go to see him every day. There's nothing in that."

"What surprises me in all this is the part that Alexey Karamazov is taking in it. His brother's going to be tried to-morrow or next day for such a crime, and yet he has so much time to spend on sentimentalities with boys."

"There's no sentimentality about it. Here you are going yourself now to make up with Ilusha."

"Make up? A ridiculous expression! Besides, I allow no one to analyse my actions."

"And how pleased Ilusha will be to see you! He has no idea that you are coming. Why was it, why was it you wouldn't come all this time?" Smurov cried with sudden heat.

"My dear boy, that's my business, not yours. I am going of my own accord because I choose to, but you've all been hauled there by Alexey Karamazov — there's a difference, you know. And how do you know? I may not be going to make up at all. A stupid expression."

"It's not Karamazov at all; it's not his doing. Our fellows began going there of themselves. Of course, they went with Karamazov at first. And there's been nothing of that sort — no silliness. First one went, and then another. His father was awfully pleased to see us. You know he will simply go out of his mind if Ilusha dies. He sees that Ilusha's dying. And he seems so glad we've made it up with Ilusha. Ilusha asked after you, that was all. He just asks and says no more. His father will go out of his mind or hang himself. He behaved like a madman before. You know he is a very decent man. We made a mistake then. It's all the fault of that murderer who thrashed him then."

"Karamazov's a riddle to me all the same. I might have made his acquaintance long ago, but I like to have a proper pride in some cases. Besides, I have a theory about him which I must work out and verify."

Kolya subsided into dignified silence. Smurov, too, was silent. Smurov, of course, wor-shipped Krasotkin and never dreamed of putting himself on a level with him. Now he was tremendously interested at Kolya's saying that he was "going of his own accord" to see Ilusha. He felt that there must be some mystery in Kolya's suddenly taking it into his head to go to him that day. They crossed the market-place, in which at that hour were many loaded wagons from the country and a great number of live fowls. The market women were selling pretzels, thread, etc., in their booths. These Sunday assemblies were naïvely called "fairs" in the town, and there were many such fairs in the year.

Perezvon ran about in the wildest spirits, sniffing about first on one side, then on the other. When he met other dogs he zealously sniffed them according to the rules of canine etiquette.

"I like to watch such realistic scenes, Smurov," said Kolya suddenly. "Have you noticed how dogs sniff at one another when they meet? It seems to be a law of their nature."

"Yes; it's a funny habit."

"No, it's not funny; you are wrong there. There's nothing funny in nature, however funny it may seem to man with his prejudices. If dogs could reason and criticise us they'd be sure to find just as much that would be funny to them, if not far more, in the social relations of men, their masters — far more, indeed. I repeat that, because I am convinced that there is far more foolishness among us. That's Rakitin's idea — a remarkable idea. I am a socialist, Smurov."

"And what is a socialist?" asked Smurov.

"That's when all are equal and all have property in common, there are no marriages, and every one has any religion and laws he likes best, and all the rest of it. You are not old enough to understand that yet. It's cold, though."

"Yes, twelve degrees below zero. Father looked at the thermometer just now."

"Have you noticed, Smurov, that in the middle of winter we don't feel so cold, even when there are fifteen or eighteen degrees below zero as we do now, in the beginning of winter, when there is a sudden frost of twelve degrees, especially when there is not much snow? It's because people are not used to it. Everything is habit with men, everything even in their social and political relations. Habit is the great motive-power. What a funny-looking peasant!"

Kolya pointed to a tall peasant, with a good-natured countenance, in a long sheepskin coat, who was standing by his wagon, clapping together his mittened hands to warm them. His long fair beard was all white with frost.

"That peasant's beard's frozen," Kolya cried in a loud provocative voice as he passed him.

"Lots of people's beards are frozen," the peasant replied, calmly and sententiously.

"Don't tease him," observed Smurov.

"It's all right; he won't be cross; he's a nice fellow. Good-bye, Matvey."

"Good-bye."

"Is your name Matvey?"

"Yes. Didn't you know?"

"No, I didn't. It was a guess."

"You don't say so! You are a schoolboy, I suppose?"

"Yes."

"You get whipped, I expect?"

"Nothing to speak of — sometimes."

"Does it hurt?"

"Well, yes, it does."

"Ech, what a life!" The peasant heaved a sigh from the bottom of his heart.

"Good-bye, Matvey."

"Good-bye. You are a nice chap, that you are."

The boys went on.

"That was a nice peasant," Kolya observed to Smurov. "I like talking to the peasants, and am always glad to do them justice."

"Why did you tell a lie, pretending we are thrashed?" asked Smurov.

"I had to say that to please him."

"How do you mean?"

"You know, Smurov, I don't like being asked the same thing twice. I like people to understand at the first word. Some things can't be explained. According to a peasant's notions, schoolboys are whipped, and must be whipped. What kind of a schoolboy would he be, if he were not whipped? And suddenly I tell him that they don't whip us, why, he'd be pained. But you don't understand that. One has to know how to talk to the peasants."

"Only don't tease them, please, or you'll get into another scrape as you did about that goose."

"So you're afraid?"

"Don't laugh, Kolya. Of course, I'm afraid. My father would be awfully cross. I am strictly forbidden to go out with you."

"Don't be uneasy, nothing will happen this time. Hullo, Natasha!" he shouted to a market woman in one of the booths.

"Call me Natasha! What next! My name is Marya," the middle-aged market woman shouted at him.

"I am so glad it's Marya. Good-bye!"

"Ah, you young rascal! A brat like you to carry on so!"

"I'm in a hurry. I can't stay now. You shall

tell me next Sunday." Kolya waved his hand at her, as though she had accosted him and not he her.

"I've nothing to tell you next Sunday. You set upon me, you impudent young monkey. I didn't say anything," bawled Marya. "You want a whipping, that's what you want, you saucy jackanapes!"

There was a roar of laughter among the other market women round her. Suddenly an angry man darted out from the arcade of shops close by. He was a young man, not a native of the town, with dark, curly hair and a long pale face, marked with smallpox. He wore a long blue coat and a visored cap, and looked like a merchant's clerk. He was in a state of stupid excitement and immediately started brandishing his fists at Kolya.

"I know you," he cried angrily, "I know you!"

Kolya stared at him. He could not recall when he could have had a row with the man. But he had been in so many rows in the street that he could hardly remember them all.

"Do you?" he asked ironically.

"I know you! I know you!" the man repeated idiotically.

"So much the better for you. Well, I haven't any time. Good-bye!"

"You are up to mischief again?" cried the man. "You are at it again? I know, you are at it again!"

"It's not your business, brother, if I am at it again," said Kolya, stopping and scanning him.

"Not my business?"

"No; it's not your business."

"Whose then? Whose then? Whose then?"

"It's Trifon Nikitich's business, not yours."

"What Trifon Nikitich?" asked the fellow,

staring with loutish amazement at Kolya, but still as angry as ever.

Kolya looked him gravely up and down.

"Have you been to the Church of the Ascension?" he suddenly asked him, sternly and emphatically.

"What Church of Ascension? What for? No, I haven't," said the fellow, somewhat taken aback.

"Do you know Sabaneyev?" Kolya went on even more emphatically and severely.

"What Sabaneyev? No, I don't know him."

"Well, then you can go to the devil," said Kolya, cutting short the conversation, and turning sharply to the right he strode quickly on his way as though he disdained further conversation with a dolt who did not even know Sabaneyev.

"Stop, hey! What Sabaneyev?" The young man recovered from his momentary stupefaction and was as agitated as before. "What did he say?" He turned to the market women with a silly stare. The women laughed.

"He's a deep 'un, that boy," said one of them.

"What Sabaneyev did he mean?" the fellow repeated, still furious and brandishing his right arm.

"It must be the Sabaneyev who worked for the Kuzmichovs, that's who it must be," one of the women suggested.

The fellow stared at her wildly.

"For the Kuzmichovs?" repeated another woman. "But his name wasn't Trifon. His name's Kuzma, not Trifon; but the boy said Trifon Nikitich, so it can't be the same."

"His name is not Trifon and not Sabaneyev, it's Chizhov," suddenly put in a third woman, who had hitherto been silent, listening gravely.

"Alexey Ivanovich is his name. Chizhov, Alexey Ivanovich."

"Not a doubt about it, it's Chizhov," a fourth woman emphatically confirmed the statement.

The bewildered fellow looked from one to another.

"But what did he ask for, what did he ask for, good people?" he cried almost in desperation. " 'Do you know Sabaneyev?' says he. And who the devil's to know who Sabaneyev is?"

"You're a senseless fellow. I tell you it's not Sabaneyev, but Chizhov, Alexey Ivanovich Chizhov, that's who it is!" one of the women shouted at him impressively.

"What Chizhov? Who is he? Tell me, if you know."

"That tall, snivelling fellow who used to sit in the market in the summer."

"And what the devil's your Chizhov to do with me, good people, eh?"

"How can I tell what he's to do with you?" put in another. "You ought to know yourself what you want with him, if you make such a clamour about him. He spoke to you, he did not speak to us, you stupid. Don't you really know him?"

"Know whom?"

"Chizhov."

"The devil take Chizhov and you with him. I'll give him a hiding, that I will. He was laughing at me!"

"Give Chizhov a hiding! More likely he will give you one. You are a fool, that's what you are!"

"Not Chizhov, not Chizhov, you spiteful, mischievous woman. I'll give the boy a hiding. Catch him, catch him, he was laughing at me!"

The women guffawed. But Kolya was by now a good way off, marching along with a triumphant air. Smurov walked beside him, looking back at the shouting group far behind. He, too, was in high spirits, though he was still afraid of getting into some scrape in Kolya's company.

"What Sabaneyev did you mean?" he asked Kolya, foreseeing what his answer would be.

"How do I know? Now there'll be a hubbub among them all day. I like to stir up fools in every class of society. There's another blockhead, that peasant there. You know, they say 'there's no one stupider than a stupid Frenchman,' but a stupid Russian shows it in his face just as much. Can't you see it written all over his face that he is a fool, that peasant, eh?"

"Let him alone, Kolya. Let's go on."

"Not for anything, now I'm started. Hey, good-morning, peasant!"

A sturdy-looking peasant, with a round, simple face, and grizzled beard, who was walking by, and seemed already to have had a drop too much, raised his head and looked at the boy. "Good-morning, if you are not joking," he said deliberately in reply.

"And if I am?" laughed Kolya.

"Well, a joke's a joke. Laugh away. I don't mind. There's no harm in a joke."

"I apologise, brother, it was a joke."

"Well, God forgive you!"

"Do you forgive me, too?"

"I quite forgive you. Go along."

"I say, you seem a clever peasant."

"Cleverer than you," the peasant answered unexpectedly with the same gravity.

"I doubt it," said Kolya, somewhat taken aback.

411

"It's true though."

"Perhaps it is."

"It is, brother."

"Good-bye, peasant!"

"Good-bye!"

"There are all sorts of peasants," Kolya observed to Smurov, after a brief silence. "How could I tell I had hit on a clever one? I am always ready to recognise intelligence in the peasantry."

In the distance the cathedral clock struck half-past eleven. The boys made haste and they walked as far as Captain Snegiryov's lodging, a considerable distance, quickly and almost in silence. Twenty paces from the house Kolya stopped and told Smurov to go on ahead and ask Karamazov to come out to him.

"One must sniff round a bit first," he observed to Smurov.

"Why ask him to come out?" Smurov protested. "You go in; they will be awfully glad to see you. What's the sense of getting acquainted out here in the cold?"

"That's my business, why I want to see him out here in the cold," Kolya cut him short in the despotic tone he was fond of adopting with "small boys," and Smurov ran to do his bidding.

## CHAPTER IV
### THE LOST DOG

KOLYA leaned against the fence with an air of importance, waiting for Alyosha to appear. Yes, he had long wanted to meet him. He had heard a great deal about him from the boys, but hitherto he had always maintained an appearance of disdainful indifference when he was mentioned, and he had even "criticised" Alyosha as he listened to what he was told about him. But secretly he had a great long-ing to make his acquaintance; there was something sympathetic and attractive in all he was told about Alyosha. So the present moment was important: to begin with, he had to show himself at his best, to show his independence. "Or he'll think of me as thirteen and take me for a boy like the rest of them. And what are these boys to him? I shall ask him when I get to know him. It's a pity I am so short, though. Tuzikov is younger than I am, yet he is half a head taller. But I have an intelligent face. I am not good-looking. I know I'm hideous, but I've an intelligent face. I mustn't talk too freely; if I throw myself into his arms all at once, he may think . . . Faugh! how horrible if he should think . . . !"

Kolya was thus agitated while he was doing his utmost to assume the most independent air. What distressed him most was his being so short; he did not mind his "hideous" face so much as being so short. At home on the wall in a corner he had the year before made a pencil mark to show his height, and every two months since, he had anxiously measured himself against it to see how much he had grown. But, alas! he was growing very slowly, and this sometimes reduced him almost to despair. His face was in reality by no means "hideous"; on the contrary, it was rather attractive, with a fair, pale skin, freckled. His small, lively grey eyes had a fearless look, and often glowed with feeling. He had rather high cheekbones; small lips, very red, but not very thick; his nose was small and unmistakably turned up. "I've a regular pug nose, a regular pug nose," Kolya used to mutter to himself when he looked in the mirror, and he always left it with indignation. "But perhaps I haven't got an intelligent face?" he sometimes thought, doubtful even of that. But it must not be supposed that his mind was wholly preoccupied with his face and his height. On the contrary, however bitter the moments before the looking-glass were to him, he quickly forgot them, and forgot them for a long time, "abandoning himself entirely to ideas and to real life," as he formulated it to himself.

Alyosha came out quickly and hurriedly went up to Kolya. Before he reached him, Kolya could see that he looked delighted. "Can he be so glad to see me?" Kolya wondered, feeling pleased. We may note here, in passing, that Alyosha's appearance had undergone a complete change since we saw him last. He had abandoned his cassock and was wearing now a well-cut coat, a soft, round hat, and his hair had been cropped short. All this was very becoming to him, and he looked quite handsome. His charming face always had a good-humoured expression; but there was a gentleness and serenity in his good-humour. To Kolya's surprise, Alyosha came out to him just as he was, without an overcoat. He had evidently come in haste. He held out his hand to Kolya at once.

"Here you are at last! How anxiously we've all been waiting for you!"

"There were reasons which you shall know directly. Anyway, I am glad to make your acquaintance. I've long been hoping for an opportunity, and have heard a great deal about you," Kolya muttered, a little breathless.

"We should have met anyway. I've heard a great deal about you, too; but you've been a long time coming here."

"Tell me, how are things going?"

"Ilusha is very ill. He will surely die."

"How awful! You must admit that medicine is a fraud, Karamazov," cried Kolya heatedly.

"Ilusha has mentioned you often, very often, even in his sleep, in delirium, you know. One can see that you used to be very, very dear to him . . . before the incident . . . with the knife. . . . Then there's another reason. . . . Tell me, is that your dog?"

"Mine. Perezvon."

"Not Zhuchka?" Alyosha looked at Kolya with eyes full of pity. "Is she lost for ever?"

"I know you would all like it to be Zhuchka. I've heard all about it." Kolya smiled mysteriously. "Listen, Karamazov, I'll tell you all about it. That's what I came for; that's what I asked you to come out here for, to explain the whole episode to you before we go in," he began with animation. "You see, Karamazov, Ilusha came into the preparatory class last spring. Well, you know what our preparatory class is — a lot of small boys. They began teasing Ilusha at once. I am two classes higher up, and, of course, I only look on at them from a distance. I saw the boy was weak and small, but he wouldn't give in to them; he fought with them. I saw he was proud, and his eyes were full of fire. I like them like that. And they teased him all the more. The worst of it was he was horribly dressed at the time, his breeches were too small for him, and there were holes in his boots. They teased him about that, too; they shamed him. No, that I don't like. I stood up for him at once, and gave it to them hot. I beat them, but they adore me, do you know, Karamazov?" Kolya bragged impulsively; "generally, I am fond of children. I've two chicks on my hands at home now — that's what detained me to-day. So they left off beating Ilusha and I took him under my protection. I saw the boy was proud. I tell you that, the boy was proud; but in the end he became slavishly devoted to me; he did my slightest bidding, obeyed me as though I were God, tried to copy me. In the intervals between classes he used to run to me at once, and we'd walk together. On Sundays, too. In our school they always laugh when an older boy makes friends with a younger one like that; but that's a prejudice. If it's my fancy, that's enough, isn't that so? I teach him, develop him. Why shouldn't I develop him if I like him? Here you, Karamazov, have taken up with all these young ones. I see you want to influence the younger generation — to develop them, to be of use to them, and I assure you this trait in your character, which I knew by hearsay, interests me more than anything. But let's get to the point, though. I noticed that there was a sort of softness and sentimentality coming over the boy, and you know I am a positive enemy of this sheepish sentimentality, and I have been since I was born. There were contradictions in him, too: he was proud, but he was slavishly devoted to me; he was slavishly devoted and yet all at once his eyes would flash and he'd refuse to agree with me; he'd argue, fly into a rage. I used sometimes to propound certain ideas; I could see that it was not so much that he disagreed with the ideas, but that he was simply rebelling against me, because I was cool in responding to his sentimentalities. And so, in order to harden him properly, the tenderer he was, the colder I became. I did it on purpose: that was my conviction. My object was to form his character, to lick him into shape, to make a man of him . . . and then . . . no doubt, you understand me without further words. Suddenly I noticed that for three days in succession he was downcast and dejected, not because of my coldness, but because of something else, something higher, more important.

I wondered what the tragedy was. I pumped him and found out that he had somehow got to know Smerdyakov, the servant of your late father — it was before his death, of course — and he taught the little fool a silly trick — that is, a brutal, nasty trick. You take a piece of bread, stick a pin in it, and throw it to one of those curs who are so hungry that they swallow anything without chewing it, and then watch and see what happens. So they prepared a piece of bread like that and threw it to Zhuchka, that shaggy dog there's been such a fuss about. The people of the house it belonged to never fed it at all, though it barked all day. (Do you like that stupid barking, Karamazov? I can't stand it.) So it rushed at the bread, swallowed it, and began to squeal; it turned round and round and ran away, squealing as it ran out of sight. That was Ilusha's own account of it. He confessed it to me, and cried bitterly. He hugged me, shaking all over. He kept on repeating, 'He ran away squealing, he ran away squealing': the sight haunted him. Well, I see: remorse. I took it seriously. I had been wanting to give him a lesson for other things as well. So I must confess I wasn't quite straightforward, and pretended to be more indignant perhaps than I really was. 'You've done a nasty thing,' I said, 'you are a scoundrel. I won't tell of it, of course, but I shall have nothing more to do with you for a time. I'll think it over and let you know through Smurov (that's the boy who's just come with me and who has always been devoted to me) whether I will have anything to do with you in the future or whether I give you up for good as a scoundrel.' He was tremendously upset. I must own I felt I'd gone too far as I spoke, but there was no help for it. I did what I thought best at the time.

The day after, I sent Smurov to tell him that I would not speak to him again. That's what we call it when two schoolfellows refuse to have anything more to do with one another. Secretly I only meant to send him to Coventry for a few days and then, if I saw signs of repentance, to hold out my hand to him again. That was my firm intention. But what do you think happened? He heard Smurov's message, his eyes flashed. 'Tell Krasotkin from me,' he cried, 'that I will throw bread with pins in it to all the dogs — all — all of them!' 'So,' I thought, 'this is revolt. We must smoke it out of him.' And I began to treat him with complete contempt: whenever I met him I turned away or smiled ironically. And just then that affair with his father happened, the 'bath-mop,' you remember? You must realise that he was fearfully worked up by what had happened already. The boys, seeing I'd given him up, set on him and taunted him, shouting, 'Bath-mop, bath-mop!' It was then that those fights began, for which I am terribly sorry, because they seem to have given him one very bad beating. One day he flew at them, all in the court-yard as they were coming out of school. I stood ten paces off, looking on. And, I swear, I don't remember that I laughed then; it was quite the other way, I felt awfully sorry for him, in another minute I would have run up to take his part. But he suddenly met my eyes. I don't know what he fancied; but he pulled out a penknife, rushed at me, and struck at my thigh, here, my right leg. I didn't budge. I don't mind owning I am plucky sometimes, Karamazov. I simply looked at him contemptuously, as though to say, 'This is how you repay all my kindness! Do it again, if you like, I'm at your service.' But he didn't stab me again; he broke down, he was frightened at what he had done, he threw away the knife, burst out crying, and ran away. I did not sneak on him, of course, and I made them all keep quiet, so it shouldn't come to the ears of the masters. I didn't even tell my mother till it had healed up. And the wound was a mere scratch. And then I heard that the same day he'd been throwing stones and had bitten your finger — but you understand now what a state he was in! Well, it can't be helped: it was stupid of me not to come and forgive him — that is, to make it up with him — when he was taken ill. I am sorry for it now. But I had a special reason. So now I've told you all about it . . . but I'm afraid it was stupid of me."

"Oh, what a pity," exclaimed Alyosha, with feeling, "that I didn't know before what terms you were on with him, or I'd have come to you long ago to beg you to go to him with me. Would you believe it, when he was feverish he talked about you in his delirium. I didn't know how much you were to him! And you've really not succeeded in finding that dog? His father and the boys have been hunting all over the town for it. Would you believe it, since he's been ill, I've three times heard him repeat with tears, 'It's because I killed Zhuchka, father, that I am ill now. God is punishing me for it.' He can't get that idea out of his head. And if the dog were found and proved to be alive, one might almost fancy the joy would resurrect him. We have all rested our hopes on you."

"Tell me, what made you hope that I should be the one to find him?" Kolya asked, with great curiosity. "Why did you reckon on me rather than any one else?"

"There was a report that you were looking for the dog, and that you would bring it when you'd found it. Smurov said something of the sort. We've all been trying to persuade Ilusha that the dog is alive, that it's been seen. The boys brought him a live hare: he just looked at it, with a faint smile, and asked them to set it free in the fields. And so we did. His father has just this moment come back, bringing him a mastiff pup, hoping to comfort him with that; but I think it only made it worse."

"Tell me, Karamazov, what sort of man is the father? I know him, but what do you make of him — a mountebank, a buffoon?"

"Oh, no; there are people of deep feeling who have been somehow crushed. Buffoonery in them is a form of resentful irony against those to whom they daren't speak the truth, through having been for years humiliated and intimidated by them. Believe me, Krasotkin, that sort of buffoonery is sometimes tragic in the extreme. His whole life now is centred in Ilusha, and if Ilusha dies, he will either go mad with grief, or kill himself. I feel almost certain of that when I look at him now."

"I understand you, Karamazov. I see you understand human nature," Kolya added, with feeling.

"And as soon as I saw you with a dog, I thought it was Zhuchka you were bringing."

"Wait a bit, Karamazov, perhaps we shall find him yet; but this is Perezvon. I'll let him go in now and perhaps he will amuse Ilusha more than the mastiff pup. Wait a bit, Karamazov, you will learn something in a minute. But, good heavens, I am keeping you here!" Kolya cried suddenly. "You've no overcoat on in this bitter cold. You see what an egoist I am. Oh, we are all egoists, Karamazov!"

"Don't trouble; it is cold, but I don't often catch cold. Let us go in though, and, by the way, what is your name? I know you are called Kolya, but what else?"

"Nikolay — Nikolay Ivanovich Krasotkin, or, as they say in official documents, 'son of Krasotkin.'" Kolya laughed for some reason, but added suddenly, "Of course I hate my name Nikolay."

"Why so?"

"It's so trivial, so ordinary."

"You are thirteen?" asked Alyosha.

"No, fourteen — that is, I shall be fourteen very soon, in a fortnight. I'll confess one weakness of mine, Karamazov, just to you, since it's our first meeting, so that you may understand my character at once. I hate being asked my age, I more than hate it . . . and in fact . . . there's a libellous story going about me, that last week I played robbers with the 'preparatory' boys. It's a fact that I did play with them, but it's a perfect libel to say I did it for my own amusement. I have reasons for believing that you've heard the story; but I wasn't playing for my own amusement, it was for the sake of the children, because they couldn't think of anything to do by themselves. But they've always got some silly tale. This is an awful town for gossip, I can tell you."

"But what if you had been playing for your own amusement, what's the harm?"

"Come, I say, for my own amusement! You don't play horses, do you?"

"But you must look at it like this," said Alyosha, smiling. "Grown-up people go to the theatre and there the adventures of all sorts of heroes are represented — sometimes there are robbers, and battles, too — and isn't that just the same thing, in a different form, of course? And young people's games of soldiers or robbers in their play-time are also art in its first stage. You know, they spring from the growing artistic instincts of the young. And some-

times these games are much better than performances in the theatre; the only difference
is that people go there to look at actors, while
in these games the young people are the actors
themselves. But that's only natural."

"You think so? Is that your conviction?"
Kolya looked at him intently. "Oh, you know,
that's rather an interesting notion. When I go
home, I'll think it over. I'll admit I thought
I might learn something from you. I've come
to learn of you, Karamazov," Kolya concluded, in a voice full of spontaneous feeling.

"And I of you," said Alyosha, smiling and
pressing his hand.

Kolya was much pleased with Alyosha.
What struck him most was that he treated him
exactly like an equal and that he talked to him
just as if he were "quite grown up."

"I'll show you something directly, Karamazov; it's a theatrical performance, too,"
he said, laughing nervously. "That's why I've
come."

"Let us go first to the landlord's, on the left.
All the boys leave their coats in there, because
the room is small and hot."

"Oh, I'm only coming in for a minute. I'll
keep on my overcoat. Perezvon will stay here
in the passage and play dead. *Ici*, Perezvon,
lie down and play dead! You see he's dead.
I'll go in first and reconnoitre, then I'll whistle
to him when I think fit, and, you'll see, he'll
dash in like mad. Only Smurov must not forget to open the door at the right moment. I'll
arrange it all and you'll see a trick."

## CHAPTER V
### AT ILUSHA'S BEDSIDE

THE room inhabited by the family of the retired captain Snegiryov is already familiar to
the reader. It was close and crowded at that
moment with numerous visitors. Several boys
were sitting with Ilusha and though all of
them, like Smurov, were prepared to deny that
it was Alyosha who had brought them and reconciled them with Ilusha, it was really so. All
the art he had used had been to take them, one
by one, to Ilusha, without "sheepish sentimentality," appearing to do so casually and
without design. It was a great consolation to
Ilusha in his suffering. He was greatly touched
by seeing the almost tender affection and
sympathy shown him by these boys, who had
been his enemies. Krasotkin was the only one
missing and his absence was a heavy load on
Ilusha's heart. Perhaps the bitterest of all his
bitter memories was his stabbing Krasotkin,
who had been his one friend and protector.
Clever little Smurov, who had been the first to
make it up with Ilusha, thought it was so. But
when Smurov hinted to Krasotkin that Alyosha wanted to come and see him about something, the latter cut him short, bidding Smurov tell "Karamazov" at once that he knew
best what to do, that he wanted no one's advice, and that, if he went to see the patient,
he would choose his own time for he had "his
own reasons."

That was a fortnight before this Sunday.
That was why Alyosha had not been to see
him, as he had meant to. But though he waited,
he sent Smurov to him again twice. Both
times Krasotkin met him with a curt, impatient refusal, sending Alyosha a message not to
bother him any more, adding that if he came
himself, he, Krasotkin, would not go to Ilusha at all. Up to the very last day, Smurov
did not know that Kolya meant to go to Ilusha that morning, and only the evening before, as he parted from Smurov, Kolya
abruptly told him to wait at home for him

next morning, for he would go with him to the Snegiryovs, but warned him on no account to say he was coming, as he wanted to drop in casually. Smurov obeyed. Smurov's fancy that Kolya would bring back the lost dog was based on the words Kolya had dropped that "they must be asses to be unable to find the dog, if it was alive." When Smurov, waiting for an opportunity, timidly hinted at his guess about the dog, Krasotkin flew into a violent rage. "I'm not such an ass as to go hunting about the town for other people's dogs when I've got a dog of my own! And how can you imagine a dog could be alive after swallowing a pin? Sheepish sentimentality, that's what it is!"

For the last fortnight Ilusha had not left his little bed under the ikons in the corner. He had not been to school since the day he met Alyosha and bit his finger. He was taken ill the same day, though for a month afterwards he was sometimes able to get up and walk about the room and the passage. But latterly he had become so weak that he could not move without help from his father. His father trembled over him. He even gave up drinking and was almost insane with terror that his boy would die. And often, especially after leading him round the room on his arm and putting him back to bed, he would run to a dark corner in the passage and, leaning his head against the wall, he would break into paroxysms of violent weeping, stifling his sobs that they might not be heard by Ilusha.

Returning to the room, he would usually begin doing something to amuse and comfort his precious boy: he would tell him stories, funny anecdotes, or would mimic comic people he had happened to meet, even imitate the funny howls and cries of animals. But

Ilusha could not bear to see his father fooling and playing the buffoon. Though the boy tried not to show how he disliked it, he saw with an aching heart that his father was an object of contempt, and he was continually haunted by the memory of the "bath-mop" and that "terrible day."

Nina, Ilusha's gentle, crippled sister, did not like her father's buffoonery either (Varvara had been gone for some time past to Petersburg to study at the University). But the half-imbecile mother was greatly diverted and laughed heartily when her husband began capering about or performing. It was the only thing that amused her; all the rest of the time she was grumbling and complaining that now every one had forgotten her, that no one treated her with respect, that she was being slighted and so on. But during the last few days she had completely changed. She began looking constantly at Ilusha's bed in the corner and seemed lost in thought. She was more silent, quieter, and, if she cried, she cried quietly so as not to be heard. The captain noticed the change in her with bitter perplexity. The boys' visits at first only angered her, but later on their merry shouts and stories began to divert her, and at last she liked them so much that, if the boys had given up coming, she would have felt terribly dreary. When the children told some story or played a game, she laughed and clapped her hands. She called some of them to her and kissed them. She was particularly fond of Smurov.

As for the captain, the presence in his room of the children, who came to cheer up Ilusha, filled his heart from the first with ecstatic joy. He even hoped that Ilusha would now get over his depression, and that that would hasten his recovery. In spite of his alarm about Ilusha, he had not, till lately, felt one minute's doubt of his boy's ultimate recovery.

He met his little visitors with homage, waited upon them hand and foot, he was ready to be their horse and even began letting them ride on his back, but Ilusha did not like the game and it was given up. He began buying little things for them, gingerbread and nuts, gave them tea, and buttered sandwiches for them. It must be noted that all this time he had plenty of money. He had taken the two hundred roubles from Katerina Ivanovna just as Alyosha had predicted he would. And afterwards Katerina Ivanovna, learning more about their circumstances and Ilusha's illness, visited them herself, made the acquaintance of the family and succeeded in fascinating the half-imbecile mother. Since then she had been lavish in helping them, and the captain, terror-stricken at the thought that his boy might die, forgot his pride and humbly accepted her charity.

All this time Dr. Herzenstube, who was called in by Katerina Ivanovna, came punctually every other day, but little was gained by his visits and he dosed the invalid mercilessly. But on that Sunday morning a new doctor was expected, who had come from Moscow, where he had a great reputation. Katerina Ivanovna had sent for him from Moscow at great expense, not expressly for Ilusha, but for another purpose of which more will be said in its place hereafter. But, as he had come, she had asked him to see Ilusha as well, and the captain had been told to expect him. He hadn't the slightest idea that Kolya Krasotkin was coming, though he had long wished for a visit from the boy for whom Ilusha was yearning.

At the moment when Krasotkin opened the door and came into the room, the captain and all the boys were round Ilusha's bed, looking at a tiny mastiff pup, which had been born only the day before, though the captain had bespoken it a week ago to comfort and amuse Ilusha, who was still longing for the lost and probably dead Zhuchka. Ilusha, who had heard three days before that he was to be presented with a puppy, but not an ordinary puppy, but a real pedigree mastiff (an enormously important point, of course), tried from delicacy of feeling to pretend that he was pleased. But his father and the boys could not help seeing that the puppy only served to recall to his little heart the thought of the unhappy dog he had destroyed. The puppy lay beside him feebly moving and he, smiling morbidly, stroked it with his thin, pale, wasted hand. Clearly he liked the puppy, but . . . it wasn't Zhuchka; if he could have had Zhuchka and the puppy, too, then it would have been complete happiness.

"Krasotkin!" cried one of the boys suddenly. He was the first to see him come in.

Krasotkin's entrance made a general sensation, the boys moved away and stood on either side of the bed, so that he could get a full view of Ilusha. The captain ran eagerly to meet Kolya.

"Please, please, come in . . . you are most welcome!" he mumbled. "Ilusha, Mr. Krasotkin has come to see you!"

But Krasotkin, shaking hands with him hurriedly, instantly showed his complete knowledge of the manners of good society. He turned first to the captain's wife, who was sitting in her armchair, and who was very ill-humoured at the moment, grumbling that the boys stood between her and Ilusha's bed and did not let her see the new puppy. With the greatest courtesy he made her a bow, scraping his foot, and then turning to Nina, he made her, as the only other lady present, a similar bow.

This polite behaviour made an extremely favourable impression on the deranged lady.

"There, you can see at once he is a young man who has been well brought up," she commented aloud, throwing up her hands; "but as for our other visitors, they come in riding on each other's backs."

"How do you mean, mamma, riding on each other's backs, how is that?" muttered the captain affectionately, though a little anxious on her account.

"That's how they ride in. They get on each other's shoulders in the passage and prance in like that on a respectable family. Strange sort of visitors!"

"But who's come in like that, mamma?"

"Why, that boy came in riding on that one's back and this one on that one's."

Kolya was already at Ilusha's bedside. The sick boy turned visibly paler. He raised himself in the bed and looked intently at Kolya. Kolya had not seen his little friend for two months, and he was overwhelmed at the sight of him. He had never imagined that he would see such a wasted, yellow face, such enormous, feverishly glowing eyes, and such thin little hands. He noted, with grieved surprise, Ilusha's rapid, hard breathing and dry lips. He stepped close to him, held out his hand, and, almost overwhelmed, he said:

"Well, old man . . . how are you?" But his voice failed him, he couldn't achieve an appearance of ease; his face suddenly twitched and the corners of his mouth quivered. Ilusha smiled a pitiful little smile, still unable to utter a word. Something moved Kolya to raise his hand and pass it over Ilusha's hair.

"Never mind!" he murmured softly to him to cheer him up, or perhaps not knowing why he said it. For a minute they were silent again.

"Hullo, so you've got a new puppy?" Kolya said suddenly, in a most callous voice.

"Ye-es," answered Ilusha in a long whisper, gasping for breath.

"A black nose, that means he'll be fierce, a good watch-dog," Kolya observed gravely and stolidly, as if the only thing he cared about was the puppy and its black nose. But in reality he still had to do his utmost to control his feelings so as not to burst out crying like a little one, and do what he would he could not control them. "When it grows up, you'll have to keep it on the chain, I'm sure."

"He'll be a huge dog!" cried one of the boys.

"Of course he will," "a mastiff," "large," "like this," "as big as a calf," shouted several voices.

"As big as a calf, as a real calf," chimed in the captain. "I got one like that on purpose, one of the fiercest breed, and his parents are huge and very fierce, they stand as high as this from the floor. . . . Sit down here, on Ilusha's bed, or here on the bench. You are very welcome, dear visitor, we've been hoping to see you a long time. . . . You were so kind as to come with Alexey Fyodorovich?"

Krasotkin sat on the edge of the bed, at Ilusha's feet. Though he had perhaps prepared a free-and-easy opening for the conversation on his way, now he completely lost the thread of it.

"No . . . I came with Perezvon. I've got a dog now, called Perezvon. A Slavonic name. He's out there . . . if I whistle, he'll run in. I've brought a dog, too," he said, addressing Ilusha all at once. "Do you remember Zhuchka, old man?" He suddenly fired the question at him.

A spasm passed over Ilusha's little face. He looked with an agonised expression at Kolya. Alyosha, standing at the door, frowned and signed to Kolya not to speak of Zhuchka, but he did not or would not notice.

"Where . . . is Zhuchka?" Ilusha asked in a broken voice.

"Oh, well, my boy, your Zhuchka, whew! —he's lost and done for!"

Ilusha did not speak, but he fixed an intent gaze once more on Kolya. Alyosha, catching Kolya's eye, signed to him vigorously again, but again he turned away his eyes pretending not to have noticed.

"It must have run away somewhere and perished. It must have perished after a meal like that," Kolya rapped out pitilessly, though it seemed as though something had begun to choke him. "But I've got a dog, Perezvon . . . A Slavonic name. . . . I've brought him to show you."

"I don't want him!" said Ilusha suddenly.

"No, no, you really must see him . . . it will amuse you. I brought him on purpose. . . . He's the same sort of shaggy dog. . . . You allow me to call in my dog, madam?" He suddenly addressed Madame Snegiryov, with inexplicable and obvious excitement in his manner.

"I don't want him, I don't want him!" cried Ilusha, with a mournful break in his voice. There was a reproachful light in his eyes.

"You'd better . . ." the captain started up from the chest by the wall on which he had just sat down, "you'd better . . . another time," he muttered, but Kolya could not be restrained. He hurriedly shouted to Smurov,

"Open the door," and as soon as it was open, he blew his whistle. Perezvon dashed headlong into the room.

"Jump, Perezvon, beg! Beg!" shouted Kolya, jumping up, and the dog stood erect on its hind legs by Ilusha's bedside. What followed was a surprise to every one: Ilusha started, lurched violently forward, bent towards Perezvon and gazed at him, faint with suspense.

"It's . . . Zhuchka!" he cried suddenly, in a voice breaking with joy and suffering.

"And who did you think it was?" Krasotkin shouted with all his might, in a ringing, happy voice, and bending down he seized the dog and lifted him up to Ilusha.

"Look, old man, you see, blind of one eye and the left ear is torn, just the marks you described to me. It was by those marks that I found him. I found him directly. He did not belong to anyone!" he explained, turning quickly to the captain, to his wife, to Alyosha, and then again to Ilusha. "He used to stay in the Fedotovs' back yard. Though he made his home there, they did not feed him. He was a stray dog that had run away from some farm . . . I found him. . . . You see, old man, he couldn't have swallowed what you gave him. If he had, he must have died, he must have! So he must have spat it out, since he is alive. You did not see him do it. But the pin pricked his tongue, that is why he squealed. He ran away squealing and you thought he'd swallowed it. He might well squeal, because the skin of dogs' mouths is so tender . . . tenderer than in men, much tenderer!" Kolya cried impetuously, his face glowing and radiant with delight. Ilusha could not speak. White as a sheet, he gazed open-mouthed at Kolya, with his great eyes almost starting out of his head. And if Krasotkin, who had no suspicion of it, had known what a disastrous and fatal effect such a moment might have on the sick child's health, nothing would have induced him to play such a trick on him. But Alyosha was perhaps the only person in the room who realised it. As for the captain he had himself turned, as it were, into a small boy.

"Zhuchka! So it's Zhuchka!" he cried in a blissful voice. "Ilusha, this is Zhuchka, your Zhuchka! Mamma, this is Zhuchka!" He was almost weeping.

"And I never guessed!" cried Smurov sorrowfully. "Bravo, Krasotkin, I said he'd find the dog and here he's found him."

"Here he's found him!" another boy repeated gleefully.

"Krasotkin's a brick!" cried a third voice.

"He's a brick, he's a brick!" cried the other boys, and they began clapping.

"Wait, wait," Krasotkin did his utmost to shout above them all. "I'll tell you how it happened, that's the whole point. I found him, I took him home and hid him at once. I kept him locked up at home and did not show him to any one till to-day. Only Smurov has known for the last fortnight, but I assured him this dog was called Perezvon and he did not guess. And meanwhile I taught the dog all sorts of tricks. You should only see all the things he can do! I trained him so as to bring you a well-trained dog, in fine fettle, old man, so as to be able to say to you, 'See, old man, what a fine dog your Zhuchka is now!' Haven't you a bit of meat? — he'll show you a trick that will make you die with laughing. A piece of meat, haven't you got any?"

The captain dashed across the passage to the landlady, where their cooking was done. Not to lose precious time, Kolya, in desperate haste, shouted to Perezvon, "Dead!" And the dog immediately turned round and lay on his back with its four paws in the air. The boys laughed, Ilusha looked on with the same suffering smile, but the person most delighted with the dog's performance was "mamma." She laughed at the dog and began snapping her fingers and calling it, "Perezvon, Perezvon!"

"Nothing will make him get up, nothing!" Kolya cried triumphantly, proud of his success. "He won't move for all the shouting in the world, but if I call to him, he'll jump up in a minute. *Ici*, Perezvon!" The dog leapt up and bounded about, squealing with delight. The captain ran in with a piece of cooked beef.

"Is it hot?" Kolya inquired hurriedly, with a businesslike air, taking the meat. "Dogs don't like hot things. No, it's all right. Look, everybody, look, Ilusha, look, old man; why aren't you looking? He does not look at him, now I've brought him."

The new trick consisted in making the dog stand motionless with his nose out and putting a tempting morsel of meat just on his nose. The luckless dog had to stand without moving, with the meat on his nose, as long as his master chose to keep him so, without a movement, perhaps for half an hour. But he kept Perezvon only for a brief moment.

"Take it!" cried Kolya, and the meat passed in a flash from the dog's nose to his mouth.

The audience, of course, expressed enthusiasm and surprise.

"Can you really have put off coming all this time simply to train the dog?" exclaimed Alyosha, with an involuntary note of reproach in his voice.

"Simply for that!" answered Kolya, with

ILUSHA SICK

perfect simplicity. "I wanted to show him in all his glory."

"Perezvon! Perezvon," called Ilusha suddenly, snapping his thin fingers and beckoning to the dog.

"What is it? Let him jump up on the bed! *Ici*, Perezvon!" Kolya slapped the bed and Perezvon darted up to Ilusha. The boy threw both arms round his head and Perezvon instantly licked his cheek. Ilusha crept close to him, stretched himself out in bed and hid his face in the dog's shaggy coat.

"Dear, dear!" the captain kept exclaiming. Kolya sat down again on the edge of the bed.

"Ilusha, I can show you another trick. I've brought you a little cannon. You remember, I told you about it before and you said how much you'd like to see it. Well, here, I've brought it to you."

And Kolya hurriedly pulled out of his satchel the little brass cannon. He hurried, because he was happy himself. Another time he would have waited till the sensation made by Perezvon had passed off, now he hurried on regardless of all propriety. "You are all happy now," he felt, "so here's something to make you happier!" He was himself completely intoxicated.

"I've had my eye on this thing for a long while; for you, old man, for you. It belonged to Morozov, the official, it was no use to him, he had it from his brother. I swopped a book from father's bookcase for it, 'A Kinsman of Mahomet or Salutary Folly,' a scandalous book published in Moscow a hundred years ago, before they had any censorship. And Morozov has a taste for such things. He was grateful to me, too. . . ."

Kolya held the cannon in his hand so that all could see and enjoy it. Ilusha raised him-self, and, with his right arm still round the dog, he gazed enchanted at the toy. The sensation was even greater when Kolya announced that he had gunpowder, too, and that it could be fired off at once "if it won't alarm the ladies." "Mamma" immediately asked to look closer at the toy and her request was granted. The little brass cannon on wheels delighted her immensely and she began rolling it to and fro on her lap. She readily gave permission for the cannon to be fired, without any idea of what she had been asked. Kolya showed the powder and the shot. The captain, as a former military man, undertook to load it, putting in a minute quantity of powder. He asked that the shot might be put off till another time. The cannon was placed on the floor, aiming at an empty part of the room, three grains of powder were thrust into the touch-hole and a match was put to it. A magnificent explosion followed. Mamma was startled, but at once laughed with delight. The boys gazed in speechless triumph. But the captain, looking at Ilusha, was more enchanted than any of them.

Kolya picked up the cannon and immediately presented it to Ilusha, together with the powder and the shot.

"I got it for you, for you! I've been keeping it for you for a long time," he repeated once more in his delight.

"Oh, give it to me! No, give the cannon to me!" Mamma began begging like a little child. Her face showed a piteous fear that she would not get it. Kolya was embarrassed. The captain fidgeted uneasily.

"Mamma, mamma," he ran to her, "the cannon's yours, of course, but let Ilusha have it, because it's a present to him, but it's just as good as yours. Ilusha will always let you play with it, it shall belong to both of you, both of you."

"No, I don't want it to belong to both of us, I want it to be mine altogether, not Ilusha's," persisted mamma, who was on the point of tears.

"Take it, mother, here, keep it!" Ilusha cried. "Krasotkin, may I give it to my mother?" He turned to Krasotkin with an expression of entreaty, as though he were afraid he might be offended at his giving his present to some one else.

"Of course, you may," Krasotkin assented heartily, and, taking the cannon from Ilusha, he handed it himself to mamma with a polite bow. She burst into tears with emotion.

"Ilusha, the darling, he's the one who loves his mamma!" she said tenderly, and at once began wheeling the cannon to and fro on her lap again.

"Mamma, let me kiss your hand." The captain darted up to her at once and did so.

"And I never saw such a charming fellow as this nice boy," said the grateful lady, pointing to Krasotkin.

"And I'll bring you as much powder as you like, Ilusha. We make the powder ourselves now. Borovikov found out how it's made — twenty-four parts of saltpetre, ten of sulphur and six of birchwood charcoal. It's all pounded together, mixed into a paste with water and rubbed through a skin — that's how it's done."

"Smurov told me about your powder, only father says it's not real gunpowder," responded Ilusha.

"Not real?" Kolya flushed. "It burns. I don't know, of course."

"No, I didn't mean that," put in the captain, with a guilty face. "I only said that real

powder is not made like that, but that's nothing, it can be made so."

"I don't know, you know best. We lighted some in a pomatum pot, it burned splendidly, it all burned away leaving only a tiny ash. But that was only the paste, and if you rub it through a skin . . . but of course you know best, I don't know. . . . And Bulkin's father thrashed him on acount of our powder, did you hear?" He turned to Ilusha.

"Yes," answered Ilusha. He listened to Kolya with immense interest and enjoyment.

"We had prepared a whole bottle of it and he used to keep it under his bed. His father saw it. He said it might explode, and thrashed him on the spot. He was going to make a complaint against me to the masters. He is not allowed to go about with me now, no one is allowed to go about with me now. Smurov is not allowed to either, I've got a bad name with every one. They say I'm a 'desperate character.'" Kolya smiled scornfully. "It all began with what happened on the railway."

"Ah, we've heard of that exploit of yours, too," cried the captain. "How could you lie still there? Is it possible you weren't the least afraid, lying there under the train? Weren't you frightened?"

The captain was abject in his flattery of Kolya.

"N-not particularly," answered Kolya carelessly. "What's blasted my reputation more than anything here was that cursed goose," he said, turning again to Ilusha. But though he assumed an unconcerned air as he talked, he still could not control himself and was continually missing the note he tried to keep up.

"Ah! I heard about the goose!" Ilusha laughed, beaming all over. "They told me, but I didn't understand. Did they really take you to court?"

"The most stupid, trivial affair, they made a mountain of a mole-hill as they always do," Kolya began self-confidently. "I was walking through the market-place here one day, just when they'd driven in the geese. I stopped and looked at them. All at once a fellow, who is an errand boy at Plotnikovs', looked at me and said, 'What are you staring at the geese for?' I looked at him, he was a stupid, moon-faced fellow of twenty. I am always on the side of the people, you know. I like talking to peasants. . . . We've dropped behind the people — that's an axiom. I believe you are laughing, Karamazov?"

"No, heaven forbid, I am listening attentively," said Alyosha with a most good-natured air, and the sensitive Kolya was immediately reassured.

"My theory, Karamazov, is clear and simple," he hurried on again, looking pleased. "I believe in the people and am always glad to give them their due, but I am not for spoiling them, that is a *sine qua non*. . . . But I was telling you about the goose. So I turned to the fool and answered, 'I am wondering what the goose thinks about.' He looked at me quite stupidly. 'And what does the goose think about?' he asked. 'Do you see that cart full of oats?' I said. 'The oats are dropping out of the sack, and the goose has put its neck right under the wheel to gobble them up — do you see?' 'I see that quite well,' he said. 'Well,' said I, 'if that cart were to move on a little, would it break the goose's neck or not?' 'It'd be sure to break it,' and he grinned all over his face, highly delighted. 'Come on then,' said I, 'let's try.' 'Let's,' he said. And it did not take us long to arrange: he stood at the bridle

without being noticed, and I stood on one side to direct the goose. And the owner wasn't looking, he was talking to some one, so I had nothing to do, the goose thrust its head in after the oats of itself, under the cart, just under the wheel. I winked at the lad, he tugged at the bridle, and crack! The goose's neck was broken in half. And, as luck would have it, all the peasants saw us at that moment and they kicked up a shindy at once. 'You did that on purpose!' 'No, not on purpose.' 'Yes, you did, on purpose!' Well, they shouted, 'Take him to the justice of the peace!' They took me, too. 'You were there, too,' they said, 'you helped, you're known all over the market!' And, for some reason, I really am known all over the market," Kolya added conceitedly. "We all went off to the justice's, they took the goose, too. The fellow was crying in a great funk, simply blubbering like a woman. And the farmer kept shouting that you could kill any number of geese like that. Well, of course, there were witnesses. The justice of the peace settled it in a minute, that the farmer was to be paid a rouble for the goose, and the fellow to have the goose. And he was warned not to play such pranks again. And the fellow kept blubbering like a woman. 'It wasn't me,' he said, 'it was he egged me on,' and he pointed to me. I answered with the utmost composure that I hadn't egged him on, that I simply expressed the fundamental thought, that I had spoken hypothetically. The justice of the peace smiled and was vexed with himself at once for having smiled. 'I'll complain to your masters of you, so that in the future you mayn't waste your time on such hypotheses, instead of sitting at your books and learning your lessons.' He didn't complain to the masters, that was a joke, but the matter was

425

noised abroad and came to the ears of the authorities. Their ears are long, you know! The classical master, Kolbasnikov, was particularly aroused by it, but Dardanelov got me off again. But Kolbasnikov has a grudge against every one now like a green ass. Did you know, Ilusha, he just got married, got a dowry of a thousand roubles, and his bride's a regular fright of the first rank and the last degree? The third class fellows wrote an epigram on it.

*Astounding news has reached the class:*
*Kolbasnikov has won a lass!*

And so on, awfully funny, I'll bring it to you later on. I say nothing against Dardanelov, he is a man of learning, there's no doubt about it. I respect men like that and it's not because he stood up for me."

"But you took him down about the founders of Troy!" Smurov put in suddenly, unmistakably proud of Krasotkin at such a moment. He was particularly pleased with the story of the goose.

"Did you really take him down?" the captain inquired, in a flattering way. "On the question of who founded Troy? We heard of it, Ilusha told me about it at the time."

"He knows everything, father, he knows more than any of us!" put in Ilusha; "he only pretends to be like that, but really he is at the top in every subject . . ."

Ilusha looked at Kolya with infinite happiness.

"Oh, that's all nonsense about Troy, a trivial matter. I consider that an unimportant question," said Kolya with haughty humility. He had by now completely recovered his dignity, though he was still a little uneasy. He felt that he was greatly excited and that he had talked about the goose, for instance, with

too little reserve, while Alyosha had looked serious and had not said a word all the time. And the vain boy began by degrees to have a rankling fear that Alyosha was silent because he despised him, and thought he was showing off before him. If he dared to think anything like that Kolya would . . .

"I regard the question as quite a trivial one," he rapped out again, proudly.

"And I know who founded Troy," a boy, who had not spoken before, said suddenly, to the surprise of every one. He was a taciturn, shy, handsome boy of about eleven, called Kartashov. He was sitting right near the door. Kolya looked at him with dignified amazement.

The fact was that the identity of the founders of Troy had become a mystery for the whole school, a mystery which could be penetrated only by reading Smaragdov, and no one had Smaragdov but Kolya. One day when Kolya's back was turned, Kartashov had hastily opened Smaragdov, which lay among Kolya's books, and had lighted directly on the passage relating to the founders of Troy. This had happened some time ago, but he felt uneasy and could not bring himself to announce publicly that he, too, knew who had founded Troy, afraid of what might happen and of Krasotkin's somehow putting him to shame over it.

But now he couldn't resist saying it. He had been longing to do it for ages.

"Well, who did found it?" asked Kolya, turning to him with haughty superciliousness. He saw from the boy's face that he really did know and, of course, at once prepared for the consequences. There was, so to speak, a discordant note in the general harmony.

"Troy was founded by Teucer, Dardanus,

THE LITTLE BRONZE CANNON

Ilius, and Tros," the boy rapped out at once, and in the same instant he blushed, blushed so that it was pitiful to look at him. But the boys stared at him, stared at him for a whole minute, and then all the staring eyes turned at once and were fastened upon Kolya, who was still scanning the audacious boy with disdainful composure.

"In what sense did they found it?" he deigned to comment at last. "And what is meant by founding a city or a state? What did they do — did they go and each lay a brick, do you suppose?"

There was laughter. The offending boy turned from pink to crimson. He was silent and on the point of tears. Kolya held him so for a minute.

"Before you talk of a historical event like the foundation of a nationality, you must first understand what you mean by it," he admonished him in stern incisive tones. "But I attach no consequence to these old wives' tales and I don't think much of universal history in general," he added carelessly, addressing the company generally.

"Universal history?" the captain inquired, looking almost scared.

"Yes, universal history! It's the study of the successive follies of mankind and nothing more. The only subjects I respect are mathematics and natural science," said Kolya. He was showing off and he stole a glance at Alyosha, his was the only opinion he was afraid of there. But Alyosha was still silent and still serious as before. If Alyosha had said a word it would have stopped him, but Alyosha was silent and "it might be the silence of contempt" and that finally irritated Kolya.

"Again, take the classical languages . . . they are simply insanity, nothing more. You

seem to disagree with me again, Karamazov?"

"I don't agree," said Alyosha, with a faint smile.

"The study of the classical languages, if you ask my opinion, is simply a police measure, that's the only reason why it has been introduced into our schools." By degrees Kolya began to get breathless again. "They were introduced because they are a bore and because they stupefy the intellect. It was dull before, so what could they do to make things duller? It was senseless enough before, so what could they do to make it more senseless? So they invented the classical languages. That's my opinion, I hope I shall never change it," Kolya finished abruptly. His cheeks were flushed.

"That's true," assented Smurov suddenly, in a ringing tone of conviction. He had listened attentively.

"And yet he is first in Latin himself," cried one of the group of boys suddenly.

"Yes, father, he says that and yet he is first in Latin," echoed Ilusha.

"What of it?" Kolya thought fit to defend himself, though the praise was very sweet to him. "I am fagging away at Latin, because I have to, because I promised my mother to pass my examination, and I think that whatever you do should be done well. But at heart I have a profound contempt for the classics and all that fraud. . . . You don't agree, Karamazov?"

"Why 'fraud'?" Alyosha smiled again.

"Well, all the classical authors have been translated into all languages, so it was not for the sake of studying the classics they introduced Latin, but solely as a police measure, and to stupefy the intelligence. So what can one call it but a fraud?"

427

"Why, who taught you all this?" cried Alyosha, surprised at last.

"In the first place, I am capable of thinking for myself without being taught. Besides, what I said just now about the classics being translated our teacher Kolbasnikov has said to the whole of the third class."

"The doctor has come!" cried Nina, who had been silent till then.

A carriage belonging to Madame Hohlakov drove up to the gate. The captain, who had been expecting the doctor all morning, rushed headlong out to meet him. "Mamma" pulled herself together and assumed a dignified air. Alyosha went up to Ilusha and began setting his pillows straight. Nina, from her invalid chair, anxiously watched him making the bed tidy. The boys hurriedly took leave. Some of them promised to come again in the evening. Kolya called Perezvon and the dog jumped off the bed.

"I won't go away, I won't go away," Kolya said hastily to Ilusha. "I'll wait in the passage and come back when the doctor's gone, I'll come back with Perezvon."

But by now the doctor had entered, an important-looking person with long, dark whiskers and a shiny, shaven chin, wearing a bearskin coat. As he crossed the threshold he stopped, taken aback; he probably fancied he had come to the wrong place. "How is this? Where am I?" he muttered, not removing his coat nor his peaked sealskin cap. The crowd, the poverty of the room, the washing hanging on a line in the corner, puzzled him. The captain, bent double, was bowing low before him.

"It's here, sir, here, sir," he muttered cringingly; "it's here, you've come to the right place, you were coming to us . . ."

"Sne-gi-ryov?" the doctor said loudly and pompously. "Mr. Snegiryov — is that you?"

"That's me, sir!"

"Ah!"

The doctor looked round the room with a squeamish air once more and threw off his coat, displaying to all eyes the grand decoration round his neck. The captain caught the fur coat in the air, and the doctor took off his cap.

"Where is the patient?" he asked loudly and emphatically.

## CHAPTER VI
### PRECOCITY

"WHAT do you think the doctor will say to him?" Kolya asked quickly. "What a repulsive mug though, hasn't he? I can't endure medicine!"

"Ilusha is dying. I think that's certain," answered Alyosha mournfully.

"They are rogues! Medicine's a fraud! I am glad to have made your acquaintance though, Karamazov. I have wanted to know you for a long time. I am only sorry we meet under such sad circumstances."

Kolya had a great inclination to say something even warmer and more demonstrative, but he felt ill at ease. Alyosha noticed this, smiled, and pressed his hand.

"I've long learnt to respect you as a rare person," Kolya muttered again, faltering and uncertain. "I have heard you are a mystic and have been in the monastery. I know you are a mystic but . . . that hasn't put me off. Contact with real life will cure you. . . . It's always so with characters like yours."

"What do you mean by mystic? Cure me of what?" Alyosha was rather astonished.

"Oh, God and all the rest of it."

"What, don't you believe in God?"

428

"On the contrary, I've nothing against God. Of course, God is only a hypothesis, but . . . I admit that He is needed . . . for order, for universal order and all that . . . and that if there were no God He would have to be invented," added Kolya, beginning to blush. He suddenly fancied that Alyosha might think he was trying to show off his knowledge and to prove that he was "grown up." "I haven't the slightest desire to show off my knowledge to him," Kolya thought indignantly. And all of a sudden he felt horribly annoyed.

"I must confess I can't endure entering on such discussions," he said with a final air. "It's possible for one who doesn't believe in God to love mankind, don't you think so? Voltaire didn't believe in God and loved mankind." ("I am at it again," he thought to himself.)

"Voltaire did believe in God, though not very much, I think, and I don't think he loved mankind very much either," said Alyosha quietly, gently, and quite naturally, as though he were talking to some one of his own age, or even older. Kolya was particularly struck by Alyosha's apparent diffidence about his opinion of Voltaire. He seemed to be leaving the question for him, little Kolya, to settle.

"Have you read Voltaire?" Alyosha finished.

"No, not to say read. . . . But I've read *Candide* in a Russian translation . . . in an absurd, grotesque, old translation." . . . ("At it again! again!")

"And did you understand it?"

"Oh, yes, everything. . . . That is . . . Why do you suppose I shouldn't understand it? There's a lot of salaciousness in it, of course. . . . Of course I can understand that it's a philosophical novel and written to advocate an idea. . . ." Kolya was getting confused by now. "I am a socialist, Karamazov, I am an incorrigible socialist," he announced suddenly, apropos of nothing.

"A socialist?" laughed Alyosha. "But when have you had time to become one? Why, I thought you are only thirteen?"

Kolya winced.

"In the first place, I am not thirteen, but fourteen, fourteen in a fortnight" — he flushed angrily — "and in the second place, I am at a complete loss to understand what my age has to do with it. The question is, what are my convictions, not what is my age, isn't it?"

"When you are older, you'll understand for yourself the influence of age on convictions. I fancied, too, that you were not using your own words," Alyosha answered serenely and modestly, but Kolya interrupted him hotly:

"Come, you want obedience and mysticism. You must admit that the Christian religion, for instance, has only been of use to the rich and the powerful to keep the lower classes in slavery, that's so, isn't it?"

"Ah, I know where you read that, and I am sure some one taught you this!" cried Alyosha.

"I say, what makes you think I read it? And certainly no one taught it to me. I can think for myself. . . . I am not opposed to Christ, if you like. He was an altogther humane person, and if He were alive to-day, He would be found in the ranks of the revolutionists, and would perhaps play a conspicuous part. . . . There's no doubt about that."

"Oh, where, where did you get that from? What fool have you made friends with?" exclaimed Alyosha.

"Come, the truth will out! Of course, it happens that I have often talked to Mr. Rakitin, but . . . old Belinsky said that, too, so they say."

"Belinsky? I don't remember. He hasn't written that anywhere."

"If he didn't write it, they say he said it. I heard that from a . . . but never mind."

"And have you read Belinsky?"

"Well, no . . . I haven't read all of him, but . . . I read the passage about Tatyana, asking why she didn't go off with Onyegin."

"Didn't go off with Onyegin? Surely you don't . . . understand that already?"

"Why, you seem to take me for little Smurov," said Kolya, with a grin of irritation. "But please don't suppose I am such a revolutionist. I often disagree with Mr. Rakitin. Though I mention Tatyana, I am not at all for the emancipation of women. I acknowledge that women are a subject race and must obey. *Les femmes tricottent*, as Napoleon said." Kolya, for some reason, smiled. "And on this subject at least I am quite of one mind with that pseudo-great man. I think, too, that to leave one's own country and escape to America is mean, worse than mean — stupid. Why go to America when one may be of great service to humanity here? Now especially. There's a perfect heap of fruitful activity open to us. That's what I answered."

"What do you mean? Answered whom? Has some one suggested your going to America already?"

"I must own, they've been at me to go, but I declined. That's between ourselves, of course, Karamazov; do you hear, not a word to any one. I say this only to you. I am not at all anxious to fall into the clutches of the secret police and take lessons at the Chain bridge,

*Long will you remember
The house at the Chain bridge.*

Do you remember? It's splendid. Why are you laughing? You don't suppose I am fibbing, do you?" ("What if he should find out that I've only that one number of *The Bell*\* in father's bookcase, and haven't read any more of it?" Kolya thought with a shudder.)

"Oh, no, I am not laughing and don't suppose for a moment that you are lying. No, indeed, I can't suppose so, for all this alas! is perfectly true. But tell me, have you read Pushkin, Onyegin, for instance? . . . You spoke just now of Tatyana."

"No, I haven't read it yet, but I want to read it. I have no prejudices; I want to hear both sides. What makes you ask?"

"Oh, nothing."

"Tell me, Karamazov, have you an awful contempt for me?" Kolya rapped out suddenly and drew himself up before Alyosha, as though he were on drill. "Be so kind as to tell me, without beating about the bush."

"I have a contempt for you?" Alyosha looked at him wonderingly. "What for? I am only sad that a charming nature such as yours should be perverted by all this crude nonsense before you have begun life."

"Don't be anxious about my nature," Kolya interrupted, not without complacency. "But it's true that I am stupidly sensitive, crudely sensitive. You smiled just now, and I fancied you seemed to . . ."

"Oh, my smile meant something quite different. I'll tell you why I smiled. Not long ago I read the opinion of a German who had lived in Russia, about our present-day student-body. 'Show a Russian schoolboy,' he writes, 'a map of the stars, which he knows nothing about, and he will give you back the map next day with corrections on it.' No knowledge

\* A review published abroad under Herzen's editorship, and smuggled into Russia. *Editor's note.*

430

and unbounded conceit — that's what the German meant to say about the Russian school-boy."

"Yes, that's perfectly right," Kolya laughed suddenly, "exactly so! Bravo, German! But the numbskull did not see the good side, what do you think? Conceit — maybe, that comes from youth, that will be corrected if need be, but, on the other hand, there is an independent spirit almost from childhood, boldness of thought and conviction, and not the spirit of these sausage-makers, grovelling before authority. . . . But the German was right all the same. Bravo, German! But Germans want strangling all the same. Though they are so good at science and learning, they must be strangled."

"Strangled, what for?" smiled Alyosha.

"Well, perhaps I am talking nonsense, I agree. I am awfully childish sometimes, and when I am pleased about anything I can't restrain myself and am ready to talk stuff. But, I say, we are chattering away here about trifles, and that doctor has been in there a long time. But perhaps he's examining 'mamma' and that poor crippled Nina. I liked that Nina, you know. She whispered to me suddenly as I was coming away, 'Why didn't you come before?' And in such a voice, so reproachfully! I think she is awfully kind and pitiful."

"Yes, yes! Well, you'll be coming often, you will see what she is like. It would do you a great deal of good to know people like that, to learn to value a great deal which you will find out from knowing these people," Alyosha observed warmly. "That would have more effect on you than anything."

"Oh, how I regret and how I blame myself for not having come sooner!" Kolya exclaimed, with bitter feeling.

"Yes, it's a great pity. You saw for yourself how delighted the poor child was to see you. And how he was fretting, waiting for you to come!"

"Don't tell me! You make it worse! But it serves me right. What kept me from coming was my conceit, my egoistic vanity, and the beastly wilfulness, which I never can get rid of, though I've been struggling with it all my life. I see that now. I am a beast in lots of ways, Karamazov!"

"No, you have a charming nature, though it's been distorted, and I quite understand why you have had such an influence on this generous, morbidly sensitive boy," Alyosha answered warmly.

"And you say that to me!" cried Kolya; "and would you believe it, I thought — I've thought several times since I've been here — that you despised me! If only you knew how I prize your opinion!"

"But are you really so sensitive? At your age! Would you believe it, just now, when you were telling your story, I thought, as I watched you, that you must be very sensitive!"

"You thought so? What an eye you've got, I say! I bet that was when I was talking about the goose. That was just when I was fancying you had a great contempt for me for being in such a hurry to show off, and for a moment I quite hated you for it, and began talking like a fool. Then I fancied — here, just now — when I said that if there were no God He would have to be invented, that I was in too great a hurry to display my information, especially as I got that phrase out of a book. But I swear I wasn't showing off out of vanity, but just so, I really don't know why, because I was so overjoyed, yes, I believe it was because I was so overjoyed . . . though it's perfectly disgraceful for any one to be gushing directly they are pleased, I know that. But I am convinced now that you don't despise me; it was all my imagination. Oh, Karamazov, I am profoundly unhappy. I sometimes fancy all sorts of things, that every one is laughing at me, the whole world, and then I feel ready to destroy the whole order of things."

"And you torment every one about you," smiled Alyosha.

"Yes, I torment every one about me, especially my mother. Karamazov, tell me, am I very ridiculous now?"

"Don't think about that, don't think of it at all!" cried Alyosha. "And what does ridiculous mean? Isn't every one constantly being or seeming ridiculous? Besides, nearly all clever people now are fearfully afraid of being ridiculous, and that makes them unhappy. All I am surprised at is that you should be feeling that so early, though I've observed it for some time past, and not only in you. Nowadays the very children have begun to suffer from it. It's almost a sort of insanity. The devil has taken the form of that vanity and entered into the whole generation; it's simply the devil," added Alyosha, without a trace of the smile that Kolya, staring at him, expected to see. "You are like every one else," said Alyosha, in conclusion, "that is, like very many others. Only you must not be like everybody else, that's all."

"Even if every one is like that?"

"Yes, even if every one is like that. You be the only one not like it. You really are not like every one else, here you are not ashamed to confess to something bad and even ridiculous. And who will admit so much in these days? No one. And people have even ceased to feel the impulse to self-criticism. Don't be like every one else, even if you were the only one."

"Splendid! I was not mistaken in you. You know how to console one. Oh, how I have longed to know you, Karamazov. I've long been eager for this meeting. Can you really have thought about me, too? You said just now that you thought of me, too?"

"Yes, I'd heard of you and had thought of you, too . . . and if it's partly vanity that makes you ask, it doesn't matter."

"Do you know, Karamazov, our talk has been like a declaration of love," said Kolya, in a bashful and melting voice. "That's not ridiculous, is it?"

"Not at all ridiculous, and if it were, it wouldn't matter, because it's been a good thing." Alyosha smiled serenely.

"But do you know, Karamazov, you must admit that you are a little ashamed yourself, now. . . . I see it by your eyes." Kolya smiled slyly but with a kind of happiness.

"Why ashamed?"

"Well, why are you blushing?"

"It was you made me blush," laughed Alyosha, and he really did blush. "Oh, well, I am a little, goodness knows why, I don't know . . ." he muttered, almost embarrassed.

"Oh, how I love you and value you at this moment just because you, too, are rather ashamed! Because you are just like me," cried Kolya, in positive ecstasy. His cheeks glowed, his eyes beamed.

"You know, Kolya, you will be very unhappy in your life," something made Alyosha say suddenly.

"I know, I know. How you know it all beforehand!" Kolya agreed at once.

"But you will bless life on the whole, all the same."

"Just so, hurrah! You are a prophet. Oh, we shall be friends, Karamazov! Do you know, what delights me most, is that you treat me quite like an equal. But we are not equals, no, we are not, you are better! But we shall be friends. Do you know, all this last month I've been saying to myself, 'either we shall be friends at once, for ever, or we shall part enemies to the grave!'"

"And saying that, of course, you loved me." Alyosha laughed gaily.

"I did. I loved you awfully. I've been loving you and dreaming of you. And how do you know it all beforehand? Ah, here's the doctor. Goodness! What will he tell us? Look at his face!"

## CHAPTER VII
### ILUSHA

THE doctor came out of the room again, muffled in his fur coat and with his cap on his head. His face looked almost angry and disgusted, as though all the time he were afraid of being soiled. He cast a cursory glance round the passage, and looked sternly at Alyosha and Kolya as he did so. Alyosha waved from the door to the coachman, and the carriage that had brought the doctor drove up. The captain darted out after the doctor, and, bent over, almost wriggling before him, stopped him to get the last word. The poor fellow looked utterly crushed; there was a scared look in his eyes.

"Your Excellency, your Excellency . . . is it possible?" he began, but could not go on and struck his hands together in despair. Yet he still gazed imploringly at the doctor, as though a word from him might still change the verdict concerning the poor boy.

"What can I do! I am not God!" the doctor answered offhand, though with the customary impressiveness.

"Doctor . . . your Excellency . . . and will it be soon, soon?"

"You must be prepared for anything," said the doctor in emphatic and incisive tones, and, dropping his eyes, he was about to cross the threshold and step into the coach.

"Your Excellency, for Christ's sake," the terror-stricken captain stopped him again. "Your Excellency! but can nothing, absolutely nothing save him now?"

"It's not in my hands now," said the doctor impatiently, "but h'm . . ." He stopped suddenly. "If you could, for instance . . . send . . . your patient . . . at once, without delay" (the words "at once, without delay" the doctor uttered with an almost wrathful sternness that made the captain start), "to Syracuse, the change to the new be-ne-ficial climatic conditions might possibly affect . . ."

"To Syracuse!" cried the captain, unable to grasp what was said.

"Syracuse is in Sicily," Kolya jerked out suddenly in explanation. The doctor looked at him.

"Sicily! your Excellency," faltered the captain, "but you've seen" — he spread out his hands, indicating his surroundings — "and what about mamma and the family?"

"N-no, Sicily is not the place for the family, the family should go to the Caucasus in the early spring . . . your daughter must go to the Caucasus, and your spouse . . . after a course of the waters in the Caucasus for her rheumatism . . . must be sent straight to Paris to the mental specialist Lepelletier; I could give you a note to him, and then . . . there might be a change . . ."

"Doctor, doctor! But you see!" The captain flung wide his hands again despairingly, indicating the bare wooden walls of the passage.

"Well, that's not my business," grinned the doctor. "I have only told you the answer of medical science to your question as to possible treatment. As for the rest, to my regret . . ."

"Don't be afraid, apothecary, my dog won't bite you," Kolya rapped out loudly, noticing the doctor's rather uneasy glance at Perezvon, who was standing in the doorway. There was a wrathful note in Kolya's voice. He used the word apothecary instead of doctor on purpose, and, as he explained afterwards, "I used it to insult him."

"What's that?" The doctor flung up his head, staring with surprise at Kolya. "Who's this?" He addressed Alyosha, as though demanding an accounting from him.

"It's Perezvon's master, don't worry about my person, apothecary," Kolya said incisively again.

"Perezvon,"* repeated the doctor, perplexed.

"He hears the bell, but where it is he cannot tell. Good-bye, apothecary, we shall meet in Syracuse."

"Who's this? Who's this?" The doctor flew into a terrible rage.

"He is a schoolboy, doctor, he is a mischievous boy; take no notice of him," said Alyosha, frowning and speaking quickly. "Kolya, hold your tongue!" he cried to Krasotkin. "Take no notice of him, doctor," he repeated, rather impatiently.

"He wants a thrashing, a good thrashing!" The doctor stamped in a perfect fury.

"And you know, apothecary, my Perezvon might bite!" said Kolya, turning pale, with

* *i.e.*, a chime of bells.

quivering voice and flashing eyes. "*Ici*, Perezvon!"

"Kolya, if you say another word, I'll break with you for ever," Alyosha cried peremptorily.

"Apothecary, there is only one man in the world who can command Nikolay Krasotkin —this is the man" (Kolya pointed to Alyosha). "I obey him, good-bye!"

He dashed from the spot and, opening the door, quickly went into the room. Perezvon flew after him. The doctor stood still for five seconds in amazement, looking at Alyosha; then he suddenly spat and went out quickly to the carriage, repeating aloud, "This is . . . this is . . . I don't know what it is!" The captain darted forward to help him into the carriage. Alyosha followed Kolya into the room. He was already at Ilusha's bedside. The sick boy was holding his hand and calling for his father. A minute later the captain, too, came back.

"Father, father, come . . . we . . ." Ilusha faltered in violent excitement but, apparently unable to go on, he flung his wasted arms round his father and Kolya, uniting them in one embrace, and hugging them as tightly as he could. The captain suddenly began to shake with dumb sobs, and Kolya's lips and chin twitched.

"Father, father! How sorry I am for you!" Ilusha moaned bitterly.

"Ilusha . . . darling . . . the doctor said . . . you would be all right . . . we shall be happy . . . the doctor . . ." the captain began.

"Ah, father! I know what the new doctor said to you about me . . . didn't I see!" cried Ilusha, and again he hugged them both with all his strength, hiding his face on his father's shoulder.

KRASOTKIN AND HIS SON

"Father, don't cry, and when I die get a good boy, another one . . . choose one of them all, a good one, call him Ilusha and love him instead of me . . ."

"Hush, old man, you'll get well," Krasotkin cried suddenly, as though getting angry.

"But don't ever forget me, father," Ilusha went on, "come to my grave . . . and, father, bury me by our big stone, where we used to go for our walk, and come to me there with Krasotkin in the evening . . . and Perezvon . . . I shall expect you. . . . Father, father!"

His voice broke. They were all three silent, still embracing.

Nina was crying quietly in her chair, and at last, seeing them all crying, "mamma," too, burst into tears.

"Ilusha! Ilusha!" she exclaimed.

Krasotkin suddenly released himself from Ilusha's embrace.

"Good-bye, old man, mother expects me back to dinner," he said quickly. "What a pity I did not tell her! She will be dreadfully anxious. . . . But after dinner I'll come back to you for the whole day, for the whole evening, and I'll tell you all sorts of things, all sorts of things. And I'll bring Perezvon, but now I will take him with me, because he will begin to howl when I am away and bother you. Good-bye!"

And he ran out into the passage. He didn't want to cry, but in the passage he burst into tears. Alyosha found him crying.

"Kolya, you must be sure to keep your word and come, or he will be in agony," Alyosha said emphatically.

"I will! Oh, how I curse myself for not having come before," muttered Kolya, crying, and no longer ashamed of it.

At that moment the captain flew out of the room, and at once closed the door behind him. His face looked frenzied, his lips were trembling. He stood before the two lads and flung up his arms.

"I don't want a good boy! I don't want another boy!" he muttered in a wild whisper, clenching his teeth. "If I forget thee, Jerusalem, may my tongue . . ." He broke off with a sob and sank on his knees before the wooden bench. Pressing his fists against his head, he began sobbing with absurd whimpering cries, doing his utmost that his cries should not be heard in the room.

Kolya ran out into the street.

"Good-bye, Karamazov! Will you come yourself?" he cried sharply and angrily to Alyosha.

"I will certainly come in the evening."

"What was that he said about Jerusalem? . . . What did he mean by that?"

"It's from the Bible. 'If I forget thee, Jerusalem,' that is, if I forget all that is most precious to me, if I let anything take its place, then may . . ."

"I understand, that's enough! Mind you come! *Ici*, Perezvon!" he cried with positive ferocity to the dog, and with rapid strides he went home.

# BOOK XI

## IVAN

### CHAPTER I
#### AT GRUSHENKA'S

ALYOSHA went towards the cathedral square to the widow Morozov's house to see Grushenka, who had sent Fenya to him early in the morning with an urgent message begging him to come. On questioning Fenya, Alyosha learnt that her mistress had been particularly distressed since the previous day. During the two months that had passed since Mitya's arrest, Alyosha had called frequently at the widow Morozov's house, both because of his own inclination and in order to take messages for Mitya. Three days after Mitya's arrest, Grushenka was taken very sick and was ill for nearly five weeks. For one whole week she was unconscious. She was very much changed — thinner and a little sallow, though she had for the past fortnight been well enough to go out. But to Alyosha her face was even more attractive than before, and he liked to meet her eyes when he went in to her. A look of firmness and intelligent purpose had developed in her face. There were signs of a spiritual transformation in her, and a steadfast, fine, and humble determination that nothing could shake could be discerned in her. There was a small vertical wrinkle between her brows which gave her charming face a look of concentrated thought, almost austere at the first glance. There was scarcely a trace of her former frivolity.

It seemed strange to Alyosha, too, that in spite of the calamity that had overtaken the poor woman, betrothed to a man who had been arrested for a terrible crime, almost at the instant of their betrothal, in spite of her illness and the almost inevitable sentence hanging over Mitya, Grushenka had yet not lost her youthful cheerfulness. There was a soft light in the once proud eyes, though at times they gleamed with the old sinister fire when she was visited by one worry which had become stronger than ever in her heart. The object of that uneasiness was the same as ever — Katerina Ivanovna, of whom Grushenka had even raved when she lay in delirium. Alyosha knew that she was fearfully jealous of her, in spite of the fact that Katerina Ivanovna had not once visited Mitya in prison, though she might have done it whenever she liked. All this made a difficult problem for Alyosha, for he was the only person to whom Grushenka opened her heart and from whom she was continually asking advice. Sometimes he was unable to say anything.

Full of anxiety he entered her lodging. She was at home. She had returned from seeing Mitya half an hour before, and from the rapid movement with which she leapt up from her

436

chair to meet him he saw that she had been waiting for him with great impatience. A pack of cards dealt for a game of "fools" lay on the table. A bed had been made up on the leather sofa on the other side of the table and Maximov lay, half reclining, on it. He wore a dressing-gown and a cotton nightcap, and was evidently ill and weak, though he was smiling blissfully. When the homeless old man had returned with Grushenka from Mokroye two months before, he had simply stayed on and was still staying with her. Having come with her through rain and mud, he had sat down on the sofa, drenched and scared, and gazed mutely at her with a timid, appealing smile. Grushenka, who was in terrible grief and in the first stage of fever, almost forgot his existence in all she had to do the first half-hour after her arrival. Suddenly she looked at him closely: he gave a pitiful, helpless little titter. She called Fenya and told her to give him something to eat. All that day he sat in the same place, almost without stirring. When it got dark and the shutters were closed, Fenya asked her mistress:

"Is the gentleman going to stay the night, mistress?"

"Yes; make him a bed on the sofa," answered Grushenka.

Questioning him in more detail, Grushenka learnt from him that he had literally nowhere to go, and that "Mr. Kalganov, my benefactor, told me straight that he wouldn't receive me again and gave me five roubles."

"Well, God bless you, you'd better stay then," Grushenka decided in her anguish, smiling compassionately at him. Her smile wrung the old man's heart and his lips twitched with grateful weeping. And so the wandering pensioner had stayed with her ever since. He did not leave the house even when she was ill. Fenya and her grandmother, the cook, did not turn him out, but went on serving him meals and making up his bed on the sofa. Grushenka had grown used to him, and coming back from seeing Mitya (whom she had begun to visit in prison before she was really well), she would sit down and begin talking to "Maximushka" about trifling matters, to keep her from thinking of her sorrow. The old man turned out to be a good story-teller on occasion, so that at last he became necessary to her. Grushenka saw scarcely any one else besides Alyosha, who did not come every day and never stayed long. Her old merchant lay seriously ill at this time, "at his last gasp," as they said in the town, and he did, in fact, die a week after Mitya's trial. Three weeks before his death, feeling the end approaching, he made his sons, their wives and children, come upstairs to him at last and bade them not leave him again. From that moment he gave strict orders to his servants not to admit Grushenka and to tell her if she came, "The master wishes you long life and happiness and tells you to forget him." But Grushenka sent almost every day to inquire after him.

"You've come at last!" she cried, flinging down the cards and joyfully greeting Alyosha, "and Maximushka's been scaring me that perhaps you wouldn't come. Ah, how I need you! Sit down at the table. What will you have — coffee?"

"Yes, please," said Alyosha, sitting down at the table. "I am very hungry."

"That's right. Fenya, Fenya, coffee," cried Grushenka. "It's been boiling a long time, it's waiting for you. And bring some little pies, and mind they are hot. Do you know, we've had a storm over those pies to-day. I took them to the prison for him, and, would you believe it, he threw them back at me: he would not eat them. He flung one of them on the floor and stamped on it. So I said to him: 'I shall leave them with the warden; if you don't eat them before evening, it will mean that you feed on your venomous spite!' With that I went away. We quarrelled again, would you believe it? Whenever I go we quarrel."

Grushenka said all this in one breath in her agitation. Maximov, suddenly grown timid, smiled with downcast eyes.

"What did you quarrel about this time?" asked Alyosha.

"I didn't expect it in the least. Only fancy, he is jealous of the Pole. 'Why are you keeping him?' he said. 'So you've begun keeping him.' He is jealous, jealous of me all the time, jealous eating and sleeping! He even took it into his head to be jealous of Kuzma last week."

"But he knew about the Pole before?"

"Yes, but there it is. He has known about him from the very beginning, but to-day he suddenly got up and began scolding about him. I am ashamed to repeat what he said. Fool! Rakitin went in as I came out. Perhaps Rakitin is egging him on. What do you think?" she added absent-mindedly, as it were.

"He loves you, that's what it is; he loves you so much. And now he is particularly irritable."

"I should think he might be, with the trial to-morrow. And I went to him to say something about to-morrow, for I dread to think what's going to happen then. You say that he is irritable, but how irritable I am! And he talks about the Pole! What a fool! He is not jealous of Maximushka yet, anyway."

"My wife was dreadfully jealous of me, too," Maximov put in his word.

"Jealous of you?" Grushenka laughed in spite of herself. "Of whom could she have been jealous?"

"Of the servant girls."

"Hold your tongue, Maximushka, I am in no laughing mood now, I feel angry. Don't ogle the pies. I shan't give you any; they are not good for you, and I won't give you any vodka either. I have to look after him, too, just as though I kept an alms-house," she laughed.

"I don't deserve your kindness. I am a worthless creature," said Maximov, with tears in his voice. "You would do better to spend your kindness on people of more use than me."

"Ah, every one is of use, Maximushka, and how can we tell who's of most use. If only that Pole weren't there at all, Alyosha. He's taken it into his head to fall ill, too, to-day. I've been to see him also. And I shall send him some pies, too, on purpose. I hadn't sent him any, but Mitya accused me of it, so now I shall send some on purpose! Ah, here's Fenya with a letter! Yes, it's from the Poles — begging again!"

Pan Musialowicz had indeed sent an extremely long and, as usual, high-flown letter in which he begged her to lend him three roubles. In the letter was enclosed a receipt for the sum, with a promise to repay it within three months, signed by Pan Wróblewski as well. Grushenka had received many such letters, accompanied by such receipts, from her former lover during the fortnight of her convalescence. But she knew that the two Poles had been to ask after her health during her illness. The first letter Grushenka got from them was a long one, written on large note-paper and with a big family crest on the seal. It was so obscure and rhetorical that Grushenka put it down before she had read half, unable to make head or tail of it. She could not attend to letters then. The first letter was followed next day by another in which *Pan* Musialowicz begged her for a loan of two thousand roubles for a very short period. Grushenka left that letter, too, unanswered. A whole series of letters had followed — one every day — all as pompous and rhetorical, but the loan asked for, gradually diminishing, dropped to a hundred roubles, then to twenty-five, to ten, and finally Grushenka received a letter in which both the Poles begged her for only one rouble and included a receipt signed by both.

Then Grushenka suddenly felt sorry for them, and at dusk she went round herself to their lodging. She found the two Poles in great poverty, almost destitution, without food or fuel, without cigarettes, in debt to their landlady. The two hundred roubles they had carried off from Mitya at Mokroye had soon disappeared. But Grushenka was surprised at their meeting her with arrogant dignity and self-assertion, with the greatest formality and pompous speeches. Grushenka simply laughed, and gave her former admirer ten roubles. Then, laughing, she told Mitya of it and he was not in the least jealous. But ever since, the Poles had attached themselves to Grushenka and bombarded her daily with requests for money and she had always sent them small sums. And now that day Mitya had taken it into his head to be fearfully jealous.

"Like a fool, I went round to him just for a minute, on the way to see Mitya, for he is ill, too, my Pole," Grushenka began again with nervous haste. "I was laughing, telling Mitya about it. 'Fancy,' I said, 'my Pole had the happy thought of singing his old songs to me to the guitar. He thought I would be touched and marry him!' Mitya leapt up swearing. . . . So, there, I'll send them the pies! Fenya, is it that little girl they've sent? Here, give her three roubles and wrap a dozen pies up in a paper and tell her to take them. And you, Alyosha, be sure to tell Mitya that I did send them the pies."

"I wouldn't tell him for anything," said Alyosha, smiling.

"Oh! You think he is unhappy about it. Why, he's jealous on purpose. He doesn't care," said Grushenka bitterly.

"On purpose?" queried Alyosha.

"I tell you you are silly, Alyosha. You understand nothing about it, with all your cleverness. I am not offended because he is jealous of a girl like me. I would be offended if he were not jealous. I am like that. I am not offended by jealousy. I have a fierce heart, too. I can be jealous myself. Only what offends me is that he doesn't love me at all. I tell you he is jealous now *on purpose*. Am I blind? Don't I see? He began talking to me just now of that woman, of Katerina, saying she was this and that, how she had called in a doctor from Moscow for the trial, to try and save him; how she had sent for the best counsel, the most learned one, too. So he loves her, if he'll praise her to my face, more shame to him! He's guilty before me himself, so he attacked me, to make out I was in fault first and to put it all on me. 'You were with your Pole before I came, so I can't be blamed for Katerina,' that's what it amounts to. He wants to put the whole blame on me. He attacked me on purpose, on purpose, I tell you, but I'll . . . ."

Grushenka did not finish saying what she would do. She hid her eyes in her handkerchief and broke into violent sobs.

"He doesn't love Katerina Ivanovna," said Alyosha firmly.

"Well, whether he loves her or not I'll soon find out for myself," said Grushenka, with a menacing note in her voice, taking the handkerchief from her eyes. Her face was distorted. Alyosha saw sorrowfully that from being mild and serene it had become sullen and spiteful.

"Enough of this foolishness," she said suddenly; "it's not for that I sent for you. Alyosha, darling, to-morrow — what will happen to-morrow? That's what worries me! And it's only me it worries! I look at every one and no one is thinking of it. No one cares about it. Are you thinking about it even? To-morrow he'll be tried, you know. Tell me, how will he be tried? You know it's the valet, the valet killed him! Good heavens! Can they condemn him in place of the valet and will no one stand up for him? They haven't troubled the valet at all, have they?"

"He's been severely cross-examined," observed Alyosha thoughtfully; "but every one came to the conclusion it was not he. Now he is lying very ill. He has been ill ever since that attack. Really ill," added Alyosha.

"Oh, dear! Couldn't you go to that counsel yourself and tell him the whole thing in private? He's been brought from Petersburg for three thousand roubles, they say."

"We gave these three thousand together — Ivan, Katerina Ivanovna, and I — but she paid two thousand for the doctor from Moscow herself. The counsel Fetyukovich would have charged more, but the case has become known all over Russia; it's in all the newspapers and reviews. Fetyukovich agreed to come more for the glory, because the case has become so notorious. I saw him yesterday."

"Well? Did you talk to him?" Grushenka put in eagerly.

"He listened and said nothing. He told me that he had already formed his opinion. But he promised to give my words consideration."

"Consideration! Ah, they are swindlers! They'll ruin him. And why did she send for the doctor?"

"As an expert. They want to prove that Mitya's mad and committed the murder when he didn't know what he was doing"; Alyosha smiled gently; "but Mitya won't agree to that."

"Yes; but that would be the truth if he had killed him!" cried Grushenka. "He was mad then, perfectly mad, and that was my fault, wretch that I am! But, of course, he didn't do it, he didn't do it! And they are all against him, saying he is the murderer, the whole town. Even Fenya's evidence went to prove he had done it. And the people at the shop, and that official, and at the tavern, too, before, people had heard him say so! They are all, all against him, all crying out against him."

"Yes, there's a fearful accumulation of evidence," Alyosha observed grimly.

"And Grigory — Grigory Vasilyevich — sticks to his story that the door was open, insists that he saw it — there's no shaking him. I went and talked to him myself. He's rude about it, too."

"Yes, that's perhaps the strongest evidence against him," said Alyosha.

"And as for Mitya's being mad, he certainly seems like it now," Grushenka began with a peculiarly anxious and mysterious air. "Do you know, Alyosha, I've been wanting to talk to you about it for a long time. I go to him every day and simply wonder at him. Tell me, now, what do you suppose he's always talking about? He talks and talks and I can make nothing of it. I fancied he was talking of something intellectual that I couldn't understand in my foolishness. Only he suddenly began talking to me about a babe — that is, about some child. 'Why is the babe poor?' he said. 'It's for that babe I am going to Siberia now. I did not kill, but I must go to Siberia!' What that meant, what babe, I couldn't tell for the life of me. Only I cried when he said it, because it was so fine the way he said it. He cried himself, and I cried, too. He suddenly kissed me and made the sign of the cross over me. What did it mean, Alyosha, tell me? What is this babe?"

"It must be Rakitin, who's been going to see him lately," smiled Alyosha, "though . . . that's not Rakitin's doing. I didn't see Mitya yesterday. I'll see him to-day."

"No, it's not Rakitin; it's his brother Ivan Fyodorovich upsetting him. It's his going to see him, that's what it is," Grushenka began, and suddenly broke off.

Alyosha gazed at her in amazement. "Ivan's going? Has he been to see him? Mitya told me himself that Ivan hasn't been once."

"There . . . there! What a girl I am! Blurting things out!" exclaimed Grushenka, confused and suddenly blushing. "Wait, Alyosha, hush! Since I've said so much I'll tell the whole truth — he's been to see him twice, the first time directly he arrived. He galloped here from Moscow at once, of course, before I was taken ill; and the second time was a week ago. He told Mitya not to tell you about it, under any circumstances; and not to tell any one, in fact. He came secretly."

Alyosha sat plunged in thought, considering. The news evidently astonished him.

"Ivan doesn't talk to me of Mitya's case,"

he said slowly. "He's said very little to me these last two months. And whenever I go to see him, he seems vexed at my coming, so I've not been to him for the last three weeks. H'm! . . . if he was there a week ago . . . there certainly has been a change in Mitya this week."

"There has been a change," Grushenka assented quickly. "They have a secret, they had a secret! Mitya told me himself there was a secret, and such a secret that Mitya can't rest. Before then, he was cheerful — and, indeed, he is cheerful now — but when he begins shaking his head like that, you know, and strides about the room and keeps pulling at the hair on his right temple with his right hand, I know there is something on his mind worrying him. . . . I know! He was cheerful before, though, indeed, he is cheerful to-day."

"But you said he was irritable."

"Yes, he is irritable and yet cheerful. He keeps on being irritable for a minute and then cheerful and then irritable again. And you know, Alyosha, I am constantly wondering at him — with this awful thing hanging over him, he sometimes laughs at such trifles as though he were a baby himself."

"And did he really tell you not to tell me about Ivan? Did he say 'don't tell him'?"

"Yes, he told me 'don't tell him.' It's you that Mitya's most afraid of. Because it's a secret: he said himself it was a secret. Alyosha, darling, go to him and find out what their secret is and come and tell me," Grushenka besought him with sudden eagerness. "Set my mind at rest that I may know the worst that's in store for me. That's why I sent for you."

"You think it's something to do with you? If it were, he wouldn't have told you there was a secret."

"I don't know. Perhaps he wants to tell me, but doesn't dare to. He warns me. There is a secret, he tells me, but he won't tell me what it is."

"What do you think yourself?"

"What do I think? It's the end of me, that's what I think. They all three have been plotting my end, for Katerina's in it. It's all Katerina, it all comes from her. She is this and that, which means I am not this and that. He tells me that beforehand — warns me. He is planning to throw me over, that's the whole secret. They've planned it together, the three of them — Mitya, Katerina, and Ivan Fyodorovich. Alyosha, I've been wanting to ask you a long time. A week ago he suddenly told me that Ivan was in love with Katerina, because he often goes to see her. Did he tell me the truth or not? Tell me, on your conscience, knife me."

"I won't tell you a lie. Ivan is not in love with Katerina Ivanovna, I think."

"Oh, that's what I thought! He is lying to me, shameless deceiver, that's what it is! And he was jealous of me just now, so as to put the blame on me afterwards. He is stupid, he can't cover his traces; he is so open, you know. . . . But I'll give it to him, I'll give it to him! 'You believe I killed,' he said. He said that to me, to me. He reproached me with that! God forgive him! You wait, I'll make it hot for Katerina at the trial! I'll just say a word then . . . I'll tell everything then!"

And again she cried bitterly.

"This I can tell you for certain, Grushenka," Alyosha said, getting up. "First, that he loves you, loves you more than any one in the world, and you only, believe me. I know. I do know. The second thing is that I don't want to worm his secret out of him, but if

he'll tell me of himself to-day, I shall tell him straight out that I have promised to tell you. Then I'll come to you to-day and tell you. Only . . . I fancy . . . Katerina Ivanovna has nothing to do with it, and that the secret is about something else. That's certain. It isn't likely it's about Katerina Ivanova, it seems to me. Good-bye for the present."

Alyosha shook hands with her. Grushenka was still crying. He saw that she put little faith in his consolation, but she was better for having poured her sorrow out, for having spoken of it. He was sorry to leave her in such a state of mind, but he was in haste. He had a great many things to do.

## CHAPTER II
### THE INJURED FOOT

THE first of these things was at the house of Madame Hohlakov, and he hurried there to get it over as quickly as possible and not be too late for Mitya. Madame Hohlakov had been slightly ailing for the last three weeks: her foot had for some reason swollen up, and though she was not in bed, she lay all day half reclining on the couch in her boudoir, in fascinating but decorous *déshabillé*. Alyosha had once noted with innocent amusement that, in spite of her illness, Madame Hohlakov had begun to be rather dressy — little caps, ribbons, *négligés*, had made their appearance, and he had an inkling of the reason, though he dismissed such ideas from his mind as idle. During the last two months the young official, Perhotin, had become a regular visitor at the house.

Alyosha had not called for four days and he was in haste to go straight to Lise, as it was with her he had to speak, for Lise had sent a maid to him the previous day, specially asking him to come to her "about something very important," a request which, for certain reasons, interested Alyosha. But while the maid went to take his name in to Lise, Madame Hohlakov heard of his arrival from some one, and immediately sent to beg him to come to her "just for one minute." Alyosha reflected that it was better to accede to the mamma's request, or else she would be sending down to Lise's room every minute that he was there. Madame Hohlakov was lying on a couch. She was dressed very festively and was evidently in a state of extreme nervous excitement. She greeted Alyosha with cries of rapture.

"It's ages, ages, perfect ages since I've seen you! It's a whole week — only think of it! Ah, but you were here only four days ago, on Wednesday. You have come to see Lise. I'm sure you meant to slip into her room on tiptoe, without my hearing you. My dear, dear Alexey Fyodorovich, if you only knew how worried I am about her! But of that later, though that's the most important thing, of that later. Dear Alexey Fyodorovich, I trust you implicitly with my Lise. Since the death of Father Zosima — God rest his soul!" (she crossed herself) — "I look upon you as a monk, though you look charming in your new suit. Where did you find such a tailor in these parts? No, no, that's not the chief thing — of that later. Forgive me for sometimes calling you Alyosha; an old woman like me may take liberties," she smiled coquettishly; "but that will do later, too. The important thing is that I shouldn't forget what is important. Please remind me of it yourself. As soon as my tongue runs away with me, you just say, 'The important thing?' Ah! how do I know now what is of most importance? Ever since Lise took back her promise — her childish promise,

Alexey Fyodorovich — to marry you, you've realised, of course, that it was only the playful fancy of a sick child who had been so long confined to her chair — thank God, she can walk now! . . . that new doctor Katya sent for from Moscow for your unhappy brother, who will to-morrow . . . But why speak of to-morrow? I am dying at the very thought of to-morrow. Dying of curiosity. . . . In a word, that doctor was here yesterday and saw Lise. . . . I paid him fifty roubles for the visit. But that's not the point, that's not the point again. You see, I'm mixing everything up. I am in such a hurry. Why am I in a hurry? I don't understand. It's awful how I seem growing unable to understand anything. Everything seems mixed up in a sort of tangle. I am afraid you are so bored you will jump up and run away, and that will be all I shall see of you. Goodness! Why are we sitting here and no coffee? Yulia, Glafira, coffee!"

Alyosha made haste to thank her, and said that he had only just had coffee.

"Where?"

"At Agrafena Alexandrovna's."

"At . . . at that woman's? Ah, it's she has brought ruin on every one. I know nothing about it though. They say she has become a saint, though it's rather late in the day. She had better have done it before. What use is it now? Hush, hush, Alexey Fyodorovich, for I have so much to say to you that I am afraid I shall tell you nothing. This awful trial . . . I shall certainly go, I am making arrangements. I shall be carried there in my chair; besides I can sit up. I shall have people with me. And, you know, I am a witness. How shall I speak, how shall I speak? I don't know what I shall say. One has to take an oath, hasn't one?"

"Yes; but I don't think you will be able to go."

"I can sit up. Ah, you put me out! Ah! this trial, this savage act, and then they are all going to Siberia, others get married, and all this so quickly, so quickly, everything's changing, and at last — nothing. All grow old and have death to look forward to. Well, so be it! I am tired. This Katya, *cette charmante personne*, has blasted all my hopes. Now she is going to follow one of your brothers to Siberia, and your other brother is going to follow her, and will live in the nearest town, and they will all torment one another. It drives me out of my mind. Worst of all — the publicity. The story has been told a million times over in all the papers in Moscow and Petersburg. Ah! yes, would you believe it, they've written about me, too, that I was 'a dear friend' of your brother's ———, I can't repeat the horrid word. Just fancy, just fancy!"

"Impossible! Where did it appear? What did it say?"

"I'll show you directly. I got the paper and read it yesterday. Here, in the Petersburg paper *Rumour*. The paper began coming out this year. I am awfully fond of gossip, and I take it in, and now it pays me out — this is what gossip comes to! Here it is, here, this passage. Read it."

And she handed Alyosha a sheet of newspaper which had been under her pillow.

It was not exactly that she was upset, she seemed overwhelmed, and perhaps everything really was mixed up in a tangle in her head. The newspaper notice was very typical, and must have been an annoyance to her, but, fortunately perhaps, she was unable to keep her mind fixed on any one subject at that moment, and so might race off in a minute to something else and quite forget the newspaper.

Alyosha was well aware that the story of the terrible case had spread all over Russia. And, good heavens! what wild rumours about his brother, about the Karamazovs, and about himself he had read in the course of those two months, among other equally credible items. One paper had even stated that he had gone into a monastery and become a monk, in horror at his brother's crime. Another contradicted this, and stated that he and his elder, Father Zosima, had broken into the monastery chest and "made tracks from the monastery." The present paragraph in the paper *Rumour* was under the heading, "The Karamazov Case at Skotoprigonyevsk."* (That, alas! was the name of our little town. I had hitherto kept it concealed.) It was brief, and Madame Hohlakov was not directly mentioned in it. No names appeared, in fact. It was merely stated that the criminal, whose approaching trial was making such a sensation — retired army captain, a swagger, an idler, and a retrograde bully — was continually involved in amorous intrigues, and particularly popular with certain ladies "who were bored with solitude." One such lady, a bored widow, who tried to seem young though she had a grown-up daughter, was so fascinated by him that only two hours before the crime she had offered him three thousand roubles, on condition that he would elope with her to the gold-mines. But the criminal, counting on escaping punishment, had preferred to murder his father to get the three thousand, rather than go off to Siberia with the middle-aged charms of his bored lady. This playful notice wound up, of course, with an outburst of high-minded in-

* The name suggests a cattle-pen, or something of the sort. *Editor's note.*

dignation at the wickedness of parricide and of the lately abolished institution of serfdom. Having read it with curiosity, Alyosha folded up the paper and handed it back to Madame Hohlakov.

"Well, that must be me," she hurried on again. "Of course I am meant. Scarcely more than an hour before, I suggested gold-mines to him, and here they talk of 'middle-aged charms' as though that were my motive! He writes that out of spite! God Almighty forgive him for the middle-aged charms, as I forgive him! You know it's . . . Do you know who it is? It's your friend Rakitin."

"Perhaps," said Alyosha, "though I've heard nothing about it."

"It's he, it's he! No 'perhaps' about it. You know I turned him out of the house. . . . You know that whole story, don't you?"

"I know that you asked him not to visit you in future, but why it was I hadn't heard . . . from you, at least."

"Ah, then you've heard it from him! He abuses me, I suppose, abuses me dreadfully?"

"Yes, he does; but then he abuses every one. But why you've closed your doors to him I haven't heard from him either. I meet him very seldom now, indeed. We are not friends."

"Well, then, I'll tell you all about it. There's no help for it, I'll confess, for there is one point in which I was perhaps to blame. Only a little, little point, so little that perhaps it doesn't count. You see, my dear boy" — Madame Hohlakov suddenly looked arch and a charming, though enigmatic, smile played about her lips — "you see, I suspect . . . You must forgive me, Alyosha. I am like a mother to you. . . . No, no; quite the contrary. I speak to you now as though you were my father — mother's quite out of place. Well,

it's as though I were confessing to Father Zosima, that's just it. I called you a monk just now. Well, that poor young man, your friend, Rakitin (Mercy on us! I can't be angry with him. I feel cross, but not very), in a word, that frivolous young man, would you believe it, seems to have taken it into his head to fall in love with me. I only noticed it later, later. At first — that is, a month ago — he began to come oftener to see me, almost every day; though, of course, we were acquainted before. I knew nothing about it . . . and suddenly it dawned upon me, and I began to notice things with surprise. You know, two months ago, that modest, charming, excellent young man, Pyotr Ilyich Perhotin, who's in the service here, began to be a regular visitor at the house. You've met him here ever so many times yourself. And he is a worthy, earnest young man, isn't he? He comes once every three days, not every day (though I should be glad to see him every day), and always so well dressed. Altogether, I love young people, Alyosha, talented, modest, like you, and he has almost the mind of a statesman, he talks so charmingly, and I shall certainly, certainly try and get promotion for him. He is a future diplomat. On that awful day he almost saved me from death by coming in the night. And your friend Rakitin comes in such boots, and always stretches them out on the carpet. . . . In a word, he began hinting at his feelings, in fact, and one day, as he was going, he squeezed my hand terribly hard. My foot began to swell directly after he pressed my hand like that. He had met Pyotr Ilyich here before, and, would you believe it, he is always gibing at him, growling at him, for some reason. I simply looked at the way they went on together and laughed inwardly. So I was sitting here alone

— no, I was laid up then. Well, I was lying here alone and suddenly Rakitin comes in, and only fancy! brought me some verses of his own composition — a short poem, on my bad foot: that is, he described my foot in a poem. Wait a minute — how did it go?

*This little foot, for heaven's sake!*
*Has suddenly commenced to ache.*

It began somehow like that. I can never remember poetry. I've got it here. I'll show it to you later. But it's a charming thing — charming; and, you know, it's not only about the foot, it had a good moral, too, a charming idea, only I've forgotten it; in fact, it was just the thing for an album. So, of course, I thanked him, and he was obviously flattered. I'd hardly had time to thank him when in comes Pyotr Ilyich, and Rakitin suddenly looked as black as night. I could see that Pyotr Ilyich was in the way, for Rakitin certainly wanted to say something after giving me the verses. I had a presentiment of it; but Pyotr Ilyich came in. I showed Pyotr Ilyich the verses and didn't say who was the author. But I am convinced that he guessed, though he won't own it to this day, and declares he had no idea. But he says that on purpose. Pyotr Ilyich began to laugh at once, and fell to criticising it. 'Wretched doggerel,' he said it was, 'some divinity student must have written it,' and with such vehemence, such vehemence! Then, instead of laughing, your friend flew into a rage. 'Good gracious!' I thought, 'they'll fly at each other.' 'It was I who wrote it,' said he. 'I wrote it as a joke,' he said, 'for I think it degrading to write verses. . . . But they are good poetry. They want to put a monument to your Pushkin for writing about women's feet, while I wrote with a moral pur-

pose, and you,' said he, 'are an advocate of serfdom. You've no humane ideas,' said he. 'You have no modern, enlightened feelings, you are uninfluenced by progress, you are a mere official,' he said, 'and you take bribes.' Then I began screaming and imploring them. And, you know, Pyotr Ilyich is anything but a coward. He at once took up the most gentlemanly tone, looked at him sarcastically, listened, and apologised. 'I'd no idea,' said he. 'I shouldn't have said it, if I had known. I should have praised it. Poets are all so irritable,' he said. In short, he laughed at him under cover of the most gentlemanly tone. He explained to me afterwards that it was all sarcastic. I thought he was in earnest. Only as I lay there, just as before you now, I thought, would it, or would it not, be the proper thing for me to turn Rakitin out for shouting so rudely at a visitor in my house? And, would you believe it, I lay here, shut my eyes, and wondered, would it be the proper thing or not, and I couldn't decide, and I kept worrying and worrying, and my heart began to beat, and I couldn't make up my mind whether to make an outcry or not. One voice seemed to be telling me, 'Cry out,' and the other, 'No, don't cry out.' And no sooner had the second voice said that than I cried out, and fainted. Of course, there was a fuss. I got up suddenly and said to Rakitin, 'It's painful for me to say it, but I don't wish to see you in my house again.' So I turned him out. Ah! Alexey Fyodorovich, I know myself I did wrong. I was putting it on. I wasn't angry with him at all really; but I suddenly fancied — that was what did it — that it would be such a fine scene. . . . And yet, believe me, it was quite natural, for I really shed tears and cried for several days afterwards, and then suddenly, one afternoon,

446

I forgot all about it. So it's a fortnight since he's stopped coming, and I kept wondering whether he would come again. I wondered even yesterday, then suddenly last night came this issue of *Rumour*. I read it and gasped. Who could have written it? He must have written it. He went home, sat down, wrote it on the spot, sent it, and they printed it. It was a fortnight ago, you see. But, Alyosha, it's awful how I keep talking and don't say what I want to say. Ah! the words come of themselves!"

"It's very important for me to be in time to see my brother to-day," Alyosha faltered.

"To be sure, to be sure! You bring it all back to me. Listen, what is an aberration?"

"What aberration?" asked Alyosha, wondering.

"In the legal sense. An aberration in which everything is pardonable. Whatever you do, you will be acquitted at once."

"What do you mean?"

"I'll tell you. This Katya . . . Ah! she is a charming, charming creature, only I never can make out who it is she is in love with. She was with me some time ago and I couldn't get anything out of her. Especially as she won't talk to me except superficially now. She is always talking about my health and nothing else, and she takes such a tone with me, too. I simply said to myself, 'Well, so be it. I don't care.' . . . Oh, yes. I was talking of aberration. This doctor has come. You know a doctor has come? Of course you know it — the one who discovers madmen. You sent for him. No, it wasn't you, but Katya. It's all Katya's doing. Well, you see, a man may be sitting there perfectly sane and suddenly have an aberration. He may be conscious and know what he is doing and yet be in a state of aberration. And

there's no doubt that Dmitri Fyodorovich had an aberration. They found out about aberration as soon as the law courts were reformed. It's all the good effect of the reformed law courts. The doctor has been here and questioned me about that evening, about the goldmines. 'How did he seem then?' he asked me. He must have been in a state of aberration. He came in shouting, 'Money, money, three thousand! Give me three thousand!' and then went away and immediately committed the murder. 'I don't want to kill,' he said, 'I don't want to,' and he suddenly went and killed. That's why they'll acquit him, because he resisted the impulse and yet killed."

"But he didn't kill," Alyosha interrupted rather sharply. He was increasingly overcome by anxiety and impatience.

"I know, it was that old man Grigory committed the murder."

"Grigory?" cried Alyosha.

"Yes, yes; it was Grigory. He lay where Dmitri Fyodorovich struck him down, and then got up, saw the door open, went in and killed Fyodor Pavlovich."

"But why, why?"

"Got an aberration. When he recovered from the blow Dmitri Fyodorovich gave him on the head, he got an aberration: then he went and killed. As for his saying he didn't, he very likely doesn't remember. Only, you know, it'll be better, ever so much better, if Dmitri Fyodorovich committed the murder. And that's how it must have been, though I say it was Grigory. It certainly was Dmitri Fyodorovich, and that's better, ever so much better! Oh! not better that a son should have killed his father, I don't admire that. On the contrary, children ought to honour their parents, and yet it would be better if it were he, as you'd have nothing to cry over then, for he did it when he was unconscious or rather when he was conscious, but did not know what he was doing. Let them acquit him — that's so humane, and would show what a blessing reformed law courts are. I knew nothing about it, but they say they have been so a long time. And when I heard it yesterday, I was so struck by it that I wanted to send for you at once. And if he is acquitted, make him come straight from the law courts to dinner with me, and I'll have a party of friends, and we'll drink to the reformed law courts. I don't believe he'd be dangerous; besides, I'll invite a great many friends, so that he could always be led out if he did anything. And then he might be made a justice of the peace or something in another town, for those who have been in trouble themselves make the best judges. And, besides, who isn't suffering from aberration nowadays? — you, I, all of us are in a state of aberration, and there are ever so many examples of it: a man sits singing a song, suddenly something annoys him, he takes a pistol and shoots the first person he comes across, and no one blames him for it. I read that lately, and all the doctors confirm it. Nowadays doctors are always confirming; they confirm anything. Why, my Lise is in a state of aberration. She made me cry again yesterday, and the day before, too, and to-day I suddenly realised that it's all due to aberration. Oh, Lise grieves me so! I believe she's quite mad. Why did she send for you? Did she send for you or did you come of yourself?"

"Yes, she sent for me, and I am going to her directly." Alyosha got up resolutely.

"Oh, my dear, dear Alexey Fyodorovich, perhaps that's what's most important," Madame Hohlakov cried, suddenly bursting into tears. "God knows I trust Lise to you with all my heart, and it's no matter her sending for you on the sly, without telling her mother. But forgive me, I can't trust my daughter so easily to your brother Ivan Fyodorovich, though I still consider him the most chivalrous young man. But only fancy, he's been to see Lise and I knew nothing about it!"

"How? What? When?" Alyosha was terribly surprised. He had not sat down again and listened standing.

"I will tell you, that's perhaps why I asked you to come, for I don't know now why I did ask you to come. Well, Ivan Fyodorovich has been to see me twice, since he came back from Moscow. First time he came as a friend to call on me, and the second time Katya was here and he came because he heard she was here. I didn't, of course, expect him to come often, knowing what a lot he has to do as it is, *vous comprenez, cette affaire et la mort terrible de votre papa*. But I suddenly heard he'd been here again, not to see me but to see Lise. That's six days ago now. He came, stayed five minutes, and went away. And I didn't hear of it till three days afterwards, from Glafira, so it was a great shock to me. I sent for Lise directly. She laughed. 'He thought you were asleep,' she said, 'and came in to me to ask after your health.' Of course, that's how it happened. But Lise, Lise, mercy on us, how she distresses me! Would you believe it, one night, four days ago, just after you saw her last, and had gone away, she suddenly had a fit, screaming, shrieking hysterics! Why is it I never have hysterics? Then next day another fit and the same thing on the third, and yesterday, too, and then yesterday that aberration. She suddenly screamed out, 'I hate Ivan Fyodorovich. I demand that you do not receive him, that you refuse him the house.' I was struck dumb at these amazing words, and answered, 'On what grounds could I refuse to see such an excellent young man, a young man of such learning, too, and so unfortunate,' for all this business is a misfortune, isn't it? She suddenly burst out laughing at my words, and so rudely, you know. Well, I was pleased, I thought I had amused her and the fits would pass off, especially as I wanted to refuse to see Ivan Fyodorovich anyway on account of his strange visits without my consent, and meant to ask him for an explanation. But early this morning Lise waked up and flew into a passion with Yulia and, would you believe it, slapped her in the face. That's monstrous, I am always polite to my servants. And an hour later she was hugging and kissing Yulia's feet. She sent a message to me, that she wasn't coming to me at all, and would never come and see me again, and when I dragged myself down to her, she rushed to kiss me, crying, and, as she kissed me, she pushed me out of the room without saying a word, so I couldn't find out what was the matter. Now, dear Alexey Fyodorovich, I rest all my hopes on you, and, of course, my whole life is in your hands. I simply beg you to go to Lise and find out everything from her, as you alone can, and come back and tell me — me, her mother, for you understand it will be the death of me, simply the death of me, if this goes on, or else I shall run away from the house. I can stand no more. I have patience; but I may lose it, and then . . . then something awful will happen. Ah, dear me! At last, Pyotr Ilyich!" cried Madame Hohlakov, beaming all over as she saw Perhotin enter the room. "You are late, you are late! Well, sit down, speak, put us out of suspense. What does the counsel say? Where are you off to, Alexey Fyodorovich?"

"To Lise."

"Oh, yes. You won't forget, you won't forget what I asked you? It's a question of life and death!"

"Of course, I won't forget, if I can . . . but I am so late," muttered Alyosha, beating a hasty retreat.

"No, be sure, be sure to come in; don't say 'if you can.' I shall die if you don't," Madame Hohlakov called after him, but Alyosha had already left the room.

## CHAPTER III
### THE IMP

GOING in to Lise, he found her half reclining in the invalid chair, in which she had been wheeled when she was unable to walk. She did not move to meet him, but her sharp keen eyes simply bored into his face. There was a feverish look in her eyes, her face was pale and yellow. Alyosha was amazed at the change that had taken place in her in three days. She was positively thinner. She did not hold out her hand to him. He touched the thin, long fingers which lay motionless on her dress, then he sat down facing her, without a word.

"I know you are in a hurry to get to the prison," Lise said curtly, "and mamma's kept you there for hours, she's just been telling you about me and Yulia."

"How do you know?" asked Alyosha.

"I've been eavesdropping. Why do you stare at me? I want to eavesdrop and I do eavesdrop, there's nothing bad about that. I don't apologise."

"You are upset about something?"

"On the contrary, I am very happy. I've only just been reflecting for the thirtieth time what a good thing it is I refused you and shall not be your wife. You are not fit to be a husband. If I were to marry you and give you a note to take to the man I loved after you, you'd take it and be sure to give it to him and bring an answer back, too. If you were forty, you would still go on carrying my love-letters for me."

She suddenly laughed.

"There is something spiteful and yet open-hearted about you." Alyosha smiled at her.

"The open-heartedness consists in my not being ashamed before you. What's more, I don't want to feel ashamed before you, just before you. Alyosha, why is it I don't respect you? I am very fond of you, but I don't respect you. If I respected you, I shouldn't talk to you without shame, should I?"

"No."

"But do you believe that I am not ashamed before you?"

"No, I don't believe it."

Lise laughed nervously again; she spoke rapidly.

"I sent some sweets to your brother, Dmitri Fyodorovich, in prison. Alyosha, you know, you are very handsome! I shall love you awfully for having so quickly allowed me not to love you."

"Why did you send for me to-day, Lise?"

"I wanted to tell you of a desire I have. I should like some one to torture me, marry me and then torture me, deceive me and go away. I don't want to be happy."

"You are in love with disorder?"

"Yes, I want disorder. I keep wanting to set fire to the house. I keep imagining how I'll creep up and set fire to the house on the sly, it must be on the sly. They'll try to put it out, but it'll go on burning. And I shall know and say nothing. Ah, what silliness! And how bored I am!"

She waved her hand with a look of repulsion.

"It's your luxurious life," said Alyosha softly.

"Is it better then to be poor?"

"Yes, it is better."

"That's what your deceased monk taught you. That's not true. Let me be rich and all the rest poor. I'll eat sweets and drink cream and not give any to any one else. Ah, don't speak, don't say anything," she shook her hand at him, though Alyosha had not opened his mouth. "You've told me all that before, I know it all by heart. It bores me. If I am ever poor, I shall murder somebody, and even if I am rich, I may murder some one, perhaps — why do nothing? But do you know, I should like to reap, reap rye? I'll marry you, and you shall become a peasant, a real peasant; we'll keep a colt, shall we? Do you know Kalganov?"

"Yes."

"He is always wandering about, dreaming. He says, why endure real life, it's better to dream. One can dream the jolliest things, but real life is a bore. But he'll be married soon for all that, he's been making love to me already. Can you spin tops?"

"Yes."

"Well, he's just like a top: he wants to be wound up and set spinning and then to be lashed, lashed, lashed with a whip. If I marry him, I'll keep him spinning all his life. You are not ashamed to be with me?"

"No."

"You are awfully cross, because I don't talk about holy things. I don't want to be holy. What will they do to one in the next world for the greatest sin? You must know all about that."

"God will condemn you." Alyosha was watching her steadily.

"That's just what I should like. I would go up and they would condemn me and I would burst out laughing in their faces. I should dreadfully like to set fire to the house, Alyosha, to our house, you still don't believe me?"

"Why not? There are children twelve years old who have a longing to set fire to something and they do set things on fire, too. It's a sort of disease."

"That's not true, that's not true, there may be children like that, but that's not what I mean."

"You mistake evil for good; it's a passing crisis, it's the result of your illness, perhaps."

"You do despise me though! It's simply that I don't want to do good, I want to do evil, and it has nothing to do with illness."

"Why do evil?"

"So that nothing may be left anywhere. Ah, how nice it would be if nothing were left anywhere! You know, Alyosha, I sometimes think of doing a fearful lot of harm and everything bad, and I should do it for a long while on the sly and suddenly every one would find it out. All would stand round and point their fingers at me and I would look at them all. That would be very pleasant. Why would it be so pleasant, Alyosha?"

"Just so. It's a craving to destroy something good or, as you say, to set fire to something. It happens sometimes."

"I not only say it, I shall do it."

"I believe you."

"Ah, how I love you for saying you believe me. And you are not lying one little bit. But perhaps you think that I am saying all this on purpose to tease you?"

"No, I don't think that . . . though per-

haps there is a little desire to do that in it, too."

"There is a little. I never can tell lies to you," she declared, with a strange fire in her eyes.

What struck Alyosha above everything was her earnestness. There was not a trace of humour or jesting in her face now, though, formerly, fun and gaiety had never deserted her even at her most "earnest" moments.

"There are moments when people love crime," said Alyosha thoughtfully.

"Yes, yes! You have uttered my thought, they love crime, every one loves crime, they love it always, not at some 'moments.' You know, it's as though people long ago made an agreement to lie about it and have lied about it ever since. They all say that they hate evil, but secretly they all love it."

"And are you still reading nasty books?"

"Yes, I am. Mamma reads them and hides them under her pillow and I steal them."

"Aren't you ashamed to destroy yourself?"

"I want to destroy myself. There's a boy here who lay down between the rails when the train was passing. Lucky fellow! Listen, your brother is being tried now for murdering his father and every one loves his having killed his father."

"Loves his having killed his father?"

"Yes, loves it, every one loves it! Everybody says it's awful, but secretly they simply love it. I for one love it."

"There is some truth in what you say about every one," said Alyosha softly.

"Oh, what ideas you have!" Lise shrieked with delight. "And you a monk, too! You wouldn't believe how I respect you, Alyosha, for never telling lies. Oh, I must tell you a funny dream of mine. I sometimes dream of devils. It's night, I am in my room with a candle and suddenly there are devils all over the place, in all the corners, under the table, and they open the doors, there's a crowd of them behind the doors and they want to come and seize me. And they are just coming, just seizing me. But I suddenly cross myself and they all draw back, afraid, though they don't go away altogether, they stand at the doors and in the corners, waiting. And suddenly I have a frightful longing to revile God aloud, and so I begin, and then they come crowding back to me, delighted, and seize me again and I cross myself again and they all draw back. It's awful fun, it takes one's breath away."

"I've had the same dream, too," said Alyosha suddenly.

"Really?" cried Lise, surprised. "I say, Alyosha, don't laugh, that's awfully important. Could two different people have the same dream?"

"It seems they can."

"Alyosha, I tell you, it's awfully important," Lise went on, with really excessive amazement. "It's not the dream that's important, but your having the same dream as I. You never lie to me, don't lie now: is it true? You are not laughing?"

"It's true."

Lise seemed extraordinarily impressed and for half a minute she was silent.

"Alyosha, come and see me, come and see me more often," she said suddenly, in a supplicating voice.

"I'll always come to see you, all my life," answered Alyosha firmly.

"You are the only person I can talk to, you know," Lise began again. "I talk to no one but myself and you. Only you in the whole world. And to you more readily than to myself. And

I am not a bit ashamed before you, not a bit. Alyosha, why am I not ashamed before you, not a bit? Alyosha, is it true that at Easter the Jews steal children and slaughter them?"

"I don't know."

"There's a book here in which I read about the trial of a Jew, who took a four-year-old boy and cut off the fingers from both hands, and then crucified him on the wall, hammered nails into him and crucified him, and afterwards, when he was tried, he said that the child died soon, within four hours. That was 'soon'! He said the child moaned, kept on moaning, and he stood gloating over it. That's good!"

"Good?"

"Good. I sometimes imagine that it was I who did the crucifying. He would hang there moaning and I would sit opposite him eating pineapple compote. I am awfully fond of pineapple compote. Do you like it?"

Alyosha looked at her in silence. Her pale, sallow face was suddenly contorted, her eyes burned.

"You know, after I read about that Jew I shook with sobs all night. I kept fancying how the little thing cried and moaned (a child four years old understands, you know) and all the while the thought of pineapple compote haunted me. In the morning I wrote a letter to a certain person, begging him to come and see me *without fail*. He came and I suddenly told him all about the boy and the pineapple compote. *All* about it, *all*, and said that it was good. He laughed and said it really was good. Then he got up and went away. He was here only five minutes. Did he despise me? Did he? Tell me, tell me, Alyosha, did he despise me or not?" She sat up on the couch, with flashing eyes.

452

THE IMP

"Tell me," Alyosha asked anxiously, "did you send for that person yourself?"

"Myself."

"Did you send him a letter?"

"Yes."

"Simply to ask about that, about that child?"

"No, not about that at all. But when he came, I asked him about that at once. He answered, laughed, got up and went away."

"That person behaved honourably," Alyosha murmured.

"And did he despise me? Did he laugh at me?"

"No, for perhaps he believes in the pine-apple compote himself. He is very ill now, too, Lise."

"Yes, he does believe in it," said Lise, with flashing eyes.

"He doesn't despise any one," Alyosha went on. "Only he does not believe any one. If he doesn't believe in people, of course, he does despise them."

"Then he despises me, me?"

"You, too."

"That's good." Lise seemed to grind her teeth. "When he went out laughing, I felt that it was good to be despised. The boy with his fingers cut off is good and to be despised is good. . . ."

And she laughed in Alyosha's face, a feverish, malicious laugh.

"Do you know, Alyosha, do you know, I should like . . . Alyosha save me!" She suddenly jumped from the couch, rushed to him and seized him with both hands. "Save me!" she almost groaned. "Is there any one in the world I could tell what I've told you? I've told you the truth, the truth. I shall kill myself, because I loathe everything! I don't want

to live, because I loathe everything! I loathe everything, everything. Alyosha, why don't you love me in the least?" she finished in a frenzy.

"But I do love you!" answered Alyosha hotly.

"And will you weep over me, will you?"

"Yes."

"Not because I won't be your wife, but simply weep for me?"

"Yes."

"Thank you! It's only your tears I want. Every one else may punish me and trample me under foot, every one, every one, not excepting *any one*. For I don't love any one. Do you hear, not any one! On the contrary, I hate them! Go, Alyosha, it's time you went to your brother." She tore herself away from him suddenly.

"How can I leave you like this?" said Alyosha, almost in alarm.

"Go to your brother, the prison will be shut, go, here's your hat. Kiss Mitya, go, go!"

And she almost forcibly pushed Alyosha out the door. He looked at her with pained surprise, when he was suddenly aware of a letter in his right hand, a tiny letter folded up tight and sealed. He glanced at it and instantly read the address "To Ivan Fyodorovich Karamazov." He looked quickly at Lise. Her face had become almost menacing.

"Give it to him, give it to him without fail!" she ordered him, trembling and beside herself. "To-day, at once, or I'll poison myself! That's why I sent for you."

And she slammed the door quickly. The bolt clicked. Alyosha put the note in his pocket and went straight downstairs, without going back to Madame Hohlakov, forgetting her, in fact. As soon as Alyosha had gone, Lise unbolted the door, opened it a little, put her finger in the crack and slammed the door with all her might, pinching her finger. Ten seconds after, releasing her hand, she walked softly, slowly to her chair, sat up straight in it and looked intently at her blackened finger and at the blood that oozed from under the nail. Her lips were quivering and she kept whispering rapidly to herself:

"I am vile, vile, vile, vile!"

## CHAPTER IV
### A HYMN AND A SECRET

It was quite late (days are short in November) when Alyosha rang at the prison gate. Already dusk was falling. But Alyosha knew that he would be admitted without difficulty. Things were managed in our little town, as everywhere else. At first, of course, on the conclusion of the preliminary inquiry, relatives and a few other persons could obtain interviews with Mitya only by going through certain inevitable formalities. But later, though the formalities were not relaxed, exceptions were made for some, at least, of Mitya's visitors. So much so, that sometimes the interviews with the prisoner in the room set aside for the purpose were practically *tête-à-tête*.

Exceptions, however, were made for only a few, namely, Grushenka, Alyosha, and Rakitin. But the captain of the police, Mihail Mihailovich, was very favourably disposed towards Grushenka. His abuse of her at Mokroye weighed on the old man's conscience, and when he learned the whole story, he completely changed his view of her. And, strange to say, though he was firmly persuaded of Mitya's guilt, yet, after the latter was once in prison, the old man came to take a more and more lenient view of him. "He was a man of good heart, perhaps," he thought, "who had come to grief through drinking and dissipation." His first horror had been succeeded by pity. As for Alyosha, the police captain was very fond of him and had known him for a long time. Rakitin, who had of late taken to coming very often to see the prisoner, was one of the most intimate acquaintances of the "police captain's young ladies," as he called them, and was always hanging about their house. Also, he gave lessons in the house of the prison superintendent, who, though scrupulous in the performance of his duties, was a kind-hearted old man. Again, Alyosha had an intimate acquaintance of long standing with the superintendent, who was fond of talking to him, generally on edifying subjects. He respected Ivan Fyodorovich, and, indeed, stood in awe of his opinions, though he was a great philosopher himself; a "homespun" one, of course. But Alyosha had an irresistible attraction for him. During the last year the old man had taken to studying the Apocryphal Gospels, and constantly talked over his impressions with his young friend. He used to come to see him in the monastery and argued for hours together with him and with the monks. So even if Alyosha was late at the prison, he had only to go to the superintendent and everything was made easy. Besides, every one in the prison, down to the humblest watchman, had grown used to Alyosha. The sentry, of course, did not trouble him so long as the authorities were satisfied.

When Mitya was summoned from his cell, he always went downstairs, to the place set aside for interviews. As Alyosha entered the room he came upon Rakitin, who was just taking leave of Mitya. They were both talking loudly. Mitya was laughing heartily as

XI: BROTHER IVAN FYODOROVICH

he saw him out, while Rakitin seemed grumbling. Rakitin did not like meeting Alyosha, especially of late. He scarcely spoke to him, and bowed to him stiffly. Seeing Alyosha enter now, he frowned more than usual and looked away, as though he were entirely absorbed in buttoning his big, warm, fur-trimmed overcoat. Then he began looking at once for his umbrella.

"I must mind not to forget my belongings," he muttered, simply to say something.

"Mind you don't forget other people's belongings," said Mitya, as a joke, and laughed at once at his own wit. Rakitin fired up instantly.

"You'd better give that advice to your own family, who've always been a serf-owning lot, and not to Rakitin," he cried, suddenly trembling with anger.

"What's the matter? I was joking," cried Mitya. "Damn it all! They are all like that," he turned to Alyosha, nodding towards Rakitin's hurriedly retreating figure. "He was sitting here, laughing and cheerful, and all at once he boils up like that. He didn't even nod to you. Have you broken with him completely? Why are you so late? I've not been simply waiting, but thirsting for you the whole morning. But never mind. We'll make up for it now."

"Why does he come here so often? Surely you are not such great friends?" asked Alyosha. He, too, nodded at the door through which Rakitin had disappeared.

"Great friends with Rakitin? No, not as much as that. Is it likely — a pig like that? He considers I am . . . a blackguard. They can't understand a joke either, that's the worst of such people. They never understand a joke, and their souls are dry, dry and flat; they re-

mind me of prison walls when I was first brought here. But he is a clever fellow, very clever. Well, Alexey, it's all over with me now."

He sat down on the bench and made Alyosha sit down beside him.

"Yes, the trial's to-morrow. Are you so hopeless, brother?" Alyosha said, with an apprehensive feeling.

"What are you talking about?" said Mitya, looking at him rather uncertainly. "Oh, you mean the trial! Damn it all! Till now we've been talking of things that don't matter, about this trial, but I haven't said a word to you about the chief thing. Yes, the trial is to-morrow; but it wasn't the trial I meant, when I said it was all over with me. Why do you look at me so critically?"

"What do you mean, Mitya?"

"Ideas, ideas, that's all! Ethics! What is ethics?"

"Ethics?" asked Alyosha, wondering.

"Yes; is it a science?"

"Yes, there is such a science . . . but . . . I confess I can't explain to you what sort of science it is."

"Rakitin knows. Rakitin knows a lot, damn him! He's not going to be a monk. He means to go to Petersburg. There he'll go in for criticism of an elevating tendency. Who knows, he may be of use and make his own career, too. Ugh! they are first-rate, these people, at making a career! Damn ethics. I am done for, Alexey, I am, you man of God! I love you more than any one. It makes my heart quake to look at you. Who was Karl Bernard?"

"Karl Bernard?" Alyosha was surprised again.

"No, not Karl. Wait, I made a mistake.

Claude Bernard. What was he? Chemist or what?"

"He must be a savant," answered Alyosha; "but I confess I can't tell you much about him, either. I've heard of him as a savant, but what sort I don't know."

"Well, damn him, then! I don't know either," Mitya cursed. "A scoundrel of some sort, most likely. They are all scoundrels. And Rakitin will make his way. Rakitin will get on anywhere; he is another Bernard. Ugh, these Bernards! They are all over the place."

"But what is the matter?" Alyosha asked insistently.

"He wants to write an article about me, about my case, and so begin his literary career. That's what he comes for; he said so himself. He wants to prove some theory. He wants to say 'he couldn't help murdering his father, he was corrupted by his environment,' and so on. He explained it all to me. He is going to put in a tinge of socialism, he says. But there, damn the fellow, he can put in a tinge, if he likes, I don't care. He can't bear Ivan, he hates him. He's not fond of you, either. But I don't turn him out, for he is a clever fellow. Awfully conceited though. I said to him just now, 'The Karamazovs are not blackguards, but philosophers; for all true Russians are philosophers, and though you've studied, you are not a philosopher — you are a churl.' He laughed, so maliciously. And I said to him, *de thoughtibus non est disputandum.*' Isn't that rather good? I, too, can set up for being a classical scholar, you see!" Mitya laughed suddenly.

"Why is it all over with you? You said so just now," Alyosha interposed.

"Why is it all over with me? H'm! . . . The fact of it is . . . if you take it as a whole, I am sorry to lose God — that's what it is."

"What do you mean by 'sorry to lose God'?"

"Imagine: inside, in the nerves, in the head — that is, these nerves are there in the brain . . . (damn them!) — there are sort of little tails, the little tails of those nerves, and as soon as they begin quivering . . . that is, you see, I look at something with my eyes and then they begin quivering, those little tails . . . and when they quiver, then an image appears . . . it doesn't appear at once, but an instant, a second, passes . . . and then something like a moment appears; that is, not a moment — devil take the moment! — but an image; that is, an object, or a happening, damn it! That's why I see and then think, because of those tails, not at all because I've got a soul, and that I am some sort of image and likeness. All that is nonsense! Rakitin explained it all to me yesterday, brother, and it simply bowled me over. It's magnificent, Alyosha, this science! A new man's arising — that I understand. . . . And yet I am sorry to lose God!"

"Well, that's a good thing, anyway," said Alyosha.

"That I am sorry to lose God? It's chemistry, brother, chemistry! There's no help for it, your reverence, you must make way for chemistry. And Rakitin does dislike God. Ugh! doesn't he dislike Him! That's the sore point with all of them. But they conceal it. They tell lies. They pretend. 'Will you preach this in your reviews?' I asked him. 'Oh, well, if I did it openly, they wouldn't let it through,' he said. He laughed. 'But what will become of men then?' I asked him, 'without God and the hereafter? In that case everything is lawful now, one can do everything?' 'Didn't you know it?' he said, laughing, 'a clever man can do what he likes,' he said. 'A clever man knows his way about, but you committed a murder and got in bad, and now you are rotting in prison.' He says that to my face! A regular swine! I used to kick such people out, but now I listen to them. He talks a lot of sense, too. And he writes cleverly. He began reading me an article last week. I copied out three lines of it. Wait a minute. Here it is."

Mitya hurriedly pulled out a piece of paper from his vest-pocket and read:

" 'In order to settle this question, it is above all essential to place one's personality counter to one's reality.' Do you understand that?"

"No, I don't," said Alyosha. He looked at Mitya and listened to him with curiosity.

"I don't understand either. It's dark and obscure, but intellectual. 'Every one writes like that now,' he says, 'it's the effect of their environment.' They are afraid of the environment. He writes poetry, too, the rascal. He's celebrated Madame Hohlakov's foot. Ha, ha, ha!"

"I've heard about it," said Alyosha.

"And have you heard the poem?"

"No."

"I've got it. Here it is. I'll read it to you. You don't know — I haven't told you — there's quite a story about it. The rogue! Three weeks ago he began to tease me. 'You've got yourself into a mess, like a fool, for the sake of three thousand, but I'm going to collar a hundred and fifty thousand. I am going to marry a widow and buy a stone house in Petersburg.' And he told me he was courting Madame Hohlakov. She hadn't much brains in her youth, and now at forty she had lost what she had. 'But she's awfully sentimental,' he says; 'that's how I shall get hold of her. When I marry her, I shall take her to Peters-

burg and there I shall start a newspaper.' And his mouth was simply watering, the beast, not for the widow, but for the hundred and fifty thousand. And he made me believe it. He came to see me every day. 'She is coming round,' he declared. He was beaming with delight. And then, all of a sudden, he was turned out of the house. Perhotin's carrying everything before him, bravo! I could kiss the silly old noodle for turning him out of the house. And he had written this doggerel. 'It's the first time I've soiled my hands with writing poetry,' he said. 'It's for the sake of seduction, so it's in a useful cause. When I get hold of the silly woman's fortune, I can be a great civic utility.' They have this civic justification for every nasty thing they do! 'Anyway it's better than your Pushkin's poetry,' he said, 'for I've managed to inject civic feeling even in that.' I understand what he means about Pushkin, I quite see that, if he really was a man of talent and yet wrote only about women's feet. But wasn't Rakitin stuck up about his doggerel! The vanity of these fellows! 'Lines on the recovery of the swollen foot of the object of my affections' — he thought of that for a title. The wag!

*A captivating little foot,*
*Though swollen, red and tender!*
*The doctors come and plasters put,*
*But still they cannot mend her.*

*Yet 'tis not for her feet I pine —*
*A theme for Pushkin, not for me —*
*I fear to note the sad decline*
*Of intellectuality!*

*For as her foot swells, strange to say,*
*Her intellect is on the wane —*
*Oh, for some remedy I pray*
*That may restore both foot and brain!*

457

He is a swine, a regular swine, but he's very arch, the rascal! And he really has put in a civic idea. And wasn't he angry when she kicked him out! He was gnashing his teeth!"

"He's taken his revenge already," said Alyosha. "He's gotten a notice published about Madame Hohlakov."

And Alyosha told him briefly about the notice in *Rumour*.

"That's his doing, that's his doing!" Mitya assented, frowning. "That's him! These notices . . . I know . . . the nasty things that have been written about Grushenka, for instance. . . . And about the other one, about Katya, too. . . . H'm!"

He walked across the room with a harassed air.

"Brother, I cannot stay long," Alyosha said, after a pause. "To-morrow will be a great and awful day for you, the judgment of God will be accomplished . . . I am amazed at you, you walk about here, talking of I don't know what . . ."

"No, don't be amazed at me," Mitya broke in hotly. "Am I to talk of that stinking dog? Of the murderer? We've talked enough of him. I don't want to say more of the stinking son of Stinking Lizaveta! God will kill him, you will see. Hush!"

He went up to Alyosha excitedly and kissed him. His eyes glowed.

"Rakitin wouldn't understand it," he began in a sort of exaltation; "but you, you'll understand it all. That's why I was thirsting for you. You see, there's so much I've been wanting to tell you for ever so long, here, within these peeling walls, but I haven't said a word about what matters most; it was as though the time hadn't come. Now I need wait no longer. I must pour out my heart to you.

Brother, these last two months I've felt a new man within me. A new man has risen up in me. He was hidden in me, but would never have come to the surface, if it hadn't been for this blow from heaven. It's fearful! And what do I care if I spend twenty years in the mines, hammering out the ore? I am not a bit afraid of that — it's something else I am afraid of now: that that new man may leave me. Even there, in the mines, underground, I may find a human heart in another convict and murderer by my side, and I may make friends with him, for even there one may live and love and suffer. One may arouse and revive in that convict a lifeless heart, one may wait upon him for years, and at last bring up from the dark depths a lofty soul, a feeling, suffering creature; one may revive an angel, raise up a hero! There are so many of them, hundreds of them, and we are all to blame for them. Why was it I dreamed that 'babe' at such a moment? 'Why is the babe so poor?' That was a prophecy to me at that moment. It's for the babe I will go. Because we are all responsible for all. For all the 'babes,' for there are big children as well as little children. All are 'babes.' I go for all, because some one must go for all. I didn't kill father, but I've got to go. I accept it. It's all come to me here, here, within these peeling walls. There are numbers of them there, hundreds of them underground, with hammers in their hands. Oh, yes, we shall be in chains and there will be no freedom, but then, in our great sorrow, we shall rise again to joy, without which man cannot live nor God exist, for God gives joy: it's His privilege — a great one. Lord, let man be dissolved in prayer! How shall I exist there underground without God? Rakitin's lying! If they drive God from the earth, we shall shelter

Him underground. A convict cannot exist without God; it's even more impossible for him than for those who are not convicts. And then we men underground will raise from the bowels of the earth a tragic hymn to God, with Whom is joy. Hail to God and His joy! I love Him!"

Mitya was almost gasping for breath as he uttered his wild speech. He turned pale, his lips quivered, and tears rolled down his cheeks.

"No, life is full, there is life even underground," he began again. "You wouldn't believe, Alexey, how I want to live now, what a thirst for existence and consciousness has sprung up in me within these peeling walls. Rakitin doesn't understand that; all he cares about is building a house and letting flats. But I've been longing for you. And what is suffering? I am not afraid of it, even if it were beyond reckoning. I am not afraid of it now. I was afraid of it before. Do you know, perhaps I won't answer at the trial at all. . . . And I seem to have such strength in me now, that I think I could stand anything, any suffering, only to be able to say and to repeat to myself every moment, 'I am.' In thousands of agonies — I am. I'm tormented on the rack — but I am! Though I sit alone in a dungeon — I am! I see the sun, and if I don't see the sun, I know it's there. And to know that the sun is there, why, that's all of life. Alyosha, my angel, all these philosophies are the death of me. Damn them! Brother Ivan . . ."

"What of brother Ivan?" interrupted Alyosha, but Mitya did not hear.

"You see, I never had any of these doubts before, but it was all hidden away in me. It was perhaps just because unrealised ideas were raging up in me, that I used to drink and fight and carry on. It was to quench them in myself, to still them, to smother them. Ivan is not a Rakitin, there is an idea in him. Ivan is a sphinx and is silent; he is always silent. And as for me, God torments me. That's the only thing that's tormenting me. What if He doesn't exist? What if Rakitin's right — that it's an artificial idea produced by mankind? Then, if He doesn't exist, man is the ruler of the earth, of the universe. Magnificent! Only how is he going to be virtuous without God? That's the question. I always come back to that. For, whom is man going to love then? To whom will he be thankful? To whom will he sing the hymn? Rakitin laughs. Rakitin says that one can love humanity without God. Well, only a snivelling idiot can maintain that. I can't understand it. Life's easy for Rakitin. 'You'd better think about the extension of civic rights,' he says to me to-day, 'or even of keeping down the price of meat. You will show your love for humanity more simply and directly by that, than by philosophy.' I answered him, 'Well, but you, without a God, are more likely to raise the price of meat, if it suits you, and make a rouble on every copeck.' He lost his temper. But after all, what is virtue? Answer me that, Alexey. Virtue is one thing with me and another with a Chinaman, so it's a relative thing. Or isn't it? Is it not relative? A treacherous question! You won't laugh if I tell you it's kept me awake two nights. I only wonder now how people can live and think nothing about it. Vanity! Ivan has no God. He has an idea. It's beyond me. But he is silent. I believe he is a freemason. I asked him, but he is silent. I wanted to drink from his spring — he was silent. But once he did drop a word."

"What did he say?" Alyosha took it up quickly.

"I said to him, 'Then everything is lawful, if it is so?' He frowned. 'Fyodor Pavlovich, our papa,' he said, 'was a pig, but he reasoned correctly enough.' That was what he dropped. That was all he said. That was going one better than Rakitin."

"Yes," Alyosha assented bitterly. "When did he come to see you?"

"Of that later, now I must speak of something else. I have said nothing about Ivan to you before. I put it off to the last. When my business here is over and the verdict has been pronounced, then I'll tell you something. I'll tell you everything. We've something terrible on hand. . . . And you shall be my judge in this matter. But don't begin about that now; mum's the word. You talk of to-morrow, of the trial; but, would you believe it, I know nothing about it."

"Have you talked to the counsel?"

"What's the use of the counsel? I told him all about it. He's a soft, city-bred rogue — a Bernard! But he doesn't believe me — not a bit of it. Only imagine, he believes that I killed. I see it. 'In that case,' I asked him, 'why have you come to defend me?' Hang them all! They've got a doctor down, too, want to prove I'm mad. I won't have that! Katerina Ivanovna wants to do her 'duty' to the end, whatever the strain!" Mitya smiled bitterly. "The cat! Hard-hearted creature! She knows that I said of her at Mokroye that she was a woman of 'great wrath.' They repeated it to her. Yes, the facts against me have grown numerous as the sands of the sea. Grigory sticks to his point. Grigory's honest, but a fool. Many people are honest because they are fools: that's Rakitin's idea. Grigory's my enemy. And there are some people whom it's better to have as foes than as friends. I mean Katerina Ivanovna. I am

afraid, oh, I am afraid she will tell how she bowed to the ground after that four thousand five hundred. She'll pay it back to the last farthing. I don't want her sacrifice; they'll put me to shame at the trial. I wonder how I can stand it. Go to her, Alyosha, ask her not to speak of that in court, can't you? But damn it all, it doesn't matter! I shall get through somehow. I don't pity her. It's her own doing. It serves her right. I shall have my own story to tell, Alexey." He smiled bitterly again. "Only . . . only Grusha, Grusha! Good Lord! Why should she have such suffering to bear?" he exclaimed suddenly, with tears. "Grusha's killing me; the thought of her's killing me, killing me. She was here just now . . ."

"She told me she was very much grieved by you to-day."

"I know. Confound my temper! It was jealousy. As she was leaving, I repented, I kissed her. I didn't ask her forgiveness."

"Why didn't you?" exclaimed Alyosha.

Suddenly Mitya laughed almost mirthfully.

"God preserve you, my dear boy, from ever asking forgiveness for a fault from a woman you love. From one you love especially, however greatly you may have been in fault. For a woman — devil only knows what a woman is! I know something about them, anyway. But try acknowledging you are in fault to a woman. Say, 'I am sorry, forgive me,' and a shower of reproaches will follow! Nothing will make her forgive you simply and directly, she'll humble you to the dust, bring forward things that have never happened, recall everything, forget nothing, add something of her own, and only then forgive you. And even the best, the best of them do it. She'll scrape up all the scrapings and load them on your head. They are ready to flay you alive, I tell you, every one of them, all these angels without whom we cannot live! I tell you plainly and openly, dear boy, every decent man ought to be under some woman's thumb. That's my conviction — not conviction, but feeling. A man ought to be magnanimous, and it's no disgrace to a man! No disgrace to a hero, not even a Cæsar! But don't ever beg her pardon all the same for anything. Remember that rule given you by your brother Mitya, who's come to ruin through women. No, I'd better make it up to Grusha somehow, without begging pardon. I worship her, Alexey, worship her. Only she doesn't see it. No, she still thinks I don't love her enough. And she tortures me, tortures me with her love. The past was nothing! In the past it was only those infernal curves of hers that tortured me, but now I've taken all her soul into my soul and through her I've become a man myself. Will they marry us? If they don't, I shall die of jealousy. I imagine something every day. . . . What did she say to you about me?"

Alyosha repeated all Grushenka had said to him that day. Mitya listened, made him repeat things, and seemed pleased.

"Then she is not angry at my being jealous?" he exclaimed. "She is a regular woman! 'I've a fierce heart myself!' Ah, I love such fierce hearts, though I can't bear any one's being jealous of me. I can't endure it. We shall fight. But I shall love her, I shall love her infinitely. Will they marry us? Do they let convicts marry? That's the question. And without her I can't exist . . ."

Mitya walked frowning across the room. It was almost dark. He suddenly seemed terribly worried.

"So there's a secret, she says, a secret? We have got up a plot against her, and Katya is mixed up in it, she thinks. No, my good Grushenka, that's not it. You are very wide of the mark, in your foolish feminine way. Alyosha, darling, well, here goes! I'll tell you our secret!"

He looked round, quickly went close up to Alyosha, who was standing before him, and whispered to him with an air of mystery, though in reality no one could hear them: the old watchman was dozing in the corner, and not a word could reach the ears of the soldiers on guard.

"I will tell you our whole secret," Mitya whispered hurriedly. "I meant to tell you later, for how could I decide on anything without you? You are everything to me. Though I say that Ivan is superior to us, you are my angel. It's your word will decide it. Perhaps it's you who are superior and not Ivan. You see, it's a question of conscience, a question of the higher conscience — the secret is so important that I can't deal with it alone, and I've put it off till I could speak to you. But anyway it's too early to decide now, for we must wait for the verdict. As soon as the verdict is pronounced, you shall decide my fate. Don't decide it now. I'll tell you now. You listen, but don't decide. Stand there and keep quiet. I won't tell you everything. I'll only tell you the idea, without details, and you keep quiet. Not a question, not a movement. You agree? But, Lord, what shall I do with your eyes? I'm afraid your eyes will tell me your decision, even if you don't speak. Oo! I'm afraid! Alyosha, listen! Ivan suggests my *escaping*. I won't tell you the details: it's all been thought out: it can all be arranged. Hush, don't decide. I should go to America with Grusha. You know I can't live without

461

Grusha! What if they won't let her follow me to Siberia? Do they let convicts get married? Ivan thinks not. And without Grusha what should I do there underground with a hammer? I should only smash my head with the hammer! But, on the other hand, my conscience? I should have run away from suffering. A sign was granted, I rejected the sign. There was a way of salvation and I turned my back on it. Ivan says that in America, 'with good inclinations,' one can be of more use than underground. But where then will our underground hymn be? What's America? America is vanity again! And there's a lot of swindling in America, too, I expect. I should have run away from crucifixion! I tell you this, you know, Alexey, because you are the only person who can understand this. There's no one else. To others, it's folly, madness, all I've told you of the hymn. They'll say I'm out of my mind or a fool. I am not out of my mind and I am not a fool. Ivan understands about the hymn, too. He understands, only he doesn't answer — he doesn't speak. He doesn't believe in the hymn. Don't speak, don't speak. I see how you look! You have already decided. Don't decide, spare me! I can't live without Grusha. Wait till after the trial!"

Mitya was beside himself as he finished. He held Alyosha by his shoulders, and his yearning, feverish eyes were fixed on his brother's.

"They don't let convicts marry, do they?" he repeated for the third time in a supplicating voice.

Alyosha listened with extreme surprise and was deeply shaken.

"Tell me one thing," he said, "does Ivan insist on it, and whose idea was it?"

"His, his, and he insists on it. He didn't come to see me at first, then he suddenly came a week ago and he broached the subject straight away. He is awfully keen on it. He doesn't ask me, but orders me to escape. He doesn't doubt of my obeying him, though I turned my heart inside out before him as I have before you, and told him about the hymn, too. He told me he'd arrange it; he's found out about everything. But of that later. He's simply set on it. It's all a matter of money: here, he says, is ten thousand for your escape and twenty thousand for America. And he says we can arrange a magnificent escape for ten thousand."

"And he told you on no account to tell me?" Alyosha asked again.

"To tell no one, and especially not you; on no account to tell you. He is afraid, no doubt, that you'll stand before me as my conscience. Don't tell him I told you. Don't tell him, for anything."

"You are right," Alyosha pronounced; "it's impossible to decide anything before the verdict. After the trial you'll decide for yourself. Then you'll find that new man in yourself and he will decide."

"A new man, or a Bernard who'll decide à la Bernard, for I believe I'm a contemptible Bernard myself," said Mitya, with a bitter grin.

"But, brother, have you no hope then of being acquitted?"

Mitya shrugged his shoulders nervously and shook his head.

"Alyosha, darling, it's time you were going," he said, with sudden haste. "There's the superintendent shouting in the yard. He'll be here directly. We are late; it's irregular. Embrace me quickly. Kiss me! Make the sign of the cross over me, darling, for the cross I have to bear to-morrow."

They embraced and kissed.

"Ivan," said Mitya suddenly, "suggests my escaping; but, of course, he believes that I killed."

A mournful smile came to his lips.

"Have you asked him whether he believes it?" asked Alyosha.

"No, I haven't. I wanted to, but I couldn't. I hadn't the courage. But I saw it from his eyes. Well, good-bye!"

Once more they kissed hurriedly, and Alyosha was just going out, when Mitya suddenly called him back.

"Stand facing me! That's right!" And again he seized Alyosha, putting both hands on his shoulders. His face became suddenly quite pale, so that it was dreadfully apparent, even through the gathering darkness. His lips twitched, his eyes fastened upon Alyosha.

"Alyosha, tell me the whole truth, as you would before the Lord God. Do you believe that I killed, or don't you believe it? Do you, do you yourself, believe it or not? The whole truth, don't lie!" he cried frantically.

Everything seemed heaving before Alyosha, and he felt something like a stab at his heart.

"Hush! What do you mean?" he faltered helplessly.

"The whole truth, the whole, don't lie!" repeated Mitya.

"I've never for one instant believed that you were the murderer!" broke suddenly in a shaking voice from Alyosha, and he raised his right hand, as though calling God to witness his words.

Mitya's whole face was lighted up with bliss.

"Thank you!" he articulated slowly, as though sighing after a swoon. "Now you have given me new life. Would you believe it, till this moment I've been afraid to ask you, you, even you. Well, go! You've given me strength for to-morrow. God bless you! Come, go along! Love Ivan!" was Mitya's last word.

Alyosha went out in tears. Such distrustfulness in Mitya, such lack of confidence even in him, in Alyosha — all this suddenly opened before Alyosha an unsuspected abyss of hopeless grief and despair in the soul of his unhappy brother. Intense, infinite compassion overwhelmed him instantly and tortured him. There was a poignant ache in his torn heart. "Love Ivan" — he suddenly recalled Mitya's words. And he was going to Ivan. He had wanted to see Ivan badly since morning. He was as much worried about Ivan as about Mitya, and more than ever now.

## CHAPTER V
### NOT YOU, NOT YOU!

ON the way to Ivan he had to pass the house where Katerina Ivanovna was living. There was light in the windows. He suddenly stopped and resolved to go in. He had not seen Katerina Ivanovna for more than a week. But now it struck him that Ivan might be with her, especially on the eve of the terrible day. Having rung the bell and mounted the staircase, which was dimly lighted by a Chinese lantern, he saw a man coming down, and as they met he recognised his brother. So he was just coming from Katerina Ivanovna.

"Ah, it's only you," said Ivan drily. "Well, good-bye! You are going to her?"

"Yes."

"I don't advise you to; she's upset and you'll upset her more."

A door was instantly flung open above, and a voice cried suddenly:

"No, no! Alexey Fyodorovich, have you come from him?"

"Yes, I have been with him."

"Has he sent me any message? Come up, Alyosha, and you, Ivan Fyodorovich, you must come back, you must. Do you hear?"

There was such a peremptory note in Katya's voice that Ivan, after a moment's hesitation, made up his mind to go upstairs again with Alyosha.

"She was eavesdropping," he murmured angrily to himself, but Alyosha heard it.

"Excuse my keeping my greatcoat on," said Ivan, going into the drawing-room. "I won't sit down. I won't stay more than a minute."

"Sit down, Alexey Fyodorovich," said Katerina Ivanovna, though she remained standing. She had changed very little during this time, but there was an ominous gleam in her dark eyes. Alyosha remembered afterwards that she had struck him as particularly beautiful at that moment.

"What did he ask you to tell me?"

"Only one thing," said Alyosha, looking her straight in the face, "that you would spare yourself and say nothing at the trial of what" (he hesitated a little) ". . . passed between you . . . at the time of your first acquaintance . . . in that town."

"Ah! that I bowed down to the ground for that money!" She broke into a bitter laugh. "Why, is he afraid for me or for himself? He asks me to spare — whom? Him or myself? Tell me, Alexey Fyodorovich!"

Alyosha watched her intently, trying to understand her. "Both yourself and him," he answered softly.

"I am glad to hear it," she snapped out maliciously, and she suddenly blushed.

"You don't know me yet, Alexey Fyodorovich," she said menacingly. "And I don't know myself yet. Perhaps you'll want to trample me under foot after my testimony tomorrow."

"You will give your evidence honestly," said Alyosha; "that's all that's wanted."

"Women are often dishonest," she said, grinding her teeth. "Only an hour ago I was thinking I was horrified at the thought of touching that monster . . . as though he were a reptile . . . but no, he is still a human being to me! But did he kill? Is he the murderer?" she cried, all of a sudden, hysterically, turning quickly to Ivan. Alyosha saw at once that she had asked Ivan that question before, perhaps only a moment before he came in, and not for the first time, but for the hundredth, and that they had ended by quarrelling.

"I've been to see Smerdyakov. . . . It was you, you who persuaded me that he murdered his father. It's only you I believed!" she continued, still addressing Ivan. He gave her a sort of strained smile. Alyosha was startled to note that she addressed him familiarly. He had not suspected such intimacy between them.

"Well, that's enough, anyway," Ivan cut short the conversation. "I am going. I'll come to-morrow." And turning at once, he walked out of the room and went straight downstairs.

With an imperious gesture, Katerina Ivanovna seized Alyosha by both hands.

"Follow him! Overtake him! Don't leave him alone for a minute!" she said, in a hurried whisper. "He's mad! Don't you know that he's mad? He is in a fever, nervous fever. The doctor told me so. Go, run after him. . . ."

Alyosha jumped up and ran after Ivan, who was not fifty paces ahead of him.

"What do you want?" He turned quickly on Alyosha, seeing that he was running after him. "She told you to run after me, because I'm mad. I know it all by heart," he added irritably.

"She is mistaken, of course; but she is right that you are ill," said Alyosha. "I was looking at your face just now. You look very ill, Ivan." Ivan walked on without stopping. Alyosha followed him.

"And do you know, Alexey Fyodorovich, how people go out of their mind?" Ivan asked, his voice suddenly quiet, without a trace of irritation, in a tone of the simplest curiosity.

"No, I don't. I suppose there are all kinds of insanity."

"And can one observe that one's going mad oneself?"

"I imagine one can't see oneself clearly in such circumstances," Alyosha answered with surprise.

Ivan paused for half a minute.

"If you want to talk to me, please change the subject," he said suddenly.

"Oh, while I think of it, I have a letter for you," said Alyosha timidly, and he took Lise's note from his pocket and held it out to Ivan. They had just come up to a lamp-post. Ivan recognised the handwriting at once.

"Ah, from that imp!" he laughed maliciously, and, without opening the envelope, he tore it into bits and threw it to the wind. The bits were scattered.

"She's not sixteen yet, I believe, and already offering herself," he said contemptuously, striding along the street again.

"How do you mean, offering herself?" exclaimed Alyosha.

"As loose women offer themselves, to be sure."

"How can you, Ivan, how can you?" Alyosha cried hotly and sorrowfully. "She is a child; you are insulting a child! She is ill; she is very ill, too. She is on the verge of insanity, too, perhaps . . . I couldn't help handing her letter to you . . . I had hoped to hear something from you . . . that would save her."

"You'll hear nothing from me. If she is a child I am no nurse for her. Be quiet, Alexey. Don't go on about her. I am not even thinking about it."

They were silent again for a moment.

"She will be praying all night now to the Mother of God to show her how to act to-morrow at the trial," he said sharply and angrily again.

"You . . . you mean Katerina Ivanovna?"

"Yes. Whether she's to save Mitya or ruin him. She'll pray for light from above. She can't make up her mind for herself, you see. She has not had time to prepare herself yet. She takes me for her nurse, too. She wants me to sing lullabies to her."

"Katerina Ivanovna loves you, brother," said Alyosha sadly.

"Perhaps; but I am not very keen on her."

"She is suffering. Why do you . . . sometimes say things to her that give her hope?" Alyosha went on, with timid reproach. "I know that you've given her hope. Forgive me for speaking to you like this," he added.

"I can't behave to her as I ought — break off altogether and tell her so straight out," said Ivan irritably. "I must wait till sentence is passed on the murderer. If I break off with her now, she will avenge herself on me by ruining that scoundrel to-morrow at the trial, for she hates him and knows she hates him.

It's all a lie — lie upon lie! As long as I don't break off with her, she goes on hoping, and she won't ruin that monster, knowing how I want to get him out of trouble. If only that damned verdict would come!"

The words "murderer" and "monster" echoed painfully in Alyosha's heart.

"But how can she ruin Mitya?" he asked, pondering on Ivan's words. "What evidence can she give that would ruin Mitya?"

"You don't know that yet. She's got a document in her hands, in Mitya's own writing, that proves conclusively that he did murder Fyodor Pavlovich."

"That's impossible!" cried Alyosha.

"Why is it impossible? I've read it myself."

"There can't be such a document!" Alyosha repeated hotly. "There can't be, because he's not the murderer. It's not he murdered father, not he!"

Ivan suddenly stopped.

"Who is the murderer then, according to you?" he asked, with apparent coldness. There was even a supercilious note in his voice.

"You know who," Alyosha pronounced in a low, inward voice.

"Who? You mean the story about the crazy idiot, the epileptic, Smerdyakov?"

Alyosha suddenly felt himself trembling all over. "You know who," broke helplessly from him. He could scarcely breathe.

"Who? Who?" Ivan cried almost fiercely. All his restraint suddenly vanished.

"I know only one thing," Alyosha went on, still almost in a whisper, "*it wasn't you* killed father."

"Not you! What do you mean by 'not you'?" Ivan was thunderstruck.

"It was not you killed father, not you!" Alyosha repeated firmly.

The silence lasted for half a minute.

"I know I didn't. Are you raving?" said Ivan, with a pale, distorted smile. His eyes were riveted on Alyosha. They were standing again beside a lamp-post.

"No, Ivan. You've told yourself several times that you are the murderer."

"When did I say so? I was in Moscow.... When have I said so?" Ivan faltered helplessly.

"You've said so to yourself many times, when you've been alone during these two dreadful months," Alyosha went on softly and distinctly as before. Yet he was speaking now, as it were, not of himself, not of his own will, but obeying some irresistible command. "You have accused yourself and have confessed to yourself that you are the murderer and no one else. But you didn't do it: you are mistaken: you are not the murderer. Do you hear? It was not you! God has sent me to tell you so."

They were both silent. The silence lasted a whole long minute. They were both standing still, gazing into each other's eyes. They were both pale. Suddenly Ivan began trembling all over, and clutched Alyosha's shoulder.

"You've been in my room!" he whispered hoarsely. "You've been there at night, when he came.... Confess ... have you seen him, have you seen him?"

"Whom do you mean — Mitya?" Alyosha asked bewildered.

"Not him, damn the monster!" Ivan shouted, in a frenzy. "Do you know that he visits me? How did you find out? Speak!"

"Who is *he*? I don't know whom you are talking about," Alyosha faltered, beginning to be alarmed.

"Yes, you do know . . . or how could you . . .? It's impossible that you shouldn't know." Suddenly he seemed to check himself. He stood still and seemed to reflect. A strange grin contorted his lips.

"Brother," Alyosha began again, in a shaking voice, "I have said this to you because you'll believe my word, I know that. I tell you once and for all, it's not you. You hear, once for all! God has put it into my heart to say this to you, even though it may make you hate me from this hour."

But by now Ivan had apparently regained his self-control.

"Alexey Fyodorovich," he said, with a cold smile, "I can't endure prophets and epileptics — God's messengers especially — and you know that only too well. I break off all relations with you from this moment and probably for ever. I beg you to leave me at this turning. It's the way to your lodgings, too. You'd better be particularly careful not to come to me to-night! Do you hear?"

He turned and walked on with a firm step, not looking back.

"Brother," Alyosha called after him, "if anything happens to you to-night, turn to me before any one!"

But Ivan made no reply. Alyosha stood beside the lamp-post at the cross-roads, till Ivan had vanished into the darkness. Then he turned and walked slowly homewards. Both Alyosha and Ivan were living in lodgings; neither of them was willing to live in Fyodor Pavlovich's empty house. Alyosha had a furnished room in the house of some simple people. Ivan lived quite a distance from him. He had taken roomy and fairly comfortable quarters in the wing of a fine house that belonged to a well-to-do lady, the widow of an official. But his only attendant was a deaf and rheumatic old crone who went to bed at six o'clock

every evening and got up at six in the morning. Ivan had become remarkably indifferent to his comforts of late, and very fond of being alone. He did everything for himself in the one room he lived in, and rarely entered any of the other rooms in his lodging.

He reached the gate of the house and had his hand on the bell, when he suddenly stopped. He felt that he was trembling all over with anger. Suddenly he let go of the bell, spat, turned back, and walked with rapid steps in the opposite direction. He walked a mile and a half to a tiny, crooked, wooden house, almost a peasant hut, where Marya Kondratyevna, the neighbour who used to come to Fyodor Pavlovich's kitchen for soup and to whom Smerdyakov had once sung his songs and played on the guitar, was now lodging. She had sold their little house, and was now living here with her mother. Smerdyakov, who was ill — almost dying — had been with them ever since Fyodor Pavlovich's death. It was to him Ivan was now going, moved by a sudden and irresistible prompting.

## CHAPTER VI
### THE FIRST INTERVIEW WITH SMERDYAKOV

THIS was the third time that Ivan had been to see Smerdyakov since his return from Moscow. The first time he had seen him and talked to him after the catastrophe was on the first day of his arrival, then he had visited him once more, a fortnight later. But his visits had ended with that second one, so that it was now over a month since he had seen him. And he had scarcely heard anything of him.

Ivan had only returned five days after his father's death, so that he had not been present at the funeral, which took place the day before he came back. The cause of his delay was that

Alyosha, not knowing his Moscow address, had to apply to Katerina Ivanovna to telegraph to him, and she, not knowing his correct address either, had telegraphed to her sister and aunt, reckoning on Ivan's going to see them as soon as he arrived in Moscow. But he had not gone to them till four days after his arrival. When he got the telegram, he had of course, set off post-haste for our town. The first to meet him was Alyosha, and Ivan was greatly surprised to find that, in opposition to the general opinion of the town, he refused to entertain a suspicion against Mitya, and pointed unhesitatingly to Smerdyakov as the murderer. Later on, after seeing the police captain and the prosecutor, and hearing the details of the charge and the arrest, he was still more surprised at Alyosha, and ascribed his opinion only to his exaggerated brotherly feeling and sympathy with Mitya, of whom Alyosha, as Ivan knew, was very fond.

By the way, let us say a word or two of Ivan's feeling towards his brother Dmitri. He positively disliked him, at most, felt pity for him sometimes, and even that was mixed with great contempt, almost repugnance. Mitya's whole personality, even his appearance, was extremely unattractive to him. On Katerina Ivanovna's love for his brother Ivan looked with indignation. Yet he went to see Mitya on the first day of his arrival, and that interview, far from shaking Ivan's belief in his guilt, positively strengthened it. He found his brother agitated, morbidly excited. Mitya was talkative, but very absent-minded and incoherent. He used violent language, accused Smerdyakov, and was fearfully muddled. He talked principally about the three thousand roubles, which he said had been "stolen" from him by his father.

"The money was mine, it was my money," Mitya kept repeating. "Even if I had stolen it, I should have had the right."

He hardly contested the evidence against him, and if he tried to turn a fact to his advantage, it was in an absurd and incoherent way. He hardly seemed to wish to defend himself before Ivan or any one else. Quite the contrary, he was angry and proudly scornful of the charges against him; he was abusing every one and was in a continual rage. He only laughed contemptuously at Grigory's evidence about the open door, and declared that it was "the devil that opened it." But he could not bring forward any coherent explanation of the fact. He even succeeded in insulting Ivan during their first interview, telling him sharply that it was not for people who declared that "everything was lawful" to suspect and question him. Altogether he was anything but friendly with Ivan on that occasion. Immediately after that interview with Mitya, Ivan had gone for the first time to see Smerdyakov.

In the railway train on his way from Moscow, he kept thinking of Smerdyakov and of his last conversation with him on the evening before he went away. Many things seemed to him puzzling and suspicious. But when he gave his evidence to the examining magistrate Ivan said nothing, for the time, of that conversation. He put that off till he had seen Smerdyakov, who was at that time in the hospital.

Dr. Herzenstube and Varvinsky, the doctor he met in the hospital, confidently asserted, in reply to Ivan's persistent questions, that Smerdyakov's epilepsy was unmistakably genuine, and were surprised indeed at Ivan's asking whether he might not have been shamming on the day of the catastrophe. They gave him to

"BROTHER, TURN TO ME!"

understand that the attack was an exceptional one, the fits persisting and recurring several times, so that the patient's life was positively in danger, and it was only now, after they had taken measures, that they could assert with confidence that the patient would survive. "Though it might well be," added Dr. Herzenstube, "that his reason would be impaired for a considerable period, if not permanently." On Ivan's asking impatiently whether that meant that he was now mad, they told him that this was not yet the case, in the full sense of the word, but that certain abnormalities were perceptible. Ivan decided to find out for himself what those abnormalities were.

At the hospital he was at once allowed to see the patient. Smerdyakov was lying on a cot in a separate ward. There was only one other bed in the room, occupied by a tradesman of the town, swollen with dropsy, who was obviously going to die the following day or the day after that; he could be no hindrance to their conversation. Smerdyakov grinned distrustfully on seeing Ivan, and for the first instant seemed to be taken aback, as it were. So at least Ivan fancied. But that was only momentary. For the rest of the time he was struck, on the contrary, by Smerdyakov's composure. From the first glance Ivan had no doubt that he was very ill. He was very weak; he spoke slowly, seeming to move his tongue with difficulty; he had grown thin and sallow. Throughout the interview, which lasted twenty minutes, he kept complaining of a headache and of aches in all his limbs. His thin eunuch's face seemed to have become so tiny; the hair on his temples was ruffled, and his crest of curls in front stood up in a thin tuft. But the left eye, which was screwed up and seemed to be insinuating something, be-

trayed the old Smerdyakov. "A clever man is worth talking to." Ivan was reminded of that at once. He sat down on the stool at his feet. Smerdyakov, with a painful effort, shifted his position in bed, but he was not the first to speak. He remained silent, and did not even look much interested.

"Can you talk to me?" asked Ivan. "I won't tire you much."

"Certainly I can," mumbled Smerdyakov, in a faint voice. "Have you been back long, sir?" he added condescendingly, as though encouraging an embarrassed visitor.

"I arrived only to-day. . . . To clear up the mess you are in here."

Smerdyakov sighed.

"Why do you sigh? You knew of it all along," Ivan blurted out.

Smerdyakov was stolidly silent for a while.

"How could I help knowing, sir? It was clear beforehand. But how could I tell it would turn out like that?"

"What would turn out? Don't try to wriggle out! You foretold, didn't you, that you'd have a fit, on the way down to the cellar, you know. You mentioned the very spot."

"Have you said so at the examination yet?" Smerdyakov queried with composure.

Ivan felt suddenly angry.

"No, I haven't yet, but I will, without fail. You must explain a great deal to me, my man, and let me tell you, I am not going to let you play with me!"

"Why should I play with you, sir, when I put my whole trust in you, as in God Almighty?" said Smerdyakov, with the same composure, only for a moment closing his little eyes.

"In the first place," began Ivan, "I know that epileptic fits can't be foretold beforehand.

I've inquired, don't try to wriggle out of it. You can't foretell the day and the hour. How was it you told me the day and the hour beforehand, and about the cellar, too? How could you tell that you would fall down the cellar stairs in a fit, if you didn't sham a fit on purpose?"

"I had to go to the cellar, sir, anyway, several times a day, sir, indeed," Smerdyakov drawled deliberately. "I fell from the garret just in the same way a year ago. It's quite true you can't foretell the day and hour of a fit beforehand, but you can always have a presentiment of it."

"But you did foretell the day and the hour!"

"In regard to my epilepsy, sir, you had much better inquire of the doctors here. You can ask them whether it was a real fit or a sham; it's no use my saying any more about it."

"And the cellar? How could you know beforehand about the cellar?"

"You don't seem able to get over that cellar! As I was going down to the cellar, I was in terrible dread and doubt. What frightened me most was losing you and being left without protection in the whole world. So I went down into the cellar thinking, 'Here, it'll come on directly, it'll strike me down directly, shall I fall or not?' And it was through this fear that I suddenly felt the spasm in my throat that always comes . . . and so I went flying. All that and all my previous conversation with you at the gate the evening before when I told you how frightened I was and spoke of the cellar, I told all that to Dr. Herzenstube and Nikolay Parfenovich, the examining magistrate, and it's all in the record. And the doctor here, Mr. Varvinsky, maintained to all of

them that it was just the thought of it brought it on, the apprehension that I might fall. It was just then that the fit seized me. And so they've written it down, that that's just how it must have happened, simply because of my fear."

As he finished, Smerdyakov drew a deep breath, as though exhausted.

"Then you have said all that in your evidence?" said Ivan, somewhat taken aback. He had meant to frighten him with the threat of repeating their conversation, and it appeared that Smerdyakov had already reported it all himself.

"What have I to be afraid of? Let them write down the whole truth," Smerdyakov pronounced firmly.

"And have you told them every word of our conversation at the gate?"

"No, not exactly every word."

"And did you tell them that you can sham fits, as you boasted then?"

"No, I didn't tell them that either."

"Tell me now, why did you send me to Chermashnya that time?"

"I was afraid you'd go away to Moscow, Chermashnya is nearer, anyway."

"You are lying, you suggested my going away yourself; you told me to get out of the way of trouble."

"That was simply out of affection and my sincere devotion to you, sir, foreseeing trouble in the house, to spare you, sir. Only I wanted to spare myself even more. That's why I told you to get out of harm's way, sir, that you might understand that there would be trouble in the house, and would remain at home to protect your father."

"You might have said it more directly, you blockhead!" Ivan suddenly fired up.

"How could I have said it more directly then? It was simply my fear that made me speak, sir; and besides, you might have gotten angry, too. I might well have been apprehensive that Dmitri Fyodorovich would make a scandal and carry away that money, for he considered it as good as his own, but who could tell that it would end in a murder like this? I thought that he would only carry off the three thousand that lay under the master's mattress in the envelope, and you see, he's murdered him. How could you guess it either, sir?"

"But if you say yourself that it couldn't be guessed, how could I have guessed and stayed at home? You contradict yourself!" said Ivan, pondering.

"You might have guessed from my sending you to Chermashnya and not to Moscow."

"How could I guess it from that?"

Smerdyakov seemed much exhausted, and again he was silent for a minute.

"You might have guessed from the fact of my asking you not to go to Moscow, but to Chermashnya, sir, that I wanted to have you nearer, for Moscow's a long way off, and Dmitri Fyodorovich, knowing you are not far off, would not be so bold. And if anything had happened, you might have come to protect me, too, for I warned you of Grigory Vasilyevich's illness, and that I was afraid of having a fit. And when I explained those knocks to you, by means of which one could go in to the deceased, and that Dmitri Fyodorovich knew them all through me, I thought that you would guess yourself that he would be sure to do something, and so you wouldn't go to Chermashnya even, but would stay."

"He talks very coherently," thought Ivan, "though he does mumble; what's the derangement of his faculties that Herzenstube talked of?"

"You are playing a double game with me, damn you," he exclaimed, getting angry.

"But I thought at the time that you quite guessed," Smerdyakov parried with the most naïve air.

"If I'd guessed, I should have stayed," cried Ivan.

"Why, I thought that it was because you guessed that you went away in such a hurry, sir, only to get out of trouble, only to run away and save yourself in your fright."

"You thought that every one was as great a coward as yourself?"

"Forgive me, sir, I thought you were like me."

"Of course, I ought to have guessed," Ivan said in agitation, "and I did guess there was some mischief brewing on your part . . . only you are lying, you are lying again," he cried, suddenly recollecting. "Do you remember how you went up to the carriage and said to me, 'A clever man is worth talking to'? So you were glad I went away, since you praised me?"

Smerdyakov sighed again and again. A trace of colour came into his face.

"If I was pleased," he articulated rather breathlessly, "it was simply beeause you agreed not to go to Moscow, but to Chermashnya. For it was nearer, anyway. Only when I said those words to you, it was not by way of praise, but of reproach, sir. You didn't understand it, sir."

"What reproach?"

"Why, that foreseeing such a calamity you deserted your own parent, and would not protect us, for I might have been taken up any time on the charge of having stolen that three thousand."

"Damn you!" Ivan swore again. "Wait, did you tell the prosecutor and the examining magistrate about those knocks?"

"I told them everything just as it was."

Ivan wondered inwardly again.

"If I thought of anything then," he began again, "it was solely of some dirty trick on your part. Dmitri might kill, but that he would steal — I did not believe that then. . . . But I was prepared for any dirty trick from you. You told me yourself you could sham a fit. What did you say that for?"

"It was just through my simplicity, and I never have shammed a fit on purpose in my life. And I only said so then to boast to you. It was just foolishness, sir. I liked you so much then, and was open-hearted with you."

"My brother plainly accuses you of having killed and stolen."

"What else is left for him to do?" said Smerdyakov, with a bitter grin. "And who will believe him with all the evidence against him? Grigory Vasilyevich saw the door open. What can he say after that, sir? But, well, God help him! He is trembling for his own skin."

He was quiet for a while, and suddenly, as though on reflection, added:

"And look here again, sir: he wants to lay the blame on me and make out that it is the work of my hands — I've heard that already, sir. But as to my being clever at shamming a fit: should I have told you beforehand that I could sham one, if I really had had such a design against your father? If I had been planning such a murder could I have been such a fool as to give such evidence against myself beforehand? And to his own son, too! Upon my word! Is that likely? As if that could be, such a thing has never happened. No one hears

this talk of ours now, except Providence itself, and if you were to tell of it to the prosecutor and Nikolay Parfenovich you might defend me completely by doing so, for who would be likely to be such a criminal, if he is so open-hearted beforehand? Any one can see that."

"Well," and Ivan got up to cut short the conversation, struck by Smerdyakov's last argument, "I don't suspect you at all, and indeed I think it's absurd to accuse you. On the contrary, I am grateful to you for setting my mind at rest. Now I am going, but I'll come again. Meanwhile, good-bye. Get well. Is there anything you want?"

"I am very thankful for everything, sir. Marfa Ignatyevna does not forget me, and provides me with whatever I want, in her kindness. Good people visit me every day."

"Good-bye. But I shan't say anything of your being able to sham a fit, and I don't advise you to, either," something made Ivan say suddenly.

"I quite understand. And if you don't speak of that, I shall say nothing of our whole conversation at the gate."

Then it happened that Ivan went out, and only when he had gone a dozen steps along the corridor, he suddenly felt that there was an insulting significance in Smerdyakov's last words. He was almost on the point of turning back, but it was only a passing impulse, and muttering, "Nonsense!" he went out of the hospital.

His chief feeling was one of relief at the fact that it was not Smerdyakov, but Mitya, who had committed the murder, though he might have been expected to feel the opposite. He did not want to analyse the reason for this feeling, and even felt a positive repugnance

472

at prying into his sensations. He felt as though he wanted to make haste to forget something. In the following days he became convinced of Mitya's guilt, as he acquainted himself with all the evidence against him. There was the evidence of people of no importance, Fenya and her mother, for instance, but the weight of it was almost overpowering, let alone the testimony of Perhotin, the people at the tavern, and at Plotnikovs' shop, as well as that of the witnesses at Mokroye. It was the details that were so damning. The secret knocks impressed the lawyers almost as much as Grigory's evidence as to the open door. Grigory's wife, Marfa, in answer to Ivan's questions, declared that Smerdyakov had been lying all night the other side of the partition, "He was not three paces from our bed," and that although she was a sound sleeper she waked several times and heard him moaning, "He was moaning the whole time, moaning continually."

Talking to Herzenstube, and giving it as his opinion that Smerdyakov was not mad, but only rather weak, Ivan only evoked from the old man a subtle smile.

"Do you know how he spends his time now?" he asked, "learning lists of French words by heart. He has an exercise-book under his pillow with the French words written out in Russian letters for him by some one, he, he, he!"

Ivan ended by dismissing all doubts. He could not think of Dmitri without repulsion. Only one thing was strange, however. Alyosha persisted that Dmitri was not the murderer, and that "in all probability" Smerdyakov was. Ivan always felt that Alyosha's opinion meant a great deal to him, and so he was disturbed by it now. Another thing that was

strange was that Alyosha did not make any attempt to talk about Mitya with Ivan, that he never began on the subject and only answered his questions. This, too, struck Ivan particularly.

But he was very much preoccupied at this time with something quite apart from that. On his return from Moscow, he had abandoned himself hopelessly to his mad and consuming passion for Katerina Ivanovna. This is not the place to begin to speak of this new passion of Ivan's, which left its mark on the rest of his life: this would furnish the subject for another story, another novel, which I may perhaps never undertake. But I cannot omit to mention here that when Ivan, on leaving Katerina Ivanovna with Alyosha, as I've related already, told him, "I am not keen on her," it was an absolute lie: he loved her madly, though at times he hated her so that he could have murdered her. Many causes helped to bring about this feeling. Shattered by what had happened to Mitya, on Ivan's return she rushed to meet him as her one salvation. She was hurt, insulted, humiliated. And here the man had come back to her, who had loved her so ardently before (oh, she knew that very well), and whose heart and intellect she considered so superior to her own. But the stern girl did not abandon herself altogether to the man, in spite of the Karamazov violence of his passions and the great fascination he had for her. She was continually tormented at the same time by remorse for having deserted Mitya, and in moments of discord and violent anger (and they were numerous) she told Ivan so plainly. This was what he had called to Alyosha "lies upon lies." There was, of course, much that was false in it, and that angered Ivan more than anything. . . .

But of all this later.

In a word, for a time he almost forgot Smerdyakov's existence, and yet, a fortnight after his first visit to him, he began to be tormented by the same strange thoughts as before. It's enough to say that he was continually asking himself why it was that on that last night in Fyodor Pavlovich's house he had crept out on to the stairs like a thief and listened to hear what his father was doing below. Why had he recalled that afterwards with repulsion; why, next morning, had he been suddenly so depressed on the journey; why, as he reached Moscow, had he said to himself, "I am a scoundrel"? And now he almost fancied that these tormenting thoughts would make him even forget Katerina Ivanovna, so completely did they take possession of him again. It was just after fancying this that he met Alyosha in the street. He stopped him at once, and put a question to him:

"Do you remember when Dmitri burst in after dinner and gave father a beating, and afterwards I told you in the yard that I reserved for myself 'the right to desire' . . . tell me, did you think then that I desired father's death or not?"

"I did think so," answered Alyosha softly.

"It was so, too; it was not a matter of guessing. But didn't you fancy then that what I wished was just that 'one reptile should devour another'; that is, just that Dmitri should kill father, and as soon as possible . . . and that I myself was even prepared to help to bring that about?"

Alyosha turned rather pale, and looked silently into his brother's eyes.

"Speak!" cried Ivan. "I want above everything to know what you thought then. I want the truth, the truth!"

He drew a deep breath, looking angrily at Alyosha in anticipation of his answer.

"Forgive me, I did think that, too, at the time," whispered Alyosha, and ceased, without mentioning a single mitigating circumstance.

"Thanks," snapped Ivan, and, leaving Alyosha, he went quickly on his way. From that time on Alyosha noticed that Ivan obviously began to avoid him and seemed even to have taken a dislike to him, so much so that Alyosha gave up going to see him. Immediately after that meeting with him, Ivan, instead of going home, went straight to Smerdyakov again.

## CHAPTER VII
### THE SECOND VISIT TO SMERDYAKOV

By that time Smerdyakov had been discharged from the hospital. Ivan knew his new lodging, the dilapidated little wooden house, divided in two by a passage, on one side of which lived Marya Kondratyevna and her mother, and on the other, Smerdyakov. No one knew on what terms he lived with them, whether as a friend or as a lodger. It was supposed afterwards that he had come to stay with them as Marya Kondratyevna's betrothed, and was living there for a time without paying for board or lodging. Both mother and daughter had the greatest respect for him and looked upon him as greatly superior to themselves.

Ivan knocked, and, on the door's being opened, went into the passage. By Marya Kondratyevna's directions he went straight to the better room on the left, occupied by Smerdyakov. There was a tiled stove in the room and it was extremely hot. The walls were gay with blue paper, which was a good deal worn, however, and in the cracks under it cockroaches swarmed in amazing numbers, so that they made a continual rustling. The furniture was very scanty: two benches along the walls and two chairs by the table. The table of plain wood was covered with a cloth with a pink pattern. There was a pot of geranium at each of the two little windows. In the corner there was an ikon-case. On the table stood a little copper samovar with many dents in it, and a tray with two cups. But Smerdyakov had finished tea and the samovar was out. He was sitting at the table on a bench. He was looking at an exercise book and drawing lines with a pen. There was an inkwell by him and a short iron candlestick, but with a stearin candle. Ivan saw at once from Smerdyakov's face that he had completely recovered from his illness. His face was fresher, fuller, his hair stood up jauntily in front and was plastered down on his temples. He was sitting in a parti-coloured, wadded dressing-gown, rather dirty and frayed, however. He had spectacles on his nose, which Ivan had never seen him wear before. This trifling circumstance suddenly redoubled Ivan's irritation: "A creature like that and wearing spectacles!"

Smerdyakov slowly raised his head and looked intently at his visitor through his spectacles; then he slowly took them off and rose from the bench, but by no means respectfully, almost lazily, solely to preserve the most elementary civility. All this struck Ivan instantly, he took it all in and noted it at once — most of all the look in Smerdyakov's eyes, positively malicious, churlish, and even haughty. "Why are you barging in here?" it seemed to say; "we settled everything then, why have you come again?" Ivan could scarcely control himself.

"It's hot here," he said, still standing, and unbuttoned his overcoat. "Take off your coat," Smerdyakov conceded.

Ivan took off his coat and threw it on a bench. With trembling hands he took a chair, moved it quickly to the table and sat down. Smerdyakov managed to sit down on his bench before him.

"To begin with, are we alone?" Ivan asked sternly and impulsively. "Can they overhear us in there?"

"No one can hear anything. You've seen for yourself: there's a passage."

"Listen, my good fellow, what was that you babbled, as I was leaving the hospital, that if I said nothing about your being a past master at shamming fits, you wouldn't tell the examining magistrate our whole conversation at the gate? What do you mean by the *whole* conversation? What could you mean by it? Were you threatening me? Have I entered into some sort of compact with you? Do you suppose I am afraid of you?"

Ivan said this in a perfect fury, giving him to understand with obvious intention that he scorned any subterfuge or indirectness and meant to show his cards. Smerdyakov's eyes gleamed resentfully, his left eye winked, and he at once gave his answer, with his habitual composure and deliberation: "You want to have everything above-board, very well, you shall have it," he seemed to say.

"This is what I meant then, and this is why I said what I did: I meant that you, knowing beforehand of this murder of your own parent, left him to his fate, and that people might afterwards think evil of your feelings and perhaps of something else, too — that's what I promised then not to tell the authorities."

Though Smerdyakov spoke without haste and was obviously controlling himself, yet there was in his voice something determined and emphatic, resentful and insolently defiant. He stared impudently at Ivan. A mist passed before Ivan's eyes for the first moment.

"How? What? Are you out of your mind?"

"I'm in perfect possession of all my faculties."

"Do you suppose I *knew* of the murder?" Ivan cried at last, and he brought his fist down violently on the table. "What do you mean by 'something else, too'? Speak, scoundrel!"

Smerdyakov was silent and still scanned Ivan with the same insolent stare.

"Speak, you stinking rogue, what is that 'something else, too'?" he shouted.

"The 'something else' I meant was that you probably, too, were very desirous of your parent's death."

Ivan jumped up and struck him with all his might on the shoulder, so that he fell back against the wall. In an instant his face was bathed in tears, and saying, "It's a shame, sir, to strike a sick man," he suddenly covered his eyes with his very dirty blue-check cotton handkerchief and sank into quiet weeping. A minute passed.

"That's enough! Leave off," Ivan said peremptorily, sitting down again. "Don't put me out of all patience."

Smerdyakov took the rag from his eyes. Every line of his puckered face reflected the insult he had just received.

"So you thought then, you scoundrel, that together with Dmitri I meant to kill my father?"

"I didn't know what thoughts were in your mind then," said Smerdyakov in an injured tone; "and so I stopped you then at the gate to sound you on that very point."

"To sound me, how?"

"Why, as to that very circumstance, whether or not you wanted your father to be murdered?"

What infuriated Ivan more than anything was the aggressive, insolent tone which Smerdyakov persisted in using.

"You murdered him!" he cried suddenly. Smerdyakov smiled contemptuously.

"That it wasn't I who murdered him you know for a fact, yourself. And I should have thought that there was no need for a sensible man to speak of it again."

"But why, why had you such a suspicion about me at the time?"

"As you know already, it was simply from fear. For I was in such a position, that, shaking with fear, I suspected everyone. I resolved to sound you, too, for I thought if you wanted the same thing that your brother did, then the business was as good as settled and I should be crushed like a fly, too."

"Look here, you didn't say that a fortnight ago."

"I meant that when I talked to you in the hospital, only I thought you'd understand without wasting words, and that being such a sensible man you didn't care to talk of it openly."

"What next! Come, answer, answer, I insist: what was it . . . what could I have done to put into your vile soul a suspicion so degrading to me?"

"As for the murder, you couldn't have done that and didn't want to, but as for wanting some one else to do it, that was just what you did want."

"And how coolly, how coolly he speaks! But why should I have wanted it, what grounds had I for wanting it?"

"What grounds had you? What about the

476

inheritance?" said Smerdyakov sarcastically, and as it were vindictively. "Why, after your parent's death, sir, there was at least forty thousand to come to each of you, and very likely more, but if Fyodor Pavlovich had got married then to that lady, Agrafena Alexandrovna, she would have had all his capital made over to her directly after the wedding, for she's plenty of sense, sir, so that your parent would not have left you two roubles among the three of you. And were they far from a wedding, either? Not a hair's-breadth: that lady had only to lift her little finger, sir, and he would have run after her to church, with his tongue out."

Ivan restrained himself with effort.

"Very good," he commented at last, "you see, I haven't jumped up, I haven't knocked you down, I haven't killed you. Speak on. So, according to you, I had fixed on Dmitri to do it, I was reckoning on him?"

"How could you help reckoning on him, sir? If he killed him, then he would lose all the rights of a nobleman, his rank and property, and would go off to exile, so his share of the inheritance would come to you, sir, and your brother Alexey Fyodorovich, in equal parts, so you'd each have not forty, but sixty thousand. There's not a doubt, sir, you did reckon on Dmitri Fyodorovich."

"What I put up with from you! Listen, scoundrel, if I had reckoned on any one then, it would have been on you, not on Dmitri, and I swear I did expect some dirty trick from you . . . at the time . . . I remember my impression!"

"I thought, too, for a minute, at the time, that you were reckoning on me as well," said Smerdyakov, with a sarcastic grin. "So that it was just by that more than anything else that you gave yourself away. For if you had a foreboding about me and yet went away, you as good as said to me, 'You can murder my parent, I won't hinder you!'"

"You scoundrel! So that's how you understood it!"

"It was all that going to Chermashnya. Why! You were meaning to go to Moscow, sir, and refused all your father's entreaties to go to Chermashnya — and simply at a foolish word from me, sir, you consented at once! What reason had you to consent to go to Chermashnya? Since you went to Chermashnya with no reason, simply at my word, it shows that you must have expected something from me, sir."

"No, I swear I didn't!" shouted Ivan, grinding his teeth.

"You didn't? Then you ought, as your father's son, to have had me taken to the lock-up, sir, and thrashed at once for my words then . . . or at least to have given me a punch in the face on the spot, but you were not a bit angry, if you please, and at once in a friendly way acted on my foolish word and went away, which was utterly absurd, sir, for you ought to have stayed to save your parent's life. How could I help drawing my conclusions?"

Ivan sat scowling, both his fists convulsively pressed on his knees.

"Yes, I am sorry I didn't punch you in the face," he said with a bitter smile. "I couldn't have taken you to the lock-up just then. Who would have believed me and what charge could I bring against you? But the punch in the face . . . oh, I'm sorry I didn't think of it. Though blows are forbidden, I should have pounded your ugly phiz to a jelly."

Smerdyakov looked at him almost with delight.

"On ordinary occasions, sir," he said in the same complacent and sententious tone in which he had taunted Grigory and argued with him about religion at Fyodor Pavlovich's table, "on ordinary occasions, blows on the face are forbidden nowadays by law and people have given them up, but on exceptional occasions people still resort to blows, sir, not only among us but all over the world, be it even the fullest Republic of France, just as in the time of Adam and Eve, and they never will leave off, but you, sir, even in an exceptional case, did not dare."

"What are you learning French words for?"

Ivan nodded towards the exercise book lying on the table.

"Why shouldn't I learn them, sir, and so improve my education, supposing that I may myself chance to go some day to those happy parts of Europe?"

"Listen, monster." Ivan's eyes flashed and he trembled all over. "I am not afraid of your accusations, you can say what you like about me on the witness stand, and if I don't beat the life out of you, it's simply because I suspect you of that crime and I'll drag you to justice. I'll unmask you."

"To my thinking, you'd better keep quiet, sir, for what can you say against me, considering my absolute innocence; and who would believe you? Only if you begin, I shall tell everything, too, sir, for I must defend myself."

"Do you think I am afraid of you now?"

"If the court doesn't believe all I've said to you just now, sir, the public will, and you will be put to shame, sir."

"That's as much as to say 'A clever man is worth talking to,' eh?" snarled Ivan.

"You hit the mark, indeed, sir. And you'd better be sensible, sir."

Ivan got up, shaking all over with indignation, put on his coat, and without replying further to Smerdyakov, without even looking at him, walked quickly out of the cottage. The cool evening air refreshed him. There was a bright moon in the sky. A nightmare of ideas and sensations filled his soul. "Shall I go at once and give information against Smerdyakov? But what information can I give? He is not guilty, anyway. On the contrary, he'll accuse me. And as a matter of fact, why did I set off for Chermashnya then? What for? What for?" Ivan asked himself. "Yes, of course, I was expecting something and he is right . . ." And he remembered for the hundredth time how, on that last night in his father's house, he had listened on the stairs. But he remembered it now with such anguish that he stood still on the spot as though he had been stabbed. "Yes, I expected it then, that's true! I wanted the murder, I did want the murder! Did I want the murder? Did I want it? I must kill Smerdyakov! If I don't dare kill Smerdyakov now, life is not worth living!"

Ivan did not go home, but went straight to Katerina Ivanovna, alarming her by his appearance. He was like a madman. He repeated his whole conversation with Smerdyakov, every syllable of it. He couldn't be calmed, however much she tried to soothe him: he kept pacing the room, speaking strangely, disconnectedly. At last he sat down, put his elbows on the table, leaned his head on his hands and pronounced this strange aphorism: "If it's not Dmitri, but Smerdyakov who's the murderer, I share his guilt, for I put him up to it. Whether I really did, I don't know yet. But if he is the murderer, and not Dmitri, then, of course, I am the murderer, too."

When Katerina Ivanovna heard that, she got up from her seat without a word, went to her writing-table, opened a box standing on it, took out a sheet of paper and laid it before Ivan. This was the document of which Ivan spoke to Alyosha later on as a "mathematical proof" that Dmitri had killed their father. This was the letter written by Mitya to Katerina Ivanovna when he was drunk, on the very evening he met Alyosha at the cross-roads on the way to the monastery, after the scene at Katerina Ivanovna's, when Grushenka had insulted her. Then, parting from Alyosha, Mitya had rushed to Grushenka. It is not known whether he saw her, but in the evening he was at the "Metropolis," where he got thoroughly drunk. Then he asked for pen and paper and wrote a document of weighty consequences to himself. It was a wordy, disconnected, frantic letter, a drunken letter in fact. It was like the talk of a drunken man, who, on his return home, begins with extraordinary heat telling his wife or one of his household how he has just been insulted, what a rascal has just insulted him, what a fine fellow he is, on the other hand, and how he will pay that scoundrel out; and all that at great length, incoherently and excitedly, with drunken tears and blows on the table. The letter was written on a dirty piece of ordinary paper of the cheapest kind. It had been provided by the tavern and there were figures scrawled on the back of it.

There was evidently not space enough for his drunken verbosity and Mitya had not only filled the margins but had written the last lines right across the rest. The letter ran as follows:

"FATAL KATYA! To-morrow I will get the money and repay your three thousand, and farewell, woman of great wrath, but farewell, too, my love! Let us make an end! To-morrow I shall try and get it from every one, and if I can't get it, I give you my word of honour I shall go to my father and break his head and take the money from under the pillow, if only Ivan has gone. If I have to go to Siberia for it, I'll give you back your three thousand. And farewell. I bow down to the ground before you, for I've been a scoundrel to you. Forgive me! No, better not forgive me, you'll be happier and so shall I! Better Siberia than your love, for I love another woman and you got to know her too well to-day, so how can you forgive? I will murder the man who's robbed me! I'll leave you all and go to the East so as to know no one. Not *her* either, for you are not my only tormentor, she is, too. Farewell!"

"P.S. — I write my curse, but I adore you! I hear it in my heart. One string is left, and it vibrates. Better tear my heart in two! I shall kill myself, but first of all the cur. I shall tear three thousand from him and fling it to you. Though I've been a scoundrel to you, I am not a thief! You can expect three thousand. The cur keeps it under his mattress, in pink ribbon. I am not a thief, but I'll murder my thief. Katya, don't look disdainful. Dmitri is not a thief; but a murderer! He has murdered his father and ruined himself to hold his ground, rather than endure your pride. And he doesn't love you.

"P.P.S. — I kiss your feet, farewell! P.P.P.S. — Katya, pray to God that some one'll give me the money. Then there will be no blood on me, and if no one does — there will! Kill me! Slave and enemy,

D. KARAMAZOV."

Having read this "document," Ivan rose convinced. So then it was his brother who killed, not Smerdyakov. And if not Smerdyakov, then not he, Ivan. This letter at once assumed in his eyes the aspect of a mathematical proof. There could be no longer the slightest doubt of Mitya's guilt. The suspicion never occurred to Ivan, by the way, that Mitya might have committed the murder with Smerdyakov as an accomplice, and indeed such a theory did not fit in with the facts. Ivan was completely reassured. The next morning he thought of Smerdyakov and his gibes only with contempt. A few days later he positively wondered how he could have been so horribly distressed at his suspicions. He resolved to dismiss him with contempt and forget him. So passed a month. He made no further inquiry about Smerdyakov, but twice he happened to hear that he was very ill and out of his mind.

"He'll end in madness," the young doctor, Varvinsky, observed about him and Ivan remembered this. During the last week of that month Ivan himself began to feel very ill. He went to consult the Moscow doctor who had been sent for by Katerina Ivanovna just before the trial. And just at that time his relations with Katerina Ivanovna became acutely strained. They were like two enemies in love with each other. Katerina Ivanovna's "returns" to Mitya, that is, her brief but violent revulsions of feeling in his favour, drove Ivan to perfect frenzy. Strange to say, until that last scene described above, when Alyosha came from Mitya to Katerina Ivanovna, Ivan had never once, during that month, heard her express a doubt of Mitya's guilt, in spite of those "returns" that were so hateful to him. It is remarkable, too, that while he felt that he hated Mitya more and more every day, he

realised that it was not on account of Katya's "returns" that he hated him, but just *because he was the murderer of his father*. He was conscious of this and fully recognised it.

Nevertheless, he went to see Mitya ten days before the trial and proposed to him a plan of escape — a plan he had obviously conceived a long time ago. He was partly impelled to do this by a sore place still left in his heart by a phrase of Smerdyakov's, that it was to his, Ivan's, advantage that his brother should be convicted, as that would increase his inheritance and Alyosha's from forty to sixty thousand roubles. He determined to sacrifice thirty thousand on arranging Mitya's escape. On his return from seeing him, he was very mournful and dispirited; he suddenly began to feel that he was anxious for Mitya's escape, not only to heal that sore place by sacrificing thirty thousand, but for another reason. "Is it because I am as much a murderer at heart?" he asked himself. Something very deep down seemed burning and rankling in his soul. His pride above all suffered cruelly all that month. But of that later. . . .

When, after his conversation with Alyosha, Ivan suddenly decided with his hand on the bell of his lodging to go to Smerdyakov, he obeyed a sudden and peculiar impulse of indignation. He suddenly remembered how Katerina Ivanovna had only just cried out to him in Alyosha's presence: "It was you, you alone, persuaded me of his" (that is, Mitya's) "guilt!" Ivan was thunderstruck when he recalled it. He had never once tried to persuade her that Mitya was the murderer; on the contrary, he had suspected himself in her presence, that time when he came back from Smerdyakov. It was *she*, she, who had produced that "document" and proved his brother's guilt. And now she suddenly exclaimed: "I've been at Smerdyakov's myself!" When had she been there? Ivan had known nothing of it. So she was not at all so sure of Mitya's guilt! And what could Smerdyakov have told her? What, what, had he said to her? His heart burned with violent anger. He could not understand how he could, half an hour before, have let those words pass and not have cried out at the moment. He let go of the bell and rushed off to Smerdyakov. "I shall kill him perhaps this time," he thought on the way.

## CHAPTER VIII
### THE THIRD AND LAST
### INTERVIEW WITH SMERDYAKOV

WHEN he had gone half-way, the keen dry wind that had been blowing early that morning rose again, and a fine dry snow began falling thickly. It did not stay on the ground, but was whirled about by the wind, and soon there was a regular snowstorm. There were scarcely any street-lamps in the part of the town where Smerdyakov lived. Ivan strode through the darkness, unconscious of the storm, instinctively picking his way. His head ached and there was a painful throbbing in his temples. He felt that his hands were twitching convulsively. Not far from Marya Kondratyevna's cottage, Ivan suddenly came upon a solitary drunken little peasant. He was wearing a coarse and patched coat, and was walking in zigzags, grumbling and swearing to himself. Then suddenly he would begin singing in a husky drunken voice:

*"Ah, Vanka's gone to Petersburg*
*I won't wait till he comes back."*

But he broke off every time at the second line and began swearing again; then he would be-

gin the same song again. Ivan felt an intense hatred for him without even thinking about him at all. Suddenly he realised his presence and felt an irresistible impulse to knock him down. At that moment they met, and the peasant with a violent lurch fell full tilt against Ivan, who pushed him back furiously. The peasant went flying backwards and fell like a log on the frozen ground. He uttered one plaintive "O-oh!" and then was silent. Ivan stepped up to him. He was lying on his back, without movement or consciousness. "He will freeze to death," thought Ivan, and he went on his way to Smerdyakov's.

In the passage, Marya Kondratyevna, who ran out to open the door with a candle in her hand, whispered that Smerdyakov was very ill; "it's not that he's laid up, but it's as though he has gone out of his mind, and he even told us to take the tea away; he wouldn't have any."

"Why, has he been making a row?" asked Ivan coarsely.

"Oh, dear, no, quite the contrary, he's very quiet. Only please don't talk to him too long," Marya Kondratyevna begged him. Ivan opened the door and stepped into the room.

It was overheated as before, but there were changes in the room. One of the benches at the side had been removed, and in its place had been put a large old mahogany sofa, upholstered in leather, on which a bed had been made up, with fairly clean white pillows. Smerdyakov was sitting on the sofa, wearing the same dressing-gown. The table had been brought out in front of the sofa, so that there was hardly room to move. On the table lay a thick book in a yellow cover, but Smerdyakov was not reading it. He seemed to be sitting doing nothing. He met Ivan with a slow silent look, and was apparently not at all surprised at his coming. There was a great change in his face; he was much thinner and sallower. His eyes were sunken and his lower lids were blue.

"So you are really ill, eh!" Ivan stopped short. "I won't keep you long, I won't even take off my coat. Where can one sit down?"

He went to the other end of the table, moved up a chair and sat down on it.

"Why do you look at me without speaking? I've only come with one question, and I swear I won't go without an answer. Has the young lady, Katerina Ivanovna, been to see you?"

Smerdyakov still remained silent, looking quietly at Ivan as before. Suddenly, with a motion of his hand, he turned his face away.

"What's the matter with you?" cried Ivan.

"Nothing."

"What do you mean by 'nothing'?"

"Well, she has. It doesn't matter to you. Let me alone."

"No, I won't let you alone. Tell me, when was she here?"

"Why, I'd quite forgotten about her," said Smerdyakov, with a scornful smile, and, turning his face to Ivan again, he stared at him with a look of frenzied hatred, the same look that he had fixed on him at their last interview, a month before.

"You seem very ill yourself, your face is pinched; you don't look like yourself," he said to Ivan.

"Never mind my health, answer my question."

"But why are your eyes so yellow? The whites are quite yellow. Are you so tormented?" He smiled contemptuously and suddenly laughed outright.

"Listen, I've told you I won't go away without an answer!" Ivan cried.

"Why do you keep pestering me? Why do you torment me?" said Smerdyakov, with a look of suffering.

"Damn it! I've nothing to do with you. Just answer my question and I'll go away."

"I've no answer to give you," said Smerdyakov, looking down again.

"You may be sure I'll make you answer!"

"Why are you so uneasy?" Smerdyakov stared at him, not simply with contempt, but almost with a kind of repulsion. "Is this because the trial begins to-morrow? Nothing will happen to you, can't you believe that at last? Go home, go to bed and sleep in peace, don't be afraid of anything."

"I don't understand you. . . . What have I to be afraid of to-morrow?" Ivan articulated in astonishment, and suddenly a chill breath of fear did in fact pass over his soul. Smerdyakov measured him with his eyes.

"You don't understand?" he drawled reproachfully. "It's a strange thing a clever man should care to play such a farce!"

Ivan looked at him, speechless. The startling, incredibly supercilious tone of this man, who had once been his valet, was extraordinary in itself. He had not taken such a tone even at their last interview.

"I tell you, you've nothing to fear. I won't say anything about you, there's no evidence against you. I say, how your hands are trembling. Why are your fingers twitching like that? Go home, *you* did not kill."

Ivan started. He remembered Alyosha.

"I know it was not I," he faltered.

"Do you?" Smerdyakov caught him up again.

Ivan jumped up and seized him by the shoulder. "Say everything, you reptile! Say everything!"

482

Smerdyakov was not in the least scared. He only riveted his eyes on Ivan with insane hatred.

"Well, it was you who murdered him, if that's the case," he whispered furiously.

Ivan sank back in his chair, as though pondering something. He grinned angrily.

"You mean my going away. What you talked about last time?"

"You stood before me last time and understood it all, and you understand it now, too."

"All I understand is that you are mad."

"Aren't you tired of it? Here we are face to face; what's the use of fooling each other and keeping up a farce? Are you still trying to put it all on me, to my face? *You* killed; you are the real murderer, I was only your accomplice, your faithful servant, and it was at your word I did it."

"*Did* it? Why, did you kill?" Ivan turned cold.

Something seemed to give way in his brain, and he shuddered all over with a cold shiver. Then Smerdyakov himself looked at him wonderingly; probably the genuineness of Ivan's horror struck him.

"You don't mean to say you really did not know?" he faltered mistrustfully, looking with a crooked smile into his eyes. Ivan still stared at him, and seemed unable to speak.

*Ah, Vanka's gone to Petersburg*
*I won't wait till he comes back,*

suddenly echoed in his head.

"Do you know, I am afraid that you are a dream, a ghost sitting before me," he muttered.

"There's no ghost here, sir, but only us two and one other. No doubt he is here, that third, between us."

"Who is he? Who is here? What third person?" Ivan cried in alarm, looking about him, his eyes hastily searching every corner.

"That third is God Himself, sir, Providence. He is the third beside us now. Only don't look for him, sir, you won't find him."

"It's a lie that you killed him!" Ivan cried madly. "You are mad, or teasing me as you did last time!"

Smerdyakov, as before, watched him curiously, with no sign of fear. He could still scarcely get over his incredulity; he still fancied that Ivan knew everything and was merely pretending in order to "put it all on him to his face."

"Wait a minute, sir," he said at last in a weak voice, and suddenly bringing up his left leg from under the table, he began tucking up his trouser leg. He was wearing long white stockings and slippers. Without haste Smerdyakov took off his garter and thrust his fingers down into his stocking. Ivan stared at him, and suddenly shuddered in a paroxysm of terror.

"He's mad!" he cried, and, rapidly jumping up, he drew back, so that he knocked his back against the wall and stood up against it, stiff and straight. He looked with insane terror at Smerdyakov, who, entirely unaffected by his terror, continued fumbling in his stocking, as though he were making an effort to get hold of something with his fingers and pull it out. At last he got hold of it and began pulling it out. Ivan saw that it was a piece of paper, or perhaps a roll of papers. Smerdyakov pulled it out and laid it on the table.

"Here, sir," he said quietly.

"What is it?" responded Ivan, trembling.

"Kindly look at it, sir," Smerdyakov answered, still in the same low tone.

Ivan stepped up to the table, took up the

483

roll of paper and began unfolding it, but suddenly he drew back his fingers, as though from contact with a loathsome, fearful reptile.

"Your hands keep twitching, sir," observed Smerdyakov, and he deliberately unfolded the bundle himself. In the wrapper were three packets of hundred-rouble notes.

"They are all here, sir, all the three thousand roubles; you need not count them. Take them, sir," Smerdyakov suggested to Ivan, nodding at the notes. Ivan sank back in his chair. He was as white as a handkerchief.

"You frightened me . . . with your stocking," he said, with a strange grin.

"Can you really not have known till now?" Smerdyakov asked once more.

"No, I did not know. I kept thinking of Dmitri. Brother, brother! Ah!" He suddenly clutched his head in both hands. "Listen. Did you kill him alone? With my brother's help or without?"

"It was only with you, sir, together with you, I killed him, and Dmitri Fyodorovich is quite innocent."

"All right, all right. Talk about me later. Why do I keep on trembling? I can't speak properly."

"You were bold enough then, sir. You said 'everything is permitted,' and how frightened you are now," Smerdyakov muttered in surprise. "Won't you have some lemonade? I'll order some at once. It's very refreshing. Only I must hide this first."

And again he motioned towards the notes. He was just going to get up and call at the door to Marya Kondratyevna to make some lemonade and serve it, but, looking for something to cover up the notes that she might not see them, he first took out his handkerchief, and, as it turned out to be very dirty, took up

the big yellow book that Ivan had noticed at first lying on the table, and put it over the notes. The book was "The Sayings of our Holy Father Isaac the Syrian." Ivan read the title mechanically.

"I won't have any lemonade," he said. "Of me later. Sit down and tell me how you did it. Tell me all about it."

"You'd better take off your greatcoat, sir, or you'll be too hot." Ivan, as though he'd only just thought of it, tore off his coat, and, without getting up from his chair, threw it on the bench. "Speak, please, speak."

He seemed calmer. He waited, feeling sure that Smerdyakov would tell him *all* now.

"How it was done?" sighed Smerdyakov. "It was done in a most natural way, sir, in accordance with your very words."

"Of my words later," Ivan broke in again, apparently with complete self-possession, speaking firmly, and not shouting as before. "Only tell me in detail how you did it. Everything, as it happened. Don't forget anything. The details, above everything, the details, I beg you."

"You'd gone away, sir, then I fell into the cellar."

"In a fit or did you sham?"

"I shammed, naturally. I shammed it all. I went quietly down the steps to the very bottom and lay down quietly, and as I lay down I gave a scream, and struggled, till they carried me out."

"Wait! And were you shamming all along, afterwards, and in the hospital?"

"No, not at all. Next day, in the morning, before they took me to the hospital, I had a real attack, and a more violent one than I've had for years. For two days I was quite unconscious."

LAST INTERVIEW WITH SMERDYAKOV

"All right, all right. Go on."

"They laid me on this cot. I knew I'd be the other side of the partition, for whenever I was ill Marfa Ignatyevna used to put me there, near them. She's always been very kind to me from my birth up. At night I moaned, but quietly. I kept expecting Dmitri Fyodorovich to come."

"Expecting him? To come to you?"

"Not to me. I expected him to come into the house, for I'd no doubt that he'd come that night, for being without me and getting no news, he'd be sure to come and climb over the fence, as he used to and do something or other."

"And if he hadn't come?"

"Then nothing would have happened, sir. I should never have brought myself to it without him."

"All right, all right . . . speak more intelligibly, don't hurry; above all, don't leave anything out!"

"I expected him to kill Fyodor Pavlovich. I thought that was certain, for I had prepared him for it . . . during the last few days. . . . He knew about the knocks, that was the chief thing. With his suspiciousness and the fury which had been growing in him all those days, he was bound to get into the house by means of those taps. That was inevitable, so I was expecting him, sir."

"Wait," Ivan interrupted, "if he had killed him, he would have taken the money and carried it away; that's how you must have reasoned. What would you have got by it afterwards? I don't see."

"But he would never have found the money. That was only what I told him, that the money was under the mattress. But that wasn't true, sir. At first it was lying in a drawer, that's how it was. And afterwards I suggested to Fyodor Pavlovich, as I was the only person he trusted, to hide the envelope with the notes in the corner behind the ikons, for no one would have guessed that place, especially if he came in a hurry. So that's where the envelope lay, in the corner behind the ikons, sir. It would have been absurd to keep it under the mattress, the drawer, anyway, could be locked. But everybody here believes it was under the mattress. A stupid idea. So if Dmitri Fyodorovich had committed the murder, finding nothing, he would either have run away in a hurry, afraid of every sound, as always happens with murderers, or he would have been arrested. So I could always have clambered up to the ikons and have taken away the money next morning or even that night, and it would have all been blamed on Dmitri Fyodorovich. I could reckon. upon that."

"But what if he would not have killed him, but only stunned him?"

"If he would not have killed him, of course, I would not have dared to take the money, and nothing would have happened. But I calculated that he would beat him senseless, and I should have time to take it then, and then I'd make out to Fyodor Pavlovich that it was no one but Dmitri Fyodorovich who had taken the money after giving him a thrashing."

"Stop . . . I am getting mixed. Then it was Dmitri after all who killed him, you only took the money?"

"No, he didn't kill him, sir. Of course, I could tell you even now that he is the murderer. . . . But I don't want to lie to you now, because . . . because if you really haven't understood till now, as I see for myself, and have not been pretending, so as to put your guilt on me to my very face, you are still responsible for it all, sir, since you knew of the murder and charged me to do it, and went away knowing all about it. And so I want to prove to your face this evening that you are the chief murderer in the whole affair, and I am the merest accomplice, although it was I who did the killing. It is you who are the rightful murderer."

"Why, why, am I the murderer? Oh, God!" Ivan cried, unable to restrain himself at last, and forgetting that he had put off discussing himself till the end of the conversation. "You still mean that Chermashnya business? Wait, tell me, why did you want my consent, if you really took Chermashnya for consent? How will you explain that now?"

"Assured of your consent, I should have known that you wouldn't have made an outcry over those three thousand being lost, even if the authorities had suspected me, instead of Dmitri Fyodorovich, or as his accomplice; on the contrary, you would have protected me from others. . . . And when you got your inheritance you could have rewarded me now and again, all the rest of your life. For you'd have received your inheritance through me, seeing that if he had married Agrafena Alexandrovna, you'd have gotten nothing."

"Ah! Then you intended to pester me all my life afterwards," snarled Ivan. "And what if I hadn't gone away then, but had informed against you?"

"What could you have said? That I persuaded you to go to Chermashnya? That's all nonsense. Besides, after our conversation you would either have gone away or have stayed. If you had stayed, nothing would have happened. I should have known that you didn't want it done, and should have attempted nothing. As you went away, it meant you assured me that you wouldn't dare to inform against me at the trial, and that you'd overlook my having the three thousand. And, indeed, you couldn't have prosecuted me afterwards, because then I should have told it all in the court; that is, not that I had stolen the money or killed him — I shouldn't have said that — but that you'd put me up to the theft and the murder, though I didn't consent to it. That's why I needed your consent, so that you couldn't have cornered me afterwards, for what proof could you have had? I could always have cornered you, revealing your eagerness for your father's death, and I give you my word the public would all have believed it, and you would have been ashamed for the rest of your life."

"Was I so eager then, was I?" Ivan said again, gnashing his teeth.

"To be sure you were, and by your consent, sir, you silently permitted me to do the deed." Smerdyakov looked resolutely at Ivan. He was very weak and spoke softly and wearily, but some hidden inner force urged him on. He evidently had some design. Ivan felt that.

"Go on," he said. "Go on telling me what happened that night."

"What more is there to tell! I lay there and I thought I heard the master shout. And before that Grigory Vasilyevich had suddenly got up and came out, and he suddenly gave a scream, and then all was silence and darkness. I lay there waiting, my heart beating; I couldn't bear it. I got up at last, went out. I saw the window open on the left into the garden, and I stepped to the left to listen and find out whether he was alive there, and I heard the master moving about, sighing, so I knew he was alive. Well! I thought. I went to the window and shouted to the master, 'It's I.' And he shouted to me, 'He's been, he's been; he's run away.' He meant Dmitri Fyodorovich had been there. 'He's killed Grigory!' 'Where?' I whispered. 'There, in the corner,' he pointed. He was whispering, too. 'Wait a bit,' I said. I went to the corner of the garden to look, and there I came upon Grigory Vasilyevich lying by the wall, covered with blood, senseless. So it's true that Dmitri Fyodorovich has been here, was the thought that came into my head, and I determined on the spot to make an end of it, as Grigory Vasilyevich, even if he were alive, would see nothing of it, as he lay there senseless. The only risk was that Marfa Ignatyevna might wake up. I felt that at the moment, but this desire seized me, till I could scarcely breathe. I went back to the window to the master and said, 'She's here, she's come; Agrafena Alexandrovna has come, wants to be let in.' He started like a baby. 'Where is she, where?' he fairly gasped, but couldn't believe it. 'She's standing there,' said I, 'open.' He looked at me through the window, half believing and half distrustful, but afraid to open. 'Why, it's me he is afraid of now,' I thought. And here is a funny thing: I had the idea of tapping on the window frame before his eyes, the taps that meant, as we'd agreed, that Grushenka had come. He didn't seem to believe my words, but as soon as he heard the taps, he ran at once to open the door. He opened it. I would have gone in, but he stood in the way to prevent me passing. 'Where is she? Where is she?' He looked at me, all of a tremble. Well, thought I, if he's so frightened of me as all that, it's a bad look-out! And my legs went weak with the fear that he wouldn't let me in or would call out, or Marfa Ignatyevna would run up, or something else might

happen. I don't remember now, but I must have stood pale, facing him. I whispered to him, 'Why, she's there, there, under the window, how is it you don't see her?' I said. 'Bring her then, bring her.' 'She's afraid,' said I, 'she was frightened at the noise, she's hidden in the bushes; go and call to her yourself from the study.' He ran to the window, put the candle in the window. 'Grushenka,' he cried, 'Grushenka, are you there?' Though he cried that, he didn't want to lean out of the window, he didn't want to move away from me, for he was panic-stricken; he was so afraid of me that he didn't dare to move away from me. 'Why, here she is,' said I. I went up to the window and leaned right out of it. 'Here she is, she's in the bushes, smiling at you, don't you see her?' He suddenly believed it; he was all of a shake — he was so madly in love with her — and he leaned right out of the window. I snatched up that iron paper weight from his table — do you remember it, sir? — weighing about three pounds. I swung it and hit him on the pate with the corner of it. He didn't even cry out. He only sank down suddenly, and I hit him again and a third time. And the third time I knew I'd broken his skull. He suddenly rolled on his back, face upwards, covered with blood. I looked round. There was no blood on me, not a spot. I wiped the paper weight, put it back, went up to the ikons, took the money out of the envelope, and flung the envelope on the floor and the pink ribbon beside it. I went out into the garden all of a tremble, straight to the apple tree with a hollow in it — you know that hollow. I'd marked it long before and had a rag and a piece of paper ready in it. I wrapped all the notes in the paper and then in the rag and stuffed it deep down into the hole. And there it stayed for over a fortnight. I took it out later, when I came out of the hospital. I went back to my bed, lay down and thought in fear, 'If Grigory Vasilyevich has been killed outright, it may be a bad job for me, but if he is not killed and recovers, it will be first rate, for then he'll bear witness that Dmitri Fyodorovich has been here, and so he must have killed him and taken the money.' Then I began groaning with suspense and impatience, so as to wake Marfa Ignatyevna as soon as possible. At last she got up, and she rushed to me, but when she saw Grigory Vasilyevich was not there, she ran out, and I heard her scream in the garden. And that set it all going and put my mind at rest."

He stopped. Ivan had listened all the time in dead silence without stirring or taking his eyes off him. As he told his story Smerdyakov glanced at him from time to time, but for the most part kept his eyes averted. When he had finished he was evidently agitated and was breathing hard. The perspiration stood out on his face. But it was impossible to tell whether it was remorse he was feeling, or what.

"Wait," cried Ivan, pondering. "What about the door? If he only opened the door to you, how could Grigory have seen it open before? For Grigory saw it before you went."

It was remarkable that Ivan spoke quite amicably, in a different tone, not angry as before, so if any one had opened the door at that moment and peeped in at them, he would certainly have concluded that they were talking peaceably about some ordinary, though interesting, subject.

"As for that door and Grigory Vasilyevich's having seen it open, that's only his fancy," said Smerdyakov, with a wry smile. "He is not a man, I assure you, but an obstinate nag. He didn't see it, but fancied he had seen it,

and there's no shaking him. It's just your luck and mine that he took that notion into his head, for they can't fail to convict Dmitri Fyodorovich after that."

"Listen . . ." said Ivan, beginning to seem bewildered again and making an effort to grasp something. "Listen. There are a lot of questions I want to ask you, but I forget them . . . I keep forgetting and getting mixed up. Yes. Tell me this at least, why did you open the envelope and leave it there on the floor? Why didn't you simply carry off the envelope? . . . When you were telling me, I thought you spoke about it as though it were the right thing to do . . . but why, I can't understand . . ."

"I did that for a good reason, sir. For if a man had known all about it, as I did for instance, if he'd seen those notes before, and perhaps had put them in that envelope himself, and had seen the envelope sealed up and addressed, with his own eyes, if such a man had done the murder, what should have made him tear open the envelope afterwards, especially in such desperate haste, since he'd know for certain the notes must be in the envelope? No, if the robber had been some one like me, he'd simply have put the envelope straight in his pocket without opening it and got away with it as fast as he could. But it'd be quite different with Dmitri Fyodorovich. He only knew about the envelope by hearsay; he had not seen it, and if he'd found it, for instance, under the mattress, he'd have torn it open as quickly as possible to make sure the notes were in it. And he'd have thrown the envelope down, without having time to think that it would be evidence against him. Because he was not an habitual thief and had never directly stolen anything before, for he is a gentleman born, and if he did bring himself to steal, it would not be regular stealing, but simply taking what was his own, for he'd told the whole town he meant to before, and had even bragged aloud before every one that he'd go and take his property from Fyodor Pavlovich. I didn't say that openly to the prosecutor when I was being examined, but quite the contrary, I brought him to it by a hint, as though I didn't see it myself, and as though he'd thought of it himself and I hadn't prompted him; so that Mr. Prosecutor's mouth positively watered at my suggestion."

"But can you possibly have thought of all that on the spot?" cried Ivan, overcome with astonishment. He looked at Smerdyakov again with alarm.

"Mercy on us! Could any one think of it all in such a desperate hurry? It was all thought out beforehand."

"Well . . . well, it was the devil helped you!" Ivan cried again. "No, you are not a fool, you are far cleverer than I thought . . ."

He got up, obviously intending to walk across the room. He was in terrible distress. But as the table blocked his way, and there was hardly room to pass between the table and the wall, he only turned round where he stood and sat down again. Perhaps the impossibility of moving irritated him, as he suddenly cried out almost as furiously as before.

"Listen, you miserable, contemptible man! Don't you understand that if I haven't killed you, it's simply because I am keeping you to answer to-morrow at the trial? God sees," Ivan raised his hand, "perhaps I, too, was guilty; perhaps I really had a secret desire for my father's . . . death, but I swear I was not as guilty as you think, and perhaps I didn't urge you on at all. No, no, I didn't urge you

on! But no matter, I will give evidence against myself to-morrow, at the trial. I'm determined to! I shall tell everything, everything. But we'll make our appearance together. And whatever you may say against me at the trial, whatever evidence you give, I'll face it, I am not afraid of you. I'll confirm it all myself! But you must confess, too! You must, you must, we'll go together. That's how it shall be!"

Ivan said this solemnly and forcefully, and from his flashing eyes alone it could be seen that it would be so.

"You are ill, sir, I see, you are quite ill. Your eyes are yellow, sir," Smerdyakov commented, without the least irony, with apparent sympathy in fact.

"We'll go together," Ivan repeated. "And if you won't go, no matter, I'll confess alone."

Smerdyakov paused as though pondering.

"There'll be nothing of the sort, and you won't go, sir," he concluded at last with finality.

"You don't understand me," Ivan exclaimed reproachfully.

"You'll be too much ashamed, if you confess it all. And, what's more, it will be no use at all, for I shall say straight out that I never said anything of the sort to you, and that you are either ill (and it looks like it, too), or that you're so sorry for your brother that you are sacrificing yourself to save him and have invented it all against me, for you've always thought no more of me than if I'd been a fly and not a human being. And who will believe you, and what single proof have you got?"

"Listen, you showed me those notes just now to convince me."

Smerdyakov lifted the book off the notes and laid it on one side.

"Take that money away with you," Smerdyakov sighed.

"Of course I shall take it. But why do you give it to me, if you committed the murder for the sake of it?" Ivan looked at him with great surprise.

"I don't want it," Smerdyakov articulated in a shaking voice, with a gesture of refusal. "I did have an idea of beginning a new life with that money in Moscow or, better still, abroad. I did dream of it, chiefly because 'everything is permitted.' That was quite right what you taught me, sir, for you talked a lot to me about that. For if there's no infinite God, there's no such thing as virtue, and there's no need of it. You were right there. So that's how I looked at it."

"Did you reach that conclusion by yourself?" asked Ivan, with a wry smile.

"With your guidance, sir."

"And now, I suppose, you believe in God, since you are giving back the money?"

"No, I don't believe," whispered Smerdyakov.

"Then why are you giving it back?"

"Leave off . . . that's enough!" Smerdyakov waved his hand again. "You used to say yourself that everything was lawful, so now why are you so upset, too? You even want to go and give evidence against yourself. . . . Only there'll be nothing of the sort! You won't go to give evidence," Smerdyakov decided with conviction.

"You'll see," said Ivan.

"It isn't possible. You are very clever. You are fond of money, I know that. You like to be respected, too, for you're very proud; you are far too fond of female charms, too, and you care most of all about living in undisturbed comfort, without having to depend on any one

— that's what you care most about. You won't want to spoil your life for ever by taking such a disgrace on yourself. You are like Fyodor Pavlovich, you are more like him than any of his children; you've the same soul as he had."

"You are not a fool," said Ivan, as though struck. The blood rushed to his face. "I used to think you were a fool. You are serious now!" he observed, looking suddenly at Smerdyakov with a different expression.

"It was your pride made you think I was a fool. Take the money."

Ivan took the three rolls of notes and put them in his pocket without wrapping them in anything.

"I shall show them at court to-morrow," he said.

"Nobody will believe you, as you've plenty of money of your own; you may simply have taken it out of your cash-box and brought it to court."

Ivan rose from his seat.

"I repeat," he said, "the only reason I haven't killed you is that I need you for to-morrow, remember that, don't forget it!"

"Well, kill me. Kill me now," Smerdyakov said, all at once looking strangely at Ivan. "You won't dare do that even!" he added, with a bitter smile. "You won't dare to do anything, you, who used to be so bold!"

"Till to-morrow," cried Ivan, and moved to go out.

"Wait a moment. . . . Show me those notes again."

Ivan took out the notes and showed them to him. Smerdyakov looked at them for ten seconds. "Well, you can go," he said, with a wave of his hand. "Ivan Fyodorovich!" he called after him again.

"What do you want?" Ivan turned without stopping.

"Farewell!" "Till to-morrow!" Ivan cried again, and he walked out of the cottage.

The snowstorm was still raging. He walked the first few steps boldly, but suddenly began staggering, as it were. "It's something physical," he thought, with a grin. Something like joy was springing up in his heart. He was conscious of unbounded resolution; he would make an end of the wavering that had so tortured him of late. His determination was taken, "and now it will not be changed," he thought with happiness. At that moment he stumbled against something and almost fell down. Stopping short, he made out at his feet the peasant he had knocked down, still lying senseless and motionless. The snow had covered his face. Ivan seized him and lifted him in his arms. Seeing a light in the little house to the right he went up, knocked at the shutters, and asked the man to whom the house belonged to help him carry the peasant to the police-station, promising him three roubles. The man got ready and came out. I won't describe in detail how Ivan succeeded in his object, bringing the peasant to the police-station and arranging for a doctor to see him at once, providing with a liberal hand for the expenses. I will only say that this business took a whole hour, but Ivan was well content with it. His mind wandered and worked incessantly.

"If I had not taken my decision so firmly about to-morrow," he reflected with delight, "I should not have stayed a whole hour to look after the peasant, but should have passed by, without caring about his being frozen. I am quite capable of watching myself, by the way," he thought at the same instant, with still greater delight, "although they have de-

cided that I am going out of my mind!"

Just as he reached his own house he stopped short, asking himself suddenly hadn't he better go at once now to the prosecutor and tell him everything. He decided the question by turning back to the house. "Everything together to-morrow!" he whispered to himself, and, strange to say, almost all his gladness and self-satisfaction passed in one instant.

As he entered his own room he felt something like a touch of ice on his heart, like a recollection or, more exactly, a reminder, of something agonising and revolting that was in that room now, at that moment, and had been there before. He sank wearily on his sofa. The old woman brought him a samovar; he made tea, but did not touch it. He sent the old woman away for the night. He sat on the sofa and felt giddy. He felt that he was ill and helpless. He was beginning to drop asleep, but got up uneasily and walked across the room to shake off his drowsiness. At moments he fancied he was delirious, but it was not illness that he thought of most. Sitting down again, he began looking round, as though searching for something. This happened several times. At last his eyes were fastened intently on one point. Ivan smiled, but an angry flush suffused his face. He sat a long time in his place, his head propped on both arms, though he looked sideways at the same point, at the sofa that stood against the opposite wall. There was evidently something, some object, that irritated him there, worried him and tormented him.

## CHAPTER IX
### THE DEVIL. IVAN'S NIGHTMARE

I AM not a doctor, and yet I feel that the moment has come when I positively must give the reader some account of the nature of Ivan

Fyodorovich's illness. Anticipating events, I shall say at least one thing: he was at that moment on the very eve of an attack of brain fever. Though his health had long been affected, it had offered a stubborn resistance to the fever which in the end gained complete mastery over it. Though I know nothing of medicine, I venture to hazard the suggestion that he really had perhaps, by a terrible effort of will, succeeded in delaying the attack for a time, hoping, of course, to check it completely. He knew that he was unwell, but he loathed the thought of being ill at that fatal time, at the approaching crisis in his life, when he needed to have all his presence of mind, to say what he had to say boldly and resolutely and "to justify himself to himself."

He had, however, consulted the new doctor, who had been brought from Moscow thanks to a fantastic notion of Katerina Ivanovna's, to which I have referred already. After listening to him and examining him the doctor came to the conclusion that he was actually suffering from some disorder of the brain, and was not at all surprised by an admission which Ivan had reluctantly made him. "Hallucinations are quite likely in your condition," the doctor opined, "though it would be better to verify them . . . you must have yourself treated seriously at once, without a moment's delay, or things will go badly with you." But Ivan did not follow this judicious advice and did not take to his bed to be nursed. "I am still on my feet, I am still strong enough; if I drop, it'll be different then, any one may treat me who likes," he decided, dismissing the subject with a wave of the hand.

And so he was sitting almost conscious himself of his delirium and, as I have said already, looking persistently at some object on the sofa against the opposite wall. Suddenly some one proved to be sitting there, though goodness knows how he had come in, for he had not been in the room when Ivan came into it, on his return from Smerdyakov. This was a man or, more accurately speaking, a Russian gentleman of a certain kind, no longer young, *qui frisait la cinquantaine*, as the French say, with rather long, still thick, dark hair, slightly streaked with grey, and a small pointed beard. He was wearing a brownish jacket, evidently made by a good tailor though already shabby, made perhaps three years ago and quite out of fashion, so that smart and well-to-do people had not been wearing this style for the last two years. His linen and his long neck-tie in the form of a scarf were all such as are worn by gentlemen who aim at being stylish, but on closer inspection his linen was not over-clean and his wide scarf was very threadbare. The visitor's check trousers fitted admirably, but were too light in colour and too tight for the present fashion. His soft fluffy white hat was out of keeping with the season.

In brief, there was every appearance of gentility on straitened means. It looked as though the gentleman belonged to that class of lily-handed landowners who used to flourish in the days of serfdom. He had unmistakably been, at some time, in fashionable society, had once had good connections, had possibly preserved them indeed, but, after a gay youth, becoming gradually impoverished on the abolition of serfdom, he had sunk into the position of a hanger-on of the better class, wandering from one good old friend to another and received by them for his companionable and accommodating disposition and as being, after all, a gentleman who could be asked to sit down with any one, though, of course, not in

IVAN AND THE DEVIL

a place of honour. Such hangers-on, gentlemen of accommodating temper, who can tell a story, take a hand at cards, and who have a distinct aversion for any commissions if they are forced upon them, are usually solitary creatures, either bachelors or widowers. Sometimes they have children, but, if so, the children are always being brought up at a distance, at some aunt's, to whom these gentlemen never allude in good society, as though somewhat ashamed of the relationship. They gradually lose sight of their children altogether, though at intervals they receive a birthday or Christmas letter from them and sometimes even answer it.

The countenance of the unexpected visitor was not so much good-natured as accommodating and ready to assume any amiable expression as occasion might arise. He had no watch, but he had a tortoise-shell lorgnette on a black ribbon. On the middle finger of his right hand was a massive gold ring with a cheap opal stone in it.

Ivan was angrily silent and would not begin the conversation. The visitor waited and sat exactly like a dependant who had come down from his room to keep his host company at tea, and was discreetly silent, seeing that his host was frowning and preoccupied. But he was ready for any affable conversation as soon as his host should begin it. All at once his face expressed a sudden solicitude.

"I say," he began to Ivan, "excuse me, I only mention it to remind you. You went to Smerdyakov's to find out about Katerina Ivanovna, but you came away without having found out anything about her, you probably forgot . . ."

"Ah, yes," broke from Ivan and his face grew gloomy with care. "Yes, I'd forgotten . . . but it doesn't matter now, never mind, let it all wait till to-morrow," he muttered to himself; "and you," he added, addressing his visitor, "I should have remembered that myself in a minute, for that was just what was tormenting me! Why did you pop up, do you think I'm going to believe that you prompted me, and that I didn't remember it of myself?"

"Don't believe it then," said the gentleman, smiling affably, "what's the good of forcing yourself to believe? Besides, proofs do not help one to believe, especially material proofs. Thomas believed, not because he saw Christ risen, but because he wanted to believe, before he saw. Look at the spiritists, for instance. . . . I am very fond of them . . . only fancy, they imagine that they are serving the cause of religion, because the devils show them their horns from the other world. That, they say, is a material proof, so to speak, of the existence of the hereafter. The hereafter and material proofs, tra-la-la! And if you come to that, does proving there's a devil prove that there's a God? I want to join a society of idealists, I'll lead the opposition in it, I'll say I am a realist, and not a materialist, he-he!"

"Listen." Ivan suddenly got up from the table. "I seem to be delirious . . . I am delirious, in fact, talk any nonsense you like, I don't care! You won't drive me to fury, as you did last time. But I feel somehow ashamed . . . I want to walk about the room . . . I sometimes don't see you and don't even hear your voice as I did last time, but I always guess what you are gabbling, for it's I, *I myself speaking, not you.* Only I don't know whether I was dreaming last time or whether I really saw you. I'll wet a towel and put it on my head and perhaps you'll vanish into thin air."

Ivan went into the corner, took a towel, and

did as he said, and with a wet towel on his head began walking up and down the room.

"I am so glad that from the first we have been on terms of familiarity," the visitor began.

"Fool," laughed Ivan, "do you suppose I should stand on ceremony with you? I am in good spirits now, though I've a pain in my temple . . . and in the top of my head . . . only please don't talk philosophy, as you did last time. If you can't take yourself off, talk of something amusing. Give me some gossip, you are a hanger-on, you ought to gossip. What a nightmare to have! But I am not afraid of you. I'll get the better of you. I won't be taken to a mad-house!"

"*C'est charmant*, hanger-on. Yes, I am in my natural shape. For what am I on earth but a hanger-on? By the way, I am listening to you and am rather surprised to find you are actually beginning to take me for something real, not simply your fancy, as you persisted in declaring last time . . ."

"Never for one minute have I taken you for reality," Ivan cried with a sort of fury. "You are a lie, you are my illness, you are a phantom. It's only that I don't know how to destroy you and I see I must suffer for a time. You are my hallucination. You are the incarnation of myself, but only of one side of me . . . of my thoughts and feelings, but only the nastiest and stupidest of them. From that point of view you might be of interest to me, if only I had time to be bothered with you . . ."

"Excuse me, excuse me, I'll show you up. When you flew out at Alyosha at the lamppost this evening and shouted to him, 'You learnt it from *him!* How do you know that *he* visits me?' you were thinking of me then. So for one brief moment you did believe that

I really exist." The gentleman laughed blandly.

"Yes, that was a moment of weakness . . . but I couldn't believe in you. I don't know whether I was asleep or awake last time. Perhaps I was only dreaming then and didn't see you really at all . . ."

"And why were you so harsh with Alyosha just now? He is a dear; I've wronged him over Father Zosima."

"Don't talk of Alyosha! How dare you, you flunkey!" Ivan laughed again.

"You scold me, but you laugh — that's a good sign. But to-night you are ever so much more polite to me than you were last time and I know why: that great resolution of yours."

"Don't speak of my resolution," cried Ivan savagely.

"I understand, I understand, *c'est noble, c'est charmant*, you are going to defend your brother to-morrow and to sacrifice yourself . . . *C'est chevaleresque.*"

"Hold your tongue, I'll kick you!"

"I shan't be altogether sorry, for then my object will be attained. If you kick me, you must believe in my reality, for people don't kick ghosts. Joking apart, it doesn't matter to me, scold if you like, though it's better to be a trifle more polite even to me. 'Fool, flunkey!' what words!"

"Scolding you, I scold myself," Ivan laughed again, "you are myself, myself, only with a different mug. You just say what I am thinking . . . and are incapable of saying anything new!"

"If my way of thinking agrees with you, it's all to my credit," the gentleman declared, with delicacy and dignity.

"You pick out only my worst thoughts, and what's more, the stupid ones. You are stupid and vulgar. You are awfully stupid. No, I can't bear you! What am I to do, what am I to do!" Ivan said through his clenched teeth.

"My friend, above all things I want to be a gentleman and to be recognised as such," the visitor began in an access of the good-humoured and conciliatory pride typical of a dependant. "I am poor, but . . . I won't say very honest, but . . . it's an axiom generally accepted in society that I am a fallen angel. By God! I can't conceive how I can ever have been an angel. If I was, it must have been so long ago that there's no sin in forgetting it. Now I prize only my reputation as a well-bred person and live as I can, trying to make myself agreeable. I love men genuinely, I've been much maligned! When from time to time I settle here among you, my life gains a kind of reality and that's what I like most of all. You see, like you, the fantastic makes me suffer, and so I love your earthly realism. Here, with you, everything is circumscribed, here everything is formula, geometry, while with us it's all indeterminate equations! I wander about here dreaming. I love dreaming. Besides, on earth I become superstitious. Please don't laugh, that's just what I like, to become superstitious. I adopt all your habits here: I've grown fond of going to the public baths, would you believe it, and I enjoy steaming myself with merchants and priests. My dream is to become incarnate once for all and irrevocably in the form of some merchant's wife weighing two hundred and fifty pounds, and to believe all she believes. My ideal is to go to church and offer a candle in simple-hearted faith, I swear by God it is. Then there would be an end to my sufferings. I like being doctored, too; in the spring there was an outbreak of smallpox and I went and was vac-

cinated in a foundling hospital — if only you knew how I enjoyed myself that day. I subscribed ten roubles to the cause of the Slavs! . . . But you are not listening. Do you know, you are not yourself to-night," the gentleman said, after a pause. "I know you went yesterday to that doctor . . . well, what about your health? What did the doctor say?"

"Fool!" Ivan snapped out.

"But you're a clever one. You are scolding again? I didn't ask out of sympathy, but just like that. You needn't answer. Now rheumatism has come in again . . ."

"Fool!" repeated Ivan.

"You keep saying the same thing; but I had such an attack of rheumatism last year that I still remember it."

"The devil has rheumatism?"

"Why not, if I sometimes become incarnate? I become incarnate and I take the consequences. Satan *sum et nihil humanum a me alienum puto*."

"What, what? Satan *sum et nihil humanum* . . . that's not bad for the devil!"

"I am glad I've pleased you at last."

"But you didn't get that from me." Ivan stopped suddenly, seeming struck. "That never entered my head, that's strange."

"*C'est du nouveau, n'est ce pas?* This time I'll act honestly and explain it to you. Listen, in dreams and especially in nightmares, from indigestion or whatever it may be, a man sometimes has such artistic dreams, so complex and realistic, so full of events, even a whole world of events, woven into such a plot, with such unexpected details from the most exalted matters to the last button on a cuff, as I swear Leo Tolstoy will never invent. Yet such dreams are sometimes dreamed not by novelists, but by the most ordinary people, officials, journalists, priests. . . . The subject is a complete enigma. A statesman confessed to me, indeed, that all his best ideas came to him when he was asleep. Well, that's how it is now, too, though I am your hallucination, yet, just as in a nightmare, I say original things which had not entered your head before. So I don't repeat your ideas, yet I am only your nightmare, nothing more."

"You are lying, your aim is to convince me you have an existence of your own, and are not my nightmare, and now you are asserting you are a dream."

"My dear fellow, I've adopted a peculiar method to-day, I'll explain it to you afterwards. Wait, where did I break off? Oh, yes! I caught cold then, only not here but yonder."

"Where is yonder? Tell me, will you be here long? Can't you go away?" Ivan exclaimed almost in despair. He ceased walking to and fro, sat down on the sofa, leaned his elbows on the table again and held his head tight in both hands. He pulled the wet towel off and flung it away in vexation. It was evidently of no use.

"Your nerves are out of order," observed the gentleman, with a carelessly easy, though perfectly friendly, air. "You are angry with me even for being able to catch cold, though it happened in a most natural way. I was hurrying to a diplomatic *soirée* at the house of a lady of high rank in Petersburg, who was aiming at influence in the Ministry. Well, evening dress, white tie, gloves, though I was God knows where and had to fly through space to reach your earth. . . . Of course, it took only an instant, but you know a ray of light from the sun takes a full eight minutes, and fancy in evening dress and open waistcoat. Spirits don't freeze, but when one is incarnate, well

. . . in brief, I acted rashly, and set off, and you know in those ethereal spaces, in the waters that were above the firmament, there's such a frost . . . at least one can't call it frost, you can fancy, 150° below zero! You know the game the village girls play — they invite the unwary to lick an axe when it's 30° below, the tongue instantly freezes to it and the dupe tears the skin off, so it bleeds. But that's only when it's 30°, when it's 150° I imagine it would be enough to put your finger on the axe and it would be the end of it . . . if only there could be an axe there."

"And can there be an axe there?" Ivan interrupted, absent-mindedly and squeamishly. He was exerting himself to the utmost not to believe in the delusion and not to sink into complete insanity.

"An axe?" the guest interrupted in surprise.

"Yes, what would become of an axe there?" Ivan cried suddenly, with a sort of savage and insistent obstinacy.

"What would become of an axe in space? *Quelle idée!* If it were far enough away, it would begin, I think, to revolve round the earth without knowing why, like a satellite. The astronomers would calculate the rising and the setting of the axe, Gatzuk would put it in his almanac, that's all."

"You are stupid, awfully stupid," said Ivan peevishly. "Lie more cleverly or I won't listen. You want to get the better of me by realism, to convince me that you exist, but I don't want to believe you exist! I won't believe it!"

"But I am not lying, it's all the truth; the truth is unhappily hardly ever amusing. I see you persist in expecting something big of me, and perhaps something fine. That's a great pity, for I only give what I can . . ."

"Don't talk philosophy, you ass!"

"Philosophy, indeed, when all my right side is numb and I am moaning and groaning. I've tried the whole medical faculty: they can diagnose beautifully, they have the whole of your disease at their finger-tips, but they've no idea how to cure you. There was an enthusiastic little student here, 'Even if you die,' said he, 'you'll know perfectly well what disease you died of!' And then this way they have of sending you to specialists. 'We only diagnose,' they say, 'but go to such-and-such a specialist, he'll cure you.' The old doctor who used to cure all sorts of diseases has completely disappeared, I assure you, now there are only specialists and they all advertise in the newspapers. If anything is wrong with your nose, they send you to Paris: there, they say, is a European specialist who cures noses. If you go to Paris, he'll look at your nose; I can cure only your right nostril, he'll tell you, for I don't cure the left nostril, that's not my specialty, but go to Vienna, there there's a specialist who will cure your left nostril. What are you to do? I fell back on popular remedies, a German doctor advised me to rub myself with honey and salt in the bath-house. Solely to get an extra bath I went, smeared myself all over, and it did me no good at all. In despair I wrote to Count Mattei in Milan. He sent me a book and some drops, bless him, and, only fancy, Hoff's malt extract cured me! I bought it by accident, drank a bottle and a half of it, and I was ready to dance, it took it away completely. I made up my mind to write to the papers to thank him, I was prompted by a feeling of gratitude, and, only fancy, it led to no end of bother: not a single paper would take my letter. 'It would be very reactionary,' they said, 'no one will believe it. *Le diable n'existe*

*point.* You'd better print it anonymously,' they advised me. What use is a letter of thanks if it's anonymous? I laughed with the men at the newspaper office. 'It's reactionary to believe in God in our days,' I said, 'but I am the devil, so I may be believed in.' 'We quite understand that,' they said. 'Who doesn't believe in the devil? Yet it won't do, it might injure our reputation. Perhaps as a joke, if you like.' But I thought as a joke it wouldn't be very witty. So it wasn't printed. And do you know, I have felt sore about it to this day. My best feelings, gratitude, for instance, are literally denied me simply because of my social position."

"Philosophical reflections again?" Ivan snarled with hatred.

"God forbid, but one can't help complaining sometimes. I am a slandered man. You upbraid me every moment with being stupid. One can see you are young. My dear fellow, intelligence isn't the only thing! I have naturally a kind and merry heart. 'I also write vaudevilles of all sorts.' You seem to take me for Hlestakov* grown old, but my fate is a far more serious one. Before time was, by some decree which I could never make out, I was predestined 'to deny' and yet I am genuinely good-hearted and not at all inclined to negation. 'No, you must go and deny, without denial there's no criticism and what would a journal be without a department of criticism?' Without criticism it would be nothing but one 'hosannah.' But nothing but hosannah is not enough for life, the hosannah must be tried in the crucible of doubt and so on, in the same style. But I don't meddle in that, I am not the creator, I am not answerable. Well, they've

* The hero of Gogol's "Inspector-General." *Editor's note.*

chosen their scapegoat, they've made me head the department of criticism and so life was made possible. We understand that comedy; I, for instance, simply ask for annihilation. No, live, I am told, for there'd be nothing without you. If everything on earth were sensible, nothing would happen. There would be no events without you, and there must be events. So against the grain I serve so that there may be events, and do what's unreasonable because I am commanded to. For all their indisputable intelligence, men take this farce as something serious, and that is their tragedy. They suffer, of course . . . but then they live, they live a real life, not a fantastic one, for it is suffering that is life. Without suffering what would be the pleasure of it? It would be transformed into an endless church service; it would be holy, but tedious. But what about me? I suffer, but still, I don't live. I am $x$ in an indeterminate equation. I am a sort of phantom in life who has lost all beginnings and ends, and who has even forgotten his own name. You are laughing — no, you are not laughing, you are angry again. You are for ever angry, all you care about is intelligence, but I repeat again that I would give away all this super-stellar life, all the ranks and honours, simply to be transformed into the soul of a merchant's wife weighing two hundred and fifty and set candles before God's shrine."

"Then even you don't believe in God?" said Ivan, with a smile of hatred.

"That is, — how shall I put it? — if only you are in earnest . . ."

"Is there a God or not?" Ivan cried with the same savage persistence.

"Ah, then you are in earnest! My dear fellow, upon my word I don't know. There! I've said it now!"

"You don't know, but you see God? No, you are not some one apart, you are myself, you are I and nothing more! You are rubbish, you are my fancy!"

"Well, if you like, we have the same philosophy, that would be true. *Je pense, donc je suis*, I know that for a fact, all the rest, all these worlds, God and even Satan — all that is not proved, to my mind. Does all that exist of itself, or is it only an emanation of myself, a logical development of my ego which alone has existed for ever: but I make haste to stop, for I believe you will be jumping up to beat me directly."

"You'd better tell me some anecdote!" said Ivan miserably.

"There is an anecdote precisely on our subject, or rather a legend, not an anecdote. You reproach me with unbelief, you say that I see, yet don't believe. But, my dear fellow, I am not the only one like that. We are all in a muddle over there now and all through your science. As long as there were atoms, five senses, four elements, everything hung together somehow. There were atoms in the ancient world even, but since we've learnt that you've discovered the chemical molecule and protoplasm and the devil knows what, we put our tails between our legs. It was just chaos, and, above all, superstition, scandal; there's as much scandal among us as among you, you know; a little more in fact, and indeed, we have informers, for we, too, have a place where certain 'information' is welcome. Well, this wild legend belongs to our middle ages — not yours, but ours — and no one believes it even among us, except the merchants' wives weighing two hundred and fifty pounds, not your merchants' wives I mean, but ours. Everything you have, we have, too, I am revealing one of our secrets out of friendship for you; though it's forbidden. This legend is about Paradise. There was, they say, here on earth a thinker and philosopher. He rejected everything, 'laws, conscience, faith,' and, above all, the future life. He died; he expected nothing but darkness and death and he found a future life before him. He was astounded and indignant. 'This is against my principles!' he said. And he was punished for that . . . that is, you must excuse me, I am just repeating what I heard myself, it's only a legend . . . he was sentenced to walk a quadrillion kilometres in the dark (we've adopted the metric system, you know) and when he had finished that quadrillion, the gates of heaven would be opened to him and he would be forgiven . . ."

"And what tortures have you in the other world besides the quadrillion kilometres?" asked Ivan, with a strange eagerness.

"What tortures? Ah, don't ask. In the old days we had all sorts, but now they have taken chiefly to moral punishments — 'remorse' and all that nonsense. We got that, too, from you, from the softening of your manners. And who's the better for it? Only those who have got no conscience, for how can they be tortured by remorse when they have no conscience? But decent people who have a conscience and a sense of honour suffer for it. Reforms, when the ground has not been prepared for them, especially if they are institutions copied from abroad, do nothing but mischief! The ancient hell-fire was better. Well, this man, who was condemned to the quadrillion kilometres, stood still, looked round, and lay down across the road. 'I won't go, I refuse on principle!' Take the soul of an enlightened Russian atheist and mix it with the soul of the prophet

Jonah, who sulked for three days and nights in the belly of the whale, and you get the character of that thinker who lay across the road."

"What did he lie on there?"

"Well, I suppose there was something to lie on. You are not laughing?"

"Bravo!" cried Ivan, still with the same strange eagerness. Now he was listening with an unexpected curiosity. "Well, is he lying there now?"

"That's the point, that he isn't. He lay there almost a thousand years and then he got up and went on."

"What an ass!" cried Ivan, laughing nervously and still seeming to be pondering something intently. "Does it make any difference whether he lies there for ever or walks the quadrillion kilometres? It would take a billion years to walk it?"

"Much more than that. I haven't got a pencil and paper or I could work it out. But he got there long ago and that's where the story begins."

"What, he got there? But how did he get the billion years to do it?"

"Why, you keep thinking of our present earth! But our present earth may have been repeated a billion times. Why, it became extinct, froze, cracked, broke to bits, disintegrated into its elements, again 'the waters above the firmament,' then again a comet, again a sun, again an earth from the sun — and the same sequence may have been repeated endlessly and exactly the same to every detail. How disgustingly boring . . ."

"Well, well, what happened when he arrived?"

"Why, the moment the gates of Paradise were open and he walked in, before he had been there two seconds, by his watch (though to my thinking his watch must have long dissolved into its elements in his pocket on the way), he cried out that those two seconds were worth walking not a quadrillion kilometres but a quadrillion of quadrillions, raised to the quadrillionth power! In fact, he sang 'hosannah' and overdid it so that some persons there of a nobler way of thinking wouldn't shake hands with him at first — he'd become too rapidly reactionary, they said. The Russian temperament. I repeat, it's a legend. I offer it for what it's worth. So that's the sort of ideas we have on such subjects even now."

"I've caught you!" Ivan cried, with an almost childish delight, as though he had succeeded in remembering something at last. "That anecdote about the quadrillion years, I made up myself! I was seventeen then, I was at high school. I made up that anecdote and told it to a schoolfellow called Korovkin, it was in Moscow. . . . The anecdote is so characteristic that I couldn't have taken it from anywhere. I thought I'd forgotten it . . . but I've unconsciously recalled it — I recalled it myself — it was not you telling it! Thousands of things are unconsciously remembered like that even when people are being taken to execution . . . it's come back to me in a dream. You are that dream! You are a dream, you don't exist!"

"From the vehemence with which you deny my existence," laughed the gentleman, "I am convinced that you believe in me."

"Not in the slightest! I haven't a hundredth part of a grain of faith in you!"

"But you have the thousandth of a grain. Homeopathic doses perhaps are the strongest. Confess that you have faith even to the ten-thousandth of a grain."

"Not for one minute," cried Ivan furiously.

"But I should like to believe in you," he added strangely.

"Aha! There's an admission! But I am good-natured. I'll come to your assistance again. Listen, it was I caught you, not you me. I told you your anecdote you'd forgotten, on purpose, so as to destroy your faith in me completely."

"You are lying. The object of your visit is to convince me of your existence!"

"Just so. But hesitation, suspense, conflict between belief and disbelief — is sometimes such torture to a conscientious man, such as you are, that it's better to hang oneself. Knowing that you are inclined to believe in me, I administered some disbelief by telling you that anecdote. I lead you to belief and disbelief in turn, and in doing it I have a purpose of my own. It's the new method. As soon as you disbelieve in me completely, you'll begin assuring me to my face that I am not a dream but a reality. I know you. Then I shall have attained my object, which is an honourable one. I shall sow in you only a tiny grain of faith and it will grow into an oak-tree — and such an oak-tree that, sitting on it, you will long to enter the ranks of 'the hermits in the wilderness and the saintly women,' for that is what you are secretly longing for. You'll dine on locusts, you'll drag yourself into the wilderness to save your soul!"

"Then it's for the salvation of my soul you are working, is it, you scoundrel?"

"One must do a good deed sometimes. You are ill-humoured, I see."

"Clown! Did you ever tempt those holy men who ate locusts and prayed seventeen years in the wilderness till they were overgrown with moss?"

"My dear fellow, I've done nothing else.

One forgets the whole world and all the worlds, and sticks to one such saint, because he is a very precious diamond. One such soul, you know, is sometimes worth a whole constellation. We have our own arithmetic, you know. The conquest is priceless! And some of them, on my word, are not inferior to you in culture, though you won't believe it. They can contemplate such depths of belief and disbelief at the same moment that sometimes it really seems that they are within a hair's-breadth of being 'turned upside down,' as the actor Gorbunov says."

"Well, did you get your nose pulled?"*

"My dear fellow," observed the visitor sententiously, "it's better to get off with your nose pulled than without a nose at all. As an afflicted marquis observed not long ago (he must have been treated by a specialist) in confessing to his spiritual father — a Jesuit. I was present, it was simply charming. 'Give me back my nose!' he said, and he beat his breast. 'My son,' said the priest evasively, 'all things are accomplished in accordance with the inscrutable decrees of Providence, and what seems a misfortune sometimes leads to extraordinary, though unapparent, benefits. If stern destiny has deprived you of your nose, it's to your advantage that as long as you live no one will dare say that he will pull your nose for you.' 'Holy father, that's no comfort,' cried the despairing marquis. 'I'd be delighted to have my nose pulled every day of my life, if it were only in its proper place.' 'My son,' sighed the priest, 'you can't ask for all the blessings at once. That would be murmuring against Providence, who even in this has not forgotten you, for if you cry out as you cried

* Literally: "Did you get off with a nose?" — meaning, "Did you fail?" *Editor's note.*

out just now, declaring you'd be glad to have your nose pulled for the rest of your life, your desire has already been fulfilled indirectly, for when you lost your nose, you were led by the nose.' "

"Faugh, how stupid!" cried Ivan.

"My dear friend, I only wanted to amuse you. But I swear that's the genuine Jesuit casuistry and I swear that it all happened word for word as I've told you. It happened lately and gave me a great deal of trouble. The unhappy young man shot himself that very night when he got home. I was by his side till the very last moment. As for those Jesuit confessionals, they are really my most delightful diversion at melancholy moments. Here's another incident that happened only the other day. A little blonde Norman girl of twenty — a buxom, unsophisticated beauty who would make your mouth water — comes to an old priest. She bends down and whispers her sin through the grating. 'Why, my daughter, have you fallen again already?' cries the priest. 'O Sancta Maria, what do I hear! Not the same man this time, how long will this go on? Aren't you ashamed!' '*Ah, mon père,*' answers the sinner with tears of penitence, '*ça lui fait tant de plaisir, et à moi si peu de peine!*' Fancy, such an answer! I drew back. It was the cry of nature, better than innocence itself, if you like. I absolved her sin on the spot and was turning to go, but I was forced to return. I heard the priest at the grating making an appointment with her for the evening — though he was an old man hard as flint, he fell in an instant! It was nature, the truth of nature asserted its rights! What, you are turning up your nose again? Angry again? I don't know how to please you . . ."

"Leave me alone, you are throbbing in my

brain like a haunting nightmare," Ivan moaned miserably, helpless before his apparition. "I am bored with you, agonisingly and insufferably. I would give anything to be able to shake you off!"

"I repeat, moderate your expectations, don't demand of me 'everything great and noble' and you'll see how well we shall get on," said the gentleman impressively. "You are really angry with me for not having appeared to you in a red glow, with thunder and lightning, with scorched wings, and for showing myself in such a modest guise. You are wounded, in the first place, in your æsthetic feelings, and, secondly, in your pride. How could such a vulgar devil visit such a great man as you! Yes, there is that romantic strain in you, that was so derided by Belinsky. I can't help it, young man, as I got ready to come to you I did think of appearing as a joke in the form of a retired general who had served in the Caucasus, with a star of the Lion and the Sun on my coat. But I was positively afraid to do it, for you'd have thrashed me for daring to pin the Lion and the Sun on my coat, instead of, at least, the Polar Star or the Sirius. And you keep on saying I am stupid, but, mercy on us! I make no claim to be equal to you in intelligence. Mephistopheles declared to Faust that he desired evil, but did only good. Well, he can say what he likes, it's quite the opposite with me. I am perhaps the one man in all creation who loves the truth and genuinely desires good. I was there when the Word, Who died on the Cross, rose up into heaven bearing on His bosom the soul of the penitent thief. I heard the glad shrieks of the cherubim singing and shouting hosannah and the seraphim's thunderous shout of rapture which shook heaven and all creation, and I swear to you by all that's sacred I longed to join the chorus and shout hosannah with them all. The word had almost escaped me, had almost broken from my lips . . . you know how susceptible and æsthetically impressionable I am. But common sense — oh, a most unhappy trait in my character — kept me in due bounds and I let the moment pass! For what would have happened, I reflected, what would have happened after my hosannah? Everything on earth would have been extinguished at once and no events could have occurred. And so, solely from a sense of duty and because of my social position, I was forced to suppress the good impulse and to stick to my nasty task. Somebody takes all the credit for goodness to himself, and nothing but nastiness is left for me. But I don't covet the honour of leading a cheat's life, I am not ambitious. Why am I, of all creatures in the world, doomed to be cursed by all decent people and even to be kicked, for if I put on mortal form I am bound to take such consequences sometimes. I know, of course, there's a secret in it, but they won't tell me the secret for anything, for then perhaps, seeing the meaning of it, I might bawl hosannah, and the indispensable minus would disappear at once and good sense would reign supreme throughout the whole world. And that, of course, would mean the end of everything, even of magazines and newspapers, for who would take them in? I know that at the end of all things I shall be reconciled. I, too, shall walk my quadrillion and learn the secret. But till that happens I shall sulk and fulfil my destiny though it's against the grain — that is, ruin thousands for the sake of saving one. How many souls have had to be ruined and how many honourable reputations destroyed for the sake of that one righteous man,

Job, over whom they made such a fool of me in the old days. Yes, till the secret is revealed, there are two sorts of truths for me — one, their truth, yonder, which I know nothing about so far, and the other my own. And there's no knowing which will turn out the better. . . . Are you asleep?"

"I might well be," Ivan groaned angrily. "All my stupid ideas — outgrown, thrashed out long ago, and flung aside like a dead carcass — you present to me as something new!"

"There's no pleasing you! And I thought I should fascinate you by my literary style. That hosannah in the skies really wasn't bad, was it? And then that ironical tone *à la* Heine, eh?"

"No, I was never such a flunkey! How then could my soul beget a flunkey like you?"

"My dear fellow, I know a most charming and attractive young Russian gentleman, a young thinker and a great lover of literature and art, the author of a promising poem entitled 'The Grand Inquisitor.' I was only thinking of him!"

"I forbid you to speak of 'The Grand Inquisitor,'" cried Ivan, crimson with shame.

"And the 'Geological Cataclysm.' Do you remember? That was a poem, now!"

"Hold your tongue, or I'll kill you!"

"You'll kill me? No, excuse me, I will speak. I came to treat myself to that pleasure. Oh, I love the dreams of my ardent young friends, quivering with eagerness for life! 'New men are there,' you decided last spring, when you were meaning to come here, 'they propose to destroy everything and begin with cannibalism. Stupid fellows! they didn't ask my advice! I maintain that nothing need be destroyed, that we need to destroy only the idea of God in mankind; that's how we have

set to work. That's what one should begin with. That's what, that's what one should begin with. Oh, blind race of men who have no understanding! As soon as men have all of them denied God — and I believe that period, analogous with geological periods, will come to pass — the old conception of the universe will fall of itself without cannibalism and, what's more, the old morality, and everything will begin anew. Men will unite to take from life all it can give, but only for joy and happiness in the present world. Man will be lifted up with a spirit of divine Titanic pride and the man-god will appear. From hour to hour extending his conquest of nature infinitely by his will and his science, man will feel such lofty joy from hour to hour in doing it that it will make up for all his old hopes of attaining the joys of heaven. Every one will know that he is wholly mortal, that there is no resurrection, and will accept death proudly and serenely like a god. His pride will teach him that it's useless for him to murmur because life is but a moment, and he will love his brother without need of reward. Love will be sufficient unto the moment of life, but the very consciousness of its momentariness will intensify its fire, which now is dissipated in dreams of eternal love beyond the grave' . . . and so on and so on in the same style. Very charming!"

Ivan sat with his eyes on the floor and his hands pressed to his ears, but he began trembling all over. The voice continued.

"The question now is, my young thinker reflected, is it possible that such a period will ever come? If it does, everything is determined and humanity is settled for ever. But as, owing to man's inveterate stupidity, this cannot come about for at least a thousand years, every one who recognises the truth even now may legitimately order his life as he pleases, on the new principles. In that sense, 'everything is permitted' for him. What's more, even if this period never comes to pass, since there is anyway no God and no immortality, the new man may well become the man-god, even if he is the only one in the whole world, and, promoted to his new rank, he may lightheartedly overstep all the barriers of the morality of the old slave-man, if necessary. There is no law for God. Where God stands, the place is holy. Where I stand will be at once the foremost place . . . 'everything is permitted' and that's the end of it! That's all very charming; but if you want to swindle, why do you want a moral sanction for doing it? But that's our modern Russian all over. He can't bring himself to swindle without a moral sanction. He is so in love with truth . . ."

The visitor talked, obviously carried away by his own eloquence, speaking louder and louder and looking ironically at his host. But he did not succeed in finishing; Ivan suddenly snatched a glass from the table and flung it at the orator.

"*Ah, mais c'est bête enfin*," cried the latter, jumping up from the sofa and shaking the drops of tea off himself. "He has remembered Luther's inkstand! He takes me for a dream and throws glasses at a dream! It's like a woman! I suspected you were only pretending to stop up your ears, but you were listening to me."

A loud, persistent knocking was suddenly heard at the window. Ivan jumped up from the sofa. "Do you hear? You'd better open," cried the visitor; "it's your brother Alyosha with the most interesting and surprising news, I'll be bound!"

"Be silent, deceiver, I knew it was Alyosha, I felt he was coming, and of course he has not come for nothing; of course he brings 'news,' " Ivan exclaimed frantically.

"Open, open to him. There's a snowstorm and he is your brother. *Monsieur sait-il le temps qu'il fait? C'est à ne pas mettre un chien dehors.*"

The knocking continued. Ivan wanted to rush to the window, but something seemed to fetter his arms and legs. He strained every nerve to break his chains, but in vain. The knocking at the window grew louder and louder. At last the chains were broken and Ivan leapt up from the sofa. He looked round him wildly. Both candles had almost burnt out, the glass he had just thrown at his visitor stood before him on the table, and there was no one on the sofa opposite. The knocking on the window frame went on persistently, but it was by no means so loud as it had seemed in his dream; on the contrary, it was quite subdued. "It was not a dream! No, I swear it was not a dream, it all happened just now!" cried Ivan. He rushed to the window and opened the movable pane.

"Alyosha, I told you not to come," he cried fiercely to his brother. "In two words, what do you want? In two words, do you hear?"

"An hour ago Smerdyakov hanged himself," Alyosha answered from the yard.

"Come round to the steps, I'll open at once," said Ivan, and went to open the door to Alyosha.

# CHAPTER X
### "IT WAS HE WHO SAID THAT"

ALYOSHA, coming in, told Ivan that a little over an hour ago Marya Kondratyevna had come to his rooms and informed him that

Smerdyakov had taken his own life. "I go in to clear away the samovar and I see he is hanging on a nail in the wall." On Alyosha's inquiring whether she had informed the police, she answered that she had told no one, "but I flew straight to you, I've run all the way." She was like one crazed, Alyosha reported, and was shaking like a leaf. When Alyosha ran with her to the cottage, he found Smerdyakov still hanging. On the table lay a note: "I destroy my life of my own will and desire, so as to put no blame on any one." Alyosha left the note on the table and went straight to the police captain and told him all about it. "And from him I've come straight to you," said Alyosha, in conclusion, looking intently into Ivan's face. He had not taken his eyes off him while he told his story, as though struck by something in his expression.

"Brother," he cried suddenly, "you must be terribly ill. You stare and don't seem to understand what I tell you."

"It's a good thing you came," said Ivan, as though brooding, and not hearing Alyosha's exclamation. "I knew he had hanged himself."

"From whom?"

"I don't know. But I knew. Did I know? Yes, he told me. He told me so just now."

Ivan stood in the middle of the room, and still spoke in the same brooding tone, looking at the ground.

"Who is *he?*" asked Alyosha, involuntarily looking round.

"He's slipped away."

Ivan raised his head and smiled softly.

"He was scared of you, of you, the dove. You are a 'pure cherub.' Dmitri calls you a cherub. Cherub! . . . the seraphim's thunderous shout of rapture. What are seraphim? Perhaps a whole constellation. But perhaps that constellation is only a chemical molecule. Is there a constellation of the Lion and the Sun? Do you know?"

"Brother, sit down," said Alyosha in alarm. "For goodness' sake, sit down on the sofa! You are delirious; put your head on the pillow, that's right. Would you like a wet towel on your head? Perhaps it will do you good."

"Give me the towel: it's here on the chair. I just threw it down there."

"It's not here. Don't worry yourself. I know where it is — here," said Alyosha, finding a clean towel, folded up and unused, by Ivan's dressing-table in the other corner of the room. Ivan looked strangely at the towel: recollection seemed to come back to him for an instant.

"Wait" — he got up from the sofa — "an hour ago I took that new towel from there and wetted it. I wrapped it round my head and threw it down here . . . How is it it's dry? There was no other."

"You put that towel on your head?" asked Alyosha.

"Yes, and walked up and down the room an hour ago . . . Why have the candles burnt down so? What's the time?"

"Nearly twelve."

"No, no, no!" Ivan cried suddenly. "It was not a dream. He was here; he was sitting here, on that sofa. When you knocked at the window, I threw a glass at him . . . this one. Wait a minute. I was asleep last time, but this dream was not a dream. It has happened before. I have dreams now, Alyosha . . . yet they are not dreams, but reality. I walk about, talk, and see . . . though I am asleep. But he was sitting here, on that sofa there. . . . He is frightfully stupid, Alyosha, frightfully stupid." Ivan laughed suddenly and began pacing about the room.

"Who is stupid? Of whom are you talking, brother?" Alyosha asked anxiously again.

"The devil! He's taken to visiting me. He's been here twice, almost three times. He taunted me with being angry at his being a simple devil and not Satan, with scorched wings, in thunder and lightning. But he is not Satan: that's a lie. He is an impostor. He is simply a devil — a paltry, trivial devil. He goes to the baths. If you undressed him, you'd be sure to find he had a tail, long and smooth like a Danish dog's, a yard long, dun colour. . . . Alyosha, you are cold. You've been out in the snow. Would you like some tea? What? Is it cold? Shall I tell her to bring some? *C'est à ne pas mettre un chien dehors . . .*"

Alyosha ran to the wash-stand, wetted the towel, persuaded Ivan to sit down again, and put the wet towel round his head.

"What were you telling me just now about Lise?" Ivan began again. (He was becoming very talkative.) "I like Lise. I said something nasty about her. It was a lie. I like her . . . I am afraid for Katya to-morrow. I am afraid for her most of all. On account of the future. She will cast me off to-morrow and trample me under foot. She thinks that I am ruining Mitya from jealousy on her account! Yes, she thinks that! But it's not so. To-morrow the cross, but not the gallows. No, I shan't hang myself. Do you know, I can never commit suicide, Alyosha. Is it because I am base? I am not a coward. Is it because of the thirst for life? How did I know that Smerdyakov had hanged himself? Yes, it was *he* told me so."

"And you are quite convinced that there has been some one here?" asked Alyosha.

"Yes, on that sofa in the corner. You would have driven him away. You did drive him away: he disappeared when you arrived. I love your face, Alyosha. Did you know that I love your face? And *he* is myself, Alyosha. All that's base in me, all that's mean and contemptible. Yes, I am a romantic. He noticed it . . . though it's a libel. He is frightfully stupid; but that's his advantage. He has cunning, animal cunning — he knew how to infuriate me. He kept taunting me with believing in him, and that was how he made me listen to him. He fooled me like a boy. He told me a great deal that was true about myself, though. I should never have owned it to myself. Do you know, Alyosha," Ivan added in an intensely earnest and confidential tone, "I should be awfully glad to think it was *he* and not I."

"He has worn you out," said Alyosha looking compassionately at his brother.

"He's been teasing me. And you know he does it so cleverly, so cleverly. 'Conscience! What is conscience? I make it up myself. Why am I tormented by it? Out of habit. Out of the seven-thousand-year-old universal human habit. So let us give it up, and we shall be as gods.' It was he said that, it was he said that!"

"And not you, not you?" Alyosha could not help crying, looking frankly at his brother. "Never mind him, anyway; have done with him and forget him. And let him take with him all that you curse now, and never come back!"

"Yes, but he is spiteful. He laughed at me. He was insolent, Alyosha," Ivan said, with a shudder of offense. "But he slandered me, slandered me in many ways. He told lies about me to my face. 'Oh, you are going to perform an act of heroic virtue: to confess you murdered your father, that the valet murdered him at your instigation.'"

"Brother," Alyosha interposed, "restrain yourself. It was not you who murdered him. It's not true!"

"That's what he says, he, and he knows it. 'You are going to perform an act of heroic virtue, and you don't believe in virtue; that's what tortures you and makes you angry, that's why you are so vindictive.' He said that to me about myself and he knows whereof he speaks."

"It's you say that, not he," exclaimed Alyosha mournfully, "and you say it because you are ill and delirious, tormenting yourself."

"No, he knows whereof he speaks. 'You are going out of pride,' he says. 'You'll stand up and say it was I who killed, and why do you writhe with horror? You are lying! I despise your opinion, I despise your horror!' He said that about me. 'And do you know you are longing for their praise — "He is a criminal, a murderer, but what a generous soul; he wanted to save his brother and he confessed."' That's a lie, Alyosha!" Ivan cried suddenly, with flashing eyes. "I don't want the low rabble to praise me, I swear I don't! That's a lie! That's why I threw the glass at him and it broke against his ugly face."

"Brother, calm yourself, stop!" Alyosha entreated him.

"Yes, he knows how to torment one. He's cruel," Ivan went on, unheeding. "I had an inkling from the first as to what he came for. 'Granting that you go out of pride, still you had a hope that Smerdyakov might be convicted and sent to Siberia, and Mitya would be acquitted, while you would only be condemned *morally*' (Do you hear? he laughed then) — 'and some people will praise you. But now Smerdyakov's dead, he has hanged himself, and who'll believe you alone? But yet you are going, you are going, you'll go all the same, you've decided to go. What are you going for now?' That's awful, Alyosha. I can't

endure such questions. Who dares ask me such questions?"

"Brother," interposed Alyosha — his heart sank with terror, but he still seemed to hope to bring Ivan to reason — "how could he have told you of Smerdyakov's death before I came, when no one knew of it and there was no time for any one to know of it?"

"He told me," said Ivan firmly, refusing to admit a doubt. "It was all he did talk about, if you come to that. 'And it would be all right if you believed in virtue,' he said. ' "No matter if they disbelieve me, I am going for the sake of a principle." But you are a little pig like Fyodor Pavlovich and what is virtue to you? Why do you want to go meddling if your sacrifice is of no use to any one? Because you don't know yourself why you go! Oh, you'd give a great deal to know yourself why you go! And can you have made up your mind? You've not made up your mind. You'll sit all night deliberating whether to go or not. But you will go; you know you'll go. You know that whichever way you decide, the decision does not depend on you. You'll go because you won't dare not to go. Why won't you dare? You must guess that for yourself. That's a riddle for you!' He got up and went away. You came and he went. He called me a coward, Alyosha! *Le mot de l'énigme* is that I am a coward. 'It is not for such eagles to soar above the earth.' It was he added that — he! And Smerdyakov said the same. He must be killed! Katya despises me. I've seen that for a month past. Even Lise will begin to despise me! 'You are going in order to be praised.' That's a brutal lie! And you despise me, too, Alyosha. Now I am going to hate you again! And I hate the monster, too! I hate the monster! I don't want to save the monster. Let him rot in Siberia! He's begun singing a hymn! Oh, to-morrow I'll go, stand before them, and spit in their eyes!"

He jumped up in a frenzy, flung off the towel, and fell to pacing the room again. Alyosha recalled what he had just said. "I seem to be sleeping awake. . . . I walk, I speak, I see, but I am asleep." It seemed to be just like that now. Alyosha did not leave him. The thought passed through his mind to run for a doctor, but he was afraid to leave his brother alone: there was no one to whom he could leave him. By degrees Ivan lost consciousness completely at last. He still went on talking, talking incessantly, but quite incoherently, and even articulated his words with difficulty. Suddenly he staggered violently; but Alyosha was in time to support him. Ivan let him lead him to his bed. Alyosha undressed him somehow and put him to bed. He sat watching over him for another two hours. The sick man slept soundly, without stirring, breathing softly and evenly. Alyosha took a pillow and lay down on the sofa, without undressing.

As he fell asleep he prayed for Mitya and Ivan. He began to understand Ivan's illness. "The anguish of a proud determination. An earnest conscience!" God, in Whom he disbelieved, and His truth were gaining mastery over his heart, which still refused to submit. "Yes," the thought floated through Alyosha's head as it lay on the pillow, "yes, if Smerdyakov is dead, no one will believe Ivan's evidence; but he will go and give it." Alyosha smiled softly. "God will conquer!" he thought. "He will either rise up in the light of truth, or . . . he'll perish in hate, revenging on himself and on every one his having served the cause he does not believe in," Alyosha added bitterly, and again he prayed for Ivan.

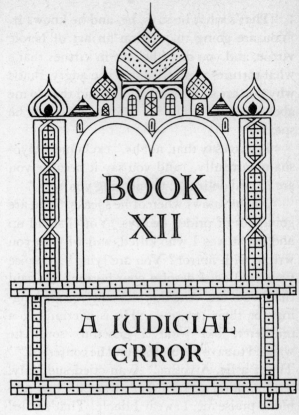

# BOOK XII

# A JUDICIAL ERROR

## CHAPTER I
### THE FATAL DAY

At ten o'clock in the morning of the day following the events I have described, the trial of Dmitri Karamazov began in our district court.

I hasten to emphasize the fact that I am far from esteeming myself capable of reporting all that took place at the trial in full detail, or even in proper order. I imagine that to recall everything, and to explain it all duly, would fill a whole volume, even a very large one. And so I trust I may not be reproached for confining myself to what struck me personally, and what I specially remembered. I may have mistaken what was of secondary importance for the main thing, and may have omitted the most prominent and essential features. But I see I shall do better not to apologise. I will do my best and the reader will see for himself that I have done all I can.

And, to begin with, before we enter the court-room, I will mention what surprised me most on that day. Indeed, as it appeared later, every one was surprised at it, too. We all knew that the affair had aroused great interest, that every one was burning with impatience for the trial to begin, that it had been a subject of talk, conjecture, exclamation, and surmise for the last two months in local society. Every one knew, too, that the case had become known throughout Russia, and yet we had not imagined that it had aroused such burning, such intense, interest in all and sundry, not only among ourselves, but everywhere. This became evident at the trial that day.

Visitors had arrived not only from the chief town of our province, but from several other Russian cities, as well as from Moscow and Petersburg. There came lawyers, several distinguished personages, and also some ladies. Every ticket of admission had been snatched up. A special place behind the table at which the court sat was set apart for the most distinguished and important of the male visitors; a row of armchairs had been placed there — something which had never been allowed before. A large proportion — not less than half of the public — were ladies. So many lawyers had arrived that they did not know where to seat them, for all the tickets had long since been distributed, or obtained by pleading and entreaty. I saw at the end of the room, behind the platform, a special partition hurriedly put up, behind which all these lawyers were admitted, and they thought themselves lucky to have standing room there, for all chairs had been removed to gain space, and the crowd behind the partition stood throughout the case closely packed, shoulder to shoulder.

Some of the ladies, especially those who came from a distance, made their appearance in the gallery very smartly dressed, but the majority of the ladies were oblivious even to dress. Their faces betrayed hysterical, eager, almost morbid, curiosity. A peculiar fact — established afterwards by many observations — that almost all the ladies, or, at least the vast majority of them, were on Mitya's side and in favour of his being acquitted. This was perhaps chiefly owing to his reputation as a heart-breaker. It was known that two women who were rivals were to appear in the case. One of them — Katerina Ivanovna — was an object of particular interest. All sorts of extraordinary tales were told about her, amazing anecdotes of her passion for Mitya, in spite of his crime. Her pride and "aristocratic connections" were particularly insisted upon (she had called upon scarcely any one in the town). People said she intended to petition the Government for leave to accompany the criminal to Siberia and to be married to him somewhere in the mines, underground. The appearance of Grushenka in court, as Katerina Ivanovna's rival, was awaited with no less agitation. The public was looking forward with anxious curiosity to the meeting of the two rivals — the proud aristocratic girl and "the hetaira." But Grushenka was a more familiar figure to the ladies of the district than Katerina Ivanovna. They had already seen "the woman who had ruined Fyodor Pavlovich and his unhappy son," and all, almost without exception, wondered how father and son could be so in love with "such a very common, ordinary Russian girl, who was not even pretty."

In brief, there was a great deal of talk. I know for a fact that there were several serious family quarrels on Mitya's account in our town. Many ladies quarrelled violently with their husbands because of differences of opinion about the dreadful case, and it was only natural that the husbands of these ladies should enter the court-room not only unfavourably disposed towards the accused, but actually full of bitter hostility towards him. In fact, one may say positively that the masculine, as distinguished from the feminine, part of the audience was biased against the accused. There were numbers of severe, frowning, even vindictive, faces. Mitya, indeed, had managed to offend many people during his stay in the town. Some of the visitors were, of course, in excellent spirits and quite unconcerned as to the fate of Mitya personally. But all were interested in the trial, and the majority of the men were certainly hoping for the conviction of the criminal, except perhaps the lawyers, who were interested in the legal, so to speak, rather than the moral aspect of the case.

Everybody was excited by the presence of the celebrated Fetyukovich. His talent was known everywhere, and this was not the first time he had appeared for the defence in notorious criminal cases in the provinces. And when he did, such cases became celebrated and long remembered all over Russia. There were stories, too, about our prosecutor and about the presiding judge. It was said that our prosecutor was trembling at the thought of meeting Fetyukovich, and that they had been inveterate enemies from the beginning of their careers in Petersburg, that our touchy Ippolit Kirillovich, who always considered that he had been offended by some one in Petersburg because his talents had not been properly appreciated, was keenly excited over the Karamazov case, and was even dreaming of rebuilding his flagging fortunes by means of it, but that Fetyukovich was his one anxiety. But these rumours were not quite justified. Our prosecutor was not one of those men who lose heart in the face of danger. On the contrary, his self-confidence increased with the increase of danger. It must be noted that our prosecutor was in general too hasty and morbidly impressionable. He would put his whole soul into some case and work at it as though his whole fate and his whole fortune depended on its result. This was the subject of some ridicule in the legal world, for just by this characteristic our prosecutor had gained a wider notoriety than could have been expected from his modest position. People laughed particularly at his passion for psychology. In my opinion, they were wrong, and our prosecutor was, I believe, a character of greater earnestness than was generally supposed. But because of his morbidity he had failed to impress himself on people at the outset of his career or at any time later.

As for the presiding judge, I can only say that he was a humane and cultured man, who had a practical knowledge of his work and the most advanced views. He was rather ambitious, but did not concern himself greatly about his career. The great aim of his life was to be a progressive. He had, too, connections with wealth. He felt, as we learnt afterwards, rather strongly about the Karamazov case,. but not in any personal way. He was interested in it as a social phenomenon, in its classification and its character as a product of our social conditions, as typical of the national character, and so on, and so on. His attitude to the personal aspect of the case, to its tragic significance and the persons involved in it, including the prisoner, was rather indifferent and abstract, as was perhaps fitting, indeed.

The court-room was packed to overflowing long before the judges made their appearance. Our court-room is the best hall in the town — spacious, lofty, and with good acoustics. On the right of the judges, who were on a raised platform, a table and two rows of chairs had been placed for the jury. On the left was the place for the defendant and his counsel. In the middle of the court, near the judges, was a table with the "material evidence." On it lay Fyodor Pavlovich's white silk dressing-gown, stained with blood; the fatal brass pestle with which the supposed murder had been committed; Mitya's shirt, with a bloodstained sleeve; his coat, stained with blood in patches over the pocket in which he had put his handkerchief; the handkerchief itself, stiff with blood and by now quite yellow; the pistol loaded by Mitya at Perhotin's with a view to suicide, and taken from him on the sly at Mokroye by Trifon Borisovich; the envelope in which the three thousand roubles had been kept ready for Grushenka, the narrow pink ribbon with which it had been tied, and many other articles which I don't remember. Some distance farther back in the room were the seats for the public. But in front of the balustrade a few chairs had been placed for witnesses who were to be retained in court after giving their evidence.

At ten o'clock the three judges arrived — the presiding judge, one honorary justice of the peace, and one other. The prosecutor, of course, entered immediately after. The presiding judge was a short, stout, thick-set man of fifty, with a dyspeptic complexion, dark hair turning grey and cut short, and a red rib-

bon, of what Order I don't remember. The prosecutor struck me and the others, too, as looking particularly pale, almost green. His face seemed to have grown suddenly thinner, perhaps in a single night, for I had seen him looking as usual only two days before. The presiding judge began by asking the court attendant whether all the jurymen were present.

But I see I can't go on like this, partly because many things I did not hear, others I did not grasp, and others I have forgotten, but most of all because, as I have said before, I have literally no time or space to mention everything that was said and done. I only know that neither side objected to many of the jurymen. I remember the twelve jurymen — four were petty officials of the town, two were merchants, and six peasants and local townspeople. I remember, long before the trial, questions were continually asked with some surprise, especially by ladies, "Can such a delicate, complex and psychological case be submitted for decision to petty officials and even peasants?" and "What can an official, still more a peasant, understand in such an affair?" All the four officials on the jury were, in fact, men of no consequence and of low rank. Except for one who was rather younger, they were grey-headed men, little known in society, who had vegetated on a pitiful salary, and who probably had elderly, unpresentable wives and crowds of children, perhaps even without shoes and stockings. At best, they spent their leisure over cards and, of course, had never read a single book. The two merchants looked respectable, but were strangely silent and stolid. One of them had shaved his beard, and was dressed in European style; the other had a small, grey beard, and wore a red ribbon with some sort of medal upon it on h neck. There is no need to speak of the towns-people and the peasants. Our townspeople are almost peasants, and even work on the land. Two of them also wore European dress, and, perhaps for that reason, were dirtier and more uninviting-looking than the others. So that one might well wonder, as I did as soon as I had looked·at them, "what men like that could possibly make of such a case?" Yet their faces wore a strangely imposing, almost menacing, expression; they were stern and frowning.

At last the presiding judge opened the case of the murder of Fyodor Pavlovich Karama-zov, retired titular councillor. I don't quite remember how he expressed himself. The court attendant was told to bring in the prisoner, and Mitya made his appearance. There was a hush in the court. One could have heard a fly. I don't know how it was with others, but Mitya made a most unfavourable impression on me. He looked an awful dandy in a brand-new frock-coat. I heard afterwards that he had ordered it in Moscow expressly for the occa-sion from his own tailor, who had his measure. He wore immaculate black kid gloves and elegant linen. He walked in with his yard-long strides, looking stiffly straight in front of him, and sat down in his place with a most unper-turbed air.

At the same moment the counsel for the de-fence, the celebrated Fetyukovich, entered, and a sort of subdued hum passed through the court. He was a tall, spare man, with long thin legs, with extremely long, thin, pale fingers, clean-shaven face, rather short hair, demurely brushed, and thin lips that were at times curved into something between a sneer and a smile. He looked about forty. His face would have been pleasant, if it had not been for his ~~~es, which, in themselves small and inex-

pressive, were set remarkably close together, with only the thin, long nose as a dividing line between them. In fact, there was something strikingly birdlike about his face. He wore a frock-coat and white tie.

I remember the presiding judge's first ques-tion to Mitya, about his name, his status, and so on. Mitya answered sharply, and his voice was so unexpectedly loud that it made the judge start and look at the prisoner almost with surprise. Then followed the reading of a list of persons who had been summoned to take part in the trial — that is, as witnesses and experts. It was a long list. Four of the wit-nesses did not appear — Miüsov, who had testified at the preliminary inquiry, but was now in Paris; Madame Hohlakov and Maxi-mov, who were absent through illness; and Smerdyakov, through his sudden death, a po-lice certificate of which was presented. The news of Smerdyakov's death produced a sud-den stir and whisper in the court. Many in the audience, of course, had not heard of the sud-den suicide. What struck people most was Mitya's sudden outburst. As soon as the state-ment of Smerdyakov's death was made, he cried out aloud from his place:

"The dog died like a dog!"

I remember how his counsel rushed to him, and how the presiding judge addressed him, threatening to take stern measures if such ir-regular behaviour repeated itself. Mitya nodded and in a subdued voice repeated sev-eral times abruptly to his counsel, with no show of regret:

"I won't again, I won't. It escaped me. I won't do it again."

And, of course, this brief episode did him no good with the jury or the public. His char-acter was displayed, and it spoke for itself. It

TRIAL FOR MURDER

was under the influence of this incident that the court clerk read the bill of indictment. It was rather short, but circumstantial. It contained only the chief reasons why so-and-so had been arrested, why he must be tried, and so on. Yet it made a great impression on me. The clerk read it loudly and distinctly. The whole tragedy was suddenly unfolded before us, in concentrated form, in bold relief, in a fatal and pitiless light. I remember how, immediately after it had been read, the presiding judge asked Mitya in a loud, impressive voice:

"Prisoner, do you plead guilty?"

Mitya suddenly rose from his seat.

"I plead guilty to drunkenness and dissipation," he exclaimed, again in a startling, almost frenzied, voice, "to idleness and debauchery. I meant to become an honest man for good, just at the moment when I was cut down by fate. But of the death of the old man, my enemy and my father, I am not guilty. But of robbing him, no, no, I am not guilty! I could not be. Dmitri Karamazov is a scoundrel, but not a thief."

Having shouted thus, he sat down, visibly trembling all over. The presiding judge again briefly, but impressively, admonished him to answer to the point, and not to go off into irrelevant exclamations. Then he ordered the case to proceed. All the witnesses were led up to take the oath. Here I saw them all together. The brothers of the accused were, however, allowed to give evidence without taking the oath.

After an exhortation from the priest and the presiding judge, the witnesses were led away and were seated as far apart from one another as possible. Then they began calling them up one by one.

## CHAPTER II
### DANGEROUS WITNESSES

I do not know whether the witnesses for the defence and for the prosecution were separated into groups by the presiding judge, and in what order they were to be called. But no doubt some arrangement existed. I only know that the witnesses for the prosecution were called first. I repeat I don't intend to describe all the questioning step by step. Besides, my account would be to some extent superfluous, because in the speeches of the prosecutor and the counsel for the defence all the testimony presented was brought together and set in a strong and significant light, and I took down parts of those two remarkable speeches in full, and will quote them in due time, and I shall also describe one extraordinary and quite unexpected episode, which occurred before the final speeches, and undoubtedly influenced the sinister and fatal outcome of the trial.

I will only observe that from the first moments of the trial one peculiar characteristic of the case was conspicuous and observed by all, that is, the overwhelming strength of the prosecution as compared with the arguments and means at the disposal of the defence. Every one realised it from the first moment when in this stern court-room the facts began to accumulate round a single point, and the whole horrible and bloody crime was gradually revealed. Every one, perhaps, felt from the first that the case was beyond dispute, that there was no doubt about it, that there could be really no discussion, and that the arguing would be only a matter of form, and that the criminal was guilty, obviously and conclusively guilty. I imagine that even the ladies, who were so impatiently longing for the acquittal of the interesting prisoner, were at the same time, without exception, convinced of his guilt. What's more, I believe they would have been mortified if his guilt had not been so firmly established, as that would have lessened the effect of the closing scene of the criminal's acquittal. That he would be acquitted all the ladies, strange to say, were firmly persuaded up to the very last moment. "He is guilty, but he will be acquitted, from motives of humanity, because of the new ideas, the new sentiments that have come into fashion," and so on, and so on. And that was why they had crowded into the court so impatiently. The men were more interested in the contest between the prosecutor and the famous Fetyukovich.

All were wondering and asking themselves what could even a talent like Fetyukovich's make of such a lost cause; and so they followed his achievements, step by step, with concentrated attention.

But Fetyukovich remained an enigma to all up to the very end, up to his speech. Persons of experience suspected that he had a system, that he had some design, that he was working towards some object, but it was almost impossible to guess what it was. His confidence and self-reliance were unmistakable, however. Every one noticed with pleasure, moreover, that, after so short a stay, not more than three days, perhaps, among us, he had so wonderfully succeeded in mastering the case and "had studied it to a nicety." People described with relish, afterwards, how cleverly he had "taken down" all the witnesses for the prosecution, and as far as possible perplexed them and, what's more, had aspersed their reputation and so depreciated the value of their evidence. But it was supposed that he did this

rather by way of sport, so to speak, for professional glory, to show nothing had been omitted of the accepted methods, for all were convinced that he could do no real good by such disparagement of the witnesses, and that he probably was more aware of this than any one, having some idea of his own in the background, some concealed weapon of defence, which he would suddenly reveal when the time came. But meanwhile, conscious of his strength, he seemed to be playing and gambolling.

So, for instance, when Grigory, Fyodor Pavlovich's old servant, who had given the most damning piece of evidence about the open door, was examined, the counsel for the defence positively pounced upon him when his turn came to question him. It must be noted that Grigory entered the hall with a composed and almost stately air, not the least disconcerted by the majesty of the court or the vast audience listening to him. He testified with as much confidence as though he had been talking with his Marfa, only perhaps more respectfully. It was impossible to confuse him. The prosecutor questioned him first in detail about the family life of the Karamazovs. The family picture stood out in lurid colours. It was plain to ear and eye that the witness was guileless and impartial. In spite of his profound reverence for the memory of his deceased master, he yet bore witness that he had been unjust to Mitya and "hadn't brought up his children as he should. He'd have been devoured by lice when he was little, if it hadn't been for me," he added, describing Mitya's early childhood. "It wasn't fair either of the father to wrong his son over his mother's property, which was by right his."

In reply to the prosecutor's question what

grounds he had for asserting that Fyodor Pavlovich had wronged his son in their money relations, Grigory, to the surprise of every one, had no proof at all to bring forward, but he still persisted that the arrangement with the son was "unfair," and that he ought "to have paid him several thousand roubles more." I must note, by the way, that the prosecutor asked this question whether Fyodor Pavlovich had really kept back part of Mitya's inheritance with marked persistence of all the witnesses who could be asked it, not excepting Alyosha and Ivan, but he obtained no exact information from any one; all alleged that it was so, but were unable to bring forward any clear proof. Grigory's description of the scene at the dinner-table, when Dmitri had burst in and given his father a beating, threatening to come back to kill him, made a sinister impression on the court, especially as the old servant told his story quietly, without more words than necessary, and using a peculiar phraseology, so that it was all very eloquent. He observed that he was not angry with Mitya for having knocked him down and struck him on the face; he had forgiven him long ago, he said. Of the deceased Smerdyakov he observed, crossing himself, that he was a lad of ability, but stupid and afflicted with disease, and, worse still, an unbeliever, and that it was Fyodor Pavlovich and his elder son who had taught him atheism. But he defended Smerdyakov's honesty almost with warmth, and related how Smerdyakov had once found the master's money in the yard, and, instead of concealing it, had taken it to his master, who had rewarded him with a "gold-piece" for it, and trusted him implicitly from that time forward. He maintained obstinately that the door into the garden had been open. But he

was asked so many questions that I can't recall them all.

At last the counsel for the defence began to cross-examine him, and the first question he asked was about the envelope in which Fyodor Pavlovich was supposed to have put three thousand roubles for "a certain person." "Have you ever seen it, you, who were for so many years in close attendance on your master?" Grigory answered that he had not seen it and had never heard of the money from any one "till everybody was talking about it." This question about the envelope Fetyukovich put to every one who could conceivably have known of it, as persistently as the prosecutor asked his question about Dmitri's inheritance, and got the same answer from all, that no one had seen the envelope, though many had heard of it. From the beginning every one noticed Fetyukovich's insistence on this subject.

"Now, with your permission I'll ask you a question," Fetyukovich said, suddenly and unexpectedly. "Of what was that balsam, or, rather, decoction, made, which, as we learn from the preliminary inquiry, you used on that evening to rub your lame back, in the hope of curing it?"

Grigory looked blankly at the questioner, and after a brief silence muttered "there was saffron in it."

"Nothing but saffron? Don't you remember any other ingredient?"

"There was plantain in it, too."

"And pepper perhaps?" Fetyukovich queried.

"Yes, there was pepper, too."

"And so on. And all soaked in vodka?"

"In spirits."

There was a faint sound of laughter in the court.

515

"You see, in spirits. After rubbing your back, I believe, you drank what was left in the bottle with a certain pious prayer, known only to your spouse, didn't you?"

"I did."

"Did you drink much? Roughly speaking, a wine-glass or two?"

"It might have been a tumblerful."

"A tumblerful, even. Perhaps a tumbler and a half?" Grigory did not answer. He seemed to see what was meant.

"A glass and a half of neat spirits — is not at all bad, don't you think? You might see the gates of heaven open, not only the door into the garden?"

Grigory remained silent. There was another laugh in the court. The presiding judge stirred.

"Do you know for a fact," Fetyukovich persisted, "whether you were awake or not when you saw the open door?"

"I was on my legs."

"That's not a proof that you were awake." (There was again laughter in the court.) "Could you have answered at that moment, if any one had asked you a question — for instance, what year it is?"

"That I don't know."

"And what year is it, what year of our era, Anno Domini, do you know?"

Grigory stood with a perplexed face, looking straight at his tormentor. Strange to say, it appeared he really did not know what year it was.

"But perhaps you can tell me how many fingers you have on your hand?"

"I am a servant," Grigory said suddenly, in a loud and distinct voice. "If the authorities think fit to make game of me, it is my duty to suffer it."

Fetyukovich was a little taken aback, and the presiding judge intervened, reminding him that he must ask more relevant questions. Fetyukovich bowed with dignity and said that he had no more questions to ask of the witness. The public and the jury, of course, were left with a grain of doubt in their minds as to the evidence of a man who might, while undergoing a certain cure, have seen "the gates of heaven," and who did not even know what year he was living in, so that the lawyer to some extent achieved his purpose. But before Grigory left the box another episode occurred. The presiding judge, turning to the accused, asked him whether he had any comment to make on the evidence of the last witness.

"Except about the door, all he has said is true," cried Mitya, in a loud voice. "For combing the lice off me, I thank him; for forgiving my blows, I thank him. The old man has been honest all his life and as faithful to my father as seven hundred poodles."

"Prisoner, choose your words," the judge admonished him.

"I am not a poodle," Grigory muttered.

"All right, it's I am a poodle myself," cried Mitya. "If it's an insult, I take it on myself and I beg his pardon. I was a beast and cruel to him. I was cruel to Æsop, too."

"What Æsop?" the judge asked sternly again.

"Oh, Pierrot . . . my father, Fyodor Pavlovich."

The judge again and again warned Mitya impressively and very sternly to be more careful in his language.

"You are injuring yourself in the opinion of your judges."

The counsel for the defence was equally clever in dealing with the evidence of Rakitin.

I may remark that Rakitin was one of the leading witnesses and one to whom the prosecutor attached great significance. It appeared that he knew everything; his knowledge was amazing, he had been everywhere, seen everything, talked to everybody, knew every detail of the biography of Fyodor Pavlovich and all the Karamazovs. Of the envelope, it is true, he had only heard from Mitya himself. But he described minutely Mitya's exploits at the "Metropolis," all his compromising doings and sayings, and told the story of Captain Snegiryov's "bath-mop." But even Rakitin could say nothing positive about Mitya's inheritance, and confined himself to contemptuous generalities.

"Who could tell which of them was to blame, and which was in debt to the other, with their crazy Karamazov way of muddling things so that no one could make head or tail of it." The tragedy of the crime he presented as the product of the ancient way of living based on serfdom and the disorderly state of Russia, due to the lack of proper institutions. He was, in fact, allowed some latitude of speech. This was the first occasion on which Rakitin showed what he could do, and attracted notice. The prosecutor knew that the witness was preparing a magazine article on the case, and afterwards in his speech, as we shall see later, quoted some ideas from the article, showing that he had seen it already. The picture drawn by the witness was a gloomy and sinister one, and greatly strengthened the case for the prosecution. Altogether, Rakitin's discourse fascinated the public by its independence and the extraordinary nobility of its ideas. There were even two or three outbreaks of applause when he spoke of serfdom and the disorderly state of Russia.

But Rakitin, in his youthful ardour, made a slight blunder, of which the counsel for the defence at once adroitly took advantage. Answering certain questions about Grushenka, and carried away by the loftiness of his own sentiments and his success, of which he was, of course, conscious, he went so far as to speak somewhat contemptuously of Agrafena Alexandrovna as "Samsonov's kept woman." He would have given a good deal to take back his words afterwards, for Fetyukovich caught him out over it at once. And it was all because Rakitin had not reckoned on the lawyer's having been able to become so intimately acquainted with every detail in so short a time.

"Allow me to ask," began the counsel for the defence, with the most affable and even respectful smile, "you are, of course, the same Mr. Rakitin whose pamphlet, 'The Life of Father Zosima, the Elder, Deceased in the Lord,' published by the diocesan authorities, full of profound and religious reflections and preceded by an excellent and devout dedication to the Bishop, I have just read with such pleasure?"

"I did not write it for publication . . . it was published afterwards," muttered Rakitin, for some reason fearfully disconcerted and almost ashamed.

"Oh, that's excellent! A thinker like you can, and indeed ought to, take the broadest view of every social phenomenon. Your most instructive pamphlet has been widely circulated through the patronage of the Bishop, and has been of appreciable service. . . . But this is the chief thing I should like to learn from you. You stated just now that you were very intimately acquainted with Madame Svyetlov."

(It must be noted that Grushenka's surname was Svyetlov. I heard it for the first time that day, during the trial.)

"I cannot answer for all my acquaintances. . . . I am a young man . . . and who can be responsible for every one he meets?" cried Rakitin, flushing all over.

"I understand, I quite understand," cried Fetyukovich, as though he, too, were embarrassed and in haste to excuse himself. "You, like any other, might well be interested in an acquaintance with a young and beautiful woman who would readily entertain the *élite* of the youth of the neighbourhood, but . . . I only wanted to know . . . it has come to my knowledge that Madame Svyetlov was particularly anxious a couple of months ago to make the acquaintance of the younger Karamazov, Alexey Fyodorovich, and promised you twenty-five roubles if you would bring him to her in his monastic dress. And that actually took place on the evening of the day on which the terrible crime, which is the subject of the present investigation, was committed. You brought Alexey Karamazov to Madame Svyetlov, and did you receive the twenty-five roubles from Madame Svyetlov as a reward, that's what I wanted to hear from you?"

"It was a joke. . . . I don't see of what interest that can be to you. . . . I took it for a joke . . . meaning to give it back later . . ."

"Then you did take . . . But you have not given it back yet . . . or have you?"

"That's of no consequence," muttered Rakitin, "I refuse to answer such questions. . . . Of course I shall give it back."

The judge intervened, but Fetyukovich declared he had no more questions to ask of the witness. Mr. Rakitin left the witness-box not absolutely without a stain upon his character. The effect left by the lofty idealism of his speech was somewhat marred, and Fetyukovich's expression, as he watched him walk away, seemed to suggest to the public, "this is a specimen of the lofty-minded persons who accuse him." I remember that this incident, too, did not pass off without an outbreak from Mitya. Enraged by the tone in which Rakitin had referred to Grushenka, he suddenly shouted, "Bernard!" When, after Rakitin's cross-examination, the judge asked the prisoner if he had anything to say, Mitya cried loudly:

"Since I've been arrested, he has borrowed money from me! He is a contemptible Bernard and careerist, and he doesn't believe in God; he cheated the Bishop!"

Mitya, of course, was pulled up again for the intemperance of his language, but Rakitin was done for. Captain Snegiryov's testimony was a failure, too, but for quite a different reason. He appeared in ragged and dirty clothes, muddy boots, and in spite of the vigilance exercised and preliminary examination by an expert, he turned out to be hopelessly drunk. On being asked about Mitya's attack upon him, he refused to answer.

"God bless him. Ilusha told me not to. God will make it up to me yonder."

"Who told you not to tell? Of whom are you talking?"

"Ilusha, my little son. 'Father, father, how he insulted you!' He said that at the stone. Now he is dying . . ."

The captain suddenly began sobbing, and plumped down on his knees before the judge. He was hurriedly led away amidst the laughter of the public. The effect prepared by the prosecutor did not come off at all.

Fetyukovich went on making the most of every opportunity, and amazed people more and more by his minute knowledge of the case. Thus, for example, Trifon Borisovich made a great impression, of course, very prejudicial to Mitya. He calculated almost on his fingers that on his first visit to Mokroye, Mitya must have spent three thousand roubles, "or very little less. Just think what he squandered on those gipsy girls alone! And as for our lousy peasants, it wasn't a case of flinging half a rouble in the street, he made them presents of twenty-five roubles each, he didn't give them less. And what a lot of money was simply stolen from him! And if any one did steal, he did not leave a receipt. How could one catch the thief when he was flinging his money away all the time? Our peasants are robbers, you know; they have no care for their souls. And the way he went on with the girls, our village girls! They're completely set up since then, I tell you, they used to be poor." He recalled, in fact, every item of expense and added it all up. So the theory that only fifteen hundred had been spent and the rest had been put aside in a little bag seemed inconceivable.

"I saw three thousand as clear as a penny in his hands, I saw it with my own eyes; I should think I ought to know how to reckon money," cried Trifon Borisovich, doing his best to please "the authorities."

When it was Fetyukovich's turn to cross-examine him, he scarcely tried to refute his evidence, but began asking him about an incident at the first carousal at Mokroye, a month before the arrest, when Timofey and another peasant called Akim had picked up on the floor in the passage a hundred roubles dropped by Mitya when he was drunk, and had given them to Trifon Borisovich, and received a rouble each from him for doing so. "Well," asked the lawyer, "did you give that hundred roubles back to Mr. Karamazov?" Trifon Borisovich shuffled in vain. . . . He was obliged, after the peasants had been examined, to admit the finding of the hundred roubles, only adding that he had religiously returned it all to Dmitri Fyodorovich "in perfect honesty, and it's only because his honour was in liquor at the time, he wouldn't remember it." But, as he had denied the incident of the hundred roubles till the peasants had been called to prove it, his evidence as to returning the money to Mitya was naturally regarded with great suspicion. So one of the most dangerous witnesses brought forward by the prosecution was again discredited.

The same thing happened with the Poles. They assumed an attitude of pride and independence; they asserted loudly that they had both been in the service of the Crown, and that "*Pan* Mitya" had offered them three thousand "to buy their honour," and that they had seen a large sum of money in his hands. *Pan* Musialowicz introduced a terrible number of Polish words into his sentences, and seeing that this only raised him in the eyes of the judge and the prosecutor, grew more and more pompous, and ended by talking in Polish altogether. But Fetyukovich caught them, too, in his snares. Trifon Borisovich, recalled, was forced, in spite of his evasions, to admit that *Pan* Wróblewski had substituted another pack of cards for the one he had provided, and that *Pan* Musialowicz had cheated during the game. Kalganov confirmed this, and both the Poles left the witness-box with damaged reputations, amidst laughter from the public.

Then exactly the same thing happened with almost all the most dangerous witnesses. Fetyukovich succeeded in casting a slur on all of them, and dismissing them with a certain de-

519

rision. Both the amateurs and the professional lawyers were lost in admiration, and were only puzzled as to what good purpose could be served by it, for all, I repeat, felt that the case for the prosecution could not be refuted, but was growing more and more tragically overwhelming. But from the confidence of the "great magician" they saw that he was serene. They waited, feeling that "such a man" had not come from Petersburg for nothing, and that he was not a man to return unsuccessful.

## CHAPTER III
### THE MEDICAL EXPERTS AND
### A POUND OF NUTS

THE evidence of the medical experts, too, was of little use to the accused. And it appeared later that Fetyukovich had not reckoned much upon it. The medical line of defence had only been taken up through the insistence of Katerina Ivanovna, who had sent for a celebrated doctor from Moscow on purpose. The case for the defence could, of course, lose nothing by it and might, with luck, gain something from it. There was, however, an element of comedy about it, owing to the difference of opinion among the doctors. The medical experts were the famous doctor from Moscow, our doctor, Herzenstube, and the young doctor, Varvinsky. The two latter appeared also as witnesses for the prosecution.

The first to be called in the capacity of expert was Dr. Herzenstube. He was a grey and bald old man of seventy, of middle height and sturdy build. He was much esteemed and respected by every one in the town. He was a conscientious doctor and an excellent and pious man, a Herrnhuter or Moravian brother, I am not quite sure which. He had been living amongst us for many years and behaved with extraordinary dignity. He was a kind-hearted and humane man. He treated the sick poor and peasants for nothing, visited them in their slums and huts, and left money for medicine, but he was as obstinate as a mule. If once he had taken an idea into his head, there was no shaking him. Almost every one in the town was aware, by the way, that the famous doctor had, within the first two or three days of his presence among us, made some extremely offensive remarks as to Dr. Herzenstube's qualifications. Though the Moscow doctor asked twenty-five roubles for a visit, several people in the town were glad to take advantage of his arrival, and rushed to consult him regardless of expense. All these had, of course, previously been patients of Dr. Herzenstube's, and the celebrated doctor had criticised his treatment with extreme harshness. Finally, he had asked the patients as soon as he saw them, "Well, who has been cramming you with nostrums? Herzenstube? He, he!" Dr. Herzenstube, of course, heard all this, and now all the three doctors made their appearance, one after another, to be examined.

Dr. Herzenstube roundly declared that the abnormality of the prisoner's mental faculties was self-evident. Then giving his grounds for this opinion, which I omit here, he added that the abnormality was not only evident in many of the prisoner's actions in the past, but was apparent even now at this very moment. When he was asked to explain how it was apparent now at this moment, the old doctor, with simple-hearted directness, pointed out that the prisoner on entering the court had "an extraordinary air, remarkable under the circumstances"; that he had "marched in like a soldier, looking straight before him, though it would have been more natural for him to look to the left where, among the public, the ladies were sitting, seeing that he is a great admirer of the fair sex and must be thinking much of what the ladies are saying of him now," the old man concluded in his peculiar language.

I must add that he spoke Russian readily, but somehow every sentence was formed in the German manner, which did not, however, trouble him, for it had always been a weakness of his to believe that he spoke Russian perfectly, better indeed than Russians. And he was very fond of using Russian proverbs, always declaring that the Russian proverbs were the best and most expressive sayings in the whole world. I may remark, too, that in conversation, through absent-mindedness, he often forgot the most ordinary words, which sometimes went out of his head, though he knew them perfectly. The same thing happened, though, when he spoke German, and at such times he always waved his hand before his face as though trying to catch the lost word, and no one could induce him to go on speaking till he had found the missing word. His remark that the accused ought to have looked at the ladies on entering roused a whisper of amusement in the audience. All our ladies were very fond of our old doctor; they knew, too, that, having been a bachelor all his life and a chaste, religious man, he looked upon women as superior and ideal creatures. And so his unexpected observation struck every one as very queer.

The Moscow doctor, being questioned in his turn, definitely and emphatically affirmed that he considered the prisoner's mental condition abnormal in the highest degree. He talked at length and with erudition of "aberration" and "mania," and argued that, from all the facts collected, the prisoner had undoubtedly been in a condition of aberration for several days before his arrest, and, if the crime had been committed by him, it must, even if he were conscious of it, have been almost involuntary, as he had not the power to control the morbid impulse that possessed him.

But apart from temporary aberration, the doctor diagnosed mania, which promised, in his words, to lead to complete insanity in the future. (It must be noted that I report this in my own words, the doctor made use of very learned and technical language.) "All his actions are in contravention of common sense and logic," he continued. "Not to refer to what I have not seen, that is, the crime itself and the whole catastrophe, the day before yesterday, while he was talking to me, he had an unaccountably fixed look in his eye. He laughed unexpectedly when there was nothing to laugh at. He showed continual and inexplicable irritability, using strange words, 'Bernard!' 'Ethics!' and others equally inappropriate." But the doctor detected mania, above all, in the fact that the accused could not even speak of the three thousand roubles, of which he considered himself to have been cheated, without extraordinary irritation, though he could speak comparatively lightly of other misfortunes and grievances. According to all accounts, he had even in the past, whenever the subject of the three thousand roubles was touched on, flown into a perfect frenzy, and yet he was reported to be a disinterested and not grasping man.

"As to the opinion of my learned colleague," the Moscow doctor added ironically in conclusion, "that on entering the court, the accused would have naturally looked at the ladies and not straight before him, I will only say that, apart from the playfulness of this theory, it is radically unsound. For though I fully agree that the accused, on entering the court where his fate will be decided, would not naturally look straight before him in that fixed way, and that that may really be a sign of his abnormal mental condition, at the same time I maintain that he would naturally not look to the left at the ladies, but, on the contrary, to the right to find his legal adviser, on whose help all his hopes rest and on whose defence his fate depends." The doctor expressed his opinion resolutely and emphatically.

But the unexpected pronouncement of Dr. Varvinsky gave the last touch of comedy to the difference of opinion between the experts. In his opinion the accused was now, and had been all along, in a perfectly normal condition, and, although he certainly must have been in a nervous and exceedingly excited state before his arrest, this might have been due to several perfectly obvious causes, jealousy, anger, continual drunkenness, and so on. But this nervous condition would not involve the mental aberration of which mention had just been made. As to the question whether the accused should have looked to the left or to the right on entering the court, "in his modest opinion," the accused would naturally look straight before him on entering the court, as he had in fact done, as that was where the judges, on whom his fate depended, were sitting. So that it was just by looking straight before him that he showed his perfectly normal state of mind at present. The young doctor concluded his "modest" testimony with some heat.

"Bravo, doctor!" cried Mitya, from his seat, "just so!"

Mitya, of course, was checked, but the young doctor's opinion had a decisive influence on the judges and on the public, and, as ap-

peared afterwards, every one agreed with him. But Dr. Herzenstube, when called as a witness, was quite unexpectedly of use to Mitya. As an old resident in the town who had known the Karamazov family for years, he furnished some facts of great value for the prosecution, and suddenly, as though recalling something, he added: "But the poor young man might have had a very different life, for he had a good heart both in childhood and after childhood, that I know. But the Russian proverb says, 'If a man has one head, it's good, but if another clever man comes to visit him, it would be better still, for then there will be two heads and not only one.'"

"One head is good, but two are better," the prosecutor put in impatiently. He knew the old man's habit of talking slowly and deliberately, regardless of the impression he was making and of the delay he was causing, and highly prizing his flat, dull, and always gleefully complacent German wit. The old man was fond of making jokes.

"Oh, yes, that's what I say," he went on stubbornly. "One head is good, but two are much better, but he did not meet another head with wits, and his wits went. Where did they go? I've forgotten the word." He went on, passing his hand before his eyes, "Oh, yes, *spazieren*."

"Wandering?"

"Oh, yes, wandering, that's what I say. Well, his wits went wandering and fell in such a deep hole that he lost himself. And yet he was a grateful and sensitive boy. Oh, I remember him very well, a little chap so high, left neglected by his father in the back yard, when he ran about without boots on his feet, and his little breeches hanging by one button."

A note of feeling and tenderness suddenly

HE SAT RIGID IN HIS PLACE

came into the honest old man's voice. Fetyuko-vich positively started, as though scenting something and caught at it instantly.

"Oh, yes, I was a young man then. . . . I was . . . well, I was forty-five then, and had only just come here. And I was so sorry for the boy then; I asked myself why shouldn't I buy him a pound of . . . a pound of what? I've forgotten what it's called. A pound of what children are very fond of, what is it, what is it?" The doctor began waving his hands again. "It grows on a tree and is gath-ered and given to every one . . ."

"Apples?"

"Oh, no, no. You have a dozen of apples, not a pound. . . . No, there are a lot of them, and all little. You put them in the mouth and crack."

"Nuts?"

"Quite so, nuts, I say so," the doctor re-peated in the calmest way as though he had been at no loss for a word. "And I bought him a pound of nuts, for no one had ever bought the boy a pound of nuts before. And I lifted my finger and said to him, 'Boy, *Gott der Vater.*' He laughed and said, '*Gott der Vater.*' . . . '*Gott der Sohn.*' He laughed again and lisped, '*Gott der Sohn.*' '*Gott der heilige Geist.*' Then he laughed and said as best he could, '*Gott der heilige Geist.*' I went away, and two days after I happened to be passing, and he shouted to me of himself, 'Uncle, *Gott der Vater, Gott der Sohn,*' and he had only for-gotten '*Gott der heilige Geist.*' But I reminded him of it and I felt very sorry for him again. But he was taken away, and I did not see him again. Twenty-three years passed. I am sitting one morning in my study, a white-haired old man, when there walks into the room a bloom-ing young man, whom I should never have

recognised, but he held up his finger and said, laughing, '*Gott der Vater, Gott der Sohn,* and *Gott der heilige Geist.* I have just arrived and have come to thank you for that pound of nuts, for no one else ever bought me a pound of nuts; you are the only one that ever did.' And then I remembered my happy youth and the poor child in the yard, without boots on his feet, and my heart was touched and I said, 'You are a grateful young man, for you have remembered all your life the pound of nuts I bought you in your childhood.' And I em-braced him and blessed him. And I wept. He laughed, but he wept, too . . . for the Rus-sian often laughs when he ought to be weep-ing. But he did weep; I saw it. And now, alas!"

"And I am weeping now, German, I am weeping now, too, you saintly man," Mitya cried suddenly.

In any case the anecdote made a certain favourable impression on the public. But the chief sensation in Mitya's favour was created by the evidence of Katerina Ivanovna, which I will describe directly. Indeed, when the witnesses *à décharge,* that is, called by the defence, began giving evidence, fortune seemed all at once markedly more favour-able to Mitya, and, what was particularly striking, this was a surprise even to the coun-sel for the defence. But before Katerina Iva-novna was called, Alyosha was examined, and he recalled a fact which seemed to furnish positive evidence against one important point made by the prosecution.

## CHAPTER IV
### FORTUNE SMILES ON MITYA

IT came quite as a surprise even to Alyosha himself. He was not required to take the oath, and I remember that both sides addressed him very gently and sympathetically. It was evident that his good reputation had preceded him. Alyosha gave his evidence modestly and with restraint, but his warm sympathy for his unhappy brother was unmistakable. In answer to one question, he sketched his brother's character as that of a man, violent-tempered perhaps and carried away by his passions, but at the same time honourable, proud, and generous, capable of self-sacrifice, if necessary. He admitted, however, that, through his passion for Grushenka and his rivalry with his father, his brother had been of late in an intolerable position. But he repelled with indignation the suggestion that his brother might have committed a murder with intent to rob, though he recognised that the three thousand roubles had become almost an obsession with Mitya; that he had looked upon them as part of the inheritance he had been cheated of by his father, and that, indifferent as he was to money as a rule, he could not even speak of that three thousand without fury. With regard to the rivalry of the two "ladies," as the prosecutor expressed it — that is, of Grushenka and Katya — he spoke evasively and was even unwilling to answer one or two questions altogether.

"Did your brother tell you, anyway, that he intended to kill your father?" asked the prosecutor. "You can refuse to answer if you think necessary," he added.

"He did not tell me so directly," answered Alyosha.

"How so? Did he indirectly?"

"He spoke to me once of his hatred for our father and of his fear that in an extreme moment . . . in a moment of disgust, he might perhaps murder him."

"And you believed him?"

"I am afraid to say that I did. But I never doubted that some higher feeling would always save him at the fatal moment, as it has indeed saved him, for *it was not he* killed my father," Alyosha said firmly, in a loud voice that was heard throughout the court.

The prosecutor started like a warhorse at the sound of a trumpet.

"Let me assure you that I fully believe in the complete sincerity of your conviction and do not explain it by or identify it with your affection for your unhappy brother. Your peculiar view of the whole tragic episode is known to us already from the preliminary investigation. I won't attempt to conceal from you that it is highly subjective and contradicts all the other evidence collected by the prosecution. And so I think it essential to press you to tell me what facts have led you to this conviction of your brother's innocence and of the guilt of another person whom you clearly indicated at the preliminary inquiry?"

"At the preliminary inquiry I only answered the questions which I was asked," replied Alyosha, slowly and calmly. "For my own part, I made no accusation against Smerdyakov."

"Yet you pointed to him?"

"I was led to do so by my brother Dmitri's words. Already before the inquiry I was told what took place at his arrest and how he had then pointed to Smerdyakov. I believe absolutely that my brother is innocent, and if he didn't commit the murder, then . . ."

"Then Smerdyakov? Why Smerdyakov? And why are you so completely persuaded of your brother's innocence?"

"I cannot help believing my brother. I know he wouldn't lie to me. I saw from his face he wasn't lying."

"Only from his face? Is that all the proof you have?"

"I have no other proof."

"And of Smerdyakov's guilt have you no proof whatever but your brother's word and the expression of his face?"

"No, I have no other proof."

The prosecutor dropped the examination at this point. The impression left by Alyosha's evidence on the public was most disappointing. There had been talk about Smerdyakov before the trial; some one had heard something, some one had pointed out something else, it was said that Alyosha had gathered together some extraordinary proofs of his brother's innocence and Smerdyakov's guilt, and after all there was nothing, no evidence except certain moral convictions so natural in a brother.

But Fetyukovich began his cross-examination. On his asking Alyosha when it was that the accused had told him of his hatred for his father and that he might kill him, and whether he had heard it, for instance, at their last meeting before the catastrophe, Alyosha started as he answered, as though only just recollecting and grasping something.

"I remember one circumstance now which I'd quite forgotten myself. It wasn't clear to me at the time, but now . . ."

And, obviously only now for the first time struck by an idea, he recounted eagerly how, at his last interview with Mitya that evening under the tree, on the road to the monastery, Mitya had struck himself on the breast, "the upper part of the breast," and had repeated several times that he had a means of restoring his honour, that that means was here, here on his breast. "I thought, when he struck himself on the breast, he meant that it was in his heart," Alyosha continued, "that he might find in his heart strength to save himself from some awful disgrace which was awaiting him and which he did not dare confess even to me. I must own I did think at the time that he was speaking of our father, and that the disgrace he was shuddering at was the thought of going to our father and doing some violence to him. Yet it was just then that he pointed to something on his breast, so that I remember the idea struck me at the time that the heart is not in that part of the breast, but below, and that he struck himself much too high, just below the neck, and kept pointing to that place. My idea seemed silly to me at the time, but he was perhaps pointing then to that little bag in which there were sewn up these fifteen hundred roubles!"

"Just so," Mitya cried from his place. "That's right, Alyosha, it was the little bag I struck with my fist."

Fetyukovich flew to him in hot haste entreating him to keep quiet, and at the same instant pounced on Alyosha. Alyosha, carried away himself by his recollection, warmly expressed his theory that this disgrace was probably just that fifteen hundred roubles on him, which he might have returned to Katerina Ivanovna as half of what he owed her, but which he had yet determined not to repay her and to use for another purpose: to enable him to elope with Grushenka, if she consented.

"It is so, it must be so," exclaimed Alyosha, in sudden excitement. "My brother cried several times that half of the disgrace, half of it (he said *half* several times) he could free himself from at once, but that his character was unhappily so weak that he wouldn't do it . . . that he knew beforehand he was incapable of doing it!"

"And you clearly, confidently remember that he struck himself just on this part of the breast?" Fetyukovich asked eagerly.

"Clearly and confidently, for I thought at the time, 'Why does he strike himself up there when the heart is lower down?' and the thought seemed foolish to me at the time . . . I remember its seeming foolish . . . it flashed through my mind. That's what brought it back to me just now. How could I have forgotten it till now! It was that little bag he meant when he said he had the means but wouldn't give back that fifteen hundred. And when he was arrested at Mokroye he cried out — I know, I was told it — that he considered it the most disgraceful act of his life that when he had the means of repaying Katerina Ivanovna half (half, note!) of what he owed her, he yet could not bring himself to repay the money and preferred to remain a thief in her eyes rather than part with it. And what torture, what torture that debt has been to him!" Alyosha exclaimed in conclusion.

The prosecutor, of course, intervened. He asked Alyosha to describe once more how it had all happened, and several times insisted on the question, had the prisoner seemed to point to anything. Perhaps he had simply struck himself with his fist on the breast?

"But it was not with his fist," cried Alyosha; "he pointed with his fingers and pointed here, very high up. . . . How could I have so completely forgotten it till this moment!"

The judge asked Mitya what he had to say about this evidence. Mitya confirmed it, saying that he had been pointing to the fifteen hundred roubles which were on his breast, just below the neck, and that that was, of course, the disgrace. "A disgrace I cannot deny, the most shameful act of my whole life," cried Mitya. "I might have repaid it and didn't repay it. I preferred to remain a thief in her eyes rather than give it back. And the most shameful part of it was that I knew beforehand I shouldn't give it back! You are right, Alyosha! Thanks, Alyosha!"

So Alyosha's cross-examination ended. What was important and striking about it was that one fact at least had been found, and even though this were only one tiny bit of evidence, a mere hint at evidence, it did go some little way towards proving that the bag had existed and had contained fifteen hundred roubles and that the prisoner had not been lying at the preliminary inquiry when he alleged at Mokroye that those fifteen hundred roubles were "his own." Alyosha was glad. With a flushed face he moved away to the seat assigned to him. He kept repeating to himself: "How was it I forgot! How could I have forgotten it! And what made it come back to me now?"

The examination of Katerina Ivanovna began. As she appeared there was a great commotion in the court-room. The ladies clutched their lorgnettes and opera-glasses. There was a stir among the men: some stood up to get a better view. Everybody alleged afterwards that Mitya had turned "white as a sheet" on her entrance. All in black, she advanced modestly, almost timidly. It was impossible to tell from her face that she was agitated; but there was a resolute gleam in her dark and gloomy eyes. I may remark that many people mentioned that she looked particularly handsome at that moment. She spoke softly but clearly, so that she was heard all over the court. She expressed herself with composure, or at least tried to appear composed. The presiding judge began his examination discreetly and respectfully, as though afraid to touch "certain chords," and showing consideration for her great misfortune. But in answer to one of the first questions Katerina Ivanovna replied firmly that she had been betrothed to the accused "until he left me of his own accord . . ." she added quietly. When they asked her about the three thousand she had entrusted to Mitya to post to her relations, she said firmly, "I didn't give him the money simply to send it off. I felt at the time that he was in great need of money. . . . I gave him the three thousand with the understanding that he should post it within the month if he cared to. There was no need for him to worry himself about that debt afterwards."

I am not repeating all the questions asked her and all her answers word for word. I am only giving the substance of her testimony.

"I was firmly convinced that he would send off that sum as soon as he got money from his father," she went on. "I have never doubted his disinterestedness and his honesty . . . his scrupulous honesty . . . in money matters. He felt quite certain that he would receive three thousand roubles from his father, and spoke to me several times about it. I knew he had a feud with his father and have always believed that he had been unfairly treated by his father. I don't remember any threat uttered by him against his father. He certainly never uttered any such threat in my presence. If he had come to me at that time, I should have at once relieved his anxiety about that wretched three thousand, but he had given up coming to see me . . . and I myself was put in such a position . . . that I could not invite him. . . . And I had no right, indeed, to be exacting about that money," she added suddenly, and there was a ring of resolution in her voice. "I once received a loan from him

of more than three thousand, and I accepted it, although I could not at that time foresee that I should ever be in a position to repay my debt."

There was a note of defiance in her voice. It was then Fetyukovich began his cross-examination.

"Did that take place not here, but at the beginning of your acquaintance?" Fetyukovich suggested cautiously, feeling his way, instantly scenting something favourable. I must mention in parenthesis that, though Fetyukovich had been brought from Petersburg partly at the instance of Katerina Ivanovna herself, he knew nothing about the episode of the five thousand roubles given her by Mitya, and of her "bowing to the ground to him." She concealed this from him and said nothing about it, and that was strange. It may be pretty certainly assumed that she herself did not know till the very last minute whether she would speak of that episode in court, and waited for the inspiration of the moment.

No, I can never forget those moments. She began telling her story. She told everything, the whole episode that Mitya had told Alyosha, and her bowing to the ground, and her reason. She told about her father and her going to Mitya, and did not in one word, in a single hint, suggest that Mitya had himself, through her sister, proposed they should "send him Katerina Ivanovna" to fetch the money. She generously concealed that and was not ashamed to make it appear as though she had of her own impulse run to the young officer, hoping for something . . . to beg him for the money. It was something tremendous! I turned cold and trembled as I listened. The court was hushed, trying to catch every word. It was something unexampled. Even from

527

such a self-willed and contemptuously proud girl as she was, such an extremely frank avowal, such sacrifice, such self-immolation, seemed incredible. And for what, for whom? To save the man who had deceived and insulted her and in however small a degree to help save him, by creating a strong impression in his favour. And, indeed, the figure of the young officer who, with a respectful bow to the innocent girl, handed her his last five thousand roubles — all he had in the world — was thrown into a very sympathetic and attractive light, but . . . my heart contracted painfully! I felt that calumny might come of it later (and it did, in fact, it did). It was repeated all over the town afterwards with spiteful laughter that the story was perhaps not quite exact — that is, in the statement that the officer had let the young lady depart "with nothing but a respectful bow." It was hinted that something was omitted here.

"And even if nothing had been omitted, if this were the whole truth," the most highly respected of our ladies maintained, "even then it's very doubtful whether it was creditable for a young girl to behave in that way, even for the sake of saving her father."

And can Katerina Ivanovna, with her intelligence, her morbid sensitiveness, have failed to understand that people would talk like that? She must have understood it, yet she made up her mind to tell everything. Of course, all these nasty little suspicions as to the truth of her story arose only afterwards and at the first moment all were deeply impressed by it. As for the judges and the lawyers, they listened in reverent, almost shamefaced silence to Katerina Ivanovna. The prosecutor did not venture upon even one question on the subject. Fetyukovich made a low bow to her. Oh, he was almost triumphant! Much ground had been gained. For a man to give his last five thousand on a generous impulse and then for the same man to murder his father at night for the sake of robbing him of three thousand — the idea seemed too incongruous. Fetyukovich felt that now the charge of theft, at least, was as good as disproved. "The case" was thrown into quite a different light. There was a wave of sympathy for Mitya. As for him . . . I was told that once or twice, while Katerina Ivanovna was giving her evidence, he jumped up from his seat, sank back again, and hid his face in his hands. But when she had finished, he suddenly cried in a sobbing voice:

"Katya, why have you ruined me?" and his sobs were audible all over the court. But he instantly restrained himself, and cried again:

"Now I am condemned!"

Then he sat rigid in his place, with his teeth clenched and his arms across his chest. Katerina Ivanovna remained in court and sat down in her place. She was pale and sat with her eyes cast down. Those who were sitting near her declared that for a long time she shivered all over as though in a fever. Grushenka was called.

I am approaching the sudden catastrophe which was perhaps the final cause of Mitya's ruin. For I am convinced, so is every one — all the lawyers said the same afterwards — that if the episode had not occurred, the accused would at least have received a light sentence. But of that later. A couple of words first about Grushenka.

She, too, was dressed entirely in black, with her magnificent black shawl on her shoulders. She walked to the witness-box with her smooth, noiseless tread, with the slightly swaying gait common in women of full figure. She looked steadily at the presiding judge, turning her eyes neither to the right nor to the left. To my thinking she looked very handsome at that moment, and not at all pale, as the ladies alleged afterwards. They declared, too, that she had a concentrated and spiteful expression. I believe that she was simply irritated and painfully conscious of the contemptuous and inquisitive eyes of our scandal-loving public. She was proud and could not stand contempt. She was one of those people who flare up, angry and eager to retaliate, at the mere suggestion of contempt. There was an element of timidity, too, of course, and inward shame at her own timidity, so it was not strange that her tone kept changing. At one moment it was angry, contemptuous, and rude, and at another there was a sincere note of self-condemnation. Sometimes she spoke as though she were taking a desperate plunge; as though she felt, "I don't care what happens, I'll say it. . . ." Apropos of her acquaintance with Fyodor Pavlovich, she remarked curtly, "That's all nonsense, and was it my fault that he would pester me?" But a minute later she added, "It was all my fault. I was laughing at them both — at the old man and at him, too — and I brought both of them to this. It was all on account of me it happened."

Samsonov's name came up somehow. "That's nobody's business," she snapped at once, with a sort of insolent defiance. "He was my benefactor; he took me when I went barefoot, when my family had turned me out." The presiding judge reminded her, though very politely, that she must answer the questions directly, without going off into irrelevant details. Grushenka crimsoned and her eyes flashed.

The envelope with the notes in it she had not seen, but had only heard from "that wicked wretch" that Fyodor Pavlovich had an envelope with three thousand in it. "But that was all foolishness. I was only joking. I wouldn't have gone there for anything."

"To whom are you referring as 'that wicked wretch'?" inquired the prosecutor.

"The lackey, Smerdyakov, who murdered his master and hanged himself last night."

She was, of course, at once asked what grounds she had for such a definite accusation; but it appeared that she, too, had no grounds for it.

"Dmitri Fyodorovich told me so himself; you can believe him. The woman who came between us has ruined him; she is the cause of it all, let me tell you," Grushenka added. She seemed to be quivering with hatred, and there was a vindictive note in her voice.

She was again asked to whom she was referring.

"The young lady, Katerina Ivanovna there. She sent for me, offered me chocolate, tried to fascinate me. There's not much true shame about her, I can tell you that . . ."

At this point the presiding judge checked her sternly, begging her to moderate her language. But the jealous woman's heart was burning, and she did not care what she did.

"When the prisoner was arrested at Mokroye," the prosecutor asked, "every one saw and heard you run out of the next room and cry out: 'It's all my fault. We'll go to Siberia together!' So you already believed him to have murdered his father?"

"I don't remember what I felt at the time," answered Grushenka. "Every one was crying out that he had killed his father, and I felt that it was my fault, that it was on my account he had murdered him. But when he said he wasn't guilty, I believed him at once, and I believe him now and always shall believe him. He is not the man to tell a lie."

Fetyukovich began his cross-examination. I remember that among other things he asked about Rakitin and the twenty-five roubles "you paid him for bringing Alexey Fyodorovich Karamazov to see you."

"There was nothing strange about his taking the money," sneered Grushenka, with angry contempt. "He was always coming to me for money: he used to get thirty roubles a month at least out of me, chiefly for luxuries: he had enough to keep him without my help."

"What led you to be so liberal to Mr. Rakitin?" Fetyukovich asked, in spite of an uneasy movement on the part of the presiding judge.

"Why, he is my cousin. His mother was my mother's sister. But he's always begged me not to tell any one here of it, he is so dreadfully ashamed of me."

This fact was a complete surprise to every one; no one in the town nor in the monastery, not even Mitya, knew of it. I was told that Rakitin turned purple with shame where he sat. Grushenka had somehow heard before she came into court that he had given evidence against Mitya, and so she was angry. The whole effect on the public, of Rakitin's speech, of his noble sentiments, of his attacks upon serfdom and the political disorder of Russia, was this time finally ruined. Fetyukovich was satisfied: it was another godsend. Grushenka's cross-examination did not last long and, of course, there could be nothing particularly new in her testimony. She left a very disagreeable impression on the public; hundreds of contemptuous eyes were fixed upon her, as she finished giving her evidence and sat down again in the court-room, at a good distance from Katerina Ivanovna. Mitya was silent throughout her testimony. He sat as though turned to stone, with his eyes fixed on the ground.

Ivan was called to give evidence.

## CHAPTER V
### A SUDDEN CATASTROPHE

I MAY note that he had been called before Alyosha. But the court attendant announced to the presiding judge that, owing to an attack of illness or some sort of fit, the witness could not appear at the moment, but was ready to give his evidence as soon as he recovered. But no one seemed to have heard it and it only came out later.

His entrance was at first almost unnoticed. The principal witnesses, especially the two rival women, had already been questioned. Curiosity was satisfied for the time; the public was feeling almost fatigued. Several more witnesses were still to be heard, who probably had little information to give after all that had been given. Time was passing. Ivan walked up with extraordinary slowness, looking at no one, and with his head bowed, as though plunged in gloomy thought. He was irreproachably dressed, but his face made a painful impression, on me at least: there was an earthy look in it, a look like a dying man's. His eyes were lusterless; he raised them and looked slowly round the court. Alyosha jumped up from his seat and moaned "Ah!" I remember that, but it was hardly noticed.

The presiding judge began by informing him that he was a witness not on oath, that he might answer or refuse to answer, but that, of course, he must bear witness according to his conscience, and so on and so on. Ivan listened and looked at him blankly, but his face gradually relaxed into a smile, and just as the judge, looking at him in astonishment, finished, he suddenly laughed outright.

"Well, and what else?" he asked in a loud voice.

There was a hush in the court; there was a feeling of something strange. The judge showed signs of uneasiness.

"You . . . are perhaps still unwell?" he began, seeking the attendant with his eyes.

"Don't trouble yourself, your Excellency, I am well enough and can tell you something interesting," Ivan answered with sudden calmness and respectfulness.

"You have some special communication to make?" the judge went on, still mistrustfully.

Ivan looked down, waited a few seconds, and, raising his head, answered, almost stammering:

"No . . . I haven't. I have nothing particular to say."

They began asking him questions. He answered, as it were, reluctantly, with extreme brevity, with a sort of disgust which grew more and more marked, though he answered rationally. To many questions he answered that he did not know. He knew nothing of his father's money relations with Dmitri. "I wasn't interested in the subject," he added. Threats to murder his father he had heard from the accused. Of the money in the envelope he had heard from Smerdyakov.

"It's all the same thing over and over again," he interrupted suddenly, with a look of weariness. "I have nothing particular to tell the court."

"I see you are unwell and understand your feelings," the judge began.

He turned to the prosecutor and the counsel for the defence to invite them to examine the witness, if necessary, when Ivan suddenly asked in an exhausted voice:

"Let me go, your Excellency, I feel very ill."

And with these words, without waiting for permission, he turned to walk out of the court. But after taking four steps he stood still, as though he had reached a decision, smiled slowly, and went back.

"I am like that peasant girl, your Excellency . . . you know. How does it go? 'I'll stand up if I like, and I won't if I don't.' They were trying to put on her sarafan to take her to church to be married, and she said, 'I'll stand up if I like, and I won't if I don't.' . . . It's in some book about the peasantry."

"What do you mean by that?" the judge asked severely.

"Why, this," Ivan suddenly pulled out a roll of notes. "Here's the money . . . the notes that lay in that envelope" (he nodded towards the table on which lay the material evidence) "for the sake of which our father was murdered. Where shall I put them? Here, officer, take them."

The court attendant took the whole roll and handed it to the judge.

"How could this money have come into your possession if it is the same money?" the judge asked wonderingly.

"I got it from Smerdyakov, from the murderer, yesterday. . . . I was with him just before he hanged himself. It was he, not my brother, killed our father. He did the killing, and I instructed him to do it. . . . Who doesn't desire his father's death?"

"Are you in your right mind?" broke involuntarily from the judge.

"I should think I am in my right mind . . . in the same nasty mind as all of you . . . as all these . . . ugly faces." He turned suddenly to the audience. "My father has been murdered and they pretend they are horrified," he snarled, with furious contempt. "They keep up the sham before one another. Liars! They all desire the death of their fathers. One reptile devours another. . . . If there hadn't been parricide, they'd have been angry and gone home ill-humoured. It's circuses they want! Bread and circuses! Though I am one to talk! Have you any water? Give me a drink for Christ's sake!" He suddenly clutched his head.

The attendant at once approached him. Alyosha jumped up and cried, "He is ill. Don't believe him: he has brain fever." Katerina Ivanovna rose impulsively from her seat and, rigid with horror, gazed at Ivan. Mitya stood up and greedily looked at his brother and listened to him with a wild, strange smile.

"Don't disturb yourselves. I am not mad, I am only a murderer," Ivan began again. "You can't expect eloquence from a murderer," he added suddenly for some reason and laughed crookedly.

The prosecutor leaned over to the presiding judge in obvious dismay. The two other judges whispered to each other in agitation. Fetyukovich pricked up his ears as he listened: the hall was hushed in expectation. The presiding judge seemed suddenly to recollect himself.

"Witness, your words are incomprehensible and impossible here. Calm yourself, if you can, and tell your story . . . if you really have something to tell. How can you confirm your statement . . . if indeed you are not delirious?"

"That's just it. I have no proof. That cur Smerdyakov won't send you proofs from the other world . . . in an envelope. You think of nothing but envelopes — one is enough. I've no witnesses . . . except one, perhaps," he smiled thoughtfully.

"Who is your witness?"

"He has a tail, your excellency, and that would be irregular! *Le diable n'existe point!* Don't pay attention: he is a paltry, pitiful devil," he added suddenly. He ceased laughing and spoke, as it were, confidentially. "He is here somewhere, no doubt — under that table with the material evidence on it, perhaps. Where should he sit if not there? You see, listen to me. I told him I didn't want to keep quiet, and he talked about the geological cataclysm . . . idiocy! Come, release the monster . . . he's been singing a hymn. That's because his heart is light! It's like a drunken man in the street bawling how 'Vanka went to Petersburg,' and I would give a quadrillion quadrillions for two seconds of joy. You don't know me! Oh, how stupid all this business is! Come, take me instead of him! I didn't come for nothing. . . . Why, why is everything so stupid? . . ."

And he began slowly, and as it were reflectively, looking round him again. But the court was all excitement by now. Alyosha rushed towards him, but the court attendant had already seized Ivan by the arm.

"What are you about?" he cried, staring into the man's face, and, suddenly seizing him by the shoulders, he flung him violently to the floor. But the police were on the spot and he was seized. He screamed furiously. And all the time he was being removed, he yelled and screamed something incoherent.

The whole court was thrown into confusion. I don't remember everything just as it happened. I was excited myself and could not follow. I only know that afterwards, when everything was quiet again and every one understood what had happened, the court attendant came in for a reprimand, though he very reasonably explained that the witness had been quite well, that the doctor had seen him an hour ago, when he had a slight attack of giddiness, but that, until he had come into court, he had talked quite sensibly, so that nothing could have been foreseen — that he had, in fact, insisted on giving evidence. But before all had completely regained their composure and recovered from this scene, it was followed by another. Katerina Ivanovna had an attack of hysterics. She sobbed, shrieking loudly, but refused to leave the court-room, struggled, and besought them not to remove her. Suddenly she cried to the presiding judge:

"There is more evidence I must give at once . . . at once! Here is a document, a letter . . . take it, read it quickly, quickly! It's a letter from that monster . . . that man there, there!" she pointed to Mitya. "It was he killed his father, you will see that directly. He wrote to me how he would kill his father! But the other one is ill, he is ill, he is delirious! For the past three days I've seen that he was delirious!" she kept crying out, beside herself.

The court attendant took the document she held out to the judge, and she, dropping into her chair, hiding her face in her hands, began convulsively and noiselessly sobbing, shaking all over, and stifling every sound for fear she should be ejected from the court-room. The document she had handed up was that letter Mitya had written at the "Metropolis" tavern, which Ivan had spoken of as a "mathematical proof." Alas! its mathematical con-

clusiveness was recognised, and had it not been for that letter, Mitya might have escaped his doom or, at least, that doom would have been less terrible. It was, I repeat, difficult to follow the details. What ensued is still confused to my mind. The presiding judge must, I suppose, have at once passed on the document to the judges, the jury, and the lawyers on both sides. I only remember how they began examining the witness. On being gently asked by the presiding judge whether she had recovered sufficiently, Katerina Ivanovna exclaimed impetuously:

"I am ready, I am ready! I am quite able to answer you," she added, evidently still afraid that for some reason she would not be listened to. She was asked to explain in detail what this letter was and under what circumstances she had received it.

"I received it the day before the crime was committed, but he wrote it the day before that, at the tavern — that is, two days before he committed the crime. Look, it is written on some sort of bill!" she cried breathlessly. "He hated me at that time, because he had behaved contemptibly and had run after that creature . . . and because he owed me that three thousand. . . . Oh! he was humiliated by that three thousand on account of his own meanness! This is how it happened with that three thousand. I beg you, I beseech you, to hear me out! One morning, three weeks before he murdered his father, he came to me. I knew he was in want of money, and what he wanted it for. Yes, yes — to seduce that creature and carry her off. I knew then that he had been false to me and meant to abandon me, and it was I, I, who gave him that money, who offered it to him on the pretext of his sending it to my sister in Moscow. And as I gave it him, I

533

looked him in the face and said that he could send it when he liked, 'in a month's time would do.' How, how could he have failed to understand that I was practically telling him to his face, 'You want money to be false to me with your creature, so here's the money for you. I give it to you myself. Take it, if you have so little honour as to take it!' I wanted to show him in his true colours, and what happened? He took it, he took it, and carried it off, and squandered it with that creature in one night. . . . But he understood, he understood that I knew it all. I assure you he understood, too, that I gave him that money to test him, to see whether he was so dishonourable as to take it from me. I looked into his eyes and he looked into mine, and he understood it all and he took it — he carried off my money!"

"That's true, Katya," Mitya roared suddenly, "I looked into your eyes and I knew that you were dishonouring me, and yet I took your money. Despise me as a scoundrel, despise me, all of you! I've deserved it!"

"Prisoner," cried the presiding judge, "another word and I will order you to be removed."

"That money was a torment to him," Katya went on with impulsive haste. "He wanted to repay it. He wanted to, that's true; but he needed money for that creature, too. So he murdered his father, but he didn't repay me, and went off with her to that village where he was arrested. There, again, he squandered the money he had stolen from his father, whom he had murdered. And a day before the murder he wrote me this letter. He was drunk when he wrote it. I saw it at once, at the time. He wrote it from spite, and feeling certain, positively certain, that I should never show it to any one, even if he did kill him. Or else he wouldn't have written it. For he knew I shouldn't want to revenge myself and ruin him! But read it, read it carefully — more carefully, please — and you will see that he had described it all in his letter, all beforehand, how he would kill his father and where the old man's money lay. Look, please, don't overlook that, there's one phrase there, 'I shall kill him as soon as Ivan has gone away.' So he thought it all out beforehand how he would kill him," Katerina Ivanovna prompted the court venomously and malignantly. Oh! it was clear she had read the fatal letter with the closest attention and had studied every line of it. "If he hadn't been drunk, he wouldn't have written to me; but, look, everything is described there in advance, point by point, just as he committed the murder afterwards, the whole programme!"

She exclaimed thus, frantically, reckless now of all consequences to herself, though, no doubt, she had foreseen them even a month ago, for even then, perhaps, shaking with anger, she had pondered whether to show the letter at the trial or not. Now she had taken the fatal plunge.

I remember that the letter was read aloud by the clerk, directly afterwards, I believe. It made an overwhelming impression. They asked Mitya whether he admitted having written the letter.

"It's mine, mine!" cried Mitya. "I wouldn't have written it, if I hadn't been drunk! . . . We've hated each other for many things, Katya, but I swear, I swear I loved you even while I hated you, and you didn't love me!"

He sank back on his seat, wringing his hands in despair. The prosecutor and the counsel for the defence began cross-examining her, chiefly to ascertain what had induced her to conceal such a document and to give her evidence in quite a different tone and spirit just before.

"Yes, yes. I was telling lies just now. I was lying against my honour and my conscience, but I wanted to save him, for he has hated and despised me so!" Katya cried like a madwoman. "Oh, he has despised me horribly, he has always despised me, and do you know, he despised me from the very moment that I bowed down to him for that money. I saw that. . . . I felt it at once at the time, but for a long time I wouldn't believe it. How often I have read in his eyes, 'you came of yourself, though.' Oh, he didn't understand, he had no idea why I ran to him, he can suspect nothing but baseness, he judged me by himself, he thought every one was like himself!" Katya hissed furiously, in a perfect frenzy. "And he only wanted to marry me because I'd inherited a fortune, because of that, because of that! I always suspected it was because of that! Oh, he is a beast! He was always convinced that I should be trembling with shame all my life before him, because I went to him then, and that he had a right to despise me for ever for it, and so to be superior to me — that's why he wanted to marry me! That's so, that's all so! I tried to conquer him by my love — a love that knew no bounds. I even tried to forgive his faithlessness; but he understood nothing, nothing! How could he understand indeed? He is a monster! I received that letter only the next evening: it was brought me from the tavern — and only that morning, only that morning I wanted to forgive him everything, everything — even his treachery!"

The presiding judge and the prosecutor, of course, tried to calm her. I can't help thinking that they felt ashamed of taking advantage of her hysteria and of listening to such avowals.

I remember hearing them say to her, "We understand how hard it is for you; be sure we are able to feel for you," and so on, and so on. And yet they dragged the evidence out of the raving, hysterical woman. She described at last with extraordinary clearness, which is so often manifested, though only for a moment, even in such overwrought states, how Ivan had been driven nearly out of his mind during the last two months trying to save "the monster and murderer," his brother.

"He tortured himself," she exclaimed, "he was always trying to minimise his brother's guilt and confessing to me that he, too, had never loved his father, and perhaps desired his death himself. Oh, he has a deep, deep conscience! His conscience simply ravaged him! He told me everything, everything! He came every day and talked to me as his only friend. I have the honour to be his only friend!" she cried suddenly with a sort of defiance, and her eyes flashed. "He had been twice to see Smerdyakov. One day he came to me and said, 'If it was not my brother, but Smerdyakov who committed the murder (for the legend was circulating everywhere that Smerdyakov had done it), perhaps I, too, am guilty, for Smerdyakov knew I didn't like my father and perhaps believed that I desired my father's death.' Then I brought out that letter and showed it him. He was entirely convinced that his brother had done it, and he was overwhelmed by it. He couldn't endure the thought that his own brother was a parricide! Only a week ago I saw that it was making him ill. During the last few days he has talked incoherently in my presence. I saw his mind was giving way. He walked about, raving; he was seen muttering in the streets. The doctor from Moscow, at my request, examined him the day before yesterday and told me that he was on the eve of brain fever — and all on his account, on account of this monster! And last night he learnt that Smerdyakov was dead! It was such a shock that it drove him out of his mind . . . and all through this monster, all for the sake of saving the monster!"

Oh, of course, such an outpouring, such an avowal is possible only once in a lifetime — at the hour of death, for instance, on the way to the scaffold! But it was in Katya's character, and it was such a moment in her life. It was the same impetuous Katya who had thrown herself on the mercy of a young profligate to save her father; the same Katya who had just before, in her pride and chastity, sacrificed herself and her maidenly modesty before all these people, telling of Mitya's generous act, in the hope of softening his fate a little. And now, again, she sacrificed herself; but this time it was for another, and perhaps only now — perhaps only at this moment — she felt and knew how dear that other was to her! She had sacrificed herself in terror for him, conceiving all of a sudden that he had ruined himself by his confession that it was he who had committed the murder, not his brother, she had sacrificed herself to save him, to save his good name, his reputation!

And yet one terrible doubt occurred to the audience — was she lying in her description of her former relations with Mitya? — that was the question. No, she had not intentionally slandered him when she cried that Mitya despised her for her bowing down to him! She believed it herself. She had been firmly convinced, perhaps ever since that bow, that the simple-hearted Mitya, who then still adored her, was laughing at her and despising her. She had conceived for him an hysterical, "lacer-

ated" love only because of pride, wounded pride, and that love was not like love, but more like revenge. Oh! perhaps that lacerated love would have grown into real love, perhaps Katya longed for nothing more than that, but Mitya's faithlessness had wounded her to the bottom of her heart, and her heart could not forgive him. The moment of revenge had come upon her suddenly, and all that had been accumulating so long and so painfully in the offended woman's breast burst out all at once and unexpectedly. She betrayed Mitya, but she betrayed herself, too. And no sooner had she given full expression to her feelings than the tension, of course, was over and she was overwhelmed with shame. Hysterics began again: she fell on the floor, sobbing and screaming. She was carried out. At that moment Grushenka, with a wail, rushed towards Mitya before they had time to prevent her.

"Mitya," she wailed, "your serpent has destroyed you! There, she has shown you what she is!" she shouted to the judges, shaking with anger. At a signal from the presiding judge they seized her and tried to remove her from the court-room. She wouldn't allow it. She fought and struggled to get back to Mitya. Mitya uttered a cry and struggled to get to her. He was overpowered.

Yes, I think the ladies who came to see the spectacle must have been satisfied — the show had been a rich one. Then I remember the Moscow doctor appeared on the scene. I believe the presiding judge had previously sent the court attendant to arrange for medical aid for Ivan. The doctor announced to the court that the patient was suffering from a dangerous attack of brain fever and that he must be at once removed. In answer to questions from the prosecutor and the counsel for the defence he said that the patient had come to him of his own accord the day before yesterday and that he had warned him that he had such an attack coming on, but he had not consented to be looked after. "He was certainly not in a normal state of mind: he told me himself that he saw visions when he was awake, that he met several persons in the street, who were dead, and that Satan visited him every evening," said the doctor, in conclusion. Having given his evidence, the celebrated doctor withdrew. The letter produced by Katerina Ivanovna was added to the material evidence. After some deliberation, the judges decided to proceed with the trial and to enter both the unexpected pieces of evidence (given by Ivan and Katerina Ivanovna) into the record.

But I will not detail the evidence of the other witnesses, who only repeated and confirmed what had been said before, though all with their characteristic peculiarities. I repeat, all was brought together in the prosecutor's speech, to which I shall pass directly. Every one was excited, every one was electrified by the last incident, and with burning impatience all were awaiting the dénouement, that is, the speeches of the prosecutor and the counsel for the defence, and the verdict. Fetyukovich was obviously shaken by Katerina Ivanovna's evidence. But the prosecutor was triumphant. When all the evidence had been taken, the court was adjourned for almost an hour. Finally the presiding judge resumed the trial. I believe it was just eight o'clock when our prosecutor, Ippolit Kirillovich began his speech.

## CHAPTER VI
### THE PROSECUTOR'S SPEECH.
#### CHARACTERIZATION

IPPOLIT KIRILLOVICH began his speech trembling with nervousness, with cold sweat on his forehead and temples, feeling chills and fever all over by turns. He described this himself afterwards. He regarded this speech as his *chef d'œuvre*, the *chef d'œuvre* of his whole life, his swan-song. He died, it is true, nine months later of consumption, so that he would have had the right, had he had a presentiment of his end, to compare himself to a swan singing his last song. He had put his whole heart and all the brain he had into that speech. And he unexpectedly revealed that civic sentiment and a feeling for "the accursed questions" lay concealed in him, at least to the degree possible to our poor Ippolit Kirillovich. Where his speech really excelled was in its sincerity. He genuinely believed in the prisoner's guilt; he was accusing him not only as a matter of form and of official duty, and in calling for vengeance he quivered with a genuine desire to "save society." Even the ladies in the audience, though they remained hostile to Ippolit Kirillovich, admitted that he made an extraordinary impression on them. He began in a cracked, broken voice, but it soon gained strength and filled the court to the end of his speech. But as soon as he had finished, he almost fainted.

"Gentlemen of the jury," began the prosecutor, "this case has made a stir throughout Russia. But what is there to wonder at, what is there so peculiarly horrifying in it for us? We are people accustomed to all this! That's what's so horrible, that such dark deeds have ceased to horrify us. What ought to horrify us

537

is that we are so accustomed to it, and not this or that isolated crime. What are the causes of our indifference, our lukewarm attitude to such deeds, to such signs of the times, auguring an unenviable future? Is it our cynicism, is it the premature exhaustion of intellect and imagination in a society that is sinking into decay, in spite of its youth? Is it that our moral principles are shattered to their foundations, or is it, perhaps, a complete lack of such principles among us? I cannot answer such questions; nevertheless they are disturbing, and every citizen not only must, but ought to be harassed by them. Our young and still timid press has done good service to the public already, for without it we should never have heard of the horrors of unbridled violence and moral degradation which are continually made known by the press, not merely to those who attend the new public courts vouchsafed to us in the present reign, but to every one. And what do we read almost daily? Of things beside which the present case grows pale, and seems almost commonplace. But what is most important is that the majority of our national crimes of violence bear witness to a widespread evil that has struck such deep root among us that it is difficult to contend against it.

"One day we see a brilliant young officer of high society, at the very outset of his career, in a cowardly underhand way, without a pang of conscience, murdering an official who had once been his benefactor, and the servant girl, to steal his own IOU and what ready money he could find on him; 'it will come in handy for my pleasures in the fashionable world and for my career in the future.' After knifing them, he puts a pillow under the head of each of his victims, and goes away. Next, a young hero 'decorated for bravery' kills the mother of his chief and benefactor, like a highwayman, and to urge his companions to join him he asserts that 'she loves him like a son, and so will follow all his directions and take no precautions.' Granted that he is a monster, yet I dare not say in these days that he is unique. Another man will not kill, but will feel and think like him: his soul is equally dishonourable. In silence, alone with his conscience, he asks himself perhaps, 'What is honour, and isn't the condemnation of bloodshed a prejudice?'

"Perhaps people will cry out against me that I am morbid, hysterical, that it is a monstrous slander, that I am raving, exaggerating. Let them say so — and heavens! I should be the first to rejoice if it were so! Oh, don't believe me, think of me as morbid, but remember my words; if only a tenth, if only a twentieth part of what I say is true — even so it's horrible! Look how our young people commit suicide: they do not ask themselves the Hamletic question, 'What is there beyond?' — there is no sign of such a question, as though the whole matter of our soul and what awaits us beyond the grave had long since been erased from their nature and buried under the sands. Look at our dissoluteness, at our sensualists. Fyodor Pavlovich, the luckless victim in the present case, is almost an innocent babe compared with many of them. And yet we all knew him, 'he lived among us!' . . .

"Yes, one day perhaps the leading intellects of Russia and of Europe will study the psychology of Russian crime, for the subject is worth it. But this study will come later, at leisure, when all the tragic topsy-turvydom of to-day is farther behind us, so that it's possible to examine it with more insight and more impartiality than such men as I have. Now we

538

are either horrified or pretend to be horrified, though we really gloat over the spectacle, and love strong and eccentric sensations which tickle our cynical, pampered idleness. Or, like little children, we brush the dreadful ghosts away and hide our heads in the pillow so as to return to our sports and merriment as soon as the terrible spectre has vanished. But we must one day begin life in sober earnest, we, too, must look upon ourselves as a society; it's time we tried to grasp something of our interests as a group, or at least to make a beginning in that direction.

"A great writer* of the last epoch, comparing Russia to a swift troika galloping towards an unknown goal, exclaims at the close of his greatest work, 'Oh, troika, birdlike troika, who invented thee!' and adds, in proud ecstasy, that all the peoples of the world stand aside respectfully to make way for the recklessly galloping troika. That may be, they may stand aside, respectfully or no, but in my poor opinion the great writer ended his book in this way either in an access of childish and naïve optimism, or simply in fear of the censorship of the day. For if the troika were drawn by his heroes, Sobakevich, Nozdryov, Chichikov, it could reach no rational goal, whoever might be driving it. And those were the steeds of old, ours are worse specimens still . . ."

At this point Ippolit Kirillovich's speech was interrupted by applause. The Liberal significance of the reference to the Russian troika was appreciated. The applause was, it's true, of brief duration, so that the judge did not think it necessary to caution the public, and only looked severely in the direction of the offenders. But Ippolit Kirillovich was encouraged; he had never been applauded before—

* Gogol is meant. *Translator's note.*

fore! He had been all his life unable to get a hearing, and now he suddenly had an opportunity of securing the ear of all Russia.

"What, after all, is this Karamazov family, which has gained such sad notoriety throughout Russia?" he continued. "Perhaps I am exaggerating, but it seems to me that certain general fundamental features of the educated class of to-day flash upon the eye, as it were, in the picture of this family,—oh, not all and only, of course, in miniature, reflected 'like the sun in a small drop of water.' Nevertheless, they are reflected, they do show themselves. Think of that unhappy, dissolute, unbridled old man, this head of a family, who has met with such a melancholy end! Born into the nobility, but from the first a poverty-stricken dependent, he comes into a small fortune, through an unexpected marriage. A petty knave, a toady and buffoon, of fairly good, though undeveloped, intelligence, he is, above all, a usurer. As the years pass, and his little capital increases, he grows bolder. His abjectness and servility disappear, there remains only a sarcastic and malicious cynic and sensualist. The spiritual side is entirely obliterated, but his thirst for life is excessive. He sees nothing in life but sensual pleasure, and he brings his children up to do likewise. He has no sense of his spiritual duties as a father. He ridicules those duties. He leaves his little children to the servants, and is glad to be rid of them, forgets about them completely. The old man's maxim is *après moi le déluge.* He embodies the very opposite of what is meant by a citizen, he represents the most complete divorce from, and, indeed, hostility to, society. 'The world may burn for aught I care, so long as I am at my ease,' and he is at his ease; he is content, he is eager to go on living in the same way for another twenty or thirty years. He swindles his own son and with that money which he withholds from him, his maternal inheritance, tries to get his mistress away from him, from his own son. No, I don't intend to leave the prisoner's defence altogether to my talented colleague from Petersburg. I will speak the truth myself, I can well understand what resentment he had heaped up in his son's heart against him.

"But enough, enough of that unhappy old man; he has paid the penalty. Let us remember, however, that he was a father, and one of the typical fathers of to-day. Am I unjust, indeed, in saying that he is typical of many modern fathers? Alas! many of them differ only in not openly professing such cynicism, for they are better educated, more cultured, but their philosophy is essentially the same as his. Perhaps I am a pessimist, but you have agreed to forgive me. Let us agree beforehand, you need not believe me, but let me speak. Let me say what I have to say, and remember something of my words.

"Now for the children of this father, this head of a family. One of them is the prisoner before us, all the rest of my speech will deal with him. Of the other two I will speak only in passing.

"The elder is one of those modern young men of brilliant education and vigorous intellect, who has lost all faith in everything. He has denied and rejected much already, like his father. We have all heard him, he was a welcome guest in local society. He never concealed his opinions, quite the contrary in fact, which justifies me in speaking rather openly of him now, of course, not as a private person, but as a member of the Karamazov family. Another person closely connected with the case died here by his own hand last night. I mean a sickly idiot, a former servant, and possibly the illegitimate son of Fyodor Pavlovich — Smerdyakov. At the preliminary inquiry, he told me with hysterical tears how the young Ivan Karamazov had horrified him by his spiritual unrestraint. 'Everything in the world is permitted according to him, and nothing must be forbidden in the future — that is what he always taught me.' I believe that idiot was driven out of his mind by this thesis which he had been taught, though, of course, the epileptic attacks from which he suffered, and this terrible catastrophe, have helped to unhinge his mind. But he dropped one very interesting observation, which would have done credit to a more intelligent observer, and that is, indeed, why I've mentioned it, 'If there is one of the sons that is like Fyodor Pavlovich in character, it is Ivan Fyodorovich.'

"With that remark I conclude my sketch of his character, feeling it indelicate to continue further. Oh, I don't want to draw any further conclusions and croak like a raven over the young man's future. We've seen to-day in this court that there are still good impulses in his young heart, that family feeling has not been destroyed in him by lack of faith and moral cynicism, which has come to him rather by inheritance than by the exercise of independent thought.

"Then the third son. Oh, he is a devout and modest youth, who does not share his elder brother's gloomy and destructive theory of life. He has sought to cling to the 'folk ideals,' or to what goes by that name in some circles of our intellectual class. He clung to the monastery, and was within an ace of becoming a monk. He seems to me to have betrayed unconsciously, and so early, that timid despair which leads so many in our unhappy society, who dread cynicism and its corrupting influences, and mistakenly attribute all the mischief to European enlightenment, to cast themselves upon their 'native soil,' as they say, into the motherly embraces of their native land, like children frightened by ghosts, yearning to fall asleep on the withered bosom of their decrepit mother, and to sleep there for ever, only to escape the horrors that terrify them.

"For my part I wish the excellent and gifted young man every success; I trust that his youthful idealism and his striving towards the ideals of the people may never degenerate, as often happens, on the moral side into gloomy mysticism, and on the civic side into obtuse chauvinism — two evils which are even a greater menace to Russia than the premature decay, due to misunderstanding and to the gratuitous adoption of European enlightenment, from which his elder brother is suffering."

Two or three people clapped their hands at the mention of chauvinism and mysticism. Ippolit Kirillovich had, indeed, been carried away by his own eloquence. All this had little to do with the case in hand, to say nothing of the fact of its being somewhat vague, but the sickly and consumptive man was overcome by the desire to express himself once in his life. People said afterwards that he was actuated by unworthy motives in his criticism of Ivan, because the latter had on one or two occasions got the better of him in argument, and Ippolit Kirillovich, remembering it, tried now to take his revenge. But I don't know whether it was true.

All this was only introductory, however, and the speech passed to more direct consideration of the case.

"But to return to the eldest son," Ippolit Kirillovich went on. "He is in the dock before us. We have his life and his actions, too, before us; the fatal day has come and all has come out into the open. While his brothers seem to stand for 'Europeanism' and 'the principles of the people,' he seems to represent Russia in its spontaneity. Oh, not all Russia, not all! God preserve us, if it were! Yet, here we have her, our mother Russia, the very scent and sound of her. Oh, we are spontaneous, we are a marvellous mingling of good and evil, we are a lover of culture and Schiller, yet we brawl in taverns and pluck out the beards of our boon companions. Oh, we, too, can be good and noble, but only when all goes well with us. What is more, we can be carried off our feet, positively carried off our feet by noble ideals, but only if they come of themselves, if they fall down to us from heaven, if they are gratuitous, gratuitous, if they need not be paid for. We hate paying for anything, but are very fond of receiving, and that's so with us in everything. Oh, give us every possible good that life can offer (we couldn't be content with less), and put no obstacle in our way, and we will show that we, too, can be noble. We are not greedy, no, but we must have money, a great deal of money, and you will see how generously, with what scorn of filthy lucre, we will fling it all away in the reckless dissipation of one night. But if the money is not handed to us, we will show what we can do to get it when we want it badly. But of this later, let us take events in their chronological order.

"First, we have before us a poor abandoned child, running about the back yard, 'without boots to his feet,' as our worthy and esteemed fellow citizen, of foreign origin, alas! expressed it just now. I repeat it again, I yield to no one the defence of the criminal. I am here to accuse him, but to defend him also. Yes, I, too, am human; I, too, can weigh the influence of home and childhood on the character. But the boy grows up and becomes an officer; on account of a duel and other reckless conduct he is exiled to one of the remote frontier towns of our prosperous Russia. There he leads a wild life as an officer. And, of course, a big ship must travel far. We need money, money before all things, and so after prolonged wrangling he comes to a settlement with his father, and the last six thousand is sent him. A letter is in existence in which he practically gives up his claim to the rest and settles his dispute with his father over the inheritance on the payment of this six thousand.

"Then comes his meeting with a young girl of lofty character and brilliant education. Oh, I do not venture to repeat the details; you have only just heard them. Honour, self-sacrifice were displayed there, and I am silent. The figure of the young officer, frivolous and dissolute, but bowing before true nobility and a lofty ideal, was shown in a very sympathetic light before us. But the other side of the medal was unexpectedly turned to us immediately after in this very court. Again I will not venture to conjecture why it happened so, but there were causes. The same lady, bathed in tears of long-concealed indignation, has declared to us that he, he of all men, was the first to despise her for her impulse, which, though incautious, reckless perhaps, was still dictated by lofty and generous motives. He, he, the girl's betrothed, looked at her with that smile of mockery, which was more insufferable from

him than from any one. And knowing that he had already deceived her (he had deceived her, believing that she was bound to endure everything from him, even treachery), she intentionally offers him three thousand roubles, and clearly, too clearly, lets him understand that she is offering him money with which to betray her. 'Well, will you take it or not, are you so lost to shame?' is the dumb question in her scrutinising eyes. He looks at her, sees clearly what is in her mind (he's admitted here before you that he understood it all), appropriates that three thousand unconditionally, and squanders it in two days with the new object of his affections.

"What are we to believe then? The first legend of the young officer sacrificing his last farthing in a noble impulse of generosity and doing reverence to virtue, or this other revolting picture? As a rule, between two extremes one has to find the mean, but in the present case this is not true. The probability is that in the first case he was genuinely noble, and in the second as genuinely base. And why? Precisely because we have the broad Karamazov nature — that's just what I am leading up to — capable of combining the most incongruous contradictions, and capable of contemplating at once the two abysses: the abyss above us, the abyss of the highest ideals, and the abyss below us, the abyss of the lowest and foulest degradation. Remember the brilliant remark made by a young observer who has seen the Karamazov family at close quarters — Mr. Rakitin: 'The sense of their own degradation is as essential to these reckless, unbridled natures as the sense of the highest nobility.' And that's true, they need continually this unnatural mixture. Two abysses, gentlemen, two abysses at the same moment, or we are miserable and dissatisfied and our existence is incomplete. We are wide, wide as mother Russia; we include everything and put up with everything.

"By the way, gentlemen of the jury, we've just touched upon that three thousand roubles, and I will venture to anticipate a little. Can you conceive that a man like that, on receiving that sum and in such a way, at the price of such shame, such disgrace, such utter degradation, could have been capable that very day of setting apart half that sum, that very day, and sewing it up in a little bag, and would have had the firmness of character to carry it about with him for a whole month afterwards, in spite of every temptation and his extreme need of it! Neither in drunken debauchery in taverns, nor when he was flying into the country, trying to get from God knows whom the money so essential to him to remove the object of his affections from being tempted by his father, did he bring himself to touch that little bag! Why, if only to avoid exposing his mistress to being tempted by the old man of whom he was so jealous, he would have been certain to have opened that bag and to have stayed at home to keep watch over her, awaiting the moment when she would say to him at last, 'I am yours,' so as to fly with her far from their fatal surroundings.

"But no, he does not touch his talisman, and what is the reason he gives for it? The primary reason, as I have just said, was that when she would say, 'I am yours, take me where you will,' he might have the wherewithal to take her. But that first reason, in the prisoner's own words, paled beside the second. While I have that money on me, he said, I am a scoundrel, not a thief, for I can always go to my insulted betrothed, and, laying down half the sum I have fraudulently appropriated, I can always say to her, 'You see I've squandered half your money, and shown I am a weak and immoral man, and, if you like, a scoundrel' (I use the prisoner's own expressions), 'but though I am a scoundrel, I am not a thief, for if I had been a thief, I shouldn't have brought you back this half of the money, but should have appropriated it as I did the other half!' A surprising explanation! This frantic, but weak man, who could not resist the temptation of accepting the three thousand roubles at the price of such disgrace, this very man suddenly develops the most stoical firmness, and carries about thousands of roubles without daring to touch them. Does that fit in at all with the character we have analysed? No, and I venture to tell you how the real Dmitri Karamazov would have behaved in such circumstances, if he really had brought himself to sew up the money in a little bag.

"At the first temptation — for instance, to entertain the woman with whom he had already squandered half the money — he would have ripped open his little bag and have taken out some hundred roubles, for why should he have taken back precisely half the money, that is, fifteen hundred roubles; why not fourteen hundred? He could just as well have said then that he was not a thief, because he brought back fourteen hundred roubles. Then a little later he would have ripped it open again and taken out another hundred, and then a third, and then a fourth, and before the end of the month he would have taken the last note but one, feeling that if he took back only a hundred it would answer the purpose, for a thief would have stolen it all. And then he would have looked at this last note, and have said to himself, 'It's really not worth while to give back one hundred; let's spend that, too!' That's how the real Dmitri Karamazov, as we know him, would have behaved. One cannot imagine anything more incongruous with the actual facts than this legend of the little bag. Nothing could be more inconceivable. But we shall return to that later."

After touching upon what had come out in the proceedings concerning the financial relations of father and son, and arguing again and again that it was utterly impossible, from the facts known, to determine which was in the wrong, Ippolit Kirillovich passed to the evidence of the medical experts in reference to Mitya's fixed idea about the three thousand owing him.

## CHAPTER VII
### AN HISTORICAL SURVEY

"THE medical experts have striven to convince us that the prisoner is out of his mind and, in fact, a maniac. I maintain that he is in his right mind, but it's just this that's worst of all: if he had not been, he would have behaved more cleverly. As for his being a maniac, that I would agree to, but only as regards one point, that is, his fixed idea about the three thousand that his father had failed to pay up. Yet I think one might find a much more plausible explanation of his frenzy over the money than his tendency to insanity. For my part I agree thoroughly with the young doctor who maintained that the prisoner's mental faculties have always been normal, and that he has only been irritable and exasperated. The reason for the prisoner's continual and violent anger was not the sum itself; there was a special motive at the bottom of it. That motive is jealousy!"

Here Ippolit Kirillovich described at length the prisoner's fatal passion for Grushenka. He began from the moment when the prisoner went to the "young person's" lodgings "to give her a beating" — "I use his own expression," the prosecutor explained — "but instead of beating her, he remained at her feet. That was the beginning of this passion. At the same time the old man, the father of the accused, casts his eye upon the same person — a strange and fatal coincidence, for they both lost their hearts to her simultaneously, though both had known her before. And she inspired in both of them the most violent, characteristically Karamazov passion. We have her own confession: 'I was laughing at both of them.' Yes, the sudden desire to make mock of them came over her, formerly she had not wished this, but now suddenly the notion came into her head — it ended by both of them being conquered by her. The old man, who worshipped money as though it were God, at once set aside three thousand roubles as a reward for one visit from her, but soon after that, he would have been happy to lay his property and his name at her feet, if only she would become his lawful wife. We have good evidence of this. As for the prisoner, his tragedy is plain; it is before us. But such was the young person's 'game.' The enchantress gave the unhappy young man no hope until the last moment, when he knelt before her, stretching out hands that were already stained with the blood of his father and rival. It was in that position that he was arrested. 'Send me to Siberia with him, I have brought him to this, I am most to blame,' the woman herself cried, in genuine remorse, at the moment of his arrest.

"The talented young man, who took it upon himself to describe the present case, Mr.

Rakitin, to whom I have referred already, characterised this heroine in a few brief and graphic terms: 'Early disillusionment, early betrayal and fall, abandonment by her betrothed, who had seduced her; then poverty, repudiation by her respectable family, and finally, the protection of a wealthy old man, whom she still, however, considers as her benefactor. There was perhaps much that was good in her young heart, but it was embittered too early. She became prudent and saved money. She grew sarcastic and revengeful towards society.' After this sketch of her character it may well be understood that she might laugh at both of them simply from mischief, from malice.

"During this month of hopeless love and moral degradation, when he betrayed his betrothed and appropriated money entrusted to his honour, the prisoner was driven almost to frenzy, almost to madness by continual jealousy — and of whom? His father! And the worst of it was that the crazy old man was trying to seduce and entice the object of his passion by means of that very three thousand roubles which the son looked upon as his own property, part of his inheritance from his mother, of which his father was cheating him. Yes, I admit it was hard to bear! It might well drive a man to madness. It was not the money, but the fact that this money was used with such revolting cynicism to ruin his happiness!"

Then the prosecutor went on to describe how the idea of murdering his father had entered the prisoner's head, and traced it by means of the evidence.

"At first we only shout about it in taverns — we shout about it all that month. Ah, we like being always surrounded with company,

and we like to tell our companions everything, even our most diabolical and dangerous ideas; we like to share every thought with others, and expect, for some reason, that those we confide in will respond to us with perfect sympathy, enter into all our troubles and anxieties, agree with us and not oppose us in anything. If not, we fly into a rage and smash up everything in the tavern." (Then followed the anecdote about Captain Snegiryov.) "Those who saw and heard the prisoner during that month began to think at last that he might mean more than threats, and that such a frenzy might turn threats into actions."

Here the prosecutor described the meeting of the family at the monastery, the conversations with Alyosha, and the abominable scene of violence when the prisoner rushed into his father's house just after dinner.

"I cannot positively assert," the prosecutor continued, "that the prisoner actually intended to murder his father before that incident. Yet the idea had several times presented itself to him, and he had deliberated on it — as regards that we have facts, the testimony of witnesses, and his own admission. I confess, gentlemen of the jury," he added, "that till to-day I have been uncertain whether to attribute to the prisoner conscious premeditation in the matter of the murder. I was firmly convinced that he had pictured the fatal moment beforehand, but had only pictured it, contemplating it as a possibility. He had not definitely considered when and how he might commit the crime.

"But I was uncertain only till to-day, till that fatal document was presented to the court just now. You yourselves heard that young lady's exclamation, 'It is the plan, the programme of the murder!' That is how she defined that miserable, drunken letter of the unhappy prisoner. And, in fact, that letter indicates a programme and a premeditated plan. It was written two days before the crime and so we know now for a fact that, forty-eight hours before the perpetration of his terrible design, the accused swore that, if he could not get money next day, he would kill his father in order to take money contained in the envelope with the pink ribbon from under his pillow, 'as soon as Ivan had left.' You hear that — 'as soon as Ivan had gone away'; so everything had been thought out, the circumstances had been weighed; and he carried it all out just as he had written it. The proof of premeditation is conclusive; the crime must have been committed for the sake of the money, that is stated clearly, that is written and signed. The accused does not deny his signature.

"I shall be told he was drunk when he wrote it. But that does not diminish the value of the letter, quite the contrary; he wrote when drunk what he had planned when sober. Had he not planned it when sober, he would not have written it when drunk. I shall be asked: Then why did he shout about his plan in the taverns? A man who premeditates such a crime holds his peace and keeps it to himself. Yes, but he talked about it before he had formed a plan, when he had only the desire, only the impulse to do it. Afterwards he talked less about it. On the evening he wrote that letter at the 'Metropolis' tavern, contrary to his custom he was silent, though he had been drinking. He did not play billiards, he sat in a corner, talked to no one. He did indeed turn a shopman out of his seat, but that was done almost unconsciously, because he could never enter a tavern without making a disturbance.

It is true that after he had taken the final decision, he must have felt apprehensive that he had talked too much about his design beforehand, and that this might lead to his arrest and prosecution afterwards. But there was nothing for it; he could not take his words back, but his luck had served him before, it would serve him again. We believed in our star, gentlemen! I must confess, too, that he did a great deal to elude the fatal moment, that he made many efforts to avoid the bloody conclusion. 'To-morrow I will try and borrow the money from every one,' as he writes in his peculiar style, 'and if they won't give it to me, there will be bloodshed.' Again, what is written when drunk is carried out when sober."

Here Ippolit Kirillovich passed to a detailed description of all Mitya's efforts to borrow the money in order to avoid the crime. He described his adventure with Samsonov, his journey to Lyagavy, everything on the basis of documentary evidence. "Harassed, jeered at, hungry, after selling his watch to pay for the journey (though he tells us he had fifteen hundred roubles on him — a likely story), tortured by jealousy at having left the object of his passion in the town, suspecting that she would go to Fyodor Pavlovich in his absence, he returns at last to the town, to find, to his joy, that she has not been near his father. He accompanies her himself to her protector, Samsonov. (Strange to say, we are not jealous of Samsonov, which is psychologically interesting.) Then he hastens back to his ambush in the back yard, and there learns that Smerdyakov is in a fit, that the other servant is ill — the coast is clear and he knows the 'signals' — what a temptation! Nevertheless he resists it; he goes off to a lady who has for some time been residing in the town, and who is highly esteemed among us, Madame Hohlakov. That lady, who had long watched his career with compassion, gave him the most judicious advice, to give up his dissipated life, his unseemly love-affair, his frequenting of taverns, the waste of his youth and vigour, and to set off to Siberia to the gold-mines: 'that would be an outlet for your turbulent energies, your romantic character, your thirst for adventure.'"

After describing the result of this conversation and the moment when the prisoner learnt that Grushenka had not remained at Samsonov's, the sudden frenzy of the luckless man, worn out with jealousy and nervous exhaustion, at the thought that she had deceived him and was now with his father, Ippolit Kirillovich concluded by dwelling upon the fatal influence of chance. "Had the maid told him that her mistress was at Mokroye with her former lover, nothing would have happened. But she lost her head, she could only swear and protest her ignorance, and if the accused did not kill her on the spot, it was only because he flew in pursuit of his false mistress.

"But note, frantic as he was, he took with him a brass pestle. Why that? Why not some other weapon? But since we had been contemplating our plan and preparing ourself for it for a whole month, we would snatch up anything like a weapon that caught our eye. We had realised for a month past that any object of the kind would serve as a weapon, so we instantly, without hesitation, recognised that it would serve our purpose. So it was by no means unconsciously, by no means involuntarily, that he snatched up that fatal pestle. And then we find him in his father's garden — the coast is clear, there are no witnesses, it's a dark night, jealousy rages. The suspicion that

she is there, with him, with his rival, in his arms, and perhaps laughing at him at that moment — takes his breath away. And it was not mere suspicion, the deception was open, obvious. She must be there, in that lighted room, she must be behind the screen; and the unhappy man would have us believe that he stole up to the window, peeped respectfully in, resigned himself decently, and discreetly withdrew, for fear something dangerous and immoral should happen. And he tries to persuade us of that, us, who know his character, who understand his state of mind at the moment, and who are aware that he knew the signals by which he could at once enter the house."

At this point Ippolit Kirillovich broke off to discuss exhaustively the suspected connection of Smerdyakov with the murder, in order to dispose of that theory once for all. He did this very circumstantially, and every one realised that, although he professed to despise that suspicion, he thought the subject of great importance.

## CHAPTER VIII
### A TREATISE ON SMERDYAKOV

"To begin with, how did this suspicion arise?" Ippolit Kirillovich began. "The first person to cry out that Smerdyakov had committed the murder was the accused himself at the moment of his arrest, yet from that time to this he has not brought forward a single fact to confirm the charge, nor the faintest suggestion of a fact. The charge is confirmed by three persons only — the two brothers of the accused and Madame Svyetlov. The elder of these brothers expressed his suspicions only to-day, when he was undoubtedly suffering from brain fever. But we know that for the last two months he has completely shared our conviction of his brother's guilt and did not attempt to combat that idea. But of that later. The younger brother has admitted that he has not the slightest fact to support his notion of Smerdyakov's guilt, and has been led to that conclusion only from the prisoner's own words and the expression of his face. Yes, that astounding piece of evidence has been brought forward twice to-day by him. Madame Svyetlov was even more astounding. 'What the accused tells you, you must believe; he is not a man to tell a lie.' That is all the evidence against Smerdyakov produced by these three persons, who are all deeply concerned in the prisoner's fate. And yet the theory of Smerdyakov's guilt has been noised about, has been and is still maintained. Is it credible? Is it conceivable?"

Here Ippolit Kirillovich found it necessary to describe the personality of Smerdyakov, "who had cut short his life in a fit of morbid derangement." He depicted him as a man of weak intellect, with a smattering of education, who had been thrown off his balance by philosophical ideas beyond his grasp and frightened by certain modern theories of duty and obligation which he learnt in practice from the reckless life of his master, who was also perhaps his father — Fyodor Pavlovich; and, theoretically, from various strange philosophical conversations with his master's elder son, Ivan Fyodorovich, who readily indulged in this diversion, probably out of boredom or wishing to amuse himself at the valet's expense. He spoke to me himself of his psychological condition during the last few days at his father's house," Ippolit Kirillovich explained; "but others, too, have borne witness to it — the accused himself, his brother, and the servant Grigory — that is, all who knew him well.

"Moreover, Smerdyakov, depressed by his attacks of epilepsy, was as cowardly as a chicken. 'He fell at my feet and kissed them,' the accused himself has told us, before he realised how damaging such a statement was to himself. 'He is an epileptic chicken,' he declared about him in his characteristic language. And it was he whom the accused chose for his confidant (we have his own word for it) and he frightened him into consenting at last to act as his spy and informer. In that capacity he deceived his master, revealing to the accused the existence of the envelope with the notes in it and the signals by means of which he could get into the house. How could he help telling him, indeed? 'He would have killed me, I could see that he would have killed me,' he said at the inquiry, trembling and shaking even before us, though the tormentor who had scared him so was by that time under arrest and could do him no harm. 'He suspected me every minute. In fear and trembling I hastened to tell him every secret to pacify him, that he might see that I had not deceived him and let me off alive.' Those are his own words. I wrote them down and I remember them. 'When he began shouting at me, I would fall on my knees.'

"He was by nature a very honest young man and enjoyed the complete confidence of his master, ever since he had restored him some money he had lost. So it may be supposed that the poor fellow suffered pangs of remorse at having deceived his master, whom he loved as his benefactor. Persons severely afflicted with epilepsy are, so the most skilful doctors testify, always prone to continual and morbid self-reproach. They are tormented by a sense of being 'guilty' of something and before somebody, they are tormented by pangs of conscience, often entirely without cause; they exaggerate and often invent all sorts of faults and crimes. And here we have a man of that type who had really been driven to wrongdoing by terror and intimidation.

"He had, besides, a strong presentiment that something bad would be the outcome of the situation that was developing before his eyes. When Ivan Fyodorovich was leaving for Moscow, just before the catastrophe, Smerdyakov besought him to remain, though he was too timid to tell him clearly and categorically what he feared. He confined himself to hints, but his hints were not understood.

"It must be observed that he looked on Ivan Fyodorovich as a protector, whose presence in the house was a guarantee that no harm would come to pass. Remember the phrase in Dmitri Karamazov's drunken letter, 'I will kill the old man, if only Ivan goes away.' So Ivan Fyodorovich's presence seemed to every one a guarantee of peace and order in the house.

"But he went away, and within an hour of his young master's departure Smerdyakov was taken with an epileptic fit. But that's perfectly intelligible. Here I must mention that Smerdyakov, oppressed by fears and a sort of despair, had felt during those last few days the possibility of an approaching epileptic attack, of the kind from which he had suffered before at moments of moral stress and strain. The day and hour of such an attack cannot, of course, be foreseen, but every epileptic can feel beforehand that he is likely to have one. So the doctors tell us. And so, as soon as Ivan Fyodorovich has left the house, Smerdyakov, depressed by his lonely and unprotected position, goes on an errand to the cellar. He walks down the stairs wondering if he will have a fit or not, and what if it is to come upon him at once. And

just because of this very mood, this very apprehension, these very questions, he is seized by the spasm in his throat that always precedes such attacks, and he falls unconscious onto the floor of the cellar. And in this perfectly natural occurrence people try to detect a suspicion, a hint that he was shamming an attack *on purpose*. But, if it were on purpose, the question arises at once, what was his motive? What was he reckoning on? What was he aiming at? I say nothing about medicine: science, I am told, may lie, science may go astray: the doctors were not able to discriminate between the counterfeit and the real. That may be so, but answer me one question: what motive had he for shamming? Is it that, having plotted the murder, he desired to attract the attention of the household by having a fit just before the crime?

"You see, gentlemen of the jury, on the night of the murder, there were five persons in Fyodor Pavlovich's house — Fyodor Pavlovich himself (but he did not kill himself, that's evident); then his servant, Grigory, but he was almost killed himself; the third person was Grigory's wife, Marfa Ignatyevna, but it would be simply shameful to imagine her murdering her master. Two persons are left — the accused and Smerdyakov. But, if we are to believe the statement of the accused that he did not do the killing, then Smerdyakov must have done it, for there is no other alternative, no one else can be found. Thus arose this 'shrewd,' colossal accusation against the unhappy idiot who committed suicide yesterday. It came about for the sole reason that no other suspect could be found. Had a shadow of suspicion rested on any one else, had there been any sixth person, I am persuaded that even the prisoner would have been ashamed to accuse

Smerdyakov, and would have accused that sixth person, for to charge Smerdyakov with that murder is perfectly absurd.

"Gentlemen, let us lay aside psychology, let us lay aside medicine, let us even lay aside logic, let us turn only to the facts and see what the facts tell us. If Smerdyakov killed, how did he do it? Alone or in collusion with the accused? Let us consider the first alternative — that he did it alone. If he had killed him it must have been with some object, for some advantage to himself. But not having a shadow of the motive that the accused had for the murder — hatred, jealousy, and so on — Smerdyakov could have murdered him only for the sake of gain, in order to appropriate the three thousand roubles he had seen his master put in the envelope. And yet he tells another person — and a person most closely interested, that is, the accused — everything about the money and the signals, where the envelope lay, what was written on it, what it was tied up with, and, above all, told him of those signals by which he could enter the house. Did he do this simply to betray himself, or in order to find a rival who would be anxious to get that envelope for himself? 'Yes,' I shall be told, 'but he spoke out of fear.' But how do you explain this? A man who could conceive such an audacious, savage act, and afterwards carry it out, tells facts which are known to no one else in the world, and which, if he held his tongue, no one in the whole world would ever have guessed!

"No, however cowardly he might be, if he had plotted such a crime, nothing would have induced him to tell any one about the envelope and the signals, for that was as good as betraying himself beforehand. He would have invented something, he would have told some

lie if he had been forced to give information, but he would have been silent about that. On the contrary, I repeat, if he had said nothing about the money but had committed the murder and stolen the money, no one in the world could have charged him with murder for the sake of robbery, since no one but he had seen the money, no one but he knew of its existence in the house. Even if he had been accused of the murder, it could only have been thought that he had committed it from some other motive. But since no one had observed any such motive in him beforehand, and every one saw, on the contrary, that his master was fond of him and honoured him with his confidence, he would, of course, have been the last to be suspected. People would have suspected first the man who had a motive, a man who had himself declared he had such motives, who had made no secret of it; they would, in fact, have suspected the son of the murdered man, Dmitri Fyodorovich. Had Smerdyakov killed and robbed him, and the son been accused of it, that would, of course, have suited Smerdyakov. Yet are we to believe that, though plotting the murder, he told that son, Dmitri, about the money, the envelope, and the signals? How logical! How clear!

"The day comes for the murder planned by Smerdyakov, and we have him falling downstairs in a *feigned* fit of epilepsy — with what object? In the first place that Grigory, who had been intending to take his medicine, might put it off and remain on guard, seeing there was no one to look after the house, and, in the second place, I suppose, that his master, seeing that there was no one to guard him, and in terror of a visit from his son, might redouble his vigilance and precaution. And, most of all, I suppose that he, Smerdyakov, disabled by the fit, might be carried from the kitchen, where he always slept, apart from all the rest, and where he could go in and out as he liked, to Grigory's room at the other end of the lodge, where he was always put, shut off by a screen three paces from their own bed. This was the immemorial custom established by his master and the kind-hearted Marfa Ignatyevna, whenever he had a fit. There, lying behind the screen, he would most likely, to keep up the sham, have begun groaning, and so keeping them awake all night (as Grigory and his wife testified). And all this, we are to believe, that he might more conveniently get up and murder his master!

"But I shall be told that he shammed illness on purpose that he might not be suspected and that he told the accused of the money and the signals to tempt him to commit the murder, and when he had murdered him and had gone away with the money, making a noise, most likely, and waking people, Smerdyakov got up, am I to believe, and went in — what for? To murder his master a second time and carry off the money that had already been stolen? Gentlemen, are you laughing? I am ashamed to put forward such suggestions, but, incredible as it seems, that's just what the accused alleges. When he had left the house, had knocked Grigory down and raised an alarm, he tells us Smerdyakov got up, went in and murdered his master and stole the money! I won't press the point that Smerdyakov could hardly have reckoned on this beforehand, and have foreseen that the furious and exasperated son would simply come to peep in respectfully, though he knew the signals, and beat a retreat, leaving Smerdyakov his booty. Gentlemen of the jury, I put this question to you in earnest; when was the moment when Smerdyakov could have committed his crime? Name that moment, for without that it's impossible to accuse him.

"But, perhaps, the epileptic fit was a real one, the sick man suddenly came to himself, heard a shout, and went out. Well — what then? He looked about him and said to himself, 'Let me go and kill the master'? And how did he know what had happened, since he had been lying unconscious till that moment? But there's a limit, gentlemen, to these flights of fancy.

" 'Quite so,' some astute people will tell me, 'but what if they were in collusion? What if they murdered him together and shared the money — what then?' A weighty suspicion, truly! And the evidence confirming it is astounding: one man commits the murder and takes all the trouble while his accomplice lies on his side shamming a fit, precisely to arouse suspicion in every one, alarm in his master and alarm in Grigory. It would be curious to know what motives could have induced the two accomplices to form such an insane plan.

"But perhaps it was not a case of active complicity on Smerdyakov's part, but only of passive acquiescence; perhaps Smerdyakov was intimidated and agreed not to prevent the murder, and, foreseeing that he would be blamed for letting his master be murdered, without screaming for help or resisting, he may have obtained permission from Dmitri Karamazov to get out of the way by shamming a fit — 'you may murder him as you like; it's nothing to me.' But as this attack of Smerdyakov's was bound to throw the household into confusion, Dmitri Karamazov could never have agreed to such a plan. I will waive that point, however. Supposing that he did agree, it would still follow that Dmitri Karamazov is the murderer, the actual murderer and the instigator, and Smerdyakov is only a passive accomplice, and not even an accomplice, but merely acquiesced against his will out of terror.

"But what do we see? As soon as he is arrested the prisoner instantly throws all the blame on Smerdyakov, not accusing him of being his accomplice, but of being himself the murderer. He did it alone, he says. He did the murdering and robbing, it was the work of his hands. Strange sort of accomplices who begin to accuse one another at once — that never happens. And think of the risk for Karamazov: he is the chief murderer, Smerdyakov is not the chief murderer, he is only the abettor, and all the time he was lying in bed behind the partition, and it is on this man that Karamazov puts the blame. But he, the man who lay in bed, might well have resented it and in self-preservation, if nothing else, might well have confessed the truth: 'We both had a hand in it, but I didn't kill, but only permitted and abetted the murder out of fear.' For he might well have seen that the court would at once estimate the degree of his guilt, and so he might well have reckoned that even if he were punished, it would be a far less severe punishment than the one meted out to the chief murderer, who wished to throw all the blame on him. But in that case he would have been certain to make a confession, yet he has not done so. Smerdyakov never hinted at their complicity, though the actual murderer persisted in accusing him and declaring that he had committed the crime alone.

"What's more, Smerdyakov at the inquiry volunteered the statement that it was *he* who had told the accused of the envelope with the money and of the signals, and that, but for

him, Karamazov would have known nothing about them. If he had really been a guilty accomplice, would he so readily have stated at the inquiry that he had himself told everything to the accused? On the contrary, he would have tried to conceal it, to distort the facts or minimise them. But he neither distorted nor minimised them. No one but an innocent man, who had no fear of being charged with complicity, could have acted as he did. And in a fit of morbid melancholy arising from his disease and this catastrophe he hanged himself yesterday. He left a note written in his peculiar style, 'I destroy myself of my own will and inclination so as to throw no blame on any one.' What would it have cost him to add: 'I am the murderer, not Karamazov'? But that he did not add. Did his conscience lead him to suicide and not to avowing his guilt?

"And what followed? Notes for three thousand roubles were brought into the court just now, and we were told that they were the same that lay in the envelope now on the table before us, and that the witness had received them from Smerdyakov the day before. But you, gentlemen of the jury, yourselves recall the painful scene which took place here. I shall not recall the details, I shall only allow myself to make comments on two or three points, selecting such trivial ones as might not be obvious at first sight to every one, and so may be overlooked. In the first place, Smerdyakov must have given back the money and hanged himself yesterday from remorse (for without remorse he would not have returned the money). And it was, of course, only last night that he confessed his guilt to Ivan Karamazov, for the first time, as the latter informs us. If it were not so, indeed, why should Ivan Fyodorovich have kept silence till now? And so he confessed, but why, I ask again, did he not avow the whole truth in the last letter he left behind, knowing that the innocent prisoner had to face this terrible ordeal the next day?

"The money alone is no proof. A week ago, quite by chance, the fact came to the knowledge of myself and two other persons in this court that Ivan Fyodorovich had sent two five per cent notes of five thousand each — that is, ten thousand in all — to the chief town of the province to be changed. I only mention this to point out that any one may have money on a given date, and that it can't be proved that these notes are the same as were in Fyodor Pavlovich's envelope.

"Ivan Karamazov, after receiving yesterday a communication of such importance from the real murderer, did not stir. Why didn't he report it at once? Why did he put it all off till morning? I think I have a right to conjecture why.

"His health had been giving way for a week past: he had admitted to a doctor and to his most intimate friends that he was seeing visions and encountering phantoms of the dead: he was on the eve of the attack of brain fever by which he has been stricken to-day. In this condition he suddenly heard of Smerdyakov's death, and at once reflected, 'The man is dead, I can throw the blame on him and save my brother. I have money. I will take a roll of notes and say that Smerdyakov gave them to me before his death.' You will say that was dishonourable: it's dishonourable to slander even the dead, even to save a brother. True, but what if he lied unconsciously? What if, finally unhinged by the sudden news of the valet's death, he imagined it really was so? You saw the recent scene: you have seen the witness's condition. He was standing up and was speaking, but where was his mind?

"Then followed the document, the prisoner's letter addressed to Madame Verhovtzev written two days before the crime and containing a complete programme of the murder. Why, then, are we looking for a programme and its authors? The crime was committed precisely according to this programme, and by no other than the writer of it. Yes, gentlemen of the jury, it went off without a hitch! No, we didn't, we didn't run respectfully and timidly away from our father's window, being besides firmly convinced that the object of our affections was with him. No, that is absurd and incredible! He went in and did the deed. Most likely he killed him in anger, burning with resentment, as soon as he looked on his hated rival. But having killed him, probably with one blow of the brass pestle, and having convinced himself, after careful search, that she was not there, he did not, however, forget to put his hand under the pillow and take out the envelope with the money, the torn envelope which lies now on the table before us.

"I mention this fact that you may note one, to my thinking, very characteristic circumstance. Had he been an experienced murderer and had he committed the murder for the sake of robbing only, would he have left the torn envelope on the floor as it was found, beside the corpse? Had it been Smerdyakov, for instance, murdering his master to rob him, he would have simply carried away the envelope with him, without troubling himself to open it over his victim's corpse, for he would have known for certain that the notes were in the envelope — they had been put in and sealed up in his presence — and had he taken the envelope with him, no one would ever have known of the robbery. I ask you, gentlemen of the jury, would Smerdyakov have behaved in that way? Would he have left the envelope on the floor?

"No, this was precisely the action of a frantic murderer, a murderer whose reason was already clouded, who was not a thief and had never stolen before that day, who snatched the notes from under the pillow, not like a thief stealing them, but as though seizing his own property from the thief who had stolen it. For that was the idea which had become almost an insane obsession with Dmitri Karamazov in regard to that money. And pouncing upon the envelope, which he had never seen before, he tore it open to make sure that the money was in it, and ran away with the money in his pocket, even forgetting to consider that he had left an astounding piece of evidence against himself in that torn envelope on the floor. All because it was Karamazov, not Smerdyakov, he doesn't think, he doesn't reflect, and how should he? He runs away; he hears behind him the servant cry out; the old man catches him, stops him, and is felled to the ground by the brass pestle.

"The accused, moved by pity, leaps down to look at him. Would you believe it, he tells us that he leapt down out of pity, out of compassion, to see whether he could do anything for him. Was that a moment to show compassion? No; he jumped down simply to make certain whether the only witness of his crime was dead or alive. Any other feeling, any other motive would be unnatural. Note that he took trouble over Grigory, wiped his head with his handkerchief, and, convincing himself he was dead, he ran like one lost to the house of his mistress, covered with blood. How was it he never thought that he was covered

with blood and would be at once detected? But the accused himself assures us that he paid no attention to the fact that he was covered with blood. That may be believed, that is very possible, that always happens at such moments with criminals. On one point they will show diabolical cunning, while another will escape them altogether. But he was thinking at that moment of one thing only — where was *she?* He had to find out at once where she was, so he ran to her lodging and learnt an unexpected and astounding piece of news — she had gone off to Mokroye to meet her former lover."

## CHAPTER IX
### PSYCHOLOGY AT FULL STEAM.
### THE GALLOPING TROIKA. THE END OF
### THE PROSECUTOR'S SPEECH

HAVING reached this moment in his speech, Ippolit Kirillovich, who had chosen the historical method of exposition, beloved by all nervous orators, since they find in its limitations a check on their own eager rhetoric, went off into a dissertation on Grushenka's "former and indubitable lover," and brought forward several interesting thoughts on this subject.

"Karamazov, who had been frantically jealous of every one, collapsed, so to speak, and effaced himself at once before this former lover. What makes it all the more strange is that he seems to have paid practically no attention to the new danger that assailed him in the person of this unexpected rival. But he had looked upon him as a remote danger, and Karamazov always lives in the present. Possibly he regarded him as a fiction. But his wounded heart grasped instantly that perhaps the woman had been concealing this new rival and deceiving him, because this newcomer was anything but a fiction and a fantasy to her, but was the one, the one hope of her life. Grasping this instantly, he resigned himself.

"Gentlemen of the jury, I cannot pass over in silence this unexpected trait in the character of the accused. He suddenly evinces an irresistible desire for justice, a respect for woman and a recognition of the rights of her heart. And all this at the very moment when he had stained his hands with his father's blood for her sake! It is true that the blood he had shed was already crying out for vengeance, for, after having ruined his soul and his earthly destiny, he was involuntarily forced to ask himself at that same instant what he meant and what he could mean *now* to her, to that being, dearer to him than his own soul, in comparison with that former and indubitable lover who had returned to the woman he had once betrayed, penitent, with new love, with honourable offers, with the promise of a reformed and happy life. And he, luckless man, what could he give her now, what could he offer her?

"Karamazov understood all this, he understood that all ways were barred to him by his crime and that he was a criminal under sentence, and not a man with life before him! This thought crushed and annihilated him. And so he instantly seizes upon one frantic plan, which, given Karamazov's character, could not but appear to him as the sole and fatal way out of his terrible position. That way out was suicide. He runs for the pistols he had left in pledge with Perhotin and on the way, as he runs, he pulls out of his pocket the money, for the sake of which he had stained his hands with his father's blood. Oh, now he needs money more than ever. Karamazov dies, Karamazov shoots himself and it will be re-

membered! It is not for nothing that we are a poet and it is not for nothing that we burnt the candle at both ends. 'To her, to her! and there, oh, there I will give a feast to the whole world, such as never was before, that will be remembered and talked of long after! In the midst of shouts of wild merriment, reckless gipsy songs and dances we shall raise the glass and drink to the woman we adore and her new-found happiness! And then, on the spot, at her feet, we shall dash out our brains before her and destroy our life! She will remember Mitya Karamazov sometimes, she will see how Mitya loved her, she will pity Mitya!'

"There is much here that is love of effect, romantic frenzy and sentimentality, the wild recklessness of the Karamazovs. Yes, but there is something else, gentlemen of the jury, something that cries out in the soul, throbs incessantly in the mind, and poisons the heart unto death — that *something* is conscience, gentlemen of the jury, its judgment, its terrible torments! But the pistol will settle everything, the pistol is the only way out! But *beyond* — I don't know whether Karamazov wondered at that moment, 'What lies beyond?' and whether Karamazov could, like Hamlet, wonder what lies beyond. No, gentlemen of the jury, they have Hamlets, but we still have Karamazovs!"

Here Ippolit Kirillovich drew a minute picture of Mitya's preparations, the scene at Perhotin's, at the shop, with the drivers. He cited numerous words, remarks, gestures, all confirmed by witnesses, and the picture made a terrible impression on the audience. What chiefly impressed people were the facts taken as a whole. The guilt of this man, frenzied and already careless of any precautions, stood out clear and incontrovertible.

"What need had he of precautions? Two or three times he almost confessed fully, hinted at it, all but spoke out." (Then followed the evidence given by witnesses.) "He even cried out to the peasant who drove him, 'Do you know, you are driving a murderer!' But it was impossible for him to speak out, he had to get to Mokroye and there to finish his romance. But what was awaiting the luckless man? Almost from the first minute at Mokroye he saw that his indubitable rival was perhaps by no means so indubitable, that the toast to their new-found happiness was not desired and would not be acceptable. But you know the facts, gentlemen of the jury, from the preliminary inquiry. Karamazov's triumph over his rival was complete and his soul passed into quite a new phase, perhaps the most terrible phase through which his soul has passed or will pass.

"One may say with certainty, gentlemen of the jury," the prosecutor exclaimed, "that outraged nature and the criminal heart bring their own vengeance more completely than any earthly justice. What's more, justice and punishment on earth positively alleviate the punishment of nature and are, indeed, necessary to the soul of the criminal at such moments, as its salvation from despair. For I cannot imagine the horror and moral suffering of Karamazov when he learnt that she loved him, that for his sake she had rejected her first lover, that she was summoning him, Mitya, to a new life, that she was promising him happiness — and when? When everything was over for him and nothing was possible!

"By the way, I will note in parenthesis a point of importance for the light it throws on the prisoner's position at the moment. This woman, this love of his, had been till the last moment, till the very instant of his arrest, a being unattainable, passionately desired by him but unattainable. Yet why did he not shoot himself then, why did he relinquish his design and even forget where his pistol was? It was just that passionate desire for love and the hope of satisfying it that restrained him. In the dizzy atmosphere of their revels he kept close to his adored mistress, who was feasting with him and was more charming and fascinating to him than ever — he did not leave her side, he filled his eyes with her, he melted before her.

"His passion might well, for a moment, stifle not only the fear of arrest, but even the torments of conscience. For a moment, oh, only for a moment. I can picture the state of mind of the criminal hopelessly enslaved by these influences — first, the influence of drink, of noise and excitement, of the thud of the dance and the scream of the songs, and of her, flushed with wine, singing and dancing and laughing to him in her drunken state! Secondly, the hope in the background that the fatal end might still be far off, that not till next morning, at least, would they come and take him. So he had a few hours and that's much, very much! In a few hours one can think up many things. I imagine that he felt something like what criminals feel when they are being taken to the gallows. They have another long, long street to ride down and at walking pace, past thousands of people. Then there will be a turning into another street and only at the end of that street the dread square! I fancy that at the beginning of the journey the condemned man, sitting on his shameful cart, must feel that he has infinite life still before him. But the houses recede, the cart moves on — oh, that's nothing, it's still far to the turning into the second street and he still looks boldly right and left at those thousands of callously curious people with their eyes fixed on him, and he still fancies that he is just such a man as they. But now comes the turning into the next street. Oh, that's nothing, nothing, there's still a whole street before him, and however many houses have been passed, he will still think there are many left. And so to the very end, to the very square.

"This I imagine is how it was with Karamazov then. 'They've not had time yet,' he must have thought, 'I may still find some way out, or, there's still time to make some plan of defence, and now, now — she is so fascinating!'

"His soul was full of confusion and dread, but he managed, however, to put aside half his money and hide it somewhere — I cannot otherwise explain the disappearance of quite half of the three thousand he had just taken from his father's pillow. He had been in Mokroye more than once before, he had caroused there for two days together already, he knew the old big house with all its passages and outbuildings. I imagine that part of the money was hidden in that house, not long before the arrest, in some crevice, under some floor, in some corner, under the roof. With what object? I shall be asked. Why, the catastrophe may take place at once, of course; he hadn't yet considered how to meet it, he hadn't the time, his head was throbbing and his heart was with *her*, but money — money was indispensable in any case! With money a man is everywhere a man. Perhaps such prudence at such a moment may strike you as unnatural? But he assures us himself that a month before, at a most exciting and fateful moment, he had withdrawn half of three thousand and sewn

it up in a little bag. And though that was not true, as we shall prove directly, it shows the idea was a familiar one to Karamazov, he had contemplated it. What's more, when he declared at the inquiry that he had put fifteen hundred roubles in a bag (which never existed) he may have invented that little bag on the inspiration of the moment, because two hours before he had removed his money and hidden it at Mokroye till morning, in case of emergency, simply not to have it on his person. Two abysses, gentlemen of the jury, remember that Karamazov can contemplate two abysses and both at once.

"We have searched the house, but we haven't found the money. It may still be there or it may have disappeared next day and be in the prisoner's hands now. In any case, he was arrested at her side, on his knees before her, she was lying on the bed, he had his hands stretched out to her and he had so entirely forgotten everything that he did not even hear the men coming to arrest him. He hadn't time to prepare any line of defence in his mind. Both he and his mind were caught unawares.

"And here he is, before his judges, the arbiters of his destiny. Gentlemen of the jury, there are moments in the execution of our duties when it is terrible for us to face a man, terrible on his account, too! Those are the moments of contemplating that animal fear, when the criminal sees that all is lost, but still struggles, still intends to offer resistance. Those are the moments when every instinct of self-preservation rises up in him at once and he, to save himself, looks at you with penetrating, questioning, and suffering eyes, studies you, your face, your thoughts, uncertain on which side you will strike, and his distracted mind frames thousands of plans in an instant, but he is still afraid to speak, afraid of giving himself away! This journey through the purgatory of the spirit, this animal thirst for self-preservation, these humiliating moments of the human soul, are awful, and sometimes arouse horror and compassion for the criminal even in the examining magistrate. And this was what we all witnessed then.

"At first he was thunderstruck and in his terror dropped some very compromising words. 'Blood! I've deserved it!' But he quickly restrained himself. He had not prepared what he was to say, what answer he was to make, he had nothing but a bare denial ready. 'I am not guilty of my father's death.' That was his fence for the moment and behind it he hoped to throw up a barricade of some sort. His first compromising exclamations he hastened to explain by declaring that he was responsible for the death of the servant Grigory only. 'Of that bloodshed I am guilty, but who has killed my father, gentlemen, who has killed him? Who can have killed him, *if not I?*' Do you hear, he asked us that, us, who had come to ask him that question! Do you hear that phrase uttered with such premature haste — 'if not I' — the animal cunning, the naïveté, the Karamazov impatience of it? 'I didn't kill him and you mustn't think I did! I wanted to kill him, gentlemen, I wanted to kill him,' he hastens to admit (he was in a hurry, in a terrible hurry), 'but still I am not guilty, it is not I murdered him.' He concedes to us that he wanted to murder him, as though to say, you can see for yourselves how sincere I am, so you'll believe all the sooner that I didn't murder him. Oh, in such cases the criminal is often amazingly frivolous and credulous.

"At that point one of the lawyers asked him, as it were casually, the simplest question, 'Wasn't it Smerdyakov killed him?' What followed, we expected: he was horribly angry at our having anticipated him and caught him unawares, before he had time to pave the way to choose and snatch the most suitable moment for bringing in Smerdyakov's name. In keeping with his character, he rushed at once to the other extreme, and began to assure us that Smerdyakov could not have killed him, was not capable of it. But don't believe him, that was only his cunning; he didn't really give up the idea of Smerdyakov; on the contrary, he would yet bring him forward again; for, indeed, he had no one else to bring forward, but he would do that later, because for the moment that line was spoiled for him. He would bring him forward perhaps next day, or even a few days later, choosing an opportunity to cry out to us, 'You see, I myself was more sceptical about Smerdyakov than you, you remember that yourselves, but now I am convinced. He killed, who but he!' And for the present he falls back upon a gloomy and irritable denial. Impatience and anger prompt him, however, to the most inept and incredible explanation of how he looked into his father's window and how he respectfully withdrew. Above all, he does not yet know the circumstances, the evidence given by Grigory.

"We proceed to search him. The search angers, but encourages him, the whole three thousand have not been found on him, only half of it. And no doubt only at that moment of angry silence and denial the notion of the little bag first enters his head. No doubt he is conscious himself of the improbability of the invention and strives painfully to make it sound more likely, to weave it into a romance that will sound plausible. In such cases the first duty, the chief task of the examining magistrates, is to prevent the criminal from preparing himself, to pounce upon him unexpectedly so that he may blurt out his cherished ideas in all their simplicity, improbability, and inconsistency. The criminal can be made to speak only by the sudden and apparently incidental communication of some new fact, of some circumstance of great importance in the case, of which he had no previous idea and could not have foreseen. We had such a fact in readiness — that was Grigory's evidence about the open door through which the prisoner had run out. He had completely forgotten about that door and had not even suspected that Grigory could have seen it.

"The effect of it was amazing. He leapt up and shouted to us, 'It was Smerdyakov murdered him, Smerdyakov!' and so betrayed his most cherished, basic idea in its most improbable shape, for Smerdyakov could have committed the murder only after he had knocked Grigory down and run away. When we told him that Grigory saw the door was open before he fell down, and had heard Smerdyakov groan behind the partition as he came out of his bedroom — Karamazov was positively crushed. My esteemed and witty colleague, Nikolay Parfenovich, told me afterwards that he was almost moved to tears at the sight of him. And to improve matters, the prisoner hastened to tell us about the famous little bag — so be it, you shall hear this tale!

"Gentlemen of the jury, I have told you already, why I consider this invention not only an absurdity, but the most improbable fiction that could have been brought forward under the circumstances. If one tried on a bet to invent the most unlikely story, one could hardly find anything more incredible. The worst of such stories is that the triumphant romancers can always be put to confusion and crushed by the very details in which real life is so rich and which these unhappy and involuntary story-tellers neglect as insignificant trifles. Oh, they have no thought to spare for such details, their minds are concentrated on their grand invention as a whole, and fancy any one daring to pull them up for a trifle! But that's how they are caught. The accused is asked the question, 'Where did you get the stuff for your little bag and who made it for you?' 'I made it myself.' 'And where did you get the linen?' The accused is already offended, he considers it almost insulting to ask him such a trivial question, and, would you believe it, his resentment is genuine! But they are all like that. 'I tore it off my shirt.' 'Very well, then we shall find that shirt among your linen to-morrow, with a piece torn off.' And only fancy, gentlemen of the jury, if we really had found that torn shirt (and how could we have failed to find it in his chest of drawers or trunk if such a shirt really existed?) that would have been a fact, a material fact in support of his statement! But he was incapable of that reflection. 'I don't remember, it may not have been off my shirt, I sewed it up in my landlady's cap.' 'What sort of cap?' 'It was an old cotton rag of hers lying about.' 'And do you remember that clearly?' 'No, I don't.' And he is angry, very angry, and yet imagine not remembering it! At the most terrible moments of a man's life, for instance when he is being led to execution, he remembers just such trifles. He will forget anything but some green roof that has flashed past him on the road, or a jackdaw on a cross — that he will remember. Obviously, when he was making that little bag he was hiding from the people in the house and he must have remembered his humiliating fear that some one might come in and find him needle in hand, how at the slightest noise he jumped up and slipped behind the partition (there is a partition in his lodgings).

"But, gentlemen of the jury, why do I tell you all this, all these details, trifles?" cried Ippolit Kirillovich suddenly. "Just because the accused still persists in these absurdities to this moment. He has not explained anything since that fatal night two months ago, he has not added one actual illuminating fact to his former fantastic statements. 'Those are all trivialities. You must believe me on my honour.' Oh, we are glad to believe it, we are eager to believe it, even if only on his word of honour! Are we jackals thirsting for human blood? Give us, show us a single fact in the prisoner's favour and we shall rejoice; but let it be a substantial, real fact, and not a conclusion drawn from the prisoner's facial expression by his own brother, or that when he beat himself on the breast he must have meant to point to the little bag, and that in the darkness, too. We shall rejoice at the new fact, we shall be the first to repudiate our charge, we shall hasten to repudiate it. But now justice cries out and we persist, we cannot repudiate anything."

Ippolit Kirillovich passed to his final peroration. He looked as though he was in a fever, he spoke of the blood that cried for vengeance, the blood of the father murdered by his son, with the base motive of robbery! He pointed to the tragic and blaring totality of the facts.

"And whatever you may hear from the talented and celebrated counsel for the defence," Ippolit Kirillovich could not resist adding, "whatever eloquent and touching appeals may be made to your sensibilities, remember that at this moment you are in a temple of justice. Remember that you are the champions of our justice, the champions of our holy Russia, of her foundations, her family, everything that she holds sacred! Yes, you represent Russia here at this moment, and your verdict not only will be heard in this hall but will reecho throughout the whole of Russia, and all Russia will hear you, as her champions and her judges, and she will be encouraged or disheartened by your verdict. Do not disappoint Russia and her expectations. Our fatal troika dashes on in her headlong flight perhaps to destruction, and for a long time throughout Russia men have stretched out imploring hands and called a halt to its furious reckless course. And if other nations stand aside from that troika that may be, not out of respect to her, as the poet would fain believe, but simply out of horror. Out of horror, perhaps out of disgust. And well it is that they stand aside, but maybe they will cease one day to do so and will form a firm wall confronting the hurrying apparition and will check the frenzied rush of our lawlessness, for the sake of saving themselves, enlightenment, and civilisation! Already we have heard voices of alarm from Europe, they already begin to sound. Do not tempt them! Do not heap up their growing hatred by a sentence justifying the murder of a father by his own son!"

In a word, though Ippolit Kirillovich was genuinely moved, he wound up his speech with this rhetorical appeal — and indeed, the effect produced by him was extraordinary. When he had finished his speech, he went out hurriedly and, as I have mentioned before, almost fainted in the adjoining room. There was no applause in the court, but serious people were pleased. The ladies were not so well satisfied, though even they were pleased with his eloquence, especially as they had no apprehensions as to the outcome of the trial and had full trust in Fetyukovich. "He will speak at last and of course carry all before him."

Every one looked at Mitya; he sat silent through the whole of the prosecutor's speech, with his hands clasped, his teeth clenched, and his head bowed. Only from time to time he raised his head and listened, especially when Grushenka was spoken of. When the prosecutor mentioned Rakitin's opinion of her, a smile of contempt and anger passed over his face and he murmured rather audibly, "The Bernards!" When Ippolit Kirillovich described how he questioned and tortured him at Mokroye, Mitya raised his head and listened with intense curiosity. At one point he seemed about to jump up and cry out, but controlled himself and only shrugged his shoulders disdainfully. People talked afterwards of the end of the speech, of the prosecutor's feat in examining the prisoner at Mokroye, and jeered at Ippolit Kirillovich. "The man could not resist boasting of his cleverness," they said.

The court was adjourned, but only for a short interval, a quarter of an hour or twenty minutes at most. There was a hum of conversation and exclamations in the audience. I remember some of them.

"A serious speech," a gentleman in one group observed frowningly.

"He unreeled too much psychology," said another voice.

"But it was all true, the absolute truth!"

"Yes, he is first rate at it."

"He summed it all up."

"Yes, he summed us up, too," chimed in another voice. "Do you remember, at the beginning of his speech, making out we were all like Fyodor Pavlovich?"

"And at the end, too. But that was all rot."

"And obscure, too."

"He was a little too much carried away."

"It's unjust, sir, it's unjust."

"No, it was smartly done, anyway. He's had long to wait, but he's had his say, ha-ha!"

"What will the counsel for the defence say?"

In another group I heard:

"He had no business to make a thrust at the Petersburg man like that: 'appealing to your sensibilities' — do you remember?"

"Yes, that was awkward of him."

"He was in too great a hurry."

"A nervous fellow."

"We laugh, but what must the accused be feeling?"

"Yes, what must it be for Mitya?"

"What will counsel for the defence say?"

In a third group:

"Who is that lady, the fat one, with the lorgnette, sitting at the end?"

"She is a general's wife, divorced, I know her."

"That's why she has the lorgnette."

"She is not good for much."

"Oh, no, she is a piquant little woman."

"Two places beyond her there is a little blonde, she is prettier."

"Clever work at Mokroye, wasn't it, eh?"

"Oh, it was clever enough. We've heard it before, how often he has told the story at people's houses!"

"And he couldn't resist doing it now. That's vanity."

"He is a man with a chip on his shoulder, he-he!"

"Yes, and quick to take offence. And there was too much rhetoric, such long sentences."

"Notice, he scares us, he kept trying to scare us. Do you remember about the troika? 'They have Hamlets, but we have, so far, only Karamazovs!' That was clever!"

"That was to get in well with the Liberals. He is afraid of them."

"Yes, and he is afraid of the lawyer, too."

"Yes, what will Fetyukovich say?"

"Whatever he says, he won't get round our peasants."

"Don't you think so?"

A fourth group:

"What he said about the troika was good, that bit about the other nations."

"And that was true what he said about other nations not standing for it."

"What do you mean?"

"Why, in the English Parliament a Member got up last week and speaking about the Nihilists asked the Ministry whether it was not high time to intervene, to educate this barbarous nation. Ippolit was thinking of him, I know he was. He was talking about that last week."

"Not an easy job."

"Not an easy job? Why not?"

"Why, we'd shut up Kronstadt and not let them have any corn. Where would they get it?"

"In America. They get it from America now."

"Nonsense!"

But the bell rang, all rushed to their places. Fetyukovich mounted the tribune.

# CHAPTER X
## THE SPEECH FOR THE DEFENCE.
### A TWO-EDGED WEAPON

ALL was hushed as the first words of the famous orator rang out. The eyes of the audience were fastened upon him. He began very simply and directly, with an air of conviction, but not the slightest trace of conceit. He did not make the slightest attempt at eloquence, at rhetoric, or at phrases ringing with emotion. He was like a man speaking in an intimate circle of sympathetic friends. He had a beautiful voice, sonorous and appealing, and there was something genuine and simple in the very sound of it. But every one realised at once that the speaker might suddenly rise to true pathos and "pierce the heart with wondrous power." His language was perhaps more irregular than Ippolit Kirillovich's, but he spoke without long phrases, and, indeed, with more precision. One thing did not please the ladies: he kept bending forward, especially at the beginning of his speech, not exactly bowing, but as though he were straining towards and darting at his listeners, bending his long narrow back in the middle, as though there were a hinge there that enabled him to bend almost at a right angle.

At the beginning of his speech he spoke rather disconnectedly, without system, one may say, dealing with facts separately, but in the end these facts formed a whole. His speech might be divided into two halves, the first consisting of criticism in refutation of the charge, sometimes malicious and sarcastic. But in the second half he suddenly changed his tone, and even his manner, and at once rose to pathos. The audience seemed on the look-out for it, and quivered with delight.

SPEECH FOR THE DEFENCE

He went straight to the point, and began by saying that although he practised in Petersburg, he had more than once visited provincial towns to defend those whom he believed to be innocent or concerning whose innocence he had a kind of presentiment. "That is what has happened to me in the present case," he explained. "From the very first accounts in the newspapers I was struck by something which strongly prepossessed me in the prisoner's favour. In a word, what interested me most was a fact which often occurs in legal practice, but rarely, I think, in such an extreme and peculiar form as in the present case. I ought to formulate that peculiarity only at the end of my speech, but I will do so at the very beginning, for it is my weakness to come to the point directly, not keeping my effects in reserve and economising impressions. That may be imprudent on my part, but then it's sincere. What I have in my mind is this: there is an overwhelming accumulation of evidence against the accused, and at the same time not one fact that will stand criticism, if it is examined separately, by itself. As I followed the case more closely in the papers and through rumours, I was more and more confirmed in my idea, and I suddenly received from the relatives of the accused a request to undertake his defence. I at once hurried here, and here I became completely convinced. It was to break down this terrible chain of facts, and to show that each piece of evidence taken separately was unproved and fantastic, that I undertook the case."

So Fetyukovich began.

"Gentlemen of the jury," he suddenly protested, "I am new to this district. I have no preconceived ideas. The accused, a man of turbulent and unbridled temper, has not insulted me, as he has insulted perhaps hundreds of persons in this town, and so prejudiced many people against him beforehand. Of course I recognise that the moral sentiment of local society is justly excited against him. The accused is of turbulent and violent temper. Yet he was received in society here; he was even welcome in the family of my talented friend, the prosecutor."

(N.B. At these words there were two or three laughs in the audience, quickly suppressed, but noticed by all. All of us knew that the prosecutor received Mitya against his will, solely because he had somehow found favour with the prosecutor's wife — a lady most virtuous and highly respected, but fanciful, capricious, and fond of opposing her husband, especially in trifles. Mitya's visits, however, had not been frequent.)

"Nevertheless I venture to suggest," Fetyukovich continued, "that in spite of his independent mind and just character, my opponent may have formed a mistaken prejudice against my unfortunate client. Oh, that is so natural; the unfortunate man has only too well deserved to be regarded with such prejudice. Outraged morality, and still more outraged taste, is often inexorable. Of course, we have, in the prosecutor's excellent speech, heard a stern analysis of the prisoner's character and conduct, and his severe critical attitude towards the case was evident. And, what's more, he went into psychological subtleties to explain the essence of the matter, subtleties into which he could not have entered, if he had the least conscious and malicious prejudice against the personality of the accused. But there are things which are even worse, even more fatal in such cases, than the most malicious and consciously unfair attitude. It is worse if we are carried away by the artistic instinct, by the desire to create, so to speak, a romance, especially if God has endowed us with psychological insight. Before I started on my way here, I was warned in Petersburg, and was myself aware, that I should find here a talented opponent whose psychological insight and subtlety had gained him peculiar renown in our legal world, which is still young. But profound as psychology is, gentlemen, it's a two-edged weapon." (Laughter among the public.) "You will, of course, forgive me my trivial comparison; I can't boast of eloquence. But I will take as an example any point in the prosecutor's speech.

"The accused, running away in the garden at night, climbs over the fence, and knocks down with a brass pestle the servant who has grabbed his leg. Then he jumps back into the garden and spends five minutes over the man, trying to discover whether he has killed him or not. Now the prosecutor refuses to believe the accused's statement that he ran to old Grigory out of pity. 'No,' he says, 'such sensibility is impossible at such a moment, that's unnatural; he ran to find out whether the only witness of his crime was dead or alive, and so showed that he had committed the murder, since he would not have run back for any other reason.'

"Here you have psychology; but let us take the same method and apply it to the case the other way round, and our result will be no less probable. The murderer, we are told, leapt down to find out, out of prudence, whether the witness was alive or not, yet he had just left in his murdered father's study, as the prosecutor himself argues, an amazing piece of evidence in the shape of a torn envelope, with an inscription that there had been three thousand roubles in it. 'If he had carried that envelope away with him, no one in the world would have known of the existence of that envelope and of the notes in it, and that the money had been stolen by the accused.' Those are the prosecutor's own words. So on one side you see a complete absence of precaution, a man who has lost his head and run away in a fright, leaving that clue on the floor, and two minutes later, when he has struck another man, we are asked to assume the most heartless and calculating prudence in him. But even admitting this was so, it is psychological subtlety, I suppose, that discerns that under certain circumstances I become as bloodthirsty and keen-sighted as a Caucasian eagle, while at the next I am as timid and blind as a mole. But if I am so bloodthirsty and cruelly calculating that when I kill a man I run back only to find out whether he is alive to bear witness against me, why should I spend five minutes looking after my victim at the risk of encountering other witnesses? Why soak my handkerchief, wiping the blood off his head so that it may be evidence against me later? If we are so cold-hearted and calculating, why not hit the servant on the head again and again with the same pestle so as to kill him outright and relieve ourself of all anxiety about the witness?

"And finally I jump down to see whether the witness is alive or not, and right there on the path I leave another witness, namely, that brass pestle which I took from the two women, and which they could always recognise afterwards as theirs, and testify that I had taken it from them. And it is not as though we had forgotten it on the path, dropped it through carelessness or haste, no, we flung away our weapon, for it was found fifteen paces from where Grigory lay. Why did we do so? Just because we were grieved at having killed a man, an old servant; and we flung away the pestle with a curse, as a murderous weapon. That's how it must have been, what other reason could we have had for throwing it so far? And if we were capable of feeling grief and pity at having killed a man, it was of course because we did not kill our father. Had we murdered him, we would never have run to another victim out of pity; then we would have felt differently; our thoughts would have been centred on self-preservation. We would have had none to spare for pity, that is beyond doubt. On the contrary, I repeat, we would have broken his skull instead of spending five minutes looking after him. There was room for pity and good-feeling just because our conscience had been clear till then. Here we have a different psychology. I have purposely resorted to this method, gentlemen of the jury, to show that you can prove anything by it. It all depends on who makes use of it. Psychology lures even most serious people into romancing, and quite unconsciously.

"I am speaking of excessive psychology, gentlemen of the jury, of the abuse of psychology, as it were."

Sounds of approval and laughter, at the expense of the prosecutor, were again audible in the court. I will not repeat the speech in detail; I will only quote some passages from it, some leading points.

## CHAPTER XI
### THERE WAS NO MONEY. THERE WAS NO ROBBERY

THERE was one point that struck every one in Fetyukovich's speech. He flatly denied the existence of the fatal three thousand roubles, and consequently the possibility of their having been stolen.

"Gentlemen of the jury," he began. "Every new and unprejudiced observer must be struck by a characteristic peculiarity in the present case, namely, the charge of robbery, and the complete impossibility of determining precisely what was stolen. We are told that money was stolen — three thousand roubles — but whether those roubles ever existed, nobody knows. Consider, how did we learn of that sum, and who has seen the notes? The only person who saw them, and stated that they had been put in the envelope with an inscription, was the servant, Smerdyakov. It was he also who had spoken of it to the accused and his brother, Ivan Fyodorovich, before the catastrophe. Madame Svyetlov, too, had been told of it. But not one of these three persons had actually seen the notes, no one but Smerdyakov had seen them.

"Here the question arises, if it's true that they did exist, and that Smerdyakov had seen them, when did he see them for the last time? What if his master had taken the notes from under his bed and put them back in his cashbox without telling him? Note, that according to Smerdyakov's story the notes were kept under the mattress; the accused must have pulled them out, and yet the bed was absolutely unrumpled; that is carefully set down in the record. How could the accused have found the notes without disturbing the bed? How could he have helped soiling with his bloodstained hands the fine and spotless linen with which the bed had purposely been made?

"But I shall be asked: what about the envelope on the floor? Yes, it's worth saying a word or two about that envelope. I was somewhat surprised just now to hear the highly talented prosecutor declare of himself — of himself, observe — that but for that envelope, but for its being left on the floor as a clue, but for the robber's not having taken it with him, no one in the world would have known of the existence of that envelope and the notes in it, and therefore of the accused's having stolen it. And so that torn scrap of paper is, by the prosecutor's own admission, the sole proof on which the charge of robbery rests, 'otherwise no one would have known of the robbery, nor perhaps even of the money.' But is the mere fact that that scrap of paper was lying on the floor a proof that there was money in it, and that that money had been stolen? Yet, it will be objected, Smerdyakov had seen the money in the envelope. But when, when had he seen it for the last time? I ask you that. I talked to Smerdyakov, and he told me that he had seen the notes two days before the catastrophe. Then why may I not suppose, for instance, that old Fyodor Pavlovich, locked up alone in impatient and hysterical expectation of the object of his adoration, may have whiled away the time by breaking open the envelope and taking out the notes. 'What's the use of the envelope,' he may have asked himself, 'she won't believe the notes are there, but when I show her the thirty rainbow-coloured notes in one roll, it will make more impression, you may be sure, it will make her mouth water.' And so he tears open the envelope, takes out the money, and flings the envelope on the floor, conscious of being the owner and untroubled by any fears of leaving evidence.

"Listen, gentlemen, could anything be more likely than such a supposition and such an action? Why is it impossible? But if anything of the sort could have taken place, the charge of robbery falls to the ground; there was no money, and therefore no robbery. If the envelope on the floor may be taken as evidence that there had been money in it, why may I not maintain the opposite, namely, that the envelope was on the floor because the money had previously been taken out of it by its owner?

"But I shall be asked, what became of the money if Fyodor Pavlovich took it out of the envelope, since it was not found when the police searched the house? In the first place, part of the money was found in a drawer, and secondly, he might have taken it out that morning or the evening before to make some other use of it, to give or send it away; he may have changed his idea, his plan of action completely, without thinking it necessary to announce the fact to Smerdyakov beforehand. And if there is the barest possibility of such an explanation, how can the prisoner be so positively accused of having committed murder for the sake of robbery, and of having actually carried out that robbery? This is encroaching on the domain of romance. If it is maintained that something has been stolen, the thing must be produced, or at least its existence must be proved beyond doubt. Yet no one had ever seen these notes.

"Not long ago in Petersburg a young man of eighteen, hardly more than a boy, who carried on a small business as a costermonger, went in broad daylight into a money-changer's shop with an axe, and with extraordinary, typical audacity killed the master of the shop and carried off fifteen hundred roubles. Five hours later he was arrested, and, except for fifteen roubles he had already managed to spend, the whole sum was found on him. Moreover, the shopman, on his return to the shop after the murder, informed the police not only of the exact sum stolen, but even of the notes and gold coins of which that sum was made up, and those very notes and coins were found on the criminal. This was followed by a full and genuine confession on the part of the murderer. That's what I call evidence, gentlemen of the jury! In that case I know, I see, I touch the money, and cannot deny its existence. Is it the same in the present case? And yet it is a question of life and death, of a man's fate.

"Yes, I shall be told, but he was carousing that night, squandering money; he was shown to have had fifteen hundred roubles — where did he get the money? But the very fact that only fifteen hundred could be found, and the other half of the sum could nowhere be discovered, shows that that money was not the same, and had never been in any envelope. By strict calculation of time it was proved at the preliminary inquiry that the accused ran straight from those women servants to Perhotin's without going home, and that he had been nowhere. So he had been all the time in company and therefore could not have divided the three thousand in half and hidden half in the town. It's just this consideration that has led the prosecutor to assume that the money is hidden in some crevice at Mokroye. Why not in the dungeons of the castle of Udolpho, gentlemen? Isn't this supposition really too fantastic and too romantic? And observe, if that supposition breaks down, the whole charge of robbery is scattered to the winds, for in that case what could have become of the other fifteen hundred roubles? By what miracle could they have disappeared, since it's proved that the accused went nowhere? And we are ready to ruin a man's life with such tales!

"I shall be told that he could not explain where he got the fifteen hundred that he had, and every one knew that he was without money before that night. Who knew it, pray? The accused has made a clear and unflinching statement of the source of that money, and if you will have it so, gentlemen of the jury, nothing can be more probable than that statement, and more consistent with the temper and spirit of the accused. The prosecutor is charmed with his own romance. A man of weak will, who had brought himself to take the three thousand so insultingly offered by his betrothed, could not, we are told, have set aside half and sewn it up, but would, even if he had done so, have opened it every two days and taken out a hundred, and so would have spent it all in a month. All this, you will remember, was put forward in a tone that brooked no contradiction. But what if the thing happened quite differently? What if you've been weaving a romance, and about quite a different kind of man? That's just it, you have invented quite a different person!

"I shall be told, perhaps, that there are witnesses that he spent on one day that whole three thousand given him by his betrothed a month before the catastrophe, so he could not have divided the sum in half. But who are these witnesses? The value of their testimony has been shown in court already. Besides, in another man's hand a crust always seems larger, and no one of these witnesses counted that money; they all judged simply at sight. And didn't the witness Maximov testify that the accused had twenty thousand in his hand? You see, gentlemen of the jury, psychology is a two-edged weapon. Let me use the other edge now and see what comes of it.

"A month before the catastrophe the accused was entrusted by Katerina Ivanovna with three thousand roubles to send off by mail. But the question is: is it true that they were entrusted to him in such an insulting and degrading way as was proclaimed just now? The first statement made by the young lady on the subject was different, absolutely different. In the second statement we heard only cries of resentment and revenge, cries of long-concealed hatred. And the very fact that the witness gave her first testimony incorrectly, gives us a right to conclude that her second piece of evidence may have been incorrect also. The prosecutor will not, dare not (his own words) touch on that story. So be it. I will not touch on it either, but will only venture to observe that if a lofty and high-principled person, such as that highly respected young lady unquestionably is, if such a person, I say, allows herself suddenly in court to contradict her first statement, with the obvious motive of ruining the accused, it is clear that this testimony has been given not dispassionately, not coolly. Have not we the right to assume that a revengeful woman might have exaggerated much? Yes, she may well have exaggerated, in particular, the insult and humiliation of her offering him the money. On the contrary, it was offered in such a way that it was possible to take it, especially for a man so easy-going as the accused; above all, as he expected to receive shortly from his father the three thousand roubles that he reckoned was owing to him. It was unreflecting of him, but it was just his irresponsible want of reflection that made him so confident that his father would give him the money, that he would get it, and so could always despatch the money entrusted to him and settle the debt.

"But the prosecutor refuses to allow that he could the same day have set aside half the money and sewn it up in a little bag. That's not his character, he tells us, he couldn't have had such feelings. But yet you cried out yourself that the Karamazov nature was broad; you cried out about the two abysses which a Karamazov can contemplate at once. Karamazov is just such a two-sided nature, fluctuating between two abysses, so that even when moved by the most violent craving for riotous gaiety, he can pull himself up, if something strikes him from another quarter. And in the other quarter is love — that new love which had flamed up in his heart, and for that love he needed money; oh, far more than for carousing with his mistress. If she were to say to him, 'I am yours, I won't have Fyodor Pavlovich,' then he must have money to seize her and carry her off. That was more important than carousing. Could a Karamazov fail to understand it? That anxiety was just what he was suffering from — what is there improbable in his laying aside that money and concealing it in case of emergency?

"But time passes, and Fyodor Pavlovich does not give the accused the expected three thousand; on the contrary, the latter hears that he means to use this sum to seduce the woman he, the accused, loves. 'If Fyodor Pavlovich doesn't hand over the money to me,' he thinks, 'I shall be put in the position of a thief before Katerina Ivanovna.' And then the idea presents itself to him that he will go to Katerina Ivanovna, lay before her the fifteen hundred roubles he still carries round his neck, and say, 'I am a scoundrel, but not a thief.' So here we have already a twofold reason why he should guard that sum of money as the apple of his eye, why he shouldn't open the little bag and spend it a hundred at a time. Why should you deny the accused a sense of honour? Yes, he has a sense of honour, granted that it's mis-directed, granted it's often mistaken, yet it exists and amounts to a passion, and he has proved that.

"But now the affair becomes even more complex; his jealous torments reach a climax, and those same two questions torture his fevered brain more and more: 'If I repay Katerina Ivanovna, where can I find the means to carry Grushenka off?' If he behaved wildly, drank, and made disturbances in the taverns in the course of that month, it was perhaps because he was wretched and strained beyond his powers of endurance. These two questions became so acute that they drove him at last to despair. He sent his younger brother to beg for the last time for the three thousand roubles, but, without waiting for a reply, burst in himself and ended by beating up the old man in the presence of witnesses. After that he had no prospect of getting it from any one; his father would not give it him after that beating.

"The same evening he strikes himself on the breast, just on the upper part of the breast where the little bag is, and swears to his brother that he has the means to prevent his being a scoundrel, but that still he will remain a scoundrel, for he foresees that he will not use that means, that he won't have the character, that he won't have the will-power to do it. Why, why does the prosecutor refuse to believe the testimony of Alexey Karamazov, given so genuinely and sincerely, so spontaneously and convincingly? And why, on the contrary, does he force me to believe in money hidden in a crevice, in the dungeons of the castle of Udolpho?

"The same evening, after his talk with his brother, the accused writes that fatal letter, and that letter is the chief, the most stupen-dous proof of the accused's having committed robbery! 'I will beg from every one, and if I don't get it I will murder my father and will take the envelope with the pink ribbon on it from under his mattress as soon as Ivan has gone.' A full programme of the murder, we are told, so it must have been he. 'It has all been done as he wrote,' cries the prosecutor.

"But in the first place, it's the letter of a drunken man and written in great irritation; secondly, he writes of the envelope what he has heard from Smerdyakov again, for he has not seen the envelope himself; and thirdly, he wrote it indeed, but how can you prove that he did it? Did the accused take the envelope from under the pillow, did he find the money, did that money exist indeed? And was it to get money that the accused ran off, if you remember? He ran off post-haste not to rob, but to find out where she was, the woman who had crushed him. He was not running to carry out a programme, to carry out what he had written, that is, not for an act of premeditated robbery, but he ran suddenly, spontaneously, in a jealous fury. Yes! I shall be told, but when he got there and murdered him he seized the money, too. But did he murder him after all? The charge of robbery I repudiate with indignation. A man cannot be accused of robbery, if it's impossible to state accurately what he has stolen; that's an axiom. But did he murder him without robbery, did he murder him at all? Is that proved? Isn't that, too, a fiction?"

## CHAPTER XII
### AND THERE WAS NO MURDER EITHER

"ALLOW me, gentlemen of the jury, to remind you that a man's life is at stake and that you must be more careful. We have heard the prosecutor himself admit that until to-day he hesitated to accuse the prisoner of a full and conscious premeditation of the crime; he hesitated till he saw that fatal drunken letter which was produced in court to-day. 'All was done as written.' But, I repeat again, he was running to her, to seek her, solely to find out where she was. That's a fact that can't be disputed. Had she been at home, he would not have run away, but would have remained at her side, and so would not have done what he promised in the letter. He ran suddenly and accidentally, and by that time very likely he did not even remember his drunken letter. 'He snatched up the pestle,' they say, and you will remember how a whole edifice of psychology was built on that pestle — why he was bound to look at that pestle as a weapon, to snatch it up as a weapon, and so on, and so on. A very commonplace idea occurs to me at this point: What if that pestle had not been in sight, had not been lying on the shelf from which it was snatched by the accused, but had been put away in a cupboard? It would not have caught the prisoner's eye, and he would have run away without a weapon, with empty hands, and then he would certainly not have killed any one. How then can I look upon the pestle as a proof of arming and of premeditation?

"Yes, but he talked in the taverns of murdering his father, and two days before, on the evening when he wrote his drunken letter, he was quiet and only quarrelled with a shopman in the tavern, because a Karamazov could not help quarrelling, forsooth! But my answer to that is, that, if he was planning such a murder in accordance with his letter, he certainly would not have quarrelled even with a shopman, and probably would not have gone into the tavern at all, because a person plotting such a crime seeks quiet and retirement, seeks to efface himself, to avoid being seen and heard, and that not from calculation, but from instinct. Gentlemen of the jury, the psychological method is a two-edged weapon, and we, too, can use it. As for all this shouting in taverns throughout the month, don't we often hear children, or drunkards coming out of taverns shout, 'I'll kill you'? but they don't murder any one. And that fatal letter — isn't that simply drunken irritability, too? Isn't that simply the shout of the brawler outside the tavern, 'I'll kill you! I'll kill the lot of you!' Why not, why could it not be that? What reason have we to call that letter 'fatal' rather than ridiculous? Because his father has been found murdered, because a witness saw 'the accused running out of the garden with a weapon in his hand, and was knocked down by him: therefore, we are told, everything was done as he had planned in writing, and the letter was not 'ridiculous,' but 'fatal.'

"Now, thank God! we've come to the real point: 'since he was in the garden, he must have murdered him.' In those few words, 'since he *was*, then he *must*,' lies the whole case for the prosecution. He was there, so he must have. And what if there is no *must* about it, even if he was there? Oh, I admit that the chain of evidence — the coincidences — are really quite eloquent. But examine all these facts separately, regardless of the way they hang together. Why, for instance, does the prosecution refuse to admit the truth of the prisoner's statement that he ran away from his father's window? Remember the sarcasms in which the prosecutor indulged at the expense of the respectful and 'pious' sentiments which suddenly came over the murderer. But

570

what if there was something of the sort, a feeling of religious awe, if not of filial respect? 'My mother must have been praying for me at that moment,' were the accused's words at the preliminary inquiry, and so he ran away as soon as he convinced himself that Madame Svyetlov was not in his father's house. 'But he could not convince himself by looking through the window,' the prosecutor objects. But why couldn't he? Why? The window opened at the signals given by the accused. Some word might have been uttered by Fyodor Pavlovich, some exclamation which showed the accused that she was not there. Why should we assume everything as we imagine it, as we make up our minds to imagine it? A thousand things may happen in reality which elude the imagination of the subtlest romancer.

" 'Yes, but Grigory saw the door open and so the prisoner certainly was in the house, therefore he killed him.' Now about that door, gentlemen of the jury. . . . Observe that we have only the statement of one witness as to that door, and he was at the time in such a condition, that . . . But supposing the door was open; supposing the accused has lied in denying it, from an instinct of self-defence, natural in his position; supposing he did go into the house — well, what then? How does it follow that because he was there he committed the murder? He might have dashed in, run through the rooms; might have pushed his father away; might have struck him; but as soon as he had made sure Madame Svyetlov was not there, he may have run away rejoicing that she was not there and that he had not killed his father. And it was perhaps just because he had escaped from the temptation to kill his father, because he had a clear conscience and was rejoicing at not having killed

him, that he was capable of a pure feeling, the feeling of pity and compassion, and leapt off the fence a minute later to the assistance of Grigory after he had, in his excitement, knocked him down.

"With terrible eloquence the prosecutor has described to us the dreadful state of the prisoner's mind at Mokroye when love again lay before him calling him to new life, while love was impossible for him because he had his father's blood-stained corpse behind him and beyond that corpse — retribution. And yet the prosecutor nevertheless did allow him love, which he explained in his own way: 'a drunken condition, a criminal taken to the gallows, the end still far off,' and so on and so on. But again I ask, Mr. Prosecutor, have you not invented a new personality? Is the accused so coarse and heartless as to be able to think at that moment of love and of dodges to escape punishment, if his father's blood was really upon him? No, no, and no! As soon as it was made plain to him that she loved him and called him to her side, promising him new happiness, oh! then, I protest he must have felt the impulse to suicide doubled, trebled, and would have killed himself without fail, if he had his father's murder on his conscience. Oh, no! he would not have forgotten where his pistols lay! I know the accused: the savage, stony heartlessness ascribed to him by the prosecutor is inconsistent with his character. He would have killed himself, that's certain. He did not kill himself just because 'his mother's prayers had saved him,' and he was innocent of his father's blood. He was troubled, he was grieving that night at Mokroye only about old Grigory and praying to God that the old man would recover, that his blow had not been fatal, and that he would not have to suffer for it. Why

571

not accept such an interpretation of the facts? What trustworthy proof have we that the accused is lying?

"But we shall be told at once again, 'There is his father's corpse! If he ran away without murdering him, who did murder him?' Here, I repeat, you have the whole logic of the prosecution. Who murdered him, if not he? There's no one to put in his place.

"Gentlemen of the jury, is that really so? Is it positively, actually true that there is no one else at all? We've heard the prosecutor count on his fingers all the persons who were in that house that night. They were five in number; three of them, I agree, could not have been responsible — the murdered man himself, old Grigory, and his wife. There are left then the accused and Smerdyakov, and the prosecutor dramatically exclaims that the accused pointed to Smerdyakov because he had no one else to fix on, that had there been a sixth person, even a phantom of a sixth person, he would have abandoned the charge against Smerdyakov at once in shame and have accused that other. But, gentlemen of the jury, why may I not draw the very opposite conclusion? There are two persons — the accused and Smerdyakov. Why can I not say that you accuse my client simply because you have no one else to accuse? And you have no one else only because you have determined to exclude Smerdyakov from all suspicion.

"It's true, indeed, Smerdyakov is accused only by the prisoner, his two brothers, and Madame Svyetlov. But there are others who point to him: there are vague rumours of a question, of a suspicion, an obscure report, a feeling of expectation. Finally, we have the evidence of a combination of facts very suggestive, though, I admit, inconclusive. In the first place, we have precisely on the day of the catastrophe that fit, the genuineness of which the prosecutor, for some reason, has felt obliged so carefully to uphold and defend. Then Smerdyakov's sudden suicide on the eve of the trial. Then the equally startling evidence given in court to-day by the elder of the accused's brothers, who until now had believed in his guilt, but who has to-day produced the money and proclaimed Smerdyakov as the murderer. Oh, I fully share the court's and the prosecutor's conviction that Ivan Karamazov is suffering from brain fever, that his statement may really be a desperate effort, planned in delirium, to save his brother by throwing the guilt on the dead man. But again Smerdyakov's name is pronounced, again there is a suggestion of mystery. There is something half-expressed here, as it were, something incomplete, gentlemen of the jury. And perhaps it may one day be stated in full. But we won't go into that now. Of that later.

"The court has resolved to go on with the trial, but, meantime, I might make a few remarks about the character sketch of Smerdyakov drawn with such subtlety and talent by the prosecutor. But while I admire his talent I cannot agree with the substance of his characterisation. I have visited Smerdyakov, I have seen him and talked to him, and he made a very different impression on me. He was weak in health, it is true; but in character, in spirit, oh, no, he was by no means the weak man the prosecutor has made him out to be. Especially, I found in him no trace of the timidity on which the prosecutor so insisted. There was no simplicity about him, either. I found in him, on the contrary, an extreme mistrustfulness concealed under a mask of naïveté, and an intelligence of considerable range. The prosecutor was too simple in taking him for weak-minded. He made a very definite impression on me: I left him with the conviction that he was a distinctly spiteful creature, excessively ambitious, vindictive, and intensely envious. I made some inquiries: he hated his origin, was ashamed of it, and would clench his teeth when he remembered that he was the son of 'Stinking Lizaveta.' He was disrespectful to the servant Grigory and his wife, who had cared for him in his childhood. He cursed and jeered at Russia. He dreamed of going to France and becoming a Frenchman. He used often to say that he hadn't the means to do so. I fancy he loved no one but himself and had a strangely high opinion of himself. His conception of culture was limited to good clothes, clean shirt fronts, and polished boots. Believing himself to be the illegitimate son of Fyodor Pavlovich (there is evidence of this), he might well have resented his position, compared with that of his master's legitimate sons. They had everything, he nothing. They had all the rights, they had the inheritance, while he was only the cook. He told me himself that he had helped Fyodor Pavlovich to put the money in the envelope. The destination of that sum — a sum which would have made his career — was, of course, hateful to him. Moreover, he saw three thousand roubles in new rainbow-coloured notes. (I asked him about that on purpose.) Oh, beware of showing an ambitious and envious man a large sum of money at once! And it was the first time he had seen so much money all at once. The sight of the rainbow-coloured notes may have made a morbid impression on his imagination, but with no immediate results.

"The talented prosecutor, with extraordinary subtlety, sketched for us all the arguments for and against the hypothesis of Smerdyakov's guilt, and asked us in particular what motive he had in feigning a fit. But he may not have been feigning at all, the fit may have happened quite naturally, but it may have passed off quite naturally, and the sick man may have recovered, not completely perhaps, but still regaining consciousness, as happens with epileptics.

"The prosecutor asks at what moment Smerdyakov could have committed the murder. But it is very easy to point out that moment. He might have waked up from deep sleep (for he was only asleep — an epileptic fit is always followed by a deep sleep) at that moment when the old man, Grigory, having grabbed the leg of the accused, who was then astride the fence, shouted at the top of his voice, 'Parricide!' That strange shout resounding in the stillness of the night may have waked Smerdyakov, whose sleep was perhaps less sound at the moment: he might naturally have begun to come out of his stupor an hour before.

"Getting out of bed, he goes almost unconsciously and with no definite motive towards the sound to see what's the matter. His head is still clouded by his attack, his mind is half asleep; but, once in the garden, he walks to the lighted windows and he hears the terrible news from his master, who would, of course, be glad to see him. His head clears up at once. He learns all the details from his frightened master, and gradually in his sick and disordered brain an idea shapes itself — terrible, but seductive and irresistibly logical: to kill the old man, take the three thousand, and throw all the blame on his young master. Who will be suspected if not the young master? Who will be accused if not the young master?

There is all this evidence; he was here. A terrible lust for money, for booty, might seize upon him together with the thought that he could act with impunity. Oh! these sudden and irresistible impulses come so often when there is a favourable opportunity, and especially with murderers who a moment earlier have had no idea of committing a murder. And Smerdyakov may have gone in and carried out his plan. With what weapon? Why, with any stone picked up in the garden. But what for, with what object? Why, the three thousand which means a career for him. Oh, I am not contradicting myself — the money may have existed. And perhaps Smerdyakov alone knew where to find it, where his master kept it. And the wrapper — the torn envelope on the floor? Just now, when the prosecutor was explaining his subtle theory that only an inexperienced thief like Karamazov would have left the envelope on the floor, and not one like Smerdyakov, who would have avoided leaving a piece of evidence against himself, I thought as I listened that I was hearing something very familiar, and, would you believe it, I have heard that very argument, that very conjecture, of how Karamazov would have behaved, precisely two days before, from Smerdyakov himself. What's more, it struck me at the time. I fancied that there was an artificial simplicity about him; that he was in a hurry to suggest this idea to me that I might fancy it was my own. He prompted me, as it were. Did he not insinuate the same idea at the inquiry and suggest it to the talented prosecutor?

"I shall be asked, 'What about the old woman, Grigory's wife? She heard the sick man moaning close by, all night.' Yes, she heard it, but that evidence is extremely unreliable. I knew a lady who complained bitterly that she had been kept awake all night by a dog in the yard. Yet the poor beast, it appeared, had yelped only once or twice in the night. And that's natural. A person is asleep and hears a groan — he wakes up, annoyed at being waked, but instantly falls asleep again. Two hours later, again a groan, he wakes up and falls asleep again; and the same thing again two hours later — three times altogether during the night. Next morning the sleeper wakes up and complains that some one has been groaning and keeping him awake all night. And it is bound to seem so to him: the intervals of two hours of sleep he does not remember, he remembers only the moments of waking, so he feels he has been kept awake all night.

"But why, why, asks the prosecutor, did not Smerdyakov confess in his last letter? Why did his conscience prompt him to one step and not to the other? But, allow me, conscience implies penitence, and the suicide may not have felt penitence, but only despair. Despair and penitence are two very different things. Despair may be vindictive and irreconcilable, and the suicide, laying hands on himself, may well have felt redoubled hatred for those whom he had envied all his life.

"Gentlemen of the jury, beware of a miscarriage of justice! What is there unlikely in all I have put before you just now? Find the error in my reasoning; find the impossibility, the absurdity. And if there is but a shade of possibility, but a shade of probability in my propositions, do not condemn him. And is there only a shade? I swear by all that is sacred, I fully believe in the explanation of the murder I have just put forward. What troubles me and makes me indignant is that of all the mass of facts heaped up by the prosecution against the accused, there is not a single one certain and irrefutable. And yet the unhappy man is to be ruined by the accumulation of these facts. Yes, the accumulated effect is awful: the blood, the blood dripping from his fingers, the bloodstained shirt, the dark night resounding with the shout 'Parricide!' and the old man falling with a broken head. And then this mass of utterances, statements, gestures, shouts! Oh! this has so much influence, it can so bias the mind; but, gentlemen of the jury, can it bias your minds? Remember, you have been given absolute power to bind and to loose, but the greater the power, the more terrible its responsibility.

"I do not draw back one iota from what I have said just now, but suppose for one moment I agreed with the prosecution that my luckless client had stained his hands with his father's blood. This is only a conjecture, I repeat; I never for one instant doubt his innocence. But, let me assume that my client is guilty of parricide. Even so, hear what I have to say. I have it in my heart to say something more to you, for I feel that there must be a great conflict in your hearts and minds. . . . Forgive my referring to your hearts and minds, gentlemen of the jury, but I want to be truthful and sincere to the end. Let us all be sincere!"

At this point the speech was interrupted by rather loud applause. The last words, indeed, were pronounced with a note of such sincerity that every one felt that he really might have something to say. But the presiding judge, hearing the applause, threatened to clear the court if such an incident were repeated. Every sound was hushed and Fetyukovich began in a voice full of feeling quite unlike the tone he had used hitherto.

## CHAPTER XIII
### A CORRUPTER OF THOUGHT

"IT's not only the accumulation of facts that threatens my client with ruin, gentlemen of the jury," he began, "what threatens my client with ruin is really one fact — the dead body of his old father. Had it been an ordinary case of murder you would have rejected the charge in view of the triviality, the incompleteness, and the fantastic character of the evidence, if you examine each part of it separately; or, at least, you would have hesitated to ruin a man's life simply from the prejudice against him which he has, alas! only too well deserved. But it's not an ordinary case of murder, it's a case of parricide. That impresses men's minds, and to such a degree that the very triviality and incompleteness of the evidence becomes less trivial and less incomplete even to an unprejudiced mind. How can such a prisoner be acquitted? What if he committed the murder and gets off unpunished? That is what every one, almost involuntarily, instinctively, feels at heart.

"Yes, it's a fearful thing to shed a father's blood — the father who has begotten me, loved me, not spared his life for me, grieved over my illnesses from childhood up, suffered all his life for my happiness, and has lived in my joys, in my successes. To murder such a father — that's inconceivable. Gentlemen of the jury, what is a father — a real father? What is the meaning of that great word? What is the great idea in that name? We have just indicated in part what a true father is and what he ought to be. In the case with which we are now so deeply occupied and over which our hearts are aching — in the present case, the father, the late Fyodor Pavlovich

575

Karamazov, did not correspond to that conception of a father to which we have just referred. That's the misfortune. And indeed some fathers are a misfortune. Let us examine this misfortune rather more closely: we must shrink from nothing, gentlemen of the jury, considering the importance of the decision you have to make. It's our particular duty not to shrink from any idea, like children or frightened women, as the talented prosecutor happily expresses it.

"But in the course of his heated speech my esteemed opponent (and he was my opponent before I opened my lips) exclaimed several times, 'Oh, I will not yield the defence of the accused to the lawyer who has come down from Petersburg. I accuse, but I defend also!' He exclaimed that several times, but forgot to mention that if this terrible accused was for twenty-three years so grateful for a mere pound of nuts given him by the only man who had been kind to him, as a child in his father's house, might not such a man well have remembered for twenty-three years how he ran in his father's back yard, 'without boots to his feet and with his little trousers hanging by one button' — to use the expression of the kindhearted doctor, Herzenstube?

"Oh, gentlemen of the jury, why need we look more closely at this misfortune, why repeat what we all know already? What did my client meet with when he arrived here, at his father's house, and why depict my client as a heartless egoist and monster? He is uncontrolled, he is wild and unruly — we are trying him now for that — but who is responsible for his fate? Whose guilt is it that in spite of his excellent disposition and his grateful and sensitive heart he received such an absurd upbringing? Did any one instruct him in the way he should go? Was he schooled in the sciences? Did any one love him ever so little in his childhood? My client was left to the care of Providence like a beast of the field. He thirsted perhaps to see his father after long years of separation. A thousand times perhaps he may, recalling his childhood, have driven away the loathsome phantoms that haunted his childish dreams and with all his heart he may have longed to embrace and to forgive his father! And what awaited him? He was met by cynical taunts, suspicions, and wrangling about money. He heard nothing but revolting talk and vicious precepts uttered daily over the cognac, and at last he saw his father trying to take his mistress away from him with his own money. Oh, gentlemen of the jury, that was cruel and revolting! And that old man was always complaining of the disrespect and cruelty of his son. He slandered him in society, injured him, calumniated him, bought up his unpaid debts to get him thrown into prison.

"Gentlemen of the jury, people like my client, who are fierce, unruly, and uncontrolled on the surface, are sometimes, most frequently indeed, exceedingly tender-hearted, only they don't show it. Don't laugh, don't laugh at my idea! The talented prosecutor laughed mercilessly just now at my client for loving Schiller — loving the beautiful and the sublime! I should not have laughed at that if I were he. Yes, such natures — oh, let me speak in defence of such natures, so often and so unjustly misunderstood — these natures often thirst for tenderness, goodness, and justice, in contrast to themselves, as it were, their unruliness, their ferocity — they thirst for it unconsciously, truly thirst. Passionate and cruel on the surface, they are painfully capable of falling in love with a woman, for instance, and loving her with a spiritual and elevated love. Again do not laugh at me, this is very often the case with such natures. But they cannot hide their passions — sometimes very coarse — and that is conspicuous and is noticed, but the inner man is unseen. All their passions are quickly satisfied; but, by the side of a noble and lofty creature that seemingly coarse and rough man seeks a new life, seeks the possibility of reforming himself, of becoming better, of becoming noble and honourable, 'sublime and beautiful,' however much the expression has been ridiculed.

"I said just now that I would not venture to touch upon my client's affair with Madame Verhovtzev. But I may say half a word. What we heard just now was not evidence, but only the outcry of a frenzied and revengeful woman, and it was not for her — oh, not for her! — to reproach him with treachery, for she has betrayed him herself! If she had had but a little time for reflection she would not have given such evidence. Oh, do not believe her! No, my client is not a monster, as she called him!

"The Lover of Mankind on the eve of His Crucifixion said: 'I am the Good Shepherd. The good shepherd lays down his life for his sheep, so that not one of them might perish.' Let not a man's soul perish through us!

"I asked just now what does 'father' mean, and exclaimed that it is a great word, a precious name. But one must use words honestly, gentlemen, and I venture to call things by their right names: such a father as old Karamazov cannot be called a father and does not deserve to be. Filial love for an unworthy father is an absurdity, an impossibility. Love cannot be created out of nothing: for only

God can create something out of nothing.

"'Fathers, provoke not your children to wrath,' the apostle writes, from a heart glowing with love. It's not for the sake of my client that I quote these sacred words, I mention them for the sake of all fathers. Who has authorised me to preach to fathers? No one. But as a man and a citizen I appeal — *vivos voco!* We are not long on earth, we do many evil deeds and say many evil words. So let us all catch a favourable moment when we are all together to say a good word to each other. That's what I am doing: while I am in this place I take advantage of my opportunity. Not for nothing is this tribune given us by the highest authority — all Russia hears us! I am not speaking only for the fathers here present, I cry aloud to all fathers: 'Fathers, provoke not your children to wrath.' Yes, let us first fulfil Christ's injunction ourselves and only then venture to expect it of our children. Otherwise we are not fathers, but enemies of our children, and they are not our children, but our enemies, and we have made them our enemies ourselves. 'What measure ye mete it shall be measured unto you again' — it's not I who say that, it's the Gospel precept, measure to others according as they measure to you. How can we blame children if they measure to us according to our measure?

"Not long ago a servant girl in Finland was suspected of having secretly given birth to a child. She was watched, and a chest of which no one knew anything was found in the corner of the loft, behind some bricks. It was opened and inside was found the body of a new-born child which she had killed. In the same chest were found the skeletons of two other babies which, according to her own confession, she had killed at the moment of their birth.

"Gentlemen of the jury, was she a mother to her children? She gave birth to them, indeed; but was she a mother to them? Would any one venture to give her the sacred name of mother? Let us be bold, gentlemen of the jury, let us be audacious even: it's our duty to be so at this moment and not to be afraid of certain words and ideas like the merchants' wives of Moscow in Ostrovsky's play, who are scared by the sound of certain words. No, let us prove that the progress of the last few years has touched us, too, and let us say plainly, the father is not merely he who begets the child, but he who begets it and does his duty by it.

"Oh, of course, there is the other meaning, there is the other interpretation of the word 'father,' which demands that my father, even though he be a monster, even though he be the enemy of his children, still remains my father simply because he begot me. But this is, so to say, the mystical meaning which I cannot comprehend with my mind, but can only accept by faith, or, better to say, *on faith*, like many other things which I do not understand, but which religion bids me believe. But in that case let it be kept outside the sphere of actual life. In the sphere of actual life, which has, indeed, its own rights, but also lays upon us great obligations, in that sphere, if we want to be humane — Christian, in fact — we must, or ought to, act only upon convictions justified by reason and experience, which have been passed through the crucible of analysis; in a word, we must act rationally, and not senselessly as though in a dream or in delirium, that we may not do harm, that we may not torment and ruin a man. Then it will be real Christian work, not only mystic, but rational and truly a work of loving-kindness. . . ."

At this juncture there was violent applause from many parts of the court, but Fetyukovich waved his hands as though imploring them to let him finish without interruption. The court relapsed into silence. The orator went on.

"Do you suppose, gentlemen of the jury, that our children as they grow up and begin to reason can avoid such questions? No, they cannot, and we will not impose on them an impossible restriction. The sight of an unworthy father involuntarily suggests tormenting questions to a youth, especially when he compares him with the excellent fathers of his companions. The conventional answer to this question is: 'He begot you, and you are his flesh and blood, and therefore you are bound to love him.' The youth involuntarily reflects: 'But did he love me when he begot me?' he asks, wondering more and more. 'Was it for my sake he begot me? He did not know me, not even my sex, at that moment, at the moment of passion, perhaps inflamed by wine, and he has only transmitted to me a propensity to drunkenness — that's the sum of his benefactions to me. . . . Why am I bound to love him, simply for begetting me when he has cared nothing for me all my life after?'

"Oh, perhaps these questions strike you as coarse and cruel, but do not expect an impossible restraint from a young mind. 'Drive nature out of the door and it will fly in at the window,' and, above all, let us not be afraid of words, but decide the question according to the dictates of reason and humanity and not of mystic ideas. How shall it be decided? Why, like this. Let the son stand before his father and ask him, 'Father, tell me, why must I love you? Father, show me that I must love you,' and if that father is able to answer him and show him good reason, we have a real, normal family, resting not on mystical prejudice, but on rational, responsible, and strictly humane foundations. But if he does not, there's an end to the family tie. He is not a father to him, and the son has a right to look upon him as a stranger, and even an enemy. Our tribune, gentlemen of the jury, ought to be a school of true and sane ideas."

Here the orator was interrupted by irrepressible and almost frantic applause. Of course, it was not the whole audience, but a good half of it applauded. Fathers applauded, and mothers. Shrieks and exclamations were heard from the gallery, where the ladies were sitting. Handkerchiefs were waved. The presiding judge began ringing his bell with all his might. He was obviously irritated by the behaviour of the audience, but did not venture to clear the court as he had threatened before. Even persons of high position, old men with stars on their frock-coats, sitting on specially reserved seats behind the judges, applauded the orator and waved their handkerchiefs. So that when the noise died down, the presiding judge confined himself to repeating his stern threat to clear the court, and Fetyukovich, excited and triumphant, continued his speech.

"Gentlemen of the jury, you remember that awful night of which so much has been said to-day, when the son jumped over the fence, entered his father's house, and stood face to face with the enemy and persecutor who had begotten him. I insist most emphatically it was not for money he ran to his father's house: the charge of robbery is an absurdity, as I proved before. And it was not to murder him he broke into the house, oh, no! If he had had that design he would, at least, have taken the precaution of arming himself beforehand. The brass pestle he caught up instinctively

without knowing why he did it. Granted that he deceived his father by tapping at the window, granted that he made his way in — I've said already that I do not for a moment believe that legend, but let it be so, let us suppose it for a moment. Gentlemen, I swear to you by all that's holy, if it had not been his father, but an ordinary enemy, he would, after running through the rooms and satisfying himself that the woman was not there, have made off, post-haste, without doing any harm to his rival. He would have struck him, pushed him away perhaps, nothing more, for he had no thought and no time to spare for that. What he wanted to know was where she was. But his father, his father! The mere sight of the father who had hated him from his childhood, who had been his enemy, his persecutor, and now his unnatural rival, was enough! A feeling of hatred came over him involuntarily, irresistibly, clouding his reason. It all surged up in one moment! It was an impulse of madness and insanity, but also an impulse of nature, irresistibly and unconsciously (like everything in nature) avenging the violation of eternal laws.

"But the accused even then did not murder him — I maintain that, I cry it aloud! — no, he only brandished the pestle in a burst of indignant disgust, not meaning to kill him, not knowing that he would kill him. Had he not had this fatal pestle in his hand, he would have only knocked his father down perhaps, but would not have killed him. As he ran away, he did not know whether he had killed the old man. Such a murder is not a murder. Such a murder is not a parricide. No, the murder of such a father cannot be called parricide. Such a murder can be reckoned parricide only out of prejudice.

"But I appeal to you again and again from the depths of my soul: did this murder actually take place? Gentlemen of the jury, if we convict and punish him, he will say to himself: 'These people have done nothing for my bringing up, for my education, nothing to improve my lot, nothing to make me better, nothing to make me a man. These people have not given me to eat and to drink, have not visited me in prison and nakedness, and here they have sentenced me to penal servitude. I am quits, I owe them nothing now, and owe no one anything for ever. They are vicious and I will be vicious. They are cruel and I will be cruel.' That is what he will say, gentlemen of the jury. And I swear, by finding him guilty you will only make it easier for him: you will ease his conscience, he will curse the blood he has shed and will not regret it. At the same time you will destroy in him the possibility of becoming a new man, for he will remain in his wickedness and blindness all his life.

"But do you want to punish him fearfully, terribly, with the most awful punishment that could be imagined, and at the same time to save him and regenerate his soul? If so, overwhelm him with your mercy! You will see, you will hear how he will tremble and be horror-struck: 'How can I endure this mercy? How can I endure so much love? Am I worthy of it?' That's what he will exclaim.

"Oh, I know, I know that heart, that wild but noble heart, gentlemen of the jury! It will bow before your mercy; it thirsts for a great act of love, it will flame up and be for ever resurrected. There are souls which, in their limitation, blame the whole world. But subdue such a soul with mercy, show it love, and it will curse its deed, for there are many good impulses in it. Such a heart will expand and see that God is merciful and that men are good and just. He will be horror-stricken; he will be crushed by remorse and the vast obligation laid upon him henceforth. And he will not say then, 'I am quits,' but will say, 'I am guilty in the sight of all men and am more unworthy than all.' With tears of penitence and burning, anguished emotion, he will exclaim: 'People are better than I, they wanted to save me, not to ruin me!' Oh, this act of mercy is so easy for you, for in the absence of anything like real evidence it will be too awful for you to pronounce: 'Yes, he is guilty.'

"Better acquit ten guilty men than punish one innocent man!* Do you hear, do you hear that majestic voice from the past century of our glorious history? It is not for an insignificant person like me to remind you that Russian justice does not exist for the punishment only, but also for the salvation of the criminal!

"Let other nations cling to punishment and the letter of the law, we will cling to the spirit and the meaning — the salvation and the reformation of the lost. If this is true, if Russia and her justice are such, then forward, Russia! And do not scare us, oh, do not scare us with your frenzied troikas from which all the nations stand aside in disgust. Not a runaway troika, but the stately chariot of Russia will move calmly and majestically to its goal. In your hands is the fate of my client, in your hands is the fate of Russian justice. You will defend it, you will save it, you will prove that there are men to watch over it, that it is in good hands!"

* An aphorism attributed to Peter the Great. *Editor's note.*

## CHAPTER XIV
### THE PEASANTS STAND THEIR GROUND

THIS was how Fetyukovich concluded his speech, and the enthusiasm of the audience burst like an irresistible storm. It was out of the question to stop it: the women wept, many of the men wept, too, even two important personages shed tears. The presiding judge submitted, and even postponed ringing his bell. "To suppress such an enthusiasm would have been an attempt on something sacred," the ladies cried afterwards. The orator himself was genuinely touched.

And it was at this moment that Ippolit Kirillovich got up to make objections. People looked at him with hatred. "What? What's the meaning of it? He positively dares to make objections," the ladies babbled. But if the whole world of ladies, including his wife, had protested, he could not have been stopped at that moment. He was pale, he was shaking with emotion, his first phrases were even unintelligible, he gasped for breath, could hardly speak clearly, lost the thread. But he soon recovered himself. But of this new speech of his I shall quote only a few phrases.

". . . . We are reproached with having woven romances. But what has the counsel for the defence done, if not pile one romance on top of another? All that was lacking was verse. Fyodor Pavlovich, while waiting for his mistress, tears open the envelope and throws it on the floor. We are even told what he said while engaged on this amazing occasion. Is not this a poetic fantasy? And what proof have we that he had taken out the money? Who heard what he said? The weak-minded idiot, Smerdyakov, transformed into a Byronic hero, revenging himself on society for his illegitimate birth — isn't this a poem in the Byronic manner? And the son who breaks into his father's house and murders him without murdering him is not even a romance, not a poem — it is a sphinx setting us a riddle which he cannot solve himself. If he killed, then he killed, and what's the meaning of his killing without having killed — who can make head or tail of this?

"Then we are informed that our tribune is a tribune of true and sane ideas and from this tribune of 'sane ideas' is heard a solemn declaration that to call the murder of a father 'parricide' is nothing but a prejudice! But if parricide is a prejudice, and if every child is to ask his father: 'Father, why should I love you?' what will become of us? What will become of the foundations of society? What will become of the family? Parricide, it appears, is only a bogey with which to scare a Moscow merchant's wife. The most precious, the most sacred foundations of the destiny and future of Russian justice are presented to us in a perverted and frivolous form, simply to attain an object — to obtain the justification of something which cannot be justified. 'Oh, crush him by mercy,' cries the counsel for the defence; but that's all the criminal wants, and to-morrow it will be seen how much he is crushed. And is not the counsel for the defence too modest in asking for only the acquittal of the prisoner? Why not demand the establishment of a Fund in honour of the parricide to immortalise his exploit both for the younger generation and for posterity? Religion and the Gospel are corrected — that's all mysticism, we are told, and ours is the only true Christianity which has been subjected to the analysis of reason and sane ideas. And so a false image of Christ is set up before us!

'What measure ye mete so it shall be meted unto you again,' cries the counsel for the defence, and instantly deduces that Christ teaches us to measure as it is measured to us — and this from the tribune of truth and sane ideas! We peep into the Gospel only on the eve of making speeches, in order to dazzle the audience by our acquaintance with what is, anyway, a rather original composition, which may be of use to produce a certain effect — should the need arise! But what Christ commands us is something very different: He bids us beware of doing this, because the wicked world does this, but we ought to forgive and to turn the other cheek, and not to measure to those who trespass against us as they measure to us. This is what our God has taught us and not that to forbid children to murder their fathers is a prejudice. And we will not from the tribune of truth and sane ideas correct the Gospel of our Lord, Whom the counsel for the defence deigns to call only 'the crucified lover of humanity,' in opposition to all orthodox Russia, which cries to Him, 'For Thou art our God!' "

At this point the presiding judge intervened and checked the over-zealous speaker, begging him not to exaggerate, not to overstep the bounds, and so on, as presiding judges always do in such cases. The audience, too, was uneasy. The public was restless: there were even exclamations of indignation. Fetyukovich did not so much as make a formal rebuttal; he only mounted the tribune to lay his hand on his heart and, in an offended voice, utter a few words full of dignity. He only touched again, lightly and ironically, on "romancing" and "psychology," and in an appropriate place quoted, "Jupiter, you are angry, therefore you are wrong," which provoked a burst of approving laughter in the audience, for Ippolit Kirillovich by no means resembled Jupiter. Then, apropos of the accusation that he allowed the young generation to murder their fathers, Fetyukovich observed, with great dignity, that he would not even answer. As for the "false image of Christ" and the prosecutor's charge that he did not deign to call Christ God, but called Him "the crucified lover of humanity," which is "contrary to orthodoxy and could not be uttered from the tribune of truth and sane ideas," Fetyukovich hinted that it was a personal insinuation and that he had expected in this court to be secure from accusations "damaging to my reputation as a citizen and a loyal subject." . . . But at these words the presiding judge pulled him up, too, and Fetyukovich concluded his remarks with a bow, amid a hum of universal approbation in the court. And Ippolit Kirillovich was, in the opinion of our ladies, "crushed for good."

Then the accused was allowed to speak. Mitya stood up, but said very little. He was fearfully exhausted, physically and spiritually. The look of strength and independence with which he had entered in the morning had almost disappeared. It seemed as though he had passed through an experience that day which had taught him for the rest of his life something very important he had not understood till then. His voice had grown weak, he did not shout as before. In his words there was a new note of humility, defeat, and submission.

"What am I to say, gentlemen of the jury? The hour of judgment has come for me, I feel the hand of God upon me! The end has come for a profligate! But, before God, I repeat to you, 'No, I am not guilty of my father's blood!' For the last time I repeat, it wasn't I

"GENTLEMEN OF THE JURY"

who killed him! I was a waster, but I loved goodness. Every instant I strove to reform, but I lived like a wild beast. I thank the prosecutor, he told me many things about myself that I did not know; but it's not true that I killed my father, the prosecutor is mistaken. I thank my counsel, too. I cried listening to him; but it's not true that I killed my father, and he needn't have supposed it. And don't believe the doctors. I am perfectly sane, only my heart is heavy. If you spare me, if you let me go, I will pray for you. I will be a better man. I give you my word, before God I will! And if you condemn me, I'll break my sword over my head myself and kiss the pieces. But spare me, do not deprive me of my God! I know myself, I shall cry out in rebellion! My heart is heavy, gentlemen . . . spare me!"

He almost fell back in his place: his voice broke: he could hardly articulate the last phrase. Then the judges proceeded to put the questions and began to ask both sides to formulate their conclusions. But I shall not describe the details. At last the jury rose to retire for consultation. The presiding judge was very tired, and so his last charge to the jury was rather feeble. "Be impartial, don't be influenced by the eloquence of the defence, but yet weigh the arguments. Remember that there is a great responsibility laid upon you," and so on and so on.

The jury withdrew and the court adjourned. People could get up, move about, exchange their accumulated impressions, refresh themselves at the buffet. It was very late, almost an hour past midnight, but nobody went away: all were so excited that they could not think of rest. All waited with sinking hearts; though that is, perhaps, too much to say, for the ladies were only in a state of hysterical im-

patience and their hearts were untroubled. An acquittal, they thought, was inevitable. They all prepared themselves for a dramatic moment of general enthusiasm. I must own there were many among the men, too, who were convinced that an acquittal was inevitable. Some were pleased, others frowned, while some were simply dejected, not wanting him to be acquitted. Fetyukovich himself was confident of his success. He was surrounded by people congratulating him and fawning upon him.

"There are," he said to one group, as I was told afterwards, "there are invisible threads binding the counsel for the defence to the jury. While one is speaking one has a presentiment as to whether or not they are being woven. I was aware of them. They exist. Our cause is won. Set your mind at rest."

"Well, I wonder what our peasants will say now?" said one stout, cross-looking, pock-marked gentlemen, a landowner of the neighbourhood, approaching a group of gentlemen engaged in conversation.

"But they are not all peasants. There are four government clerks among them."

"Yes, there are clerks," said a member of the district council, joining the group.

"And do you know that Nazaryev, the merchant with the medal, a juryman?"

"What of him?"

"He is a man with brains."

"But he never speaks."

"He is no great talker, but so much the better. There's no need for the Petersburg man to teach him: he could teach all Petersburg himself. He's the father of twelve children. Think of that!"

"Upon my word, you don't suppose they won't acquit him?" one of our young officials exclaimed in another group.

"They'll acquit him for certain," said a resolute voice.

"It would be shameful, disgraceful, not to acquit him!" cried the official. "Suppose he did murder him — there are fathers and fathers! And, besides, he was in such a frenzy. . . . He really may have done nothing but swing the pestle in the air, and so knocked the old man down. But it was a pity they dragged the valet in. That was simply a ridiculous episode! If I'd been in Fetyukovich's place, I should simply have said straight out: 'He murdered him; but he is not guilty, hang it all!'"

"That's what he did, only without saying, 'Hang it all!'"

"No, Mihail Semyonovich, he almost said that, too," put in a third voice.

"Why, gentlemen, last year during Lent an actress was acquitted in our town who had cut the throat of her lover's lawful wife."

"Oh, but she did not finish cutting it."

"That makes no difference. She began cutting it."

"What did you think of what he said about children? Splendid, wasn't it?"

"Splendid!"

"And about mysticism, too!"

"Oh, drop mysticism, do!" cried some one else; "think of Ippolit and his fate from this day forth. His wife will scratch his eyes out to-morrow on account of Mitya."

"Is she here?"

"What an idea! If she'd been here she'd have scratched them out in court. She is at home with toothache. He, he, he!"

"He, he, he!"

In a third group:

"I dare say they will acquit Mitenka, after all."

"I should not be surprised if he turns the 'Metropolis' upside down to-morrow. He will be drinking for ten days!"

"Oh, the devil!"

"The devil's bound to have a hand in it. Where should he be if not here?"

"Well, gentlemen, I admit it was eloquent. But still it's not the thing to break your father's head with a steelyard! Or what are we coming to?"

"The chariot! Do you remember the chariot?"

"Yes; he turned a cart into a chariot!"

"And to-morrow he will turn a chariot into a cart, should the need arise."

"What shrewd chaps there are nowadays. Is there any justice among us in Russia, gentlemen, or not?"

But the bell rang. The jury deliberated for exactly an hour, neither more nor less. A profound silence reigned in the court as soon as the public had taken their seats. I remember how the jurymen walked into the court. At last! I won't repeat the questions in order, and, indeed, I have forgotten them. I remember only the answer to the first and chief question of the presiding judge: "Did the accused commit the murder for the sake of robbery and with premeditation?" (I don't remember the exact words.) There was a complete hush. The foreman of the jury, the youngest of the clerks, pronounced, in a clear, loud voice, amidst the deathlike stillness of the court:

"Yes, guilty!"

And the same answer was repeated to every question: "Yes, guilty!" and without the least word of extenuation. This no one had expected; almost every one had reckoned upon a recommendation to mercy, at least. The deathlike silence in the court was not broken

— all seemed petrified: those who had desired his conviction as well as those who had been eager for his acquittal. But that was only for the first instant, and it was followed by fearful confusion. Many of the men in the audience were pleased. Some were rubbing their hands with no attempt to conceal their joy. Those who disagreed with the verdict seemed crushed, shrugged their shoulders, whispered, but still seemed unable to realise it. But good Lord! how shall I describe the state the ladies were in? I thought they would start a mutiny. At first they could scarcely believe their ears. Then suddenly the whole court rang with exclamations: "What's the meaning of it? What next?" They leapt up from their places. They seemed to fancy that the verdict might be at once reconsidered and reversed. At that instant Mitya suddenly stood up and cried in a heart-rending voice, stretching his hands out before him:

"I swear by God and the dreadful Day of Judgment I am not guilty of my father's blood! Katya, I forgive you! Brothers, friends, have pity on the other woman!"

He could not go on, and broke into a terrible sobbing wail that was heard all over the court in a strange, unnatural voice unlike his own. From the farthest corner at the back of the gallery came a piercing shriek — it was Grushenka. She had succeeded in begging admittance to the court again before the beginning of the lawyers' speeches. Mitya was taken away. The pronouncement of the sentence was deferred till next day. The whole court was in hubbub but I did not wait to hear anything further. I only remember a few exclamations I heard on the steps as I went out.

"He'll have a twenty years' spell at the mines!"

"Not less."

"Well, our peasants have stood their ground."

"And have done for our Mitya."

EPILOGUE

# CHAPTER I

### PLANS FOR SAVING MITYA

VERY early, at nine o'clock in the morning, five days after the trial, Alyosha came to Katerina Ivanovna's to talk over a matter of great importance to both of them, and to give her a message. She sat and talked to him in the very room in which she had once received Grushenka. In the next room Ivan Fyodorovich lay unconscious in a high fever. Immediately after the scene at the trial Katerina Ivanovna had ordered the sick and unconscious man to be carried to her house, disregarding the inevitable gossip and general disapproval of the public. One of the two relations who lived with her had departed to Moscow immediately after the scene at court, the other remained. But if both had gone away, Katerina Ivanovna would have adhered to her resolution, and would have gone on nursing the sick man and sitting by him day and night. Varvinsky and Herzenstube were attending him. The famous doctor had gone back to Moscow, refusing to give an opinion as to the probable outcome of the illness. Though the doctors encouraged Katerina Ivanovna and Alyosha, it was evident that they could not yet give them positive hopes of recovery.

Alyosha came to see his sick brother twice a day. But this time he had specially urgent business, and he foresaw how difficult it would be to approach the subject, yet he was in great haste. He had other and urgent business for that same morning, and there was need of haste.

They had been talking for a quarter of an hour. Katerina Ivanovna was pale and terribly fatigued, yet at the same time in a state of morbid excitement. She had a presentiment of the reason why Alyosha had come to her.

"Don't worry about his decision," she said, with confident emphasis to Alyosha. "One way or another, he is bound to accept this way out. He must escape. This unhappy man, this hero, all honour and conscience—not that one, not Dmitri Fyodorovich, but the man lying the other side of that door, who has sacrificed himself for his brother," Katya added, with flashing eyes, "told me the whole plan of escape long ago. You know he has already entered into negotiations. . . . I've told you something already. . . . You see, it will probably come off at the third halting-place, when the party of convicts is being taken to Siberia. Oh, it will take a long time yet. Ivan Fyodorovich has already visited the official in charge of the third station. But we don't know yet who will be in charge of the party, and it's impossible to find that out so long beforehand. To-morrow perhaps I will show you in detail the whole plan which Ivan Fyodorovich left me on the eve of the trial in case of need. . . . That was when—do you remember?—you found us quarrelling. He had just gone downstairs, but seeing you I made him come back; do you remember? Do you know what we were quarrelling about then?"

"No, I don't," said Alyosha.

"Of course he did not tell you. It was about that plan of escape. He had disclosed the main idea to me three days before, and we began quarrelling about it at once and quarrelled for three days. We quarrelled because when he told me that, if Dmitri Fyodorovich were convicted, he would escape abroad with that creature, I felt furious at once—I can't tell you why, I don't know myself why. . . . Oh, of course, I was furious then because of that creature, and that she, too, should go abroad with Dmitri!" Katerina Ivanovna exclaimed suddenly, her lips quivering with anger. "As soon as Ivan Fyodorovich saw that I was furious because of that woman, he instantly imagined I was jealous of Dmitri, and that I still loved Dmitri. That is how our first quarrel began. I would not give an explanation, I could not ask forgiveness. I could not bear to think that such a man could suspect me of still loving that . . . and when I myself had told him long before that I did not love Dmitri, that I loved no one but him! It was only resentment against that creature that made me angry with him. Three days later, on the evening you came, he brought me a sealed envelope, which I was to open at once, if anything happened to him. Oh, he foresaw his illness! He told me that the envelope contained the details of the escape, and that if he died or was taken dangerously ill, I was to save Mitya alone. Then he left me money, nearly ten thousand — those notes to which the prosecutor referred in his speech, having learnt from some one that he had sent them to be changed. I was tremendously impressed to find that Ivan Fyodorovich had not given up his idea of saving his brother, and was confiding this plan of escape to me, though he was still jealous of me and still convinced that I loved Mitya. Oh, that was a sacrifice! No, you cannot understand the greatness of such self-sacrifice, Alexey Fyodorovich. I wanted to fall at his feet in reverence, but I thought at once that he would take it only for my joy at the thought of Mitya's being saved (and he certainly would have imagined that!), and I was so exasperated at the mere possibility of such an unjust thought on his part that I lost my temper again, and, instead of kissing his feet, made him a scene again! Oh, I am un-

happy! It's my character, my awful, unhappy character! Oh, you will see, I shall end by driving him, too, to abandon me for another with whom he can get on better, as Dmitri did. But . . . no, I could not bear it, I should kill myself. And when you came in then, and when I called to you and told him to come back, I was so enraged by the look of contempt and hatred he turned on me that — do you remember? — I cried out to you that it was he, he alone who had persuaded me that his brother Dmitri was a murderer! I told that lie on purpose to wound him again. He had never, never tried to persuade me that his brother was a murderer. On the contrary, it was I who persuaded him! Oh, my vile temper was the cause of everything! I paved the way to that accursed scene at the trial. He wanted to show me that he was an honourable man, and that, even if I loved his brother, he would not ruin him out of revenge or jealousy. So he spoke out in court . . . I am the cause of it all, I alone am to blame!"

Katya never had made such confessions to Alyosha before, and he felt that she was now at that stage of unbearable suffering when even the proudest heart painfully crushes its pride and falls vanquished by grief. Oh, Alyosha knew another terrible reason for her present misery, though she had carefully concealed it from him during those days since the trial; but it would have been for some reason too painful to him if she had been brought so low as to speak to him now about that. She was suffering for her "treachery" at the trial, and Alyosha felt that her conscience was impelling her to confess it to him, to him, Alyosha, with tears and shrieks and hysterical writhings on the floor. But he dreaded that moment and longed to spare her. It made the commission on which he had come even more difficult. He spoke of Mitya again.

"It's all right, it's all right, don't be anxious about him!" she began again, sharply and stubbornly. "All that is only a passing thing with him, I know him, I know his heart only too well. You may be sure he will consent to escape. It's not as though it would be immediately; he will have time to make up his mind to it. Ivan Fyodorovich will be well by that time and will manage it all himself, so that I shall have nothing to do with it. Don't be anxious; he will consent to run away. He has agreed already: do you suppose he would give up that creature? And they won't let her go to Siberia, so he is bound to escape. It's you he's most afraid of, he is afraid you won't approve of his escape on moral grounds. But you must generously *allow* it, if your sanction is so necessary," Katya added viciously. She paused and smiled.

"He talks about some hymn," she went on again, "some cross he has to bear, some duty; I remember Ivan Fyodorovich told me a great deal about it, and if you knew how he talked!" Katya cried suddenly, with irrepressible emotion, "if you knew how he loved that wretched man at the moment he told me, and how he hated him, perhaps, at the same moment. And I, oh, I heard his story and his tears with sneering disdain. Brute! Yes, I am a brute. It is I who gave him that fever. But that man, the convict, is he capable of suffering?" Katya concluded irritably. "Can such a man suffer? Men like him never suffer!"

There was a note of hatred and squeamish contempt in her words. And yet it was she who had betrayed him. "Perhaps because she feels how she's wronged him she hates him at moments," Alyosha thought to himself. He

hoped that it was only "at moments." In Katya's last words he detected a challenging note, but he did not take it up.

"I sent for you this morning to make you promise to persuade him yourself. Or do you, too, consider that to escape would be dishonourable, cowardly, or something . . . unchristian, perhaps?" Katya added, even more defiantly.

"Oh, no. I'll tell him everything," muttered Alyosha. "He asks you to come and see him to-day," he blurted out suddenly, looking her steadily in the face. She started, and drew back a little from him on the sofa.

"Me? Can that be?" she faltered, turning pale.

"It can and ought to be!" Alyosha began emphatically, growing more animated. "He needs you particularly just now. I would not have broached the subject and worried you, if it were not necessary. He is ill, he is beside himself, he keeps asking for you. It is not to be reconciled with you that he wants you, but only that you should come and show yourself on his threshold. So much has happened to him since that day. He realises that he is guilty before you beyond all reckoning. He does not ask your forgiveness; 'it's impossible to forgive me,' he says himself, but only that you should show yourself in his doorway."

"It's so sudden . . ." faltered Katya. "I had a presentiment all these days that you would come with that message. I knew he would call me. It's impossible!"

"Let it be impossible, but do it. Only think, he realises for the first time how he has wounded you, the first time in his life; he had never grasped it so fully before. He said, 'If she refuses to come I shall be unhappy all my life.' Do you hear? Though he is condemned to penal servitude for twenty years, he is still planning to be happy — is not that piteous? Think — you shall visit a man who is ruined through no guilt of his own," broke like a challenge from Alyosha. "His hands are clean, there is no blood on them! For the sake of his infinite future suffering, visit him now. Go, see him off on his way into the darkness — stand at his door, that is all. . . . You must do it, you must!" Alyosha concluded, laying immense stress on the word "must."

"I must . . . but I cannot . . ." Katya moaned. "He will look at me. . . . I can't."

"Your eyes ought to meet. How will you live all your life, if you don't make up your mind to do it now?"

"Better suffer all my life."

"You must go, you must go," Alyosha repeated with merciless emphasis.

"But why to-day, why at once? . . . I can't leave the patient . . ."

"You can for a moment. It will be only a moment. If you don't come, he will be delirious by to-night. I would not tell you a lie; have pity on him!"

"Have pity on *me!*" Katya said, with bitter reproach, and she burst into tears.

"Then you will come," said Alyosha firmly, seeing her tears. "I'll go and tell him you will come directly."

"No, don't tell him so on any account," cried Katya in alarm. "I will come, but don't tell him beforehand, for perhaps I may come, but not go in . . . I don't know yet . . ."

Her voice failed her. She gasped for breath. Alyosha got up to go.

"And what if I meet any one?" she said suddenly, in a low voice, turning white again.

"That's just why you must go now, to avoid meeting any one. There will be no one there, I can tell you that for certain. We shall expect you," he concluded emphatically, and went out of the room.

## CHAPTER II

### FOR A MOMENT THE LIE BECOMES TRUTH

HE hurried to the hospital where Mitya was lying now. The day after his sentence was pronounced, Mitya had fallen ill with nervous fever, and was sent to the prison division of the town hospital. But at the request of Alyosha and many other people (Madame Hohlakov, Lise, etc.), Dr. Varvinsky had not put Mitya with other prisoners, but in a separate little room, the one where Smerdyakov had lain. It is true that there was a sentinel at the end of the corridor, and there was a grating over the window, so that Varvinsky could be at ease about the indulgence he had shown, which was not quite legal, indeed; but he was a kind-hearted and compassionate young man. He knew how hard it would be for a man like Mitya to pass at once so suddenly into the society of robbers and murderers, and that he must get used to it by degrees. The visits of relations and friends were informally sanctioned by the doctor and superintendent, and even by the police captain. But only Alyosha and Grushenka had visited Mitya. Rakitin had tried to force his way in twice, but Mitya persistently begged Varvinsky not to admit him.

Alyosha found him sitting on his bed in a hospital dressing-gown, rather feverish, with a towel, soaked in vinegar and water, round his head. He looked at Alyosha as he came in with an undefined expression, but there was a shade of something like dread discernible in it. He had become terribly thoughtful since the trial; sometimes he would be silent for half an hour together, and seemed to be pondering something heavily and painfully, oblivious to everything about him. If he roused himself from his brooding and began to talk, he always spoke with a kind of abruptness and never of what he really wanted to say. He looked sometimes with a face of suffering at his brother. He seemed to be more at ease with Grushenka than with Alyosha. It is true, he scarcely spoke to her at all, but as soon as she came in, his whole face lighted up with joy.

Alyosha sat down beside him on the bed in silence. This time Mitya was waiting for Alyosha in suspense, but he did not dare ask him a question. He felt it almost unthinkable that Katya would consent to come, and at the same time he felt that if she did not come, something utterly impossible would happen. Alyosha understood his feelings.

"Trifon Borisovich," Mitya began nervously, "has pulled his whole inn to pieces, I am told. He's taken up the flooring, pulled apart the planks, split up the whole gallery, I am told. He is seeking the treasure — the fifteen hundred roubles which the prosecutor said I'd hidden there. He began playing these tricks, they say, as soon as he got home. Serve him right, the swindler! The guard here told me yesterday; he comes from there."

"Listen," began Alyosha. "She will come, but I don't know when. Perhaps to-day, perhaps in a few days, that I can't tell. But she will come, she will, that's certain."

Mitya started, would have said something, but was silent. The news had a tremendous effect on him. It was evident that he would have liked terribly to know in detail what had been said, but he was again afraid to ask. Something cruel and contemptuous from Katya would have cut him like a knife.

"This was what she said among other things; that I must be sure to set your conscience at rest about escaping. If Ivan is not well by then she will see to it all herself."

"You've spoken of that already," Mitya observed musingly.

"And you have repeated it to Grusha," observed Alyosha.

"Yes," Mitya admitted. "She won't come this morning." He looked timidly at his brother. "She won't come till the evening. When I told her yesterday that Katya was taking measures, she was silent, but her lips twitched. She only whispered, 'Let her!' She understood that it was important. I did not dare to try her further. She understands now, I think, that Katya no longer cares for me, but loves Ivan."

"Does she?" broke from Alyosha.

"Perhaps she does not. Only she is not coming this morning," Mitya hastened to explain again; "I asked her to do something for me. You know, brother Ivan will outstrip all. He ought to live, not we. He will recover."

"Would you believe it, though Katya trembles for him, she scarcely doubts of his recovery," said Alyosha.

"That means that she is convinced he will die. It's because she is frightened she's so sure he will get well."

"Ivan has a strong constitution, and I, too, believe there's every hope that he will get well," Alyosha observed with alarm.

"Yes, he will get well. But she is convinced that he will die. She has a great deal of sorrow to bear . . ."

A silence followed. A grave anxiety was fretting Mitya.

"Alyosha, I love Grusha terribly," he said suddenly in a shaking voice, full of tears.

"They won't let her go out there to you," Alyosha put in at once.

"And there is something else I wanted to tell you," Mitya went on, with a sudden ring in his voice. "If they start beating me on the way or out there, I won't submit to it. I shall kill some one, and shall be shot for it. And this will be going on for twenty years! They begin to speak rudely to me as it is. The guards do it. I've been lying here all night, passing judgment on myself. I am not ready! I haven't the strength to accept my fate. I wanted to sing a 'hymn'; but if a guard speaks rudely to me, I have not the strength to bear it. For Grusha I would bear anything . . . anything except blows. . . . But they won't let her come *there*."

Alyosha smiled gently.

"Listen, brother, once for all," he said. This is what I think about it. And you know that I would not tell you a lie. Listen: you are not ready, and such a cross is not for you. What's more, you don't need such a martyr's cross when you are not ready for it. If you had murdered our father, it would grieve me that you should reject your punishment. But you are innocent, and such a cross is too much for you. You wanted to make yourself another man by suffering. I say, only remember that other man always, all your life and wherever you may escape to; and that will be enough for you. Your refusal of that great cross will only serve to make you feel all your life an even greater duty, and that constant feeling will do more to make you a new man, perhaps, than if you went *there*. For there you would not endure it and would rebel, and perhaps at last would say: 'I am quits.' The lawyer was right about that. Such heavy burdens are not for all men. For some they are impossible. These are my

thoughts about it, if you want them so much. If other men would have to answer for your escape, officers or soldiers, then I would not have 'allowed' you," smiled Alyosha. "But they declare — the superintendent of that station told Ivan himself — that if it's well managed there will be no great inquiry, and that they can get off easily. Of course, bribing is dishonest even in such a case, but I can't undertake to judge about it, because if Ivan and Katya commissioned me to act for you, I know I should go and give bribes. I must tell you the truth. And so I can't judge of your own action. But let me assure you that I shall never condemn you. And it would be a strange thing if I could judge you in this. Now I think I've gone into everything."

"But I shall condemn myself!" cried Mitya. "I shall escape, that was settled apart from you; could Mitya Karamazov do anything but run away? But I shall condemn myself, and I will pray for my sin for ever. That's how the Jesuits talk, isn't it? Just as we are doing?"

"Yes." Alyosha smiled gently.

"I love you for always telling the whole truth and never hiding anything," cried Mitya, with a joyful laugh. "So I've caught my Alyosha being Jesuitical. I must kiss you for that. Now listen to the rest; I'll open the other side of my heart to you. This is what I planned and decided. If I run away, even with money and a passport, and even to America, I should be cheered up by the thought that I am not running away for pleasure, not for happiness, but to another form of forced labor as bad, perhaps, as Siberia. It is as bad, Alyosha, it is! I hate that America, damn it, already. Even though Grusha will be with me. Just look at her; is she an American? She is Russian, Russian to the bone; she will be homesick for her own country, and I shall see every hour that she is suffering for my sake, that she has taken up that cross for me. And what harm has she done? And how shall I, too, put up with the rabble out there, though they may be better than I, every one of them. I hate that America already! And though they may be wonderful at machinery, every one of them, damn them, they are not my kind, they are strangers to my soul. I love Russia, Alyosha, I love the Russian God, though I am a scoundrel myself. I shall croak there!" he exclaimed, his eyes suddenly flashing. His voice was trembling with tears. "So this is what I've decided, Alyosha, listen," he began again, mastering his emotion. "As soon as I arrive there with Grusha, we will set to work at once on the land, in solitude, in some remote place, with wild bears. There must be some remote parts even there. I am told there are still redskins there, somewhere, on the edge of the horizon. So off to that country, to the 'Last of the Mohicans,' and there we'll tackle the grammar at once, Grusha and I. Work and grammar — that's how we'll spend three years. And by that time we shall speak English like any Englishman. And as soon as we've learnt it — good-bye to America! We'll flee here, to Russia, as American citizens. Don't be uneasy — we would not come to this little town. We'd hide somewhere, a long way off, in the north or in the south. I shall be changed by that time, and she will, too, in America. A doctor will make me some sort of wart on my face — it's not for nothing that they're such mechanics! — or else I'll put out one eye, let my beard grow a yard, and I shall turn grey, fretting for Russia. I dare say they won't recognise us. And if they do, let them send us to Siberia — I don't care. It

will show it's our fate. We'll work on the land here, too, somewhere in the wilds, and I'll pretend to be an American all my life. But we shall die on our native soil. That's my plan, and it shan't be altered. Do you approve?"

"Yes," said Alyosha, not wanting to contradict him. Mitya paused for a minute and said suddenly: "And how they worked it up at the trial! Didn't they work it up!"

"If they had not, you would have been convicted just the same," said Alyosha, with a sigh.

"Yes, people are sick of me here! God bless them, but it's hard," Mitya moaned miserably. Again there was silence for a minute.

"Alyosha, knife me at once!" he exclaimed suddenly. "Tell me, is she coming now, or not? Tell me? What did she say? How did she say it?"

"She said she would come, but I don't know whether she will come to-day. It's hard for her, you know." Alyosha looked timidly at his brother.

"I should think it is hard for her! Alyosha, it will drive me out of my mind. Grusha keeps looking at me. She understands. My God, calm my heart: what is it I want? I want Katya! Do I understand what I want? It's the headstrong, evil Karamazov spirit! No, I am not fit for suffering. I am a scoundrel, that's all one can say."

"Here she is!" cried Alyosha.

At that instant Katya appeared in the doorway. For a moment she stood still, gazing at Mitya with a lost look, as it were. He leapt impulsively to his feet, and a scared look came into his face. He turned pale, but a timid, pleading smile appeared on his lips at once, and with an irresistible impulse he held out both hands to Katya. Seeing it, she flew impetuously to him. She seized him by the hands, and almost by force made him sit down on the bed. She sat down beside him, and still keeping his hands pressed them violently, convulsively. Several times they both strove to speak, but stopped short and again gazed speechless with a strange smile, their eyes fastened on each other. So passed two minutes.

"Have you forgiven me?" Mitya faltered at last, and at the same moment turning to Alyosha, his face working with joy, he cried, "Do you hear what I am asking, do you hear?"

"That's what I loved you for, that you are generous at heart!" broke from Katya. "My forgiveness is no good to you, nor yours to me; whether you forgive me or not, you will always be a wound in my heart, and I in yours — and so it ought to be. . . ." She stopped to take breath. "What have I come for?" she began again frantically and hastily: "to embrace your feet, to press your hands like this, till it hurts — you remember how in Moscow I used to squeeze them — to tell you again that you are my god, my joy, to tell you that I love you madly," she moaned in anguish, and suddenly pressed her lips greedily to his hand. Tears streamed from her eyes. Alyosha stood speechless and confounded; he had never expected what he was seeing.

"Love is over, Mitya!" Katya began again, "but the past is painfully dear to me. Know that will always be so. But now let what might have been come true for one minute," she faltered, with a crooked smile, looking into his face joyfully again. "You love another woman now, and I love another man, and yet I shall love you for ever, and you will love me; do you know that? Do you hear? Love me, love me all your life!" she cried, with a quiver, almost of menace, in her voice.

"I shall love you, and . . . do you know, Katya," Mitya began, drawing a deep breath at each word, "do you know, five days ago, that same evening, I loved you. . . . When you fell down and were carried out . . . All my life! So it will be, so it will always be."

So they murmured to each other words almost meaningless, and frantic, perhaps not even true, but at that moment it was all true, and they both believed implicitly what they said.

"Katya," cried Mitya suddenly, "do you believe I killed? I know you don't believe it now, but then . . . when you testified. . . . Could you, could you have believed it?"

"I did not believe it even then. I've never believed it. I hated you, and for a moment I persuaded myself. While I was testifying I persuaded myself and believed it, but when I'd finished speaking I left off believing it at once. Don't doubt that! I have forgotten that I came here to punish myself," she said, with a new expression in her voice, quite unlike the loverly tones of a moment before.

"Woman, yours is a heavy burden," broke, as it were, involuntarily from Mitya.

"Let me go," she whispered. "I'll come again. It's more than I can bear now."

She was getting up from her place, but suddenly uttered a loud scream and staggered back. Grushenka walked suddenly and noiselessly into the room. No one had expected her. Katya moved swiftly to the door, but when she reached Grushenka, she stopped suddenly, turned as white as chalk, and moaned softly, almost in a whisper:

"Forgive me!"

Grushenka stared at her and, pausing for an instant, in a vindictive, venomous voice, answered:

"We are full of hatred, my girl, you and I! We are both full of hatred! As though we could forgive each other! Save him, and I'll worship you all my life."

"You won't forgive her!" cried Mitya, with frantic reproach.

"Don't be anxious, I'll save him for you!" Katya whispered rapidly, and ran out of the room.

"And you could refuse to forgive her when she begged your forgiveness herself?" Mitya exclaimed bitterly again.

"Mitya, don't dare to reproach her; you have no right to!" Alyosha cried hotly.

"Her proud lips spoke, not her heart," Grushenka brought out in a tone of disgust. "If she saves you I'll forgive her everything . . ."

She stopped speaking, as though suppressing something. She could not yet recover herself. She had come in, as appeared afterwards, accidentally, with no suspicion, no expectation of what she would meet.

"Alyosha, run after her!" Mitya cried to his brother; "tell her . . . I don't know . . . don't let her go away like this!"

"I'll come to you again at nightfall," said Alyosha, and he ran after Katya. He overtook her outside the hospital grounds. She was walking fast, but as soon as Alyosha caught up with her she said quickly:

"No, before that woman I can't punish myself! I asked her forgiveness because I wanted to punish myself to the bitter end. She would not forgive me. . . . I love her for that!" she added, in an unnatural voice, and her eyes flashed with fierce resentment.

"My brother did not expect this in the least," muttered Alyosha. "He was sure she would not come . . ."

"No doubt. Let us leave that," she snapped.

"Listen: I can't go with you to the funeral now. I've sent them flowers. I think they still have money. If necessary, tell them I'll never abandon them. . . . Now leave me, leave me, please. You are late as it is — the bells are ringing for the service. . . . Leave me, please!"

## CHAPTER III
### ILUSHA'S FUNERAL.
#### THE SPEECH AT THE STONE

HE really was late. They had waited for him and had already decided to bear the pretty flower-decked little coffin to the church without him. It was the coffin of poor little Ilusha. He had died two days after Mitya was sentenced. At the gate of the house Alyosha was met by the shouts of the boys, Ilusha's schoolfellows. They had all been impatiently expecting him and were glad that he had come at last. There were about twelve of them, they all had their school-bags or satchels on their shoulders. "Papa will cry, be with papa," Ilusha had told them as he lay dying, and the boys remembered it. Kolya Krasotkin was at the head of them.

"How glad I am you've come, Karamazov!" he cried, holding out his hand to Alyosha. "It's awful here. It's really painful to see it. Snegiryov is not drunk, we know for a fact he's had nothing to drink to-day, but he behaves as if he were drunk. . . . I always have a grip on myself, but this is awful. Karamazov, if I am not keeping you, one question before you go in?"

"What is it, Kolya?" said Alyosha.

"Is your brother innocent or guilty? Was it he killed your father or was it the valet? As you say, so it will be. I haven't slept for the last four nights thinking of it."

597

"The valet killed him, my brother is innocent," answered Alyosha.

"That's what I said," cried Smurov.

"So he will perish for the truth, an innocent victim!" exclaimed Kolya; "though he is ruined he is happy! I am ready to envy him!"

"What do you mean? How can you? And what for?" cried Alyosha, surprised.

"Oh, if I, too, could sacrifice myself some day for truth!" said Kolya with enthusiasm.

"But not in such a cause, not with such disgrace and such horror!" said Alyosha.

"Of course . . . I should like to die for all humanity, and as for disgrace, I don't care about that — let our names perish. I respect your brother!"

"And so do I!" the boy who had once declared that he knew who had founded Troy cried suddenly and unexpectedly and he blushed up to his ears like a peony as he had done on that occasion.

Alyosha went into the room. Ilusha lay with his hands folded and his eyes closed, in a blue coffin with a white frill round it. The features of his emaciated face were hardly altered at all, and, strange to say, there was no smell of decay from the corpse. The expression of his face was serious and, as it were, thoughtful. His hands, crossed over his breast, looked particularly beautiful, as though chiselled in marble. There were flowers in his hands and the coffin, inside and out, was decked with flowers, which had been sent early in the morning by Lise Hohlakov. But there were flowers, too, from Katerina Ivanovna, and when Alyosha opened the door, the captain had a bunch in his trembling hands and was strewing them again over his dear boy. He scarcely glanced at Alyosha when he came in, and he would not look at any one, even at his crazy weeping wife, "mamma," who kept trying to stand on her crippled legs to get a closer look at her dead boy. As for Nina, the boys had pushed her in her chair close up to the coffin. She sat with her head pressed against it and she, too, was no doubt quietly weeping. Snegiryov's face looked eager, yet bewildered and exasperated. There was something witless about his gestures and the words that broke from him. "Old man, dear old man!" he exclaimed every minute, gazing at Ilusha. It had been his habit to call Ilusha "old man" as a term of affection when he was alive.

"Father, give me a flower, too; take that white one out of his hand and give it me," the crazy mother begged, whimpering. Either because the little white rose in Ilusha's hand had caught her fancy or because she wanted one from his hand to keep in memory of him, she shifted restlessly, stretching out her hands for the flower.

"I won't give it to any one, I won't give you anything," Snegiryov cried callously. "They are his flowers, not yours! Everything is his, nothing is yours!"

"Father, give mother a flower!" said Nina, lifting her face wet with tears.

"I won't give away anything and to her less than any one! She didn't love Ilusha. She took away his little cannon and he gave it to her." The captain broke into loud sobs at the thought of how Ilusha had given up his cannon to his mother. The poor crazy creature was bathed in noiseless tears, hiding her face in her hands.

The boys, seeing that the father would not leave the coffin and that it was time to carry it out, stood round it in a close circle and began to lift it up.

"I don't want him to be buried in the

churchyard," Snegiryov wailed suddenly; "I'll bury him by the stone, by our stone! Ilusha told me to. I won't let him be carried out!"

He had been saying for the last three days that he would bury him by the stone, but Alyosha, Krasotkin, the landlady, her sister, and all the boys interfered.

"What an idea, bury him by an unholy stone, as though he had hanged himself," the old landlady said sternly. "There in the churchyard the ground is consecrated. He'll be prayed for there. One can hear the singing in church and the deacon reads so clearly and distinctly that it will reach him every time just as though it were read over his grave."

At last the captain made a gesture of despair, as though to say, "Take him where you will." The boys raised the coffin, but as they passed the mother they stopped for a moment and lowered it that she might say good-bye to Ilusha. But on seeing that precious little face, which for the last three days she had only looked at from a distance, she trembled all over and her grey head began twitching spasmodically over the coffin.

"Mother, make the sign of the cross over him, give him your blessing, kiss him," Nina cried to her. But her head still twitched like that of an automaton and with a face contorted with bitter grief she began, without a word, beating her breast with her fist. They carried the coffin past her. Nina pressed her lips to her brother's for the last time as they bore the coffin by her. As Alyosha went out of the house he begged the landlady to look after those who were left behind, but she interrupted him before he had finished. "To be sure, I'll stay with them, we are Christians, too." The old woman wept as she said it.

They had not far to carry the coffin to the church, not more than three hundred paces. It was a still clear day, with a slight frost. The church bells were still ringing. Snegiryov, distraught and forlorn, ran after the coffin, in his short old overcoat, almost as thin as a summer one, with his head bare and his soft, old, wide-brimmed hat in his hand. He seemed endlessly fretted. At one minute he stretched out his hand to support the head of the coffin and only hindered the bearers, at another he ran alongside and tried to find a place for himself there. A flower fell on the snow and he rushed to pick it up as though everything in the world depended on the loss of that flower.

"And the crust of bread, we've forgotten the crust!" he cried suddenly in terrible dismay. But the boys reminded him at once that he had taken the crust of bread already and that it was in his pocket. He instantly pulled it out and was reassured.

"Ilusha told me to, Ilusha," he explained at once to Alyosha. "I was sitting by him one night and he suddenly told me: 'Papa, when my grave is filled up crumble a piece of bread on it so that the sparrows may fly down, I shall hear and it will cheer me up not to be lying alone.'"

"That's a good thing," said Alyosha, "we must often take some."

"Every day, every day!" said the captain quickly, growing animated, as it were.

They reached the church at last and set the coffin in the middle of it. The boys surrounded it and remained reverently standing so, all through the service. It was an ancient and rather poor church. Many of the ikons were without settings but such churches are the best for praying in. During the mass Snegiryov became somewhat calmer, though at times he had outbursts of the same unconscious and, as it were, incoherent anxiety. At one moment he went up to the coffin to set straight the pall or the chaplet, when a candle fell out of the candlestick he rushed to replace it and was a fearful time fumbling over it, then he subsided and stood quietly by the coffin with a look of blank uneasiness and perplexity. After the passage from the Epistle he suddenly whispered to Alyosha, who was standing beside him, that it had not been read properly but did not explain what he meant. During the prayer, "Like the Cherubim," he joined in the singing but he did not go on to the end. Falling on his knees, he pressed his forehead to the stone floor and lay so for a long while.

At last came the funeral service itself and candles were distributed. The crazed father began fussing about again, but the touching and impressive funeral prayers moved and shook his soul. He seemed suddenly to shrink together and broke into rapid, short sobs, which he tried at first to smother, but at last he sobbed aloud. When they began taking leave of the dead and closing the coffin, he flung his arms about, as though he would not allow them to cover Ilusha, and began greedily and persistently kissing his dead boy on the lips. At last they succeeded in persuading him to come away from the step, but suddenly he impulsively stretched out his hand and snatched a few flowers from the coffin. He looked at them and a new idea seemed to dawn upon him, so that he apparently forgot his grief for a minute. Gradually he seemed to sink into brooding and did not resist when the coffin was lifted up and carried to the grave. It was an expensive one in the churchyard close to the church, Katerina Ivanovna had paid for it. After the customary rites the grave-diggers

lowered the coffin. Snegiryov with his flowers in his hands bent down so low over the open grave that the boys caught hold of his coat in alarm and pulled him back. But he did not seem to understand fully what was happening. When they began filling up the grave, he suddenly pointed anxiously at the falling earth and began trying to say something, but no one could make out what he meant, and he grew quiet suddenly. Then he was reminded that he must crumble the bread and he was awfully excited, snatched up the bread and began pulling it to pieces and flinging the morsels on the grave.

"Come, fly down, birds, fly down, sparrows!" he muttered anxiously.

One of the boys observed that it was awkward for him to crumble the bread with the flowers in his hands and suggested he should give them to some one to hold for a time. But he would not do this and seemed indeed suddenly alarmed for his flowers, as though they wanted to take them from him altogether. And after looking at the grave and, as it were, satisfying himself that everything had been done and the bread had been crumbled, he suddenly, to the surprise of every one, turned, quite composedly even, and made his way homewards. But his steps became more and more hurried, he almost ran. The boys and Alyosha kept up with him.

"The flowers are for mamma, the flowers are for mamma! We were unkind to mamma," he began exclaiming suddenly.

Some one called to him to put on his hat as it was cold. But he flung the hat in the snow as though he were angry and kept repeating, "I don't want the hat, I don't want the hat." Smurov picked it up and carried it after him. All the boys were crying, and Kolya and the boy who had discovered Troy most of all. Though Smurov with the captain's hat in his hand, was crying bitterly, too, he managed, as he ran, to snatch up a piece of red brick that lay on the snow of the path, to fling it at the flock of sparrows that was flying by. He missed them, of course, and went on crying as he ran. Half way, Snegiryov suddenly stopped, stood still for a half a minute, as though struck by something, and, suddenly turning back to the church, ran towards the deserted grave. But the boys instantly overtook him and, surrounding him, caught hold of him. Then he fell helpless on the snow as though he had been knocked down, and struggling, sobbing, and wailing, he began crying out, "Ilusha, old man, dear old man!" Alyosha and Kolya tried to lift him up, soothing and persuading him.

"Captain, give over, a brave man must bear up," muttered Kolya.

"You'll spoil the flowers," said Alyosha, "and mamma is expecting them, she is sitting crying because you would not give her any before. Ilusha's little bed is still there . . ."

"Yes, yes, mamma!" Snegiryov suddenly recollected; "they'll take away the bed, they'll take it away," he added as though afraid that they really would. He jumped up and ran homewards again. But it was not far off and they all arrived together. Snegiryov opened the door hurriedly and called to his wife, with whom he had so cruelly quarrelled just before:

"Mamma, darling, oh, your poor legs, Ilusha has sent you these flowers!" he cried, holding out to her a little bunch of flowers that had been frozen and broken while he was struggling in the snow. But at that instant he saw in the corner, by the little bed, Ilusha's little boots, which the landlady had put tidily side by side. Seeing the old, patched, rusty-looking, stiff boots he flung up his hands and rushed to them, fell on his knees, snatched up one boot and, pressing his lips to it, began kissing it greedily, crying, "Ilusha, old man, dear old man, where are your little feet?"

"Where have you taken him to? Where have you taken him?" the lunatic cried in a heart-rending voice. Nina, too, broke into sobs. Kolya ran out of the room, the boys followed him. At last Alyosha, too, went out.

"Let them weep," he said to Kolya, "it's no use trying to comfort them just now. Let us wait a minute and then go back."

"No, it's no use, it's awful," Kolya assented. "Do you know, Karamazov," he dropped his voice so that no one could hear them, "I feel dreadfully sad, and if it were only possible to raise him from the dead, I'd give anything in the world to do it."

"Ah, so would I," said Alyosha.

"What do you think, Karamazov, had we better come back here to-night? He'll be drunk, you know."

"Perhaps he will. Let us come together, you and I, that will be enough, to spend an hour with them, with the mother and Nina. If we all come together we shall remind them of everything again," Alyosha suggested.

"The landlady is laying the table for them now — there'll be a funeral feast or something, the priest is coming; shall we go back to it, Karamazov?"

"Of course," said Alyosha.

"It's all so strange, Karamazov, such sorrow and suddenly pancakes, it all seems so unnatural the way we do it, according to our religion."

"They are going to have salmon, too," the boy who had discovered Troy observed in a loud voice.

"I beg you most earnestly, Kartashov, not to interrupt again with your idiotic remarks, especially when one is not talking to you and doesn't care to know whether you exist or not!" Kolya snapped out irritably. The boy flushed crimson but did not dare to make any reply.

Meantime they were strolling slowly along the path and suddenly Smurov exclaimed:

"There's Ilusha's stone, under which they wanted to bury him."

They all stood still by the big stone. Alyosha looked and the whole picture of what Snegiryov had described to him that day, how Ilusha, weeping and hugging his father, had cried, "Papa, papa, how he insulted you," rose at once before his imagination. Something suddenly shook his soul, as it were. With a serious and grave expression he looked from one to another of the dear, bright faces of Ilusha's school-fellows, and suddenly said to them:

"Boys, I should like to say one word to you, here on this spot."

The boys stood round him and at once bent attentive and expectant eyes upon him.

"Boys, we shall soon part. I shall be for some time with my two brothers, of whom one is going to Siberia and the other is lying at death's door. But soon I shall leave this town, perhaps for a long time, so we shall part. Let us make a compact, here, at Ilusha's stone, that we will never forget first, Ilusha, and, second, each other. And whatever happens to us later in life, even if we don't meet for twenty years, let us always remember how we buried the poor boy at whom we once threw stones — do you remember, by the bridge? — and afterwards we all grew so fond of him. He was a fine boy, a kind-hearted, brave boy, he felt for his father's honour and resented the cruel insult to him and stood up for him. And so, in the first place, we will remember him, boys, all our lives. And even if we are occupied with most important things, if we attain to honour or meet with great misfortune — still let us remember how good it was once here, when we were all together, united by a good and kind feeling which made us, for the time we were loving that poor boy, better perhaps than we are in reality. My little doves — let me call you so, for you are very like them, those pretty blue birds, at this minute as I look at your good dear faces. My dear children, perhaps you won't understand what I am saying to you, because I often speak very unintelligibly, but you'll remember it all the same and will agree with my words some day. You must know that there is nothing higher and stronger and more wholesome and useful for life in after years than some good memory, especially a memory connected with childhood, with home. People talk to you a great deal about your education, but some fine, sacred memory, preserved from childhood, is perhaps the best education. If a man carries many such memories with him into life, he is safe to the end of his days, and if we have only one good memory left in our hearts, even that may sometime be the means of saving us. Perhaps we may even grow wicked later on, may be unable to refrain from a bad action, may laugh at men's tears and at those people who say as Kolya did just now, 'I want to suffer for all men,' and may even jeer spitefully at such people. But however bad we may become — which God forbid — yet, when we recall how we buried Ilusha, how we loved him in his last days, and how we have been talking like friends all together, at this stone, then the cruellest and most mock-

"HURRAH FOR KARAMAZOV!"

ing of us — if we do become so — will not dare to laugh inwardly at having been kind and good at this moment! What's more, perhaps, that one memory may keep him from great evil and he will reflect and say, 'Yes, I was good and brave and honest then!' Let him laugh to himself, that's no matter, a man often laughs at what's good and kind. That's only out of frivolity. But I assure you, boys, that as he laughs he will say at once in his heart, 'No, I do wrong to laugh, for that's not a thing to laugh at.'"

"That will be so, I understand you, Karamazov!" cried Kolya, with flashing eyes.

The boys were excited and they, too, wanted to say something, but they restrained themselves, looking with intentness and emotion at the speaker.

"I say this in case we become bad," Alyosha went on, "but there's no reason why we should become bad, is there, boys? Let us be, first and above all, kind, then honest, and then let us never forget each other! I say that again. I give you my word for my part that I'll never forget one of you. Every face looking at me now I shall remember even for thirty years. Just now Kolya said to Kartashov that we did not care to know whether he exists or not. But I cannot forget that Kartashov exists and that he is not blushing now as he did when he discovered Troy, but is looking at me with his jolly, kind, dear little eyes. Boys, my dear boys, let us all be generous and brave like Ilusha, intelligent, brave, and generous like Kolya (though he will be ever so much more intelligent when he is grown up), and let us all be as modest, as clever and sweet as Kartashov. But why am I talking about those two! You are all dear to me, boys, from this day forth, I shall shut you all in my heart, and I beg you to shut me within your hearts! Well, and who has united us in this kind, good feeling which we shall remember and intend to remember all our lives? Who, if not Ilusha, the good boy, the dear boy, precious to us for ever! Let us never forget him. May his memory live for ever in our hearts from this time forth and for evermore!"

"Yes, yes, for ever, for ever!" the boys cried in their ringing voices, with softened faces.

"Let us remember his face and his clothes and his poor little boots, his coffin and his unhappy, sinful father, and how boldly he stood up for him alone against the whole school."

"We will remember, we will remember," cried the boys. "He was brave, he was good!"

"Ah, how I loved him!" exclaimed Kolya.

"Ah, children, ah, dear friends, don't be afraid of life! How good life is when one does something good and true!"

"Yes, yes," the boys repeated enthusiastically.

"Karamazov, we love you!" a voice, probably Kartashov's, cried impulsively.

"We love you, we love you!" they all caught it up. There were tears in the eyes of many of them.

"Hurrah for Karamazov!" Kolya shouted ecstatically.

"And may the dead boy's memory live for ever!" Alyosha added again with feeling.

"For ever!" the boys chimed in again.

"Karamazov," cried Kolya, "can it be true what's taught us in religion, that we shall all rise again from the dead and shall live and see each other again, all, Ilusha, too?"

"Certainly we shall all rise again, certainly we shall see each other and shall tell each other with joy and gladness all that has happened!"

Alyosha answered, half laughing, half enthusiastic.

"Ah, how splendid it will be!" broke from Kolya.

"Well, now we will finish talking and go to his funeral feast. Don't be put out at our eating pancakes — it's an old, old custom and there's something good in that!" laughed Alyosha. "Well, let us go! And now we go hand in hand."

"And always so, all our lives hand in hand! Hurrah for Karamazov!" Kolya cried once more rapturously, and once more the boys took up his exclamation.